CAGE
OF
SOULS

ADRIAN TCHAIKOVSKY is a keen
live role-player and occasional
actor, fantasy author and winner
of the Arthur C. Clarke Award.

ALSO BY ADRIAN TCHAIKOVSKY

SHADOWS OF THE APT
Empire in Black and Gold
Dragonfly Falling
Blood of the Mantis
Salute the Dark
The Scarab Path
The Sea Watch
Heirs of the Blade
The Air War
War Master's Gate
Seal of the Worm

TALES OF THE APT
Spoils of War
A Time for Grief
For Love of Distant Shores
The Scent of Tears

ECHOES OF THE FALL
The Tiger and the Wolf
The Bear and the Serpent
The Hyena and the Hawk

Guns of the Dawn
Children of Time
Children of Ruin
Spiderlight
Ironclads
Feast and Famine (collection)
Dogs of War
Cage of Souls

The Private Life of Elder Things (with Keris McDonald and Adam Gauntlett)

ADRIAN TCHAIKOVSKY

CAGE OF SOULS

HEAD
of ZEUS

First published in the UK in 2019 by Head of Zeus Ltd
This paperback edition published in the UK in 2019 by Head of Zeus Ltd

9 7 6 8

A catalogue record for this book is available from
the British Library.

ISBN (PB): 9781788547383
ISBN (E): 9781788547239

Typeset by Divaddict Publishing Solutions Ltd.

Printed and bound in Great Britain by
CPI Group (UK) Ltd, Croydon CR0 4YY

Head of Zeus Ltd
First Floor East
5–8 Hardwick Street
London EC1R 4RG

WWW.HEADOFZEUS.COM

ACKNOWLEDGEMENTS

Enormous thanks to Emma Newman, who was kind enough to act as my beta-reader and made a number of invaluable suggestions which have immeasurably improved the manuscript. Thanks also to my agent Mr Simon Kavanagh, and to my editor Nicolas Cheetham and all at Head of Zeus.

PART THE FIRST

IN WHICH I ARRIVE
AT THE ISLAND

1

A Game of Chess

Where to begin?

Not with the rioting crowd hurling stones and screaming, blood on their fingernails.

Or the white desert, and the things that deal death amongst the ruins.

The caverns of Underworld; the mad genius who was the subject of his own experiment, in hiding from the sun. No.

And not with the cells of the dock, shoulder to shoulder with all the scum they could scrape from the streets. Thieves, murderers, debtors and me. Not yet.

I might as well begin with a jaunt on the river; sounds jolly enough, no?

There was a boat, a metal-hulled antique some forty feet long. Shadrapar was its birthplace, as it is mine, but it took us east down the river into the unmappable and hungry jungles. The thump of its engine was a constant companion to all of us aboard her. We dreamed in time to its artificial heartbeat.

I take you to the point in time when that indefatigable engine proved mortal after all, and was stilled.

Some several of the crew and passengers came out on deck to consider this development. For those passengers, it was the first sunlight they had seen since setting off. The crew, armed, formed a semicircle before the boat's captain. The passengers, a ragged, stinking sample of seven from the various vintages chained below, were the focus of their hostile attention. Convicts all, bound for a final exile, and your narrator one of them.

There are extenuating circumstances.

The boat was listing as the current took it gently towards the bank behind us, and the river – my first sight of it – was wider than I had expected. It was opaque, brown with silt, loose vegetation and the reflection of the jungle.

I had never seen it before, this vast living thing in whose guts we were stewing. It had been a constant idea on the fringes of my mind: the wild eastern marches, festering in the heat of their own decay. The jungle was life, ravenous and abundant. There was no sharp line between land and water: the river glinted still between the boles of trees with roots like reaching fingers. The leaves were huge and drooped with their own weight and the whole smelled of rot and death. What struck me most was the darkness. It never got beyond twilight under that dank canopy. It scared me. I felt that it was one living thing, and that it was watching me. The relentless sun boiled down like the eye through which the jungle's presence was focused. There was no wind and it was humid enough to stick my clothes to my skin from the first moment on deck.

Everywhere there were animals.

Animals had no place in my home of Shadrapar. We were civilised. Life was humanity; animals belonged in books. The fecundity of the jungle was a rioting horror. Birds with necks like serpents hunched on branches at the water's edge, watching the boat sourly. The air whined with insects. I was bitten within a moment of stepping outside and the biters themselves were prey to larger bugs that darted and zigzagged over the water.

4

Some were as large as my hand. A lizard a man's-length long caught my eye, basking in the oppressive heat, its head decorated by a crest of lurid red. Wherever there was nothing to be seen, there was the suggestion of life: a sound, a movement. The trees thronged with unseen man-eaters.

"What's the problem?" asked the one man there who was neither convict nor crew.

"Weeds have choked the prop," said the captain. He was a solid, brutal-looking man. Anyone would have to be half-mad to start with, to make a living shipping into those fetid stews.

"Good," his questioner said, and then, after some reflection, "And that means what?"

"It means this batch of the cargo gets to go down there and cut it loose."

I was better educated than either of them and knew what a prop was. The idea of being lowered into that poisonous river made me feel ill. On land, no matter what the beast, there is a chance, a warning. In the water it is different. A sudden tug, some expanding ripples, then nothing to show that a man was ever there. I knew some of what was supposed to live this far east. There were a dozen separate volumes of Trethowan's *Bestiary* that I had dragged my way through at the Academy. Trethowan himself had never returned from his thirteenth expedition.

The passenger – the lone non-convicted passenger – stepped forwards, looking us over like a man going through a pauper's personal effects. "Any of you wretches play chess?" he asked, wrinkling his nose. At the captain's raised eyebrow he added, "Look, I know this is what you *do*, but I am so *bored* on your boat, and I have a chess set." His expression, turned back to us, was not optimistic.

I played chess.

I recall raising my hand timidly, because even that early on I had learned that, for prisoners, singling yourself out was seldom wise. At the passenger's prompting look I admitted that, yes, I did play chess. On such small matters are lives bought and sold.

"Fine. That one doesn't go," the passenger said confidently. "He'll be my catamite."

I choked. A moment later I saw that he had not the faintest idea what a catamite was. Neither did the captain, but the passenger had given the word such authority that it would have been unthinkable to challenge him.

Two of the boat's crew were preparing a hoist at the stern, a shaky platform which could be winched down to water level to let the chosen men hack away at the weed that tangled our propeller.

"Get them on!" the captain ordered gruffly, and the three of us watched as the tattered band, my erstwhile fellows, was driven onto the platform. A riverman threw a bag on there with them, and I watched their blank faces as one opened it. It contained big, saw-edged knives.

The captain had clearly done all this before. "Listen to me, you bastards," he said. He used the word as though it was the correct technical term for prisoners drafted in as weed-cutters. "We'll send you down, and you get to cut us free. Cut off anything that's snagged on the machinery below the water. Then we'll haul you up and you can hand over those toys before we take you back on."

The prisoners stared narrowly at him, wondering where the flaw in his plan was. None were well-read enough to realise just how far we all were from home.

"Do I make myself clear?" the captain demanded. The mumbles he received in reply seemed to satisfy him. More pertinent in the prisoners' minds, no doubt, were the crossbows in the hands of three rivermen. A fourth even had a flintlock musket. They just held the weapons loosely in plain sight, pragmatic men who were not being paid to bring any of us back. Even so, I was sure that at least one of the work party would make a break for the shore. For myself, I knew that I was the equal of these men in fate and impotence, but I was monstrously, guiltily glad not to be going with them. I was not ready, then, to co-exist with the water and the living jungle.

"All right, chess-man. Might as well give me your name," the passenger said. "Mine's Peter Drachmar." As though I might have heard of him. As so often in these unequal relationships, he was far less aware of the gulf that separated us than I was. That would change, where we were going.

"Stefan Advani," for such am I. I'd have you picture a man of aristocratic feature, as of a good family: a long face, dark straight hair and brown-olive skin. A high forehead – a sign of intellect and not just, as Helman always claimed, receding hairline. The nose is finely shaped but, even in the owner's opinion, a trifle long. Eternally clean-shaven, a gift from my genes, my loose, ill-fitting clothing is dirty grey and does not flatter. This is your narrator contemplating the fate that was so nearly his, something I have made a career of.

Peter Drachmar, seen there on deck, is quite a different sight. His hair is the colour of wet sand and there are laughter lines on his face even when he is not laughing. He has broader shoulders than I and wears clothes from a far better tailor. Luckily for his future employment, black is his preferred hue for a shirt. His trousers are of mustard colour and he has a short half-cloak of burgundy red that was the height of fashion the year before last. It is edged with gold trim that has faded slightly. If my description of him is more accurate, remember that, from this point on, I seldom crossed paths with a mirror.

The man Peter Drachmar, my benefactor and someone who was to loom so large in my future, stood between me and the hell of the river, and I was desperate to bind myself to him even closer. Sadly, for me, this meant pedantry, and I asked him, "Just for information, what do you think a catamite is?" The squeak of the hoists sounded over my words.

"A servant, isn't it?" he said. "Some kind of servant."

I told him what a catamite was. He raised his eyebrows thoughtfully.

"Right. Learn something new every day, don't you?" He went to lean on the rail overlooking the stern and I joined him. Work was progressing slowly as the platform tipped and tilted on the water, and the men had to lean in almost up to their shoulders to cut at the weed. For a moment, as I stood barefoot on the hot metal deck with the air drenching me with sweat, it looked cooling.

We were all men, we convicts, and apart from that and our incarceration we had little in common. Many were thieves, some were killers, others abusers of women. Still more were forgers, agitators, dismissed officials and political enemies of the Shadrapar Authority. No doubt a few were even innocent. Reduced to a common state of servitude it was impossible to tell which had killed a wife and which had only stolen a piece of fruit. I realised then (it had been long in coming) that, aside from my place on deck, I, too, was inseparable from the toiling wretches. Pluck me from thence and place me on the waterline and who could have picked me out? Who would care enough to?

"You can go down if you want," Peter suggested.

"Excuse me?"

"You were looking so damn miserable I assumed you were missing the exercise. I'm only keeping you around 'cos being a guard on the Island sounds hellish dull, and I could use a chess-foil."

"It's going to be a fair sight duller for me," I said immediately, without thinking, and Peter replied, "Really? Because you sound like a very educated type, and I think your life's going to be more interesting than you'll want, after we fetch up." His look to me reminded me that I was going to eke out my days in penal servitude, whereas Peter Drachmar was staff. For reasons of his own, as complicated and personal as mine, he was to be the newest Warden of the Island.

8

The captain stomped over to look down at the workers and shouted, "Well? How is it? If you bastards haven't done by the time we touch the bank then I'll have the lot of you shot and get some more bastards up from below. You think anyone cares how many I turn up with each trip? Marshal'd thank me for taking your worthless corpses off his hands."

There was a sullen silence from the working men until one of the rivermen sliced a crossbow bolt into the water beside the platform, which prompted someone to say that they were nearly done.

"About bloody time, you lazy bastards," the captain shouted down to them. "Could have done it with my bare hands in less."

It happened then, just as one or another of the workers was no doubt about to invite him to join them. Something reared out of the water by the platform.

It was like a serpent, with an arrow-shaped head that was almost entirely a mouth filled with back-curving teeth. Grey-green and dead-looking, it seemed to have no eyes. I caught the faint ripple that showed where its huge, turtle-like body was hanging in the water.

The workmen had time for a confused babble of fear before the head struck at them like a fisherman's spear. By some miracle it failed to snag any of them, although one man was sent crying back with blood on his arm. A crossbow bolt flitted across the thing's face like one of the ubiquitous insects, and then the musket spoke with a short, dry sound. The musketeer was firing into the water at the monster's body, and must have hit something because the head reared up at us. It really was nothing more than a set of jaws on a neck. I have no idea how it found its prey. Trethowan had neglected to mention it in the bestiary.

A crossbow bolt was abruptly flowering from behind that head, and the monster decided that the odds were bad. It submerged all at once, swamping the workmen, and was gone in an instant. Throughout the attack it had made not a sound. It was as the crossbowmen and the musketeer reloaded their weapons that the captain called out, "One of the bastards is gone."

However bad I might have thought life on the Island would be, nothing would have persuaded me to make a break through those vile waters. I think I would rather have been summarily shot than try what that man tried. He must have known that crossbows and muskets take a deal of reloading, and he swam well. Even so, he could not have got to the shore before the rivermen were ready to shoot again.

It did not even come to that. Whether the eyeless creature took him, or some other unseen river horror, I never knew, but it was just as I imagined. The sudden break in the man's swimming, the moment of confusion, and then he was gone and there were only the ripples.

The workmen were looking up, expecting to be hoisted. "Don't you slack now," the captain warned them. "If I were you I'd finish up before that thing comes back."

I turned away. It was not pity for the workmen, but merely for myself. I might be safe whilst Peter had a voyage to whittle down with chess games, but the lot of those workmen would be my lot soon enough, when we reached the Island.

The five remaining workers were hauled up and sent below again, without further complaints, and the engines were coaxed into life. They would get choked twice more on the voyage, and the same labour would be herded out to clear them. No more men were taken by monsters, but the worker whose arm had been gashed would die three days later of some contamination. There was nothing in that jungle that was not hostile to human life.

So, in the aftermath of that, picture those same two men sitting across a small table, playing chess, I thinking only that if I so much as displeased the man across from me I would be back in the company of my fellow prisoners.

No amount of pretence could disguise our circumstances. The air around us rumbled constantly with the muted shake of the engines and the walls were bare rusted metal, pocked with rivets. There was the swell, as the boat wallowed in the river current, and the smell. An ageing, badly-maintained riverboat has a smell all its own: failing metal, oil, sweat and the stale urine of ages. Our one steel-rimmed window, round as a plate, was so crusted with grime that we might as well be underwater. Peter had hung a lantern up so that we could see to play.

Peter Drachmar had one quality that annoyed me from the very moment we met and persisted throughout our acquaintance. Sitting across from him, I knew myself to be his superior in education, in breeding, in understanding and in knowledge. Peter, on the other hand, had an unrefined, pragmatic intelligence that gave him the edge with people and with chess. He was beating me five games to nothing.

"That's your move then?" he asked idly.

"I was just adjusting the piece."

"Then you should say," Peter said pleasantly. "It's the rules. Otherwise it counts as your move," and he reached over and took a piece with one of his Soldiers. That was the other thing about him, of course. Whilst I examined the board and remembered my lessons and ran every permutation of moves through my mind, Peter cheated whenever possible and took every chance to put himself ahead. This went for life as well as chess. Despite this, he was one of the most easy-going and good-natured men I ever met. Perhaps there is a lesson there somewhere.

I pushed one of my Villeins forward. My tutors had been emphatic that the secret of the game was in these unassuming little pieces, simple squares of wood. They had never elaborated on this and all my lowly little chessmen seemed to do was get in each other's way whilst Peter's Soldiers butchered mine. I think my problem was that I was thinking too far ahead. Also I have a very bad face for strategy. My eyebrows are especial giveaways.

11

It was a cold game, because of our circumstances and because we had known each other for all of half an hour. From the start the matching of wills across the board was all we had in common save our surroundings. Even as Peter pondered his next move, the water bullied our craft a little and the whole room tilted, making us clutch the table, which someone had seen fit to bolt to the floor. One of my Nobles, being the tallest pieces, skittered from its place and rolled away.

"That's lost," Peter declared.

"Excuse me?"

"If a piece falls off the board it's counted as lost," he explained.

"That's news to me." It had never come up in the tutorials.

"It represents random death due to disease," Peter told me, mimicking my speech. "Or, seeing as it was a Noble, inbreeding."

You must not think me a coward, but he was bigger than me, and I did not know him. Later I would understand that I could challenge him quite freely, and that he would think the better of me for it. At the time I let him have the point. I was so close to losing the game that it would make little difference. He eliminated my remaining Nobles in three moves and sat back, satisfied.

"You're a fine player," he said, and took a flask from somewhere within his shirt. It was copper and embossed with the figure of a woman.

"I've lost six games," I pointed out.

"That's my favourite kind of player," he said easily. "If only you'd bet something, I'd be rich."

"If only I had something to bet," I pointed out.

"Well that goes the same for me," he promised. I looked at his clothes and wondered, but he failed to go into details. It was a long time before Peter Drachmar let any of his past out of the bag.

"Another game," he offered, adding, "You nearly had me that time." It was so big a lie that even he could lend little credibility to it.

I considered the options and began replacing the pieces in their starting positions. "Anything in that flask for me?" I asked, emboldened by the stifling room. The heat from the engine mixed with the heat of the outside made the air sticky and thick.

Peter, generous in victory, handed the flask over without a second thought. The liquid inside was decidedly inferior Maiden's Kiss, but it was enough for a thirsty man, and I took a decent sized swig before surrendering the flask. By then Peter had completed setting the board. As loser, I began, and shuffled a doomed Villein forward to start.

This time round I gave up playing to win and just stalled him for as long as possible. By this I found out a useful thing about Peter Drachmar: he got bored quickly and then started taking chances. I still maintain that I would have won that game had we driven it to its conclusion. We were some thirty moves into that tedious match, however, when the timbre of the engines changed subtly. Peter noticed it before I did, looking up sharply, one finger poised on a Villein.

"Is that your move, then?" I pressed, because by then I was getting bolder. A moment later I had caught up, and knew the engine had choked once more. I was in instant terror. Surely he had tired of me. Surely he would return me to the hold – or to that new work party even now being assembled. You cannot know, if you have not been in such a place, how it is to have your entire life suspended by the threads of other people's whims.

"Captain can deal with it," he said, waving away the fact that we were drifting towards an alien shore yet again. Casually, he upset the board with his elbow as he turned back, destroying all my hard work. "New game?" he offered brightly.

The third time that the engines choked and died, Peter and I went up on deck again. The sky was darkening by then, and the men on the platform worked faster, wanting even less to be near the water with night drawing on. As we watched, something caught my eye at the water's edge. It was a dwelling, or something like it. A little domed construction of wicker that actually sat in the water, and perhaps could only be entered from beneath. There were other poles and struts standing out in the river, and I now know that these were fish traps. At the time all I could do was stare. Peter noticed too, and frowned, and I saw that he had no idea either.

"They call them web-children," the captain told us shortly.

"Who calls what web-children?" Peter asked.

"Them things that built that," the captain explained. "They live out here."

"People live in this jungle?" Peter wondered.

"Ain't people." There was something in the captain's voice that made it clear that he was not just being prejudiced against some race of mankind. At that moment I saw something moving between the trees, half-hidden and watching the boat. There was a manlike quality in the way it moved but it was not human. I wanted very much to go below again, after that, and Peter must have felt the same. I was no stranger to horror, even then, but I knew that this place would test me beyond all bearing, and I really did not think that I could survive it. There are so many deaths in the jungles, after all.

I lost the next three games to Peter. It didn't make things better. I slept, packed into another man's armpit in the hold, and when I awoke, we had arrived.

2

An Undesirable Residence

They dragged us all out into the morning to look at it, because it was a vital part of breaking our spirits. Here was our new home, and our mass grave.

To a citizen of Shadrapar, the Island was nothing but an idea. It was where criminals go, and most people thought that this was a good thing. I had thought so myself, before I began to hold opinions unpopular with the state. The details were not known to the general populace. The understanding that the Island was a long way away in the jungles of the east; that no escapee has ever made it back to trouble the law-abiding; that it killed off prisoners as fast as it received them, and was thus never full, these facts were as much as anyone wanted to know. I had never speculated how such a place might work before my fall from grace. Even when I hid in the blighted Underworld, companion to beggars and beasts, I gave it little thought. On the boat, when they had finally caught me, I tried to envisage my destination and found that, after such a long period of avoiding the question, my imagination failed me. I would never have been able to hit upon the truth.

The jungle was more of a swamp now, and the water spread on all sides, a glistening wetland choked with reeds and knotted trees. The air was rank with flies. The boat moved slowly through what must have been the only channel deep enough to take its draft, and ahead of us the water broadened out into a lake. It was half mud, and strange plants thrust out from its shallows at intervals like the hands of drowning men. At the heart of this lake was the Island.

Everyone's first glance at the Island was the same: one took it for its namesake. In the middle of this lake, you assumed, there is a hill, and the hill has been covered by the structure. The Island was roughly square, with the top two floors of decreasing size and the lower three all of the same dimensions. It was made of wood and cane, as though the entire building was a barred cell. The higher levels had a few spaces of solid wall, so that the staff could steal a little privacy. The lower levels were all of reinforced slats, cane bars and a vast webwork of rope that held it all together. It was possible to see clean through the Island, if one picked the correct opening. The eye's path took you through a dozen intervening slatted walls and out to the foul waterscape on the other side, past a hundred sullen inmates. As the boat approached we could see a few of those inmates, shadowed figures behind the bars. They gave us a sense of scale. The lake was larger than we thought. The Island was far larger than we thought. It was larger than any castle, and the prisoners within must have numbered over a thousand. We would vanish in that mass of the deprived and the lawless, and never surface. Our faces would be lost to the powerless mob.

I pride myself in thinking that I was one of the first to make out the last demoralising thing about the Island. I saw that it was misnamed. As the boat chugged closer, finally breaking onto the open waters, we bobbed in the swell that troubled the lake. I watched as we rose and fell against the line of trees, and saw that the Island, too, rose and fell. It was a moment before I could separate real movement from the illusion caused by our own, but then I knew. The Island was afloat, however impossible that might be. Either there was some great portion of it below the water, and the lake was far deeper than I had guessed, or... I knew the truth, I think, even before we pulled closer and heard the dull and muffled thumping of machinery from the nearest corner. Some constant effort was keeping the whole construction afloat, and I could foresee even then how that would shape the lives of those aboard. It was not an island at all, but the most perilous of boats.

Some of my fellow prisoners swore, and some cursed, but most just stared. From this moment, so we all saw, there would be no privacy, no dignity, no escape from the flies or from each other. The hold of the prison boat would be like a palace to us. There were about twenty-five of us when the voyage began. Now one was dead, another with a wound that would kill him. Before the year was out there would be less than twelve of us left. The Island was a living thing worse than the jungle, and it ate humanity. It roasted men in its furnaces, sweated them in its machines, digested them in the swamp waters and ground up their bones.

The rivermen themselves were oblivious. Their attention was on the prisoners not the prison. All this was some part of their obligation to their employers. The new arrivals must be allowed to see their destination from the outside. It was an effective lesson for us to learn. Beyond the crew's impassive faces and levelled weapons, I saw Peter. He was standing aloof from us, of course. From his bearing and his clothes he could almost have been the ship's owner. I saw his expression, though, and it was not the face of a happy man. He might not be going under lock and key but he would be a prisoner of this godforsaken place as much as we.

There was a small boat coming round the side of the Island, a wide-beamed dinghy without oars or sail, but I heard nothing of the engine. At first I assumed that it was hidden beneath the sullen growl of our own but, as the craft drew nearer, I saw that there were crooked arms that reached into the water at sides and rear. A constant play of droplets hung in a mist about these devices, and every so often a fish would leap up out of the water

17

and away from them. It stirred vague memories in me of things learned once and long forgotten, but by then my attention was taken with the craft's occupants. There were three, including the steersman. They were all in black: jackets with grotesquely high collars rising almost to the level of their ears at the back; trousers belted with a club and a knife; boots and gloves of shiny rubber or plastic. Their hair was shaved close to the skull. The man at the prow also wore a headband that marked him out as a leader of men. Beneath it, he was almost bald, without even the stubble of the others. He had narrow eyes and a face that defied expression. In all the time I knew the Marshal – for it was he – I never saw any real flicker of thought betray itself on his face.

"How many?" His voice was very sharp and thin, a good fit for his slot of a mouth. The captain told him our number and never mentioned the dead man that the river creature had taken. Perhaps nobody mentioned him, and the Island went unaware that it was one life short. I feel sure that the Marshal would not have cared. He made his feelings about the prisoners quite clear from the start.

Our prison boat cut its engines a hundred yards or so from the Island and coasted most of the rest of the way. When it was close enough, a few men in convict grey threw ropes to the crew, who made them fast. We watched our fellows on the Island haul with aching arms to drag us the last few feet until the blunt nose of the boat touched the splintered timber. There was a kind of dock there, a wooden platform ringed with cane, with another handful of black-clad Wardens watching suspiciously. One of them was armed with some kind of gun that I did not recognise.

"Get your worthless hides off the boat!" the Marshal screamed at us, and the captain backed him up with, "You heard him, bastards! Move!" After a few blows from the clubs of the rivermen we began heading forward in a reluctant, uncooperative mass.

Although the boat had been secured, there was still a gap between it and the Island that changed size constantly as the swell rocked us. We were forced to jump across, with the water to catch us if we fell. I nearly did, but the man behind me caught my shoulder, so that I was able to make it across with a long step. The simple, wordless act of kindness surprised me. I had looked upon my fellow inmates with the horror of a well-bred Academy man. Joining the growing huddle of criminals in the square, I examined them with new eyes. They were not just a mass of grey-clad malice now, but individuals as nervous and scared as I. I took a good look at the man who had helped me as he joined us, dark and unassuming save for the mark that ran from one ear almost to the point of his chin. I thought it was a birthmark but later I discovered that it had been scored in by an energy blade during a fight. Whether he was lucky to have survived, given his current position, was an interesting philosophical point.

"Stefan," I told him.

"Shon," he replied. His eyes were on the guards and I could see that he, like Peter, was a man of action. He never tensed enough to make me think that he was going to try something, though. Where would he go? Aside from a dive into the water or onto the hostile boat, there was only one exit, a narrow, dark doorway that led into the body of the Island. We would go there soon enough without any fighting. There was no need to hurry matters.

I saw Peter get off the boat with a graceful little step and stand away from us, at the water's edge. One of the guards went over to him and inspected his papers. The inmates who had tied the prison boat fast were now reappearing, carrying heavy sacks that they handed down to the rivermen.

"What do they make here? What can you export from a prison?" I whispered, but Shon just waved me silent with a hand that was missing most of its little finger.

The morning sun was rising from behind the trees like a bloated red mushroom. The mists that hung about the jungle were the colour of blood. I have heard that the sun is dying by degrees, swelling up with some illness and parching the land into the lifeless deserts you find to the west of the city. For the first time, in those jungles, I looked up and saw that it was true. In that disease-ridden place even the sky looked unhealthy.

We were kept waiting for some time beneath that relentless sun. A few tried to sit down but guards came with black, dense clubs and struck them until they staggered to their feet. I was beginning to feel slightly faint by then. The mounting heat of the morning was beginning to tell on me. I glanced again at Peter and saw him waiting still, standing as we were. He had no baggage, nothing but those slightly fancy clothes he stood up in.

There was a thump from behind me, and I turned to see that one of my fellows had fainted. There was a bruise on his temple that a riverman or a Warden had put there. I expected him to be kicked into either wakefulness or concussion, but the guards were ignoring him. They had other things to watch for. The Marshal had disembarked from his boat and was coming up to us. I learned later that he always escorted the new arrivals in: he was a man for whom control was an absolute and realisable dream, and it manifested itself even to such absurd lengths.

"Line up!" he shouted even as he appeared. We stared at him dumbly and the Wardens moved in. It only took a few blows to have us in two uneven ranks facing him. He was not a tall man, the Marshal: a few inches below me, and I am not the tallest. He stood before us like a drill officer, with a Warden on either side.

"I am the Marshal," he said. "I command here. I am the Governor's right hand. This is the Island. You will spend the rest of your lives here," his voice rang out flatly. "In order for the rest of your lives to be any length you will need to understand the One Rule." I could hear the capital letters.

"The One Rule is this," he continued implacably. "You will always obey. If we tell you to work, you will work. If we tell you to sleep, you will sleep. If we tell you to bend over then you will get buggered. This is the only way it will be."

He left a long pause, staring at us, looking for troublemakers. His gaze passed over me and I felt chilled. There was murder in those eyes. I could not imagine that any inmate of the Island would ever look as bloody and brutal as the Marshal did then. Of course, that was before I met Gaki, perhaps the only man alive who surpassed the Marshal in sheer bloodymindedness.

"I will show you why this rule is obeyed here," the Marshal resumed. "It is a good reason, and a persuasive one." He held out a hand to one of his subordinates, who passed him a stick perhaps three feet long, sheathed in metal to the midpoint and wrapped in layered leather below that. The men either side of me tensed instinctively, but the Marshal would have to take a good few steps forward before he could strike anyone. I noticed that Shon had changed his pose: from a loose acceptance of his situation he was abruptly like a taut wire. The few inmates still present after loading up the boat were rigid. They knew what was coming.

The Marshal stared at us with his lack of expression sitting heavy on his face, and then pointed the lance in a lazy kind of way. I thought I saw the smallest movement at the corner of his mouth before it went off. There was a crack, although perhaps it was just a light so bright and sudden that it seemed like a sound. The man on Shon's other side was thrown backwards into the men behind, and when they got out of his way he was just a limp corpse on the floor. His face and chest were charred black. In the aftermath of that strike the air between us and the Marshal boiled and sizzled. That was the second time that random chance passed me by when there was a death to be doled out.

"I do not know who he was, nor do I care," the Marshal said. Nothing in his hard voice had changed with the man's death. "That was an example. You are less than nothing to me and my staff, and we will kill any one of you without a second thought. If you wish to remain alive you will do everything in your power to avoid angering us, and even that may not be sufficient. You have no rights. You are nothing more than vermin and the boat

21

brings more of you every month. I could have the lot of you killed here and now, and not want for workers." For a moment he paused and I thought that he was seriously considering it.

"You will be taken to your new homes. Answer to your names when they are called. Any man left when the roster is finished will join the example on the floor there, so if anybody is hoping to get it over with then they can stay behind. You may or may not get on with your cell mates. They may do my job for me and dispose of you themselves. If so, I will be delighted, because it will give me an excuse to kill them. The slightest excuse is all I ask. Remember that."

He turned from us, dismissing us utterly from his mind, and walked over towards Peter, who had watched everything that went on as expressionlessly as the Marshal himself. One of the Wardens began to call out names.

"Jof Chodan!"

A big, bearded man shambled forwards and was taken away. I never saw him again.

"Kelroy the Thief!" The names were obviously in no order. The roster had probably been made man by man as we embarked for the voyage. Thinking on that, I glanced at the boat to see one of the rivermen casting off the ropes and then jumping back on board. They fended the Island off with poles until the boat's nose was pointing halfway towards the direction we had come from. Then the deep cough of the engine started again, to underscore the dragging list of names, and the prison boat began its long homeward trek.

"Paulus Forestar!" the Warden called. Nobody answered. Presumably he must have been one of our casualties. I saw Peter nod and greet the Marshal, who was looking at him without pleasure. A moment later, a few words passed between them and the Marshal punched Peter in the stomach, hard enough for us to hear the impact and Peter's surprised grunt. He doubled over and fell to his knees, and the Marshal clouted him hard across the side of the head, sending him to the ground. He stared up,

22

angry and astonished. The Marshal was teaching him a similar lesson. He would brook no disobedience.

"Shon Roseblade!" the Warden shouted. Shon stepped forwards, with a brief glance for the dead man. He spared me a second too, with the faintest smile. A steadying hand and a few words. A chess game. How fragile are the foundation stones of our most important friendships? I first met Helman Cartier, one of the closest of my old city friends, because I was owed money. Now I had tenuous links to a Warden and a fellow inmate. In a place like the Island you took all the friends you could get.

"Julio!"

Peter was being led away by a Warden who was hopefully treating him more sympathetically than his fellows were treating us. I wished him luck, inwardly, and also prayed that he would feel the need for a game or two of chess in the near future.

"Stefan Advani!"

I almost missed my own name as I considered Peter's fate. Just as the Warden was about to start on the next I stepped forwards. He regarded me narrowly. "Advani?" he asked. I nodded. Speaking to Wardens was probably a deadly offence in this place. I was not taking any chances.

Another of the staff gripped my arm hard enough to cut the blood off and dragged me away towards the dark doorway to the interior. He was perhaps twice my bulk, and he obviously enjoyed throwing smaller men around. Looking back, I saw the prison boat manoeuvre out of the lake, onto the river that led to Shadrapar, the home that I assumed I would never see again.

I made no vows. I swore no vengeance. I had no divine destiny, but I had unfinished business and an enemy yet living. These are the things that draw the fabric of the world together.

I would see Shadrapar once more, before the end.

3

Conversations with a Madman

The corridors and walkways of the Island were gloomy and shadowed. My first impression was that it was a wonder anyone could see anything in that confusion of darkness and sheer shafts of light. The profusion of lamps and dark patches led to everyone's sight adjusting quickly. After a week or so I would have the "Island eyes" the same as everyone else. Even in the Underworld I never had such adaptable vision.

The bulky guard beside me could obviously find his way about without any problem at all. Further down the corridor I saw the first lamp. It was a pale hemisphere of something cloudy that seemed to illuminate nothing but itself and my prison greys. The guard beside me was almost invisible save for the pasty skin of his face. I realised that the Island must have a generator, and was a little impressed. Most buildings in Shadrapar no longer produced their own power, and we had oil and wood and waste for light and heat. The Island really was a little oasis of technical sophistication, albeit one forever on the point of breaking down.

We descended a flight of uneven stairs, the fourth of which was broken through. They all creaked dangerously under my captor's weight. "Have to get someone to fix that," the big man murmured as we reached the bottom. I had the distinct impression that he said the same thing every time he went down them. He stopped for a moment and squinted up at the lamp above us, and then lifted his free arm up to it. I saw a twist of reed in his hand, and with a certain deftness that belied his size he applied the end of the reed to the lamp and waited. In my experience, most artificial light is cold and done with something the books call "Bioluminance". The lights within the Island were different: after a slow count of twenty the end of the reed sparked into fire, and the Warden inhaled the smoke down its hollow length.

We were amongst the inmates here. As my eyes grew accustomed to the poor light I saw that, beyond the barred walls on each side, there were prisoners. Three had been watching us silently all this time. One was facing away. One lay on the interleaved canes of the floor and appeared to be dead. There were surprisingly few of them.

The Warden took another long suck at his reed and then pulled me onwards again. The smoke seemed to have eased his temper. His grip was less painful and after a while he looked at me and said, "Midds."

"Excuse me?" I whispered. I still hardly dared speak to the man.

"The name's Midds," he told me.

I nodded, wide-eyed.

"What's yours again? Ardvard or something?"

"Advani," I said, and he had to strain to hear me. "Stefan Advani," I elaborated, perhaps a little too loud.

"Posh name," he reflected. "You sound like an Academy boy."

I stared at him for some time and he shrugged, jogging my arm. "We get all types here. Lowlives, merchants, Academy boys, even a few high-ups. We had a councillor three year ago. Didn't last ten days." He stared at me almost good-humouredly and took another pull at the reed. "Academy boy. You must be crapping yourself."

I suspect my expression confirmed his words.

"You sing? Tell stories? Jokes? Ever learn to dance?"

I twisted in his grasp to look at him and asked him incredulously if he wanted me to dance.

"Just wondered. Things go better for everyone if you can do a trick. Keeps people happy," the man called Midds explained. It was my first introduction to the Island economy, in which I would be given a more formal grounding later. At the time I was too frightened to take it in.

We had come to a stretch of corridor that looked just like the last, but Midds nodded and said, "This is my patch, for now. They move us around every ten days. Stops us getting attached."

There were almost no prisoners in the cells here, and I began to worry whether this was a particularly fatal section of the Island. When I asked, Midds just laughed.

"They're all hard at work," he said. "Anyone that can, does. You're lucky. You get a day off."

Midds had reached a particular cell – one I was to know intimately soon enough – and was unlocking the door. The lock was large and simple, as was its key. Midds had only the one visible about him, and I realised that all of the doors on his beat must have the same lock. The real walls of the prison were made from the hostile jungle and the Marshal's brutal rules.

"Your new home," Midds told me. I looked in to see a room of a little over ten feet to a side. There were no bunks or any other furnishings, save for a wooden bucket in the centre of the floor whose use was obvious. On three walls, and above and below, there were other cells, with no barrier but the cane bars. If some incontinent prisoner on high were to miss the bucket, we'd all know it. And it did happen.

There was a man lying motionless there, along one wall. From the doorway the only thing I could discern about him was that he was wearing the same drab grey clothes as I was.

"What's wrong with him?" I wanted to know, and Midds told me that he was sick and couldn't work.

"I'm surprised that you haven't killed him then."

26

Midds shrugged his rounded shoulders. "Maybe some of the others would have. Me, I think he's really ill. My stretch, my choice. When I was a kid I was brought up by Compassionates. You know, all life is one life, and that stuff?"

"So what if the Marshal told you to kill me?" I asked him.

"Oh, I'd kill you right where you stood," Midds assured me. "Like I said, it was when I was a kid. The Marshal's a mad bastard but he does make this place run."

At that point someone called, "Hey Middsy! I'll tell him you called him that!" Above our heads, on the next floor up, there was another Warden looking down.

"You say anything and I'll kick your arse all the way to Shadrapar," Midds called back easily. It was just banter, I realised, but Midds was certainly big enough to do it. Inside that sagging, paunchy frame were a lot of big bones.

"You're not here for..." I began, once the other man had moved on, and then trailed to a halt awkwardly, wondering how to put it.

"Religious reasons?" Midds finished for me. "Hell no. Got a girl in trouble. It was here or the desert. Now, how about you get into your cell and save me having to do things my folks wouldn't have approved of?"

I stepped in reluctantly, and he closed and locked the door behind me. "There'll be food before dusk, and your cell mates will be coming back around then, too."

"Who are my cell mates?" I asked, and he screwed up his face for a moment, thinking.

"Can't remember. I'm sure they'll tell you," and then he was making his way down the corridor. The next lamp threw every detail of him into sharp relief and then he was gone.

I approached the still form of my current cell mate. He was lying on his side, facing the bars of the wall, and I could hear his scratchy breathing as I drew near. He sounded like some of the worst cases in the Underworld, the people who had come down to die. He was older than I expected, and small of build. I leant against the wall to get a view of his face, and saw it lined and square-chinned. His hair was grey and had been fashionably cut once. Strangely, I felt that I knew him from somewhere. He was still as a stone, and only his faint, wheezing breath told me that he was alive.

"He has the fever," a voice told me. "It's common enough that they call it Island Fever. About one in five die from it. He will be unlucky."

I turned slowly, because the voice sounded as though the speaker was standing right at my shoulder. Instead, I saw a man within the latticed shadows of the next cell. I cast my mind back, and it seems that even then I saw something unusual about him, all the trouble that he had caused and would cause. Everyone else I spoke to told me they felt just the same. He had an aura about him that gave some part of your mind a window onto his horrible, dark soul. This was Gaki. Whilst I have served my time with monsters, killers, madmen, even the Macathars of the desert, I will say without reservation that Gaki was the worst of them all. He scared parts of me I did not even know existed.

"He caught it when he came in, three months ago," he continued, "And then he seemed to recover, but he was worked too hard and treated too badly. He relapsed. Now he'll die." Gaki had a quiet, dry voice that could always be heard no matter how much noise was being made. It was a pleasant voice, fit for a Master of the Academy.

"Who are you?" I asked, because, however much I sensed the danger in him, there was a wall between us.

"People call me Gaki," he acknowledged. "It's not much of a name, but it'll do."

"Are you ill as well?"

He laughed lightly. "Not in the way you mean."

"But you're not put to work?"

"I do not choose to work," he said simply and, although I tried to put another question to him on the subject, somehow I could not phrase the words. He could always do that. When

28

Gaki chose to close a subject, nobody could force it open again. He was one of the best examples of the principle that power is at its greatest when not actually being used.

"My name is Stefan Advani," I told him, and then, because the silence following it was awkward, I added needlessly, "I'm new here." Gaki nodded politely.

"You sound like an educated man, Stefan Advani," he observed. "I am always fond of intelligent conversation." The innocuous words at last gave me a concrete reason to pin my misgivings on. I had been in this situation before. An education is a strange thing. It can save you when nothing else can, but it can tie you to some very undesirable characters. Gaki was not the first human horror to pick my brains for idle amusement. It might be noted that he was more human, and also more horrible, than some.

He stepped forward into a strip of light and I saw that he was no taller than I, and little broader across the shoulders. He was naked from the waist up and his body was lean and well-muscled, the frame of a fit man. He had a sharp face with a pointed chin, and very calm eyes. Those eyes never became excited, even in the heat of his worst savageries. They were impartial, objective observers to his violent life. His head was shaved like those of the Wardens – a sanitary measure, by the way. Lice and other parasites would soon be my constant companions. The prisoners were not allowed razors, for obvious reasons, but Gaki's head was always closely shaved. Whether his stubble never grew out, or whether he just cut it down when nobody was watching, is a mystery to me.

"I don't suppose you know Sandor's *Lying in State*, by any chance?" he asked.

As it happened, I did. It was no great coincidence. Sandor is one of the wittiest of the modern writers, and his treatise on corruption in the Shadrapar body politic is a masterpiece, for all that it probably cost him his life. Every Academy student knows at least part of it, and social science is one of my fortes. So it

29

came to pass that I spent the best part of a morning discussing literature and philosophy with a convicted murderer. I cannot say whether he knew the calming effect it would have on me, or whether the whole exercise was only for his own amusement. It did me a power of good, though. It pains me to be indebted to Gaki for anything, after all that he did later, but I owe him that small gratitude.

We were interrupted eventually by the sick man, who had awoken and was calling out, "Water..." in a voice like dry leaves. I looked around, but Gaki was shaking his head.

"They bring food and water at dawn and dusk," he said. "If you work, you get something at midday. If not: nothing."

"He's ill, though. He needs water, food. He needs help," I said.

"He's on the long road to death, and needs no more than a push," Gaki quoted. I recognised the words but could not place them.

"Can't I do anything?" I asked.

"Tell him a story. Recite a poem," Gaki suggested. "If you want, you could save some of your food and water for him, but then you'll get weak, and what will you do when you get the fever?"

I went over to the sick man and stared down at him helplessly. He was looking up, but his eyes focused on nothing I could see. "Water..." he said again, but there was none to be had. Even fallen in upon itself, his face retained a classical dignity and I knew I recognised him. Like Gaki's quote, I could not place him.

I tried to talk to him, but he could not seem to hear me, and his replies were just mumbles. He lapsed back into something like sleep soon after, although he was never completely still, twitching and gasping and crying out. Gaki had withdrawn into the depths of his cell, and I tried to strike up a conversation with him but never quite managed. Just by willing it, he had ended the discussion.

I hoped Shon Roseblade was having a better time of it than I was. I must have sat in silence for an hour, trying to count my blessings, before Gaki spoke again. "I knew him, you know," he said.

"This man? Who is he?" I asked, thinking he meant my cell mate.

"Sandor," Gaki said quietly. There was an extra quality in his voice as it lifted from the shadows. "Sandor the writer and philosopher. I knew him."

Sandor had died before I started at the Academy, and for a moment I was brim-full of questions about the great man. What was he like? Was he as witty in real life as in his writings? Who was the lover he wrote poems for? How did he die?

In his unique way, Gaki had conveyed his meaning to me without ever saying it, and what I actually said was, "You killed him."

"I knew him," Gaki repeated, and I wondered whether it had been a random act of violence or a hired assassination, and came down on the side of the latter. Sandor's book had made a lot of enemies in high places.

There was a long silence in which I could not speak because I knew that Gaki had not finished. "I knew him," he eventually said again, but slower, and tinged with something that would be sadness in other men. I think it was the only thing that he ever regretted. There has always been a lot of speculation about the work that Sandor was partway through when he died. It is quite lost, although purported fragments surface every so often, and I saw a whole page of it in the Underworld. I sometimes try to picture the nights that Sandor and Gaki spent together, the great writer elaborating on his new project, his murderer-to-be listening. Perhaps it was Sandor, posthumously, that reworked Gaki from a normal killer into the creature I knew.

At the Academy we were taught that life is made of patterns that repeat themselves, that certain numbers are significant for certain people. The number four was surely my blessing and curse. Four deaths I narrowly missed, following my arrest (two behind me, at this point in the narrative, and two yet to come).

31

Four of us banded together in Shadrapar to challenge the way the world thought. Three other like-minded desperate cases in the Underworld to join me in my time of need. Finally this official quartet: the full complement of a cell in the Island. The sick man I had met already. The other two appeared towards dusk as the working day ended.

The first I knew of my cell mates was Midds. He came down his section and opened all the doors. Had I been tempted to make a break for it, there were Wardens at either end of the corridor, and besides, there would be nowhere to go. Even later, when I learned that the swamp was not entirely deadly to human life, I never made the attempt. Almost nobody did. It really would have been an all-or-nothing bid. The Marshal, who had killed just to set an example, would have no mercy on a failed escapee.

All of a sudden there were two men coming in through the door, one large, one small. I shuffled back from them, and they both stared at me. Behind them, Midds passed back down the corridor, locking it all up again.

The large man was bigger in all dimensions than I, and his bare arms were knotty with muscles. He carried with him a sharp, chemical smell that I would soon recognise as the smell of the vats. He bore down on me until he was almost nose to nose, if he looked down and I craned my neck back. His face was square, literally, with a flat chin rising straight to meet lumpy, angular temples. His eyes were lost somewhere within the creases of their sockets.

"New boy," he pronounced. I could tell that something unpleasant was about to happen to me and tried to summon my inner energies to resist it.

"What're you in for?" the large man demanded.

"My name is Stefan Advani, and I was convicted of agitation, subversion and attempting to evade the course of justice," I said promptly. When under pressure I had two distinct faults, before the Island cured me of them. Firstly, my voice became

32

high and shrill and ostentatiously posh. Secondly, I used to blurt the truth out before I could think of a good fabrication. I think that if I had told him I was a murderer he might have thought twice before hitting me. Instead, he hit me. It was so quick and businesslike that I had no chance to do anything with all the inner energies I had been summoning. I just had time to turn my head away slightly so that his rock-hard fist slammed across my cheek rather than into my nose. I blacked out for a fraction of a second and was lying painfully on the barred floor when I awoke.

"Now you know what's what," he told me in some satisfaction. "I'm in charge here. Don't you forget."

I caught sight of Gaki. He had watched everything quite calmly; he had no more interest in me than in my ailing cell mate.

The large man was named Onager. Perhaps he was not an evil man by nature. He had been taken from a rough life on the streets of Shadrapar to this place, and the Marshal had taught him that violence breeds control, and that control was a good thing. He was only aping his keepers, and a single blow from Onager was better than being killed by the Marshal. The other man was Lucian Corek, and he was a good four inches shorter than me, and slightly hunched. After I had picked myself up, he came over to me. He had a broken nose, I noticed, and I recognised Onager's calling card.

Lucian was a strange little man, but friendly, which was a rare commodity on the Island. Whilst Onager lapsed into sullen silence once he had made his point, Lucian talked. His talk was one of the most peculiar things about him: there was a vast amount of it that seemed to have no real purpose or function, and none of it was memorable. At the end of a conversation with Lucian I could remember in general what subjects he had covered, but not one of his actual words would stay with me. I will try and simulate his mode of speech for you, but I will only be writing things that sound like Lucian. The actual words were gone forever the moment they fled his lips.

33

He told me almost at once that he was here for forgery and bad debts. The status of bad debts in Shadrapar, where many people wore them like medals, is something I will talk of in the proper place. As for the other, he had forged official documents, and I assume that he had not been terribly good at it. He claimed to be a good hand with a bent printing press and, had I met him in the street, I could no doubt have made use of him. In the Island he provided another service. As long as he rattled on, the background awfulness of the place did not weigh so heavily on me. When he stopped, the dread quiet was almost unbearable.

"Tell me about him," I asked, when I could get a word in, indicating the sick man. Here is my best attempt at Lucian's reply.

"That poor fellow he's not at all well, you know, he was never strong, I told them they shouldn't make him do a full shift his second time round with it you see hasn't even been here long, some people are just so unlucky but then that's the way the world turns and you never know, so it's as well to be prepared as I'm sure he'd say if only he was lucid, mind you he wasn't too lucid before, came in not so long ago, two months maybe three, you lose track of time in a place like this you see, and the days are mostly one the same as the next, and that one the same as the next, although he hasn't seen so many as I have what with being here only a few months, and already with the Island Fever twice, once when he first came like everyone gets and..." But you get the idea. And then he was going over to reassure the ailing man that everything was going to be fine, only at much greater length. He called the fever victim 'Valentin'.

"Valentin?" I queried, and the name rang the same bells that the man's face had. Lucian's lengthy opinion was that the man was named something like Valentin Mildew.

"Valentin Miljus," I said flatly, and Lucian thought for a blessedly silent moment and then confirmed that it was very probably something quite like that, very likely, yes indeed.

I went over to look at the sick man again and recognised him at last as Valentin Miljus. Not a friend, or even anyone I had met, but a face I knew. A large, leaden hand clamped across my shoulder, and Onager craned past, staring.

"You know him?" the big man asked.

"Know of him," I admitted. I guessed that Valentin Miljus had kept himself to himself, even in his hale and hearty days. "He was the Lord Financier, last I heard," I noted.

I heard Onager's whistle of surprise and, because I had knowledge to impart, I forgot that he had knocked me down, and even forgot that we were all prisoners. I am always happiest when I can tell people things that they do not know. Perhaps that is why I am writing this.

"He was very high up in the Lord President's staff," I explained. "I saw him a few times at the Academy. He was a good speaker. Then he just dropped out of sight. Someone said that he'd been taken ill and had gone to his house in the suburbs to recover. Who dreamt that he had been dragged off here? I wonder what happened."

It was around then that Midds turned up with the food. My first meal in the Island and there were a few unpleasant surprises awaiting me. Midds shoved four small wooden bowls and a jug through the largest gap between the bars and then walked on, pushing a makeshift trolley. Lucian darted over to take charge of them and handed one each to Onager and myself. I looked down and saw that it was part-full of some sort of stew in which unidentified things floated. There were strands of plant, and segments of something that must have been water reed. There were chunks of something white as well that fell into flakes when I prodded them. It looked like nothing I had ever seen before.

"Fish," Onager said, and watched my horrified reaction.

"I'm supposed to eat a dead animal?" I demanded. In Shadrapar we ate what we grew in the ground. Raising animals for food was a disgusting process abandoned in ancient times. The idea of consuming the flesh of another creature was vile and

35

turned my stomach. Worse, the whole concoction was warm, despite the heat all around us. Back home we would not dream of eating anything warmer than room temperature, and the rich had their food and drink chilled.

Onager had my fish, and also Valentin's entire meal, since Valentin was in no condition to eat. Lucian assured me that my resolve against eating meat would last two days. He said that on the first day I would refuse it, on the second I would eat, but be unable to keep it down, and on the third I would be an omnivore like everybody else.

I was just getting Valentin to take some water when Lucian explained to me where the food came from. To paraphrase, the various pumps that, amongst other tasks, kept the Island afloat, took in a lot of lake water. The lake water wasn't exactly sparkling clear, and so there were sieves, which we inmates had to take out and clear. Everything that ended up in a sieve would end up in the pot, and from there to our bowls. Lucian suggested that the system had the virtue of variety.

"Everything," I asked him weakly, "that goes into the sieves?"

His enthusiastic list included fish, frogs, snails, voles, insects, waterweed. Apparently there was a great deal of nature you could eat if you boiled it long enough.

The next morning I would wolf down everything they put in front of me, and throw some of it up as Lucian predicted. After that I would adjust.

4

Father Sulplice and His Machines

"You probably have no idea what this is," the old man said. He had a tired, sad voice and it went with the rest of him. His hair was white and sparse and even his beard was mostly gone, although he still had a lopsided moustache. He was halfway up a ladder propped against a huge, silent machine.

"It's a pump," I told him, which made his day.

"You understand the machinery?" he asked, and I wondered what answer would serve me best.

"Ye-es," I tried. "A little. I'm not fond of machines, actually." An understatement. "Does this keep the Island afloat?"

Some of his joy left him, and Father Sulplice was not a vessel that could hold much joy at any time. "You might notice," he said, "that you can hear my voice. If this was working then you wouldn't be able to do that. If one of the *big* pumps *stopped* working you'd know about it because the floor would be tilting and your feet would be getting wet."

"But it is a pump," I pressed, holding on to my one victory. "What does it pump?"

"Come up here and have a look," said Father Sulplice.

We were in the machine room, and there was plenty of noise to go around even if one pump had stopped. There were about a dozen huge engines standing about, and slightly over half of

37

them were thumping away at different speeds. No two were alike and all of them showed signs of frequent makeshift repair. The floor was swarming with convicts serving out their time. They lugged great tanks across the floor and connected them to machines. They hauled the empty tanks away again when the machines were done with them. A few took the broken machines apart and tried to work out why they would not go. Men unshipped the infamous sieves and took them away to the cooking vats in another room. Others took smaller sieves from the smaller pumps and took them to drying racks, and others still took the dried contents and decanted them into sacks. Everyone toiled on with a driven intensity you would never find with volunteers. There were at least seven Wardens in attendance, and they had clubs and whips which they used with a free hand, singling out slackers and anyone they personally disliked. It had been an eventful morning. I had already seen one man beaten to unconsciousness, and another lose three fingers to a machine that suddenly started off when he was trying to unclog it. A third man had been stung by something poisonous that had come in with the lakewater. I have no idea whether any of the three survived.

I had been assigned first to a team that was hauling the filled sacks to a storeroom. It was heavy work, and the sacks reeked sharply of various chemicals. The function of everything I saw bewildered me. Nothing like this existed in Shadrapar. After a morning's worth of mindlessly dragging the sacks twenty yards down a corridor, one of the Wardens had grabbed me by the shoulder and asked me my name. On learning it he had dragged me off far more easily than I had dragged the sacks. I was sure for a moment that I was going to be executed.

Instead I was shown to the little old man, Father Sulplice, and told to do what I could to help him. It was a monstrous relief, but I had no idea what was going on until I met Peter again and was given a few more pieces of the puzzle.

Father Sulplice was the oldest inhabitant of the Island by

some years, a bent, grandfatherly man whose head came to the level of my shoulders. One instinctively pictured him as a cheery toymaker in some unlikely romance. I assumed that he was a poisoner or a molester of small children. In conversation even these outside chances fell away, and I was left wondering what on earth he had done to land him here.

Father Sulplice also occupied an ambiguous position in the Island's hierarchy. On the one hand he was a prisoner, and therefore had no rights and was scum like the rest of us. On the other he was a very skilled artificer, certainly the most skilled I ever met. He was a magician with any kind of mechanism and the Island literally rested on machines. Father Sulplice was the most valued of a small coterie of prisoners whom even the Wardens respected.

I joined him up the ladder and handed him tools from a wicker basket when he asked for them. I got two out of three right first time, which kept him happy. In between tinkering and swearing (in an old-fashioned and genteel way) at the pump, he explained a little more of the Island economy.

"You see, I know machines, and that means that when something important breaks, they call for Father Sulplice. It doesn't matter whether it's something like this, that nobody needs right now, or whether it's one of the great pumps, or even the Governor's mirror. They come to me first. I get results. That means I get taken care of. Even the Marshal doesn't want to see me worked to death. Who would fix his little boat then? Now I'm guessing you're a man of some education."

I replied that I was.

"Well then maybe someone will find some use for you. To survive here, son, you have to find somebody who cares whether you live or die. That's the touchstone, you see. Just one Warden will do. That way, the others know that they'll at least have a question to answer if they club you to death. I'm not saying it's foolproof. Nothing works every time as every artificer'll tell you. It's all you've got, though. Feel free to make friends amongst the

39

other inmates, but they won't be able to help you if one of the Wardens puts the boot in, is all I'm saying."

I thought about Peter Drachmar and prayed that he remembered me, little knowing that my very presence at Father Sulpice's side was proof of his continued goodwill.

"You take a look at this, son," the old man said, and handed down a crooked little piece of metal. "Now you run down to the store and get me something that looks like that, but straight. If you can't get a match, bring me something near and I'll just work on it. You think you can do that?"

I said that it was probably within my capabilities and shimmied down the ladder. I had to go back up to ask him where the storeroom was, which further lessened his opinion of me, but then I was off across the machine room floor. The storeroom turned out to be a wooden crate filled with assorted pieces of metal, none of which looked much like Father Sulpice's example. The crate was at the back of a heap of sacks, and prisoners were constantly in and out of the room, depositing more. So it was that whilst I tried to find a match, someone tapped me on the shoulder. I spun around, terrified that a guard would proceed to beat me into oblivion, but instead it was a face I knew: Shon Roseblade, whom I had met the day before as we disembarked.

"Stefan." He sounded genuinely surprised I had survived that long.

"Haven't killed me yet," I confirmed. I saw a new bruise on his face, and he saw Onager's work on mine. Shon had got the better of his engagement and was now top man in his cell, at least for the moment.

"I'll find you again," he said. "There's a break to eat soon." I grabbed a piece of metal at random and ran it over to Father Sulpice.

The old man seemed satisfied with it. Still balanced on the ladder he took out a knife and, with a few easy movements, whittled the part into shape. When I expressed surprise, he beckoned me up the ladder again.

"Take a look, son," he invited. The knife had a dull metal handle but its blade was almost transparent.

"It's a diamond," Father Sulplice explained. "Darned thing cuts anything to size. This is the only one on the whole of the Island, and they trust me enough to give it to me. Says a lot, doesn't it."

"I wonder that the other prisoners let you keep it," I ventured.

I thought the old man would elbow me off the ladder. "Now you're new here so I'll let that go by, but let me learn you a few rules that'll help you stay healthy. One is that nobody touches me, because if the big pumps seize up without me to fix'em then everyone goes down with the ship. Secondly, this isn't some place where the prisoners go against the Wardens. The Wardens are too strong and they kill far too easily. In this place, if someone's got a Warden as a friend you stick right close to'em. Last off, take a look at the knife."

He showed me the handle of the knife. There was a circle of some lighter metal there, sunk into the butt.

"All the Wardens' stuff that could get into the wrong hands has one of these sunk into it. Knives, clubs, anything. They've got two machines that detect these, and if something goes missing then they may well kill everyone in the cell where they detect it. I know. I keep those detectors working. It's in my interests to preserve the status quo, son. I'm an old man and I don't want any riots or revolutions to trouble me and mine. Be warned, the Marshal'd be happy to kill every last man on the Island, and by 'happy' I don't just mean he'd do it. He'd enjoy it."

Eventually I asked him the question that had been nagging at me all day: what was the work that went on here, and what was it in aid of. The answer surprised me.

"This here swamp in which we're sat is a mine," Father Sulplice said. "It may just look like muck and water to you, son, but it's packed with minerals, different ones at different points all over the place. They send boats out that fill their tanks with water, then trek the tanks back here, where we distil the minerals from'em. Works a treat most of the time. This pump here is part of that process. The minerals we ship back home and they get used for all sorts. Weapons, medicines, science, cosmetics, even as flavourings for food. Who back home'd think they relied on their prison for so many things, eh?"

I would have made some socially relevant comment, but right then a quartet of prisoners heaved a huge tank across the machine room floor, and one bellowed up at the old man, "The tank's broke. Needs fixing. Marshal says to do it first."

I could see Father Sulplice's wrinkled face developing new lines as he frowned. "How can a tank be broken?" he demanded. "What's wrong with it?"

"Blocked," the other replied, and I could see Father Sulplice working up to some scathing comment when the source of the blockage made itself apparent.

It was a snake, and it forced its way from the broad opening of the tank all in a rush, faster than I would have believed. The four prisoners holding the tank dropped it really fast and made a run for it, but the snake struck one of them, sinking its fangs into his leg, and he went down screaming. The others were trying to get out of its way as it reared up. It was thirty foot long and must have filled the tank almost completely, green and black in irregular mottlings. Very little that lived out in the swamp looked pleasant.

Its head was level with mine as it swung around, and I was up the ladder. I saw that the Wardens were standing idly back, waiting to see what it would do. If it killed a few of us and then made its getaway they would probably have been happy. Unfortunately the machine room had a solid floor, unlike most of the Island. There was nowhere the snake could go save past us.

It made a determined push in one direction, and the prisoners scattered. I saw Lucian, a small man of no athletic prowess, pelt across the room with a speed that should have won medals. I chose that point to get off the ladder to prepare for my own getaway.

It was a mistake. The serpent turned its head sharply even as my feet hit the ground, and I saw that, like the river monster, it had no eyes, though it knew I was there. I heard Father Sulplice whisper, "Bugger off, son. I don't want that thing coming anywhere near me."

Its jaws were directed straight at me, and when I took the smallest step to one side it followed me and swayed closer. I tried to muster my inner energies, but was too scared to hold them together, and besides, I had no idea whether they would work against a snake. The jaws opened slightly and I saw two fangs as long as my fingers, coloured a dirty yellow. I resolved to make a break for it.

That very instant, before I could make a fatal mistake, the snake's head whipped away from me as Shon charged into the room. Charged is the wrong word, really. He was swinging in wide circles, one of the sacks held in both outstretched arms. His feet moved in a complex pattern which turned him about on the spot faster and faster until he gave out a great cry and let the heavy sack fly away from him. It struck the serpent on the nose and exploded in a cloud of red powder and a sharply acrid smell.

The snake recoiled, literally, twisting and writhing in knots on the floor as it tried to scrape the foul chemicals away. Shon was beckoning frantically, and I bolted for him. I felt it through the floor as the snake suddenly stopped twisting and snapped up again, and I knew it was focused on me. I recall quite clearly expecting those fangs to sink deep into my back and jerk me high in the air. Terrified by the thought I cannoned into Shon and we both went down. The snake loomed high over us.

There were three light steps on the wood of the floor, and a shape launched through the air to cling to the serpent's neck. I saw a blade flash once and the head of the creature was cut cleanly off, the body flinging itself in great agonised loops across the room. My unexpected saviour landed awkwardly, but was quickly on his feet, dusting red powder from his knees. It was Peter Drachmar, of course.

"Bloody hell," Shon muttered, and pushed me off him. He and I struggled to our feet even as the other Wardens moved in.

One of them said, "You want to watch yourself. The Marshal doesn't like heroics. He'd rather twenty of them died than one of us."

Peter shrugged.

"You want to deal with him?" the Warden enquired, pointing at Shon with his club.

Peter looked at him blankly.

"You want to beat him?" the Warden pressed. "He needs beating. That's a whole sack of produce he's wasted with that stunt. He's yours if you want him."

Peter stared at the man with the same blank expression, as though dazed. Finally he said, "Don't be stupid."

The other Warden gaped at him. "What?"

"Don't be stupid," Peter told him again.

"Well if you won't do it, I will," the Warden promised.

"No you won't," Peter said quietly, so that I could hardly hear him. The Warden looked murderous, but something in Peter's face obviously warned him off, because he walked away, trying to make it look as though nothing had happened. Peter and Shon regarded each other coolly, but Shon nodded eventually, conceding the point. At the last, Peter shot me the smallest grin and went on his way.

I knew then that either Peter or Shon had recognised the other, but they were too busy sizing each other up for me to work out who knew who.

The man who had been bitten was quite dead. The eyeless serpents were not uncommon in the swamps and their bite was invariably fatal.

The rest of the working day passed uneventfully. When I returned to the cell, I discovered that Valentin Miljus, former Lord Financier, was awake.

He stared at us and at his surroundings in a raw, frightened way, a damaged man. I could see that he was burning up with the fever, and the wheeze in his voice could be heard across the corridor. Gaki was hunched like a vulture at the latticed wall of his cell, and I think it was his presence that had sent Miljus into such a fear-ridden state. Lucian and Onager both kept away from him; a dying madman was capable of anything. I had the impression that this kind of thing had happened before, and that the results had been bloody. The final stages of Island Fever could be spectacular, enough that my cell mates were content to sit right up against Gaki's adjoining wall just to stay away from the feverish man.

Being unversed in the ways of the Island, I went to him; a risk I would not take today. Valentin Miljus had no thoughts of violence, though. He needed to talk. He had a lot to get off his chest. He had no idea who I was and would not have recognised his own mother, but there was a story coiled inside him like the snake had been within the tank, and I came close enough to trigger the strike.

"Harweg came to me," he said, without any introduction, "And he told me they were coming for me and that I had to prepare." It was some time before I intuited that this Harweg must be our Lord President. "He told me just what was going to happen to me. I didn't know why. I didn't understand."

A pause, with his eyes fixed on some point in the cell where his memories were invisibly inscribed.

"The Authority met a week before and everything had been slightly out of line," he continued. "When I made my reports, nobody would meet my gaze. Everyone said how well I'd done but their voices were hollow. Only the Prelate and the Lord Justiciar were silent. When I look back I can see someone with them, who was not there when we met. I think it must be their guilt. I think they must be responsible. I didn't realise at the time. How can everything be so much clearer when I think back. Why was I blind then when I can see so clearly now?"

There was another pause and I was tempted to answer, but I had no answers and he surely would not have heard.

"They'll have forgotten about me now. That's the reason for this place. People who come here are forgotten instantly. They pass from the mind of the city. This is the oubliette, the cage of souls. The whole city knew my name once."

Another blank pause. Aside from the movement of his lips, no part of his face had any life or motion in it. He may not even have blinked. He had become cadaverous through his sickness. Even in repose he looked as though he was screaming inside.

"I talked with Alarisse, in that week," he continued. "We were repairing all the wounds that had been made between us. I met with Misa. She is going to the Academy. She had not spoken to me for half a year before. My family was coming together just as everything else was fraying apart. My family was speaking to me and everyone in the Authority was suddenly strange. They all had to think about their answers when I questioned them. The Prelate and the Lord Justiciar. I had never done anything to them. I had never curbed their spending or torn open their accounts. I can think of no reason that they should have sent me here. All I did was support Harweg."

He stopped again, and something more lucid passed behind his eyes. One bony hand gripped my wrist hard enough to leave white marks. His next words were heavy with destiny.

"It's all falling apart," he said through gritted teeth. "The Prelate and the Lord Master and the Justiciar and Harweg, and I was caught in the middle. I was too caught up in my figures. I didn't notice what was going on. I was only doing my job, and suddenly that was the wrong thing to do.

"Harweg came to me," he told me again. "He said that soldiers were coming to take me to the Island and I didn't believe him. I thought he had come to warn me, so that we could get together and turn things around, but he was there to accuse me. They had met, the Authority had met without me and decided I was guilty of something. I only did my job. I only did what they told me to do. I thought Harweg would help me. I was always a friend of his. Instead he talked to me whilst the soldiers came. I could have run then, but I never thought of it. I was just thinking about how we could make a victory out of a defeat, just like we had always done. Then the door opened and two Angels were standing there, and they took me away from my home, and then it was on the boat and away without ever being able to defend myself. People must have missed me, but only until I arrived here. Now they've forgotten. I am nothing but a lost dream of Shadrapar."

The last long pause came here. It stretched for some time, but it was obvious that he had something more to say. Onager and Lucian were staring at me, and I wondered how much they had heard. In the end, Lucian came over, having decided that Miljus was no danger to him. He said quietly that he had never known that Miljus was a minister of state, and who'd have thought it. He also said that some fever victims grew worse than this and still recovered, but even Lucian's rambling and eternally optimistic delivery lacked conviction on that point. Lucian, who routinely expected to be shipped off home on each boat that came in, had given Valentin Miljus up for lost.

"I spoke to my daughter," the failing man said at last. "But I couldn't think of anything important to say to her. I didn't have any advice. We just made idle conversation. We never spoke of our disagreements, or of her mother, or any of the important things that I wanted to talk to her about. Now it's too late, and she doesn't remember her daddy, and she'll go through life with a gap in her life and always wonder who it used to be."

That was the last will and testament of Valentin Miljus, such as it was. He lapsed back into silence, and there was no more from him that night, or ever. The idea that the inmates of the Island are forgotten by their former friends and foes in the city is a common one amongst prisoners and Wardens alike. After all, nobody returns from the Island. Sending an enemy to the Island was as good as killing him. Better, because the Island could deal out years of suffering. Miljus, however, spoke of such blanket forgetfulness as though it was a literal, physical thing, and although he was deranged and dying, his words cut far too close to my heart. Sitting in that cell with him as he wheezed his last hours away, I could feel my presence eroding, the desert wind smoothing over all the footprints I had ever made.

5

Symptoms of the Fever Victim

What happened next, of course, was that I came down with the same fever that had just finished off Miljus, and of the next week or more on the Island I can tell you very little. I took scant heed of my surroundings and had nothing intelligent to say. At the beginning and at the close of my invalidity I was hot and cold all over, shivering, coughing, cramped in my lungs and my bowels. In the middle I was oblivious to my pains as I was to the rest of the world. From one perspective it might be called the most peaceful time I ever spent at the Island.

Perhaps I should go straight to the moment when I finally recognised a human face again, although since that face was Lucian's it hardly seems worth it. Instead, I will try to give an account of the things that I saw around me in the throes of the fever. My mind has imbued them with a spurious significance, and this is my account.

I was playing chess. At the beginning I was back in the prison boat, facing across from Peter Drachmar, and everything was as I remembered it. I recall that the throb of the engine changed as we played, so that it became more and more like a heartbeat. Peter noticed nothing but I could see the metal walls of the room suddenly flushed rust-red with blood. They sucked in and bulged out with the rhythm of the cardiac engine, and I knew that if the boat felt us within it, it would vomit us out into the toxic river.

I faded out from this scene of game-playing many times, but always returned to it across the days of my fever. As the illness grew more intense, the room in which we sat changed in bizarre ways. The walls receded, leaving us stranded at the tiny table in a vast and vaulted hall, baroque with carvings, all of it worked from the rusted, rivet-pocked metal. The worse my condition became, the larger and more byzantine the room, until I was surrounded by an artificial forest, insanely detailed and intricate, where the gaps between figures opened onto further halls that were darker and more detailed still. Of all the things that I saw in my delirium, that cathedral-like place was not stolen from any memory of mine, and I cannot tell from where I might have drawn it.

My opponent changed too. From Peter, the shadows drew other faces. The fever tried on the shapes of fellow prisoners, but Lucian, Onager, even Shon were not credible behind a chessboard. Instead the sickness delved deep into my mind to find others, and those others brought their contexts with them. In my weakened state I was swept along by a tide of memories run mad. I played chess across from Jon de Baron, my old Academy friend, and then I was running through the streets of Shadrapar trying to save him, even as the crowd roared and the Angels loaded their weapons. Poor Jon: wit, socialite and wastrel who never deserved what happened to him. Then I was running, not towards, but away. The white sand of the desert was beneath my heels and I could feel the vast, deceptive footfalls of the Macathar as it bore down on me. Its shadow blotted out the sun as its house-sized body loomed above me.

Then the chessboard was back, and the fever tried to show me the face of my beloved Rosanna, but it was too painful and I refused to play until she was taken away. The fever took me away instead, back to the city, in the shadow of the Weapon, desperate to tell her something but never able to find her. There were others, some close, some that I had barely known, all sitting in sequence across that chessboard from me. Even the Lord President, Harweg, although I would barely recognise the man in waking hours. The game unfolded, and I felt that it was getting away from me. The pieces seemed to have their own agendas. I was losing control of the game.

I began to play against people I had known in the Underworld, my ragged compatriots in hiding. There were friends at first, the cartographer, the bibliophile, even the creature known as Faith, but the dreams took me inevitably to the Transforming Man, and again I tried to turn away. This must have been close to the height of my fever. He hunched across and around the chessboard as horribly as he had ever held court back beneath the city.

Some time later, I was trying to play against Gaki and losing horribly, and I began to realise that if I lost the game then I would never see the sun again, never even see the Island's walls. I tried to understand what was happening on the board, and the silent, cold-eyed Gaki moved his pieces like clockwork. In time he was gone within the darkness of a cowled cloak, as the game reached its most desperate point. I avoided that hooded visage for fear that I should catch sight of it and find it to be Valentin Miljus, personifying death by fever. I would rather have seen a naked skull than his genteel, wasted features.

I must have begun to pull out of the fever at that point, because the game turned around and I started to win for a change. The shadow of death retreated from my opponent, who tried on other faces from my past, each less painful than the last. At the end I recall playing against Peter again in the prison boat cabin, just as we had in real life. In the dream, though, I beat him. I never did in waking games. After that it was only a brief step to recovery.

I have Lucian to thank for keeping me alive, or so he told me. He made sure that I ate and drank when I was able, and he probably talked to me as well, although thankfully I heard none of it. All I know is that one day the game was gone, and I was awake in the cell, surrounded by fading pieces of my past.

The next day, on the basis that I was well enough to recognise my own name, I was set to work. I tried to take things as easily as I could, terrified of the kind of fatal relapse that had claimed Valentin Miljus. In going slowly I was nearly whipped for slacking, which would have finished me off. Father Sulplice was out of the prison, apparently, mending a boat that had become stranded. It was the first time I realised that the prisoners were let out of the cage. Even though I had been told of the chemical harvesting expeditions, I had not thought that we, the inmates, would be the harvesters. Wardens accompanied each boat with orders to kill at the first sign of a mutiny but, as always, where was there to go? The swamp had a hundred ways of killing a lone man, and very few of feeding and sheltering him. Besides, there were worse things than beasts out there. I still recalled the mysterious web-children and wondered. I would know soon enough.

I spent most of the day cleaning floors. I learned that chemical spills do not come out of wood, and neither does blood unless you reach it very quickly. There followed a meagre supper of marsh weed and pond insects, after which a Warden turned up at our cell and shouted out, "Advani!"

I went through the usual palaver about being executed on the spot, and then noticed that the caller was Peter. He let me out, and I was marched off away from my fellows as though death awaited. Instead, though, our path led gradually upwards, through a maze of hanging, latticed corridors, until something unfamiliar opened before me. It was the sky.

I think I might have fallen to my knees. Perhaps I wept. I saw the sky for the first time in what seemed like forever, and it was sunset, the clouds all bruised purples and fierce reds. It was the most beautiful thing I ever saw. I actually dashed outside to find myself on that selfsame square that the boat had docked at. Peter stepped out after me and waited for me to calm down.

The first part of our conversation was a welter of thanks from me: for saving me from the snake, for not having Shon beaten, for placing me with Father Sulpice and especially, over and over, for letting me see the sky again. When all that had dragged out, I was left feeling slightly embarrassed. "So," I said at last. "How about you?"

He shrugged, uncharacteristically quiet, or perhaps I had monopolised all the talk there was to be had. He stepped over and stared out across the bloody water of the lake.

"Is it how you expected?" I pressed. "Are you regretting choosing to work here?"

He looked back at me and there was something in his eyes that alarmed me.

"You didn't choose it," I decided. "You had to come here. Like Midds. Why?"

"Just a love of adventure," he said. It rang hollow. "This is the great frontier, isn't it? Fortunes and reputations for the taking. They say the same thing about the deserts, don't they? Ever been there?"

I had, which surprised him. "I'd rather the deserts than this place," he said. "I was there five days and never saw a Macathar, or any of the other stuff."

"The expedition I was on was a shambles," I told him. "And believe me, I saw a Macathar. I'd rather be whipped by the Marshal every day than go back. Everything people say about them is true."

He shrugged. "I might be up for a game of chess later on," he suggested.

I felt that I had been getting more than my share of chess, but I had to keep on his good side and told him that chess sounded great. "You played a lot of chess back home, then, to get so good." A little toadying is never amiss, and then, "How have you settled in?" as though I was his mother.

53

Something reared up, near the edge of the lake. I thought it might be one of the eyeless monsters, and shuddered. A similar shudder went through Peter and did not stop when the creature submerged once again.

"The punch in the gut kind of prepared me for the way things are around here," he told me flatly. "After you lot got herded down below, I got the Marshal all to myself. 'That's your first lesson,' he said to me. 'I rule here. I rule under the Governor, but he doesn't like to get his hands dirty, so I rule here. Got that?'

"I told him that he and I saw eye to eye, and he told me that no, we didn't, and as far as he was concerned I was just one rung up from the prisoners. He took me to where the Wardens live, and it isn't much better than you get."

I must have been unable to keep my scepticism silent, because he round on me.

"Don't forget that you were condemned to this, but I'm staff. I thought that I'd be doing better. I get a room the size of your cell, and the only privacy's from these rotting curtains, crawling with bugs. You can hear everything the other Wardens are doing, and some of them are doing some revolting things, I can tell you.

"The next thing the Marshal showed me was a head, or it had been somebody's head once. The Wardens have a common room, and the head's over the door, looking down. 'This,' says the Marshal, 'is your second lesson. Guess what he did.'"

I guessed that he had mutinied or something, and I guessed wrong.

"'He got himself captured by the enemy,' the Marshal told me. 'He got himself held for ransom by some new boy who didn't know the rules. You get yourself in a compromising position with a prisoner and this is what happens to you. You lose your privileges. You become one with the scum. I killed him. I killed the man who was holding him. I killed that man's cell mates. It's the only way to deal with them. They aren't human. If they put one foot out of line, you go straight ahead and whip the life out of them, or you get them moved down Below. If they put two feet out of line, if they answer you back or show any signs of defiance, then kill them flat out. They are here to work and obey. If they fail on either count then they are better dead than alive and causing trouble. Understand me, Drachmar?'"

"I bet the other Wardens all hate his guts, though," I put in.

"Yeah, right, camaraderie of my fellows," Peter spat. "No such luck. We should have been thick as thieves, but you get extra rations and a real pat on the head if you inform on someone. The only way to stop a guy ratting on you's to kick hell out of them. Fighting's common enough there's a rota, and the rest take bets. I've spent a week here laying into pretty much anyone who looked funny at me, broke a really big man's jaw and after that they left me alone a bit."

"But after that…" I couldn't imagine.

"There's no friends where any day the Marshal could be looking for a scapegoat. When we're not punching each other, it's civil, careful between us. Most of 'em just have something they do, with the time. Some have religion, and one watches birds. He actually looks out and watches different kinds of birds. Beats the hell out of me. So I beat the hell out of him, same thing in the end. Just because you like birds doesn't mean you're a soft touch."

He sank into silence then, and I tried to enjoy the sky, but the great hulk below us had hooks in my mind. *How long before we go back down below?* "What will you tell them, about this, about me? What will they think, if it's like that?"

He gave me a look, eyebrows raised, a bit of a smile at last. "They'll think you're my catamite. Don't tell me a Warden's not picked you up yet, nice-looking Academy boy like you?" and, while I stammered that I was yet to have that pleasure, "Hey, you know the Governor?"

"We've not been introduced."

"Weirdest little thing I ever saw. But someone said – what was it? Do you do something that's called Old School Shorthand? That sounds like educated stuff to me."

Yes, I was familiar with Old School Shorthand. No, I had not expected anybody to enquire about it since my being exiled from civilisation.

Peter bobbed his head. "Might have something for you. No promises. Back to me, anyway, just to put you in the frame. Soon after I found my feet here, I made the great decision to help you and your mate out in the machine room. Turns out I should have beaten all hell out of you two for busting the sack. I should have let the snake have you. Marshal had me whipped. Nine lashes, which may not sound much, but just you try it. He did it himself. He enjoyed it."

"Oh." I couldn't find any more to say than that.

"I just want to tell you that I really doubt that I'll be doing that again any time soon, so you look after yourself. You hear me?"

His gaze returned to the water, which still held the last traces of the sunset. Some noisy leviathan bellowed furiously out there amidst the eyeless monsters and the web-children and whatever other horrors the place held. The thought of the Marshal's blind hatred was far more frightening, and I wanted more of the sun. Father Sulplice had spoken of the boats that put out to harvest the swamp waters and I determined that I would find a place on one sooner or later. Death by monster was better than rotting in darkness. It was an uncharacteristically adventurous resolution.

Peter and I played a few desultory games of chess then, which he won without really trying. For me, it was all too close to the fever dreams. I kept looking at the walls and wondering whether they were moving outwards. I couldn't concentrate.

"Your game has gone all to hell," Peter remarked after his second victory. He must have seen in my face the fear that he would go off and get another opponent, because he followed it up with, "You should practise more. I'll try to come by more often."

There was a meditative pause as we set the board up for

another game. It was the same set that we had used aboard ship, ergo Peter's own.

"You've found any decent sorts amongst the inmates?" he asked casually.

"A few," I thought, thinking of Shon and Father Sulplice, even of Lucian. "A mixed bag, really."

"Then you're doing a whole lot better than I am," Peter admitted. "You're the only person in this whole place that I can talk to. Who's the prisoner, then?"

6

Master of All He Surveys

The third time my head hit the bars I confessed that I was not so hungry after all. It is amazing how appetite can leave you when a man twice your size has a knee in your back and is bouncing your face off the wall.

Pickings from the sieves had been lean for a day or so. The waters beneath the Island had become sparsely populated. Lucian explained that the outside swamp would serve to fill our watery larder in a few days, but in the meantime we were all on short commons. All except Onager. Onager, as a thug and a brute, had to keep his strength up. He had a strange code of conduct. He would only take our food with permission, which he exacted with skilfully applied violence.

During my feverish period, Valentin's body had been removed, and only three bowls were delivered by the duty Warden. A few days after my recovery, the spring dried up and Onager took to his regime of tax and tithe. Sometimes Lucian and I ate, sometimes we did not. Lucian put up no fight at all, just a constant resentful undercurrent of his usual babble. I tried to hold out on the first two days, for the principle of the thing, but Onager was a persuasive man, and larger than Lucian and I combined.

When I was helping Father Sulplice, life was easier, because the tasks were at least nominally interesting. When I was scrubbing the floors, or carting sacks around, my stomach gnawed at me. I began to feel that I, who was not eating, was instead being eaten from within by some parasite from the swamp. I had never been really hungry before, even in the Underworld.

Because I was hungry, I was weak. Because I was weak, I stumbled and was struck by the guards. Once I crashed into Onager whilst we carried a sack apiece, and he floored me with a quick right and continued on his way. It was not that he did not like me, or that I was the butt of the Island's jokes. I was just in the wrong place at the wrong time. Crude fate was stamping on me.

Luck was absent from my side for twelve days of measured starvation, during which the thought of a return to the fever obsessed my waking hours and my dreams. I did not see Shon or Peter, and even Father Sulplice was little help. He was selfish, in an old man's introverted way. He was determined to live, and had nothing to spare for me. Moreover, he managed to get himself into trouble during this time. When one of the larger machines fell apart all over the factory floor, he got into a row with one of the Wardens. No other prisoner would have lived through it, and even he failed to get away unpunished. The Warden – a tall, skinny man with a shock of ginger hair whom the others called 'Red' – gave him fair warning. Father Sulplice snapped back that he was a man who cared about machines, and if Red wanted to make an issue of it then he could just sink with the rest when the pumps stopped working. Red took this in his stride and simply said that in that case, Father Sulplice's son would drown too, and how about that? I had heard no hint that the old man had a descendant penned in with us damned souls, but it was obviously true. Father Sulplice got right down to work without any more trouble and refused to answer any of my questions. It was obviously a touchy subject.

I was probably on the point of starving to death when one of the Wardens came for me, some stranger who had taken over our corridor. He called out my name and dragged me out of the cell with his free hand about the hilt of his knife. Onager was lounging at the back like the cat that got all the food, and perhaps the Warden was worried that he might make a break for it. From my point of view, Onager had a good deal: all the food he could eat and plenty of exercise getting it. The Warden was not to know that, however. He locked the door sharply behind him and then pushed me down the corridor. He was a stone-faced creature, angular and awkward, and he walked in the dead centre between the cells, so that no prisoner could reach out to grab him. It was a madness that gripped some Wardens that had been there too long, or were too weak of mind. The humdrum cruelties that each day drew from them mounted up on their consciences until they broke beneath the weight. They saw the wheel of retribution come thundering down on them. They became obsessed with the debt of wrong that they had accrued. Many of them took their own lives in the end. Those who were not yet so desperate, such as the man escorting me, were constantly guarding themselves against any number of real or imagined dangers, convinced the world was going to get them.

If I had known all of this at the time I would have kept my mouth shut, because a single wrong word and that stone-faced man might have knifed me, sure that I was some insidious threat. Instead, I was hungry and desperate.

"Tell me," I said, "Do you do a last meal here, for a condemned man?"

My captor said nothing.

"If you do, I think I might try for a capital crime. It shouldn't be so hard here. I'd rather be executed on a full stomach than starve. What do you say?"

He just pushed me again. I stumbled over the lattice of the floor and fell to my knees. The Warden was dragging me to my feet even as I registered the pain. On either side, the mute faces of other prisoners looked out at me like ghosts from the shadows, speculating about what my punishment was to be.

We hit some stairs next, although not the stairs Peter had taken me to. I was going to the Wardens' level. Perhaps the man just wanted a "nice-looking Academy boy" for a tryst after all. It happened. It was a good way of earning favour with the Wardens, in fact: all part of the prison economy. Looking at my captor, I didn't think that was it, though. He had something else in mind. It was said that they took prisoners up and tortured them, or made them fight for sport. Or maybe I was just going to be executed as a tutelary exercise of the Marshal's.

"If it's all the same to you," I managed, "I'd rather die here. I know my place. What difference does it make, after all?"

The Warden grabbed me by the collar of my prison greys and pushed me back onto the stairs. The uneven wood of the steps dug into me from my heels to my neck. He stared grimly down at me and said, "I want to kill you. I want to kill you right now. It isn't my choice. Think about that."

He hauled me to my feet again and forced me onwards, and I did indeed think about it. It occupied my thoughts so much that I only realised after the event that we had ascended clean beyond the Warden's dingy quarters and were now on the uppermost level of the Island. I was made aware of this by the change in the quality of the light. There was still a lot of lattice work here in the ceiling, and I could see the old dark blue of the late evening sky, but much of it had been reinforced so that the natural darkness was kept at bay by an artificial darkness, touched only by artificial light. Someone lived here who could have owned the sky, but instead closeted themselves away and blotted it out.

The one lit lamp showed that there were at least five others left dark. By the time I had registered this, the Warden had gone, and I thought that I was alone in this great empty space. Had I come here straight from the city I would have found it cramped and low-ceilinged. Now, it was a vast, almost boundless expanse; a great dark netherworld of indistinct shapes. It reminded me of the gloom of the Underworld. There, though, the shapes had been ragged beggars, fugitives, madmen and dreamers. Here the shapes were nothing more or less than furniture.

There were chairs, insofar as I could make out, and what might have been a gaming table (already I was dreading more chess). Against one wall something threw back the weak lamplight, and I knew that must be a mirror of some sort. There was a contraption some distance from me that I could really not make anything of, but which looked like a partly-folded wading bird. There was a screen of the kind that elegant ladies undressed behind. There was a man.

I had stared at him for some time before I realised. I was trying to work out why anyone would make a coatstand so short and then put it in the middle of the room, quite overburdened with clothes. Then I caught the lamp reflecting in his eyes and I realised.

My own eyes were slowly accustoming themselves to the dimness. There was more light coming through gaps in the floor than there was from the room itself. I could see my companion as a short man in the kind of gown that rich people of leisure wore in Shadrapar.

He was the baldest man I have ever known. This may seem a trite and malicious thing to say, but it is quite literally true. There was not a hair on his body. When he saw that I had seen him, he took a step forward to observe me better, and the lamp shone dimly on the dome of his scalp. He had no eyebrows or even eyelashes. There was not a single hair on head or body. This was a modification that he had ordained before coming here, an extreme hygienic measure, so that even the most opportunistic of lice and bugs would find him as inhospitable as the deadly deserts. A faint trace of insecticide hung close to him. I suspect he sweated it.

"You must be the Governor," I said calmly. When even the lowliest guard has full power of life or death over you, you find that higher grades of authority lose their sting. Indeed, I felt that the Governor was far less likely to demand my instant execution than the Marshal and his underlings.

His eyes, reptilian in their unblinking, lash-less gaze, remained locked on my face.

"You have been Academy-trained, have you not?" he asked. His voice was soft and slightly unpleasant in some way I could not name.

It was not the most encouraging start to a conversation, but he was the Governor and I could only go where he led. "I am," I confirmed. "I passed my Reds with honours three years ago."

He turned away and began padding off towards the far wall. I realised that the solid flooring I had noted was actually carpeted. The Governor had imported a peculiar selection of luxuries.

"Come here," his voice whispered to me. "I want to see if you're any use at all." It seemed to come from right beside me despite the fact that he was across the room. He was heading for that strange arrangement of folded legs that had puzzled me earlier. With a resigned shrug I did the same.

A section of wall some ten feet wide had been slid back, opening out onto the darkness of a night sky in which the stars were just appearing. There were a few wisps of cloud out there, but nothing else, not even a moon. The dark that was sky could not be divided from the darknesses that were land and water.

"It will be cool tonight," the Governor observed to himself, "Which is good. On a really cool night you can see forever."

I thought that he was talking nonsense for a moment, but then I saw that the instrument was a telescope. It was perhaps the finest example of its kind I have ever seen, far exceeding anything the Academy had to offer. It was mostly bound in brass, and I think the body itself was hand-crafted and organic. There was a secondary lens fastened to one side that looked as though it could be used to measure starlight, which was something nobody did these days. Nobody but the Governor. There was a whole discipline of astronomy that had fallen into disuse over the centuries, and I am prepared to believe that the Governor was its last practitioner.

"The stars are one of my passions," he told me softly, as he adjusted the telescope. "Do you know anything about their study?"

I admitted that I knew very little.

"All too common," he said, wistfully. "When the world was young, or so we are taught, men believed that events were guided by the stars, which dictated the fates of individuals and nations. People believed that the stars were a secret language the future was written in. When the world was older and more sensible, it was believed that the stars *were* our future. Men made machines to take them beyond this world, did you know that? We peopled the stars with creatures like us, and set out to meet them. Such boundless optimism." He fidgeted with the telescope's mechanisms again. "It was all in vain, of course, the machines, the boats and vessels and birds and devices that were thrown up into the night sky," he murmured. "For the stars are very far away, and however fast our machines carried us, it was not fast enough. The gaps between stars are so great that nothing can cross them quickly, not even light, which is fastest of all. We never found a way to skip between the stars, to meet the people we were sure awaited us there. That broke the back of our optimism. The spirit of man was crushed by the distances between the stars."

He invited me to look into the telescope. I had to stoop, for he was shorter than I, and I saw very little. There was a star there, and perhaps the shadow of a planet or moon across it, and there were numbers and readings above and below that I could not interpret. Behind me, the quiet, sad voice of the Governor continued.

"The one thing we learned is that stars die," he said sepulchrally. "Stars waste away or bloat or become fierce and feverish, just as men do when they are ill. And like all men, stars die eventually. Thus the earliest stargazers were proved right after all. The fate of the world is written in the stars, for just as the stars bloat and burst and wither and die, so does our sun, which is no more than a star, after all."

I stood back from the telescope and he took my place and spent perhaps half an hour moving it about the pinpricked sky. He made notes, too, for all that it was too dark to see. In the end I asked him what he was studying, because I could not go on in ignorance.

"We have no future here," the Governor told his telescope, for he still had his back to me. "The sun may be a million years in dying, but we will not live to see its end. We are the last remains of a once-great people and we do not look into the sky because we have no wish, now, to see what the future holds. We study the past, instead, and make up stories about how things used to be. The historians do not realise, when they look into the sky, they are looking into the past. The light from those stars is older than you or I, and some of it is older than the Earth. When I turn my lens on a star I see the past, the universe as it was countless years ago. Perhaps I am seeing reflected light shed by our sun once upon a time. I am studying the past because when one is at the end of a road, the only way to look is backwards."

I had no answer to that, save to tell myself that the Governor was at least the quiet kind of madman, as opposed to the Marshal, who was the aggressive kind. I began to wonder whether I had been dragged up here for the sole reason of hearing the sort of rambling I had done my best to avoid in my Academy days. All this nonsense about men living on the stars was a notion to which I had been introduced in my junior classes, and to be honest it never really interested me.

I will confess that much of this fine thought came retrospectively. At the time, as the Governor studied the stars, I became suddenly aware of a nearby side-table on which a bowl of little dried fruits had been placed, possibly for ornamental purposes. Whilst a man who had the power of life or death over me regarded the cosmos, I stole and consumed every one of his little fruits in utter silence. It was a small enough bounty for a hungry man, and he could have had me executed for it as easily as blinking, but I was a slave to my shrunken stomach. I could have done nothing else. I wonder whether he even noticed their loss.

The Governor finally left the telescope alone and crossed the room again. I stayed by the window to catch every last breath of fresh air and openness. If you have never been confined then you cannot know what it means to have an open window beside you and nothing between you and the sky, no matter how dark.

The darkness was something that was about to change, because some action of the Governor brought all the other lamps up to full fire, leaving us both blinking for a moment. When my vision cleared I had a far better view of the Governor than I wished. He was truly a bizarre little man, like a baby that had grown to full size without ever losing its infantile skin. There were no lines even around the eyes, but where they might be expected to look guileless, instead there was an ingrained corruption there that nothing could hide. Such grotesquery was a fashion in Shadrapar. The very rich would use the old medical sciences to augment their children and their bloodlines: longer lives, resistance to disease, improved brains, stronger bodies. Like every other innovation of the rich, though, this tinkering gained its power from being seen and admired. Every inner change had an outer transformation to signal it. The practice was widespread enough that the first son of a family might be given a hunchback or a club foot and be much admired for it. The fashion of selective deformity could be told at a glance from the natural defects the poor had to make do with, and so advertised to the whole world that the bearer was one of the elite. So it was with the Governor.

"I tell you this because I need to tell people from time to time," the Governor said. He was not looking at me. He very seldom did. "You will at least understand my words, if not my motives. This is not your purpose however." He found a bureau and opened a drawer reverently, and despite myself, I crowded closer for a look.

"You have heard, of course, of the explorer Trethowan," the Governor noted. "Do say yes, because you are no earthly use otherwise."

I replied, promptly and truthfully, that I had. Trethowan's twelve-volume bestiary had terrified me long before I was actually condemned to the horrible places that he had described.

"Look at this." The Governor dumped a stack of papers on the bureau top. It was not a particularly thick stack, but he seemed to find it an effort. He was surely weaker than me but I never considered overpowering him. There was a horrible soft quality to him, as though he might have no bones, nothing more than a pale, smooth fungus in the shape of a man.

I stole over to skim the top page of his papers and was immediately caught by it. You have probably guessed that they were written by Trethowan, and I knew the handwriting well enough. The printed copies of his books in the Academy library had been annotated by his own hand before his final, terminal excursion into the great unknown.

A lost Trethowan book. To any scholar, whether biology was his field or no, this was worth the Governor's weight in any currency you care to name. Even though the papers were few, perhaps under forty sheets, the writing was so thick that there was more dark ink than yellow parchment to be seen. As Peter had intimated, it was all in Old School Shorthand, which is fiendishly difficult to master, but brutally efficient for someone with little time or paper. Even so, he had found room for some of his elegant illustrations of new beasts and plants that had caught his eye. Three pages down I found the eyeless monster that had attacked the riverboat, caught exactly as in life. Trethowan's perennial enthusiasm for the living world was scattered through the whole document, but he seemed to have other things on his mind when he wrote it. Much seemed to read like a philosophical text.

I felt I had to ask, and so I said, "Why does the Island have such a treasure?"

"You know of Trethowan's fate."

"I know that he never returned from his last expedition."

"Then you do not know," the Governor told me. "Perhaps nobody does, outside the Island. Trethowan was one of the charges of my predecessor. He died here, as all prisoners do. There was no last expedition."

"What did he do?" I wondered aloud. The Governor shot me a slightly annoyed look.

"I am not here to busy myself with what the wards have done. We ask no questions here. Trethowan's crime is locked up in the offices of the Justiciar and I have no interest in it. His last words, however, have aroused some curiosity in me. These papers have been here since I took up office," the Governor said, almost petulantly. "I have no clerk here. I can make nothing of them. I was told that you could."

I agreed that I could. I have never managed to write in Old School, but at a pinch I can decipher it.

"Good," said the Governor. "For a few hours a week you will be allowed out of your cell to unravel Trethowan. I am sure that this will be ample recompense for your services."

I felt almost indecently lucky. I resolved to see if there was any kind of favour I could do Peter in return. Even a lowly inmate must be able to do something to show his gratitude.

"Do you want me to start now?" I asked, almost greedily. He gave me a disdainful look.

"No. You will wait until I send for you again." There was more to that sentence when he embarked on it, but a change came over his face, part-guilt, and part leering anticipation, so naked on his bare face that I turned my eyes away.

In doing so, I saw the woman. She was standing in a narrow doorway that I had not marked, and she was breathtaking, tall and elegant, with raven-dark hair and an astonishingly full figure that would have turned the head of a machine.

It was obvious that she was waiting on the Governor's pleasure, but at the same time, she commanded him too. Something about the way it was between them felt unhealthy, festering. I felt that I should get out of the room right there and then or catch some horrible, consuming disease.

Thankfully, the Governor was already dismissing me, and I backed out of the room over the carpeted floor until I was in the corridor beyond where the Warden grabbed me and marched me back to my cell. When I returned there I suddenly regained my hunger, which had quite left me in the Governor's quarters. Those little fruits had not gone very far. On such an insistent empty stomach I fell prey to some particularly bizarre and unwelcome dreams in which I had not left the upper levels at the right time, and instead was forced to watch the Governor and his strange mistress as they came together. It was a sight that awoke me three times in succession, and each time in a cold sweat.

7

The Fairer Sex

Thanks to the Island finding fresher pastures, my enforced hunger strike let up soon after, and the vile slop that we were served was like ambrosia. In short, I found a fly in my soup and counted myself lucky.

Onager and Lucian were both curious about my excursion. I kept it to myself, still trying to work out what was going on. The Governor's celestial obsessions, Trethowan's manuscript, the sinister mistress, all these things turned in my head like the gears of a machine, never interlocking to any useful purpose. During the next day I wondered if I should push my luck with the Wardens. I thought that the Governor might have told them not to kill me, because of the service only I could render him. I never quite plucked up the nerve to try it, and possibly just as well. The next boatload of convicts could have been packed to the bilges with Academy drop-outs suckled on Old School Shorthand. Besides, you will have noticed by now that I am not the most courageous of men. Cowardice has been my lifelong companion. When I have let my innately craven nature guide me, I have seldom gone wrong.

Now I think about it, most of the serious mistakes in my life come from taking a stand. One of the Academy Masters once said that nobody ever made a statue of a man running away. My answer to that is that very few living men get statues.

Of course, I had reached the limit of running away. I had the luxury of running ten feet in any direction. I had been forced, at this late stage, into taking a stand. If I had my way, it would be a stand behind someone larger than I was.

I met up with Shon shortly afterwards, in the brief lunch break between the punishing morning shift and the grind of the afternoon. Even he had heard that people in high places were taking an interest in me.

"Think you can do anything for me? You know how this place works," he said idly. "Governor's favour, you must be able to pimp in exchange for something. Better food, more space in your cell, sexual favours, whatever…"

"Sexual favours…" For a moment I thought of the strange woman, but of course Shon was talking about other prisoners. Again, all part of the local economy.

Shon shrugged. "No worse than goes on back home," he opined.

"You're obviously a man of the world. Were you a career criminal?"

He laughed at that. "Depends on who you ask," he said. "I was a lawyer."

I looked upon him narrowly. "No," I decided.

"Yes," he said simply. "I worked for a big shady merchant cartel with a lot going on. I went in and talked to the representatives of other big, shady cartels. We made alliances, contracts. Sometimes I appeared in the Courts to defend cartel leaders. It was a living. It paid well."

"You strike me more as a man of action," I said dubiously.

"Well, when deals like that go bad, they go bad all at once and usually when you're right in the middle of them. That's where I got this scar." He traced the thin ear-to-chin mark. "The other side went for me with an electric knife just as we were about to sign on the line. Or there's some third party who doesn't want

71

any kind of deal to come through, and they always go for the advocates first. That's how come I'm here. Someone set me up for bad debts, contraband and taxes. I'd at least have liked to be sent here for something I did."

It was almost a disappointment to discover that Shon was something so pedestrian. A lawyer, even a brawling lawyer who looks like a pirate, is at least within spitting distance of my own estate.

"What about Peter?" I asked idly. "Was he a lawyer too?"

"Who's Peter?"

"The Warden who killed the snake. I thought you might know him, from the way you looked at him."

"Oh." Shon nodded. "I bet on him once. He was a duellist. This is a good few years back but I won a lot of money, so I remember him. Not a show duellist, either."

Two kinds of men fought for the amusement of a crowd. Show duellists were cheats, basically. Their moves were mostly worked out in advance. They fought to surrender or sometimes first blood. It was easy entertainment for the masses. The other category, into which Shon was placing Peter, was that of the blood duellist. They fought for real and usually to the death. It was a profession nobody stayed in long. The successful retired and, of the failures, what needs to be said? I wondered what had driven Peter to choose such a desperate course, and how it had led to this distant exile. Lunch break was over, though. The Wardens were kicking us back to work.

That evening I sat with my hands about my belly and tried to wish it smaller, so that it would not complain so much. Onager had decanted about half of my portion into his own bowl, with my forced permission. To add insult to injury, Lucian was in a more than usually talkative mood.

He had his one customary topic of conversation, which was his departure. To hear him say it you would think that he had a place reserved on the next boat home. Lucian had plentiful, generous and wealthy friends back in Shadrapar who were even now working to have him freed. They would petition the President. They would cry to the Justiciar's office. They would make a great nuisance of themselves until the word was cried from the valleys to the mountains that Lucian Corek must be released. He also talked of how he would live when he returned to the city: turning a new leaf, setting up an honest trade, rewarding his friends. He talked of freeing Onager and myself. In his wildest moments he even suggested taking up a position as the Island's next Governor, instituting a sweeping series of reforms to end the tyranny of this place forever.

When I had first heard this tune I had been impressed, because I was naive then and did not know that Lucian had been in the Island for almost seven years. Lucian, however, could never be persuaded that freedom was not just around the corner. He lived from day to day in the assurance that the days of captivity before him were numbered and few. If seven years in the Island could not dent his confidence, what good could a few rational arguments do?

He was just beginning to enumerate the high public officials who knew him by name and would surely be pining for his company (there were seventeen of them, and by then I knew them by heart) when a Warden stopped outside our cell. He was not alone. It was the stone-faced, hostile man that had conveyed me to the Governor, and there was a big shape in greys behind him. Lucian went quiet, and all three of us looked up as the key was turned in the lock.

"Company," the Warden hissed. His hand was on his knife again and he was standing so that he could keep an eye on both us and the newcomer. He hauled the door open and said, "In." The stranger lumbered into the doorway, and practically filled it. The door was shut and locked the moment that the newcomer was out of its way. The Warden beat a quick retreat.

Onager stood up and measured his height against that of our new companion. He was perhaps an inch or so taller but several stone lighter. Our new cell mate was solid and broad enough that the floor creaked with every footfall. Lucian and I chose opposite corners and resolved to stay well out of the way.

Onager threw his shoulders back and took the step or two needed to confront the newcomer. With customary speed and accuracy his rock-hard fist slammed into the stranger's face with a dull sound. The stranger fell back a pace and then slapped Onager across the side of the head so hard that they must have heard it up on the Wardens' level. That was when things got interesting. The slap had been mostly reflex and Onager got in two or three more good blows before the newcomer had really worked out what was going on. One went to the head and might have done some good. Any strike to the body was surely wasted. There was so much padding there that Onager's punches failed even to make a sound. Then the stranger decided to up the ante and smashed a fist solidly down across Onager's jaw, staggering him. He kicked out and hit his opponent solidly in the stomach, a futile gesture. The newcomer waded forward a pace and backhanded him flatly across the face, knocking him into the bars.

I will say this for Onager: he was determined. He bounced straight back and laid at least four hard fists on his antagonist, mostly around the face. He received a meaty palm that struck under the chin and hurled him into the wall again. Both of them had bloody noses by now, and they would surely have every colour of bruise once the morning came. The prisoners across the way and on one side were cheering, mostly for Onager. On the other side, Gaki watched narrowly, hunched like a spider in the corner of his cell. As for me, I have never seen violence as a spectator sport, and this was violence of the crudest and dullest kind.

There was more of the same, and Lucian and I had to run ourselves ragged about the little cell to avoid catching any of the fallout. In the end there was no real winner, although I would say Onager got the worst of it. He ended up sitting in one corner, panting and bleeding and spitting out the occasional tooth. The new arrival, on seeing that he had mostly given up his attack, sat down across from him. A pair of small, beady eyes, mounted in a fat, flat square face, fixed on Lucian and myself.

"So," came the voice. "Either of you two boys want to try anything?"

There was a long silence from everybody. Even Onager stopped spitting and looked up with a horrified expression on his face. The spectators in the other cells gave us an appreciative hush.

It was clearly a woman's voice. The stranger was massively built, huge and sloped like a mountain, sporting a flat face with small features, threatening as a fist. And besides, we were all, to a man, men. Nobody had even considered the matter to be in question. And yet that voice, though low for a woman, left no room for doubt.

Lucian and I assured her that neither of us had anything we wanted to try.

"We're both the quiet type," I explained nervously. If she had slapped me lightly across the cheek she would have put my jaw out of its socket. "I'm Stefan Advani, and this is Lucian Corek. The gentleman you were fighting goes by the name of Onager."

She stared at me for longer than I was comfortable with. "You're having me on. Nobody really talks like that."

"*I'm* having *you* on?" I said before I could stop it. It was true, though, that I had been unconsciously been giving her my very best Cultured Tones, brought out when I was particularly frightened by something. Her ill-tempered stare bore into me. To break the gathering tension and defuse any attempt on my life, I offered, "So, what should we call you, Miss?"

I think the Miss was a mistake. I probably came closer than I ever knew to getting stuffed through the cracks in the floor. After a glowering moment, however, she said, "Hermione," and then, "Something amusing you?" with deliberate provocation, because my face must have been a picture. I shook my head silently.

There followed an hour without conversation as both Onager and Hermione nursed their wounds. After that, the big woman wanted to know when we were being fed, and I plucked up the courage to explain to her how things worked around here, which went a way towards bridging the gap between us. In any other place I would fear repercussions, but Onager had been dethroned, and until he was reinstated he would not be in any position to order Lucian and myself around. Thankfully, Hermione was new to the Island and we guessed that she would not understand that she would be expected to bully us in his place. We had a few weeks' grace, we decided, before we were under anyone's yoke again.

There was another lengthy silence of readjustment, as all four of us reset our mental parameters, and then the question that was burning in my mind finally forced its way out of me.

"I've got to say I'm surprised," I said. "You're only the second woman I've seen on the Island. It begs the question."

This drew a fair amount of speculation, because for most of my audience, Hermione was the first woman they had seen there. Hermione herself turned a surly scowl on me, an expression that her face was tailor-made for.

"I wasn't good enough for them," she said sourly.

"For whom?" I enquired politely.

"There was me, and there was another woman, and they took us up to the top level, and we stood around for hours while the men got put away, and then this bitch came out to look us over. You could tell straight away there was something wrong with her, like she was poison. She had some kind of eunuch with her, some flabby little baldy man. They both looked us over, and the other woman got taken in. This bitch looked at me, and she said all kinds of things that I wouldn't take from anyone. If there hadn't been guards there I'd have had her. I'd have put her

76

through the wall…" She stopped, thinking. Her face, when not being actively used for speaking or scowling, simply relaxed into a characteristic sullen brooding. No trace of her thoughts (and Hermione's thoughts were complex and deep) ever showed on it.

"Maybe I wouldn't have," she eventually conceded. "There was something about the bitch that I wouldn't have wanted to touch."

Of course I recognised both 'bitch' and 'eunuch' from my own encounter.

"She said that I wasn't a woman in her book. I was…" She stopped again, obviously unwilling to repeat the criticisms. "She said that if I looked that much like a man I should go and live with the men."

"So there are other women prisoners on the Island?" I pressed. I had the full attention of everyone in earshot. Hermione just shrugged, though, and Lucian took the chance to put in that there were certainly women on the Island, only not very many, and they were all kept separate at the top, for the personal pleasures of the Wardens.

"I suppose I'm for the personal pleasure of the prisoners, then," Hermione said with grim satisfaction. "I'll take personal pleasure in breaking the neck of anyone that tries." She was clearly getting the hang of the way things worked.

I learned later that there were about fifty women on the Island at any one time, which worked out to around five per cent of the inmate population. I have three theories to explain this: women are genuinely less prone to criminal activities; alternatively the crimes they commit are not generally covered by laws or punished by exile; thirdly they are as venal and nasty as men, but just get away with it more often. I leave you to make up your own mind.

The general conversation in the surrounding cells had turned to the subject of how lucky the Wardens were, what with women on tap and capital punishment at their fingertips, when a new voice spoke up. It was Gaki's.

"I am afraid the Wardens have no more access to the fairer sex than you do," he said airily. "The women here are the personal property of the Governor's mistress."

Hermione gave Gaki a level look. "How do you know, then?"

"Oh, I hear things," he said, idly. "I get around."

"Who's the Governor's mistress?" someone asked, and Gaki pointed out that Hermione had already described her.

"She is known as Lady Ellera," he said softly, although his voice must have carried six cells in every direction. "She is the one person in the Island that I would not like to have as an enemy. Perhaps I keep quiet and cooperate with the Wardens to avoid attracting her notice and displeasure. The women are her domain. She has uses for them. She is a scientist of the flesh, you understand. She is one of those whose study is themselves." He saw my twitch. "Yes, Stefan, I see you have met others of the trade. Her work requires materiel, to provide for her treatments, and that materiel is kept penned above for when she needs renewal and refinement. She may have insulted you, and despised you," he said to Hermione, "but I am sure that you will live far longer here, in misery, than you would in comfort up there. Lady Ellera's women slaves are treated with all kindness. It is often so with sacrificial victims, or so I am told."

There was a chill silence after Gaki's words. Only Hermione, who did not yet know his horrible reputation, looked him in the eye. She was the only person not to find something terrible in his gaze. Fear was absent from her make-up.

She was imprisoned for the simple crime of murder. She had killed her employer, his foreman and two jeering onlookers after some minor dispute about pay. It was not that she was short-tempered, anything but. A woman with an ogre's strength and looks, she had taken a thousand blows until the thousand-and-first had finally triggered her deep-buried anger. Within the bizarre and artificial structure of the Island she fitted perfectly.

8

A Night at the Races

Three days later, the unexpected happened. I was awoken some time after dark by the scratching of a key in the lock of our cell, and then the door was eased open. I had a whirl of wild speculations, from a secret cull of the inmates by the Wardens to the stealthy entrance of Gaki (but somehow I thought he would not need a key). Then I saw that there was a prisoner at the door, a man unknown to me. Lucian and Onager were up and ready, and a strange and exciting thought hit me.

"Is it a breakout?" I asked them. "Are we free?"

There was general laughter and derision, and Lucian explained it to me. Essentially, one of the prisoners had got hold of the keys to this stretch of cells. It happened sporadically. Sometimes the keys were stolen, but, more often, a Warden leant the keys out in return for some service, or perhaps something uncovered in the swamps. This place had been a city, long ago in the unremembered depths of time, and valuables could still be found. The Wardens, on leave in Shadrapar, would sell these trinkets for a little extra cash. In return, one section of the Island would get a night's freedom; a chance to brawl and gamble and gossip and do all the things the prisoners liked to do. This was all strictly against the Marshal's rules, of course, and if he decided to come down and investigate then somebody would be for it. For this reason, according to Lucian, he tacitly allowed it to happen. They gave him an excuse to destroy any particular individual he felt deserved it, or to order some random deaths. Not that he needed a pretext, but he was a man who loved rules and laws and due process, however nonsensical and self-imposed. I suspect it made him feel righteous to catch us in the act of defiance.

Each Outing, as they were called, was a lottery, depending on whether the Marshal knew and whether he was feeling withdrawal from murderous tyranny. With the Wardens and even the Marshal in on this peculiar arrangement, I think only the Governor, way up on the top floor, was ignorant of the business.

You might think that, with this risk hanging over every such gathering, the inmates would not chance it. You have probably not been caged up like we were; it was worth it for just a little freedom. Our stretch of cellway was sealed off by other doors, to which we did not have the keys, but maybe half a hundred prisoners were abruptly free to gather in a largish storeroom and talk, and mingle, and play games.

The Island had an ecosystem; every place does. On the bars and slats of the Island there grew a kind of tough, greenish mould or lichen that was too hard to scrape off with a fingernail. It was soft enough to make food for a variety of little mites and silverfish. These, in turn, were stalked by amphibious beetles the size of my little finger's top joint. These were the prey of whip-scorpions and spiders the size of my thumb, and of a kind of mantis-thing that could change colour to match the lichen perfectly. All of these invertebrate predators went to feed a kind of gecko that had huge black eyes in a wedge-shaped head and could cling upside down to ceilings. The lizard was food for the prisoners, who were in turn food for a number of lice species and several internal parasites I do not wish to talk about. In addition, the lizard was a good pastime, or so I was assured.

The mantids, spiders and whip-scorpions were all pressed into service as duellists: placed in a ring in pairs and not allowed out until they had found each other and grappled in mortal combat. The winner got a meal. The winner's owner, and anyone who bet on it, got their share of whatever was being bet. Sometimes it was food, sometimes services. Sometimes it was just a favour in the future. There was a great deal of deficit spending, but that was endemic in our culture.

The geckos, we raced. If you saw a promising-looking beast and there was an Outing in the near future, you swiped it and hid it. They were docile enough to be stored down the trousers, and if the Outing was cancelled one could always eat the prospective racer. Some inmates had developed a keen eye for a good bet, and would spend ages sizing a reptile up before plucking it from its roost.

The little athletes would be placed at equal distance from a set point, and shown some morsel, usually an insect with most of its legs pulled off. Released, they would be off. Even if you had nothing to bet, it was quite gripping to see a dozen lizards of various colours making a determined dash for a crippled bug. I may not have mentioned it, but we were starved for entertainment. It was a time-honoured tradition to release the winners at the end of the night. The losers were frequently used to pay off debts, consumed or freed as the new owners willed it.

It was all a far cry from Shadrapar, where animals of all kinds were absent or exterminated as vermin. Here on the Island, surrounded and invaded by nature, we used it to our advantage.

Of course, at the beginning of my first Outing it was all I could do to accept that I could go out of my cell. Hermione, too, took a bit of persuading, and Lucian had to go through the whole rigmarole of explanation again before she believed it. Lucian was being very attentive to Hermione, sensing a softer touch than Onager.

I wandered into the storeroom and saw the end of a brutal fight to the death between a pair of largish spiders. There was a great deal of rejoicing from over half the watchers, and the others

81

grumbled and paid up or made promises. Just as in real life, of course, debts were only as good as your means of enforcement. Just as in real life, again, debts could be used as currency. If someone owed you something, then you could pay your own debt by passing on the debt that was owed to you. It was a good idea to pay quickly, because you never knew who would end up holding your marker. I think that was another reason that Lucian made so much of Hermione. He wanted people to see that he had a big, strong friend to pass bad debts on to.

After the fight, I was introduced to our benefactor, the holder of the keys, a young-looking man named Thelwel. At the time I noted him only very briefly, seeing a neat, decent-looking man distinctly out of place amongst the riot of gambling inmates. He had a perpetually hairless face, like me – a modification fashionable back home, so that my hair was past my shoulders by then, but my chin was as smooth as a child's. If Thelwel looked like anything, it was a junior librarian. He will have a particularly important part to play in my story, and he had an unusual secret, which I will eventually share with you, but when I first met him it was only in passing. All I understood was that he had been out on the boats all week and found a few artefacts that our Warden liked. I wondered at that, because it was the stone-faced man who hated us all very much. Perhaps stone-face had his own debts to pay. Perhaps he was just trying to work off his evil karma with a gesture of generosity. I never knew.

I, of course, had nothing to wager, caught off guard by the whole business. I did not participate in any of the games but watched several. Lucian introduced me to various curious inmates as "The Professor" but I put a stop to that as quickly as I could. I didn't see why I should be lumbered with "The Professor" just because I had an education.

I did not see Shon. He was on a different stretch and had not been released. Gaki was also notably absent. I suspect that his cell had not been unlocked, although I did not check. Gaki was quite capable of coming and going as he pleased. He didn't need charity from the Wardens.

Several of the prisoners had heard in some vague way that I was of interest to the Governor. They had never met him; he was a kind of legend built from misinformation and invention. The inmates mostly believed that he had it in his power to free any prisoner with a word and a gesture. As someone apparently in with the Governor, I was therefore courted assiduously. I received a wide variety of offers, some dubious and others salacious. Even those that I might have accepted, I took with a pinch of salt. I know all about bad debts, after all. I was hardly of a physique to enforce any service that was promised to me.

Hermione was also the subject of some attention, and I don't doubt that she had some interesting offers too. About half an hour into the Outing she floored one overenthusiastic inmate with a single slap and after that she was mostly left alone. She obviously considered everyone, with the possible exception of Lucian and myself, as her enemies. Thelwel told me later that he and Hermione had quite a conversation at around this point. He was always a good listener, though, and if anyone could win Hermione's trust then it was him.

I became absorbed in the first of the great lizard races, then, and found it mildly enjoyable. Compared to most of my Island activities it was the height of culture. In the back of my mind, however, the last work of Trethowan festered, demanding attention. I wondered if the great man himself had raced lizards across this floor in his time. It would have been in character, from what I knew of him.

In all, it was rather a pleasant way to spend a night. No matter that we would all be sluggish and bleary-eyed the next morning (and many of us beaten because of it). No matter, too, the dire end of this night's Outing. In all, it was good. It reminded me of Peter's words concerning the Wardens and their lack of cameraderie. I will not claim that we were all brothers together, we prisoners, but in some strange way we had a better standard of living. We were already in as much trouble as we could be without actually being dead, and therefore could take ourselves less seriously.

There was a bout of mantis-baiting, and then another lizard race in which the winner won by more than a body length. The owner made a lot of his acquisition, and speculated idly about finding an equally fast lady lizard and setting up the first ever gecko-breeding stables. Someone else asked how you were supposed to tell a lady lizard anyway. Hermione put in that they were the ones that were too smart to get caught in the first place.

Bets were being taken for the next race. The winner of the previous one was entered quickly, at flat odds, and there was a battery of hopefuls ready to test themselves against him. It was actually quite a sharp game, because each time a lizard won, it ate, and the more it ate the less interested it was in running for the next meal, so a winner's form declined through the evening, whilst a loser gained an extra edge from hunger. Betting on foot races was a common practice amongst Academy intellectuals, but I think even those dons would have been hard put to weigh the odds in our little games in the Island.

For some time I amused myself by trying to use my mental energies to fix the outcome of lizard races. It had no discernible effect. I could not at the time decide whether the lizards' brains were too small; or whether I was not concentrating properly; or whether the entire business was just sham and hokery. The city and my studies seemed so far away. At around that time the fight started.

I had been bending my will on a small, yellow-spotted specimen, attempting to make up for its poor track record so far, when the first punch was thrown. It was considered very bad form to make trouble there, for reasons that will become obvious. Onager, however, was not a great respecter of traditions. The Outing had given him an opportunity too good to miss.

Onager, in common with all large and thuggish men, had a couple of large and thuggish friends on the same stretch as us, and of course they were out mingling just as we were. Also like all men of his size and temperament he had no compunctions about stacking the odds in his favour. One of his friends was a particularly ugly man named Tallan, and the other had a shock of dung-coloured hair, and I have entirely forgotten his name. Their target, needless to say, was Hermione. The extent of the plan, to my knowledge, was for all three to jump her and beat her senseless.

Even the simplest plans go wrong, especially when put together by the simplest people, and Onager was no Academy graduate. Anyone intending to start a small localised brawl in a room full of convicts is just asking for trouble. Trouble, naturally, came running at the call.

I am told that Onager threw the first punch, and that Tallan and friend were intended to hold Hermione's arms behind her back to best receive it. I am dearly sorry that I missed the repercussions of this. Thelwel assured me that no sooner had Onager's blow thudded dully against Hermione's cheek than she woke up to what was going on and hit Onager with his own henchmen, sweeping her arms from behind her back, and taking the two men with her. All three fell in a heap, and Hermione wisely decided to kick one very hard in a delicate area. It was the shock-headed man, who would be unmistakable for the next week owing to his pronounced limp.

Of course, you could not have thrown a stone in that room without hitting two or three inmates, and three large convicts took a lot of other people with them. Most of those decided to hit whoever seemed most responsible. Many hit people who had been doing nothing save watching a race or cheering on a whip-scorpion. In a few moments, everyone had a piece of the action whether they wanted one or not. I sincerely hoped that the lizards and other assorted wildlife took the chance to creep into the gaps in the floor, because there was a great deal of trampling going on. Some of the prisoners were professional thugs, duellists and killers, and others were fiercely defending their amateur status. Still more, such as Lucian and myself, were just doing our level best not to be stomped. I think that I must have run literally from one end of the room to the other some ten or twelve times to keep out of harm's way. All around me people were venting their aggression on any target that presented itself. A quiet den of gambling and vice had become a battlefield in the blink of an eye.

I remember seeing Lucian getting elbowed in the back of the head accidentally as some fighter geared up for another punch. Tallan, Onager's ugly henchman, was hit in the eye by someone else. At least four people tried their luck with Hermione and got floored for it.

Thelwel, a pacifist, came through it all without landing a blow. He passed through the fray like a dancer and nobody laid a finger on him.

I remember being backed into one corner of the storeroom as Onager pounded away at someone. All around on the floor prisoners were shaking their heads groggily, or just playing dead and hoping not to be stepped on. From somewhere there was the distinctive sharp clap as Hermione slapped someone across the side of the head. Onager dropped whoever he was working on and turned to face her furiously. He had a cut above one eye and the bruises from the previous night had a new complement of friends. I expected him to lunge at her full length across the room. Instead he stopped dead still. So did everyone else. Hermione looked from Onager to the doorway almost disinterestedly, and folded her arms. I crept out from Onager's shadow and saw that we had acquired an audience.

It was the Marshal, and he had with him some half-dozen Wardens. All of them had guns of one type or another, from shiny new flintlocks to older and deadlier devices I could not place. The expression on the Marshal's face meant death.

It was a specific death, though. It was around now that the third of my near-death experiences occurred.

Shameless and spurious suspense, I know. I had not so much as met the Marshal since my induction into the Island. He had his mind on bigger prey. His hawkish eyes raked over us all and he said, "Lorgry."

A man I had never noted before, a broad, bearded and anonymous creature, snapped his head up. I just had time to see the expression of hate and fear on his face before the Marshal shot him. It was a simple chemical projectile gun, of the kind that the ancients were so good at making. It made a mess of his head, certainly. The thought, inane as it was, came to me that it was a terrible thing to die with such a twisted expression on one's face. That one look was his last will and testament.

"Well," said the Marshal, almost in good humour. "I think that deals with the ringleader." Needless to say, Lorgry had played no great part in any of the preceding events that I was aware of. He had simply attracted the prior ire of the Marshal and this brawl had given the Marshal the opportunity to call in that debt. I never did find out what he had done to seal his fate.

"Get these men back to their cells," the Marshal ordered, and then held up a hand to stop the Wardens even as they moved in. "No. Fighting. Socialising. Forbidden things. I think we had best set some kind of example to prevent further chaos. Get me a troublemaker."

The Wardens exchanged glances and one was about to ask the Marshal to specify when his gloved hand stabbed out blindly. It could have fallen on anyone standing, and I was close to the front now. Curiosity had gotten the better of me. When that deadly finger pointed my way my heart froze. But of course it was not me. Some quirk of fate had conspired to let a little justice into the stale heart of the Island. The Marshal was pointing at Onager.

The big man was obviously going to make a fight of it, although I would have thought he would have had enough of being beaten. One of the Wardens jammed the barrel of a pistol underneath his chin, the flint drawn back and a tense finger on the trigger. All the fight went out of Onager right away. He had that much sense.

"Take him Below," was the Marshal's cryptic sentence, and Onager was led away. Only later, when Lucian regained consciousness, would I understand what that meant. Only later still would I see why it was so terrible. Certainly, I would never see Onager again.

9

The Great Disaster

"Going Below" turned out to be literal. There were three floors of prisoners in the Island, with the Wardens and then the Governor above. An inmate who was sent Below was rehoused on the lowest floor. When you were Below, you were right on the lake. The floor was at least three inches down through cold, slimy water with things in it. It was dark there, and it was always damp. Disease was rife, especially a kind of fungus that grew on anything, including people. Inmates Below were advised to sleep sitting up to avoid drowning. Also there were other dangers. The water below our feet was populated by monsters, and it was not unknown for one to force its way through the floor and supplement its diet.

All this we had from Lucian, who claimed to have done a few weeks Below once. He said that it was for refusing to submit to some degrading punishment, but I suspect that he just really annoyed a Warden with his ceaseless chatter. God knows, if I could have sent Lucian Below every time he annoyed me, he would have had webbed feet by the end of my first month's imprisonment.

A Warden might send a man Below for a short while. The Marshal sent men Below forever. He did not believe in half measures.

It is never pleasant to find that a bad situation has further nuances that one had not appreciated. I had assumed that the deal with the Wardens was that if they did not actually kill us, then their punishments were at least immediate and soon over. A beating hurts, but it hurts less the following morning. This Below-ing was an unwelcome development.

"I've been Below." The voice made Lucian and me start. It was Gaki's, of course. He could sit silent for a whole day, so that you forgot that he was there. The mind was always trying to forget Gaki. One word would bring it all back to you, then. You would suddenly be reminded that you were sharing a world with him.

"I pass by there sometimes, at night," he explained. He was in a pensive mood. "When everyone is asleep, sometimes I need the extra darkness." He was huddled in the shadows against the wall of our cell. "In the dead of night, you can hear things speaking to one another. Things that were never human." Gaki was a master of the human. He could crawl inside anyone's head and make trouble there. The idea of a non-human intellect clearly disturbed him.

We waited for a while to see if there was any more. Neither Lucian or I would willingly interrupt Gaki. Hermione, on the other hand, was new.

"Who are you?" she asked bluntly, and Gaki told her. Then she wanted to know why he had a cell to himself.

"Because I do not work well with others," he said softly. Hermione grunted in surprise.

"Is that all?" she said. "Neither do I. I want a cell to myself too." Gaki regarded her curiously.

Lucian was at Hermione's elbow, whispering urgently that Gaki was special, even the Marshal was scared of him.

"Hmf," Hermione said. "Special." Then the dreaded words, "Prove it."

The smile stretched a little wider on Gaki's pale visage. "Stefan," he whispered. "Step a little closer, would you?"

The Marshal never scared me as much as Gaki did. As a long-time coward, I have been a connoisseur of fear in my time and fear of Gaki was definitely a superior vintage. I stepped forwards. It only took one step, in that little cell, to see what he wanted me to see.

I will stress that the cell was gloomy to the extreme. The lamps in the corridor, and above and below, were dim, and the shadows fell in confusing patterns that could make anybody doubt their eyes. It was always hard to judge shape and distance in those latticed rooms.

When I stepped forward, I had one of those little changes of perspective. They happen all the time: at first glance one thing is close and tiny, but then you realise that it is huge and far away. Alternatively, something that looked as though it was behind, turns out to be in front. Gaki was in the cell with us.

I have no explanation that I would bet my life on. All I can assume is that we had grown so used to him being there, just on the other side of those bars, in the dark, in the gloom, that when he slipped from his own cell as we worked, and secreted himself in ours, we simply did not see the difference. True, he might have squeezed through the tiny gaps in the bars. He might have stepped mystically from the shadows on one side to the shadows on the other. I, who have seen and done enough strange things in my life, prefer not to believe in a world of such prodigies. I would prefer not to believe in a world with Gaki in it at all, but he was difficult to ignore.

Our food had been delivered a moment before, as luck would have it. Lucian had been holding forth about Below as a kind of pre-dinner conversation. Now he earned my lasting admiration by politely asking Gaki if he cared to eat with us, and proffering his own bowl.

"I don't mind if I do," said Gaki, and promptly erased Lucian from his notice, which suited Lucian just fine. On the basis that I was keeping as close to Lucian as I could, he also paid me no more heed. I tried, and failed, to imagine a mind that could know to the smallest detail that I would see him if I stood up and moved one pace towards him, and would not see him clearly otherwise, even when he was speaking to us. That degree of control frightened me. Then again, you will have noticed that I am not the hardest man to frighten.

Gaki himself, now that he was our guest, was interested in Hermione. It was a new experience, I think, to meet someone who did not instinctively keep out of his way. Hermione obviously did not feel the shudder that everyone from myself to the Marshal felt in Gaki's presence. She did not lower her eyes when their gazes locked. More, when Gaki left a topic pointedly unfinished, Hermione waded straight through his privacy and wanted answers. She fascinated him. It had been so long since Gaki had ever come up against someone so insensitive to menace. As Lucian and I shared my bowl of stew, he and the huge woman asked questions of each other. Gaki's answers were too soft to hear, and doubtless evasive. Hermione's showed that an exceptional person can still try to lead an unexceptional life. I think that, if she had been anyone other than a twenty-nine-stone, six-foot-five woman, then she would have passed through history without leaving a ripple.

Later on that night, the two of them were playing some kind of game I did not know. Gaki had scratched concentric circles onto the largest piece of flat floor, and they were moving splinters between them with great concentration. They reminded me bizarrely of children. They had the same complete absorption in what they were doing. They were both murderers, and Gaki was by far the least-human human being I have ever come across. For that quiet moment, though, they were innocents at play.

I remember thinking that I would never get to sleep with Gaki in the cell, but I did sleep, and when I awoke he was back on his side of the divide, leaving only a few circles scratched into the floor.

★

Where to begin?

That was the way Trethowan had chosen to start his last work. I liked it so much that I plagiarised it for my own.

Not strictly true. Trethowan had actually written ">?" which indicated that he was not sure how to progress. Old School Shorthand is so difficult because the translator must also be an eloquent writer to make sense of the rigidly abbreviated text. Hence no two translators would give the same result. The information would be identical but the styles would be quite different. For my part, I had read enough of Trethowan to give a fair approximation of his own words. I like to think that I did him justice.

I had been given a little room to myself, a cell not currently in use. Here the Governor had ordered to be placed the roughest desk I had ever worked at, a flat piece of tree nailed to another piece of tree. Obviously, within the ranks of the prisoners, there was not one halfway decent carpenter. Perhaps it was a particularly law-abiding profession. I had hoped to work at the Governor's own desk, but he apparently did not want me in his chambers again. The disappointment was acute. I had been hoping to ogle a few of the famed women prisoners.

So there I was with a makeshift desk, and another piece of tree to sit on. On one hand I had the precious stack of Trethowan's last thoughts and on the other a ream of fine paper and pens of various sizes, all at the Governor's expense. I was happier than I had been for a long time. I looked once upon that first symbol, that ">?", and knew that Trethowan was thinking, "Where to begin?" as surely as I would when I came to my own memoirs.

Trethowan and I had the same way of going about things. He, too, eschewed the rigmarole of place and history and breeding. I suspect that he knew his time was short and he needed to communicate this last lesson before his fate met him. I have always wondered what circumstances surrounded him being allowed to write this down, in a scholar's code indecipherable to his captors. Perhaps that was his last revenge on them, his little rebellion.

My own first act of rebellion comes here. It is characteristic of my life that it is a scholarly bit of work, inspired only by a love of useless knowledge. It is the ant scrawling graffiti on the ankle of the giant. Still, it shows at least a splinter of defiance, and for that reason I cling to it.

I realised that, while I was transcribing, nobody was keeping an eye on me. None could tell whether I was doing the task I had been set to or simply scrawling down nonsense. One writing man looks much the same as another. Hence, I made the Governor's pristine copies, but I made my own too. Not the whole manuscript, but I made copies of those parts that seemed important, those parts where Trethowan was most lucid, scribbled down in the original Old School to save time and space. Of the pages I omitted, most concerned themselves with natural history, Trethowan's passion. I feel justified in passing on them because, as Trethowan pointed out, they were becoming obsolete even then. The pages that I wished to keep I concealed within the mass of copies I had made, and at the most opportune moment, I slipped them into my prison greys. I accumulated quite a collection over all the time of my work, and I have them with me now, creased and stained as they are.

Later on, when I had gained in confidence, I began this journal too, telling my own little story in the shadow of Trethowan's philosophising. I crammed my meagre tribulations onto spare pages and hid them away, chapter by chapter, starting as he had started and recording a past that crept up on my present each time I added to it.

You have seen how I set out. Here, in contrast, is the very first page of Trethowan's last words, as rendered into proper language by yours truly. To give you an example of Old School Shorthand, the first two sentences together were formed of nine characters in the original, and were only that long because he had to define "ecologist".

Where to begin?

My name is Ignaz Trethowan and I am what was once called an ecologist. I made it my business to study the interrelations between living things and their environments. I have written twelve books on the subject misfiled as bestiaries by librarians with no imagination. Reference to them may be useful, if you can find copies. The annotated versions in the Academy vaults would be the most illuminating.

To the reader: herewith is the result of my last researches. These words are my legacy, and the most important things I will ever write. Take them seriously! They point the way to the future.

Your education may not cover the idea of ecology. I am perhaps the last person alive who has made that old science his business. I will use some of my little store of time to explain to you why this is so important. This should have been the work of years with scribes and copyists at my beck and call. Instead I write in shorthand in adverse circumstances, so forgive me, deride me, but at least read to the end.

Ecology is of no interest to my people, who lock themselves from the world. It is hardly surprising when the world has grown so hostile. The sun is dying slowly, and wreaks havoc on us as we circle round it. Our world is being changed and poisoned and everything that was is passing. My home is the last vestige of a long string of civilisations that have waxed and waned on the Earth. We ran out of resources and space and will. Now we sit in a single city and play games while the world is hammered on the anvil of the sun. [He wrote this out in full.] *It was believed by ecologists nine generations back that the living world was being destroyed by this hammering. This theory ended the serious study of the science. It is wrong. That is the most important thing I have to tell you. Just because we cease to look does not mean the world stands still. I have been into the jungle twelve times to gather my data and I am convinced of my conclusions. In the distant past, our ancestors seemed to be obsessed with the extinction of species. They measured time by the number of types of creature they destroyed. After this wholesale destruction came a general disinterest in the outside world because there was so little of it left. My colleagues ask, if that was so, how is there such abundant swamp and jungle at our very doorstep? I reply that evolution is not what it was. Every time I ventured into the jungle there has been a new ecology waiting for me. Evolution works in our jungles almost fast enough to see. As the world becomes unliveable, so life throws up things that can survive in it, faster and faster. One ancient theory was that the planet was aware, a great living world-mind. If so, then that mind has woken up. Life is teeming in the world as never before, changing and changing in the hope of finding a form that can last, and it is not just insensate, animal urges that are being churned up by this flood. There is intelligence out there. We are no longer alone.*

Do I have your interest yet?

So ran the introduction to Trethowan's work. It took me a whole afternoon to work out, and when the Warden came to return me to my cell I was desperate to learn more. As I walked back, something Trethowan had written recurred to me: He spoke of scribes and copyists. A cunning plan began to form in my head regarding the favour-economy practised amongst the prisoners. I think this marks the point when I really began to think like an Islander.

My plan would have to wait though. It would be pushed from my head by the Great Disaster.

When it happened, past midnight, I was suddenly awake with the knowledge that something was wrong. I could not place it, for I had not been on the Island long enough, but something had changed. I raised my head and saw that Lucian was also awake and looking around him, lamplight glittering from his wide eyes.

It was the quiet. That was what was different. Some distinctive sound that I had taken for granted was gone. I opened my mouth to phrase the question and realised before I spoke. The pumps. Something was different about the pumps. I could still hear the steady throbbing, but it was fainter than usual. With a slow, queasy feeling in my stomach I realised that the pump closest to us had stopped.

I did not know what the procedure was. Would it be looked at in the morning? Could the Island manage on only three pumps? Could I detect even then a faint tilt in the floor as the unsupported corner of the Island sagged into the water?

Then the shouting broke out. It was relatively distant at first, and below us, but it spread fast until there was a general uproar coursing through the Island in an attempt to get the notice of the Wardens. Men in the nearest cells to us were taking up the chorus, no words, just a caterwauling to make as much noise as possible. Lucian joined in, too, howling like a beast. Against that racket there was no point trying to ask questions. I just sat tight, waiting for something to happen. Living in a cage teaches you helplessness.

Soon, even through that row, I could hear running footsteps. The prisoners in the cells overhead fell quiet. For an irrational moment I thought that they were going to evacuate the whole place. Instead, though, the Wardens above us took a single man out of the cell, then locked it again.

"What is it?" I demanded of Lucian. "What are they going to do?"

Lucian told me that I would see, and it would teach me for being so clever, which was unhelpful. At that moment, though, two or three Wardens came pounding down our stretch. "Thelwel!" shouted one. "Advani!" shouted another. Even before I could register this, our door was being unlocked and a Warden reached inside and pulled me bodily out.

"What is this? What's going on?" I asked. The idea of being sacrificed to some great pump-god was rattling around in my head. I got struck and told to shut up for my pains, and was marched along next to Thelwel, who bid me a polite good day.

"Can you tell me what's going to happen to us?" I asked him desperately.

"Certainly," he said. "I didn't realise that you were an artificer when we met the other night, or I would have spoken to you at length."

"An artificer?" I goggled at him.

"Why, yes," he confirmed. "The pump won't fix itself."

"Oh, no no no," I said, mostly to myself. I understood the situation now. Yes, I knew a little about machines. No, I was no artificer. I was just about able to pass tools to Father Sulplice best of three. I explained this to Thelwel hurriedly.

"No matter. Every little helps." In his own way, Thelwel was as remorselessly positive as Lucian.

The big pumps that kept the Island afloat extended through the bottom two levels, and the problem seemed to be with the top part, or at least that was where we were taken. By the time we were there the floor was at a definite angle, sloping towards the broken machine, so that Thelwel, our guards and I skidded and slipped over the uneven floor.

The sight was chaos. The pump was over ten feet across, a vast, lumpy cylinder with tubes, vents and wheels projecting at all angles. The entire rusty contraption was at a tilt, and steam was gusting from a broken seal, fogging the air. Below us there was a steady chorus of cries from the prisoners on the lowest level. As we arrived, a huge section of casing was levered off the pump to crash and slide on the floor. Father Sulplice, like a superannuated monkey, was hanging halfway up the machine, cursing and spitting. Thelwel broke into a run and I joined him.

There were two or three other prisoners there assisting, plus a couple of Wardens. One was the man I knew as "Red" and the other was a balding, stocky man by the name of Harkeri. Father Sulplice had obviously been making the running up until them, with everyone else just holding things for him and helping as best they could. Thelwel threw himself into the work instantly, though, and I was surprised to see Father Sulplice give place to him without a word.

"Diagnosis?" he asked.

"Blown seal, cracked secondary casing, sieve plate's gotten mangled, and there's something wedged up near the blades," Father Sulplice rattled off quickly. "I've sent someone for a new seal and some tape."

"Good." Thelwel took precisely one second to think. "Stefan, look here," he said, and I looked. It was one of the sieves that fed us, and something had gone straight through it so that pieces of mesh were stuck everywhere. I saw immediately what he wanted me to do and began prying all the broken strands from within the machinery. It was a task that fit my abilities.

"Get the casing laid out ready, lads," Father Sulplice directed. "You fancy getting the old seal out, son?" This last was to Harkeri the Warden, who obeyed without question. Everything was noticeably more at an angle now. I was hunched over part of the machinery, clinging on with my knees even as I levered the mesh away from the mechanism. The air around us was a constant clamour of shouting, escaping steam and the clattering of metal. Prisoner and Warden were forgotten in the heat of the emergency. As Thelwel checked the mechanisms nearest the seal to ensure that they had not been damaged as well, Red stood beside him with his arms up to the elbows in the works, trying to free whatever had jammed the fan blades. At around this time another prisoner arrived with a trailing rubber seal and a roll of metal tape which Thelwel descended on swiftly. He assigned someone to tape over the cracked casing, whilst he himself began to install the new seal. He worked with a cool-headed speed that was astonishing, not letting anything distract him from his task. He never cursed or lost patience with the machinery, even when the seal proved to be badly made and refused to squeeze into its groove. He just tried and tried again as the steam sprayed in his face and the world continued to list.

I, on the other hand, was cursing and digging with my fingernails at a stubborn section of mesh which was wedged good and proper between two pipes. I clawed and pried at the metal, and it came free all at once when I was least expecting it. I ended up bouncing down the inclined floor, and when I hit the lowest corner I was wet, because the water of the lake was just beginning to impinge on us. I gave out a horrified yell and got to my feet, splashing and struggling. At the pump, Red suddenly hauled a vast length of weed out from the blades and in the same breath Thelwel struck him hard across the chest, sending him hurtling towards me so that we both landed in a heap. Even as he fought to get up I heard the blades keen into life. Red's face showed the pale realisation that Thelwel had just saved his fingers.

Harkeri pounded in with a new sieve, which fit perfectly, I am pleased to say. Thelwel and Father Sulplice were forcing the new seal into place with a combination of main force and ingenuity. They worked as one, with utter concentration. Belatedly, I guessed that Thelwel must be the son of Father Sulplice, whose well-being was always being held over the old man's head.

"Ready with the casing, lads," Father Sulplice directed, and Red and I struggled up to help lift the heavy piece of metal into place. This last piece was a nightmare of slipping and lurching. The piece fitted on what was now the underside of the pump, and so we were standing on a slope trying to fit something above our heads. All the while the pump shuddered and gasped and tried to get going, and the mechanisms below us began to dredge up gallons of lakewater that gushed past us even as Thelwel and his father tried to keep it in with the casing. Red climbed past me and braced himself against it and the three of them exerted every muscle in their bodies to force the metal closed. Leaving the men on either side of me, I took up one of Father Sulplice's bigger tools, a wrench as long as my arm, and lunged at the recalcitrant casing with it, digging my toes into the slanted floor. I surely added very little to the net force that was being applied, but perhaps that little did the trick for the casing clicked shut, and Father Sulplice bolted it in place with a kind of monstrous stapler. All at once the sound of the pump changed from a tortured creaking to the firm, rhythmic thudding which had underlain our every moment in the Island. We watched the casing anxiously in case it was going to fly loose, but after a slow count of twenty it was evident that everything was working. By the time we were sure, the floor was beginning to assume its normal orientation.

I cannot tell you what it felt like in that moment. Father Sulplice and his son embraced, and Red, the Warden, clapped me on the back and grinned at me, and I grinned back. We were the men who had saved the Island. For just one moment we were all comrades, and heroes.

Then the Marshal was in the doorway. Perhaps he had always been there, calmly watching our desperate efforts.

"The emergency is over," he said in his soulless voice. "Get these men back to their cells." And that was that. Red and Harkeri became Wardens again, and everyone else reverted to being inmates. The next day, though, behind the Marshal's back, we would all be given easy duties, and other prisoners would even offer to do those for us. There was thanks to be found even in the Island, if you knew where to look.

I did not discover until a day or so later that seventeen men had drowned in the Great Disaster, and that one of those was

101

Onager. It could have been me, I thought, and was relieved. That was all I thought about it until some time later, when I realised that I had lost some part of my humanity. For all that Onager had treated me badly and made my life a misery, he was still a human being and I owed him some kind of sadness at his passing. Instead, I had felt only relief that another had been taken in my place. For the sixteen drowned men that I never knew, I felt nothing. Of course, when this revelation came to me I felt all the proper things, such a waste, such a shame, and so forth, but the memory of my initial reaction stayed with me. I am just as ashamed now, but I will still own to it. It is easy for a comfortable, free man to cry at the fall of every little bird. A prisoner in fear of his life has precious little regret to spare for anyone else.

10

Knights Errant and Gallant

Capitalising on my high stock within the Island, I chose my next scribing episode to put my cunning plan into operation. I was being watched over by Midds, who would at least probably not have me killed if he found me out. Midds was a man who tried to live each day with a minimum of effort. He had no zeal for his job and no great bitterness to take out on his charges. While I scribbled away he leant against the corridor wall and smoked his handmade herbal rollups. The vice was widespread amongst the Wardens. It brought calm and occasional visions, and was slightly addictive. The weeds themselves grew in the swamps, and boat-crews kept an eye out for them.

I worked away for about an hour, and then I called out to the Warden, who shambled in without much curiosity.

"Want me to sharpen your pencil for you?" he asked idly.

"Actually, I've had a thought," I told him. True enough, although the relevant thought had been had some days before. "This is going to take me forever. I mean, look at this." I showed him a representative page. Midds' religious education had made him a fair reader, but Old School Shorthand was beyond him.

"What do you want me to do about it?" he said.

"I need someone for me to dictate to," I told him. "If I could just read this out to someone, rather than having to do it all out longhand, I'd get this done in half the time." Actually, I honestly don't think that it would have made that much difference. It sounded reasonable, though, and Midds was not to know any different.

"I don't know about that," he said slowly.

"The Governor is very keen to read these. He's been sitting on them for years waiting for someone to come along and translate them. Now I'm here he really doesn't want to have to wait a moment more than he has to." I wasn't sure how the Wardens viewed the Governor, but he relayed his commands via the Marshal, who scared all hell out of them.

Midds looked at me suspiciously and I think he knew some trick was being pulled. As I say, though, he was not a man to exert himself needlessly. Getting me a copyist was easier than arguing it over with me, plus the outside chance of displeasing the Governor. I could virtually see the calculations on his face.

"Well, what scribe?" he said eventually. "The Governor wanted you, after all. He doesn't want any old sod to write it down for him."

"I know some of the other prisoners who have clerical backgrounds. They'll be trained to write neatly and well. Better than me, to be honest. At the Academy we had people to copy down our writings; I'm not used to doing it all myself." Any devious plan should be at least seven parts truth to three parts fabrication.

"Well…" Midds weighed the odds one final time and came down on the side of least resistance. "Who are you after?"

"Shon Roseblade. He has a scar from here to here."

Midds did not know him, but he was already won over so it was a small step to convince him to accompany me to the machine room and the workshop. I found Lucian and asked directions, and was led to Shon, who was sweeping a floor. He glanced up warily as I approached with a Warden in tow.

"There's a job for you," Midds told him. "Got to be better than this. Come on."

On the way back to my little study I explained the deal to him and he understood instantly. He grinned at me behind Midds' back and acknowledged that an Academy education was clearly good for something.

The irony was that Shon's handwriting *was* a good deal easier and clearer than mine. In the shadier end of the legal profession he had seldom been given access to secretaries and did most of his own writs. As I worked my way through Trethowan's dense code, he put down my careful sentences in an elegant hand. Midds kept out of our way for most of the time, and actually left us for about an hour to go and find something to eat. Shon and I caught up on our respective histories. I explained to him about the Outing and the Great Disaster. He told me about a man on his stretch who had gone violently mad and killed a Warden. Everyone in that cell had been shot. On the upside, Shon had won three meals in an Outing of his own. Thusly we exchanged all the minutiae of prison life.

A day or so later I received a neatly written slip telling me that the Governor was pleased by the improved quality of my work. I kept the slip with my pirate copies of Trethowan's work and my own burgeoning autobiography.

After the second successful demand for a copyist to help me, it became standard practice. Word got around the Wardens, and after a week or two whichever man was supervising me would just march me out into the machine room and let me pick my companion. I chose Shon a lot of the time, and Lucian occasionally, and Thelwel. All of these could write well and Lucian, the forger, had extraordinarily beautiful handwriting. He would have made so much more money by exploiting his talents legitimately. There were other copyists as well, mostly men to whom I owed debts from various Outings. I made sure that I only bet with men who had shown me their prowess with the pen. This was not hard. As soon as it became known that Stefan Advani could save someone a day's labour, inmates were queuing down the halls to prove their calligraphy to me.

I finally seemed to have found my niche on the Island. Change, though, as Trethowan often stressed, is endemic in every situation.

I had another chess session with Peter soon enough, which was my cultural equivalent of a night at the opera. (This is a disputed subject, so I should make it clear that I am quite fond of the opera.)

"Has the Marshal got some terminal disease?" I asked him as we set the board up.

"Hah?" Peter glanced up.

"You're whistling."

"Oh, that." He permitted himself a lopsided smile. "I've had a holiday."

"Back home? I thought that you had… reasons for leaving." I still had no idea what those reasons were and was always looking for an opportunity to bring the subject up.

"Oh, Shadrapar is quite definitely closed to me," he agreed. "The world has other places, though," he added loftily. He reached into his uniform tunic to produce his familiar flask and a couple of little metal beakers. "Try some of this," he suggested. "One of the Wardens brews it. Evil stuff."

I waited politely until he had poured us each a cupful of the sludge-coloured liquid. "So," I prompted, but he was already lifting his cup and it would have been churlish not to join him.

"So," I said again, after a sip, and then I coughed quite a lot and demanded to know what he had just poisoned me with. That drink was the Gaki of the alcoholic world.

"It depends on what Harkeri gets to ferment," Peter explained. "This is a good batch, on the basis that we can still see."

I recalled the balding, solid Harkeri, apprentice tinkerer. He had not seemed the type to be distilling moonshine. A sombre, studious man, I had thought, and said so.

"He's a religious nut," Peter explained expansively. "Have you ever heard of the Agrarians? Apparently, they have serious rituals for which getting solemnly and devoutly drunk is all part of it. They fiddle with their brains so they can drink forever without falling over. Harkeri's the quietest drunk you ever saw. He says it gives him visions. It turns you blind, but then you're supposed to be able to see something he calls 'the Geometry of God', all these weird lines and shapes. After coming here it didn't take long for him to start peddling the stuff in exchange for whatever was going. He's all right, once you get to know him. Tell the truth, I prefer the quiet ones."

I took another sip, which probably did bring me closer to God, in the sense of accelerating my liver failure. "So," I managed eventually, for the third time, "where were you travelling?"

Peter held out his hands with two pieces in them. "White starts," he suggested. I knew full well that both pieces would be black, but could not be bothered to keep calling him on it. As luck would have it, therefore, Peter had the first move.

"I got myself boat duty," he told me. "Don't know why I didn't think of it sooner. Not exactly safe, but worth it for the fresh air. I really didn't realise I'd hate being cooped up with people so much. I might have stayed to face the music if I'd known. Anyway, you remember the Marshal's little toy dinghy, when we were coming in? Well, the collecting boats are a bit like that, but much, much bigger. Most of that is the tanks: there are these great big empty tanks to suck the water into, plus some kind of machine to do the sucking. There's three things that stick down into the water and make the boat go somehow. From what I've been hearing, you're the new expert on things mechanical, so maybe you could tell me."

I confessed that I had absolutely no idea and referred him to Father Sulplice.

"Anyway," he said. "You've got all this, which takes up most of the room on the boat, and then you've got a kind of a plate stuck on the front of all the other machines which has about five different-coloured lights on it, and basically, what you do, is you cruise about the swamp until most of the lights light up, and then you take in some water into the tanks until the lights go off. I assume they're detecting things in the water, but I really am happy in my complete ignorance of the subject. So, there's me, and three of your lot. We're out there on our own for at least a day and a night, that being how long it takes to get everything properly filled, at a minimum. Every so often we need to go somewhere overgrown and everyone gets out and clears the way with sticks. Then there's getting food, where you basically eat what you find. They always send someone out who's gone before and knows what you can eat and what you can't."

"I'll bet it changes a lot," I broke in. "I'll wager the boat veterans find they have to keep changing their diet."

"That's right," Peter acknowledged. "One of them was saying just that to me. How'd you know?"

"An education's good for something," I said airily, thinking of Trethowan. "Did you see anything out there? Anything unusual?"

"You're thinking of those huts and things we saw on the way in," he guessed, although actually I had nearly forgotten. "Web-children, was it? No, to be honest. I heard plenty of stories from the others. Tribes of gill-people, snakes with human faces, stones that could speak, all the usual. I think they were just putting the frighteners on me. The new guy, you know."

"All quiet then?"

"Oh, plenty of things tried to kill me," Peter assured me, as if to say that a day was not complete without at least one attempt on his life. He then regaled me with a story about something like a lobster, large as his boat, which had decided to make snacks of Peter and his crew. I was unsure how much to believe of this, because he was prone to exaggeration and Trethowan had never mentioned anything like it. On the other hand, the world was patently stranger than I knew, and apparently getting stranger all the time. Giant lobsters were surely not an unthinkable complication. In Peter's tale, they dealt with the threat by backing the boat into it at top speed, whereby whatever mechanism propelled the boat proved unpleasant enough to the lobster to drive it away. As we skipped our pieces over the board he went on to tell of the lagoon he and his crew had discovered, uncharted by man. The eyeless monsters had raised their heads from the waters there and called to each other, washing their flippers through the waves, a waltz of the blind never before seen by human eyes. The land around the Island was filled with such secret wonders. The Governors of the Island had long given up mapping the boundaries of land and water, for such maps were never good the second time round. It was Trethowan's promise: life was indefatiguable.

Peter made the expeditions sound very attractive, and I'd already had thoughts in that direction. I would get to see the sky, after all. I would get to see what Trethowan had been so impressed by. I made up my mind to at least give it a try: another deviation from my usual character. My life on the Island was changing me even as the world changed outside.

Peter then diverted me with further tales of what he had seen away from the island; huge amphibious monsters with man-size jaws that closed only on waterweed; swimming things like scorpions with paddle tails preying on fish caught in the suction of the punps; serpents wth fur, like limbless otters that had abandoned the land forever. It seemed to me, with my limited knowledge of the subject, that the world was casting up every design from its past to see what fitted best. Beyond this there were the tales which Peter himself doubted, told to him by prisoners who had been out many times. Cities drowned in the mire, so that a boat had to pick its way through the rooftops; places of death where invisible rays from ancient machines killed any living thing with blindness and sickness; and of course the endless tales of things in the swamp that built and spoke. The web-children, always the web-children. They were said to be like fish, but others said like frogs, and still others said that they could pass for humans if they tried, except for their eyes, too wide and never blinking. Peter thought they were probably a tribe of feral people, cut off from Shadrapar generations ago, perhaps even escaped prisoners. I was more hesitant in committing myself. Trethowan had pushed back a lot of horizons.

Picture me there, then. I am enjoying a game of chess with my friend Peter Drachmar. There is a drink to hand, which improves with the tasting. I have a life that breaks up the monotony with regular intervals of study, such as I enjoy. I have a few other associates whose company is tolerable. You might say that I had rather fallen on my feet, for someone condemned to lifelong imprisonment.

Needless to say, all this was to go down the pan in short order and I have only the finer side of my nature to blame. As I have mentioned, whenever my reluctant valour creeps from hiding, disaster almost always follows.

There was another Outing. That was where the trouble started. Needless to say I was better prepared for this one, and came to the great racing meet with stock in trade: to wit, three copying sessions and a lizard. The lizard had already bitten me three times, and so I hoped that it was a goer.

With a basic grasp of the proceedings, and no Onager, it was a pleasant occasion. Word was around that I was a hero of the Great Disaster, had the power to grant favours, was in with the Governor and had at least one Warden eating out of the palm of my hand. I was hailed as a close friend by a number of people I had never even met.

I had wanted to seek out Thelwel, but Hermione was already monopolising him. Instead, I found a race that was being organised and entered my runner, who bit me once more for luck. Whenever anyone tried to bet with me I first demanded proof of handwriting, which amused the other prisoners no end. The race did not go quite as planned in the offing, on the basis that my reptile decided to attack one of its fellows and ignored the bait completely. Not only did I lose the race, but one of the other prisoners was complaining that I had fixed his lizard by setting my own onto it. Shortly thereafter I lost my racer, whose form I had begun to doubt, on a side-bet. From that point on I decided to play the odds and try to make a few decent wins on other inmates' beasts. It was surprisingly like playing chess with Peter. I sat there assured of my superior intellect and made the most calculated judgement calls, and I lost everything except my shirt. It was lamentable. There was obviously something missing in my analysis of the situation, because I was being inexplicably taken for a ride by men who would have been unable to master basic calculus. It began to eat into my good humour after a while, having lost three scribing sessions to people I was not overly fond of. One of them had not actually been all that literate, and I suspected that I would be doing the writing at that session, with an idle audience of one. That was when I went in search of better company. The wise man knows when to quit.

Better company was hard to find. Lucian was in the midst of a bit of scorpion-baiting, and Thelwel was still talking to Hermione. All would have been so different if I had just settled down to watch the races, but they irked me, and given that there was nobody I wanted to talk to who was free to talk to me, I decided to call it a night.

So, I was out of the storeroom, thinking that if the Marshal should make another appearance, at least I would be out of his way. I was not the only wanderer. Some men had gone for private liaisons of their own, others were just stretching their legs. Perhaps, I thought, I will talk to Gaki. At least he can keep up an intelligent conversation when he wants to.

That was when I heard the scuffling ahead. I froze, thinking it was the Marshal, and then unfroze, because I could see the flash of prison greys in the gloom. Just a couple of inmates having a disagreement, I decided.

As my eyes grew more accustomed to the light I saw that there were three there, and that the two larger were struggling to restrain the smaller. I recognised the two attackers as Tallan and his nameless, shock-headed friend. The lack of Onager had obviously not dampened their enthusiasm for bullying.

I was angry and tired: a good place from which to make bad decisions. Also, the attention paid to me by other prisoners, regarding the services I could provide, had gifted me with an inflated sense of my own importance in this closed-off little world.

Their victim started a renewed bout of fighting and Tallan slammed a fist in that drew a grunt of pain. The unfortunate was half the size of either of them, no bigger than I was. Then they had thrown the poor creature down, and it was plain to me that they meant grievous bodily harm at the least, murder at the worst.

And so, in strides Stefan Advani the avenger, less to see justice done than because I loathed Tallan and the other one, and I had the hilarious misconception that I could do something to help,

"Hey!" was my battle cry. "Stop that! Hey!" It struck fear into them, I'm sure.

I'd got too close already and Tallan turned, frowning, and backhanded me to the floor. His fellow took the opportunity to put the boot into their primary target, prompting a cry of pain that stopped all three of us for a second, a weirdly familiar revelation. This voice, from a more conventional vessel than Hermione's, nonetheless also belonged to a woman. It was plainly the first that any of us knew of it.

Tallan spat contemptuously at me, dismissing my presence as both surplus to requirements and irrelevant, and his friend hoisted their victim up for a better look. All the little irritations of the night suddenly condensed within me and I was abruptly resigned to what I would do next. I lurched to my feet and focused my inner energies. When I had them in a tight ball in the centre of my mind, as I had done so many times before, I reached out and pushed with them. It brought a wave of nostalgia for the old times with my academic colleagues, when we used to practise this almost as a hobby.

I was used to exerting my mind against my friend Helman, who would be pushing back just as hard against me. It had been like punching a brick wall. He had been a man of extraordinary willpower, far greater than mine. When I pushed my energies onto the shock-headed man I just felt a horrible giving sensation as I smashed into his unprepared brain. It was like clutching a stone and feeling it crumble to mould under your fingers. The shock-headed man gave out a dreadful inhalation, a harsh gasp for air that would do him no good, and then he convulsed once and flopped onto his back.

Harro. His name was Harro. I remember now.

Tallan looked at his victim, at me and at his friend's body, and then ran for it. I think that I must have looked quite imposing, with my face a death-mask and my body thrumming with guilt. All the backwash of my mental energies was coursing through me, and I was aware that I had killed. It was not as though I had run him through with a knife. That would have been circumstantial in comparison. I had felt his mind collapse beneath my touch. If you have never done this, you can never know just how hideous a feeling it is.

The next thing I knew with any certainty was that their erstwhile prey was standing before me. Possibly there were words but I was trying to keep my brain together and didn't hear them. A moment later my eyes focused and I saw before me a woman wearing ill-fitting convict greys. She was small, dark, with a fashionably heart-shaped face and the expensive beauty of the rich, now her hair was not cast forwards to hide it. Possibly she was trying to thank me; possibly she was unsure whether I had actually helped her or just turned up in time to see Harro expire of natural causes.

The obvious ramifications were hammering into me. I was a murderer. Whatever I might say about false imprisonment, I had earned my place here now. All this recrimination stopped me paying much attention to whatever she was saying, and then it was too late.

The Marshal was there, at last, with armed Wardens. He was obviously unsure of what to make of the situation. He stepped forwards to take charge and then saw something in my face that he did not like.

"Take her," he snapped, after an uncharacteristic pause. The woman was grabbed by two or three Wardens and dragged off. She did not even try to struggle, but she did look back at me.

The Marshal looked down at Harro's body, upon which there was not a mark. I had come to my senses by then and started backing away. At every pace I thought he would call me back, perhaps even have me shot. Instead I got clean away, although I could feel him staring at me until I turned the corner.

When I rejoined the other prisoners, as we began to trek back to our cells, there was a difference. Tallan had been telling stories about me. He had no inkling of what it was that I had actually done, but he knew I had done it. Most of the prisoners gave me plenty of space, and did not meet my eyes.

That night, I was chased in nightmares by the sensation of Harro's mind folding in on itself, collapsing like a house of cards.

11

Repercussions

I am driven to wonder whether the reader of this account has been assuming that all this business with mental energies and focusing was just an academic's fantasy.

Now you know.

For about three days I lived in dread and mostly in isolation. The other inmates had no wish to go anywhere near me. It was not that I was a murderer. That, after all, was not an unusual thing in the Island. It was the means. Tallan had been quite explicit about what had happened. I had stepped up behind Harro and stared at him, and Harro had died. That made me too much of an unknown factor as far as the Islanders were concerned. If I could kill with a look then I was far too dangerous to be around.

The Wardens watched me very narrowly as well. I made sure that I gave them no excuse.

The fact was that it was all a fuss over nothing. Harro had been something of a fluke, the combination of an unheralded concentration against a weak and wholly unsuspecting mind. The very fact that people were wary around me stymied any power I might have had over them. Now things had gone so far, though, I suspected that I was better keeping that a secret. There was no telling what might happen to me if people discovered I was actually defenceless.

Lucian did not talk to me, when we were locked up for the night. I would have counted this as a blessing at any other time, but I had been in silence all day, and even Lucian's prattle would have been welcome. As for Hermione, she was never very talkative.

"So you killed someone, then," she observed.

I admitted that I had.

"One of the people who hit me."

I said that this also was true.

"Good," she told me, and that was that. She had no real interest in methodology.

All the way through this, I could feel Gaki watching me. His eyes glittered through the darkness at me, but he held his peace. His expression, when the lamps lit it, was one of calculation. For two nights his silent vigil disturbed my sleep. Only on the third did he say even a few words.

"You have hidden depths, Stefan," he chided softly. The others were asleep. It was just him and me.

I made no answer.

"I might have to kill you, eventually," he told me evenly. "I do hate things that I don't understand."

I tried to meet his gaze and failed. For three days I had wanted to talk to someone and now I was mute.

"Not yet, though," he said. "I will make some attempt to understand you, first."

In the darkness I wondered whether I could force my mind on Gaki, and knew that I could not. His own must be like a knifeblade. I would shred myself against it.

"When I was with Sandor," Gaki said, "he often speculated about the powers of the mind." He left it at that, closing the subject neatly. I was left wondering just how far Gaki had gone along that road. The human mind, as I knew like no other, is a tool with a thousand uses. Helman and I had often sat up late discussing just how society might benefit from the powers of the mind.

Now I was faced with the other side of that argument. My own mind had done nothing but kill a man, and now there was a monster in the next cell pondering on how to apply his intelligence. Things did not look good for the advancement of mankind.

It was the very next day when they came for me. Two Wardens shouldered their way through the toiling prisoners, grabbed me by the arms and hauled me away. It was not even at night. I had been fearing every footstep outside my cell for nothing. Everything was in broad daylight and before a hundred witnesses, none of whom did anything to stop it.

It was a long walk, long enough for me to give full consideration to the fates awaiting me. The two Wardens escorting me did not speak, nor did they slacken their pace, and I knew neither of them. I had assumed that I would be brought up before the Marshal for swift retribution, but instead I was hoisted beyond the Wardens' level, all the way to the top. The Governor wanted to see me.

The Governor, I believed, needed me. I was working on his pet project. I should have been reassured to discover our destination. Instead, something told me that things were not going to be as simple as that.

I had run the entire gauntlet of fears by the time we arrived, from leaden dread (of an inexorable fate awaiting me) to knee-trembling terror (of immediate physical peril) through all the little shades and distinctions in between. I am something of an expert on the subject of fear, but on that long journey to judgement, I ran dry. At the end, as we mounted the final stairs, I found all fear gone from me, replaced by a fragile calm. I knew that I was in far more trouble than I had ever been in before. At the same time I knew that it was not the death of Harro that would be laid at my door. I had to try and work out what line I had crossed.

I had at least one bargaining chip. The Governor wanted Trethowan translated, and there was nobody else in the prison who could do it. It was not much. After all, he had gone for years without it. It was the smallest lever for me to exert pressure on.

The Governor's rooms in daylight were brighter than before, but not much. There was much use of drapes to keep the sun out, and a lot of the earlier gloom was still keeping him company. I wondered whether his hairless skin burned easily. I could see the man himself at the far end of the room, illuminated by something quite unlike natural light. There was a malign, flickering radiance cast across his soft face, and it came from the mirror that I had noted before.

Despite my situation I could not help but feel excited at this discovery. I knew of such devices, of course. There had even been one at the Academy, although it had not functioned in living memory. To find one in working order here was astonishing, as was the implication that another such machine must exist in the city by which the Governor could communicate with his own superiors.

My excitement dimmed somewhat when I made out what the Governor and his correspondent were saying.

"And this is what?" the Governor demanded.

"Something he produced, with a few others. It was in his file," came the reply. I could not make out the face that the mirror was displaying, the angle was too sharp, but the voice sounded slightly familiar.

"The reason for his conviction," the Governor suggested.

"Probably. I get the impression it caused a stir at the time. I really can't remember. I've had a clerk go through it for you. Nothing earth-shattering."

"What about these mind powers you mentioned?"

"Oh, they're in there," the unseen man responded. "No detail, but they're there. The entire thrust was, I am informed, that there was no future in the way we were living and we should seek out alternative lifestyles. There's a chapter on "*The Ancients' Ancients*", if you can believe that, where your man reckons that there were once civilisations that, and I quote, '*Did not require physical tools to accomplish physical tasks, instead manipulating the infinitely more powerful forces of the universe with their minds alone. These energies are implicit in the very structure of being and need only to be tapped with the correct mental manipulation. A small push can therefore trigger a prodigious result. To work through machines is to batter a door down, whereas the mind is the key that can open the lock.*' How about that?"

I recognised the words, of course. They were Helman's, although the final comparison is mine. The book they were talking about was the very volume that my friends and I had produced. They were checking up on me, and had already linked Harro's death to my studies at the Academy.

"There's more of the same, unfortunately," the man in the mirror was saying. "Then it goes into references. Various recovered ancient documents, which supposedly hint at still more ancient secrets, and so on and so forth. Various recent but highly dubious papers claiming to demonstrate the existence of these powers. At the back there's some kind of experimental log, but to be honest I can't make much of it. You know I only got my Academy Reds by bribes and good family. There's certainly nothing about using it as a weapon. Like most idealists they thought that their perfect mind-control world wouldn't need weapons."

"What about side effects?" the Governor asked. "There must be something."

"Leo, Leo, Leo, believe me. I have had some very bored clerks go over every word. It all reads like anyone else's mystic rubbish. Your man there probably just died. People do just die, especially on the Island."

"No." The Governor looked frustrated and fed up. He was quite different to the vague and distant man who had commissioned me before. "*She* is insistent, Harweg. Something happened."

"Well, I'll send the book to you on the next boat. It's only taking up space here," Harweg said through the mirror. "Anyway, that's all I can spare you. Keep up the work and all that, and I'll speak to you before the end of the week."

The mirror went abruptly dark, just after I recalled that Harweg was the name of the current Lord President. The Governor, "Leo", had friends in high places. By that time the bald man was turning on me.

"Now you," he said, as sharply as his voice would permit. "Tell me what you did."

I stared at him, trying to work out what it was he wanted. "I was just defending someone," I started uncertainly. "I know that the man died, but I didn't have any option at the time, and he was going to—"

"Enough," the Governor snapped. He looked like a man under pressure, which was odd considering that he was the master here. "I don't care how many inmates you kill. Why should that matter to me? It's not my job to count them. What did you do? What effects does it have?"

"Well..." His unpleasant, soft face was very close to my own, and I tried not to meet his eyes. "In theory it can do all manner of things. We never really worked out the limits—"

He struck me. He actually struck me. It was like being slapped with a damp cloth. He probably hurt his hand on my cheekbone far more than he hurt me. The very surprise of it was enough to silence me for a moment, and then I blurted out, "It kills. Obviously. That is what it did. It killed him."

"I know what it did to him," the Governor spelled out to me. "What about to... others? What side effects does it have? How does it contaminate?"

"Contaminate?" I asked, baffled.

"This mental radiation of yours. Does it leak? Does it creep out of your head when you're not using it? When you use it, how does it taint those around you? How does it spoil them? Answer me!"

I goggled at him, utterly bewildered. The conversation had taken a sharp turn and scuttled away from any territory I was familiar with at breakneck speed. The Governor looked as though he might hit me again, and to avoid any contact with that fungous skin I said, "I really don't understand, sir. I'm sorry."

He turned away. He was so clearly a man who had never really needed to be angry in his life. He was bad at it. He didn't think to have the Wardens beat me. He didn't think to make threats (which he was in an ideal position to enforce). He was quite out of his element. In retrospect I almost feel sorry for the man.

"There was someone else there, when you did this thing," his voice came to me, more under control now. "Two others, as it happened. There was the accomplice of the man you killed, and there was... another person there. This mental power of yours... it affected them, yes? A fallout. It contaminated them. Yes? Well?"

I really didn't think that it had; I had really never thought about it. "It doesn't seem very likely," I told him, a scholar again for just a second.

"'It doesn't seem very likely,'" he parroted back to me. "You don't even know. This unnatural power you have and you don't even know." He stomped off across the room in disgust, leaving me none the wiser. The two Wardens were still holding me by the arms, and I hung between them, trying to work it out. I began to feel that the four of us (Leo, myself and my escort) were not alone. It was partly a sense that I was being watched and partly that the whole equation was missing a piece. I started looking into the shadows and the doorways and wasted too much time thinking like a city man. In the Island you could be watched straight through the walls. Even the Governor's room had chinks and holes enough for a legion of spies. Once I had

121

considered that, I soon saw the shadow behind the latticework, and knew that it must be Lady Ellera, the Governor's mistress, whom even Gaki respected. It was she who was pressuring the Governor over this. Gaki had said that she had uses for the other women prisoners. Somehow I had interfered with such a use. Either there really was some side effect that I was not aware of, or she just thought there was. I could imagine her, secure in the considerable power she wielded, coming up against something she did not understand. I have known such people and they always throw tantrums on the rare occasions the world trips them. Personally, I did not believe any of that talk about contamination, but people fear the unknown, and those used to control fear that which they cannot.

The woman Gaki feared was afraid of me.

"What are we going to do with him?" the Governor asked, and I did not know whether he was talking to her or to himself. As it happened, he was talking to neither. There was a single light step behind me, and then I felt the cold barrel of a pistol just beneath my ear.

"Simple enough," said the Marshal.

The Governor looked at me, and at him. The man had been patiently standing in the shadows and I had not noticed him at all. All of a sudden he was about to pull the trigger. My much-vaunted brains and mental powers were going to be all over the Governor's walls and ceiling.

I think it was that thought which the Governor disliked. It was too immediate and messy. The other thing that saved me was that he was unused to dealing with prisoners face to face. His world was more civilised and far less brutal than the Marshal's. Indeed, the very brutality of the Marshal allowed him to exist in pampered isolation up in his rooftop abode. When faced with personally ordering a death sentence, as opposed to just knowing that such things went on in his name, I think he was rather shocked.

"Oh no," he said. "Wasteful. My new clerk has not arrived

yet, and I would rather not burn my bridges until I know that his replacement is up to standard."

Those words, of course, were my death sentence, whether immediate or eventual. Obviously, when the whole of Trethowan was a blank to him, he could take it or leave it. Now that I had given him a taste for it he had decided to go the whole way and hire a professional clerk out of his own pocket. My usefulness to the Governor had just evaporated like the morning dew.

"With respect, sir, I really think that we should make an example of him," the Marshal said flatly.

"Why's that? Who to?" the Governor asked, genuinely for information. There was a strained silence from behind me, and I realised that the Marshal was actually trying to find a good reason for killing me. He had never needed to justify it before.

"Because he has displeased you," was all he came up with, and even at the time I thought it was rather weak.

"No, no," the Governor said. "Waste, Marshal. Just put him somewhere until we know whether we can spare him."

The Marshal grunted. "How about Below, sir?"

"Oh, whatever," was the Governor's blithe reply. "Just put him somewhere where he won't get in the way again."

"Very well." When I was turned to look at him, the Marshal's face was the hostile mask he always wore. "Stefan Advani, you are being sentenced to an indefinite time Below for the crime of causing an affray. I invite you to provoke me into killing you."

It was said in such a flat, callous manner that I did indeed speak. Some part of me really thought, after all this time, that rational dialogue could solve anything.

"I was only trying to save her," I insisted. "I was only trying to stop it."

The Marshal raised a black-gloved hand. "Only trying to stop what?"

"You must have seen the tail end of it. You were on the scene quickly enough. I didn't think I was going to kill him. I don't know what this side effect you're talking about is. I was only trying to help her."

The Marshal and the Governor exchanged a glance I did not like.

"Help who?" the Marshal asked quietly.

"The woman they were attacking. The woman your men took away."

"There was no woman," the Marshal said, still very calm.

I stared at him. "You know there was," I told him, and for once I was just as calm and level as he was.

The Marshal permitted himself the tiniest crinkle at the side of his eyes. It meant that he was smiling. "All the women are held on this level, and they never escape. There could have been no woman there, hence you will be punished for causing an affray and killing one of your worthless fellows. If you start telling everyone that there was a woman there, and putting stupid ideas in their heads, then I will personally come and beat you every morning in your cell Below."

A long pause. "It's like that, is it?" I said.

"Just like that. Rest assured your victim's accomplice has received the same friendly warning." He looked at me dispassionately and then said, "If you will step back, sir, I'd like to try something."

Curious, the Governor put some distance between himself and me.

"I don't like this mind power nonsense. I don't believe in it. I don't like people having ideas that I don't believe in. I want to put this to rest once and for all." The Marshal's eyes narrowed slightly. "You. Advani."

I looked into those eyes and shivered. Possibly I made some tiny noise to indicate that I was paying attention.

The Marshal laid a hand on the shoulder of one of the Wardens. "Kill this man," he said.

There was a long, awkward silence. Both I and the Warden stared at him.

"You heard me," the Marshal said. "Use these mind powers. Kill this man. Or," he continued, drawing a knife, "I will stab you. Wounds go bad easily Below. You don't want to take one down there with you. Kill him, or I'll stab you."

The chosen Warden's grip on my arm was numbing.

"Just strike out at him," the Marshal suggested. "Knock him down. Eat his brain. Punch him in the head. However it works. Use your mind." The blade of the knife was long and keen, and serrated along part of the back, and I could imagine with ridiculous clarity what it would feel like sliding into me and being torn out. I could imagine sitting, half-underwater, with that wound festering in me. The Marshal brought his knife very close to my face. I folded.

I reached out with my mind against the clenched, hard mind of the Warden, and of course nothing happened. I was too drained, or he was too strong or ready for me. He did not even notice. Nothing whatsoever happened.

The Marshal knew. He saw in my eyes that I had tried, and that I had failed. That was enough to satisfy him. He was a very clever man, on a very limited range of subjects. He might not understand or believe in my mental energies, but he had their measure.

Then he stabbed me. After all, he had given himself the opportunity, so why not use it? The blade lanced into my upper arm and I cried out in pain. I cried out even more when he wrenched it out, because the serrated edge made a mess of the wound. A moment later one of the Wardens was roughly applying a tourniquet and bandage, because I was not at that moment under sentence of death. They wanted to keep me alive so that they could kill me officially later.

I can remember very little of the next moments because I was in incredible pain. I was hunched about my torn arm as the two Wardens hustled me roughly down stair after stair. One of them, probably the man I had been invited to kill, continually jogged my wound so that the entire episode exists in my memory as flashes of agony and jolting. When I came to my senses they were bundling me into a cell on the waterline.

It was as Lucian had described. The floor was awash with an inch of scummy water, and there was moss and mould crawling up the bars in a determined effort to reach the ceiling. When I splashed down, countless little leaping creatures scattered from my shadow, and I had all the fun of imagining them running over my sleeping body, and probably sucking my blood in the bargain. What Lucian had not dwelled on was the darkness. There were no lamps down Below. Sitting in the scum on the floor of my cell I could count five separate rays of daylight that filtered in through the torturous maze of the Island's interior.

In that utter gloom I stumbled to my feet and knocked my head on the ceiling. My injured arm shot out another spike of pain and I nearly blacked out. Only those thin sunbeams told me that I had not done so. The cell was tiny. There was not enough room on the floor to lie out straight on. I could touch one wall with one hand, and the opposite wall with the other. The lowness of the ceiling I had already noticed. I sat down in the water and stared at the sunbeams.

They all had faces. I had a nasty turn before I understood. Those lucky prisoners (lucky being a relative term) into whose cells the feeble light came were making the most of it. They sat with their faces illuminated by the pale rays and drank it in as best they could.

My neighbour had a sunray. His face, flat and lean and pocked with disease-scars, was lit harshly by it. It was not a face worth the lighting, I thought, but in truth he had the barest sliver of the sun and I did not, and I was jealous.

I had a few hours to build on that jealousy, in which that faint ray pined and waned into nothing, and my companion's unsavoury features were returned to the dark. In that time I sat, shivering with the damp and trying not to move because every twitch and tremor reawakened the fire in my arm. I felt that

I could stay still forever down there, in the blackness and the quiet, as the waters rose and fell and the mould grew over me. Then I heard the faintest of rustlings as the other prisoners of Below began to sit up and take notice of something. There was a light approaching. I could see the small glow of it, and the reflections from the faces and the greys of all the other prisoners as they thronged the walls of the corridor. There was no hope in those expressions. They were just trying to snatch a little more light before the night closed in on them again.

It was Peter. I saw his face floating ghostlike above his lamp. And he was plainly regretting being here, a feeling which I shared. He stopped by my cell, and turned down his lamp to the smallest glimmer.

"What the hell did you do?" he demanded in a whisper. I could barely see his lips move. To him I must have been a vague grey spectre in the darkness.

"I stopped a fight. The rest is really too complex to explain, and I don't feel like it," I said tiredly.

"I can't get you out of this," Peter warned.

"Find another chess partner. I'm sorry."

There was an unfamiliar expression on his face. I realised that it was sympathy. It had been a while since I had seen it.

"Take this, at least," he told me, and held something through the bars. I took it and knew it even as I touched it. It was his flask.

"Well God knows I could do with a drink," I said, almost absently.

"For your wound," Peter insisted. "Drink some if you need to, but pour it over your wound. Otherwise your arm will rot off you, right here."

"Rotting in prison," I murmured. "I never thought of it literally before."

"What the hell is wrong with you?" he demanded in a tight whisper. I met his eyes, or at least the lamp-glints where his eyes were.

"The worst has happened," I told him. "I'll be in this hole until the new clerk arrives, and then the Marshal will kill me. It's all over. You've been a true friend to me, and I thank you for that, but I've finally arranged my own funeral. My good side got the better of me at last."

Peter stared at me for a long time and his face twisted with helpless compassion. "I'll—" he started, and then could not think of anything that he could reasonably do. Instead, he stood and walked away. What else was left?

That night I had the fourth of my near-death experiences, and by far the most horrible. I had managed to sleep, in fits and starts, sitting back against the lumpy wall. I was terribly tired, worn out from being scared too long. My arm wound, still stinging from the alcohol, kept stabbing me awake again and again, and I would drift between sleep and wakefulness for a while before slumber dragged me down once more.

I awoke from a dream of drowning to hear screams. I was in a world of sound only, confined to my little cell whilst something terrible was happening just next door. As I crouched within my four walls, lost and bewildered, my neighbour was under attack. I could hear him shrieking and kicking and calling out desperately for help. He was dying only feet away from me and not only could I do nothing, I could not even see the manner of his death. All I knew was that it was taking far too long. He was being picked apart in there, dissected alive, screaming and struggling and throwing himself around his cell. Once, something hard and many-legged was cast from him to skitter over my own floor. It touched my hand with cold, sharp feet and I cast it back, heard it rattle from the wall and plop into the water. Still my companion continued to die by degrees.

Then there was something new: a cracking sound of torn cane and splintering wood. I heard myself whimper ever so quietly, because I knew that something was forcing itself through the floor of my neighbour's cell. There was a pause in which his cries began to fade, although he continued to fight, and then I heard the tortured snapping as something large smashed up from the water. There was one more visceral crunch, and I imagined a huge set of mandibles slicing into the luckless man's body, breaking limbs and ribs. Finally there was a scraping as the creature extricated itself from the structure of the Island and left, taking its prize with it.

Weaver crabs, the thought came to me. It was something Trethowan had written of. Weaver crabs: the hand-sized males seek out and find food, which they attack, whilst releasing a scent to attract the huge, deadly female. Trethowan had approved of their ingenuity. It had all seemed perfectly innocent on paper.

I had no reason to believe that I was not next in line. The crabs could come back and take me at their leisure. I am afraid I stood and shouted for help. I called out like a man possessed, and nobody came. The other prisoners were silent, and that told me that nobody would ever come. I called out for Peter then, but Peter was three floors up and could not hear me.

I was in the cage of souls, as Valentin Miljus had put it. I was lower than I had ever been, and would ever be. I needed hope like a drowning man needs air.

Shadrapar.

I hoped for Shadrapar. A ludicrous hope, even were I not Below. I was a prisoner of the Island for life, forever exiled. Nonetheless, I thought of Shadrapar. Like poor, deluded Lucian I began to plan what I would do when I escaped from the Island. I tried to recall all the sights and sounds of that city. I let my mind play over the faces of departed friends, because even the old pain of parting and loss was better than that deadly darkness.

I will leave myself there, in that most wretched of positions. The time has come for me to tell you about Shadrapar, last of all cities, about the place I once had in it, and about the events that destined me for the Island.

PART THE SECOND

MY LIFE IN THE CITY

12

The City at the End of the World

Shadrapar.

There have been greater cities. There have been more populous cities, more ancient cities, cities with taller buildings, with more marvellous wonders. It is to be hoped that there have been more beautiful cities in the history of the world than Shadrapar.

Still, and in spite of this, she had a distinction that none of the others could claim. Shadrapar was the last of all cities. Oh, perhaps there was some metropolis clinging to the other side of the world, but we knew nothing of any other human settlement. Shadrapar was all to us. Books tell of places known as "the Queen of Cities" or "Empress of Cities". Shadrapar was the Widow of Cities.

Looking down on her from one of the tall watchtowers that ring her, I could point out to you the four distinct districts. Those sepia stone buildings with the fantastic ornament now mostly broken off, the crumbling mansions with overgrown, overlarge gardens, that is the Old Quarter, home of most of the Old Families. There are all the winding streets of my birth, where time settles like a fat man in an armchair and every family knows the lineage of all the others; where proud and impoverished folks look down on the new money that looks down on them from the hill.

Across the river is the Steel Town, a chaotic assortment of grinding mills, machine halls, cosmetics breweries, artificer's shacks, warehouses and an infinite variety of workshops and factories. In the Steel Town it is impossible to hear yourself think, and the air is thick with the smell of the inorganic world being smashed apart and put back together. It was similar in some small ways to the smell of the machine room at the Island, but a thousand times stronger.

Close to the centre is a mound of earth, too regular to be natural, far enough from the Steel Town to avoid the stink and the roar. This is the Government District from which the city is run. Actually, very little of that hill is required to keep our decaying metropolis ticking along. Outnumbering the offices of the powers that be are the sprawling and tasteless homes of those who have come into money and power lately. Every year the Government District, with its burgeoning cargo of the newly-wealthy, bites a little deeper into the Old Quarter, those marvellous old houses torn down and replaced, or done up in the latest gaudy fashion. When the mint reprinted the notes of our currency in new and clashing colours, I remember my father saying that at last the new money suited its owners. Jealousy, of course: money was what we didn't have.

Finally, not so much a district as a slum that fills all the remaining space, there is the Poor Quarter. It runs in a strip between the Old Quarter and the Steel Town, and spreads out all around so that the Old Quarter is like an island in that sea. It even laps against the shore of the Government District, mostly in those parts that genuinely contain civic buildings. The private owners invest in large walls, not so much to keep the poor out, but so that they do not have to look at them. The Poor Quarter is a maze of houses, from tall tenements that house twenty or fifty families to shambolic ruins that house none. Much of it is abandoned. There are far more houses than people at the tail-end of time, and more and more vacant shells as you move out from the centre of Shadrapar. The outskirts are the province only of rogues, exiles and madmen. Here, the great outdoors is right on the doorstep and the threshold is often crossed. The Vermin are always active, even in daylight, and the abandoned streets are open to anything that wishes to walk out of the desert or the jungle.

Speaking of which, let me turn your eyes outwards. Looking to the east along the course of the river, you would see the land shade from wild grassland to full jungle, and of that I have written and will write further. If the notional watchtower that we share is to the west or south, then you would see a hatching of fields scratching sustenance from the drying earth, and then the desert stretching in a vast desolation of white sand to the horizon. Occasionally one can make out the ruins of buildings out there, if the sun is not too bright. When the sun is bright then there is nothing to be seen but glare.

In some old maps, those lands are picked out as grassland. Some ancient charts suggest that there might have been a sister city, a thriving trade route. The lesson is easily learned. The deserts are spreading.

There remains one compass point left. North is the sea, which I have not mentioned before, and will not again. Expeditions cross into the desert, and the jungles house the Island and its inmates, but the sea is no place for human life, even for a moment. North from Shadrapar lies a barren, rock-strewn beach leading jaggedly down to the poisoned shore. It is not water, as we understand it, that makes up that sea. It is some chemical-laced potion fatal to life, and yet inimitable to death as well. The tiny micro-animals that are responsible for decay and renewal are as averse to the sea as we are. If you ventured down to the tide's edge you would see a rolling expanse of black fluid out as far as the eye could see, and everywhere across it you would see the bodies: of fish and marine creatures, and the occasional luckless human being. The species of animal to be found floating on the tide are all extinct, and have been for millennia. There are bizarre and astonishing prodigies there that have no equal

135

anywhere on Earth. Everything is preserved in its final attitude of twisted, envenomed death, and will no doubt still be there when the sun consumes the Earth and brings the whole sad show to an end. I looked upon the sea just once in my life, and that through a telescope, and never wished to do so again.

Some who make the sea their study claim that there are things that make the waters move, and feed on those unnaturally maintained corpses. I believe none of it. The sea is death's unchanging kingdom on Earth, and it has no part in this story. My story is, despite all that has happened, one of hope, and there is no hope for the oceans.

So, now you know Shadrapar and its environs, but how little that tells you! How can I describe to you, a stranger who will never know it, the place of my birth? Try as I might, I will never give you a feel for that wondrous, shabby, intricate and overblown city. How can I know what would seem a marvel to you, what commonplace and what primitive? Shall I tell you of all our little cults and sects proliferating on every street? Each fringe tradition spoke supposedly ancient secrets. Each was a fad in its time and then was no more, save in the minds of a few die-hard worshippers. Some went publicly, and were jeered at or revered as fashion dictated. Others met stubbornly and silently and were hunted for their practices, but faith feeds on persecution. If you try to stop someone doing something, even for a perfectly obvious reason, they will assume there is some great secret you are trying to keep from them.

Shall I tell you of the Rengens, alley children abducted by the laboratories and cosmetics factories, reshaped and re-engineered into gods and goddesses and released onto the streets as living advertisements, with the factory logo emblazoned on their altered bodies? What about the Outriders, who spent their lives at war with the Vermin infesting the abandoned districts of the city?

Much else you will have gleaned from my earlier writing: the fashion amongst the idly wealthy to disfigure themselves

136

in expensive ways; our vegetable diet and abhorrence for the animal kingdom. I was born into a city of a thousand factions and customs, where the learning of the ancients was corroding unevenly from the minds of men. We had forgotten how to make new energy reactors yet still retained the science of genetic and cosmetic surgery. We were like savages picking over a vast heap of wonders, and casting off those that we had no love for. Knowledge that fell out of fashion was lost and never regained. At the same time, we were a city in which everyone told stories of the past and reinvented history to suit them. In the midst of this, the real scholars, including yours truly, had to struggle with what little information we could scrape together.

Shadrapar was ruled by a council, the wisest way to govern. The President was elected by the members of the council from amongst themselves, and each member of the council, the Lord Martial, the Lord Financier and so forth, was elected by and from the members of their department. In this way we avoided the unpredictability of a dictatorship, where so much power vested in one man will inevitably lead to tears. Also we avoided the toadying and crowd pleasing of democracy, an idea so far-fetched that I am tempted to suggest that it was never practised save by writers of fiction. Government by committee is by far a sounder political ideology. Imperfect, of course. The fever-ramblings of Valentin Miljus were my first indication of just how imperfect it was, in fact, and there were more such omens on the way.

Who am I, then? The time has come to speed through my history and genealogy as fast as decorum permits.

I was born within the Shadow of the Weapon, which will mean nothing to you. To be born within the Shadow of the Weapon means that one was born either in the Old Quarter or the Great Square that is roughly central to Shadrapar, though you could see the Weapon itself from almost anywhere in the city. It was once a great mark of distinction, wealth and power, to be born within the Shadow of the Weapon. At the time of my birth it was mostly a sign of declining fortunes as all the real wealth and power moved to the Government District.

The Weapon was the hub of Shadrapar. I will describe it as if you were even now standing in its shadow. You see an irregular, open-weave spire of metal that rises five storeys. It is multicoloured, this metal, and the colours change with angle, with light, and just quietly by themselves. It is difficult to look straight at; it always seems to have changed in shape and detail since you last saw it. That is the Weapon, most notable landmark of Shadrapar. How it worked, what precisely it did, when it was built and for what purpose, none of these things were known since long before my birth. Every Shadrapan child knew, however, that it was there to defend us. It was there to destroy the city's enemies should things ever get that dire, should our backs be pushed to the wall. In my day and age most people assumed that it would defend us against the Macathars when they ventured in force, at last, from their desert haunts.

Enough about the Weapon, more about me: Stefan Advani, child of the Old Quarter. My family had been vastly important, swaying governments with a nod or a wink, raising and quelling mobs with a well-chosen word, coining money as though it was drawn from thin air and owning more factories and land than I care to think of. All this was back in the time of my great-grandfather, in the golden reign of President Marks. Pardon me if I digress, but old Marks is worth a note. He inaugurated the Walk of Shame where, one year to the day after a government has appointed itself, all members must track through the city to suffer whatever abuse the Shadrapan populace cares to vent on them. Needless to say, Marks was the most popular president of all time, and nobody had a bad word to say about him. Later governments were not so lucky, and cursed his name roundly every time the Walk of Shame came up. It was only a few years before my time that the jeering crowds were allowed to throw things as well...

Returning to my ancestry, a subject that so obviously fails to hold my own attention, my family had indeed been great in the reign of Marks but succeeding generations had fallen on hard times, losing land, money, industries and respect until, by my birth, we really had nothing but the house. There were a couple of servants, it is true, but they stayed with us only for roof and board, and were ruthlessly insubordinate every chance they got. My father, Jon-Steel Advani, was a man terribly in debt at all times, a master of the Shadrapan game of avoiding his creditors which was practically our civic sport. He lived consistently beyond his means and somehow always managed to get away with it. He died of general excess leaving nothing but his losses. My mother, Cyrilla Centravelle, was a quiet woman who could have written the definition for long-suffering. I think that had she been given the governing of our finances then we would have at least broken even. My father was a man of immense personality, however: the one blind spot in her common sense. I have inherited rather more from him than from her, though sadly not his infallible gift for keeping out of trouble.

I was an only child; families of the Old Quarter were traditionally small. In my early childhood everything was parties and high society. My father would host balls on borrowed money, and use them as an excuse for borrowing more. I spent my free time playing by myself in the small grounds of our house, and reading. I could never get enough of reading. In that time which was not free, more often than not, I was being taught.

It may seem strange that a boy born into a house with no money – in fact with a negative amount of money – should have had a private tutor. The tutor was an old friend of my father's and even more broke than we were. He used our house as a meal ticket, a rain shelter and a hidey-hole when his own creditors were on the prowl. In return, he taught me. My father was an Academy man, of course, and he would have it no other way but that I became just as uselessly educated as he was. For that, I thank him. A vast and worthless education is the greatest gift a child can have. So it was that in my tender years I learned that ragbag clutter which is all that is preserved of a hundred thousand years of history.

The tutor's name was Alessandro Gavelle, and he was a serious scholar who would have been one of the leading lights of the Academy had he not had a penchant for gambling his life away. He was rake-thin with a winning smile, a mind full of quips and quotations and a thousand games. I idolised him and I idolised my flamboyant father, whilst my poor, unregarded mother did her desperate best to keep the household together. My childhood was utterly naive until I was eighteen.

Some two weeks after my eighteenth birthday, my father died quite suddenly; it was his heart.

The mob descended. The creditors took our house and everything in it, and my mother and I ended up on the street. Alessandro Gavelle disappeared, seeking some other protection from his own pursuers. I never did find out what happened to him.

My mother and I ended up in a tiny, squalid room in the Poor Quarter, where we learned all about the way the world works when seen from the bottom looking up. My mother had some sort of job in a factory, and I tried to work out what had happened to my dreams and ambitions. It took me some five months to decide on a plan. In this time I discovered that much of Shadrapar was virtually lawless. The poor districts were governed by cartels and gangs and mobs, who negotiated the power between themselves with the help of men like Shon Roseblade. I also discovered the existence of the Underworld, although then I only understood it as some kind of mythical and limitless subterranean world ruled by monsters and Vermin and renegades. How little I knew that I would be one of those renegades in time.

Five months, as I have said, while my poor mother sweated to work, who had never had to work before in her life. At the end of those five months I had realised two things. One: I was doing nobody any favours where I was. Two: I would have wasted every moment of my life to date if I neglected my education. This may sound frivolous, but an educated man has prospects of employment. An Academy man is welcome in the highest circles. It should have been a sound financial investment.

Which was the problem, for I had nothing to invest, my plans requiring a certain amount of capital. Denied any other route, I decided that I would have to get rich quick, and following is how I did it.

13

The Expedition

You are probably thinking that I was a self-absorbed and selfish youth, to leave my mother slaving away whilst I gadded off on spurious schemes of advancement. Probably you are right. I would offer in my defence that I felt it was what my mother would have wanted, but I am aware that lacks conviction. I think the best breast of it I can make is to plead guilty and carry on. I think I just assumed that she would manage, as she always had.

Which left me considering my options for fast money, which were few.

I could take up a life of crime, which in Shadrapar was as old and tradition-bound as any legitimate trade. A likely lad with a sharp mind could get himself apprenticed to a mobster just as easily as he could to an engineer. It was fairly obvious from the start, though, that I did not have what it would take. A career on the wrong side of the civil authorities was not for me, though later I was to dabble as an amateur.

There was the chance to join the Outriders, which was also good money. You got your kit and your training, and you got to do the city a service. You were also locked into an eleven-year contract, and two-thirds never made it. The Outriders earned their money. They spent the day and night stalking the Vermin through abandoned buildings, and the pipes and sewers of the Underworld. They fought them with gun and knife, and they burned out their nests. In return the Vermin set traps and ambushed them. Shadrapar's Vermin are an enduring and ubiquitous bunch who will outlive us, I am sure. They are hairy rodents with long tails, about half the size of a man. Their forepaws are quite like hands, and their instinctive behaviours include crafting tools, keeping possessions and leaving messages for each other. Despite this, the Masters of the Academy have issued official proclamations to state that Vermin are, without doubt, dumb animals, and therefore fair game.

I wonder what those Masters would have made of the web-children and the others. The jungle's special offspring were not common knowledge in Shadrapar. Possibly they would also have been the subject of an official proclamation. I leave you to make your own conclusions and judgements, concerning them and concerning us.

Outriding, therefore, was not a career choice I was happy with, being too much like hard work, which left only the quickest of the get-rich-quick schemes. I would join an expedition.

There were two types of expedition. There were the Academy-backed and government-funded official kind, such as took Trethowan out into the jungles for the increasing of mankind's knowledge. Alternatively there were desperate private ventures, backed by hope and borrowed money, which went out to somewhere old and pillaged it in the hope of unearthing something of value. It was a reliable way of getting either rich or dead. Almost nobody came back without something to show for it. They came back with some piece of marketable history or they failed to come back at all. It may seem a strange choice for a self-confessed coward, but it was a simple acknowledgement that I had no other choice if I was ever to get what I wanted.

There were generally half a dozen expeditions touting for business at any one time. About half never came off, for lack of funding. Some were specifically designed to take the money and run, without ever risking life and limb beyond the city. Those that tried such schemes often found that life and limb could be equally at risk within the city. I asked around until someone pointed me in the right direction, and then I sold myself to a rather severe woman as a scholar. She looked at me, all sixteen years of me, and knew exactly what kind of scholar I was. I managed to field two out of three test questions she threw at me, which was better than most. I also told her that I could fight, and that I was willing to do menial tasks. That last probably damaged my image as a serious scholar but at the same time got me my place on the expedition. Aside from a couple of experts, all the rest of the team needed to be was willing and expendable.

I must have been mad. We all must have been quite crazy. We had almost no equipment and no real historian to point us in the right direction. We were heading out into the deadly desert, a place which bred monsters and nothing else. We had two leaders. That was the real signal that the enterprise was doomed: two captains. Captain Tarent was one, a young, athletic man who was spectacularly greedy. You could see the lust in his eyes at all times. A lust for power, for wealth, for respect; a lust just to have more of any given commodity than anyone else. He was a supremely dangerous man to be around, but I was too young to realise. Opposing him on almost every decision he made was Captain Edlando, who was older and more tired. Edlando had at least been to the desert twice before and yet here he was again. The glory and success that should have attended such a hero had drained away like water into the sand, and he was left as one of life's washed-out failures. He was bitter and resentful, especially of energetic younger men such as Tarent. The fact that, without Tarent's drive, we would never have got the money together to equip us ate away at his insides like a cancer.

We met in the Shadow of the Weapon, as was traditional. I believe that originally some kind of cheering and well-wishing was involved. In my day it was just a landmark that even the most witless would-be explorer could find.

There was a vehicle there. The various parts of it had patently not been intended to make something of that particular shape. It had a cab of sorts up front, with two huge wheels, and the back was mostly canvas-covered flatbed, for personnel, equipment and loot in equal proportions. The entire business was caked with rust, armoured in grit and must have dated back to the rule of President Marks.

Our two captains were squabbling over supplies with a merchant over at the edge of the square. Of the rest of the team, one was inside the cab and three had yet to appear. Only a solitary youth of my own age was loitering about the vehicle, trying to look heroic. I discovered that he was called Jon de Baron. At the time I took little notice of him, save to see that he was wearing a very fashionable khaki get-up that had been all the rage with the socialites last season, when looking like an effete explorer was in. It was plain that the clothes did not fit him well, and had been darned in too many places, but he was making an effort. As a first impression of Jon de Baron, or Jonathan Barren as he was born, it was an accurate and telling one. He and I would be fast friends later on, once circumstance had welded us together, but he was a man vastly concerned with appearances, and not at all with what was behind them. I learned that he was not even on the expedition for the money (he told me proudly, flaunting the second-hand but nonetheless expensive clothes). According to him he was risking his life because "girls always love an explorer". I wrote him off for a complete fool. The truth was that he had been badly jilted for a man of action just a few days before, and had signed up whilst heartbroken. Like many clownish, cheerful-seeming men, Jon de Baron was capable of being deeply hurt and never showing it.

At that point our two captains returned and I got my first look at them: bronzed, grinning Tarent and weather-beaten, greying Edlando. Jon and I introduced ourselves, and the rest of the team crept out from beneath stones and out of shadows. There was a solid, bald man named something like Julphash (I misheard his name and never plucked up the courage to ask him again) who was to drive the ridiculous vehicle of ours. There was another man, heavily-built and unfashionably bearded, an ex-Outrider named Kerreth. There were two artificers: a man of Edlando's approximate age called Mental (honestly, Mental) and a woman perhaps ten years older than I was, by the name of Martlet. Mental and Martlet obviously came as a pair.

I remember looking them all over and being thoroughly unimpressed, even at age eighteen. I took a swift dislike to Tarent, which showed that I was a fair judge of character. Of the rest, only Kerreth seemed even remotely reliable, which showed that my character judgement had its flaws. I had known when I signed that it was going to be a fool's errand, however, and payment was strictly in arrears depending on what we brought back. If I wanted anything out of this sorry mess I would have to stick it out to the end.

It became clear that things were not going to go smoothly. Our rations were costing us over the odds (Tarent blamed Edlando for putting us in a poor bargaining position and not pre-ordering). We were a tent short, and there had been a misunderstanding over some of the equipment: namely that one or other of the captains had assumed that Mental and Martlet would be bringing devices such as a metal detector and a radiation counter. Mental and Martlet possessed no such devices and had been hoping that the expedition leaders would be putting up the wherewithal for them. There was a free and frank exchange of views between the artificers and the captains, and then between Tarent and Edlando. A small early morning crowd was gathering to watch. Expeditions leaving were two a penny, but street theatre was always worth the time of day.

In the end, Edlando held out for a day's delay to purchase the necessary items, and Tarent argued that every day cost us money, and who knew what new disaster tomorrow would bring to delay us even more? Mental and Martlet were with Edlando, but Kerreth, Julphash (or whatever) and Jon wanted to leave straight away and, more fool me, so did I. We tried a spontaneous exercise in the old democracy, and Tarent carried it by superior force of personality rather than reasoning or merit. This is exactly why democracy could never work as a governmental system.

There was further argument about who got to sit up front. I am quite serious. The cab was designed for two, and for three at a pinch. Edlando pointed out that he knew the way, and Tarent said that he needed to make command decisions. A further fight showed itself on the horizon before our suffering driver pointed out that they would both just fit. Hence all three of them spent the outward journey crammed in like packed fruit whilst the rest of us could relax in the back. Not only was there the extra space that one of the captains should have been taking up, there was also all the room made by our missing tent and absent equipment. It was a high price to pay for a little leg room.

The first part of the journey was dull. Mental, with an utterly self-effacing air that I still remember, could do sleight-of-hand tricks. He performed a few with such a deadpan delivery that they were not in the least entertaining. Kerreth, on the other hand, had some cards, and Jon and I both ended up owing a fair amount of notional money to him. He accepted our IOUs.

It took all morning to rattle our way to the end of the fringe of fields and out into the desert sands. Scavenging in the desert is a long and honourable tradition and the closer ruins had been picked clean long ago. Those that were visible from the watchtowers were practically household names. The Blue Tower, with its mountings at the top for a great diamond lens long since taken away; the Shattered Town; the Spire and Dish; the Light House, whose walls still sometimes skittered with dots and beads of illumination. These landmarks, like the signs of alehouses, were familiar to many of Shadrapar's citizens and of no use to us. We were on our way deep into uncharted desert. There were enough cenotaphs of mankind's defeat out there for a thousand expeditions.

Things started to go wrong almost immediately. We set up tents for the night and, when we got up in the morning, Kerreth died. He put his boots on, and a scorpion stung him, and he died. It was a stupid way to go. Mental had been up for an hour beforehand, but he had emptied his boots out. As for the rest of us, we got into the habit fast. So much for Kerreth, on whose survival I would have bet money. On the upside, at least it cleared my gambling debts.

Tarent's reaction was to say that Kerreth had known the risks (which patently he had not) and that it meant less people to share the loot with. Edlando said nothing.

We saw plenty more scorpions that day, and some would not have fitted into my boot with a crowbar. The deserts had an ecosystem, just like everywhere else. It was a barren one, though, and consisted almost entirely of scorpions and cockroaches. The scorpions, you understand, preyed on the cockroaches, and what the cockroaches ate I cannot say, but obviously there was something there for them. The strange thing was that this one-stage food chain existed in a variety of sizes. There were tiny beasts that would fit on a fingernail and could travel on the wind with the sand grains; there were nasty-looking creatures that could sit in the palm of a hand; there were lumbering articulated brutes half the size of a man, or as large as a man, or larger. The largest we saw was a cockroach that must have been three-quarters as long as the vehicle. If there was a scorpion that preyed on that, we managed to avoid it.

Towards the end of the day we saw something more. We saw, in the distance, the true lord of the desert: a Macathar.

It was striding through a ruin. It has long been known that they have an affinity for the remnants of human civilisation. Edlando ordered the vehicle stopped, and took out a telescope to have a look, and then he pointed it out to us. If he had not, we would have missed it, despite its movement. It was almost the same bright whiteness as the sand.

Mostly, it was an arthropod, ridgy and crustaceous with limbs like a crab's, rough with nodules and serrated edges. There were four of these legs, rising up to spiked elbows before arcing down. The body, slung between them, was box-like and armoured, and seemed mostly a single piece without divisions. This one had something of a hook curving underneath where a tail might be, but Macathars are all slightly different in the details of their form. There was no head, but from the fore of that lumpy, squared-off body sprang a cluster of sensory organs: huge black glassy eyes, twitching feelers, strange rods and porous cups and other receptors for senses that we can know nothing of. We saw it make its way in a strong, confident stride, oblivious of us, and Edlando sat and waited until the scale of it caught up with us. It was behind the ruins, we saw. That long-legged sand-crab monstrosity was easily the size of a two-storey house. Once that had been assimilated, none of us could look at the beast without shuddering. There was something in that appalling scale that drove home the wrongness of the creature. The way it walked, the bundle of nameless senses, the arched limbs, everything seemed unnatural. I had no idea what or even how it ate. There was no visible mouth.

The most alien thing about it was its motion. It was very similar to the motion of a creature crossing the floor of a pool. There was the same sense of it being buoyed up by some dense other medium. Each slow stride enabled ten tons of monster to coast across the sand without any apparent effort at all.

We kept very still all this while and it showed no signs of detecting our scrutiny. It stalked off across the dunes and was lost in the glare, and still we did not move or speak for some time.

It was Mental who broke the silence, just before the driver put our vehicle into motion again. "One school of thought holds that they are machines," he explained solemnly. "Machines of the ancients that are proof against time and corrosion, and that walk the lands where their masters are just so much dust."

Martlet suggested that the Macathars fed on sunlight, but found no takers. Likewise, Edlando's assertion that they fed on the wandering souls of the numberless human dead was laughed off, albeit a little nervously.

As for Edlando, he was looking more and more haggard as the days went by, as though he had a sense of his own death lurking just below the horizon. I began to be thankful that he was crammed up front with Tarent and Julphash.

The true disaster struck the next day. It was the day before we were due to arrive at the scavenging spot that Edlando had picked out, and we were getting fractious at the long wait. We had already passed quite enough ruins, and even Mental was of the opinion that they could not all have been picked clean. Edlando was obstinate and insisted we follow his plan. He gave no reasons, but merely looked at us as if to say that he was older and wiser than we were and we should know better than to argue. This, and the aura of gloom that hung about him, served to lose him even the tenuous support of Mental and Martlet. So it was that during the afternoon of that day, Captain Tarent spoke up.

"Oh to hell with this," he decided. "That's as good as any. Let's stop there." He pointed out a particularly bizarre ruin, blasted stone walls laced with strips of eroded metal.

"That is not the plan," Edlando countered stubbornly.

"It may not be your plan," Tarent said. "It'll do for me. Let's trawl this one and then we can go on to your spot. Are you worried it won't be there a day later? It's been there for millennia, I'm sure it'll wait for us."

"That is not the plan," Edlando repeated. I can still hear these words in his voice, in my head. It is all I really have left of him. It was a long time ago.

Tarent craned back to look at us, huddling close in the back. "What about you lot? Let's everyone have a say."

"I'm game," Jon said. I nodded. The two artificers were likewise minded to ply their trade here and now.

"That is not the plan," Edlando said again. Three times now, which led to one of the eerier coincidences of my life, as I shall reveal.

"Let's go fish," Tarent decided, and the driver stopped and we got out with all of our kit and went to the ruin. For a moment Edlando stayed alone in the vehicle, and I have often wondered whether he was trying to work out how to make it go. If so then the knowledge was beyond him, for he hopped out and trailed after the rest of us, the mark of doom more prominent than ever on his brow.

The ruin that Tarent had fixed on was mostly open to the sky. The walls curved outwards a little and were jagged at the top, even after so long, and at first I supposed that they were intended to support some kind of burgeoning dome. Later I guessed that there had been some kind of explosion within that had inflicted the deformation and damage.

Inside it was mostly bare and the floor was awash with sand, but that did not discourage us. One came across few complete and fully-furnished ruins in the deserts. Instead, Mental and Martlet took out the equipment that we did have and told Jon and me how to set it up so that we might best detect relics buried beneath the sand. It was something of an arduous task, due to the low quality of the equipment and the ineptitude of Jon and myself. Meanwhile Tarent and Edlando quartered the area and divided it up so that we could search methodically, each to his own system.

Jon had the first find, a timeworn gauntlet still containing the horribly desiccated hand of its last owner. Martlet declared it to be quite without value, and Jon was rather glad to be rid of it. He also found the second and third prizes, the last of which was one of the red crystals that some of the ancients used to focus the energies in their machines, which Mental declared would fetch a moderate price. As for myself, I still say that sand had gotten into my machine, for I was finding nothing.

What happened next was that Tarent and Edlando got into

yet another blazing row, this time over something as petty as how to mark out our search area. I think that Edlando was making trouble this time, feeling his grasp of the expedition fall away. As I stooped over my recalcitrant machine I could hear their raised voices echoing back and forth from the walls. By this time I had really given up hope of actually finding anything and had migrated to the westernmost wall, so I was at least within its shadow. The heat of the desert was enough to addle your brains. Jon, who had no more sense than he was born with, was still out in the sun, finding artefacts hand over fist.

The shouting was starting to give me a headache. Those old walls had marvellous acoustic qualities, so that every syllable bounded back to assault me again. This in turn made my squinting at the display of my machine painful. I decided to look up and watch the spectacle of our chain of command disintegrating.

I was struck by two things. First was the fact that only Tarent was shouting now, and indeed his had been the only voice for some time. Edlando was standing silently, staring somewhere else. There was the tiniest bitter smile on his lined face.

Second was the shadow of the wall. I saw the uneven and twisted outline cast across the white sand, and as I watched I saw it move. The broken line of shade shifted slightly, and then surged forward, so that I knew exactly what was crowding the top of the wall, looking down.

Immediately I was cramming myself back against the stone, as deep into its cover as I could go. I saw Tarent stop in mid-word as he finally took note of Edlando's expression. He looked back over his shoulder, and all life and hope went out of his face. Across the ruin I saw Mental and Martlet, similarly frozen. Jon had somehow contrived to be somewhere else, which saved his life.

The shadow of the wall moved again as the Macathar peered over it. I looked up and saw that hideous bundle of sensors projecting clear over the wall's top. The eyes were broader across than my body and blacker than darkness. Everything else was the eternal white of the desert. I saw four or five tiny arms preening and cleaning the eyes and other organs, tipped with claws and combs.

Tarent opened his mouth to say something, and the Macathar struck. Even though I had wondered what and how it ate, I had never paused to consider whether the creatures could harm us. There was something about them that promised pain and death. I saw nothing, no lash or claw or ray but, in that instant, Tarent and Edlando were thrown to the ground. For perhaps five seconds, they were writhing, making raw, agonised sounds, and then they were dead, and their skins were blotted with burns and red weals as though they had been touched by fire.

Had I been a man of action then no doubt some heroic course would have occurred to me, and I would have died in a similar manner. Instead I was a coward and I lived.

There was a spitting, crackling noise, and I saw that Julphash had leapt from the vehicle. He had a pistol in one hand, one of the old kind that spat little sizzling bolts of energy. I have never liked weapons, but this was a particularly elegant one. The energy pocked into the Macathar's shell with little explosions of dust, and I saw one bolt vanish into a huge eye and do no obvious damage. The assembly of sensors swung towards Julphash and struck him down with the same invisible power so that even as he fell his elegant pistol exploded in his grasp, scattering shrapnel through the air and through him. Meanwhile Mental had produced a more primitive projectile gun and was loosing bullets off at the monster whilst Martlet ran frantically from the ruin. I saw the great eyes focus more sharply on Mental, and he was consumed: first he fell, and then he smouldered, and then he was blasted into ash so that nothing whatsoever was left of him but his gun. There was no heat involved. I would have felt the backwash of any incinerating fiery ray, but instead there was nothing, just the terrible concentration of the Macathar and Mental's complete disintegration. I saw the great orbs swing to focus on the fleeing Martlet, now some ways distant, and they narrowed perceptibly to bring her into focus before they fried her as well.

I remained quite still and silent. Of Jon there was nothing to be seen. Of the others, the bodies or the ash spoke for them. Aside from that it was just me and the Macathar.

It stayed where it was for what seemed like a very long time, but was probably no more than ten minutes. I could still see its shadow, and the assemblage of eyes and organs projecting over the wall. If it had been human then I would say that it was thinking about what it had done. Then it lurched into motion again, and I saw in silhouette how easily it turned and was gone, poling itself away over the desert sands as easily as a feather-light insect walks over a table.

I stayed where I was for at least another ten minutes before I dared move. My back was up against one of the lead strips that laced the walls.

When I did move, it was to a silent, dead world. I was quite alone in the desert. It was enough to turn a man's brains. Hardly any wonder that I started hearing voices.

"Hello? Hello? Is there anybody there?"

I stopped dead. For some bizarre reason I thought of the souls of the dead. I thought that Edlando's superstitious soul was talking to me. It was such a tinny and distant voice, that it could easily have come from the afterlife.

"Hello? Hello? Anyone? Can anyone hear me?"

It was coming from one of the walls, which did not reassure me. I glanced about but could see no sign of the Macathar. The voice continued imploring me as I searched for it, finally finding a tiny panel that I would have missed had it not been talking to me.

"Hello? He-llo?" There was something familiar about the voice, I realised.

"Hello?" I called back at the wall, there was a thoughtful pause, and then I added, "Jon?"

"Mental?" the tiny voice of Jon crackled.

"Stefan," I corrected. "Where are you?"

"Beneath you," Jon's transcribed voice flickered. "Look, go to the wall that I was searching against. There's a catch, a kind of square button. It opens onto a chute, and I fell down here. You've got to see this, Stefan, you're not going to believe this. And bring the others."

He was not the only person with news, of course. When I had found his subterranean shelter, I told him of the fate of our comrades, and we both sat together for some time. We had only known them for a few days, of course, and more immediate in our minds was the thought that it could so easily have been us. That has been a theme of my life, as you know.

Jon's shelter turned out to contain a case of chemicals of dubious provenance, a working machine which could extract pure samples of such chemicals and several ancient personal effects, which were all good merchandise on the jewellery and cosmetic market. In addition there was an astonishingly fragile manuscript in one of the known ancient languages which was worth more than the rest put together and bought us both our scholarships to the Academy. It was in the form of an ancient parable concerning quests with terrible ends undertaken by the unprepared, and it included in it the haunting refrain, "What I tell you three times is true."

We drank a toast to the futile caution of Captain Edlando when we returned to Shadrapar. It seemed only the decent thing to do.

14

Alma Mater

The Academy covers all the land between the Wasted God Convent and the Grand Memorial. The former housed a fair proportion of its students, the latter once absorbed even more of its scholars' attention. The Grand Memorial is a stone twenty feet high inscribed with hundreds of lines of unfamiliar script. It says a lot about the practical uses of learning that scholars spent decades trying to decrypt the meanings within that ancient language. Only a few years before my entry to the Academy did someone come up with the idea that it was just a list of names.

The Academy has nineteen buildings of varying ages, squarely in the Old Quarter, within sight of the Weapon. All students are required to lodge on the grounds, and Jon and I were put into The House of the Mint, a run-down barracks of a place for people who actually had to pay their way in, as opposed to having their way paid for them. Had my father still been amongst the living I could have got better treatment. Alone, I was just another grubby little seeker after knowledge with my hand stuffed with cash. Jon, of course, was very nouveau riche, and none of his family could read let alone boast an Academy background, so he had fought his way up to the place that I had fallen down to.

I know. I'm very elitist. It's hard to shake off even after such a long time living at the bottom of the barrel. Just to enlighten you as to the general standard of learning in Shadrapar, a fair proportion of the Academy entrants could not read or write. Most of the city population was illiterate. There was simply very little call for it, unless you were going to make a career as a clerk or a scholar. The second-year Academics were depicted over the door of the Grand Hall of Learning (where we ate) as machines all travelling on parallel rails, same speed, same direction, shoulder to shoulder. I have no idea what shambolic image would best suit the first year students. Suffice it to say that the real learning only started in the second year. The first year was spent in making everyone up to the same standard, so that we had the tools necessary to take apart the vast constructs of knowledge they would feed us later. This was where my chaotic childhood came into its own, for I knew much of what they had to teach already. I took the time to learn the three styles of scholarly shorthand (New School, Cursory and the lifesaving Old School) and an extinct language or two, and I went to the memory classes that allow me, so long after, to reel off all these details without breaking stride. For me, though, there was precious little learning in that first year. I spent the time finding my feet in the world from within that protective enclave. I made friends.

My mother, incidentally, was genuinely proud of me, though you may not believe it. She may not have approved of the Academy, given the way my father had turned out, but at least I was meeting people of good – better still, of wealthy – family. I was opening a narrow window onto prosperity. Besides, there had been money left over from that disastrous expedition to make her life more comfortable. Despite the self-absorption that seems to serve as the spine for my otherwise spineless life I did at least think of her.

They were fond days, my time at the Academy. I have never been so happy, before or since. Especially since. I thank my friends for that, and there were enough of them: Jilting Helena (a new man every week), Ecarlo the Stubborn (who never paid even the smallest debt), Jon Patrellis (heir to nine factories and the largest townhouse in the Government Quarter), Illian de Gancer (a beautiful, delicate flower, and twice winner of the Academy knife-fighting belt). Above all of these colourful characters, though, there were three who were dearer to me than my own life.

You have heard of my meeting with Jon de Baron and the doomed venture that we collaborated on. I don't actually think that he intended going to the Academy at all, but by the time we got back, taking it in turns to work out how to move that cumbersome vehicle, I had sold it to him as part of the high-class dream that he was so desperate to buy into.

Jon was a singular figure in the Academy, creating his own niche between those of good but declining families, and those of rough but wealthy ones. His own genesis was decidedly the latter, but they were all driven, career people who thought of nothing but how to prostitute their learning in some trade or other. They came seeking profitable secrets, or because an education would open doors that their forebears had found locked. Jon, on the other hand, came seeking style.

He was never short of money. His half of our haul, backed by his family's own finances, meant that he could always afford to keep up with the very best. Somehow, though, when he dressed for high fashion, there was always a clashing colour or an awkward cut to prove him wrong. It should have made him a laughing stock, but you recall that studied imperfection was very much the fashion as well, and Jon's accidents were often taken as daring statements.

As soon as he had met a few of the really wealthy, with their carefully manicured grotesqueries, Jon decided that he was going to ape that too. Neither his funds or his family would allow such body-tailoring, though. Instead of mutilating himself in the name of fashion he decided on a more mechanical way to make himself grotesque. He collected somewhere near a hundred coins of no real value and stuffed his pockets with them. When he walked, it sounded as though he was wading through an invisible sea of money. In his years at the Academy he was mugged twice for the contents of his pockets, much to the disgust of thieves who found themselves with a considerable weight of nothing on their hands. It was certainly bizarre enough to get him noticed by the smart set, if only to laugh at him. Jon laughed at himself too; he seldom took himself seriously, and then only when he had fallen foul of another unsuitable liaison.

Jon and I had bought our way into the Academy with enterprise and foolish adventure. In contrast, Rosanna was shoehorned in without ever deciding to go. The name she gave was Rosanna Paramor. The truth was that the rule of the Wasted Convent mandated that those who came into its purview leave their family names behind.

The Wasted Convent bordered the Academy grounds and had a history of generous donations. This led to an arrangement whereby the Order was allowed to submit some dozen students a year who would be taught free of charge. It was an arrangement the Academy was continually trying to get out of, but the nuns of the Wasted Order were fierce and the Order was still moderately rich, so the status quo was maintained.

I should elaborate on the Wasted Order briefly. It was a religious foundation which held that God was dying, if not already dead. The world and the sun were both on their way out, and it seemed reasonable to most of Shadrapar that God was dying with them. This was essentially the standard belief for those who never really thought much about God, including myself. The Wasted Order had a chapel, on the ceiling of which God was pictured, emaciated and hollow and clearly on His last legs. The idea was an old one, and God had been on His way out for some time. Ancient writings concern themselves greatly with a distribution of God's effects after His demise, and many texts of ancient cultures depict Him as white-bearded and plainly very old, even back then. No wonder, so many millennia later, we assumed He was on His deathbed.

What a dying divinity has to do with a set of free scholarships is anybody's guess, but the Wasted Order was not going away within the foreseeable future. It took on girls of reasonable potential whose families had perished or had no need of them. They were brought up in an atmosphere of strict religious instruction, impeccable morality and abstinence. If God was too ill to have any fun, the Wasted Order proclaimed, then why should we?

Every year the Order would shovel their dozen most promising novices into the Academy to get a good (and free) education. The meeting of pure and unsullied nuns and a hive of vice like the Academy must surely have brought a smile even to a dying God's face. The Convent Madames who ran the order had a great many rules for their protégées, but after leaving the convent I believe that only the stricture about leaving names behind stuck, and that because invention is a form of lying, lying is a sin, and so the novices took pleasure in fabricating aliases. Rosanna was no exception. Like so many others brought up in strict religious purity she gambled, cheated at cards, drank stuff that made men blind, swore like an Outrider and flirted with everybody. Everybody but myself.

In my first year, on the basis that I had been fairly well educated beforehand, I held that I was very much amongst the elite when it came to holding opinions. This was before I met Helman, who knew far more than me and did not boast about it. One summer evening I was sitting with Jon and a couple of others in a little kava house we frequented when I heard a female voice advocating some theory that I found rather risible. I leant back in my chair and said something patronising to the effect that the theory (whatever it was) was an astonishing piece of doggerel. Rosanna, whose theory it was, promptly produced several further theories, none of them complimentary, on the subjects of my intellect, dress and the size of my nose. I responded in kind, for I have always loved the cut and thrust of academic debate, and a real row developed to the delight of all present. In debate I was the sort of youth who would always hit below the belt, and I had been used, from my position of superior knowledge, to getting my own way. Rosanna would not have it. We laid into each other for a good half an hour until someone shouted that there was a patrol of Angels outside and would we please shut up.

So started our peculiar relationship. We would run into one another at isolated intervals and one of us would pick a fight. It became a major spectator sport. There was much gambling on who would score more points in a given engagement. We were almost always at even odds. If someone found out that I was under the weather or that Rosanna had been given bad news or anything else that might affect our form, they kept it to themselves and used their inside knowledge to profit outrageously. We were no respecters of place or person. We silenced a respected Master by taking over his lesson with a debate on semantics. We disturbed meals, shook up the library and scandalised the Wasted Order's Year's End Reverence. Notable hosts would surreptitiously invite us both to their dinners. We were a very popular entertainment. We would argue on any subject. One of us had only to venture an idle remark and the other would instantly entrench on the opposite side. Jon once ran a book on how long, in minutes, we could sit at table before hostilities commenced.

That first time we clashed I really didn't look at Rosanna at all. I was too fired up with my own pomp. Later, when my original desire to correct and inform had regressed to an intellectual war between us, I had a great deal of time to study her. Rosanna Paramor's convent upbringing had not furnished her with any elegant deformities. Her skin was very clear and her hair was thickly curled and as dark as Master's ink (rather than the grey stuff we used). No attenuated society beauty she:

short and round and with a face full of character, rather than vacuously perfect or elaborately imperfect. Her fiercely acerbic personality radiated through every look and movement and, though I caught the sharp edges of it in our debates, I admired it even so. I looked forward to the next barrage of insults. I made sure that I had a dozen new unkind things to say about her dress, person and education every time we met. It was an odd thing to share a mutual public animosity of such rage and fury, but it gave us a place to go that was ours alone. So it fell out that one night our savage row over a minor point of translation grew so monstrous that it outstripped our audience's stamina. They left us to our argument which grew so passionate in their absence that we awoke in bed the next morning having made aggressive love for much of the night.

We kept up our public face for some months. The bickering was part of our relationship, after all. Both of us were solicitous of our peers, who took such joy in our mutual enmity. The secret slipped out when, after a particularly acrimonious confrontation at someone's dinner party, we automatically kissed afterwards. From then, the game was up. We still fought occasionally, but not in the same way. We had found too much agreeable about one another.

It would be very satisfying if I should reveal now that it was she who I saved on the Island. How balanced and convenient a story that would make, the lovers reunited after so long. But no, let me dispel any such suspicions. It was not she. I am inconstant and Rosanna was dead before I ever got on the boat.

Lastly amongst my closest friends was Helman Cartier, who is responsible for all of it, and whom I spent an idle two weeks hunting down one summer.

The evasion of creditors was considered an art form in Shadrapar, the debtor dancing lightly through the city from haunt to haunt, always one step ahead, until the creditors' own creditors caught up. The hope was that the debtor's debt to the creditors would be too small to be noticed against the creditor's own debts to those greater creditors. Hence the debtor would get off free whilst his creditor paid the just penalty for being so clumsy as to be pinned down. Being in debt was nothing to be ashamed of; being caught certainly was.

In Shadrapar, the city at the end of the world, everything was in short supply. We were running out of all commodities and the general intention was that the human race was going to make everything stretch just long enough to take us up to the end. After that, what were we saving it for? Hence, we borrowed. Because there was never enough of anything to go round, we borrowed everything we could from everyone else. If everyone in the city had decided to realise their assets at the same time, there would not be a tenth of what was needed. Everyone was overdrawn and hoping that, if they kept spending, nobody would notice. Our civilisation existed only by common consent, and that real ten per cent was borrowed, loaned, stolen, lent out, snatched back and passed from hand to hand.

You might have thought that I would have nothing at all to do with this, given the toll it had taken on my family and home. You should also recall, however, that I still cherished my father's memory as a golden ideal, hopelessly broke and yet living a life of borrowed luxury. In addition, the greatest scorn of the fashionable, and hence the wealthy and powerful, was levelled at those who did not play the game. You were a dull excuse for an Academy student if you did not venture a wager, and you were the most appalling boor if you failed to take someone up on one. To forsake gambling and indebtedness was to forsake life and society.

As it happened I had a fairly lucky first year, and the card and dice games I got into were peopled by those at least as unskilled at cheating as I was. The wagers I ventured on the knife fights or foot races turned my way more often than not and I had one week in which my choices were little short of supernatural. Of course, winning the wager or the card game was the easy part of getting rich. The loser smoothly gives you their IOU and you politely accept. Then follows the aforementioned chase as you try to pin them down later and exact your due.

So, I had won a fair amount on a fight from a student by the name of Louyere. Even more surprisingly I had managed to catch up with him at a card game just after his winning streak took a bloody nose-dive. I was given all the pleasures of righteous indignation, pointing out that he was not only gambling with my money, but losing with it. Louyere looked suitably embarrassed and had no way to weasel out of paying up.

"Look, I don't have it on me," he told me, and his happy gambling friends assured me that it was true: they had fleeced him out of it.

"I would have it," Louyere continued, "but it's tied up. Someone owes me a bundle."

This was a fairly standard tactic: the sale of one's credits to one's creditors. I bought his debt from him and declared us quits, with several sanctimonious remarks about gambling with borrowed money. Hand in hand with the debtor culture was a love of hypocrisy. It was another civic pastime.

Louyere was owed money by Helman Cartier, of course. Since I had no pressing need for the funds, and at the same time nothing else to do, I started a leisurely tracking of Helman. In the process I learned a great deal about my surrogate debtor.

Helman had been discovered by one of the Masters and allowed in free. The Academy was supposed to contain the learning of Shadrapar you see and, from about the age of five, it was evident that Helman *was* the learning of Shadrapar. Should he be barred, the Academy might as well close its doors forever.

At the Academy library I learned that Helman seldom put in an appearance any more because he had read all the books that interested him. I learned that he had digested what we had of the old social history, of the natural sciences and the mind, whilst eschewing the more fashionable literary fields. He had been in the habit of reading a weighty tome over a light lunch.

At one of the parts manufacturers I discovered that he had given over a modest sum of money for a number of devices made to his own specifications. This was what he had borrowed the money for, and not just from Louyere – he must have tapped some three or four people for similar amounts. Helman, I discovered, was the man who did not gamble. His money, and the money he cajoled out of others, was for more sober ends.

I learned at one of the bookbinders that he had just collected his latest monogram. When asked what he meant by "latest", the bookbinder assured me that Helman Cartier put out about one treatise per month. Helman was *producing*. Unlike the Academy students, unlike the Academy Masters, Helman was writing ideas down. He was reading what we had left of the ancient knowledge and building on it with theories of his own. This would explain the odd looks I had often received when asking about him. Helman scared the Academy staff because they had no idea where he was going, and it was evident that Helman was going *somewhere*.

I finally tracked him down several weeks later, curious to see this prodigy. He was in the cheapest, shabbiest room an Academy student could end up in, containing a mattress, a table and chair, several books and a machine. Also paper, lots of paper.

Helman Cartier himself was around my age, with a long, serious face. He wore simply-cut clothes of grey and black that no fashionable student would be seen dead in. On him, however, they had more style and grace than all Jon's desperate attempts. Helman Cartier had more self-possession than anyone, utterly confident in his own abilities. He had no temper and an unshakeable belief in the infallibility of reasoned argument.

"You're Stefan Advani," he told me, a moment after I entered. He had seen me arguing with Rosanna once and never forgot a face.

"Look at this," he told me, and spent some time demonstrating his machine to a total stranger. It was shaped like a human head made mostly of glass, and strange lights flicked on and off in it. He told me that it was linked to his brain, and that the lights showed him which parts of his brain were working when he thought about different things. An hour of detailed, fascinating explanation, and by the end he had linked the machine to my brain so that I could see how I thought. The lights were noticeably dimmer.

I paid off all of Helman's debts, because it was obvious he would not be able to. It put quite a strain on my resources. I never told him that I had done so. Helman had introduced me to a new concept. To do something and not try to turn it to my advantage by boasting was a novel concept. That I boast of it now shows how the world is lessened by Helman's loss.

I do not cry for the dead, as a rule, not now, so long after it all. I do not cry for poor Jon de Baron or even for Rosanna Paramor, my love, my eternal adversary. I weep for Helman, though, because he was the best of us. I weep for the lost potential that might have saved the world.

15

Saving the World

Helman was the ringleader. It was his idea that undid us all. His idea was a worthy one, but he failed to take into account that, when you set out to change things, the things you want to change push back.

He broached the concept some time in our third year at the Academy. We were in his room after a night on the town. Jon was merry and Rosanna and I were argumentative, which is to say amorous. Helman had been watching us with his most serious look on.

Then and there, without further ado, he launched into his grand explanation which was to shape our lives for the next few years.

"Our society has a problem," Helman explained. "Stagnation. There is nothing new under the sun in Shadrapar. Everything we make, we make because chance has preserved the blueprint. Everything we discover has been dug up from a past age. Everything we write is a study on something someone else wrote. Our social sciences are based on societies no longer extant. Our natural sciences are shreds and scraps that we learn by rote. When a machine breaks down and the manual is lost, we neither try to fix it nor build a new one. We are living on a rubbish-heap

167

of broken things." It was typical of Helman's speech. He had no small talk.

"We are waiting for the end of the world and assuming that enough of the past will last until that moment. Eat, drink and be merry, for tomorrow you die."

He paused again, gathering his words. "Nobody knows how long we have: a thousand, a hundred thousand years perhaps. A small fragment of the history of the world but long enough in human terms to surpass our ancestors, to find a way to mend the sun, but only if we look. If we just sit around using up everything that is left then the human race is doomed. End of story."

He put his hands palm-down on his desk, a characteristic pose. "Solutions," he said shortly.

"I was going to get around to rediscovering the old technologies," said Jon with a vague gesture, "but, you know…"

"Perhaps go back to nature," Rosanna suggested.

"No, no," I put in instantly. "A new technology. Nobody wants to be anywhere near nature."

Helman held up his hands for quiet before we could start.

"As for nature," he said mildly, "I am inclined to agree with Stefan. The human race is no longer capable. We lack the skills and knowledge to survive without civilised comforts."

"Rediscovery then," Jon pressed.

"The ancient civilisations whose learning we eke out were built on one foundation," Helman said. "They consumed the Earth's resources. Some were frugal, others wasteful, but they all burned what could be burned, mined what lay in the earth, electrolysed minerals from the waters and in all ways used up everything of value in the planet. The only reasons we have anything left is that we are so few in number that the little we use up makes no difference at all. Were we to adopt the old industry and technology we would run out of energy and materiel. We would merely accelerate our slide into the jaws of nature. Which leaves us with Stefan's contribution."

"Which was facetious," Rosanna pointed out. "All very well to say, 'a new technology'. I suspect in practice it would be somewhat more difficult."

Helman smiled slightly.

"What is it?" Rosanna pressed.

"Helman, I don't think I've followed everything up to now," Jon admitted. "You appear to be saying we're buggered. So why worry about it?"

"I'm not done," Helman said. "I'm saying that we're – buggered, if you must, only because we lack the means, yes?"

We all nodded. He smiled again, waiting patiently.

I believe it was I who said, "You've found the means, haven't you?"

Helman looked down at his hands, still smiling slightly. "The earliest periods for which we have records were themselves very concerned with those periods before them, periods we only know of because the later ancients speculated about them. I am now referring to cultures that were actually back at the dawn of man and civilisation. Forget the rise and fall of human culture, all the dark ages and renaissances. A genuine beginning."

It was a difficult idea to grasp. For us, a primitive ancient society was one that was recovering from a terrible war or plague, or some other catastrophe that had brought mankind low. Theoretically, however, there must have been a first hard struggle out of barbarism.

"One of my most treasured sources, which I believe to be very true, posits a kind of false start, an early catastrophe within a few thousand years of human history," Helman explained. "Before this catastrophe there was a height of civilisation not seen for thousands of years. Perhaps in one sense a height of civilisation never seen again. After the catastrophe there started the history that, after an unknown age of time, has resulted in us, in the state that the human race is now in."

Rosanna was nodding slowly. "I've come across the idea once, but nothing more. What of it?"

"This First Genesis, as I have called it, seems to have been quite different from all that followed it," Helman said sombrely. "The ancients who studied the First Genesis people write of the great constructions that they made: circles, pyramids, other geometrical shapes of incredible size. Their own studies convinced them that such construction was impossible with the primitive technology available to their forebears. So they concluded the First Genesis men had some secret technology that enabled them to build and create and destroy without the telltale tracks of machines and industry."

Helman paused to ensure that he had our attention.

"The First Genesis people's secret was never rediscovered in all the ages of human history. They found a set of natural laws which enabled them to manipulate the world without machines."

Rosanna was unsatisfied.

"A lovely theory," she said sharply. "So these ancient's ancients had a magic building device. It doesn't help us."

Helman smiled again.

"If you will observe my stylus over there," he suggested, pointing at his desk. The thin moulded rod lay innocently near the edge.

What I am about to say next is true: Helman concentrated on the stylus, and after a little while it moved. It twitched on the desk top and then rose into the air, ghosted across the room and fell into his hand.

We were quite silent, watching him.

"It is a long way from building pyramids, I know," he admitted. "It is all I can manage for now. I am still working to understand the natural laws behind it. What I do know, however, is this. The moving object is directed by the mind. Moving an object requires energy, and the mind contains little in real terms. The energy comes from the fabric of the universe itself and is therefore virtually limitless, if only it can be unlocked. I have managed to snag a little of that energy but there is a vast well waiting to be drawn upon."

It was one of those ideas that fire the brain once they take hold. I don't think I've ever worked so hard at something in my life, even in the Island. It was obvious that the mere fact of four Academy students having an idea was not going to change the world. Anyone who did not know Helman would be quick to point out that moving pencils was not the same as rebuilding civilisation or tinkering with the sun. At best, if we had disseminated our plan immediately, we would have been thought an engaging topic of after-dinner conversation. At worst we would have been laughed at. We needed to prepare ourselves before we took on society. This was the future of the world in the balance. We would need to ensure that it was given a fair chance before our peers.

It is a tribute to Helman's steady, careful nature that our folly was some years in the making. Had it been left to me, Rosanna or Jon, we would have fired out a half-baked piece of work in a year or two and been slapped down by public derision. Helman's perfectionism ruled us, though. For our new world to have any chance at all we would need results, data. We would need to show that one man's brain could be expanded into a world-building tool.

You might think that this is the sort of idea that students are always coming up with late at night, usually forgotten before the morning hangover. You might also be forgiven for thinking that we were a spot too ambitious. I suggest that you do not appreciate how ambitious we were. The idea of actually producing something new, a novel idea, a plan for the future, was unthinkable in Shadrapar. We picked over the past and wrote about how things once were. We talked in long words about the collected literature of people about whom we knew nothing, and borrowed their remaining words for our chapter headings. Even Sandor's *Lying in State* was a retrospective. The sun was always in our minds like a long-sick relative. The past lived, for us. The future was death and the present was merely waiting for the end.

171

We did not think of leaving records for those who were to come after. It was never believed that anybody would.

You will recall the conversation I recounted between the Island's Governor and Harweg, Lord President of Shadrapar. A book was mentioned. That book, so easily dismissed, was the fruit of all our years of labour.

We started by paraphrasing Helman's speech to us and using it as an introduction, and after that we spent an age discussing how society would need to be changed in order to put our principles to good use. This was mostly Rosanna's work, as she had more patience and was the better social historian. For myself, I was working with Helman on the practical and scientific aspects of the matter. I discovered quickly enough that moving a pencil is easier than it looks, and in terms of time and effort I might as well just pick it up with my hands. I took measurements as Helman flexed his mental faculties, and tried to extend my own mind as I have described. Helman and I used to test our brains against each other and I could feel the ability to move the force of my intellect outside my skull strengthening each time. We would sit across a chessboard and play a game, all the while keeping our minds locked together, searching for a weakness. Helman always won, but I was learning. At the beginning of my training I would fold after a minute of pressure, and then my chess game would go to pieces. At the time of publication I could comfortably keep Helman busy for two hours or more, and give him a good run at chess as well.

Such coincidences shape our lives. Had Helman suggested playing cards as we duelled with our brains, then things would have gone the worse for me later on and I would have never hooked up with Peter Drachmar.

Jon was our financier. Changing the world on a shoestring was not easy. Normally, if you needed to measure something, test something or investigate something, you would find out how the ancients had done it. In our case we knew full well that the ancients who left records had never done what we were doing. Helman personally invented several machines like his glass head to help us in our work and they all had to be newly-made to his specifications. For this, Jon gambled and borrowed around town, solicited sponsorship from anyone who looked gullible and embezzled most of his family's fortune. He also drew illustrations and a number of humorous cartoons for the final work, many of them without Helman's consent.

We did not all eat drink, breathe and sleep the project. Only Helman did that. He hovered over every stage as someone else might attend the bed of a sick child. For the rest of us, life went on above and around the great work. Rosanna and I grew closer, further apart, closer, as the tides of affection took us. We had our small spats and our grand rows and our tender reconcilliations. Jon still ploughed through every unsuitable partner he could find, and came within a hair of getting married once, had the rest of us not sabotaged the wedding by dressing up as Wasted Order nuns. My reading of ancient manuscripts suggest that, time and space do what they will, students will never change.

Our Academy days of safe seclusion drew towards their end with little incident. I won money. Rosanna won her first and only knife duel. Helman had one serious argument with a Master, and everybody thought that he would be thrown out. The Master left instead, though, because they all knew Helman was right. In the end we graduated and got our Reds mostly as expected. Helman was a Perfect, the first for eight years. Rosanna and I both scraped nearly identical Honourables, and Jon managed a High.

After that, whilst still working with Helman, we found ourselves in need of employment to put fruit on the table. Helman became tutor to one of the richest industrial families on the strength of his graduation. I became a bookmaker's clerk (in the gambling sense), an honourable trade and highly respected. Rosanna, for her part, set up a convent. It was a scam: she hired a couple of drink-sodden former nuns and convinced a dozen good families to put their children into her care. She pocketed most of the proceeds, the ex-nuns were kept in spirits and the children received a far more rounded education than they might have done from the Wasted Order.

Jon, for his part, got into a spectacularly messy relationship with a niece of the Lord Financier (not Valentin Miljus, the other one) which went wrong publicly and with vast recriminations. In response, without warning, he signed up on another expedition (this time as the accredited Academy expert) and went off into the desert for two weeks. This one went off rather better than the first and he came back with a moderate haul and no casualties.

And my mother died.

I should mention it, for those that might wonder what became of her. It is quite mundane in detail. About three weeks before we unveiled our finished project, she died. She had become ill and there had been doctors involved, which is always a presentiment of death in my experience. I was with her at the end. I tried to tell her about Helman's plan, but she was not interested. She spoke a lot about my father, alternating between savage criticism and nostalgic remembrance. She had enough left to pay the doctors and the mortician, and that was all. It shows the kind of financial planning I can only wonder at.

All through this time we were roughing out the pages of our great work, and there came a time when the end was in sight. We would have our finished product to bring to the people. Straight away, Jon began to talk himself around the printers, and similar unsavoury trades. He played in their crooked card games and gained their trust enough to propose our project to them. One of them bit, eventually, and agreed to print our book. He was a gnome-like individual by the name of Emil des Shartz, a former Academy graduate (Low Formal pass, but what of that?). I think that beneath his scowling, balding exterior he was a man with a sense of adventure. He would be publishing the first entirely new work in a hundred years, after all. He demanded most of the money we had up front, but I worked out that he must have pulled an equal amount from his own pocket to get things moving.

Rosanna took it on herself to raise the general awareness of what we were doing. Everywhere she went, every party, convention, kava house and pharmaceutical bar, she talked about Helman. She and I went back to our old ways and argued for public acclaim, debating points of Helman's theory. Rosanna paid flunkies to spread the word and badgered Emil into printing posters announcing that the world was about to change and had them put up all over town. In short, by a week before our projected date of publication you could not go anywhere fashionable without someone bringing up, "this new thing Cartier's doing". It could not be said that anyone had a clear idea what it was, but they all knew, all the Academics and socialites and people of means, that something was afoot. Bets were placed. People enjoyed the suspense. It was regarded as quite the titillating party piece on Helman's part. It was not the way he would have wished it, but at least people were talking.

There came the time when Helman finally declared the project ready. We sat with Emil in his office and ceremonially handed over to him the stack of our calculations, writings and illustrations. It looked surprisingly small to us, a single medium-sized volume.

"Brilliant," Emil said. "What's it called?"

We were momentarily struck dumb. Not one of us had given any thought to a title. Names are used to distinguish a thing from a similar thing, and in our minds there was nothing remotely comparable to our work. Emil was right, though. We needed a name.

There was a quick, free and frank exchange of views there and then, as Emil sat back and leafed through the draft. Helman held out for *Natural Principles* which, while accurate, was tedious. I was quite keen on *Bold New World*, *New Natural Order*, *The Shape of Future Things* and several other variations on the same theme. Rosanna laughed all over my ideas and put forward such mystic nonsense as *The Way*, *The Path*, *The Path and the Way*, *The Key and the Path* and endless permutations that promised everything and revealed nothing. Helman was moved to expand his suggestion to *Principles of Nature* which he thought was a bit racy. I got out of my depth with *Gateway to the Stars* and Rosanna diversified to *The Secret* but then regressed to *The Secret Key*, *The Path of Secrets* and the like.

"The Secret Path to the New World's Natural Principles," said Jon, who was not taking it seriously. Emil snickered.

"All right," I rounded on him. "You decide."

"What?" Emil said, startled.

"You're printing it. We give you the honour of naming it," I told him.

Emil thought visibly. At last he nodded to himself and said, "How to Save the World." He thought a moment more and added, "In big red letters all over the cover. With an exclamation mark."

Helman vetoed the exclamation mark. Other than that it was just as he said.

16

Repercussions

Needless to say, the result of our labours surprised us. Results, I should say. There were two distinct consequences and neither of them was expected.

Let me say that we did gear ourselves up for a fight. We were ready for the sternest resistance. We knew the academic institution far too well to think that they would take it lying down. For a quartet of students to pen a work overthrowing their entire ethos would have them swarming out of the Academy like scorpions disturbed from beneath a stone. They would come down on us crammed with disputation, and we would meet them word for word, argument for argument. We had right on our side, you see. We had the salvation of humanity at stake. We would crash through their stale, dry philosophies like a battering ram. We were young.

We went so far as to publish our presence in a certain gaming house, so that they should waste no time in finding us. We wanted to clear that first engagement of Helman versus the Establishment as soon as possible.

We were ready for other opposition as well. The President and the rest of the Authority would hardly be keen to rework the entire infrastructure of Shadrapar, even to save the species. However, we were convinced that, with the Academy and polite society on our side, we would be able to talk Harweg and Miljus and the others over.

I would remind you that we were led by Helman who, for all his excellent qualities, had an unshakeable belief in the sovereignty of human reason.

So, Emil printed *How to Save the World* in the somewhat profligate quantity of fifty copies. It rained, the day of the printing, which was a thankfully rare occurrence in Shadrapar. Rain over the city is not like the simple sky-thrown water of the jungle. It has other things in it, chemicals drawn from the poisonous air across the sea. When it rains, they put great sails up over the crops to protect them, and everyone gets indoors and stays there. After the rains there is a thin, greasy film over everything, a clear, plasticky stuff that must be scraped off. Rain is foul in Shadrapar, then as now, and thankfully it came no more than about three times a year. The fact that it rained on the very day our book was produced should have told us something. We were all rational scholars, however, and had no time for omens. Instead we retreated to our room above the gaming house to await the storm.

Which never came.

I said at the time that the one thing we had not been expecting was complete indifference. As I say, it turned out that there were actually two things that caught us out, but indifference came first.

Our book was distributed to the Academy buildings, to private libraries and convent reading rooms and the occasional tables of the fashionable. There, insofar as I am aware, it mouldered. Despite all our work, despite the great hubbub of expectation beforehand, the book fell like a stone into the utter silence of people just not caring. Oh, I'm sure that people skimmed the pages and tittered absently at Jon's cartoons. Perhaps a copy or two was actually read cover to cover, but the overwhelming public response was a lack of response. People were perhaps very mildly amused. It furnished an hour's polite conversation at the odd dinner where other topics were lacking. The Academy filed the book in the library but not a Master actually laid eyes on it. It was a silly little trifle put together overnight by students for a prank.

We sat in our room and plotted everyone's untimely demise. Occasionally we went out to dine, and nobody mentioned it, and this was not because not mentioning it would gall us. It was just that nobody thought of our project at all. Nobody took anything serious seriously in polite company. Two Masters might get into a face-slapping row over a piece of ancient manuscript, but ask them to judge a murderer or save a life, or to save everyone's future, and they laughed it off.

They laughed us off, all four of us, and then forgot us. By the end of the week Helman was heartbroken, and the rest of us were really spoiling for a fight. Which was what we got, unfortunately.

It is difficult to know how to describe the next sequence of events in order to convey them to you, the unknown reader. They are jumbled in my head, by my panic and by their sheer magnitude. Moreover, I was not there for them all. For the first significant time in my narrative (discounting Peter's swamp escapades and the like) I must break from those things which I saw with my own eyes, and report to you something that was reported to me. Emil told me, as it happened. He saw everything I missed.

Perhaps I should start with the reason I was absent. It was a dinner, that was all. An invitation had come through from an influential man of letters for one of us to sit at his table. We knew that it would be a chance to force our ideas on the elite, and we bickered over who was best suited to going. In the end, I won out. I was getting restless cooped up in our room above the gaming house and got quite fierce in my protestations. Jon folded quickly, but then there was Rosanna.

She did not argue with me. For once, the one time that it turned out to matter, she let me have my way. I am no believer in fate, but I still ask myself, "Why was this?" It seemed like nothing at the time, some silly quirk of hers that I would later use to tease her with. I never had the chance to tease her with it, or with anything.

You must forgive me my sentiment. How this writing brings it all back. My hands are shaking even now. I feel almost like praying that the Wasted God has a little strength left to lend me.

So I skipped out on my friends for a dinner party at which, needless to say, I accomplished nothing. Nobody was interested in saving the world and I even forgot about it myself, lost in the currents and counter-currents of gossip. I had been closeted with the others for some days and it was a refreshing chance to be in other company. I remember thinking just that.

Now I leave me. Now I go to Emil's testimony.

Emil's offices were opposite the gaming house. It was the reason we had chosen the place. From his first floor window he saw everything. Specifically, at around two hours before sunset, he saw groups of people gathering in the street outside. This in itself was not unheard of. These people were not the usual run that we were used to in that area. Emil told me that he had assumed someone had sent them there for a joke, told them there was a job there. They were, not to put too fine a point on it, workers. I have not spoken much of the working classes in Shadrapar yet. I had not met many of them. Our paths had seldom crossed. Only in those lean weeks after my father's death, when my mother and I had been forced to seek the cheapest and meanest haunts, had I really experienced life amongst the labourers. That life, I knew, was hard. I think that it is never an enviable position to be in, to be a manual labourer, a worker. Remember that I have done hard physical work myself since. Sergei, whom I would meet later, had a lot to say about the virtues of the working man. It is his influence that stops me degenerating into just venting my spleen. For his sake I will try to write a balanced account of the subsequent events.

Groups of labourers, factory hands and similar men (they were mostly men) began to condense in isolated islands down the street. Emil noticed them, looking out of his window, and was mildly curious, but not enough to actually ask any questions. He was dealing with his accountant's report, and the traditions and rites of that profession insist on such documents being as complex and opaque as possible. The gathering of a few workmen under his window was of no great concern to Emil at that point.

At about this moment I was just starting the main course, in a rather surly fashion. I had discovered early on that nobody was interested in our project and the small talk that I usually took such delight in was starting to bore me. It seemed smaller than usual and the novelty of new company had worn off. I was beginning to wish that I had never come.

At around the time that dessert was being trolleyed round, the small groups of factory men had aggregated into what can only be referred to as a mob. This Emil did take notice of. Mobs were uncommon in Shadrapar. They were no longer a naturally occurring formation in humanity's strata. People were too desperate (at the low end) or indolent (at the high end of society) to bother about grabbing a chair leg and going off with two hundred neighbours to complain about something. We knew in our hearts that we were doomed, and therefore why try to fight for a better tomorrow. It was the same hurdle that Helman and the rest of us had fallen at. Shadrapar had not seen an honest-to-goodness mob since before President Marks' time.

At least we had made an impression, at long last. At least our work provoked a response.

You see, we had never even thought about anyone outside our social circle having any issues with the book. After all, a good half of the people we dined with could not read. It seemed unreasonable for there to be a literary sensation amongst the factory processors and workers. We had never thought about them, their feelings. I tell a lie. Perhaps Helman had considered them, and the fact that their lives would be so much easier and less harsh when the burden of all that physical toil was lifted from their shoulders, and onto the lobes of our brains.

You might see, now, what the problem was.

The mob was relatively quiet at first, according to Emil. It blocked the street and milled about in general disorder, and it was hard for him to take it seriously. Without experience of such human phenomena all Emil saw was a slew of people blocking traffic. He rang down for one of his staff to find out what was going on. That was when he discovered that his entire staff had jumped ship. The presses were silent. He was the only person left in the building. That should have worried him. Instead it made him angry because he assumed that they were out mingling with the factory hands and not doing their jobs. In actual fact, as he discovered later, they had all got wind of what was going on and had made a run for it while they could. Emil had not endeared himself to his workforce, and so they had left him in the dark and in the lurch.

So it was that, just as I was making my excuses and leaving the tedium of the dinner table, Emil stomped downstairs onto the shopfloor and out onto the street, looking for the faces of his staff.

I think the frightening thing about a mob is that it has no brain. We are all accustomed to the idea of a vital area to strike at, a leader to convince, a simple decapitation to render the entire beast, machine or army helpless. With a mob there is no such thing. It is a kind of hive creature, a thousand small sparks combining into a great fire. There was a lot of talk about ringleaders and agitators and the like afterwards. That is nonsense. The mob simply was, without nervous system or mind to direct it, and all its component parts were expendable.

I am not suggesting that all of those men and women all decided to go look for trouble each of their own accord. There was a definite force behind it. Some factory owner or other (and I never did find out who) had got hold of a copy of *How to Save the World* and not liked what he saw. The simple fact is that if there was the slightest chance we were right then he would be out of pocket. There would be no need of factories in our future, nor exploitative profitmongers or sweatshop slave-drivers. We were inadvertently proposing devaluing the entire labour economy by removing the necessity of labour, which necessity in a fairer world might give power to the labourers, but in this one only gives power to those who control the mills and factories in which the labourers must slave. One of those magnates had obviously decided to nip us in the bud in case anyone started listening to us, so he had put rumours through his workforce that we were trying to make them obsolete. By disdaining industry and machines we were threatening their way of life, the welfare of their families, so they were told.

The mob changed when Emil came out to them. One moment it had been placid, mindless, a great directionless mass of people just waiting for a spark to animate them. Emil was that spark, and he had just started to shout for his missing staff when the mob roared with one voice (as he put it) and came for him. This might have been the first time Helman and the others became aware of what was happening.

Every worker and factory hand who could manage it surged onto Emil's shopfloor, taking Emil with them. There, seeing the accursed means of production that had churned out our heretical tome, they began to break things. Once that kind of business starts there is really no stopping it. As Emil watched, horrified, they smashed all but one of his presses (and that one was missed through carelessness – let no-one tell you a mob is thorough). They smashed him, too, when he tried to interfere. Emil was not a perceptive nor a sensitive man, and he could evidently not tell which way the wind was blowing even at gale force. When faced with a small army of thugs trashing his premises he shouted at them, ordered them to desist, and finally waded in with a jack-handle (it's some printer's machinery thing, I don't know what it's for). He got kicked about fairly badly for his pains, and they broke his nose and several ribs, and when I last saw him (long ago, before the Island) he still limped. They left him alive, though. They had not got up speed at that point. So much for Emil's testimony which, with his loss of consciousness, must end here. Thankfully for the purposes of narrative it is probably around here, give or take ten minutes, that I arrive on the scene.

In immaculate evening dress, with all my aesthetic pretensions, imagine me regarding the scene: Emil's place is broken, there is no other word for it. Only the stonework is intact. Everything that could be snapped in half or shattered to fragments has been served just so. There are perhaps three hundred solid, angry, agitated people outside the gaming house. They are shouting a name.

The name is, "Carter!"

Not Cartier, mark you. Carter. I'm not sure whether this consensual mistake on the part of the mob is deepest irony or misplaced bathos.

I stopped dead, as you would. I was unseen, for they were all looking inward, focusing on the house.

At that point, I am sure, I should have done something. I should have shouted at them. I should have attracted their attention and got them to follow me all over the city. I should have done something like that, only... Only I was scared, more frightened than I had ever been. I think that anyone who sets themselves above their fellow men, leaders, scholars, aesthetes, anyone like that has a fear of the mob at heart. A fear that the great bulk of the species that they effect to look down on will turn on them, bring them back to earth and trample them. I was afraid of that crowd. It surged and pulsed against the walls of the gaming house. It roared out that corruption of Helman's surname like a massed curse. It had no mind or direction but a limitless fount of rage and destruction that was independent of any person in it. I have never found a beast of the jungle nor of the desert that frightened me as much as that mob, not even the Macathars.

The noise the mob was making was nothing compared to the positive shriek of hatred it gave vent to when Helman appeared on the balcony above them. It was the right position for a warlord addressing his troops, a dictator his people. He had no hold on them, though. Helman of all people could never have quelled a mob. He had no common touch.

He tried to reason with them. As I say, Helman believed utterly in the power of reason over emotion. He called down to them good, logical arguments as to why they should break up and go home, and they jeered and roared and some of them threw things. I could see Helman being calm and rational in the heart of the storm, numbering points off on his fingers. Despite the situation he had no fear of them. He could not see that they wanted to tear him limb from limb because he could see no reason for it.

A lot of the mob's energy had gone into smashing Emil's place. They were working themselves up to another attack, and Helman was fuelling them. He could see that every word he spoke made things worse, and yet there was no desperation in him, nor would he give up. He just carried on in his thin, clear voice, trying to make them see what was so patently obvious to him. I should point out that the other denizens of the gaming house had fled long before out of the back door, and my friends could have done so as well, save for Helman. Helman could not bear to see such misjudgement in his fellow men. He was accused, and his nature bound him to argue his case. And the others would not leave him.

Abruptly, some restraining cord snapped within the crowd and they threw themselves against the gaming house like a tide and broke against the walls, shattered the windows, pounded at the door. Someone, probably Rosanna, had at least barred that. Helman was still advocating reason but nobody was even looking at him any more. I think I called out then, when it was too late. I think I shouted at them all to stop, as though it would have helped. Nobody heard me. The crowd was lost in its own roar. I could not even hear my own words, just the thunder of three hundred men's displeasure and the pounding against that bolted door.

That was when the Angels came. You must have Angels where you come from, though you may call them the Guard or the Gendarmes or something similar. They kept what order there was in Shadrapar, and they kept it jealously. A riot was hardly something to dodge their attention. My heart leapt when I saw them coming, and it must have been the first time in the history of Shadrapar that somebody was pleased to see the Angels. They were never popular.

They came with a big, tracked armoured car, perhaps eight of them in full gear. They had helmets and the piecemeal body armour the past had left them, but all of them had some design of shielding pack on their back. The two point generators that projected past their shoulders looked like folded wings, were often actually styled as such with carved vanes and snap-out sharp-edged feathers. They all had energy guns of one kind or another. Flanking their vehicle they came down on the mob at a run.

Perhaps there was some kind of shouted warning. I could have missed it in the general row. All I know was that the Angels opened fire as soon as they were close, lancing their bolts of energy, their needle beams of light and balls of blue flame, into the hostile crowd. Perhaps eight or nine people dropped dead on the spot, burned and charred, and the rest fell back in boiling confusion, screaming and shouting fit to wake the dead of ages. I had no wish to get caught in that rout so I slipped into Emil's place, which the mob had no more interest in. Emil himself was lying unconscious on the floor, but I had no time for him then. The crowd was still roiling outside.

I remember the next thing most clearly of all: the Angels were still loosing off shots into the crowd, and they were close enough for me to see the lack of passion in their eyes. The crowd itself was split, unsure whether to charge or retreat. The driver of the armoured car upped the speed, so that the vehicle began to forge towards the crowd like a crushing ram.

I had not seen Helman disappear from the balcony. Like everyone else I had been far too concerned with other matters. Helman, champion of reason.

He came out of the gaming house, right where his enemies wanted him. He was shouting, actually shouting, not just calling in loud tones. I had never heard him shout, save for that one argument with the Academy Master. He was shouting at the Angels. He was trying to get them not to charge the crowd.

He always did believe, right up to the end, that reasoned argument would solve everything, if only people would just sit down and listen to him. If only.

He went under the tracks of the car, my friend Helman. I think it may even have been slowing down, because it coursed to a halt with its reinforced nose cracking the timbers of the gaming house door, then reversed a step or two to allow access. That was the end of Helman Cartier: genius, philanthropist and my closest friend.

The crowd had backed off now, but it was still massed at two or three alleyways, in sight of the gaming house and its remaining prey. I saw the Angels arrange themselves around their vehicle, which had white wings painted on its dark grey sides to show who it belonged to. The real angels were supposedly flying men and women with powers of judgement. With the loss of any sciences that might make a winged man fly, we had resorted to these cold killers for our own version.

Two of them went inside, through the door that Helman had left unbarred. They had a clipped, aggressive violence in every move of theirs. They must have come for Valentin Miljus in the same businesslike way. Of all the people I have personally known, only the Marshal moved like that.

The crowd was getting restless, buzzing and murmuring angrily amongst itself, and the Angels still outside kept their weapons levelled at all times. I realised then, watching their stance, their quick looks each to each, that they were afraid themselves. Despite their weaponry, their reputation and defences, they were as scared of this monstrous composite beast as I was.

The two inside came out dragging Jon and Rosanna with them, and I remember thinking that at least they would be saved. The Angels would take them off for judgement, like their mythical forebears, but at worst they would be exiled to the Island. That would still be life.

The howl the crowd set up when they saw Rosanna and Jon was indescribable. I recall shrinking back from the broken windows, seeing the energy build between the workers and factory men. The Angels froze and their Commissar fired three shots into the air to put fear into the mob, but there was no room for fear there. They were fighting furious. They had unshakeable faith that we, Helman, Rosanna, Jon and I, were their enemies. At that moment none of them cared why, none of them asked for reasons. The blooding the Angels had given them had cowed them for a moment, but then the great beast had fed on its own wounds and grown stronger. The edge of the crowd began to surge back and forth, edging closer to the Angels and their prisoners, and eventually that cord would break again and they would crash down on their enemies with all the force that human madness and rage could give.

I could see the Angels quite clearly, and my friends as well. I could hear the coins chatter in Jon's pockets as he pulled at one of the armoured men, demanding sanctuary. Rosanna was quite quiet, staring at the blood on the car tracks, all that remained of Helman. The Angels drew tighter together. It was clear that the next shot they fired would only serve to cue the crowd's assault.

Then someone cast the first stone. It arced out of the centre of the mob and bounced off the armoured car with a dull sound.

A poor first shot of any war. The idea, coined by one wit in the mob, spread like wildfire. I could see everyone in that angry crowd stooping to pick up whatever they had: stones, bottles, chunks of glass, scattered pieces of printing press. The Angels backed up and activated their shields. The wing-like extensions over their shoulders crackled with power to form a shimmering, sightless plane before and behind them to deflect energy and missiles. As usual, about a third of them did not work, perhaps closer to half. The secrets of their maintenance had been lost.

The rain that fell on the Angels was far less kind than the toxic showers that Shadrapar was used to. Stones and bricks bounded from the vehicle and ricocheted from the energy shields. Their momentum was never quite stopped, and a solid strike would make a shielded Angel stagger with the force of it. I saw one Angel struck down to his knees, his shield failing and the generator dented by a well-aimed shot. Another rock gashed poor Jon across the forehead, knocked him into the side of the car. Rosanna went to his aid, trying to shelter him. A bottle smashed across her back. The crowd, still throwing everything that came to hand, advanced further. The Angels began to fire, but it served only to antagonise.

I heard, even above all that, the Commissar of Angels cry out an order to retreat. Almost falling over themselves, Shadrapar's police force clambered for the vehicle, those with working shields protecting those without. The feared and respected Angels had been put to flight. The armoured car backed up almost comically, smashing chunks out of the buildings behind it in its haste to reverse. I saw Jon trying to get up on it, and one of the Angels – I think it was the Commissar himself – kicked him down. He fell back and lay in the street, the coins rattling from his pockets. Rosanna crouched over him. The mob descended.

I will say no more about that. I am sure that your imagination can furnish the details better than my poor words. For me? I went into hiding. My name was on that book, under Helman's and above those of Rosanna and Jon. I was on the list.

Harweg would later say, of our project and our work, that "it caused quite a stir at the time".

I paid a ruinous rent out to the Wasted Convent, of all places, to keep me hidden. Just round the corner from all the people who knew me, I dug in and covered my head and wept. I am told I became quickly feverish and was more trouble than I was worth. I had seen my three closest friends die. Who can blame me?

By the time I was ready to leave the Wasted Convent I was out of money, which was a happy coincidence. The Convent Madames threw me out with not a grain of sympathy. Their excuse was that God was in far worse straits than I, but as far as I was concerned they were a pack of closed-minded mercenaries. I went with trepidation into Shadrapar, half-expecting to find a mob waiting silent at the convent's door.

The first thing I needed to know was what the situation was. Was I being hunted? Was my face on posters all over the city: "Wanted for threatening the livelihood of the working man"? I got hold of a hooded cloak and wore it, which I am sure made me far more conspicuous than anything else, but at least it hid my precise identity.

I had a very great need to discover just how things lay between me and the world and I could trust virtually nobody. Anyone might sell me out to the mob. In fact, I could rely on only one person in the world and that was my fellow survivor, Emil des Shartz.

He had set up in the wreck of his old premises, so it was easy to find him, although the hardest thing I ever did was to actually return to that scene. When I got there he was cranking out posters by hand: one working press, no staff. He was still mottled with bruises, nose crooked, fingers splinted. The crowd had not been gentle with him. When I saw him I was afraid that he would be furious with me. He had lost everything on our project save his life. Even as I approached him I kept one eye on the door, ready to make a run for it. When that wound-ugly face turned on me, though, there was only surprise in it.

"Stefan!" Emil gasped at me. "Since when were you still alive?"

I shrugged. There is really no answering a question like that. I mumbled something ridiculous like, "How are you?"

"Been better," Emil said. He gestured me closer, urgent. "You've been hiding up, yes? So why stop now? You think it's safe? It's not safe for you!"

Blood running cold, I huddled beneath my cloak. "I ran out of money. I don't have a penny to hide behind. Where are they looking for me?"

"All over," Emil said. "They don't think you're dead, though I was sure of it. They come here almost every week, still."

This seemed a bit organised for a mob. I was sure that I would have noticed organised search parties of factory men tearing up Shadrapar for me. "Someone must be behind them, to keep them moving like this. Otherwise they would have dispersed by now. Who wants me so badly?"

Emil looked at me blankly for a moment and then realisation dawned. "I don't mean the people, the workmen," he said. "The Angels are after you, Stefan."

"What?"

"You're a wanted man. Provoking civil unrest, sedition, causing an affray, all that kind of stuff. They don't get riots here very often. The Authority wants someone to blame and you're the only one left to pin it on."

I sat down heavily. After killing Helman and failing to protect my other friends, the Angels were now blaming me.

"What can I do?" I whispered. "I've got no money. Nobody will hide me. I can't even disappear amongst the masses. They all hate me too." Self-pity is an ugly thing in anyone.

There was a long awkward pause as Emil looked at me, and the press clacked and muttered in the background.

"All right," he said, finally. I looked at him.

"After… after it happened I was pretty much out of pocket myself. I had to take what I could get in the way of work. I had to wake up a few old contacts, do some things I wouldn't normally touch, take a few risks with the kind of people I would work for, just to keep the creditors away."

I nodded, generally uninterested.

"Here." Emil rummaged behind a stack of rubble and old boxes. "Get this."

It was a poster, roughly drawn out, that said, "WORKERS of Shadrapar, seize the Means of Production! Free Men and Women need NO LEADERS. SMASH the AUTHORITY!" with a picture of working men with linked arms. I thought they were dancing at the time, but now I know they were showing solidarity.

"What the hell is this?" I asked.

"Ironic, no? Let me give you a little background. Years ago, when I was just starting in this business, fresh out of the Academy and apprenticed, I knew someone. He had been in the Academy above me, then worked in the library. He loved his books, owned a huge collection. His creditors had their eyes on it. He owed almost everyone. He borrowed from everyone to buy his books."

I nodded again, not really caring or following him.

"Right then. Anyway, this man I knew just disappeared, at about the time I was apprenticed. I thought no more of him. Until I got a message to go meet him. He wanted to get copies of books that we were printing. He was still collecting. He paid me. I don't know how he got the money. I haven't seen him for years now. He might be dead."

"Emil—" I interrupted, but he held up a hand.

"Easy now. This man I knew, he had gone with his books into hiding. Into the Underworld."

I stared at him. I had heard enough of it in the hard weeks after my father's death. It was a legend, a place below, of renegades and criminals and… other things. Of course, I was a renegade now, and a criminal. I saw the connection.

"I met some other people through this man I knew. Some of them keep in touch. I did these posters for one, and he'll be collecting them tonight. He'll take you, if you ask him."

"Who is he?" I asked, looking at the poster.

"Not what you expect. A madman, among other things. Still, what choice have you?"

So true. I still wonder at Emil, battered and bruised, having the residual kindness to help me like that. I think he felt some misplaced guilt for Helman and the others. God knows it was not his fault.

I departed for the Underworld that night, in the company of the peculiar Sergei. Thus ends the second part of my history.

PART THE THIRD

MY FURTHER ADVENTURES ON AND OFF THE ISLAND

17

Visitors for the Condemned

On the Island, confronted with Tallan and Harro and prompted by my own ill temper, I acted. I was suffering for it now, of course. I was now sitting in a tiny box waiting to drown or be eaten. At least I had merited the punishment by some bravery of my own, though. My life was so barren of acts of courage that I had to treasure this one. If this sounds ridiculous to you, save your disbelief, for I am about to describe something that even I hardly believe, and I was there.

I suppose I should describe myself again. Some time and much pain has passed since I last did so. I am no taller, perhaps a little bowed, and all folded up in that cell, anyway. My drab prison greys are stained and torn, with a notably large bloodstain where the Marshal stabbed me. Perhaps you see some of that staining on the pages you hold, for some were there with me in the dark and the damp. I am leaner than before – too much work and too little food. I suppose that I am stronger, too, much good it ever did me.

As I crouch in that cell, then, assuming you could see through the darkness, my face is what has changed most. My hair is long, down to my shoulders and infested with wildlife, and that makes my face look even longer. I have the odd small scar. I have lines, more than you would think my face could take. They are lines of hard learning, of growing up. They came from having killed a man, which was new to me; of doing a solid day's work, which was new to me; of being thankful to someone on a daily basis for not killing me, which was also new to me. My face has aged some several long years in the months that have passed. I am no longer young.

That was the longest night of my life, that first night Below. For all that there was no further move from the swimming predators below us, I was in constant terror waiting for the feel of scuttling little monsters in my cell. I did not sleep at all, although I could tell that everyone else had nodded off as soon as the screaming had stopped. I knew that if I let myself go even slightly from that petrified crouch then I would be smashing at the bars, pleading to be let out and taken far, far away. I would have gone mad, all of a sudden and for good, had I not kept that absolute hold on myself.

On the other hand, perhaps I did sleep, and only dreamed that I spent all night clutched in on myself. Perhaps I imagined it all.

What happened was this: I saw a light. It was not the sun, nor was it the sickly lamps. It was a light in the water. Had it not been pitch dark I would not have seen it: scarcely a suggestion of a gleaming beneath me. I saw it, though, and I saw that it was moving. It swept below me several times, clearly attached to some living thing, and then I saw that it was rising through the waters to meet me.

I moved then: with one twitch I had my back pressed against one wall of my cell to get as far from it as possible. It was heading for the hole the previous monster had made. I am afraid I shut my eyes. I still had that child-part of me that insisted that, if I ignored something, then it would go away. It was a tactic that seldom worked with imaginary horrors, let alone real ones.

I heard the faint slosh of water as it surfaced through the bent floor of the next cell, and then the occasional slap and scrabble as it caught its balance.

I opened my eyes, and for a long time I could see nothing but darkness. I found myself wondering whether this new thing could slide through the slots in the wall to get at me. There were such things. Trethowan had described them.

The faint glimmerings of phosphorescence pieced themselves together one by one, and the illuminated outlines of the creature slowly made themselves known to me. I saw a large, flat head, crescent-shaped with a huge, wide mouth; a frog-like head on a thick, ribbed neck. There were forelimbs just visible, clutching at the edges of the hole in the floor, and the remainder of the creature could be seen only as fugitive gleams deeper in the water. It had swum like a snake, so I assume it was something of that serpentine shape.

I could not see whether it had eyes. There were shadowy spaces that might have housed them, but they had no light of their own. Whether it had eyes or not, it was definitely looking at me.

And then it made a sound. I was so highly strung at that point that I thought it said my name, but that is the sheerest nonsense. It spoke, though. Although I misheard its first words, it was definitely speech. The voice was soft and not of the best diction, scarcely more than a light, throaty whisper in the dark air. It was not formed with the lips – there were no lips and the broad jaws remained slightly open but unmoving. Beneath them, though, the thing's throat pulsed and wrinkled in and out with the words.

"Sowattay'infor…"

I stared at it. If it had eyes then it stared at me.

"So watta y'in for," it said again, and the words started to make a little more sense. I continued to stare. The thing shifted slightly in the water.

It repeated itself again: "So watta y'in for." I could not speak. Those wide jaws opened in a yawn that exposed the chamber of its throat, needle teeth silhouetted against the phosphorescence.

"Marshal's gonna toastya," it whispered.

"What?" I demanded, in spite of my horror at the thing.

"Marshal's gonna toastya," it said again, and then, "So watta y'in for."

It was parroting. I saw that clearly then. Here was some monster with a talent for mimicry that had hung about the Island long enough to pick up a few phrases it had heard the prisoners say. So what are you in for? The Marshal is going to toast you. An unusual beast: Trethowan would have been fascinated. I found myself slowly coming out of my rigid horror.

"Marshal's gonna toastya," it told me, and I replied, in a faint, weak voice, "Oh I know. I know."

It regarded me brightly, whether it had eyes or not. I felt more than heard the prisoner in the cell at my back stir, realised that others were awake too.

"Gotta sleep. Gotta work inna mornin," the thing ventured. "Allus gotta work inna mornin."

"Right," I said. It was like talking to some part of my mind. Perhaps it was a hallucination and that was what I was doing.

"What are you doing, man?" one of the closer prisoners whispered. "You aren't supposed to talk to them. They're wrong." There was a raw horror in his voice.

"You want to talk to me?" I asked, in the darkness. There was a silence in which the thing shifted its position again. "You don't want to talk to me?" I concluded, "then just go to sleep."

"But it's wrong," the same voice insisted. "Listen, man—"

"So what are you in for?" I snapped out. "So what are you in for? It's wrong. It's wrong. Your conversation's no better than its." Darkness made me bold. The thought of them all sitting in their stupid, apathetic silence and darkness day and night, lapping up the sunlight and growing mouldy in the dark, disgusted me far more than any echoing monster. I thought they were jealous of me disturbing their silence. I thought that they could not tell a mimic from the real thing. As the prisoner lapsed into silence I returned my attention to the monster, which had levered itself another foot out of the water.

"So watta y'in for," it gabbled again.

"I killed a man," I told it. "That's why I'm here." It seemed simpler than to reel the whole story off.

"Kilta man," it followed up. "Kilta man. Watta y'in for. Kilta man."

"That's right," I confirmed.

"Ennywun I no?"

It was looking very carefully at me, eyes or no. I had frozen up again and was dearly wishing I had heeded the warnings of my fellow.

"Ennywun I no?"

It might have just been another repeated phrase, thrown in coincidentally where it would make some sense. I suddenly doubted my theory, though.

"Watcha called? Wasya name?" it garbled out. "Watta y'in for? Wasya name?"

"S-Stefan Advani." I could not have held back the words. I felt that I needed to shut the thing up as quickly as possible, and the only way I could do it was to answer its questions.

"Stefanad Vaani," it tried. It made a better job than many of the prisoners, even getting the stress on the penultimate syllable. "Stefanad Vaani kilta man," it followed up. Then, without warning, it was gone, slipping into the waters and vanishing in a streak of phantom light. Moments later I saw the distant glow of a lamp as a Warden trekked slowly through the Below corridors. When he got close, some of the prisoners scrabbled at their doors, saying things like, "It was here again," "He was talking to it," "He was encouraging it." The Warden shone the light of his lamp onto the bloody and mangled floor of the cell next to mine, and then turned the light on me. I never saw who it was, only that painful light. He obviously did not care enough to take any action, for he was continuing his patrol a moment later. The monster did not return.

★

Prisoners Below did not work. You might think this was a blessing, but after a single night I would have done any amount of hard labour to get out of the dark. It was dank down there, gloomy and frankly very tedious. I could have gone mad there quite easily simply from having nothing to do. Nobody spoke. I learned later that the Wardens had instructions to beat anyone who started talking. We all just sat there in that rank layer of water and stared at the scattered beams of light, or at nothing.

I had no track of time. When I was in the Underworld, equally cut off from sun and air, I still had the rhythm of day and night to sustain me. Most of the denizens set their clocks according to the world above, though they inverted them. Below there was no difference. The Wardens came down at irregular times. The prisoners sat or slept as it suited them. After a while the waxing and waning of sunbeams came to mean nothing at all. There could have been people above us turning lamps off and on. It was more plausible than some huge, distant ball of fire expiring slowly for our benefit.

After some time, then, Peter came to me.

I was crunched up into one corner of my cell, folded in on myself like a spider, or that is what Peter said. Only when the footsteps stopped before my cell did I squint into the lamplight.

"Come on," he said curtly. I could not tell whether he was doing me a kindness of his own accord, or was doing me an injury on orders. I crept forward to the door and he unlocked it. Some of the prisoners nearby began taking an interest.

He let me out into the corridor, and I stretched to my full height painfully. Around us, some of the prisoners were beginning to mutter.

"Take me!" one of them suddenly piped. "You don't want him. Me! Me!"

"No! I'm the one! Take me out!"

"I've been here longest!"

"I know where things are hidden! Precious things!"

"Me!"

"No! Me!"

Peter took a step away from me and smashed his club against a few doors until he had their attention. "He's going to have the crap kicked out of him. Marshal's orders. Any volunteers?"

There were no volunteers, no sympathy either. The prisoners Below had all kinds of jealousy but the place leached the empathy out of them in short order.

"Come on," Peter said to me, and pushed me roughly forwards, so that I stumbled on the floor. He grabbed my shoulder and dragged me back so that I could see his face, made craggy by the shadows of the lamp.

I saw him wink. Peter had come through for me somehow. I breathed a little easier, if only a little. As we ascended from the damp pit of Below he whispered, "Don't get your hopes up. You're going back there. Remember to limp a little or something."

I nodded.

"There really is nothing I can do to get you out," he continued, sotto voce. "The Marshal flat out hates you. The Governor's got it in for you. Stefan, you have got *the* surefire gift for making enemies."

"I'd kill again just to get out of that cell for a minute," I said, wondering as I did whether it was true or just a figure of speech. "I know you can't pull me out for good. Just a little air. A little light."

"Maybe more than that," Peter said evasively. We were going to a part of the Island I didn't know, but we were going up. I kept having to squint as the sun broke in through the piecemeal walls.

There was someone up ahead, at the top of another flight of stairs. A large, bulky man with a faint wreathe of smoke about him.

"Middsy," Peter acknowledged.

"All clear," the big man told him. "You better be sure that the Marshal doesn't even look funny at me, Drachmar."

"I'm a proper cornucopia of secrets," assured Peter. "You keep mine and I'll keep yours. I'll take it from here. Off you go."

Midds shambled away past us, without even a glance for me.

"What do you know about him?" I asked.

"Can't tell you. Secret," Peter said, and then: "Let's just say our man Midds likes to take boats out when he shouldn't. To gather medicinal supplies. The Marshal's boat, even, when there's no other choice."

"That's all?"

"Oh the Marshal gets very possessive about his little boat. He's real keen to know who's been playing with it."

"And a cornucopia?" I pressed.

"Something you put things in, isn't it?"

"Try oubliette," I suggested. We had mounted to the doorway to a small room whose walls were hung with woven reeds. There were small boxes and packages about, and in the centre of the floor the obligatory chessboard balanced on a crate.

"Spare storeroom," Peter said. "Discovered it a while back. Not really used much now. Nice and quiet."

"I suppose your game's getting rusty," I said, going over to the board. Peter hung back in the doorway, though.

"What?" I frowned at him, and then realised, a moment later, that we were not alone.

It was the Warden's uniform. They just vanished in the shadows, whereas the prisoners' greys were brought out in stark relief by the least amount of light. When the figure in black stepped forward I was caught quite by surprise.

Jon fell in love with an Outrider once. He said he loved the sight of a woman in uniform.

It was her, done up as a Warden. It was the woman who – I want to say that I killed Harro for her, but in truth she was more a collateral beneficiary of the act. My face must have been a picture. Certainly I stopped dead and then shot a quick look back at Peter. I had the bizarre idea I was being trapped somehow, that the Marshal and his goons would suddenly appear from the woodwork and execute me for being here. The corner of Peter's mouth twitched upwards and he raised an eyebrow.

I turned back to the woman and mumbled something to the effect that I really did not know what to say. Thankfully she took the initiative from me, because God knows I didn't know what to do with it.

"I was named Kiera de Margot. Thank you for twice saving my life," she said, and held out a hand. I remembered Gaki saying that the women on the Island were given all comforts, and this was certainly a well-maintained hand, dusky of skin, neatly manicured on all six fingers.

To me it was like seeing diamond rings and golden bangles, because here was the body and gene surgery that the extremely rich went in for. Six fingers on one hand was a good indication of exceptionally wealthy family. In keeping with the hand, the rest of her was all about the sort of beauty that is paid for in family money. Her hair was darkly lustrous, falling to the small of her back in a long unfolding of blue-black. She was tall, and they had engineered for a build that was athletic and rounded in turns. Everything about her was designed to be admired, but it came to me that it was not *her* for whom that admiration was intended. She was an advertisement for her family's taste and wealth, a prisoner to the whims of the previous generation. Only her eyes were her own, alive with a sharp humour. In this only did she recall my lost Rosanna Paramor.

And about time, some readers might be thinking. All this adoration for some prison girl I barely know, and only a few pages back I was mourning my dead love. But for me, long years had passed, and the sight of this woman struck me hard. Was it love at first sight? I leave that to credulous poets to bleat of. Did I desire her? I confess it. I am inconstant. I have barely even mentioned Faith to you yet.

I took her hand; the touch of a woman's hand after that much time sent a shock right through me.

"Madam," I replied, "I was named Stefan Advani, a scholar of the Academy, and I am delighted to have been the agent of your delivery–" Something she had said caught my imagination and punctured the courtesy. "Did you say twice?"

She sat back against the chess table. "First from the prisoners and then from their master's mistress."

"Lady Ellera," I said automatically, and to my surprise I felt Peter start behind me.

"Names best not said," he muttered low, coming closer. "'Herself.' That's what the Wardens call her."

"We call her the Witch Queen," Kiera said soberly. I dared to squeeze her hand as a gesture of comfort and she smiled at me. I was overdoing it, intended charm burlesquing into mummery. "I'm sure you've heard the rumours of her, and most of them are true. Of the women I met when I came here first, a third are no longer with us."

"I've… heard as much," I admitted. "That she has… uses…"

"She has a laboratory dedicated to it," Kiera said outright. Her hand tightened on mine. "She uses us to keep her young and healthy. It's like she's taking limbs and organs from us, only it's tiny parts of us we can't even see from within our bodies, but things we can't do without. I was marked for her next companion – that's what they call it, the 'Lady's Companion'. What she didn't know was I'd found a way out of the women's quarters. I was going to steal a boat, head out into the jungle. Anywhere was better than becoming a reagent in her lab. There were complications, as you saw."

"And the Wardens took you back," I pointed out. "They're saying you never even got out, now."

"I got taken before the Witch Queen," Kiera confirmed. "She… sniffed at me, and I could tell something had upset her. She said I'd been touched by something she didn't understand. Whatever the hell you did made me unfit for her purposes."

"And for that I got stuffed down Below," I noted, a little more acidly than I had meant to.

"We're none of us doing so well," Kiera said softly. She leant in a little, and I was acutely aware of Peter's presence behind me. At that moment I really wished that he would go away.

"They were very angry with you," she said simply. "They dragged in anyone they thought knew you. The people from your cell, some other prisoners, even a couple of Wardens. That was when I saw Peter. He was different, less scared of the Marshal." I really should have taken note of that "Peter" so early on, but more fool me, I was too busy looking into her eyes.

"So I got hold of Peter," she continued simply. "They didn't find out how I escaped, so I got out the same way. Leontes really does have no imagination. He never tried to have me questioned about it, and the Marshal has some thing about women. He doesn't want to have anything to do with them.

"Who's Leontes?" Peter voiced my next question.

"The Governor," Kiera told us. "You didn't know his name?"

Peter and I exchanged looks. "I never honestly gave it a thought," I admitted. "Leontes what?"

"De Margot, actually," said Kiera de Margot. "A very distant cousin, and it helps me not a bit. If he was still in favour with the rest of the family then he would not have been posted here. He's forgotten most of everything he left behind. He only has the time for the stars and his Witch now. Certainly not for me."

"We better hurry this up," Peter said. "They'll miss you otherwise, and we're all sunk if they find us. Stefan's got to go Below again, and I've got work to do."

"Go Below?" Kiera said, astonished. "But... but I thought you were going to—"

"The Marshal hates his guts and the Governor doesn't need him. He's got some flash new Academy scribe to do whatever Stefan was doing for him," Peter said. He was abruptly on the defensive. "The next time they remember he exists it'll be for the execution. There's nothing I can do for him. For anyone. I'm sorry, Stefan."

"I know how things are," I told him, and then to Kiera, "At least I accomplished something. You're safe, now." I made it sound terribly noble and self-sacrificing. Inside I wanted to cry.

She smiled tightly. "I'm waiting for Leontes or his Witch to realise that if I'm no use to Herself then I might as well be thrown to the prisoners or the Wardens. It'll come to them eventually."

"Oh." I must have looked dejected, because abruptly my hand was held by both of hers.

"Perhaps the prisoners will be kinder." She did not believe it, I could tell from her voice. It was just meaningless brave-talk. None of us believed it, in fact, but we all let the words lie without a challenge. We bade our farewells, and just as I was about to go she pulled me back with surprising strength and touched my hand to her lips, the way wealthy women do.

I had my own sunray to light me when I returned to Below.

18

Attempted Murder

I skipped back to my cell and forgot completely about Peter's cover story of my having been beaten. I tried to explain to my fellow sufferers that I was just highly resistant to pain and that it hurt like hell on the inside, but they were having none of it. I honestly could not have cared less.

All this warm feeling lasted about an hour, insofar as I could judge, before the ubiquitous gloom of Below began to get to me. After all, I was no better off than before. Even so, some superstitious little part of me had decided that I would not have had such a meeting simply to be left to rot the next minute. I seemed to have developed a belief in destiny. Even Trethowan did not go so far as to toy with predestination, writing:

My discoveries here have proved that there is no pattern to the world save that which life makes. There is no such thing as inevitability so long as there is at least one living cell left. Whilst the unliving moves from health to decay by degrees, life is the chaos which grows and builds and moves from less to more organised forms, thus confounding the general trend of the universe towards entropy. Some ancient writers even claimed that life was the universe's attempt at self-preservation.

Trethowan, of course, was fighting against the common belief of humanity that we were doomed and so why bother? Perhaps he would have looked kindly on my sense that I was destined for something better than Below. Trethowan was a seeker after hope, after all. Hope that even with the sun expiring daily above us, things could somehow change for the better.

Later we had another visitor to Below, this one not a conversationalist.

I first became aware of it simply through the reaction of my fellow prisoners. There was a kind of ripple of alarm from the cells down the hall. It was nothing so much as an exclamation, barely even a sound. Rather, it was a sense of movement, of each man in turn shrinking back from something and freezing into complete quiet and silence. It was a prey reaction, as Trethowan would have said.

I looked into the gloom and saw nothing, even though there was a good scattering of sunbeams lancing through our perpetual dark. Still I heard the ripple of revulsion, and it was getting close to me. Then something crossed a shaft of light. All I saw was the movement, at first. Then there was another flicker, and I had the impression of something stick-like poling forward, and then another, and then...

Under the faint sunlight it looked nut-brown, and hard as a nut too, and at first it seemed suspended in mid-air until I saw the webwork of legs holding it up. There were several of them, four, six, maybe eight, and none was more than an inch or two in diameter: a network of thin, black, jointed pipes to hold up a lozenge-shaped body perhaps four feet long. As it slid through that beam of light I saw no eyes or anything else to tell it that it was giving itself away. Instead, the leading end of that body had two clasping, raptorial arms and a long, bent beak that must have been eighteen inches long. The rest of the body was hard shell above and just darkness below, where the light did not touch it. It moved with an awful deliberation, one leg at a time, rocking slightly in between steps. The span of its legs was huge, and it could have touched the corners of a room far larger than the cramped corridor. It paid us no heed, and that hard, shiny body could not have passed through the small gaps in the cell walls. It was after other prey.

It must have heard the Warden coming before I did. Perhaps those wide-spread legs felt the vibrations of his footfalls. Abruptly it stopped, and began to hoist itself into the air. One leg at once found purchase amongst the bars of the wall and on the ceiling and carefully inverted itself, until it was clinging upside down above us, only one leg crossing a sunbeam to tell of it.

I could hear the Warden approaching now, the idle scuff of bored footsteps. There was a terrible tension amongst my fellow prisoners.

The Warden rounded the corner. All I could see of him was his lamp, which was pointed mostly down to light his way. I thought of that stiletto beak and what it would do to a human body. I opened my mouth to say something, but the very suspense was weighing down on me. The fixed anticipation of dozens of my fellows charged the air, filled it, leaving no room for sound. It may seem strange to you now, but I was physically oppressed by that expectant silence. It was as if the mean, starved minds of the Below prisoners reached out and forced me back, shut me up, as if they were using the inner energies that had got me into this mess. People in desperate situations can find unexpected reserves.

The Warden came close, and I saw the one visible leg shift slightly in the light as the creature adjusted its position. In the gloom between sunbeams I saw the long, hard body lower itself down in that cradle of legs like a man climbing with ropes. I convinced myself that I could see the two grasping arms unfurled slightly, ready to strike. I imagined that lethal beak folding out. The hunter, eyeless and deadly, was ready.

The close, tense bloodlust of my fellows clamped down on me, and must have spoken to the Warden at some level because his tread faltered slightly, just short of the monster's reach. That gave me the smallest window through which to shout, "Look out! Above you!"

The Warden jerked back, and the thing struck at him. I saw very little of it, just the suggestion of movement in the dark. In my mind's eye, however, I can picture it even now: dangling down on its horrible legs, claws extended, beak raised like a dagger.

It fell short, although the Warden must have felt the air before him being cut by those grasping arms. In the next second he was out with his club, striking the creature a massive blow across the body. I heard the carapace crack, and then the creature was wobbling away, step after jerky step, trying to escape across the ceiling. The Warden stepped in calmly and struck it twice, three more times, finally knocking it to the floor, where he stamped hard on its soft underside and then continued to beat it with his club until its legs had stopped thrashing.

There was an appalled silence to follow. The Warden stood quite still over the shattered corpse of his attacker and still all we could see of him was his lamp. That beam of artificial light passed over the cells and each prisoner in turn shrank back from it, as though they, too, were lurking insects awaiting a stomping. Only I faced up to it, and I think that told him who it was that had warned him. The light pinned me for a long time, and then the man was tracking off down the corridor. When a strand of sunlight caught his head and one shoulder I realised that I did not know him.

After he had gone, I could taste the anger in the air. There was not a man down that stretch of corridor who was not hating me with a passion. They had wanted their entertainment. To make up for their sunless lot they had wanted to see a Warden die, and I had thwarted them. Not a word was said by that desperate multitude, but I could feel the sour disappointment radiating from them in waves. They would gladly have torn me apart right then, for spoiling their fun.

I didn't care. I had given up on them. I turned my back on their lethargic fellowship. I hoped.

Later, they came for me. Sometimes it was a regular circus Below. You couldn't move for Wardens and semi-aquatic carnivores.

In this case there were three of them, none of them men I knew. They marched up purposefully to my cell and opened the door, and then one of them dragged me out. I sensed that my fellow prisoners were getting their hopes up again. They would shed no tears if I were executed.

As soon as I was out of my cell, one of the Wardens grabbed my injured shoulder and another punched me hard in the stomach, doubling me over and sending me to the floor. I curled up as tightly as possible, protecting my head and my vitals, because by now I knew the drill. I got a sound and businesslike kicking from the three of them. After this long in the Island I could tell a beating on orders from a beating for reasons of personal pleasure. From the clipped efficiency with which the boots slammed into my arms, legs and back I judged that this was a special request from the Marshal, who had apparently decided to hurry my demise. A bruised and battered man is more susceptible to all manner of deaths.

After they had kicked me around a bit they hauled me to my feet. I let myself hang between them, in order to assure them that they had done me harm, and they dragged my away. I was going on another excursion.

The Wardens hauled me out of Below, and once we had started going up we just kept going. We were headed to the Governor's own rooms. I fought the rising tide of fear and bile within me and decided that I would try to face my judgement like a man.

It struck me then that the Governor's rooms were like Below, in that the sun was blotted out by hangings and tapestries and the gloom was perpetual. It also struck me that if the Governor had been a sun-lover and allowed the light in, then the entire Island would have been a brighter place. In such a way, one man's eccentricities made everyone's life a little worse.

The Marshal was there waiting for us. Even in my bruised state I noted that there was the slightest edge of agitation to him. His steel eyes flicked from my captors to myself, and back.

"Leave us," he spat out, and the three Wardens obediently turned on their heels and were gone. The Marshal and I were left quite alone.

Something was definitely wrong with him. Normally the only emotion one could read in his face or body language was that stock blind hatred that seemed to fuel his every waking moment. As I stood before him there was... a shiftiness, is the best way I can describe it. For the first time, the Marshal was going outside the rules.

It all happened faster than it takes me to tell it. He looked quickly, right and left, to make sure that we were unobserved. I think that some part of me knew what was coming then. He bared his teeth and slammed my back against a wall by my bad shoulder. There was a knife in his other hand. He was going to kill me.

The knife jerked in; an awkward, murderous motion. I tried to twist in his grasp and abruptly a gate in my mind was down and I flung everything I had at him, trying to get a hold of his brain.

It was like trying to hold a greased lead bullet, and I could not do it. His mind slipped through my concentration, streamlined and predatory as a swamp-monster. When I brushed him, though, he flinched away from me, loosed his hold on my shoulder, the knife stuttering in its strike. In a single motion, I ducked under his arm and was three steps away. When I looked into his face again it was as expressionless as ever, his attention was focused beyond me.

I heard the footsteps and turned despite myself. Had the

Marshal struck then, he would have had me, but on this one occasion he was shy of committing murder in front of witnesses.

Coming out of the doorway from the Governor's chambers was a haggard, long-faced man with a vaguely shabby look. He was distinctive only in that he was dressed neither as a prisoner nor a Warden. Beyond that, he was around my age, washed-out and faded at the edges. His long coat had been patched too often. His satchel (an academic's mainstay – I once owned a satchel just like that) was scuffed and threadbare. Everything about him had seen better days, as had he.

He turned on me a look that I had never seen on another before, but knew well from having used it myself so often. It was a blankly uncomprehending "why?" kind of a look from a man who had been kicked by the world in places he had not known existed.

Do you remember Louyere? Let me jog your memory: Louyere, mediocre student and appalling gambler, who owed me money once and redeemed his debt with Helman's marker. Louyere, that little link in the chain of my life: there he was on the Island, looking as though his penchant for losing at cards had finally caught up with him. He must have been in desperate straits to come here. It is no coincidence that the Governor could attract nothing more in the way of academic talent than Louyere. Who in his right mind would leave Shadrapar of their own free will? Louyere must have racked up the sort of debts that even God could not have bailed him out from. And now he was staring at me as he passed, bewilderment and loathing on his face. I would see him again before the end. Farewell to Louyere.

Even as he was descending the stairs to go, the Marshal and I had more company. It was Leontes himself, Governor of the Island, and behind him...

Lady Ellera's appearance wreaked exactly the same havoc as it had before. She was beautiful like the sun; exactly like the sun, because you could see the sickness in her. Being in the same room as her set the heart racing and twisted the gut all at once.

The Governor was almost stamping. He looked for all the world like a preternaturally large toddler in a foul temper. He stormed flabbily up to me and looked me up and down, his round face trying to knot itself into a scowl.

"He looks half dead," he complained to the Marshal, as though he was examining some distant image of me. "What's happened to him?"

"The lowest level is a dangerous place," the Marshal said with the smooth confidence of a man who knows his version of events will be believed.

The Governor's little eyes found mine. "You are an *annoying* man!"

I blinked at him, speechless. He had said it with real fire, as though I should have been quite hurt. In a lifetime of them, it was the most ineffectual insult I ever received.

"Honestly," he whined, "I really feel that it is a slight to this institution that I am forced to rely on the services of my own wards to accomplish even the simplest of tasks." He glared at the Marshal as though implicating him in this conspiracy. "After all we do for them, you would think that we'd rank a little higher in their esteem. But no! All they send us are shoddy little men!"

In Shadrapar, of course, the Island was nothing more than where bad people went. The Governor's demands and desires meant nothing beyond his walls. I wondered what had condemned him to this post. We were all prisoners of the Island in our ways.

"Sir, this man is a troublemaker," the Marshal stated. High praise indeed. "I still say he should be executed now. We will regret it otherwise."

"Oh, they're all troublemakers to you." The Governor was in an unhelpful mood. "Why else are they here? This is a prison, Marshal. We have to work with what we've got. I want my Trethowan!" he shouted wretchedly. I kept a carefully blank face.

"Then I'll fetch your Academy scholar again," the Marshal said. "He can do the work for you. This man is dangerous."

"It wasn't the same!" the Governor complained. "It was awful. It had no life to it. It wasn't the same as when Advani was doing it." I was content to remain a piece of furniture in this debate. That was how I was being treated by the Governor: an object that provided a service. Until he had wrung that service out of me he was loath to give me up.

All the same, hooray for Old School Shorthand, and score another point for obsolete education.

"Sir," the Marshal continued desperately, "he is a danger to you. He is a danger to your…" He wasn't looking at the Lady Ellera – the Marshal didn't like to admit to the existence of women in general or her in particular. Still, it was plain who he meant.

For a moment I saw Leontes waver. Of course, he would be remembering my supposed tainting of Kiera and the Lady Ellera's horror at it. He twitched and turned, cringing a little before her.

But her gaze was on me, not on him. "Thank you for your concern, Marshal," she murmured, putting a long-nailed hand on the Governor's rounded shoulder. "I am sure that this wretch will not harm me."

Pinned by her gaze, I felt incapable of doing anything at all.

"There you go," Leontes declared. "I want him to finish it. Marshal, you have such a small mind. It wouldn't matter to you. Trethowan had ideas. He saw a vision of the future."

The Marshal shrugged. Why should he care about the future? I was surprised the Governor was so emphatic about it. Then I remembered his obsession with the stars. He was quite a cerebral man in his way, and thank the Wasted God for that. Was ever a man saved by such a tenuous thing as a slightly superior writing style?

And all that time, the Witch Queen regarded me thoughtfully. That should have worried me more than it did.

"Put him back into his old cell!" the little bald man commanded. "Set him back to work, anything, but he has to keep on writing."

"We might as well keep him Below, sir," the Marshal started.

"No, no. It's dangerous down there. You said so. He might get eaten or something. Let him keep writing. The moment he's done you can cut him into a thousand little pieces for all I care."

I privately resolved to take as long as humanly possible over my translations.

"And while I'm about it," Leontes continued, rounding on me again, "None of this changing writing. None of this getting other people to do it. Look at this." He pulled a folded piece of paper from inside his tunic. "I want it done like this. So it looks nice."

He showed me the paper's contents and my heart skipped slightly. I was really not sure of the reaction my next words would receive.

"Excuse me... sir," I dared. "That's not actually my writing. You see I was employing another of the prisoners... I was dictating to him, you see. I thought it would be quicker. And neater, obviously..." I trailed off into silence. The Governor regarded me blankly, the Marshal furiously.

"Well do that, then. Have this man, this... who?"

"Roseblade, sir. Shon Roseblade."

"Well have this Roseblade write for you. Marshal, see that he has this man available when he writes."

"But sir—"

"You heard him. It will be quicker that way. We all want this to be over with, do we not?"

The Marshal did not trust himself to speak. If he could have forced his mind onto me then I swear I would have combusted there and then in a pillar of fire.

"Now get him to his cell and get him fed up properly," the Governor said dismissively, and then Lady Ellera was sweeping out and he was pattering behind her.

He left me alone with the Marshal again, but I didn't care. I was a charmed man at that moment. The Marshal was malevolent and hateful, but he did indeed have a tidy little mind, and it was propped up at all corners with order. He imposed it and he fed off it. Discipline, regulations, obedience: he who lives by the chain of command shall also die by it. To kill me beforehand would have been excusable. No doubt he would have been defending himself, or some such story. To kill me after the Governor had given him his orders would be to disobey his one superior. Such an act of chaos would set echoes fit to bring the Island down. I am sure that this was the way he thought.

He called the Wardens again and told them to take me back to my cell – my upper cell. For want of a better word, I was going home.

19

Further Conversations with a Madman

It turned out to be evening when they got me back to my home away from homes. The Marshal's procrastinating had made me miss a meal. With an honour guard of three Wardens I trooped down into that familiar corridor. Midds, back in charge of my stretch again, stood at the far end with his hands behind his back and his paunch hanging out.

There was a ripple of reaction through the cells, akin to the prisoners Below when the insect-monster stalked amongst them. For a second, the Island held its breath.

I had not been in favour before they hauled me off to Below. The other prisoners had been ostracising me after I killed Harro. I was not sure what reaction I would receive when I rejoined their company.

I heard a mutter spring up from man to man, cell to cell: "It's him... he's back... it's Advani... he's out..." The news leapt from mouth to mouth and gathered speed as it went. I stopped dead and the Wardens barged into me, and went no further because things were escalating still.

It was like watching a flood: all those tiny trickles and whispers feeding off each other, converging into a roaring torrent of noise like a river hurling itself upon a dam. Which burst.

All of a sudden they were on their feet, all the prisoners of my stretch. They were standing and cheering and stamping. Some of them banged their food bowls on the doors just to make a little extra noise. They were shouting, and what they were shouting was, "Varny! Varny!"

Memories? Oh, you can be sure. For a moment I was listening to that crowd of factory men chanting "Carter!" outside Emil's printing house. This was different though. The name being mangled by the mob was mine, to start with, and they were cheering it. It took a moment for me to distinguish that roar of approval from the hate-filled sounds of my memories, but at last I understood that I had somehow become a celebrity. I had scored a victory for the oppressed, and they were delighted.

I had not realised that, when the Marshal consigned someone Below forever, then forever was just what they got. Perhaps I was not the first man to bounce back from such a sentence, but I was surely the first within living memory. Even those sent Below for a week or so frequently failed to return, as Onager's absence proved. I had been cast down by the Marshal himself, never to return, and here I was. I had beaten the system.

The Wardens around me started smashing at doors, trying to get people to shut up. If the Marshal had been there he would have been killing people, and then maybe he would have got his way or maybe there would have been a riot. None of the Wardens there had guns and they were not going into any cells any time soon. At the end of the corridor, Midds stood impassively, letting the wall of sound break over him.

I have been disparaging about the roar of the crowd before now. Standing there, basking in the adulation of my peers for the very first time, I felt like a king. I saw, at long last, why people sought power over others and why they courted the popularity of the masses.

I passed down the stretch, looking for familiar faces. The mass of cheering men were indistinguishable from one another. Only those who were silent stood out. Tallan, of course: he had no reason to be overjoyed at my return. He refused to meet my eyes, and I knew that I would have trouble with him later, but he was scared of me. I caught Thelwel's eye too, not cheering but smiling, which I think is as close as he came to it. Then, of course, there was Gaki. As we approached my old home I sensed him by his very stillness. He was standing at the bars of the cell he shared with nobody and watching me, with a faint, amused smile on his face. Even Gaki approved of me, in that moment. He was always a man for a bit of chaos.

They got me to my cell, then had to wait as Midds shambled forward to unlock it. The prisoners were calming down by then, and all eyes were on me, including mine. It was only when I was pushed inside, that I turned to have a look at my escort.

They were three dissimilar men, but they could have been brothers at that moment. The same look was stamped on all three faces. They had felt the statue of authority totter for a moment, and seen a spectre of what might be. If the Marshal's control slipped, if the iron fist was found rusting, then we would be on them like a pack of animals and they knew it. And I *did* think "we".

The Wardens lost no time in putting as much distance between me and them as possible. Midds stayed on for a moment to look at me, without any noticeable expression, and then shambled off into the shadows, pausing to light one of his rollups.

Lucian was right at me with a flood of verbiage that I did not even try to follow. The gist of it was that he was happy to see me, and wanted to know everything that had happened to me, whilst simultaneously not letting me get a word in edgeways. Hermione was content to hang back and squint at me, and I am not sure I could have survived her hearty congratulations in any case. Then there was the third man. He was gangly and thin, and he had long fair hair, which was unusual for a new boy. Long hair was a result of confinement on the Island without scissors or razor, and few prisoners actually arrived with it. His face was closed beneath his high forehead and there was an intensity there I did not like. More of him later.

222

For of course they wanted to know what had happened.

I swear that I intended to play it down. I was going to brush the whole affair off in a few self-deprecating words. I am, after all, not a performer: an academic by trade and a survivor by experience, but never a man for stand-up entertainment.

Perhaps it was that I could not make a few words stretch to the task, but my version of events became more and more elaborate as I told it. It started simply enough, and I glossed over the business with Harro, but then I got into my audience with the Governor, his conversation with the President and his miraculous mirror. I let dark hints drop about the reasons for my imprisonment (*so what are you in for?*) and made myself out as a man of mystery. I let on just enough to cast myself as a daring rebel and political prisoner. I described the Marshal putting his knife into me in graphic detail, although I left out the reason why. In their minds the Marshal needed no excuses anyway. Then I descended Below again for them, and did far better than Lucian in bringing the horrors of that place into the light: the darkness, the damp, the dead souls of the prisoners and the lurking presence beneath. You could hear each slight shuffle, so intent was my audience on my every word. Every so often one of them would nod, as though remembering a similar experience and attesting to the truth. Even Midds came close enough to hear, smoking reflectively as I spoke.

I told them of the weaver crabs and how they took their victim. I told them, too, of the monster who spoke, bringing them to laughter with its "Marshal's gonna toastya," and then silencing them when the parroting stopped. There were a few nightmares of talking salamanders that night, I'm sure.

I did not mention Kiera de Margot, diverting the headlong rush of my recitation to avoid betraying her and Peter. What I did go into was my treatment at the hands of the Marshal and the Governor. I felt it wise to play down the powers of my mind and therefore (and this is the only reason, honestly) I made the Marshal's murderous attempt quite the tale of sound and fury, with me leaping hither and yon to avoid the repeated lunges of his gleaming knife. It was what my audience wanted to hear.

When it came to the reason for my release (if being moved from one cell to a better cell within a prison can count as a release) I had to go through it twice, because most of them did not follow it. The idea that the Governor (unseen and unknown by most) was so keen to read some dead man's writings that he would push the Marshal aside to save my life was bizarre to them. Perhaps it should have been more so to me. I convinced them by painting a picture of the Governor that was perhaps only slightly exaggerated: a grotesque whose strange and insular pastimes occupied all that there was of his life.

Of Lady Ellera I said nothing.

I was going into a blow-by-blow account of the defeat of the Marshal and the victory of good scholarship when the new boy struck up. To tell the truth I had forgotten about him in the heat of the moment, caught up as I was in my narrative. It came as a bit of a shock to be interrupted by this lanky, long-haired creature suddenly standing up and shouting, "*Sin*!"

I forget the precise words I had been saying because he shocked me out of them, something to do with the value of education and my own cleverness. He had gone from complete calm silence to vibrating fury without any transition and now he was standing in the centre of the cell bellowing at the top of his lungs.

"*Sin*!" he shouted again. "Most outrageous *Sin*! For is it not known that the *End* of the *World* is brought nearer every time these men of *Letters* unravel yet another piece of it. Is it not the *Truth* that the world grows tired of their constant questioning. *Sin*, I say! Nothing but *Sin* which is rank in the nostrils of God. If we are to *Save* ourselves we must cast out these false teachers, these pedants and searchers and *Evil* men who seek to *Know*. They *Pick* at the *Fabric* of the world and decay it with their never-ending questions. God does not intend us to *Question* His creation! God will return to His full health only when these *Men* of *Sin* and *Science* have been purged from the ranks of the *Right* and cast into the barren spaces."

There was more. He went on for some time and he really spoke like that, with almost random words given an absurd emphasis. The other prisoners were shouting at him to shut up, but he was louder than all of them. It looked as though my tale would rest unfinished.

Hermione loomed over the man, then, and he stared up at her defiantly. "I will not be *Silenced* by a *Mannish Witch*!" he declared. "Shall the righteous not stab at *Sin* when they see it?"

"Not here they shan't," Hermione rumbled. I was astonished that she hadn't pasted him into the floor already. As a matter of fact, on closer inspection half of the newcomer's face was purpled by a bruise the size and shape of Hermione's right hand. Now, though, she seemed wary of having another go at him. She raised one hand threateningly, and the long-haired man spat at her but he subsided.

"He bites," she told me later, when both the newcomer and Lucian were asleep. It seemed odd in such a physically powerful creature, but I think that she somehow thought his religious mania was a kind of disease that she might catch if she had too much contact with him.

"Who is he, anyway?" I asked.

"Mandrac," she rumbled. "Says he's *the* Mandrac."

"He's got religion badly," I said. Talking quietly to Hermione in that old familiar cell was infinitely comforting after all I had been through.

"Gaki says he'll deal with him," she said, which surprised me.

"Why should he care?"

"If he makes any more trouble," Hermione insisted, "Gaki said he'll deal with him."

I glanced automatically at the killer's cell, and with no real surprise saw him awake and at the bars, watching us.

"Does he trouble you, Stefan?" Gaki asked, very softly.

"I... I'm still forming a first impression," I said awkwardly.

225

That intelligent face creased with good humour. "Just say the word, Stefan. I grow rusty and must needs practise my skills."

What the Mandrac might have done had he overheard that conversation is unknown. What he actually did, in ignorance of it, was this.

Later that night I was woken roughly by someone trying to strangle me. I felt just the bony hands about my neck, but they were pressing into the muscle, rather than the windpipe, and banging the back of my head on the floor. I saw the hate-ridden face of the Mandrac above me. I realised later that he was probably shouting more about *Sin* but at the time all I heard was the rushing of blood in my ears and the smack of my head on the boards. If he had been a strangler by nature then I would have died, but he was a theologian by trade and a strangler only by circumstance. When I jerked a knee up in what can only be described as a knee-jerk reaction, his tirade stopped with a wheeze and he convulsed off me.

"*Heretic*!" he screamed. "Conniver at the world's destruction. Creature of *Sin*! You must be destroyed for the world to be *Saved*!"

I kicked him in the knee and he fell back further. Around us, other prisoners were waking up and telling him to shut his face before he brought the Marshal down on us.

"Are you *Blind* that you cannot *See*?" the Mandrac demanded. "For the *Salvation* of the *World* this heretic must be *Cleansed* from the company of the *Right*! His prying at the *Weft* of the *World* brings all our souls into *Perdition*!"

There was a chorus of jeers from the other prisoners, and one anonymous wit pointed out that nobody there was fit for the company of the right. The Mandrac stared around at them with over-wide eyes and then, faster than can be believed, he was at my throat again, trying to get a grip with his big, ill-suited hands. I went over backwards and smacked him in the eye with more force than I thought I could muster. The idea of using my mind on him never occurred to me. I was too panicked to call on it.

Then the Mandrac was hauled off me and high into the air by Hermione, and slung into one corner of the cell. He recoiled from the walls and bared his teeth at her. "Stinking *Whore!*" he declared. Lucian helped me to my feet as Hermione and the maniac faced off, and I was very aware of Gaki watching me coolly from the next cell.

"Do it," I said to him, as soft as he ever spoke and with no hesitation.

"Stefan, you surprise me," he said, with a delighted look. I slumped down so that my back was to his wall. At that moment I was battered and fed up. I forgot to be afraid of Gaki, and I forgot any conscience I might lay claim to.

"Just don't kill him here," I said bitterly. "Or they'll blame us."

"Stefan, what did they do to you down Below?" Gaki whispered. I was too tired to reply.

Gaki hunched along the wall until he was close to the Mandrac.

"You fascinate me," I heard him whisper.

"Stay away from me, demon," the Mandrac told him, showing that a madman can sometimes see more clearly than a sane one. "I *Abjure* you."

"Would you turn down a potential convert so quickly?" Gaki pressed slyly. "I, too, have seen signs and portents. Tell me of yours, for your way is surprisingly persuasive."

The Mandrac regarded him narrowly for a moment, and then said, in a calmer voice, "Surely it is common knowledge that seventy-two years ago the Lord appeared to the prophet Jarnard as he worked under the Unjust Masters of the Cosmetics Industry..." and carried on in that vein. The conversation between him and Gaki was quickly too quiet to hear, a welcome change. I heard the rhythm of question and answer as Gaki explored the man's beliefs but, despite the bruises on my throat, I slept and missed what passed between them.

The next day, of course, it was back to the grinding mill as though I had never left. I remembered Below, and found that the tough, gruelling work was no longer so terrible in comparison to enforced leisure. The story of my release had crept about the Island and prisoners from other stretches gave me nods and grins and clasps of the shoulder to show they appreciated what I had done for them.

I had done nothing for them. All I had done was save my own skin. That this could somehow become a public service still amazes me. I suppose there were few enough victories against the establishment on the Island.

I saw Shon briefly, enough to see that little had changed with him. I had no chance to tell him that he was now the Governor's personal calligrapher but that would come in time. I met up with Father Sulplice and we sweated and strained over a broken siphon together, trying to get the recalcitrant machine to stop choking on its own fluids.

"I hear you made yourself a few more enemies, son," Father Sulplice said to me. "I hear you've got yourself a charmed life."

I shrugged before both accusations and rattled a piece of pipe into the open mouth of the siphon, hoping there was nothing alive down there.

"You ought to watch yourself, son," the old man said. "Nobody lives forever. Not when the Marshal's got them on his list."

"One day at a time," I assured him.

He nodded into his moustache and the siphon abruptly started up and whisked the rod out of my hand and into the bowels of the Island.

"This place is a hazard to your health without anybody

actually wanting you dead," Father Sulplice observed. "After all, you earned yourself a death just getting sent here."

"What about Thelwel?" I asked shortly, catching him off guard as the siphon stuttered and died. I watched his lined old face close up like a shellfish.

"The problem's down the pipe. Must be a fan out of shape," he muttered.

"He's your son," I pointed out. I was sure of it as soon as his eyes narrowed. "I can't imagine him doing anything to send him here."

There was perhaps a marginal softening to the glare. "He didn't do anything, son, but I did enough for two. I don't regret it, even though it's put us both in the cage of souls for life."

"The cage of—" Valentin Miljus had died with the phrase on his lips. "Why do you call it that?"

"I heard it," said the old man, suddenly evasive.

"Who from?" Miljus seemed unlikely.

Father Sulplice began walking away, tracing the siphon pipe. "There's a thing that spoke to me once, when I was dreaming. Cage of souls. Sticks in the mind."

I hurried to catch him up but he was looking past my shoulder. "Someone wants to talk to you, son."

There was a Warden after me, picking his way through the working prisoners. He was a slope-shouldered, melancholy-faced man with tiny black-button eyes. I did not feel that he was going to beat me or kill me (and you develop a feel for that kind of thing, after a while). Instead, when he got to me, he just stood there looking at me.

Eventually he said, "Advani," and I nodded, waiting.

"You want to go out?" It was a while before I realised that it was a question, not a statement, and that he was talking about the jungles rather than Shadrapar. I weighed up the pros and cons. On the one hand there were monsters. On the other hand there was the sun. A week Below and you value the sun.

"Yes," I decided.

"Day after tomorrow, you can come," he said. He stared at me some more, and I really did not know where to put myself.

"Sauven," he added, and again it took me a while to realise that he was giving me his name. He spoke with very little inflection.

"Thank you," I said, and he turned and walked away without another word. Only then, with the light sliding off his shoulders, did I realise that he was the man I had saved Below. In a closed system like the Island, all your sins and virtues come back to you soon enough.

I had little time to think about it. There was a sudden chaos of yelling and complaining machinery from the other end of the workshop. It was that last that had Father Sulplice pelting past me on spry old legs, and I fell into step with him, hoping to reopen our conversation. Then all thought of that left me, for the men ahead of me were covered in blood. Three prisoners and a Warden, and all of them practically painted red from head to foot across their fronts. Many others were splattered too, yet nobody in my sight was hurt. We were close to one of the bigger extractor pumps, and it was still making a shearing, grinding noise, and spitting out... pieces.

People falling into the machines was not an unheard of thing in the Island, with its combination of dangerous technology and untrained workforce. This was different, though.

I was told that it was the Mandrac. I had to take the witnesses' words for that because there was surely not enough left to identify him even as a human being. Lucian told me that the Mandrac had calmly climbed up the casing of the pump and stood at the rim before anyone had realised what he was doing. There, while Wardens shouted at him to get down, he stared into the rotating blades, spinning faster than he could see, then fell into that man-wide opening without a sound.

When I was back in my cell that night, feeling sicker than I had ever felt, I saw Gaki looking at me.

230

"It really was a fascinating religion," the killer mused, in the dark spaces when everyone but the two of us seemed to be asleep. "A collector's item. Delightfully simple in dogma, and yet so complex when it came to the mythology behind it."

One of Gaki's unique pauses, into which no words could be put because he had not finished speaking.

"Easy to pull apart, though, once you have a toehold. He should have had the courage of his convictions. If he had seen all questioning as heresy he would have been proof against me, but he was too proud. He had to show off the superiority of his beliefs. His inconsistent, poorly-reasoned beliefs."

I know that swaying a zealot with reason is a feat beyond even Helman. Maniacs like the Mandrac could happily believe that black was black, white and grey all at once. But Gaki had made him see.

Gaki had murdered the Mandrac, and the murder weapon had been the man's own mind. The man had been unable to live with himself once Gaki had brought down his house of cards. I could imagine the killer's quiet voice chasing the Mandrac painstakingly along a chain of logic: if *this* is not true, then *that* cannot be true, and if *that* is not true, then what do you have left? I wondered where the first crack came, the first trivial admission of fault into which Gaki dug his nails.

And I had told him to do it. I cannot honestly say I felt sorry for the death of the Mandrac, homicidal votary that he had been. At the same time my involvement made me feel deeply queasy. After a while I realised that it was not conscience, but fear that I now owed something to Gaki. I had the impression that he, alone in the world, always collected his debts.

20

Alarums and Excursions

Most of the back of the boat was three huge tanks that I found to be full, even before we set off.

"Just plain water," Thelwel explained to me. "If they were empty, the boat's draft would be too shallow and we'd tip."

Behind the tanks, the spider-leg apparatus that propelled us clawed its three rigid arms into the water. At the end of each I could just make out a metal globe that seemed faintly familiar.

"Point generators," Thelwel again explained. "The boat works on electrostatic propulsion. The generators set up a charge differential between fore and aft, which propels us forwards. It would only work in water with high levels of dissolved mineral salts, which is why we're here in the first place. After you've been out a few times you can tell a good spot to mine just by how the boat runs." Thelwel was a regular, when it came to boats.

A boat's crew, insofar as the Island's mining operation was concerned, was composed of a single Warden, an inmate with some technical savvy and a couple of other prisoners to do the leg work. I was glad that Thelwel was providing the mechanical expertise. A broken point generator was not something I would know how to repair, if it's even possible any more.

The Warden, of course, was Sauven, my new-found debtor.

When I arrived for duty he was already in the boat. There was a metal chair set into the tanks, which kept him partly hidden from marauding monsters. He looked at me blankly when I turned up, and then nodded without any obvious recognition. He was watching Thelwel check the boat's mechanisms. As well as the three of us, there was a man named Heri Klamp, known to his cell mates as "Hairy". He was a short, stocky man with a beard that had been kept in check infrequently with workshop tools. His manner was moderately cheerful at getting a bit of fresh air. In contrast, Sauven sat on his throne like some archetypal king of melancholy, long face and bowed shoulders.

I should describe Thelwel properly now, because he is important. Suffice to say that he was a man of pleasant feature and manner, medium-dark of hair and skin. He was my height, slightly more athletic, and there was in every movement, gesture and expression a precision and awareness that I never saw in any living thing before or since.

The bright and uncompromising morning was all the brighter for my not having seen the sun for so long. It was looking fat and unwell, turned a bruised reddish-purple by the mists rising from the waters.

The space frightened me. Behind me was the solid, comfortable wall of the Island, for all that it was kept afloat by old machines and wishful thinking. Everywhere else there was open water, with the ringing trees just shadows through the mist. Strange, high calls and guttural croaks sang overhead or bounced from the water, and it was all too devoid of boundaries and bars and the comfortable human devices for making the world a manageable size. It looked a hundred times larger than it had when I arrived. I felt open to attack from all sides, from above and below. I found myself crouching, frog-like, in the bottom of the boat, trying to get low enough to hide behind the low sides.

"It will pass," Thelwel told me. "Everyone has this, the first time. It will pass, and you will be the better for it."

It did pass mostly, but through all two days of that trip outside I was on edge, constantly expecting monstrous assault. Some part of me had been maimed by my confinement.

Of course, just because I was paranoid didn't mean that there weren't monsters.

Thelwel activated the point generators and the water around the three outriggers began to bubble and hiss. The air was abruptly sharp with ozone. The controls for the boat were crude switches mounted on a simple wooden board, attached to the mechanism by tangled wires. It had probably been fixed up in half a minute by Father Sulplice ten years before.

"Spires," Sauven said without inflection.

"Spires it is," Thelwel confirmed. I had noticed earlier that they had an easy understanding born of long association.

"You come out here a lot?" I pressed Thelwel, as the boat pulled away from the Island. The motion was surprisingly uncomfortable, as if the generators made the boat vibrate at just the wrong frequency.

"As much as I can," Thelwel replied, and in response to my glance at the Warden acknowledged, "Him too. He doesn't like people."

I wondered how to take this, given that most of the Island's complement seemed to be people it was not easy to like.

And then, to my considerable surprise, Thelwel added, "I love it out here."

"What?" I asked, thinking that I had misheard.

"Nature," Thelwel said. "The living world."

"Do you – were you even born in Shadrapar?" I asked timidly. I would have believed any answer just then.

There was a moment's pause before he said, "Yes, of course. Where else is there?"

We had reached the edge of the lake, then, and Thelwel began guiding us along the perimeter, looking for a wide-enough channel. One could never know the layout of the channels and banks of the jungle because the solid land was constantly shifting, day to day. Our lake, and the river we had all arrived on, were the only constants. Our destination might stay in the same place, but everything else drifted around them and had to be found anew every time.

"What are the spires?" I asked him.

"Ruins. The jungle is dotted with them. They make good mining spots if you can find them. The chemicals from the old days still leak out and will do until the sun dies. As far as chemical waste goes, the ancients built to last."

All this talk with Thelwel was keeping my mind off the encroaching nature, but as the boat turned to slide under the shadow of the canopy the full horror of it became too much to ignore. The sheer abundance of vitality on all sides oppressed me as the prisoners Below had, a physical weight on the mind. Everywhere I looked there was riotous, fecund life. Insects tore through the air on clattering wings and consumed one another voraciously. The trees were hung with climbing lizards, red-shot serpents, long-limbed verminous things, webs the size of double doors. The water around us was in constant turmoil as things alighted on the surface and were snatched from below. Beyond all this there were the calls of all the things we could not see, a thousand beasts marking their territory, pleading for mates or triumphing over prey. And it stank. It stank of rot and rebirth enough to make me gag. The world was alive.

I was rigid, my eyes closed. Thelwel put a hand on my shoulder. "Everyone has this," he said again. I felt that there was a faint note of disappointment in his voice, and it was this that pulled me out of it. Thelwel, you see, was a peer. I had less to prove to Lucian or Shon or Peter Drachmar. You would not have found them in the halls of the elegant back in Shadrapar. In front of Thelwel I had to keep up appearances. If facing up to the crawling world of life and death and reproduction was important to him then I could do it.

The light caught the ripples deep between the trees. Everything was waterlogged. And so much for the sun, while

I am complaining about things. It was almost as dark as Below beneath the trees. Hairy, who had also been out before, lit up a spitting blue-white lamp at the prow of the boat that cast a weird benthic illumination over the murky and unquiet waters. It also glinted off eyes. Thelwel, when he looked at me, had two bluish sparks in his sockets and even Sauven's deep-set orbs gave back that artificial fire. All around us, in the violated darkness between trees, myriad points of reflected light gathered to stare at us.

It turned out that the entire enterprise was what we students used to call "a skive".

The Marshal's rules were that a mining boat had two days in which to fill its tanks. The boat had to be back at quay by dusk of the second day, and full. The Marshal, of course, was not a technical sophisticate. Whilst it was true under normal circumstances that a boat would take about two days to be glutted, there were places, such as the spires, where the job could be done in one. The second day was therefore free for wilderness lovers to relax in. When I first discovered this I felt that I would far rather have returned to the Island a day earlier. Later on, after I had stopped jumping at every sound, I conceded that life with monsters was better than life with the Marshal.

Nobody tried to escape, incidentally, or at least nobody did whilst I was there. The jungle ate people. Even with the boat, which afforded a precarious safety, people still died on mining trips. To flee into the carnivorous jungle, to head for distant Shadrapar, would be nothing short of suicide. The power of the Island was that, cruel as it was, it was the only place of safety in the world for us.

I will not go so far as to say that I enjoyed myself, on that first trip, but it was a change from the walls, the abuse and the toil. That night, Thelwel rigged up a heater from the boat's engines, and Hairy and I boiled up the roots and berries that we had collected. For the first time in months we ate like Shadrapans. The next day was spent in idling, for the tanks were full. Sauven had a little book, and wrote in it occasionally between long periods of staring into the canopy. I cannot prove anything but I suspect he was a poet. Thelwel simply kicked back and relaxed. Hairy and I played a few impromptu games that we could devise with stones and scratched lines, but for a lot of the time I joined Thelwel in watching the living world. A thousand little dramas played themselves out before us, death and rebirth, and I found that I understood them. It was Trethowan's world after all. He was another who loved it, against all the conventions of society. I could not join him in that love, but I could at least begin to understand how that love had grown.

We had a few incidents along the way. A few monsters put in an appearance, but the point generators of the boat apparently had some property which warned creatures away. There was one attack particularly deserving of mention, occurring whilst we were mining at the spires.

The spires rose out of another lake, stretching some fifteen, twenty feet into the air. Irregular, twisted pillars of pitted metal, the years had scarred and corroded them to a purplish black. They were perhaps six feet wide at their thickest, each with a multi-tined and mostly-broken tip. They were much twined with vines and plants which had worked their way into every crease and nook, yet all dying from proximity to the metal. There were perhaps nine spires together, with more through the trees. At the water line, each boasted a glossy grey platform of pure ice, despite the muggy heat of the air. Beneath, the water was startlingly clear, and the submerged roots of the spires descended an uncertain distance before they were buried in the mud.

I had the impression that what we were seeing were the very pinnacles of some vast structure beneath us, interred for all time. The spires themselves reminded me of the Weapon, centrepiece of Shadrapar; something in the twisted, irregular design hinted at a common aesthetic, as though built by the same doomed race. On some, the creeping vegetation was dotted with dead grey patches that turned to dust at a touch. On others the plants had rioted forth into chaotic and dysfunctional forms that were rotting even as they bloomed. One was covered from the tip to just off the ice by beetles the size of my hand: round, black, clumsy insects with a starling orange rosette across their domed backs. Trethowan said such colours meant poison more often than not, and I wondered if the creatures were somehow sucking up venom from the spire itself.

We had stopped the boat dead in the water, Thelwel using the point generators to produce a holding current, after some fiddling. All the little lights on the control plank had come on. The pumps were churning and complaining away, extracting the chemicals that were our lifeblood and our penance. While this was happening, until the tanks were full or the lights went off, there was precious little for us to do. Sauven sat in his chair like the Wasted God and Thelwel tinkered idly with the electrics. I was still getting over my nervousness at being in the open air. Hairy, on the other hand, had dinner on his mind. He had plucked a number of metallic blue berries which he claimed were "mostly edible," and now he was after fish. He had disembarked from the boat onto the nearest platform of ice, despite the ominous creaking, and was looking over the brink into the water.

Despite the influence of the spires, there was enough life around their bases. Peering into that startlingly transparent water I could see fish enough, and other things that swam with legs. There were things made of translucent jelly that jerked about by jet propulsion, ribbon-like serpents, spiny crawling hands and a profusion of other forms. Once something black and shapeless passed beneath us, looking like nothing so much as a glossy cloak being dragged over the mud by one corner, save that it was fully as big as the boat. Suffice to say that nobody would have caught me with my hands in it.

This was Hairy's plan, though. He lay on the ice looking down and made quick, savage grabs for anything that passed close enough. I thought he was mad, but apparently he had learned this from someone he had been out with before. It was obviously a skill that needed practise: all he was getting was wet.

I think I saw the movement first, not from the water, but from the spire behind Hairy. Something was moving in the profusion of wilting vegetation that covered it. For a moment I thought that my eyes were playing tricks on me, but then from between the dying leaves there came a familiar arrowhead shape, lean and deadly and eyeless. It was kin to the serpent that had killed a man in the machine room, the first day I had worked there, but it was dull black and larger. It had been coiled all around the spire, hidden by the vegetation, and now it was poised above Hairy.

I cried for Hairy to watch out, and I think he may even have seen the monster reflected in the water, for he rolled aside as the blind head speared down at him. It must have missed him by the thickness of his skin, and that hammer-blow broke the ice.

Abruptly, Hairy was teetering on a jagged plate a few feet across, which at every moment was trying to slide him off into the water. Above, the serpent reeled in its coils for another strike, none the worse for its collision. Sauven was going for a weapon, and I was frozen, useless to all concerned. It was Thelwel who did all the work.

As Hairy clung to his unsteady raft, Thelwel stepped neatly from the boat onto what remained of the ice and put himself between the serpent's strike and Hairy. I shouted at him, because it was obvious he would be killed. The snake's lunging descent would punch those jaws right through him in their hunt for Hairy. They did not, however. They checked their fall and gaped open a little, showing fangs longer than my fingers and a long thread of tongue.

Hairy had drifted a little closer, and with great care I reached out and grabbed the shoulder of his prison greys, hauling him in until he could clamber aboard. The entire business, his wobbling ascent and my helping him, was a slow-motion ballet because nobody wanted any sudden movement to restart the snake's attack.

The snake was trying to get round Thelwel. It quested right and left, and Thelwel kept moving to block it, as sure-footed on the broken ice as ever I was on dry land. The serpent could not sense him properly. Its darting tongue did not taste him as prey, but as some obstruction which was maddeningly in the way whichever direction it moved. By this time, Sauven had his gun levelled at the thing. It was, and there is no other way of putting it, a Big Gun, long barrelled and ugly, and he used both hands to aim it at the coiling, bemused monster.

"Count of three, Thelwel," he said softly, and Thelwel brought one hand up, without ever stopping his little deflecting dance.

He showed three fingers, then his hand flashed down and came back with two, and then again with one, and on the downbeat of that one he kicked away from the ice and dived sideways into the water. Instantly the serpent drew back, as though it had finally decided he was worth eating after all. Before it could lance after him, Sauven let fly with his gun, saturating the spire and contents with energy. I saw the snake's head blown off and its coils torn and tossed. The vegetation was blackened and blasted away but the spire simply absorbed the fusillade without showing any damage at all. Sauven only stopped when the gun died in his hands, and by then the snake was quite dead and no part of it was moving. In the silence afterwards I saw countless fish and other water-beasts flock to the surface to devour the remains.

Through the blood-cloudy water Thelwel swam, hooking his arms over the side of the boat and letting Hairy and I drag him up. He had no explanations, and his manner made it obvious that he would not part with his secrets. When he settled down to look at the broken gun, both Hairy and Sauven seemed to take it all in their stride. Only I had questions.

*

I was writing soon after that. A Warden came and told me I was wanted for "the Governor's work". We collected Shon, and then the man led the two of us, not to an unoccupied cell but all the way to the top floor. We were ensconced in one of the Governor's antechambers, which had been furnished in his characteristic piecemeal extravagance.

"You have to work here," we were told, "where we can keep an eye on you."

It was a fine idea in principle, but like most of the Governor's thoughts on the running of the Island it lacked practical application. The Warden assigned to watch us soon got bored and strayed far enough in examining the soft furnishings that we could talk openly. I clued Shon in on what we were doing, and what was likely to happen to me when the task was done. I had already given this matter some thought, and I felt I could prolong the matter beyond all reason with elaborate language whilst not losing much in style. If that would not serve, I explained to Shon, I could surely invent more Trethowan. I was familiar enough with the kind of material that he produced and, as for the style that the Governor was so happy with, it was all my own. I felt cautiously confident that I could put off the day of my execution for years.

We worked first on the botched passages that Louyere had handled and essentially redid them from scratch. After all, and despite the above sleight of hand, I had pride in my work. We made steady progress, and the Warden soon found a chair across the room and began to snore, his boots up on a table.

Then someone was speaking my name: not Shon, a woman's voice. I paused, acutely conscious of the Warden, and looked surreptitiously at both doors. They were empty. Through the gaps in the wall I saw a shadow: Kiera, of course.

Shon had already seen her and I wasted a few precious moments introducing them. He was obviously mistrustful of her, parrying her enquiries with a few terse words. I would enlighten him later. At that moment I did not want to use up what little time I could scrounge with Kiera on such matters. I wanted to talk to her about her, and about me as well, always my favourite topic of conversation.

"Are you still safe?" was the first question I asked of her.

"I am not to be thrown away just yet," she answered. "The Witch Queen has some important matter soon, some experiment or ritual. She will draw blood for it and feed it through her machines, and in its wake she will have made any decisions regarding me. If I survive that, then I am safe for a little while. But you, Stefan, you must be careful. She's interested in you."

"She wants me dead," I said blithely. "So does the Marshal. I'm holding them at bay with my pen." Oh the arrogance of the scholar!

"*My* pen," Shon put in, with strict legal accuracy.

I saw Kiera's shadow shake its head. "She's had a chance to think about things. She's *interested* in you. Beware of her, Stefan. She may be mad, but it's made her strong."

I decided that I did not want to talk about the Lady Ellera any more. It was hard to escape the idea that she would know of it somehow. Instead, to entertain Kiera, I recounted my adventures outside the Island with special reference to Thelwel. Shon continued scribing away, making a second copy of that day's material, and to the Warden it must have seemed as though we were hard at work as always, me speaking and Shon writing.

I told Kiera of my run in with the Governor, the Marshal and the Witch Queen, and how I had survived that, I confess that I made even more of a drama of it than I had before my fellow prisoners. In return Kiera told something of herself. Within the very rich families, I found, there were the kind of wars and evil doings that even the Underworld denizens would not have countenanced. Her family had been at loggerheads with at least three others of equal standing and, to hear her tell of it, her childhood was one long round of assassinations, attempted kidnappings, spies and the grease of politics. Perhaps she exaggerated as much as I did, but Kiera de Margot's past had been more than etiquette and parties.

She was moving towards the reason for her arrest, picking her way through the tangled relations between her family and two others, when she heard some noise that I missed.

"I must go," she whispered.

I had meant to say something practical, such as, "Go then. Don't reveal our secret," or some such nonsense, but instead I managed, "When will I see you again?"

I saw the silhouette shrug. "Who knows?" and with that she was gone.

I exchanged a look with Shon, who murmured, "Be careful who you trust." I ignored him, though, looking into the gloom beyond the wall and missing her already. For a while, in her company, I had felt almost free and civilised again. It was a feeling dangerously close to affection.

21

A Game of Chess

I held my breath for the next week or so, but the Island simply ground away at its own pace and nothing leapt up to torment me. Needless to say, I became complacent.

The next Outing was a memorable one, if only because numerous prisoners approached me and asked me to "touch their lizards". I initially took this as a euphemism, but it was a literal request. I was lucky, you see. I had acquired some mystical aura of fortune by surviving my hardships. Insofar as I know, the reptiles that received the benefits of my beatitude performed no better than those without, but every time one of them won it was attributed to me.

The Outing was thanks to Hairy Klamp, who had collected some of the herbs Midds and other Wardens smoked. I took note of this and resolved to make my next mining expedition more profitable.

I had wanted to question Thelwel regarding our encounter with the serpent. No sooner had I located him amongst the throng, though, Hermione barrelled up and dragged him off. I saw them later, deep in conversation. I was too far away to hear a word, but it made a fascinating study. Hermione was barely looking at him. In fact, she was looking absolutely everywhere but at him. She fidgeted, obviously finding the most roundabout and awkward way of saying things. It came to me that she had been showing an interest in Thelwel before my trip Below, and I began to fear for him. Thelwel himself was calm as ever. I saw him obviously going over several points with the air of someone breaking difficult news. I considered that if a woman spurned is to be feared, then Hermione scorned would be a terror to put out the sun. Still, if anyone could break the news to her gently it would be Thelwel.

I did not see any violence between them, so I assumed Thelwel had done his job. Instead, I started kibitzing on the lizard races and the spider trials. One prisoner had captured a monstrous, hairy arachnid that was the size of his hand, and it had an understandable winning streak. It was a repulsive little monster, but its owner handled it without fear, stroked it and spoke lovingly to it. I think it remained the victor for much of the night before retiring, stuffed with prey. Its sentimental owner let it loose, and I shuddered at the thought of the thing running about our stretch.

I found Thelwel again shortly after. Hermione was nowhere to be seen. I broached the subject as tactfully as I could, which was not particularly tactfully. "Narrow escape, then?"

He looked at me blankly, and I clarified by giving Hermione's name. Thelwel shrugged at that. "Affection in the strangest places finds its root, or so I have read," he quoted.

I had read the same. In fact, it was from *Lying in State* by Sandor, the author almost certainly killed by Gaki. He had been applying the maxim to the unsuitable kind of people who become popular presidents.

"I take it you let her down easily," I said. "I wouldn't want her angry at me. Given that I share a cell with her, I wouldn't want her angry at all."

"I simply said that I was in no position to advise her. I have no experience." He shrugged again, with an odd melancholy.

I didn't know quite how to take this. "You just kept her hanging on, then?" I could not blame Hermione, in that moment. I'd had some carnal thoughts about Thelwel myself, but he seemed to live an existence entirely devoid of such bonds, physical or emotional.

In this case, though, I was mistaken. "Oh no," he assured me. "She feels nothing for me—"

The vitally important revelation he was going to make was lost as someone dashed into the storeroom-turned-racetrack shouting that the Wardens were coming. Everyone scattered in a random spasm of guilty panic, and then bunched up again, unsure whether to make a run for it and risk facing the Marshal in the corridors.

Every face in that room was turned to me, and they were all expecting me to do something. It was a horrifying revelation to discover that popularity and responsibility go hand in hand. So I had walked free from Below, did that mean I could save a single one of them from the Marshal's wrath? No, it did not, but I had gone from being their banner to being their shield.

I do not believe in heroes or noble motives. I stood forward of the crowd of nervous prisoners because I was more afraid of their bitter revenge, should I fail them, than I was of the Wardens. This is not to say that the Wardens did not scare me. Finding myself somehow turned into a figurehead for the criminal classes, it was all I could do just to stand upright.

The first black-clad shape turned the corner outside and I tottered to the storeroom doorway, if only because it gave me something to lean on for support.

It was Midds. It was only Midds and he had no dark cohorts with him. He slouched down the corridor, unkempt and overweight as ever. "Marshal's doing a tour," he confided. "Thought I'd let you know. Don't want any trouble on my watch." Then he was ambling off, until only the tiny red star of his lit smoke could be seen, and then not even that.

Needless to say, we were all back behind closed doors before the dust had settled. The Marshal never did materialise, but I have no doubt that Midds was right and the man was prowling the unseen dark spaces of the Island, looking for victims.

During my next slice of Trethowan things started to go downhill (and given how long things had been on the level there was a lot of ground to be covered in that direction). Shon and I were working our way through a particularly dense passage in which the writer was illustrating a theory by example. The theory in question concerned the speed of evolutionary change, and started like this:

> It is difficult to state with any clarity whether a species is changing. It may be that a specimen collected later is from a related but contemporaneous species, rather than a successive variant of the original. For a long time I was convinced that this was the only process at work. The example which opened my eyes was the Parathous vine (named after Trethowan's chief Outrider, I believe – S) which I encountered on my very first journey. This white-flowered vine formed something of a landmark on our entry into the deeper reaches of the jungle and therefore can be recognised as a discrete organism, a rare thing in the jungles. On my third expedition I took a further sample of the plant and discovered that a number of changes had taken place in its structure...

The differences that Trethowan reports in the vine were very complex and I cannot say that I understood most of them. I suspect the Governor may have skipped the passage entirely.

On account of the general numbness inflicted by this technical data I was a little slow in realising that Shon had stopped writing. I only grasped that something was wrong when he stood back from the desk, giving himself room to act. I craned round and saw that Kiera's prediction had come to pass. There in the doorway was the Lady Ellera, also known as the Witch Queen.

She, whose interest consumed so much of the blood of others, looked as though it had been drawn from her. I only knew two others whose complexion was paler. She wore a long gown that was sometimes black, sometimes deep red and sometimes the rust colour of dried blood. More delicate than machined silk, it fell from below her shoulders to the floor and hung on every curve of her. Her hair was caught in a tiara of a darkly gleaming metal I did not recognise, and rings of all colours glittered on her long, pale fingers. She was a beautiful, terrible apparition and her face was the height of both qualities. Judging by appearances is a shallow trait but sometimes if a person is of strong-enough character it stamps itself on their face. The lines of it remain. Lady Ellera's face was cruel and proud, and proud of her cruelty, she who had become queen of her own kingdom despite arriving in chains. She was admirable, really. Few people have such grasp of their own destiny. Her sins shone through her face and made her radiant.

I feared her, and justifiably. The Marshal followed orders and would not kill me until the Governor lifted his prohibition. Lady Ellera owed nothing to any laws but her own. Should she kill me, she might displease her lover, but his displeasure would be finite and at the end of it I would still be dead.

"Leave us," she said to our guard, still from the doorway, and "And you," to Shon. I saw that my friend was tensed for fighting and that he, too, was afraid.

"You'd better go," I said to him. Shon looked from me to the Witch Queen, bit his lip, and then passed from the room.

The Lady Ellera fixed me with her gaze. "Come here, Stefan," she said. I rose at last from the desk, but she had to ask me again before I took a few faltering steps towards her. Seeing that I was following, she swept through the dim room beyond and into the darkness. I had no idea where she was leading me. Nonetheless, I followed. I cannot explain it now but at the time I felt I had no choice.

I found her again in a room that had been bizarrely hung with greenery. Vines and boughs were pinned in all the eight corners, giving the impression that the jungle outside was somehow reaching inwards. It broke the shape of the room and blurred any sense of the work of human hands. There was a low drawered table against one wall that boasted two tall candles, corpselight flames giving off a sweet fragrance. On the opposite wall, the light of a single lamp was dimmed and greened by a cascade of thin cloth draped over it.

In the centre of the room there was a table with familiar ornament.

"I know that you enjoy a game of chess, once in a while," came the soft voice of the Lady Ellera.

She was hovering in the gloom that enfolded most of the room, and her voice seemed to reach me by strange routes through the hanging foliage. I edged nervously to the chessboard and saw that the pieces were fantastically carved, no two the same. I imagined that it was the Governor's very own set.

"I... I'm not much of a player," I stammered.

"What a shame," she whispered, and I looked up from the board to see her weirdly tinted face hanging in the darkness. All light in the room was focused somehow on the chessboard, for as she stepped towards it every line of her body was caught by it. She did not look like a clever and opportunistic prisoner. She looked like the Witch Queen.

She sat at the table with an animal grace, and I found that I was sitting across from her, looking directly into her mesmeric eyes. The incense from the candles was affecting me in strange ways. She was waiting for me to do something, and I realised that the chess game had begun and that it was my turn. With a start I saw that the game was somewhat advanced, but I could not remember making any of the moves I saw before me. I stared wildly at the board, trying to see what strategy I had been following, but I had lost its trail completely. I looked up into her eyes again, and she was amused. Had she moved all the pieces while I was not watching? Was she trying to throw me? I was thrown. I stumbled a piece at random across the board. The green light, the smoky air with the shadows of foliage making arabesque inroads through it, it was my fever dream all over again.

"I read your little book with the amusing name," the Lady Ellera said. For an insane moment I thought she was talking about a pamphlet Jon and I had put together titled *Surly's Satires* in which we had lampooned the Academy Masters. That was surely the only little book with an amusing name that I had been guilty of. Then I saw that she was speaking so contemptuously of *How to Save the World*.

"You... you read it...?"

"When Leo had finished with it." She was moving again, and I could find no sense in the tactics of her chessmen, nor in my own. "Leo could not see the potential. I could," she confided. "You are a very clever man, Stefan Advani."

I tried to deny it. "It wasn't just me," I muttered. "The others..."

"Where are the others?" she asked.

"Dead."

"Then you are the clever one. Even here, one can live well enough. I do, Stefan. I live well because I understand the minds of people. You understand them too, but in a different way. You have something I want, Stefan."

I stared at her. In truth I was sparing little of my attention for the board. My libido and my prudence were brawling, and only the former was armed. I took a deep breath that was mostly incense and said, "What could I possibly have...?"

"You have a power," she said, and there was such a passion in her voice that I felt the heat of it. "The power to destroy, to control. Let Leo and the idiot Marshal dismiss it so easily. I have read your words and I know. Let me into your mind, Stefan. Show me how you killed that man. Show me your power."

My jaw surely hung open. "My power?" I gasped. She leant across the board to me, pushing another piece into position.

"Have you not been searching forever for one who believes?"

I tried to stare at the board, but I could not.

"Have you not grown tired of rejection, Stefan?"

Her voice, soft and insidious, was all I could hear.

"Have you not grown tired of being alone with your secret?" she whispered.

"Yes..." I managed, for suddenly it was true.

"Tell me how, Stefan. You know I will be a capable student."

I did. That was just the problem. Even as stupefied as I was, I knew that if she got her mind around Helman's secret she would find far more use for it than he or I had. I owed it to the world to stop her. Surely I did.

"Stefan, I will have such gifts for you." I stared at the board and saw that I was one move away from losing the game. When I looked up she was standing right there beside me. I shivered all through my skin. Part of me wanted to make a run for it right there, but most of my physical parts were keen to stay.

"Haven't you missed spending time with your own kind of people? You have been with the beggars and the brutes for too long, Stefan."

"Yes," I found myself saying. "Yes, I have." My world contracted to just myself and her.

"Tell me, Stefan," she said. "We shall rule this place together."

I stared at her eyes, mirrors in which one could see anything one wished. The look there could have been desire for me. I very much wanted it to be just that. It was more likely simple calculating patience, but the real and unreal were drifting closer by the second in that green-scented room.

I knew that she must not master the arts that Helman had developed. I was very clear on that point.

"Your friend was wrong, Stefan," she was saying, her lips at my ear. "This is no ancient art, but a new one. The tracts he cites were fiction. This is not the past, but the future of mankind. For the ugly, stupid masses, there is no salvation. For the gifted, though, the powers you have discovered will give us the world. You and I are gifted, Stefan. We have that power. Show me how to use it and we will have dominion over everyone. Just you and I, Stefan."

I knew that she was evil, but it is the rare prisoner given the chance to cuckold the Governor. I knew that if she took the world in her hands she would break it, but the thought occurred to me that I never asked to be the guardian of the world's virtue anyway.

Her lips brushed my skin and it was like kissing a snake. It was astonishingly erotic. I had the contradiction of the woman right there, and in that moment it was no contradiction.

Her arms about my shoulders, her lips brushing mine, she said, "Show me," and I did.

I told her everything. I gave her the clearest and most concise ever lesson on how to use the mind as a lever. I told her how Helman had moved objects and how I had killed Harro. In the light of her eager stare, even the memory of a man's mind imploding at my touch seemed somehow laudable. And she was right: never has anyone listened to me as raptly as she.

Her mind was like the hungry arrowhead of a swamp creature's, cast in diamond. I could not have scratched it. Even as I laid myself open for her I realised that she could destroy me, crush my mind as I had crushed Harro's. I had no defences left to stave her off. I had barely the will to object to it.

Nothing happened.

"Tell me the secret," she whispered again. "Tell me how to do it."

I went through everything once more for her, conniving at my own destruction. I told her what Helman had told to me, that had enabled me to break through and use my mind for the first time. I prepared myself for that fatal thrust again.

Nothing.

"What are you keeping back from me?" she demanded. Her voice had an edge to it, now. I protested my innocence. I had given her all the keys she would need to unlock her mind, but there was no keyhole. She had blocked it off, perhaps, sealed it shut while perfecting her study of herself. She had made her mind like a machine, cut away everything that might hinder her or make her weak, and somewhere amongst that discarded mental viscera was that organ or lobe that would have allowed her to unshell the world like a clam. I knew her brain would never do what she wanted it to. More, she knew that I knew. She chose to misunderstand.

The mood went downhill swiftly after that. From whispered entreaties she urged me, then she threatened me. She stood sharply and upset the chessboard. In her fury she ground one of the intricate chessmen underfoot.

I could not help her. There had not been so much as the least twitch from her mind throughout. Even Jon had done better than that. But then Jon had something the Witch Queen lacked: he had empathy. I think that was the difference.

I had made another enemy.

"What is it that holds you back?" she hissed. "Where did you get such a high opinion of yourself, that you turn me aside?" Without any warning she had a hand to my throat, and I felt the cool, clear touch of a razory blade. Her eyes were all murder now.

"Your secret will rot in your grave, Stefan, if you do not share it with me."

I did consider telling her that it was simply her own work that was to blame, rather than my nobility of spirit, but I thought that it would worsen the situation drastically. Instead I said nothing and stayed very still indeed.

The blade twitched at my throat with her impatience, and I felt a tiny drop of blood mingle with the sweat. I knew that she must be weighing the displeasure of the Governor against her own need to lash out.

"I know where your strength comes from," she said, showing that even her character judgement can be flawed. "You escaped the Marshal, you rescued the girl. You think that you are something special."

At the mention of "the girl" I kept my face carefully without reaction, and that lack of response gave her the clue she needed.

"I will take that from you, Stefan, and then perhaps you will lose a few of your inhibitions. That girl you are so proud of, the de Margot bitch. I have no need of her. I will give her to your revolting, lusting peers, Stefan. Will seeing her torn apart by those animals break your pride?"

I said nothing, but I found that I had stood up. She was looking at me venomously, but the blade had disappeared. She still wanted what I had enough to leave me alive.

I backed from the room, trying to think of some plan but finding nothing in my head but fragments.

22

Crime and Punishment

It came one evening, after just enough time had passed to take the edge off my panic. Some Wardens came down and I felt the hush descend on the prisoners further along the stretch. I saw the dark uniforms, and beyond them a glitter of green and sapphire, underwater colours. Lady Ellera had come down into the dirt for this one deed.

Only when they were almost upon us did I spot Kiera in prison greys, head down. The Wardens had her between them, and kept a distance between themselves and Lady Ellera, who was stalking like a mantis at their backs.

My look to her was mute entreaty.

"She is just one more prisoner. Where else do prisoners belong? Who shall we give her to, Stefan?" she said, loud enough for most people to hear. "Who shall have the privilege? Who hates you enough?"

I said nothing and gave no indication. Kiera was not looking at me, but circumstances were making plain that this development was my fault.

The prisoners were slowly beginning to understand what was being offered. In a place with no rewards save an early grave this was beyond all experience. I saw interest flare in many pairs of eyes. My inspiration remained silent.

"When this whore ran into this vile company before, there were two who apprehended her," Lady Ellera mused. "One of them is dead, now. But there were two. Who was the other? Which one, among you, has seen this face before?" and she grasped Kiera by the chin and forced her head up, dragging her around so all the prisoners could see.

Tallan shouted out at once, "It was me!" But then a whole chorus of prisoners were claiming to be that man. Everyone, it seemed, had been there when I killed Harro. Lady Ellera was looking only at Tallan, though, staring into his eyes to find the truth. He fell back from the bars at her scrutiny, and made no sound at all when she asked, "Was it you, then? Truly?"

She saw, though; she could read people. "It was you," she declared triumphantly, and the other prisoners fell silent.

"Throw her to the beasts," she told the Wardens, who unlocked Tallan's cell and pushed Kiera in. "Enjoy, Stefan," the Lady Ellera told me. "I will come back for your secrets and perhaps you will not be so coy, then."

She left, the Wardens reluctantly in tow. After she had gone, Hermione spat.

A number of other things happened as well. Tallan went for Kiera and she kicked him hard on the knee. The other two prisoners in his cell went for her as well and she danced out from between them. Had she been in a room twice as large, I think she might have kept them at bay. It was a small cell, though, and there were three men trying to pin her down. She kneed one savagely between the legs and caught another with a flying elbow, but Tallan grabbed her and slammed her to the floor.

"Now," I heard him say, as he got his breath back, "you and I have some unfinished business..."

And I was yelling at him, whatever came into my mind, until I had nothing left and just threatened to kill him then and there. It was a futile threat against a man in another cell, the violence that is even a weak man's last resort. Tallan's head snapped up, though, and I thought I saw some residual fear deep in those eyes.

I decided to follow through with everything I had. "If any one of you touches her, then I will kill them like I killed Harro. Tallan, you of all people know that I can."

The prisoners were suddenly very quiet. All eyes left Kiera for me. I stood, a skinny and unprepossessing creature, and faced them down, leaving no gap for fear to filter in.

"The first man to try anything with her, I will crush that man's mind like a hollowed gourd. Believe me when I say that I can do this thing. Should she be harmed in any way then I will destroy every wretched man in the cell and know no mercy. Believe me. Every man in the cell, and any other whom I even suspect."

Dear God, but to my own ears it was the least convincing performance of my life. Under the protection of Stefan the Scrawny? How ludicrous that seemed. I had no confidence that the powers of my mind could be placed at my beck and call for murder.

But they did not know the limitations of my prowess. Tallan had seen Harro die and it was written in large print all over his face. He recoiled from Kiera as though she was venomous, and it was that rather than my histrionics which made his two cellmates keep their distance.

I have looked back on that day many times. A grand gesture, no? Well, no. Honestly? No. What I remember most keenly, apart from the ripe absurdity of the whole rigmarole, was that I was motivated far more by guilt than anything else. Of course I did not want anything to happen to Kiera, but most of all I did not want it to happen and be my fault. Culpability whetted a sharper edge than empathy. My murderous threats were more born of self-loathing than love of any other.

Kiera pulled herself to her feet and put herself in the opposite corner of the cell to Tallan. An uneasy peace descended.

Lucian was looking at me in a very peculiar way, keeping his distance insofar as one could.

"You have nothing to fear from me," I said, and again the words sounded ridiculous because I was the fearful man, surely, not a man anyone had ever feared. I tried to tell him I would never use my powers against him but the words just tripped over each other.

"It is not that which gives him pause, Stefan," commented Gaki, looking as though someone had just told him a particularly good joke. "You sounded just like the Marshal," he explained lazily. "Really, it was uncanny. I begin to wonder whether you are on the right side of the bars."

I thought of the Marshal's policy of exterminating a cell for the crimes of an individual. I also realised how little it had gained me. Try as I might I could not imagine being able to keep Tallan and company in awe of me for long. I had bought some small bagful of time, but it was leaking steadily.

Of course, it happened while I was working. I was Stefan Advani, not Stefan the Terrible. Whatever fear I could instil my presence with, it would not linger long in my absence. So it was that the very next day we trooped back to the cells and I discovered Kiera had vanished.

For a second I was numb, cold. How had I imagined anything different?

What had happened to her? The obvious conclusion waited at the front of my mind. It was quite clear that Tallan had crept away as the rest of us worked, done his will and then disposed of her remains. I could see it in my mind's eye in hideous detail.

A shock went through me like someone injecting a drug. Something rose from a hitherto unused depth of my brain and sat at the controls like a toad. "You!" I snapped out harshly. It didn't sound like me at all. "Where is she?"

Tallan jumped at my voice. I think a lot of people did. I was standing at the bars of my cell, one arm jutting out into the corridor pointing straight at him.

"What?" he demanded.

"Where is she?"

"I don't know!"

"What did you do to her?" I demanded. "I warned you, Tallan."

"I didn't do nothing," he protested.

"Didn't do nothing?" I snapped back. "Sophistry! If you didn't do nothing then what did you do?" I remember this scene as though I watched someone else play it out. "I told you, didn't I? I told you what would happen if you so much as touched her." I wasn't raging. Everything in me was cold like a knifeblade. And some of me enjoyed it. I had an excuse to bully another human being and it gave me my life back, just for a moment. It might have started with Kiera but in the end it was about me.

"I didn't touch her! I didn't!" Tallan insisted. One of his friends said that they had been together all day, which was proof of nothing in my book.

In that moment I must really have achieved some utter transformation. When I look back on it, I remember nothing but calm, because the all-consuming passion that possessed me was so alien to me that it left no trace.

"I told you but you wouldn't listen…" I reached out and felt Tallan's brain, hollow as an egg.

"Ask him!" the wretch was shrieking. "Ask Gaki! He was here all the time! I didn't do it!"

I think that if I had relaxed my restraint a fraction then Tallan would have died. Instead, I rounded on Gaki with a supreme effort of will.

"Well?" I gritted.

"Don't let me stop you," Gaki said mildly. "I'm sure you and Tallan have unfinished business."

"Tell him!" Tallan almost shrieked. "It wasn't me! It wasn't me!"

"Well?" I grated out again. Gaki gave me a pitying smile.

"Why not kill him anyway? You're ready to and you'll never have a better chance. You know you'll have to deal with him eventually. Why be an academic all your life? These hard choices make one a man of action."

I stared at him, trying to keep some vestige of control.

"Kill Tallan, and then I'll tell you," suggested Gaki, in the manner of a gentleman making a sporting wager.

"Did he touch her?" I gasped out.

"Of course he didn't," Gaki said. "But who cares?"

I spun to face Tallan again, finding him cringing back in the corner of his cell. I had a hard knot of hate built up between my eyes and I was desperate to let it fly.

There was a voice saying my name. It was not Gaki's or Tallan's but only poor, harmless Lucian's. He was saying my name over and over, and asking me to please calm down, because all of this was most unlike me and to tell the truth it was scaring the hell out of him, and it would be a terrible shame if I went mad...

When I turned to face him he was ready to flinch, but it was just me, just Stefan Advani. I have no idea where all the cold hate went. "I'm sorry," I said, and then I said it again, just generally. The words rang out in the silence that had cloaked our whole stretch.

"What happened to her?" I asked Gaki, in tired, ragged tones.

"She left," Gaki said blithely.

"How? With who?" I demanded of Gaki, of whom no-one had the power to demand anything. He was in the giving vein, however.

"Of her own accord and on her own recogniscence. She escaped from her cell and, after that, for reasons that should be obvious, I lost track of her."

She had known my protection was a fruit that could not last and she had made her escape. Was she in hiding in some deserted corner of the Island, stealing food and trying to dodge the Wardens? Had she retreated to those chambers she had been cast out from, risking the further wrath of Lady Ellera? Or had she done what she was going to do when I saved her from Harro and Tallan? Had Kiera de Margot gone alone and friendless in a swamp packed with predators? Nobody could survive that. The Island's security was based on the single fact that the natural world had a lust for human flesh.

Depending on what caught her, it might be kinder than her fate on the Island. The thought did not console me. I felt the previous minutes of high adrenaline sour within me, and all that pent-up rage and fury just curdle. Abruptly I was sitting with my back against the bars, grief and rage making me their plaything.

Was this the tragic passion of the romantic hero, you ask? Did I love Kiera de Margot on such short acquaintance, that the thought of losing her rendered me inconsolable? How grand to pretend that were the case. My emotions were of a more human scale, though. I cannot even pretend that a love of justice motivated me: prisoners forcing their attentions on each other was hardly unknown, though such transactions were more often commercial than aggressive. What racked me was the thought that, if Kiera died anyway, then everything I had been through after killing Harro was for nothing. I had suffered Below and the Marshal's knife and become a murderer, all to win no more than a turn of the glass. It was a selfish grief, after all.

Two days later I was working on the factory floor when Red, the Warden with hair of that colour, stalked through calling names and punching shoulders to get attention. He was recruiting a work detail. Shon and I got punched and called out, and perhaps ten more. Red shouted for us to follow him, raising his voice over the hammer of the machines. He was heading for a storeroom.

"Get the sacks here up on deck," he said flatly. We looked at him dumbly because most of us had no idea where he meant.

"Where we came in," Shon murmured. "Follow me." He took a sack by the top corners, swung it onto his back with a grunt and lurched off with it. We followed his example, under Red's stern gaze. When it was my turn I was ready for the crushing weight. It had been a while since I had needed to move the bulky sacks around. When I hauled it across my shoulders I was surprised to find that I could move with it, rather than having to drag it across the floor. I was still worse off than Shon, but I was twice as strong as the man who arrived at the Island... how many months before?

I doggedly stomped up a flight of uneven steps, breathing through clenched teeth. The abrupt flare of sunlight caught me unawares and I stumbled and fell to one knee with a painful jar. Red was right behind me, though, and he gave me enough of a push to get me upright again. Squinting and weaving, I stepped out into the sun and air.

It was the broad open area that we had disembarked onto so long ago, and I saw again the heavy iron shape of the prison boat docked alongside it. My companions were making their way to it to load the sacks at the back, and from amidships a tired line of new arrivals was crawling, each of them too shocked by their first sight of the Island to resist its pull.

I got to the boat's stern and a sailor there tucked a hook into the neck of my burden. A wave from him and it was hoisted high in the air, then lowered gracefully through a hatch to the hold. He looked at me with contempt and I joined the plodding line of my comrades on our way back for more merchandise. I picked up my pace to put me level with Shon. "How many boats, since we arrived?"

"Seven," he told me. "This is the eighth."

I felt cold and distant for a moment. Eight boats meant eight months since we arrived on the Island. I had been exiled for a full year, and had never realised how the time had flown. Then I saw that a year was nothing, the blink of a lizard's eye. I was going to be on the Island for the rest of my life, however long or cut short that was.

We trudged down for another load and, when we emerged again, the Marshal was there to welcome the newcomers.

The captain of the prison boat, the very same foul-mouthed man who had brought me to the Island, had gone ashore with papers. I saw the Marshal open a sealed missive and scan its contents impassively. Beyond him and the new convicts I saw another man. He was a stranger, tall and elegant in very fine clothes of black and green, quite out of place. Red went over to him and asked him something, then gestured for him to step aside to await the Marshal's attention.

I nudged Shon and indicated the man. "New Warden," I suggested.

Shon stared at the newcomer thoughtfully. "Why do I think that I know that man?"

Red was striding back over, telling us to hurry it up. As we shuffled back towards the dark for our next load, I saw the Marshal call for a Warden and send him off on some errand.

When we struggled out for a third time there was a roll call in progress. I expected to see prisoners being led off, but someone had changed the procedures since I arrived, apparently. There was the obligatory dead man lying in the centre of the deck, the Marshal's trademark imposition of authority. Aside from that, one of the Wardens was reading a list of names, and each prisoner was being sent left or right, so that two groups were forming.

I was fascinated, and wanted to ask Shon about it, but he was too busy carrying heavy objects to care. I tried to see what criteria they were using to segregate the prisoners and could find none at first. Perhaps the prisoners to one side were older, on average, not quite so hairy, dirty and scarred as the others. However, arriving on a prison boat makes anyone look like a criminal.

I didn't notice the familiar face for some time. When our eyes met it was like a physical shock. He did not recognise me, but I knew him. It was one of those faces that stay with you.

Standing there in prison greys, rubbing shoulders with the thieves and the killers, was the Commissar of Angels: the very man who had mown down Helman and abandoned Jon and Rosanna to their fate. The man, too, who supervised my recapture and sent me into exile. There he was. What had brought him so low?

The names had finished, and every new prisoner bar the dead man had been assigned to left or right. The Marshal stalked over to the ship's captain and conferred in low tones, and a sailor was sent belowdecks. Moments later, three more prisoners were jostled from the hold to stand blinking in the sun. They were women, and the Marshal detailed two Wardens to herd them into line with one of the groups of prisoners – to stand alongside the Commissar.

I think I knew what would happen, then. I had unloaded my third sack, as had my comrades, but we were staying very still by the boat's side and making no move that would call attention to us. Partly we feared getting caught up in whatever was going on; partly we just wanted to watch.

Some more Wardens came up, and they had a ragbag of guns: chemical projectile weapons; ancient, verdigrised energy guns; flintlocks and matchlocks. One even had a repeating crossbow the size of a six-year-old child. Most were not known to me, but one was Sauven. He did not have his serpent-slaying weapon (Thelwel never had managed to fix it) but had found a suitable replacement. He stood in line with the others and could have been any one of them.

The prisoners crowded back against one wall, the women, the Commissar, all of them. None of them seemed to know what to do. Even the Commissar just looked old and frightened. The prisoners in the other group stood silently, no doubt each one breathing a vast sigh of relief.

"I am ordered to tell you this," the Marshal spat out to the prisoners under the gun. "'By the order of Elijah Harweg, Lord President of the Authority of Shadrapar, you have been judged to be traitors to the last bastion of the human race. You have been convicted in fair trial of conspiracy to subvert the right and proper Authority and to install a counter-Authority against the laws and regulations of Shadrapar. You also stand accused of...'" The Marshal paused. "I won't bore you," he confided. "There is a list here, and who will care if I read it or if I do not?"

He was robbing them of perhaps a minute of their lives, by sparing them that boredom.

"To resume," he continued smartly. "'The President regrets to announce that your public sentence of exile to the Island Chemical Mining Corporation Colony will not suffice to keep the loyal people of Shadrapar free of your tainted ideas, and so has deemed that you shall be executed upon your arrival at that place.'" He shook his head. "What an utter waste of words," he added, perhaps the only time he questioned anyone's orders, "But that is what I have been ordered to tell you. Shoot them down."

There was an unbreathing pause while the meaning of his last words made itself known. Even the firing squad had not been expecting such an abrupt command. One of the doomed prisoners had the chance to cry out some desperate plea for clemency.

Then the first shot was fired, and then all the other shots were fired. It was very brief. Some thirty men and three women died in mere seconds up against the Island's wall. I heard later that two prisoners had died from shots that passed straight through into the cell beyond. I am sure the Marshal considered it a bonus. Shon and I and the others just crouched there. It put the individual beatings and deaths of the Island into perspective.

Burned into my mind is the sight of the first bullets and beams striking home, the first rank of the prisoners jerking back with the explosive impact, bloody holes punched through prison greys. I saw faces that were only just becoming afraid, and too late. Who were they? What had they done? Painters, merchants, politicians, crooks? Under that fatal scrutiny all were as one. After that I looked away, but I heard the rest of the performance: brief screams and cries cut short by the gunfire, the deafening rattle and zing of the weapons. There was no time for words.

Then it was over and the echoes of the guns had died away before the last body slid down the wall to the ground. The firing squad was heading in. The surviving new prisoners were being taken to their new cells. Business was back to normal, now that little unpleasantness was out of the way.

The Marshal looked around and saw us.

"You men!" he shouted, but instead of a punishment for idling, he had a job for us.

"Put the bodies into the water. Let them feed the fish that feed us," he decided. I would rather have been whipped, just then.

The man in the fancy clothes was approaching the Marshal with papers. I was expecting him to get slugged in the gut as Peter had. Instead, the Marshal handed the man back his papers and looked him up and down. He had an air of respect that he never showed for the Governor or any living thing.

He signalled peremptorily to the nearest Warden.

"Go fetch Drachmar," he snapped out. "There's a message here for him." It was always hard to tell, but I thought he was pleased about it. This did not bode well for Peter.

I found the body of the Commissar and hauled him over my shoulder like a sack. Once I had cast off the emotional baggage associated with death then one load was like another. Whatever had characterised these people and given them their peculiarities and convictions had flown from them, and only the solid, empty prison was left to be disposed of.

The next man I grabbed I had also known. I had not noticed him in the line-up. Only now did I see whose remains I was consigning to watery consumption: Louyere the inadequate transcriber. It shook me a little. Surely justice was something I had forgotten about, but some part of me had assumed that the executed had been in some way guilty of the crime for which such an excessive punishment had been levied. Louyere had surely never been guilty of being anything other than a bad scholar. Perhaps he had become a revolutionary since leaving the Island, but I found it hard to believe. Louyere had been killed as a political dissenter, and that struck me as indicative of some deep unease back home.

I threw Louyere's familiar face into the lake with the rest of him. What else was there to do? I saw Shon hurl a dead woman after him without pause. The surgeons had made her beautiful before the guns had spoiled her. Then he stretched and wiped some sweat from his brow like any honest workman doing a day's toil.

"Damn it," he said softly. "I knew I knew him."

We looked at the newcomer. He was standing idle, watching us, watching the Wardens, watching the whole Island work. There was something about him that I had not seen for a long time. He was a free man. It was obvious to me that he had not come here to work, and so the Marshal had no more authority over him than he had over the sun.

"It is! It's Jonas Destavian!" Shon hissed.

"Who?" I asked mildly.

"What do you mean, *who*? Jonas Destavian, the one and the only." He was suddenly all excitement, a six-foot, scar-faced ten-year-old about to meet his favourite…

Oh, I thought. That was where I knew the name from. Jonas Destavian, the duellist. I had some vague notion that he was supposed to be quite good. For me to have heard of him, he would have to be quite the notable fighter.

"He's aces," Shon said definitely. "He's won twenty-one blood matches."

I looked at Jonas Destavian and saw a long-limbed man who was not, after all, as young as his movements suggested. His hair was a dark copper that had greyed slightly above the ears. His face was unlined, but there were cosmetics for that, and he could surely afford them. He had a stance about him that I had not seen before, neither the Marshal's tense aggression nor Peter's laid-back ease. Both were profoundly conscious poseurs compared to Destavian. He was ready, and that was the best way of describing him. If some lake monster had lunged for him, or an airborne predator had dived from the clouds, he would have been expecting it. The closest I had seen to it was Thelwel's strange grace, but that was a passive thing over which Thelwel had no control. Destavian was sheer, harnessed physical ability, and it was something he had honed himself into. He was a self-made man.

Peter emerged into the light cautiously, and he must have known what was going on. He stood, shielding his eyes with one hand, with that slightly deliberate relaxed pose. Destavian smiled slightly, which briefly gave his face back all the lines that cosmetics had taken away.

"Peter," he remarked, and then, self-mocking, "So we meet again."

"Jonas," acknowledged Peter carefully. He had a new black eye, which slightly spoiled his debonair. "You're here for the sights or the waters?"

"If only," Destavian said, which put an end to that. "I have been asked to call you out."

"And if I refuse?" Peter asked, following what I was sure must be an old catechism.

"I have been commissioned by Jon Anteim the Elder and licensed by the Authority to seek permission from the Governor for your execution at my hands. I am sure, though, that such procedures will not be necessary. I told my principles that Peter Drachmar never shirks a fight." Destavian looked down at the latticed floor beneath him idly. "I am sorry, for what that is worth."

"It's not worth a damn," Peter said, still the casual, easy-going man, but there was a bead of sweat above one eye that was not due to the heat.

"Oh I know," Destavian said quietly. "I know."

"What on earth is going on?" I demanded in a whisper.

"Your man's challenged to a duel," Shon said, sounding awed, "with Jonas Destavian."

"To the death?"

"Destavian wouldn't come all this way for sparring practice. Your man must have got way up some noses before coming here. I think Jon Anteim the Elder was Secretary to the Authority once." Shon shook his head slowly.

Peter shrugged as easily as he did anything and took Destavian's hand. They gripped wrist to wrist, as duellists did.

"I'm game," Peter said. "After all, 'When the swords call, you always hear it.'"

"'When once the sword has called they hear it ever'," Destavian corrected him, and both Shon and I mouthed the words, for it was from Jeffed's famous poem.

"Whatever," Peter shrugged again. "Did you bring my gear? I didn't think I'd need it here."

"I have a spare set with me. I'll have it sent to you," Destavian told him solemnly. "We must meet tomorrow, though, for the boat will wait only so long and I must be back in Shadrapar."

23

The Secret Life of Peter Drachmar

Peter came for me shortly after I had gone back to the factory floor. With barely a word he took me from my duties there (not that I was unhappy to go). We were headed up.

I tried to tell him that Kiera was probably being eaten by semi-aquatic carnivores, giving a garbled and abbreviated version of what had happened concerning her and the Lady Ellera. By this time we were on the fourth level and I realised vaguely that I had never been there before.

Peter rounded on me at that thought. "Two things," he said. "One: I have other things to think about right now. Two: it's not a problem." Then he was off again, and I found that I had entered the domain of the Wardens.

There was a large space which had probably, in some more congenial era, been intended as a common room. A scattering of Wardens were there. Two were playing some game with counters. One was writing. Another two had been having some kind of low-voiced argument. They all looked up and stared when we came in: at Peter, not me. There was an odd air of anticipation to them; it was obvious they thought Peter would not be with them much longer, about which few tears would be shed. They also evidently anticipated a modicum of entertainment in the near future.

The rooms off this common space were about twice the size of a cell, and given that only one Warden lived in each I considered them the lap of luxury. They had low, lumpy-looking beds in them, and some had a few personal touches. Many did not. There were no doors, which somehow only emphasised the similarities between guards and guarded.

"What do you mean, it's not a problem?" I whispered as Peter stalked into one room. There, he spun abruptly and faced me.

"Just what I say, Stefan," he told me, and before I could put my annoyance with him into words, I saw her.

Kiera de Margot: she was wearing a Warden's uniform again, and looking tense and harassed. I suspect that I gaped at her.

"Well," I managed, which was quite good in the circumstances.

"What's going on?" Kiera asked immediately. "They're saying someone's going to fight with you?"

"What's going on?" I echoed. "How did she get here?"

Peter, who truly had other things on his mind, looked between us. "Give me breathing space," he said. "All right. Yes, Kiera, I get to fight Jonas Destavian. Hooray for me."

Kiera started at the name, and was pale the next second. She was asking, "What? Why—?" when Peter waved his hands at her, exasperated.

"One question at a time," and, probably because mine was easier, "Stefan's turn. All right, so: yesterday, and I'd had a tough day of general brutishness and was looking forward to a good night's sleep, so that I could be just as vicious next day. I got here, into this one little place that's supposed to be my own, and here she is. She's got one of my uniforms on but she wasn't fooling anyone, and it was only a matter of time before someone else spotted her and then everything would go all to crap.

"She told me what had happened to her, all that stuff. Told me what you'd done for her, as well, which was good work. But none of it was going to matter a damn and I told her that straight. Anyway, us arguing about this sort of brought some of the others into it, and they got to see her and started asking what she was and where theirs was and pushing in to my room here and all that. And I wasn't having that, and so I told them I'd beat the living pips out of anyone who didn't just fuck off and leave us alone, just to get that out of the way. Well they looked at me, some of them looked at her, and if this place was even slightly sane they'd have kicked me to death." He shook his head, keen to be done so he wouldn't have to explain any more. "Way the Marshal runs this joint, not a man of them trusted the other, and they were all worried that if they started it then someone would rat them out. That kind of saved me cos when they came, they came without a plan and all muddled together.

"There was a scrap, anyway. Me against them and them against each other. I think I did well enough for myself, given that it was me against twenty at once. I knocked a few heads together. I kicked them about a bit. No, I didn't get the black eye then, I'm coming to that. Weird thing was that there were a couple of guys actually fighting on my side, which was nice. Middsy piled in for me, and Red as well. Anyway, there we were, most of the Island's Wardens, kicking each other to death over Kiera. Very romantic, I'm sure. That was when the Marshal came in.

"We broke up all at once. We were all very sharp for the way a room changed when it had the Marshal in it. Everyone was suddenly dusting their clothes down and pretending to have been looking at the wall when it kicked off.

"You can be sure that the Marshal wanted to know what happened, and he was pissed. He was severely mad. So, anyway, everyone kind of pointed at me, and so I got to tell the Marshal I had a girl in my room. I was very cool with him. Kiera came out as well and I think he didn't know what to make of her. He was looking from me to her to me again. Then he had me right up against the wall by my collar and he was staring into my eyes.

"'I don't like you, Drachmar,' he told me, 'but do you know, there's someone I dislike even more than you.' Right then I wouldn't have thought there could've been. He said, 'I hate Her,' and I know you know who 'Her' was. 'I hate Her' he told me, 'and I happen to know that She wanted this one to go to the scum.' That's your lot, Stefan. Anyway, he was saying, 'Now I find her with you, Drachmar, not with the scum at all. I am sure that this will make Her very unhappy. I also suspect that the scum might have gained some enjoyment from her, and they are not here to enjoy their time in my custody. Not even for the brief span it would take them to fuck this woman. Listen to me, Drachmar, I know you intend nothing but insubordination, but it happens that you have served some purpose.'" Peter really did the Marshal very well.

"Then he hit me straight in the face." Peter touched his shiner for emphasis. "'That's so you don't forget your place,' he said, the bastard. Then he let me go, and he looked around at all the other Wardens. 'This woman is in Drachmar's care, and to be maintained unharmed until I give orders otherwise. When that time comes, then Drachmar will surrender her. Will he not?'

"I didn't say anything. I didn't need to. None of the Wardens were happy with it, but the Marshal had given an order. They all knew not to cross him.

"And that's how Kiera is here right now, and I thought it would keep for a while, but then Jonas turned up and everything went out of the window."

He looked at the two of us for a moment. "I so wish that I'd never met either of you. If not for you two I'd be out of this place and into the jungle faster than you could blink at me. Rather the monsters than Jonas Destavian, believe me."

I almost pointed out that most of the time over the last few months he had been pointing out how little he could help me. Kiera looked similarly rebellious. Neither of us said anything, though, and I had to acknowledge that my life would have been far harder without Peter's company.

"Now Stefan," Peter said, "I want you to be my second."

"Does that mean I have to fight?"

"No, it means you have to argue technical points," Peter told me. "You have to wrangle, basically, about the rules."

I considered this. "I know a better man. Shon used to be a lawyer and he knows the rules already."

"I'll take you both," Peter decided. "You and this lawyer. I need all the help I can get."

"And what about me?" Kiera demanded. Peter rounded on her with surprising vehemence.

"You will be in some storeroom while Jonas and I go head to head, and if I get it, then you make tracks out into the great outdoors and don't look back. Or whatever your backup plan was."

Kiera stared at him. "That's it, is it?"

"You better be ready to do what you do as soon as Stefan gets word to you that I've lost." There was none of his easy-going humour. He was deadly serious.

"I'll come with you," I offered, although I did not really believe it. "If the worst happens we'll go together."

Kiera looked from me to Peter. "I am so sick of being rescued by people," she said sharply. "I really begin to respect the Witch Queen. At least she can look after herself."

Peter held her gaze with his own. "Will you do it? For me?"

"For you? Oh well, that makes everything all right," she said, dripping with sarcasm. "Yes, Peter. I'll do it. I bow to your logic. Just don't expect me to be overly grateful."

"Obviously," Peter replied somewhat tartly, because it was his own death he was planning for. At that moment, what could have been an interesting argument was interrupted by someone appearing in the doorway.

The intruder was a neat middle-aged man with a tuft of beard and a humorous, creased face. Behind him, a pair of Wardens were setting down three cases.

"Doctor Mandri," Peter acknowledged. "Still taking Jonas' money?"

"Indeed I am," the man acknowledged. "Nobody else's money

274

is quite so readily available." He reminded me of the better kind of Academy Master, and I took a liking to him instantly, despite circumstances.

"This is Doctor Mandri, Destavian's second, a master of law and medicine," Peter explained. "Doctor, this is Stefan Advani, scholar of the Academy and your opposite number, and this is Kiera de Margot, my..." He faltered a moment and then made matters worse by saying, "companion."

"Island life obviously has more perks than I was aware of," Doctor Mandri said. "My lady, I was named Urven Mandri, and I am at your service."

"Splendid," Kiera said levelly. "Get me out of here."

Doctor Mandri gave a single dry laugh. "Ah, if only I could, lady. Will you have another second, Peter? I would be delighted for your... companion here to grace our activities."

Peter signalled for me to speak, so I told the Doctor that we would be joined by one Shon Roseblade, attorney.

"You are obviously blessed, Peter. It is a rare man who can boast educated friends," was the Doctor's comment.

"How about you," Peter pressed. "You're on your own?"

"Sadly no," Doctor Mandri confessed. "We have brought along Bewley Anteim to watch the justice his uncle has bought. A most unpleasant young man. Jonas wanted me to stress how much he regrets being the agent of your punishment. He has no ill feelings towards you."

"So why do it?" Kiera demanded of him, and he shrugged.

"A professional cannot allow personal feelings to interpose. It is simply the way of things." He gave a small, bleak smile. "I leave you with your equipment, Peter, and your thoughts."

He bowed out, leaving us with the three cases the Wardens had brought.

"So," said Kiera after he had gone. "What did you do to upset the Anteims?"

Peter shrugged. "I guess it can't hurt if you know, now it's all come back to bite me in the arse. What you are about to hear is

275

the reason why you should never listen to a strange woman in a bar," he said, and explained as follows:

"I was down on my luck at the time, owed a lot of people, and it was getting harder to dodge them. I'd have ended up here anyway, give it enough time. I was doing prize-fighting, strong-arming, whatever I could to make ends meet, always watching for the creditors. Then this woman showed up out of nowhere. Style by the bagful, obviously good family. She just walked into the joint I was sitting in and sat right down beside me.

"'You're Peter Drachmar? I thought you'd be taller,' she said, and that was as far as introductions went. She was a looker, and I could see she was a tough one, a politico. I'd got involved in high-class infighting before and it paid well. I was happy to listen.

"It turned out that she had some political rival, and she was willing to go out of pocket to see him taken down a step. It was quite definitely the biggest money I'd seen for a long while, and half up front. With that kind of flash she could have had Destavian, but he's got more scruples than I ever did. What she really wanted was a quiet knife in an alleyway, she said it straight out. I'm not really the man for that, and besides, it's actually harder than you'd think.

"So I bargained her down and we agreed I'd find this business associate of hers and call him out. He was a bit of an amateur duellist, it turned out, and he thought he was good, which always makes things easier. She told me the places he went, who he met with. She told me his name, which was Jon Anteim the Younger. Now, sure, I'd heard of the Anteims, but I reckoned one more enemy wouldn't hurt, and that bruised pride heals soon enough. More fool me.

"I should have known something was up because I'd only insulted him once before he was at my throat. He seemed to recognise me and I began to have my doubts about the whole deal, but by then it was too late. I forget what I said about him, some comment about his way with women, but we had a fight arranged within the minute for that very afternoon. We met up in the old Red Cabin arena. He had a mob of his friends, and I had tipped off an Angel I knew to keep everything on the legal side. I was counting on staves or something, just a sporting business where I could beat him about and send him up, but he came with knives and wanting blood. Someone had been spreading the dirty about me. I found later that he thought I was sleeping with his mistress. My patroness had done her groundwork. I wouldn't have needed to prod him at all; waste of a good insult.

"We got down to cases pretty quickly after that, and I found out he was better than he was supposed to be and mad with it, which made it hard to predict him. If I'd been wanting to kill him it would have been simple. He was leaving himself open all the time because he was so keen to kill me. As it was, I just wanted to put the wind up him and I had a real tough time of it, leading him on and him getting madder and madder, and in the end it was a great big waste of my time and effort because, of course, I did kill him. He came in with a big gutting stroke and I just sidestepped and put my knife in his neck without really thinking about it. So that was that.

"Of course, there was this great fuss, and I realised, now that I had killed their first son, that I didn't want the Anteims for my enemies after all. It was all legal, a proper duel, but I knew that there were other ways of getting even. I signed up for the Island the next day. Never did see the other half of the money.

"Chasing down my patroness would have been a death sentence. I found out shortly after that she was Haelen Anteim, the dead guy's sister. She inherits the Anteim fortunes when Old Jon finally kicks it. It's her that's put Jonas onto me now, I'll bet, to shut me up. I never did tell anyone. Nobody would have believed me."

Peter tried to gauge our reactions. I had guessed it to be something of the like, although I would have worked an element of romance into it somewhere. Kiera was shaking her head.

"You surely are the most stupid man I ever heard of," she said. "I would have seen that coming from the other end of the city."

"Well, you're born to that kind of thing," Peter said irritably. "How the other half live, you know. Besides, it was legal. Anyway, I'm a Warden; it's you two who're prisoners."

"We're talking about you," Kiera said quickly.

We opened the cases next and saw the weapons that Peter would be fighting with. There were rather a lot of them.

"A proper duel between professionals is fought in three rounds," Peter explained. "Each round stops when someone gets a hit in. Yeah, someone can die before the last round, but if the fighters know what they're doing then it won't happen. Jonas will be trying to get us to the last round as fast as he can, so, Stefan, you and this Shon have to dispute any hit he lands on me. I want to drag this out and maybe figure some way of winning, 'cos I'm damned if I can see one right now. Maybe I'll even get a strike on Jonas, slow him down." He did not sound hopeful.

The first case contained a staff some five feet long, made of light wood with a copper band at each end, plus a narrow dagger with a bar handle, so that when gripped the blade would jut from between the middle fingers. The staff was dyed in bands of red and yellow, and the dagger's grip was beaded with the same colours.

"Toys," Peter said dismissively and, when I said the dagger looked dangerous enough on its own, "Anyone who gets themselves hurt with these shouldn't be in the game in the first place." Now that he had the tools of his old trade to hand there was a new quality to him. He weighed the staff thoughtfully, twirling it in the close confines of the room. Kiera smirked at that, but to me it looked casually dangerous in a way that I could never aspire to.

The next case held something that was mostly a spear: a solid metal shaft perhaps a foot shorter than the staff, bulking out into a thick, flanged mace-head before tapering to a steely point.

Again, there was red and yellow in it, stained deep into the metal. It weighed more than I could believe.

"Lead," Peter told us, hefting it. "Lead inside the head, steel everywhere else. Makes them safer, really. Easier to see coming. This is for the second round."

Kiera opened up the last case and I saw within the strangest kind of sword. It was, from pommel to tip, as long as the steel spear, but the blade was broad and almost two-dimensionally flat, seemingly made of gleaming stone. The grip had a complex guard, twisted in serpentine curves that reminded me of the Weapon, or the spires in the swamp. It was a work of art in its own right, with contours that led the eye through an intricate series of turns and then straight up the lustrous blade. The hilt was lacquered in the same colours as the other weapons, but their faded heraldry made it clear that here was the original. When I took it from its resting place it was all I could do to lift it, and it seemed impossible that anyone could fight with such a thing. On the grip itself there were stencilled four characters that read something like R O P A but not quite, and the R was backwards and quite differently drawn, so that I suspected that they were really an acronym in some other alphabet altogether.

"Careful with that," Peter cautioned.

"I know," I said. "I'm surprised that the blade hasn't snapped straight off already."

"I mean careful you don't turn it on. You'd kill yourself."

"Turn it on?" I saw then that the convolutions of the guard hid several controls, and realised that it was neither heavy nor complex for the sake of it.

Peter took the sword reverently from me, getting his arms underneath it to take the weight. "I reckon there are nineteen of these Ropa blades in Shadrapar, and most belong to the big duelling arenas. The fact that Jonas Destavian owns two shows just how good he is at this. These things are sheer death. They don't even have to cut. If I turned this on and touched your shoulder with the blade, your heart would stop or your brain would curdle. They put out a kind of a field, and it is sheer death." There was a distant look in his eyes. "They're beautiful to fight with. I only used one twice for real, but I used to go into the big arenas to practise. There's nothing like them." I think that he had resigned himself, then, to dying on the morrow, but if he died with one of those murderous devices in his hands then he would not regret it so much. Like many practical, pragmatic people, there was an artist inside of him, trying to make itself known.

The only other thing worthy of note was Shon's reaction when I asked him to second with me. I have seen men and women in the Island under every stress and pressure, but never someone quite so excited.

24

Professionals at Work

It was a grim day next, but that had not stopped the spectators turning out. Earlier, it had rained a little, which scared me. Back home that meant all kinds of liquid plastic and chemical evil. In the jungles, if you can believe it, rain was just water, which was as strange to me as anything had been. I stood with it running down my face and spotting damp on my clothes, and had nothing to connect it to, no way to relate to it. It was as though it was an experience designed by an alien species and I lacked the mindset to appreciate it.

Someone had marked out a circle on the very same deck that had seen those bloody executions the previous day. It looked remarkably small, but it still took up most of the available space. I think almost every Warden must have shirked work to watch, the Marshal included. There was a ring of black uniforms, three men deep in places. Their faces were stamped (save for the Marshal's, which was proof against stamping) with anticipation and bloodlust. It was just like any other crowd at the fights. No doubt bets were placed, but probably on how long Peter would last, not who would win.

Someone had hauled two large and ornate chairs from the top floor onto a hastily tacked-up dais to give the authorities somewhere to sit. Normally there were professional judges at these things, but here it was the Governor and Lady Ellera, neither of them looking as though they should be out in daylight. The Governor had a big, cowled cloak on to shield his hairless skin, but his mistress faced the day with such icy poise that the sun hid itself. This was the court that Shon and I, and Doctor Mandri, would be appealing to on points of law.

Peter was out already, seeming at ease and fingering the narrow blade of the punch-dagger he would be using in the first round. His was the look of a man at peace yet not moved by any great optimism.

"An old man once told me—" he started, but then the other side was coming up, and I never did find out what that old man once told him.

Doctor Mandri was looking affluently restrained in a suit of shiny metal colours. Beside him was an overweight younger man looking far more affluent and far less restrained, whom I took to be Bewley Anteim, wearing what was presumably the very fashion in Shadrapar at that moment. As swiftly as I had liked the Doctor, I took a straight dislike to the Anteim boy. Of all of us here, he was the one who wanted Peter's blood on Destavian's hands: his the vengeance and his the wherewithal to accomplish it.

Destavian was a sharp-cut image in darkly gleaming blue and green. If I had attached wings to his back you might have taken him for a dragonfly. His duelling jacket had broad sleeves to the elbow, then bands of cloth to the wrist, with semicircular padded guards over the backs of his hands. Likewise his trousers were loose and baggy to the knee then followed the muscles of his calves down to thin boots that kept the big toe separate from the others, the better to balance. He wore a headband to keep the sweat from his eyes, and his face was a study in composure. I want to digress a moment into something Trethowan wrote about predators, contrasting a cold-blooded and a warm-blooded animal as the latter took over the former's habitat. He pointed out all the advantages the warm-blood had:

282

speed, power, grace. He was unusually poetic about the subject even in shorthand. He also showed that the warm-blooded killer that usurped the older, colder species was a distinctly higher-maintenance monster, demanding more food, more space. This is what Peter and Destavian reminded me of. Peter was a touch shorter, broader, drab in the dull uniform of an Island Warden. His movements were loose and minimal. Jonas Destavian was a high society figure decked out in his personal duelling colours, and he had speed, power and grace aplenty. The crowd roared like jungle beasts themselves when they saw him.

Peter took the dagger in his left hand, the staff in his right. I would have taken it for a two-handed weapon myself, but it was light and perfectly balanced and he spun it through his fingers much as Jon de Baron could do with a pencil. He took a single, deep breath, with a ragged edge to it, and stepped into the circle. I imagined a kind of silence closing over him, as though he were going underwater. There was a bit of sun, then, and it lit us all but most especially it lit Peter's face, finding it calm, with a strange, sad smile on it. For we prisoners, the worst had happened. We had been sentenced to our hell. Peter had been falling ever since the knife had entered Jon Anteim's throat, and now he had hit bottom. Only the actual fact of the fighting was left. I think he was relieved.

Jonas Destavian stepped into the ring, moving on the balls of his feet. At the same instant, he and Peter both had their staves up over and behind their heads, points jutting towards their opponents like the tails of scorpions. I thought it was a salute, but it was the fight starting. They ran at each other full tilt, and each brought his staff down at the other with all the strength he had. The weapons clacked sharply on one another, and the daggers both lunged in, traded two or three thrusts, and then Peter and Destavian were slamming away with their staves, a rapid patter of connecting wood as fast as three men hammering a wall at speed. They constantly stepped into one another, round one another, striking at the other's back, circling continuously, feet never still and daggers always waiting for an opening. Then they broke and their circling became wider, almost to the edge of the ring. It had all been so perfectly executed that it might as well have been choreographed. It was like chess: just a standard opening, such as you often get with two experienced players who knew the best moves. All of that strike, parry and counterstrike had been nothing but a tired old mainstay.

Peter and Destavian were constantly stepping into the centre to strike at each other, gliding sideways around the riposte, staves flashing and darting like serpents, daggers held raptly still, save that the point angled like the head of a hunting thing towards the heart of the other man. Peter would dash in, arc the staff for Destavian's head, change that into a strike to the legs, then to the side, then to the head again in a whirling figure of eight, all the time trying to stay ahead of his opponent's parries. Destavian would catch his staff and flick it aside and drive back at him, his face a model of care. Then it would be Peter stepping ever backwards across the circle, shadowing Destavian's staff with his own, trying for that one parry that would turn things around. Sometimes they would lock staves, under Peter's arm or in the crook of Destavian's elbow, and then they would trade dagger-thrusts with brutal efficiency, arching backs and sucking in guts to avoid them, until one would spin away, and they would resume their pacing.

It became clear soon on that Destavian was the better. When the two of them moved, it was to his beat. When Peter attacked he was ready for it, and his own attacks seemed to be coming forever closer. He clipped Peter's shoulder once, and Doctor Mandri called out a hit, but Shon and I, at Peter's signal, denied that it had ever happened. The Governor, eager to see more substantial losses from our side, agreed with us. It was clear to me that the Lady Ellera had discovered who had taken Kiera in and she wanted Peter destroyed as much as the Anteims. The Governor was only too happy to give her her way.

Then Peter, who had just been retreating steadily in a lazy circle, took several rapid steps back to the very edge and then one forwards, bringing his staff down to the floor and vaulting with it, kicking out at the other man at near head height. Destavian slid back smoothly, but Peter was already landing right beside him in a crouch, dagger parrying dagger, one leg scything round to catch his adversary behind the knee. Destavian seemed about to fall backwards, but he balanced with his own staff and swung the kicked leg around, ending up standing, facing away from Peter. His staff flicked backwards to bounce away Peter's blade, and Peter's own staff jolted against his upper arm.

Peter scowled and stepped back crabwise, but Doctor Mandri was conceding the hit on his own fighter, and Peter shrugged at us. We could hardly dispute a hit in our favour. The Governor looked unimpressed, but waved his hand to pass it, and the first round was abruptly over. Shon showed me then that Destavian had set the whole thing up. Rather than speeding things along by striking Peter, he had forced Peter to strike him. The first round was the easiest to stall in, Shon told me, and we had lost that advantage now.

I handed the heavy mace-spear to Peter, who was looking annoyed. "Should've seen that coming," he said. He did not seem in the least out of breath although there were beads of sweat dotting his forehead and dampening his hair. "Didn't do him any damage," he continued, stripping off his uniform tunic to the iron-coloured shirt beneath. Across from us, Destavian was detaching the sleeves of his own, unwrapping the bands of cloth from his forearms. He looked over without expression and took his own weapon one-handed. Like his clothes, like his staff and dagger, it was shaded blue and green. I knew that his Ropa sword, when produced, would have in its enamels the faded exemplar of those colours.

Peter was tugging on the gloves Destavian wore already: palms lined with deep grooves for grip, and padded to absorb the shock. They stepped into the ring together, Destavian letting the heavy spear just dangle at the end of one arm, Peter gripping the haft in both hands. They stood for a moment, looking at each other, each weighing up the other. The stakes had gone up.

Destavian moved first, snapping the spear out into a point-first lunge that carried him past Peter's evasion, turning the strike into a swinging arc at Peter's back. The steel shaft of Peter's weapon deflected the tip with a high metal sound and he swept at Destavian with the heavy head, meeting an identical move with a thunderous clang of abused steel. Three times they smacked the lead-filled weights together with absurd force, then stepped away, watching one another. I think that Destavian had seen that Peter was stronger, but you could not tell it from his face. He was as still as a mantis.

I assumed that this was how it would go from now, a brutal slugging match until one of them ran out of steam. That was what the weapons seemed designed for. Instead, Destavian levelled his and approached slowly, almost delicately. Peter was trailing his spear point along the slats of the ground, feigning fatigue. He almost waited too long. Destavian was well within reach, feet inching, feeling for purchase on the uneven flooring. The champion duellist's slow advance was swaying, almost hypnotic, and when he exploded into action, I was not ready for it. He whipped the head up, spun it for momentum and brought it down hard, all in one movement. Peter had seen it coming, back-stepped a foot and a half and made a killing lunge at Destavian, hoping to find him off balance after his strike. Destavian simply bounced the head off the springy wood of the floor, knocked Peter's strike wide, and then was boring in with one of his own. Peter lost two feet of ground and they were moving in slow circles, spearpoints just touching, grating against each other, each man seeking the inside line. It was the world's most delicate dance performed with the world's most cumbersome weapons.

Then Destavian had taken his spear like a sword, both hands near the hilt, and brought it down straight at Peter's head. Peter fended it off in the same style, and then struck back and forth, lunging and swinging, with precise, heavy strokes. There was no overextension, no wild swinging: that would have been fatal with such massive weapons. Each move was brought to a shuddering halt as soon as it had missed its target, dragged into line for the next block and counter. Even through the gloves, the punishment of the weapons meeting must have been agony through every bone of their hands, but neither man showed it.

It all fell apart when Peter lunged high into Destavian's face and the other man dropped right to the ground, knee and one hand, and swept Peter's legs out with the haft of his spear.

Peter was already kicking out for purchase when Destavian came down right at him, point first. I thought that was it, that we would not have a third round, but Peter writhed out from beneath the spear, and it stuck deep into the wood of the floor. He did his best to take advantage of it, twisting up to stab raggedly at his opponent, but Destavian, rather than tugging his spear free, pulled back on the shaft, straining the point against the slats of the floor, and then released. In a remarkably executed move the butt whipped into Peter's face and struck him in the eye.

Even as he reeled back, Doctor Mandri was calling for a hit. Peter, one hand to his face, was waving at Shon and I furiously, and I knew that if he went straight into the third round like that he would die in seconds. "No hit!" Shon was calling. "I object!"

The Governor stared at him, making me very aware of the fact that we were the only ones there in prisoners' greys. Shon glanced back at me the once and then faced up to the Governor and his mistress and said, "I submit that the contact doesn't count because it was only with the butt. Although obviously it is up to the wisdom of the judge to decide, it has frequently been ruled that strikes with the butt of the weapon are not sufficient for the purposes of progressing a duel."

Doctor Mandri made the point that there had also been cases where the opposite applied, and that this was all sophistry. By this time, though, I had come up with the concept that since

Doctor Mandri had not called a hit when Destavian had pulled Peter over with the haft of his weapon, he had tacitly admitted that contact with anything other than the head did not count, or otherwise (Shon added) that Destavian had unlawfully continued the second round after a hit. I sensed that the Governor was becoming somewhat lost in the legal technicalities.

What this had done, of course, was give Peter some time to recover his wits. He had a furious red mark across his left eye socket, neatly framing the existing bruise courtesy of the Marshal. He did not seem to be blind or dazed, and he was ready when the Governor finally ruled in our favour and decreed that the second round should continue.

Destavian had spent the time in taking off his headband and replacing it with a new one. When the Governor gave his signal he was ready, and launched straight in at Peter, who spent the next dozen moves simply fending him off. They were closer now, well within distance, and the lead-weighted heads often missed by inches only. Destavian put his butt straight into Peter's stomach, taking advantage of the Governor's ruling, but Peter found it in himself to kick his opponent savagely in what should have been the groin, but was only the hip after Destavian twisted away. They parted again, and there was a long still moment, both men breathing heavily, Peter with shoulders heaving and the remains of his calm poise streaming in tatters from him. He was on the run and everyone sensed it.

He gave out a shout without warning and was at Destavian, lunging, stabbing, jabbing down, getting almost chest to chest with the spears pinned between them. He grabbed the slighter man, bore him to the ground and rolled over twice before parting with a shriek of metal. I saw a line of blood across Destavian's arm and was about to cry out in triumph for a hit when I saw the source of the blood. There was a sister line cut across Peter's left pectoral, through his shirt and into the flesh. It was shallow, but it was a hit. I think neither man could have said precisely when in that mad scramble it had occurred. Doctor Mandri barely had to say anything. Peter was already trudging over, hand held out for the Ropa blade.

Shon bundled the awkward thing over to him, and Peter took it with some effort. I wanted to see to his wound, but apparently that was not allowed until the fight was over, when – his tone seemed to say – it would be a moot point anyway. He held the blade away from us to do something to the controls, and I heard a very faint hissing from it like air leaking out of some invisible pinhole. Peter was abruptly holding the sword one-handed, as though it weighed nothing at all, making small passes with it and watching light run off the stony blade. Opposite, Destavian had his own blue-green death machine out and was handling it equally lightly.

Shon had a metal bar out, three foot long and scored every two inches. I think it came in the case. He held it far out at arm's length and gestured for me to get back. With a single fluid motion Peter brought the Ropa sword in an arc and cut six inches clean off without a sound. Destavian did the same, slicing neatly through his bar at the first two-inch marker. I understood that this was in the nature of a test.

The two duellists stepped into the circle for the final round. I saw Bewley Anteim's deep-set eyes gleam with malignant glee, assured of the outcome. Doctor Mandri straightened his collar and I sensed that, with these awesome weapons, he would always be a little worried. They were so ludicrously dangerous.

Peter and Destavian closed carefully, swords outstretched. They made a few practise feints and passes. Peter would send his blade lunging in, then drag it back to fend off the other's. As it bounced away with a sharp, electric sound, he would spin with the motion and turn it into another attack, whilst Destavian retrieved the course of his own sword and got behind it. I think I was the only person present to understand quite what it was that made the motion of the Ropa blades so bizarre, because I had studied all that was left of the old sciences. Whatever power made the blades light enough to be used rid them of weight, but not of mass. They had no bond with gravity, and the duellists could throw them every which way, but they were slow to start moving and even harder to stop. Both men kept their blades in almost constant motion, as though they were fighting with weighted chains: spinning them in deadly arcs and wheels that constantly brought them back towards the body of their opponent. When the blades touched, they bounded away from one another with a crackle and hiss, but no solid sound of contact. Perhaps they never did quite touch.

Peter tried to be the aggressor at the start, hoping to fence Destavian in behind a web of wheeling moves. He passed the blade through figures and sigils and diagrams in the air, constantly trying to home in on his nimble opponent. Destavian stepped back and away, retreating parallel to the line of the circle, his own blade passing gracefully before him to ward off Peter's. His face was blank, save that something had finally reached his eyes and they had come alive.

He fell forwards, or that is what it looked like. I was sure that he was going to go straight into the path of Peter's sword, but he had calculated the course of that ever-moving blade and it was well clear of him, with Peter trying to arrest its flight. Destavian tucked into a roll and came up turning on the ball of one foot, advancing. It was all Peter could do to keep clear of a blade that moved like a dragonfly itself, Destavian handling it with an ease and deftness that defied belief. In contrast, Peter was a lumbering amateur, barely getting out of the way of each blow and staggering, missing his footing, lurching ever backwards. Destavian's eyes were deadly now, and behind them all the cogs and springs of his brain churned out the precise moves he needed to drive in for the finish. He so nearly had it two moves later, save that Peter stumbled too far, and the blade cut close above his head. I saw a switch of Peter's fair hair go dead white with passage of that lethal field, but Peter caught his balance only to go on backing up, always backing up. When I saw his face it had been stripped of all the easy charm and carelessness. Now he was desperate. Now he wanted to live, when events had conspired to make that impossible. I wish I had never seen his face like that. I wish I had never seen Peter Drachmar afraid.

Destavian's trap was shutting on schedule. I will say this for him: there was no enjoyment in his face, just a terrible concentration. Peter fell back against the edge of the circle, against the jeering, catcalling Wardens who used to be his peers. Destavian made the killing strike.

What you must remember is Trethowan's analogy: the cold-blooded and the warm-blooded predators, and the fact that warmer blood means higher maintenance. Jonas Destavian fought in the best arenas of Shadrapar, where the audiences watched with polite appreciation as he dissected his adversaries. Peter was a backstreet pit fighter used to rough crowds and dirty play. More, Peter had been on the Island for the best part of the year, Destavian had arrived the day before. The new blue headband already black with sweat, the air around him hotter and more humid than back home. It was easy to forget the differences, after so long. The climate, the noise, the smaller confines of the circle, all of these must have contributed to what happened next.

Peter did not miraculously get in a death-stroke of his own. He fell away to one side, the only way he could escape. Destavian arrested his lunge, but the tip of the blade cut an inch of cloth from one of the spectator's jackets, and the man just died. The field of the Ropa blade did indeed stop his heart. I had not believed Peter, before.

Destavian backed away, and he must have assumed someone would halt, or at least pause the fight. He was used to civilised arenas. Instead, Peter got his sword in motion and followed it in a ridiculously clumsy move that nonetheless almost killed Destavian, who only fended it off at the last moment, and made no counterattack. I did not know the dead man but Peter must have done, and Destavian knew that he had, and that shook him. He had just killed a bystander and he was the only man who cared. Even the other Wardens were shouting for him to finish Peter, heedless of the corpse. The Marshal's regime, where no man had close friends, helped them forget their dead comrade in an instant.

Destavian tried a few more moves towards Peter, but he stopped again as Peter retreated back to the circle's edge, and I saw an understanding pass behind Peter's eyes. From that point he made free with the edge of the circle because Destavian would not follow him there. Doctor Mandri was shouting something at his comrade, but the roar of the crowd drowned his words. Destavian had a peculiar expression on his face, and I remembered Peter saying, "He's got more scruples than I ever did."

The champion made one more essay against Peter, getting some of his old form back, but Peter had got something back too: hope. He had seen that he was Destavian's superior in one way: he was meaner. He managed, with the most awkward hauling-about of his sword, to fend Destavian off, and then he went into his most desperate, most furious attack. It was pure suicide, a crazed, hacking dash that could only come to nothing when its impetus gave out. He drove Destavian back by sheer manic energy, forcing the champion to keep lightly ahead of him, sword bouncing and bounding off Destavian's in a clash and clatter of static.

I was ready for it. It happened because Destavian's focus had been broken, because he was thinking, now, of what he was doing. He was approaching the line of the circle himself. In fact, he was two good yards clear of it but unsure of the exact distance in that confused moment, with Peter so much in his face. There was a moment when he tried to check, desperate to stop some slash claiming another innocent victim. That was Peter's advantage. He knew that there were no innocents on the Island.

Peter's blade passed effortlessly into the right side of Destavian's chest and he was dead on the instant. He was looking straight into Peter's eyes when he died.

The crowd was dead silent as Destavian's body hit the floor, followed by Peter's knees and Peter's sword, because he had used everything up in that wild last gambit.

Peter touched his forehead to the wood of the ground and hugged himself, oblivious to it all. He never saw Bewley Anteim, crimson with thwarted vengeance, snatch up a knife from somewhere and launch at him. He must have felt the man's ponderous footfalls through the floor, because he looked up moments before the strike and just fell back before it, so that the blow that was intended for his neck just slashed across his collarbone, chest and shoulder. Bewley raised up the knife again, with me standing like a statue, astounded. It was Shon who scooped Peter's dropped Ropa blade up. I saw a tiny second of wonder on his face at the beauty of the way the thing moved. Then he pulled it through the air in a great flat arc and it sliced everything above the nose cleanly off Bewley's head.

25

Further Alarums and Excursions

Shon was grabbed by three or four pairs of hands right then and there. Wardens twisting his arms behind his back, forcing him to his knees. I saw the Marshal striding through the crowd as though he had been waiting for this moment all through the duel, pulling a flintlock pistol from his belt without any emotion registering on his face. I ran forward at him, shouting that Shon had only been saving Peter's life. Some anonymous Warden hit me in the nose with an elbow, and I went straight down. When I sat up, blood all down my chin, I saw Shon, struggling in his captors' grip, the Marshal putting the flintlock's long barrel to the back of his head.

Doctor Mandri gently took the barrel between forefinger and thumb and moved it some four inches up before it fired. It must have near deafened poor Shon, but it failed to explode his head. The Marshal recoiled from the intruder and snapped out at him cold as ever, "Do not interfere with the running of this Island, Doctor."

In the aftermath of the shot Mandri's calm, clear voice carried perfectly. "I am only preventing a miscarriage of justice," he said. His friend and colleague, Jonas Destavian, was lying only a few feet away, as dead as could be, but apart from a little extra gravity in his tone, you could not have told it.

"This prisoner just assaulted a free citizen of Shadrapar," the Marshal informed him. "I am afraid that it would be a poorly run prison that tolerated that."

"He is not a prisoner," Doctor Mandri said.

The Marshal stared at him.

"From the moment the duel started he became Peter Drachmar's second," the Doctor continued. "Bewley Anteim broke the law by stepping into the circle, and this man was quite within his rights. He was merely performing his duty as a second."

The Marshal tilted his head in a way that he was suggesting having Doctor Mandri executed as well, but the Doctor simply gave a tiny nod and then knelt down next to Peter. He had an old medical bag with him and he took from it some cleanser, sealant and a Universal Salve bottle. I saw why, in his position, it was important to be both a medical and a legal man.

The Wardens held onto Shon uncertainly, and for his part he stopped struggling, and they all watched the Marshal. He looked at the Doctor's back, and then at Shon. He looked for the Governor, who had left, and then at nothing at all, and I felt the wheels of his brain try to grind their way through the technicalities of the situation. Surely he could kill whoever he wanted. At the same time, he was a law-fearing man and the entrance of Destavian had extended the confines of Shadrapan law to cloak his Island. I saw his greed for control at war with his need for order, and I saw it all from the way he stood, because none of it showed on his face. I will say this for the Marshal: he must have been motivated by a genuine respect for the letter of the law, rather than fear of reprisal as most of us are. If he killed Shon then nobody would touch him for it, yet he hesitated still, then signalled for Shon to be released.

I cautiously made my way over and Doctor Mandri glanced up at me. "I think that he will live," he said, matter-of-factly.

There was far too much blood around. Most of it was Peter's and some of it was mine. The wounds left by the Ropa blade did not bleed at all.

"Is there someone to look after him?" the Doctor was asking. I thought of the hostile and uncaring Island, and then of Kiera, and said, "I really can't say."

Mandri grimaced. "Well... I'll leave something for him that should help him mend." He put a hand up, and I helped him stand. He looked tired and worn, and I think he had been arguing with the Marshal and attending to Peter as a way of taking his mind off other things.

"What now for you?" I asked.

He shrugged. "Home. There are other duellists. My services will not rust for want of use." He pressed his lips tight together for a moment. "There will not be another Jonas Destavian in my life, but what of that? One was enough. I wish you luck here, Stefan, although it seems about as luckless a place as one might find on this blasted earth. You, your friend and Peter. And his lady friend, whom I wish I could help."

Shon and Midds the Warden were looking after Peter, I saw, and nobody was paying attention to me, and so when Doctor Mandri walked to the edge of the Island and looked out at the water and the encircling trees, I went with him.

"Perhaps you are lucky after all," he said softly. "To live here, amongst this..." One hand described the man-eating jungle, the monster-haunted lake.

I said: "What?"

"I would rather stay amongst this than return to the vice and grime," Doctor Mandri told the view. His voice was sad and strange, with crests of feeling breaking at random through it. "I would rather die amongst this life here. Perhaps I should turn to crime. Did you read Trethowan, Stefan?"

I told him, with feeling, that I did.

"I always enjoyed Trethowan. He found a happiness out here, you know."

"He was committed to the Island and he died here," I told him, thus breaking a great secret open on Shadrapar.

Doctor Mandri regarded me wryly. "Well, we spoil everything, don't we? We are an ingenious people." He blinked, and I saw tears huddled in the corners of his eyes. "I loved him," he said, and did not know whether he meant as a son or a friend or a true lover. I was conscious of Destavian's body there, a bloodless slot in its chest. Doctor Mandri looked into my eyes then and saw that I could not understand why he did not have the Marshal kill the lot of us.

"He would have wanted it this way," the Doctor said. "He was a good man."

Then a Warden came to take Shon and I back below. The show was over. I never saw Doctor Mandri again.

I managed to slip away from the workshops shortly afterwards, under the pretence of going to relieve myself. The Wardens were too involved in reliving the duel to care where I was going or how long I would take. I crept from the working masses and went to the old storeroom where Kiera was holed up.

She was dressed as a Warden still, and watched me from the shadows for some time before I found her.

"So what?" she asked straight out.

"He won," I said, and then corrected it to, "Peter won."

Kiera stared at me, and then made a kind of hard shrug that flung her hair back from her face. "Pity," she said. "I was looking forward to the jungle." Her eyes were like the eyes of Doctor Mandri, though, with unacknowledged tears beading behind them. She stared at me, tough and independent, for perhaps twenty seconds more. Then, "Oh God, he actually won?"

When I nodded mutely, she flung herself at me and held me fiercely, and I put my arms around her, and tried not to think of her hair, or the way her body felt next to mine, and failed, mostly. My libido was never a respecter of occasion.

She shuddered once and I thought that the weeping would start after all, but sometimes Kiera de Margot was just as tough as she made out and she kept it all inside.

"There's more," I told her, but only as soon as she felt able to let go of me. "He was hurt."

She stared at me, waiting.

"Doctor Mandri, he said that Peter would live, but he's not going to be up and about for a while. He won't be able to... look after you. The other Wardens know this. I don't know whether you think it's safe to stay or whether you want to chance it after all."

Her eyes flicked away from me, thinking.

"What do you think, Stefan?" she asked me. "The Marshal's writ, will it still run without Peter? You know the way these people work better than I do."

I tried to imagine the Marshal and how he would be reacting to all this. I never had got my head around the way the Marshal hated Lady Ellera so much, and I considered that by beating Destavian, Peter had surely managed to infuriate the woman even more. Thanks to me, Kiera had come to symbolise rebellion against the Witch Queen's wishes. First I had supposedly tainted her with my mind, then Peter had saved her from the fate Lady Ellera had chosen for her. Now Peter had saved himself, so retaining a tenuous shield over Kiera. What a net we three were all tangled in.

"I think it will hold," I told Kiera. "I think that the Marshal will see that it holds, if only to spite Herself."

"Then I'll trust your judgement," Kiera said flatly. "I've had enough of needing people. I suppose that Peter needs me now."

We parted then, but she held my hand first, as women of good family did with their friends. I think she saw that our positions were not so different, certainly closer than we were to Peter. She made her own way back to the upper levels and I returned to the shop floor, where one of the Wardens caught me and beat me for idling, which was harsh but fair.

In the aftermath of Peter's duel the Island was quiet and thoughtful, and the next few weeks passed almost in a dream. I worked, I slept. I transcribed Trethowan for the Governor, who seemed more and more pensive as though brought bad news he could share with nobody. Hermione invented a simple word game that was briefly all the rage along our stretch. There was an Outing at which I steered well clear of Tallan and he did me the like favour. In all that time, I saw Peter and Kiera the once.

Midds came, one day, and fetched me up to see them. I never really understood Midds. Only now, recounting all of these distant adventures, do I realise how many tiny acts of kindness I owe the man for. I think his upbringing amongst the Compassionates must have been rooted deeper in him than he knew.

Anyway, Midds brought me up to the Wardens' level and there, just outside Peter's room, was Kiera. She was still in her Warden's uniform and, to my surprise, was playing chess. I came very close to just breezing straight up to her opponent and congratulating him on how well he was healing. It was not Peter at all, but balding Harkeri the artificer, who should not have been just sitting there playing chess with a female prisoner. I shut right down into subservient convict mode and waited to be acknowledged. Kiera glanced up a little too brightly, said something quietly to her adversary and gestured for me to follow her into Peter's room.

Peter was not looking particularly recovered. He was asleep, though, and breathing easily, and Doctor Mandri's medicines had obviously been working their magic on him.

I looked from Kiera to the open doorway, the chessboard beyond. "What was that about?"

She met my gaze levelly. "Give me some credit." She sat beside Peter's bedside on a chair she had borrowed from someone. "Politics is my family business, Stefan. Give me a lever and a place to stand… You, Peter and the Marshal, bless him, gave me that lever." She tried a smile but it was tired and strained. The impression of ease she had given at the gameboard was gone. "It's a matter of momentum. Peter's opposition, the Marshal's mandate, it broke their stride. There was a window in which I was not something to be abused and cast aside." By now I was wishing I could break away from her gaze, but it was impossible. "I got my fingernails into that gap. I forced it. I didn't behave like a prisoner. I didn't wear the greys. I didn't cower in Peter's room. I pretended I was free to go where I wanted. I talked to them as equals. I learned their names. It's always harder to do things to someone who knows your name. I started with Midds and Regenel – Red, they call him. I moved on to Harkeri and Gannon and Halo Phelder. I know most of them now. I was trained to remember names and faces. I could waltz out there and chat to any one of them and it would be just as though I was hosting a party back home. I smile, I flirt, I hang on an arm here and there. Who wouldn't want to be with someone like me, the society hostess?"

The odd thing was, it was when she said that that she looked most like a prisoner. She looked worn down and under tremendous pressure.

"How long do you think—?" I started, and she cut me off sharply, though her voice was too low for the Wardens outside.

"You don't need to swan in here with your Academy education to tell me that. It lasts as long as the Marshal remembers. It lasts so long as it needles the Witch enough to please him. As soon as his game's out, then my game's out too, and all those people whose names I know, Gannon, Harkeri and the rest, they'll all forget my name. They'll all pick up right where they left off. They might pause a moment, as though trying to place where they know me from, but no more. I'm living on someone else's time again, but it's the Marshal's and I can't use him—" there she stopped, but the words I think she was aiming for were *like I could use you*.

It was not as though I hadn't known or couldn't understand her position. I reached out, as gingerly as though she were venomous, and tilted her face to look at me. With the need to be bright and shining fallen from her, I could see how she would look in twenty years, if the sun left us that long. My own face probably showed how I would look when I was dead.

I won't deny that part of me was hoping that mere need might turn into something more, but there have been more romantic circumstances, I admit. In retrospect, she probably had other priorities just then.

"I survive," she said, and it could have been a motto for everyone on the Island.

It was almost a month before Peter was halfway well again. Bewley Anteim's blade had cut deep and I think he owed his life to both Kiera and Doctor Mandri. The first I knew of his recovery was seeing him across the workshop floor. He looked worn and pale still, and a lot of the lines on his face were laughter lines no longer. He was on duty though, because in the Marshal's eyes if he was well enough to walk he was well enough to work.

He came over as the midday meal was brought round, and gestured for me to go with him. In a nearby storeroom he sat heavily on a pile of sacks.

"How are you?" I asked, cautiously.

"Healing." He managed a taut smile. "Glad to be out of that bloody room, I can tell you, and away from that bloody woman. I should have been up and about a week ago, but for her."

I wasn't convinced he should have been up and about at all, but I said nothing.

"I hate being cooped up," he said, leaving me thinking that he had chosen a poor place to hide out, then. "Worse," he added, "I hate being cooped up when someone's after me."

"The Anteims."

"You can be sure." He nodded grimly. "I hear your mate, the lawman, he took Bewley right down. Not that I'm complaining, you understand. Means they'll be even keener, though, and I'm not up for another fight right now."

"If they have sent someone he'll be on the next boat," I pointed out.

"And that's due...?"

"Any day. Tomorrow maybe. That's what Lucian was saying."

"Tomorrow. Right." He mulled this over. "I'm in the mood for a gamble, Stefan. I think it would be a good idea if, when that boat pulls in, I was elsewhere."

I looked at him guardedly.

"I'm in the mood for a mining expedition," he clarified. "Maybe one that gets stuck and spends a good three, four days out away from the Island where I can't be found. That boat from the city has a schedule, after all. If it unloads a mess of duellists onto the Island, how long can they wait before they all have to go home? I can't see people like Destavian slumming it for a whole month just to get at me. Sound like a plan?"

"Something approaching a plan," I allowed.

"So are you up for it?" was his next question. "Great outdoors?"

I considered this carefully, remembering my last excursion with Sauven. "You have to bring Thelwel," I said. "If he's game, I am."

"He's good?"

"From what I've seen, indispensable."

Thelwel was game. He was fond of nature, madman that he was. He was always ready to risk his life in the jaws of a monster, just for a bit of greenery and a clear sky above him. Even now I cannot understand where he got this attitude from.

I was up early for boat duty but Thelwel was there before me, patiently coercing the craft's engines into some semblance of

302

life. He smiled as he saw me and I peered over his shoulder, hoping to understand just what he was doing. The workings of the point generators were a botched mess of repair on repair, ancient systems drawn out into a long half-life by people like Thelwel and his father.

Peter turned up shortly after that with another prisoner in tow, and it took a moment before recognition set in, because Kiera was back in her greys and it was hard to reconcile. The clothes were potent symbols. Kiera and Thelwel were introduced, and he nodded to her warily, waiting for the whole story before making judgements.

Kiera was already looking edgily at the surrounding green, at the unguessable depth of the lake. She was as artificial a creature as I was, a city creation. As Peter stowed a few tools and toys in the locker, I sat close to her. I wanted to take her hand, strictly to comfort her of course, but she kept them clasped together.

"I was not going to stay behind," she said quietly. "I didn't want the Marshal to remember me and withdraw his protection." Then, no louder, but with fierce feeling, "I'm fed up of living on someone else's sufferance."

Later I spoke to Peter, saying that I thought he had got fed up of Kiera's company during his convalescence. He looked at me with some amusement, seeing straight through me and knowing that I saw straight through him.

"I owed her this much," he pointed out. His expression was blandly good-natured.

We set off just as dawn was fingering the muddy water of the lake, and it was easier, this time, to bid goodbye to the walls and boundaries and pass into the endless shadow of the living jungle. When that line of darkness caught us, Kiera stiffened abruptly as though stabbed, and clutched the sleeve of my tunic.

"God," she gasped between clenched teeth, "It's like a nightmare." I did not know whether she meant on general

303

principles, or a specific nightmare of her own. Looking up at the vaulted and groined ceiling of green and grey and darkness, the phantom pillars of tree trunks briefly illuminated by our unhealthy ship-lights, I could only agree. It was all too close to my own fever dreams, to the Lady Ellera's green room.

We cruised softly through a vine-hung, tree-made gallery, large as a civic hall and lightless as a crypt. We were silenced by the scale of it and the boat made no sound save the faintest hum of the generators. We were at the centre of a chorus of calls and cries, croaks and rumblings, the slosh of water and the buzz of wing. Thelwel was smiling without knowing it. His eyes shone in the harsh light of the lamp. Kiera had pushed herself up beside me, shoulder to shoulder, seeking some human contact in the face of all that *other*. Her face was tugged at by fear and wonder.

Peter was untouched, not a man for imponderables.

Without ever breaking the hushed mood, something longer than the boat surfaced beside us. What it was I cannot say, for its black hide barely reflected our lights, but one small eye regarded us with a disturbing acuity, as though weighing us all in the balance. I almost expected it to speak, like that other swamp prodigy, but it just rolled away from us and was gone into the ink of the water. In all that time, none of us had made a sound.

Kiera looked to me to supply some information about our visitor, but Trethowan had not mentioned it and I could say nothing.

We found a spot to mine that was rich enough, and Peter got down to the subject of sabotage with Thelwel.

"These boats break down, don't they?" he suggested.

Thelwel, humble prisoner before a Warden, said nothing.

"Not often, but it happens," Peter continued.

Thelwel made a noncommittal noise.

"For instance, something might happen on this trip," Peter

pointed out. "The machines might go wrong and strand us for, say, three days. We can last three days out here."

Thelwel was watching him unhappily. I do not believe that Peter realised where all the blame would land if this plan of his went awry.

"So, maybe you could think of something that might pop out of joint and take just that long to fix," said Peter, now getting a little testy at the lack of response. "And maybe you could see that it happens, Thelwel, you follow me?"

"These boats go wrong enough without having to rig them," Thelwel said, not looking at him.

"That's the spirit," Peter started, and then decided that it wasn't. "Look, Thelwel, do you understand what I'm asking you?"

Thelwel's expression said that he understood all too well. Thelwel himself said nothing.

"Help me out, Stefan," Peter tried. I left Kiera to sit by Thelwel, who was looking profoundly put upon. It was not just the prospect of punishment, I saw. The idea of deliberately damaging a machine for no reason other than convenience did not sit well with him.

I told him the whole story: Peter's quarrel with the Anteims, the duel, the threat of further repercussions, also the problems that Kiera and I would face if Peter died. Through it all, his expression did not change, but at the end of it he said, "I can do it," which was what I was after. Only when I was about to thank him did he add, "I do not like the Anteim family myself."

Peter snorted. "Good man. We'll get together and plot against them some time. Kiera too. Weren't your family up against them?"

"More often than not," she agreed. "Stefan?"

"I'm a very peaceable man," I protested.

"Until a friend of yours cut most of Bewley Anteim's head off. You probably made their list for that," Peter suggested. An unpleasant thought occurred to me.

"I hope Shon's all right," I said. "I hope they don't pick on him."

Peter cursed suddenly.

I can still hear the terrible cry I gave out a moment later, when I realised what I was seeing. At first I thought it was just the humped backs of two fish moving towards us: that was all there was above the waterline. Then I looked beneath and saw that the two bumps were the raised eyes of a monster twice the length of our craft that was cruising in our direction at some speed. In form it was something like the luminous visitor to my cell Below – a long-bodied salamander with appallingly broad jaws and a powerful tail that was thrashing it through the water at us. It must have been forty feet long.

Peter dived for the lockers straight away, and Kiera grabbed the nearest loose object, one of Thelwel's tools, and threw it straight at one of the eyes.

Her aim was dead on, and the lump retracted into the creature's skull briefly in pain, but then the monster was rearing up before and over the boat, hoisting its head and forelimbs out of the water. It was high enough to blot out the light, its great semicircle of head, all streaming water and greenish hide, angling down on us. I saw those jaws gape, rimmed with needle teeth. It could have snapped any one of us up in a single gulp. The boat was rocking wildly with the swell, Kiera and I both crying out. Thelwel was scrambling towards it up the slope of the deck, waving his arms, and the monstrously huge head focused on him, each eye moving independently to track him.

It can't work, was what I was thinking. *This one has eyes, and it's far too big to be fooled by his trick*. I saw the jaws feint at him, as he stood there on the edge of the boat, balancing against the waves. The snout came within half a foot, backed, advanced again. I was crouched in the bottom of the boat, half-holding Kiera, both of us staying quite still and not giving the monster any excuse to notice us.

Thelwel was breathing very fast and his face was set and steady. He had his arms out for balance, and it looked like he was about to embrace that hideous head. The monster made a deep grumbling that vibrated through the metal hull of the boat, and hooked one foreleg over the side, tilting us towards it. Thelwel leant slowly back, still keeping his precarious footing, and that ponderous head tried to find a way round him, swinging in great baffled arcs.

Peter made a small satisfied sound, and I hoped that he had found a gun.

All of a sudden the monster pressed hard down on the side of the boat, and we all fell towards it. I saw Thelwel actually bounce back from its very lips, and Kiera and I were rolling over one another, helplessly tumbling towards that opening mouth. Past us dashed Peter, and I saw (and even in that moment I could hardly believe it) that he was leading with the point of a Ropa blade.

I think he yelled some battle cry. There was so much going on I cannot be sure. I saw the full length of the blade slide easily into the monster's flesh, somewhere above one foreleg, and the monster gave out a shrill shriek of pain, but refused to die. Even the death-field of the Ropa blade had not been able to find a vital organ in that mammoth beast. Peter had time to swear foully and take a two-handed grip on the embedded sword. The blade came free as the creature reared back, and Peter fell into a crouch, holding the weapon before him. Then the monster lunged forward. Jaws agape, it bore down as though it would swallow us all at once. I heard Peter cry out in shock, but when I looked there was another gash across the nose of the monster from the Ropa sword, and Thelwel was in its teeth. It had gripped him across the body and one arm, and I thought it would swallow him, but instead it just flung his loose body away into the trees.

Peter kicked off from his crouch and brought the blade in an arc that cut a long and bloodless line across the entire width of the monster's throat. He let the momentum of the sword carry him through, off the boat and into the water, because that vast head, suddenly and abruptly bereft of animation, was crashing down on the boat. On myself and Kiera.

That falling silhouette, large enough to mask the whole sky, was my last memory for some time.

26

Secrets of the Swamp

The first thing I saw, when consciousness returned to me, was Kiera's face. It is testament to my situation that even this failed to cheer me. I felt as though every part of me had been kicked by every Warden on the Island. It took several minutes for the preceding events to filter back into place. Before then, all I knew was that I hurt.

Kiera had a bruise over one temple and a black eye. She seemed to have come out of the whole business better than I had.

"I'm alive," I said fatuously. "You're alive. Right." I had to keep collecting my thoughts, or they would fragment and drift apart like the broken ice around the spires. I tried to sit up, and the resulting pain in my head was so thunderous I fell back instantly.

"Is Peter all right?"

Peter's own voice came to me, complaining, "I smacked my knee something wicked. There must have been a rock or something in the water. Hurts like hell."

It was obvious from the tone that he was well enough to complain. Kiera's silence was making me worried, though, and there was an undercurrent to Peter's voice I disliked. I picked over my memories of the incident and went suddenly cold.

"Thelwel! What about Thelwel?" I got out. I saw Kiera glance unhappily at something, and Peter said, "Thelwel is... fine."

Despite the pain I forced myself into a sitting position, clutching my head. I saw Peter sitting beyond Kiera, one trouser leg slit to mid-thigh. We were all sprawled across a tangle of mud and roots that passed for solid ground here in the swamp. I looked in the direction that they were unwilling to.

It took me some time to accept and understand what I was seeing: it was such a grotesque sight it quite escaped me at first. Thelwel was sitting, away from the three of us. His prison greys were torn to shreds, and I could see a faintly curving line of livid puncture-marks across his bared chest. His arm had taken the worst of it, though. It looked like one of the anatomy sketches I had seen in textbooks, and all the more so because Thelwel was methodically laying out all the various torn and damaged ends. With his left hand he was arranging the components of his right arm: the bone, the sheets of muscle, tendons and ligaments, blood vessels and serrated flaps of skin, all with the same careful patience that hung about him when he was repairing any moderately complex machine. I watched silently as he smoothed two ends of muscle together, and they knitted and joined under his practised touch. Some of the skin had already healed up, leaving bruised red-purple scar lines that looked weeks old. There was a lot of blood staining his skin and clothes, but no more forthcoming.

He looked up at me with an expression I had not previously seen on his face. Peter and Kiera he did not know, but I was a friend as much as anyone was anybody's friend on the Island. I could see fear and regret amongst the fading marks of the struggle.

There was a long silence in which his left hand continued sightlessly ordering the tissues and structures of his right. I could sense Kiera and Peter waiting for me to speak, and Thelwel also. There was a tension in the air, and I had felt it before in the mob when Helman and the others died, and many times on the

Island. It was where fear of the unknown curdled into hostility. And perhaps, in that moment only, I was the most perfect emissary to bridge the gap between the human and the artificial worlds. Thelwel was not the first such entity I had the privilege of knowing. I came to this discovery prepared.

I said, "Are you going to turn out to be a homicidal killer or a cannibal, or anything else in that vein?" I could not believe how calm I felt.

Thelwel shook his head silently.

"Then I don't care," I said. I sensed a flinch of surprise from all concerned. My head was aching, and I had no time for any kind of wasted effort. "I know you. You're the most decent man on the whole Island. You're the only one that I thought never deserved to be there. I like you. You're a friend. So you're... not what you seem. Who is? It doesn't change anything."

Still silence. Thelwel's expression was melting by degrees. It must have been a long time since he had bared this particular secret.

"You don't even have to tell us," I continued. "I'm curious, obviously. I'd love to know. I'm not going to make a big deal of it, though. Your choice."

I glanced back at Peter and Kiera, and saw that they had relaxed also. It was something of a surprise to discover that they both trusted my judgement that much.

When a man is on the rocks of emotion and about to open up some inner box of troubles, he talks about his mother. Thelwel's voice was calm and level when he said, "I had no mother, only a father."

"Father Sulplice," I prompted.

"Even he." Thelwel examined his injured arm, over which skin was creeping like mould. "He is my creator. I am a made thing."

It was so matter-of-factly said.

"Most cunningly made," Thelwel continued. "The sciences of past ages were of great span and complexity, and they had the craft to assemble the blocks of life as easily as they could stone and metal. My father is a man unparalleled as an engineer, but who never found wife, nor family. So he determined that he would fashion a son, which to him seemed simpler than wooing a woman and conceiving a child. So it was that I was brought about."

"Anyone else's son would be at the bottom of the swamp and cut in half right now," Peter pointed out.

Thelwel shrugged, and I watched the scar lines on his arm jump. "My father set out to make a human being, no more, no less," he confessed. "Being an engineer, and taking pride in his work, he decided to make some small adjustments to the original plan, so that his son would not have to suffer some of the design flaws that human flesh and blood usually owns. So it is that my tissues will heal. So it is that I can know I am hurt without being a slave to pain, and can know feeling without being a slave to emotion. I am well made, but I am still a made thing."

"So what landed you on the Island?" Kiera asked him. He looked at her warily. Father Sulplice had given him little when it came to dealing with women.

"My father's projects became known," Thelwel said. "The Authority became involved. It was not well-publicised, but there was a great commotion within the corridors of power, so my father tells me. There were old laws, from a time when the matter was more pressing, forbidding the artificial creation of human beings. They wanted me destroyed." There was a hint of real pride in his voice. "My father, they would not harm. Who else could have done what he did? The Authority could not be sure they would not need him some day. But me, they wanted destroyed. My father called in every favour and debt he had ever acquired, and spent everything he had left to hire a very skilled lawyer. The matter was settled by court and our advocate found an ingenious paradox on which to base our case.

"The paradox runs like so: if my father was guilty of creating a human being then he was indeed guilty as charged, but I was innocent, having committed no crime, and therefore I could not be disposed of without splitting open the law at the seams. On the other hand, if I was a made thing and not a human being, to be destroyed at the Authority's pleasure, my father would have committed no crime and therefore I was still his lawful property and not subject to confiscation. It was a legal fiction, but lawmakers must cling to the law even as the Marshal does. If they lay that crutch aside once it will not support them later. There was some negotiation, and we were sent here, my father and I, as a compromise." I think he was mostly recounting his father's words verbatim, or else he had rehearsed this story in the solitude of his head a very many times. I would too, if I had such a frail justification for my existence.

Eventually, Kiera asked something like, "… how long…?" and Thelwel replied, "On the Island? Fourteen years. All the life I ever had. No-one is left who knows our past and what I am, for the Island keeps no records. I would appreciate your keeping it to yourselves for obvious reasons."

The next blow was the boat, which was so completely buckled that, from the side, it described an "L" shape. The dead monster had come down that hard, flattening lockers and bursting open the tanks, releasing a thick slurry of harvested chemicals. It was the presence of those tanks, taking the brunt of the impact, that had saved Kiera and myself from instant crushing.

The question of whether Thelwel would sabotage the boat for Peter was now moot. I have often wondered whether his reluctance stemmed not just from the professional pride of an engineer, but a dislike of machines treated in such a cavalier manner. It would have been a policy that might rebound on him some day.

Peter declared that the Marshal would send another boat in search of us, although he did not sound overly happy. The Marshal, he explained, would suspect some foul play and, for that reason, the search would not stop until trace of us was found. In the meantime we would have to survive the hostile environs and the monsters, and perhaps other things.

Food and shelter were first. While Peter, Kiera and I made the world's least desirable residence from man-sized leaves we tore from the nearest tree, Thelwel got one of the boat motors running, and compromised its efficiency to the point where it was hot enough to cook on. We ate the most readily available food: grey slabs of monster steak from the beast that had wrecked our boat, cut from its half-submerged body by Peter's deadly sword.

Thelwel managed to get a lamp working too, for the gloom was growing. The spitting, bluish illumination was not cheering, but it would give us a chance to see monsters before they reached us. The chemical slick seemed to be keeping all forms of life at a healthy distance, but Peter decided that we would have to set watches. He would go first, then me, then Thelwel and then Kiera. As it fell out, by the time Peter woke me to take my turn, Thelwel was still finishing up on the boat. He had been salvaging every mechanism he could get his hands on, putting power through each in turn in search of any lingering function. He needed less sleep than we did, but that is a trait I have observed in most engineers. Whether it was a gift of his heritage I could not say.

He had made something ugly and cumbersome, like a holed metal box that had been attacked by cables and riveted copper pipes. "This," he explained to me, "is the ignition. This is the nozzle. It is a weapon."

I looked at it. It could have been a weapon; I was none the wiser. I secretly wished never to have the chance to test it.

After Thelwel had finally bedded down, the jungle resumed its busy watch over us. Insects clustered around the unhealthy lamp, and were picked off by fleet flying things that could not believe their luck. Peter snored, lying on his back with his arms outstretched, taking up as much room on our narrow root-bank as possible. Kiera was curled into a tight ball. Thelwel lay

314

peacefully on his side. There was a light mist in the air and water condensed off the leaves of our shelter and dripped on us at random. Beyond the reach of the lamp was the old, malevolent night that is always waiting for the power to die and the lamps to wink out. We fear the dark in Shadrapar, and we fear the wild, those places from whence we came.

There were monsters abroad in the jungle that night. I heard many, roaring and trumpeting their fury amongst the maze of trees, none close enough to wake my sleeping friends. I saw only one.

Out of the pitch and the shadow and the silver sheen of the mist, stepping lightly from root to root and not a toe wet in the water, came a monster in the form of a man. I must say I have no idea if this happened at all. I might so easily have slept my watch away and conjured all this up in my uneasy mind. I wish it were so. I can only tell you that this is what I remember happening.

Out of the swamp and the night came Gaki, stalking silently. The blue light shone from his bald head, from his precise and clever eyes. His expression was mildly amused, as always. He walked right up to me and it did not occur to me to use Thelwel's weapon, and just as well.

"Stefan," he said, "You appear to have had some kind of accident. How unfortunate."

"How did you get here?" I demanded. The enormity of his presence was so great that I felt I could make demands.

"I told you before," Gaki told me, in the manner of one gently remonstrating with a child. "The Island is no prison to me. I stay there because it pleases me, and I move where I will. I wanted to come and see how you were faring, Stefan."

I glanced at the others, and my intent must have been writ plain on my face, because he told me, "I do not wish to be seen, Stefan, save by you. If they should catch sight of me I will have to kill them. Best they remain sleeping."

There was not a spot of mud on him, not a drop of water, save for where the mist had condensed slightly on his scalp. His eyes

315

glittered in the artificial light. "It is astonishing, out here," he confided. "Why, if I were to dispose of you four, I could believe that I was the last man left on Earth. Have you not thought the same, Stefan?"

"The thought of being left alone here does not delight me," I told him.

He made a face. "You disappoint me. You're crippling yourself with these companions. A thug, a whore and a menial. Honestly, Stefan, you have to move in better circles. Perhaps you should not have been so quick to upset the Lady Ellera. She read your book."

"She said as much."

"Everyone's a critic, then," he said lazily. One hand flickered briefly, and he had one of the flying insectivores between his fingers, vaned wings twitching madly. He looked at it with genuine interest.

"I read your book," he said. "I stole it from Herself."

"You read—"

"You have no gift for titles," he told me. "On the other hand, the matter itself is fascinating. I have always had a fondness for the human mind."

"She wanted me to teach her," I said. "She lacked something, some quality. When I pushed against her, there was nothing in return."

Gaki smiled at the struggling flier. "Well," he said. "If I were you I would destroy her mind as you did with that other creature. Dead enemies are easier to live with."

"It… it doesn't work like that."

"When you were worried about this one," he gestured at Kiera, and the flying thing skipped from his hand unharmed and winged off into the night, "I felt your mind ready to kill Tallan. Do not tell me that it does not work like that. You have a rare gift for death, Stefan."

"I do not want any gift for death," I said. His words cut me deeper than I expected.

"Such a gift always comes unasked," he said, seeing something in his own mind that was denied to me, "and cannot be refused. Do I have it, Stefan?"

A terrible fear came over me then, of Gaki's mind like steel pincers reaching out to pierce my own. He was looking straight at me with all the murderous mildness he had, and I tried to form the force of my own brain into some kind of shield, but the fear was too great and I could not muster anything.

I felt the first slow movement, that was all. It was like watching a poisonous spider hatch, seeing the sluggish motions of its legs. Gaki was teaching himself, building on Helman's writings. I swear to this day that of the very few who actually read that damned book, not one of them meant any good. It was a cursed undertaking from the start.

Again he read my expression, and his face took on an almost childish delight. "I have it then. I will practise, Stefan. You must be ready for me. I will need a sparring partner." Abruptly he was standing, looking out into the carnivorous night.

"It would be such a crowning achievement," he mused, almost too quiet to be heard, "to be the last man on Earth. With the race in decline, who is to say it cannot be done?" His look to me was benignly predatory, a raptor that had fed enough for now. "Be ready for me, Stefan," he instructed, "when my mind needs something to gnaw on."

Then he stepped lightly away into the jungle just as he had come, and was gone into the night, and beyond. As I said, I cannot tell whether he genuinely found me in all that expanse of wild, but if there was a man to do the impossible it was Gaki. Later, I was forced to decide whether I would act upon these events as though they were real, or discard them as bad dreams. I chose the former. It is always better to be safe.

I was awoken by Peter saying, "So, how many shots can you get out of this thing?" I had a vague idea that I had passed the watch over to Thelwel at some point, but the events of the previous night were those I would rather forget.

"Nine," Thelwel said after some calculation.

"Enough for a test then." There was complicated metal sound, and I sat up to see Peter juggling the contraption that Thelwel had built, pointing the dangerous end out into the trees.

"Bang," said Peter, and slapped at the ignition switch. There was an extraordinarily violent convulsion from the machine, the noise you might hear if you eviscerated an iron giant. Something a hand's length long, visible only in retrospect, shot from the gaping nozzle and exploded the branch of a tree a hundred yards away.

"Sod me," Peter said, sounding awed. "What is it?"

"It uses the charge from one of the point generators to explosively accelerate simple fixing bolts," Thelwel replied. "I hadn't thought that it would be quite so... effective." He took the thing from Peter and examined it for damage. "It may not last the full nine shots," he said mournfully.

"You've just told every single monster in the jungle where we are," Kiera pointed out sourly.

"I've just told them not to mess with us," Peter told her, obviously happy with his noisemaker.

Peter wanted to explore then. He loaded himself up with his sword and Thelwel's creation (which he nicknamed "the Junker") and wanted us to set out into the wilderness to see what we could find. I think he had images of hidden cities, treasure, ancient artefacts. Mine were of huge toothy jaws, tentacles and poisonous stingers, but Thelwel seemed quite happy to go wandering. Kiera was strangely quiet about it all. I think she was again weighing up the odds between the mercies of the Island and those of the jungle. She let Peter and I argue until Peter inevitably won out, and we all gathered what little we had in readiness for the expedition.

"Stefan," Kiera said just as we were about to set off, voice abruptly trembling. "What are those things?"

We were being watched. When I saw what by, my heart jumped horribly. I was taken right back to the prison boat, standing on the deck with Peter, watching the forested shore; the boat's captain saying, "They call them web-children."

There were three of them, and they were very much like children of twelve or so in size and build. No living children ever looked like that, though. They were thin enough to seem starved, and we could count their too-many ribs easily through the taut skin of their narrow chests. Their heads were like skulls, their eyes huge and very dark, with no white at all. Their noses were tiny, just bumps with two raw holes, and their mouths were far too wide, stretching almost ear to ear in a constant hungry grin. Their heads were round and earless with no more hair than the Governor. They had astonishingly pallid skins, glistening slightly with a greenish tint in the light. Their limbs were long and thin. Feet ended in prehensile toes that clutched the branches on which they crouched. There were folds of skin between those toes, and between the equally long and clever fingers that were unlike a man's, the forefinger being the longest and the others declining in size to form a webbed fan with only the thumb free. It was impossible to tell if they were male or female, or if the distinction held any meaning for them. If they were children they were children of the damned, spawned here where the canopy obscured even the view of God.

It was not their caricature of human form that froze me, but their possessions. No animals these. All three had hemp-woven baldrics from which small hide pouches hung. One wore a kind of kilt of knitted reed, although the others had nothing visible to hide. Another had a band across its brow, just like Destavian or the Marshal, but made of snakeskin.

One had a simple bow, and the bone head of the arrow was levelled at Peter, the string half-drawn back. Another clutched a long and jagged shaft of rusty metal salvaged from some submerged ruin. The last held a length of cane that might have been a blowing tube for darts.

319

We stared at each other. The nonchalant half-aiming of the bow matched Peter's vague pointing of the Junker. The web-children did not seem hostile, and I am certain they did not recognise Thelwel's contraption as a weapon. Instead, they examined us avidly, huge eyes devouring every detail.

"I have seen them before," Thelwel said softly. "Never so close. They have always been here, since before I came."

"But what are they?" Kiera demanded. She sounded appalled.

"This thing is getting really heavy," Peter muttered, shifting his grip on the Junker. "Someone tell me whether I have to use it or not."

I wished I had not dawdled over my transcribing. "Trethowan mentions them two or three times, and he was obviously building to some conclusion. I haven't got that far, yet. Trethowan is too much of a showman for his own good." I cut off abruptly as one of the web-children, the one with the salvaged spear, leant forwards on its branch, staring right at me with those cavernous eyes.

"Drethouen." Its voice was high and fluting, too strange and fey to be a child's. I was abruptly back Below, listening to that speaking monster. It was not kin to these slight warriors, but there was the same sense of man's supremacy usurped.

"Trethowan," I said, dry-lipped, and the creature joined in with its "Drethouen," and then, as if to show that it was not just mimicking, it said, "How'd you know Drethouen?"

Peter, Kiera, even Thelwel, froze rigid at this prodigy. Only I had been expecting it. Had they learned our language from eavesdropping, like the thing in the water? Or perhaps, their kind had been visited by explorers from the city, by the one man who claimed the jungles as his field of expertise. Had Trethowan become a god-figure for them? Was he the spiritual father of the web-children?

"I am a friend of Trethowan," I stated, reasoning that student and friend were within arm's reach. I had spoken very slowly and deliberately, and in the aftermath one of them gave a high,

320

quick chitter that must have passed for a giggle amongst them. They seemed to think I was simple-minded.

"Drethouen," one of them told me again, speaking just as slowly and patronisingly. I heard Peter snort with amusement despite himself. The Junker had dragged at his arms enough to be pointing at the ground.

"Follow," said the web-child, cocking its head to indicate direction. All three stared at me until I nodded unwillingly. Then two of them kicked off from the branch into the water and were away, nothing more than ripples even as we tried to track them. The third lowered itself to the ground before us. The top of its head came to around the base of my ribs, and it stood stooped, back crooked, limbs held at odd angles.

"You're not seriously going to go with those things," Peter said.

I shot him an aggrieved look. "I assumed you would be going with me."

He exchanged glances with Thelwel and Kiera; none of them were happy about it. In the end, though, Kiera summed it up. "If they want to trap or kill us, then this is their place. We're in no position to stop them."

The web-child waited until we were at least moving towards it, and then it was hopping off from root to root, faster than I expected, occasionally dropping to all fours for balance.

27

Secrets of the Swamp (Part 2)

There was a tree, huge, but still a tree amongst trees, roots drowned in the murky water amidst bulges and boils of weed. There were similar deformities at the feet of some of its neighbours, and it took a long time for me to realise that they were not natural growths at all but the work of webbed hands.

They had no visible entrance. Ingress was from below the surface. Their shape, as exposed to the air, was roughly spherical, with a camouflaging irregularity about them. A boat from the Island could moor by them for a day and nobody would notice anything amiss. As our guide led us closer I saw that other random assemblages of flotsam and sticks nearby might be fish traps and nets. It took even more time to spot that the web-children were watching our approach.

They could be very still when they wanted, clinging to the bark of trees or with only their eyes out of water. At first it was difficult to see any of them, but then there seemed to be one or two everywhere I looked, solemn, silent and insatiably curious about the newcomers. The largest was little taller than our guide, and there were some that seemed adult and yet no higher than my waist. It was impossible to say how many there were in that sunken village, but fifty at least.

Our guide stopped as we stopped, watching us watch his people watch us.

"This is your home?" I asked, trying to stop myself slowing the words down.

"Not my home. Another home," I was told, and when I asked the creature why it had brought us here it looked at me as though I were an idiot and gestured for us to continue. Peter and Kiera were both thoroughly unnerved by now, shown just how much could be hidden away in a swamp so that nobody knew. How many other little communities were lurking out here? How many hundred or thousand web-children?

The village was arranged around a large pool dammed and deepened as another fish-trapping measure. We made our careful way around the edge, aware more and more of furtive movement on all sides as the web-children got over their initial caution and began to close in on us. It seemed that there was a pair of huge black eyes boring in from every direction. I found that I had backed into Kiera, who was already shoulder to shoulder with Peter, who was prudently keeping the Junker high and out of harm's way. Thelwel stood a step apart, and I saw that the web-children were not interested in him. They were close enough to reach out and take his hand but they were all looking past him to us. It was that quality he had, that detachment from the natural world. I do not know whether it was a scent or a feel or a psychic resonance, but something betrayed his origins as a made thing to them, an object rather than a creature.

"This is going to get messy," Peter whispered. The web-children were all down from their trees now, crowding forward in little knots of gangly limbs and staring eyes. They all sported the same broad and automatic smile that, in such numbers, looked only hungry.

"Easy now. Easy," Thelwel's soft voice drifted to us. "No need to make any sudden moves."

A fin-fingered hand plucked briefly at my prison greys and was snatched back. Another touched my wrist, and I felt the damp residue on my skin. Kiera jumped and pushed closer to me, and I heard Peter say, "Get!" as one of them pawed at him, which scattered them for a second before they continued their cautious advance.

Then there was a serious commotion from the largest of the mud-and-wicker dwellings. This was unusual in that it was partly up a tree, and I reckoned it for some kind of Authority Chambers or the like. There was still no visible door, but from a hidden entrance amidst the mess of its construction two or three web-children sprang out abruptly, and then leapt away to the side as something followed them out.

It was bigger than they were, and I had the impression of amorphous grey-blue hide with a rainbow sheen. It landed solidly in a shallow pool, and for a moment it was nothing but a shapeless mass. Then it unfolded upwards, a legless, flap-armed thing covered with scaled hide. Not hide belonging to the creature that wore it now, though. It was a robe, and within the baggy and ill-tailored garment there was a man.

He was tall, the more so surrounded by the web-children. His face, the only part of him exposed, was creased and re-creased with age, hook-nosed, wildly-bearded and with tufted eyebrows. His eyes, within the deeply lined recesses of their sockets, were severe and stark and aflame with rage.

He stared at the four of us and shouted out, "Kill them! Kill them all! Now!"

There was a surprised hubbub of muttering from the assembled web-children, and Peter shifted nervously. One of them was talking to the tall man, telling him something I half caught.

"Kill them!" the man cried out again, although the web-children were obviously far from convinced. "For all of our sakes! They must not know!"

The web-child – our guide, I think – spoke urgently again and I caught the last few words, "... your friends..."

"I don't have any friends!" the man snapped back.

I took a shaking step towards him through the excited web-children, and choked out, "Trethowan?"

I had seen the face, decades younger, on the inside cover of his bestiaries, doodled on and vandalised by a hundred Academy students. The nose was all that was recognisable after all those hard years.

"Listen to me!" the old man demanded of his subjects. "There's no other way! Kill them. Especially the one in black!"

"Oh you just try it!" Peter yelled back, having had enough of this. Despite Kiera trying to stop him, he levelled the Junker at the old man.

"And what the hell is that?" Trethowan bawled back at him.

"It's a *weapon!*" Peter bellowed. In some awful way he was enjoying himself.

"Peter, will you put that damned thing away!" Kiera snapped at him.

Trethowan pointed a long, bony finger practically up the Junker's barrel. "He's a Warden! I told you about them! For God's sake! Someone put an arrow in him!"

"If anyone's getting anything in him it's you, old man!" Peter roared.

"Please don't shoot Trethowan!" I begged him. "Peter! Listen to me!" All around, the web-children were getting more and more agitated. Some were joining with Trethowan's demands, and others appeared to be arguing the toss, and they were crowding all about. I made a move towards Peter, reaching for the Junker, and he yanked it away and pointed it at the sky with a snarl.

"You better be right!" he told me, and someone jogged his arm and the machine spat a long metal bolt into the sky with a shattering noise.

I actually heard, in the dead silence that followed, the bolt descend back through the canopy some distance away and splash into the water.

Then things turned nasty. All of the web-children had broken out bows, clubs and spears, and they were suddenly on the very point of tearing us to pieces. Peter had managed to do with one shot what all of Trethowan's words had failed to accomplish.

Desperately I cried out again, "Trethowan! Ignaz Trethowan!"

He rounded on me, snarling. "So what?" he demanded. "So you know my name. So what?" There was a beat in which he was scowling right into my face. Then he added, with a little edge leaving his voice, "So people still read my books, then, do they?"

"They do," I told him. "You scared me to death with all your bestiaries, long before I came here. As a matter of fact, I'm spending whole afternoons working through your Old School Shorthand even now."

The old man stepped forward, his suspicions tempered by vanity. He was far taller than I was, the third tallest man I ever met. "My notes…?" he said.

"I am working through them. For the Governor. He can't get enough of them. Can I speak, sir?"

Trethowan watched me narrowly.

"Please… we won't give you away. We won't tell anyone about you, or about them. We're all of us people that the powers of the Island would like to see dead. Even Peter there. Especially Peter. We'd gain nothing from telling your secret. We only came out here so Peter could avoid a death squad, and then a monster ate our boat, and then some of these… people came and I dropped your name, and they brought us right here. We won't do you any harm. We really won't."

Trethowan glowered at us from beneath his wild eyebrows. "I don't trust anyone. Anyone human, anyway."

"What's so special about this guy?" Peter demanded. He had a gift for picking his moment. Trethowan's eyes glittered with abruptly renewed rage.

"He's a writer," I said quickly. "A famous one. It's his work I'm transcribing on the Island. He's supposed to be dead." I looked from Peter to the old man. "You're supposed to be dead. The Governor told me."

Trethowan's lip curled into a sneer. "When surrounded by ignorance, the educated man can get away with anything. I got onto a boat and, at the opportune time, I had a monster swallow me."

"You had a what?" Peter demanded.

"Oh, you had to know just which monster to pick. A knowledge of the biological sciences isn't all theory, you know," Trethowan said airily.

"But you could not have been sure," I said thoughtfully. "Not with the way things… evolve out here."

Trethowan looked down at me and for the first time there was the trace of a smile on his craggy face: a man who has at last found someone who understands his work, even a little. "Clever boy," he said quietly. "Yes, it was a risk, but worth it." His eyes narrowed. "Who are you?"

"I was named Stefan Advani," I answered promptly, and introduced the others in turn, saying that I would vouch for them all. Especially Peter.

"If I see any hunters come through here after me…" Trethowan told me, "The children have got into the Island before. Don't think you'd be safe."

"If anyone from the Island comes through here they'll be looking for us, not you," Kiera told him. He looked at her properly for the first time, and then raised a gnarled hand to touch her chin briefly.

"The Island has changed since I was on it," he grumbled. I guessed his age at somewhere around one hundred and seventy years, but he had been born into the best families, with all the gene surgery and medication that implied.

He glanced around at the web-children who were watching attentively. "You can't let them see you!" he told them. "They wouldn't understand. They're evil, all of them. They'd come here with guns! I've told you about guns. This time we make an exception, but never again. It isn't safe."

He looked at us almost apologetically. "They're only curious," he said. "It's hard sometimes, to stop them investigating everything. The Island, our species, we fascinate them."

"You've lived with them—"

"Twenty years now. Best years of my life. My children." He glanced about him. "I suppose you should come in."

The inside of the wickerwood tree-boil was surprisingly spacious, although we all had a difficult time staying put against the sloping walls. Eventually we were all sitting with our knees touching, which was what the web-children apparently thought was comfortable.

"Bring us something to drink!" Trethowan shouted out. Some of the web-children told him to go get it himself, but another scampered out to find something.

"You are their master?" Kiera enquired.

"No such luck," Trethowan said. "If I was their master you'd be feeding the fishes. Teacher, perhaps. Mascot. Revered uncle." A thoughtful look, which from his behaviour to date I judged to be uncharacteristic, crossed his face. "Uncle. That's close enough. Nature as mother, evolution as father, but me as a favourite uncle." His features relaxed back into their scowl. "They should listen to me more. They can't go showing themselves to Islanders just because they feel like it. They don't understand how evil and violent you are."

"Not all of us," I pointed out. "We're on the same side. We have the same enemies."

"Every human being has the inclination and the capability to destroy without conscience or remorse," Trethowan declared sharply. "The only variable is how deeply it's buried. Don't look down on the thugs of the Island. You're all like that. It just takes the right stimulus."

"And what about you?" Kiera pointed out acidly.

"I'm as much of a bastard as the next man. Or woman," Trethowan shot back.

"And they're so different, are they?" she asked, jabbing a thumb at the nearest web-child which was watching her with huge, blank eyes.

Trethowan shrugged, deflating somewhat. "Oh, they can be little turds when they want to be. Murderous little shits, no innocents here. But different? Yes! Happier with what they have, willing to live with their environment, not tear it down and burn it up. And they don't have guns, and even if they did they probably wouldn't butcher anyone who looked odd to them. That's why I can't let the Island know."

"But people already know that there are web-children," I said.

"They know that some kind of strange, man-shaped animal exists, and they've borrowed the name I gave them, way back. 'So what?' they say. If they know how many, or that my children hunt and craft and build – and speak! – what then? Would they still sit around on their artificial Island and say, 'So what?' No, they would not."

"They'd be scared," Thelwel said.

"They'd be genocidal. And that's the difference, if you want it. Get a hundred Outriders with muskets out here, they'd be an extinction event for these people. A thousand web-children have been quite happy leaving the Island to fester. Bastards they may be, but not monsters like we are. Ah." Trethowan's eyes lit up a bit as a web-child entered, juggling some large gourds. "Now this makes living in a swamp the very thing, I can tell you."

The gourds contained a kind of liquor that managed to be both gaggingly bitter and sickeningly sweet in quick succession, and was as thick as engine grease. It had a tremendous kick that waited long enough that you assumed each time that you had grown immune to it. It was remarkably good after the third swallow.

I saw Peter decanting some into his little flask. "What is this stuff?" he wanted to know.

"Insides of the gourd, left in the sun, in water, seven days," a web-child told him. "Treated with oils, nine grasses, two flowers. A secret."

"You taught them to speak," I noted to Trethowan.

"I first ran into them some forty years back, on an expedition," Trethowan told me. When narrating his exploits his tone was less confrontational. "And I swear, ten years before that there wasn't anything like them. They had a language even then, basic concepts, food, fight, fear and so on – just sounds that meant things. They were ready, though. I struck out into the jungles without my assistants, just some web-children for company. I taught them words. I talked to them. The next year I came back and they were all speaking a little, and they had started making up words for things I hadn't named. It was as though I'd thrown some switch inside all of 'em at once. They were *becoming*, like some part of nature had got hold of the plans from me and was moulding itself until it could look me in the eye. They were desperate to learn, to name things. What I taught the few I met, they taught their village, and that village taught the next. When I came out here, I thought I'd be king of the swamp. I had an idea to set myself up as chief, a one-man colonisation. But they wouldn't do what I said, and then I realised that I didn't have a right to tell them. Because I'd been trying to turn them into us, and can you imagine any more stupid a goal for a man of science? They've taken what I gave them and evolved it. Did more with it than I ever had. You've read my last notes."

"I'm working my way through them," I said, and explained my arrangement with the Governor. "I'm some way from the end."

"Longer than you know. I never finished them," he said, and laughed at my horrified expression. "Just make it up. When you get that far you'll know more than anyone else in the world but me. You'll bring it to some kind of conclusion."

Peter appeared to have fallen asleep, and Kiera was leaning back, watching Trethowan narrowly. Thelwel took no real part in the discussion, which left most of the work to me. Given this, and our surroundings, the topic moved onto evolution, and Trethowan grudgingly consented to save me a lot of reading by elaborating on his theory.

"The Earth has had enough of us, Stef," he explained. "Humankind: what have we accomplished? We've hastened the end, that's all. We poisoned the Earth so much we've got one shabby city left to call our own. Some historians even think we tinkered with the sun! You hear that? Some great golden age, way back, where everything ran off sunlight, until there wasn't enough to go round and so they fooled with the sun, and that's what our problem is now. Typical human stupidity. Nobody ever looks to tomorrow. Thank God we're on the edge of extinction – not before time, pissant bloody species that we are. The world is sick of us. It's turning over in its sleep, trying to come up with something to replace us. Evolution on wingéd feet! I didn't believe it, but I'm a bloody scientist. I'm the last real scientist on Earth. When the evidence says something strongly enough, you have to believe it, even though it goes against everything all the ancients ever wrote. Bugger the ancients! They got us into this mess in the first place. Evolution, all that slow struggle, generation to generation, millions of years, all that, out of the window! The Earth knows it hasn't got much time left. It's thrown the whole machine into high gear. And you know what it's after? Intelligence! You'd think it'd have had enough of the damn stuff after our messing around, but the evolution mill is grinding towards intelligence. Everywhere you look there's something doing an impression of it. Everything is trying to be smarter. Intelligence could maybe just save life on this planet. That's why the web-children. That's why lots of things."

"Or maybe this is human work too?" I suggested. Trethowan glowered at me and spat eloquently for an answer, but I pressed on. "What if someone released something, some chemical or agent to help matters along?"

"I won't have it," he growled. "I know mankind. Man is selfish. Man will brook no competition. No man would do such a thing, at the expense of his own species."

"What if it was a man like you?" I asked, and his face went slack. I had silenced the great scholar, if only for a few heartbeats. He stared at me, and then his eyes slid over to the handful of web-children still in attendance.

"So they're noble savages gone back to a state of nature?" I suggested lazily.

Trethowan snorted. "You need to wash that Academy education out of your head, boy. "Noble? Only compared to us, argumentative little bastards. But not savages. There's only one species I reserve that for, and it's not theirs."

"They are related to us, surely," I pressed. "The web-children must be human stock. From a long time ago, obviously, but the similarities…"

"I thought that," Trethowan allowed. "Some mutant offshoot of man. No, though. They came down another road. Listen to me: their children – the web-children's children – have gills until they're grown. They regrow their teeth. They have no mammaries." He leered at Kiera. "No breasts!"

"I went to school. I know what mammaries are," she told him icily.

"Lucky you, I barely remember!" Trethowan said, and cackled at his own wit. "One thing I've missed, the last twenty years living out here. No breasts! No, Stef, the web-children aren't us. They just look like us – some kind of convergent evolution maybe? They're not the only ones getting smarter, either. They're the best, though, my web-children."

"'So what are you in for?'" I said, to myself, and he stared at me sharply.

"Who have you been talking to?" he murmured.

Kiera had picked up on my question, though. "What are you in for? What got the great Trethowan banged up?"

"My web-children." The creases and wrinkles of his face rearranged themselves into a grim and solemn look. "It was before I perfected my understanding of the worthlessness of mankind. After my twelfth expedition I tried to tell them back home what was happening. The world is changing, I said. I'd forgot what a horror of change they all had. Arguments with the Academy Masters. There might have been a fistfight, now I think about it. They had me on the prison boat so fast I barely had time to see Shadrapar recede into the distance. Didn't want to believe. Didn't want to know. Bastards. Some people just don't want to hear the truth."

"Tell me about it," I agreed, which led on to my own tale of woe, in considerably more detail than I had told it before, and somewhat the worse for drink. Trethowan found the idea of Helman's mind powers fascinating. I saw, through the alcohol and general crabbiness, the brilliant scholar whose books were still required reading.

"I would have liked to meet this Helman," he said. "He had a brain. Silly bugger. You should never show people you have a brain."

"Tell me about it," I repeated, heartfelt. A pause then, Peter snoring quietly in the background. "Trethowan—"

"Ignaz, Stef. Might as well."

"Ignaz, then... you're not how I imagined you."

"Dead, you mean?"

"I thought that you would be more... studious."

He spat again. "Bugger studious. You can't tramp about in deserts and jungles being studious. Studious is for people who stay at home and do sod all except read other people's books and write critiques. You and me, Stef, we're men of action. Practical men. 'How to Save the World' indeed. You don't save the world by being studious."

Trethowan, then: hard drinker, lecher, prone to temper tantrums, sarcasm, spite and dirty jokes and, despite all evidence to the contrary, still alive. Not as I imagined him at all.

The web-children slept in hammocks made from vines, and so did we, although not well. I remember staying up long into the night talking to Trethowan, although very little more of what was said stays with me. He continued to call me Stef, and by the end of it I think I was calling him Iggy. Even Thelwel gave up and went to sleep before I did. The drink made me forget my bruises and my predicament, and I was able to talk freely about the most abstract of subjects with someone who understood.

Of course, in the morning I had a thundering headache to worry about, and all the bruises were back. It was a very late hour when I actually fell bodily from my hammock, and then only because Peter was shaking me.

"What?" I croaked. "What is it?"

"The webbies say there's a boat scouting about. Your old man's going wild, saying we've brought the Island down on him. Get up. We need you to sweet talk him."

I felt that if I tried to sweet talk anyone my tongue would fall out, but I crawled from the building, dropped bonelessly into the puddle below and then staggered over to see what the fuss was about. Kiera and Thelwel were already up, looking alert and ready to go. I could only envy them.

"What?" I demanded, shading my eyes.

"The bloody Islanders are out in force, Stef," Trethowan snapped out. "All over the bloody place. Looking for you, are they?"

"It's too early," I complained, and before anyone could have a go at me I added, "Too early for a real search. We were due to be out two clear days, so unless I've slept longer than I think then they shouldn't be after us until this evening at the earliest. What is going on?"

"They're after something, and it better not be me," Trethowan stated. "I think you and your people better get out there and see what they want."

"Let's get moving," Peter said. "We'll flag down a boat. Come on."

"One moment," Kiera interrupted, even as Peter shouldered the Junker and hung his sword on his belt. "Mister Trethowan?"

"What is it?"

She paused a second before crossing the line. "I should like to stay here with you."

"No way," Peter said instantly, just as I was saying, "Out of the question." Trethowan's eyes narrowed suspiciously, as though he was being taken advantage of.

"If you'd listen to me," Kiera said, cutting Peter and me off. "I'm walking dead on the Island as soon as anyone cares to remember me, and you two can't protect me from either the Wardens or the inmates if I get thrown to them. Which is only a matter of time. I've been living under a sentence of death for over a month now. I can't go on with it."

"You can't survive out here," I protested.

"Trethowan does. He can show me how. I'd rather scrape out a living with the web-children than go back to face the Witch Queen."

"This is crazy," Peter complained, and rounded on Trethowan. "Will you say something, then?"

Trethowan was looking oddly uncertain, at a loss at what to do with the situation. "Not my choice," he said shortly. "Not my decision." He turned his head to look over the crowd of web-children gathered about. "They won't like it," he confided. "It'll upset them." He raised his voice abruptly. "She wants to stay with us!"

There was an instant murmur of piping voices expressing their interest. With them all talking at once, to each other and at us, it was difficult to make out what the balance of opinion was.

"There you have it. Not a chance," Trethowan declared. "You have to go back. Not a chance of it."

Even as he was saying it, there was a chorus of high complaints saying that he had it wrong and that (most of) the web-children would be only too happy to have Kiera join them. Trethowan scowled around at them, but they paid him very little heed.

"Well only until we can think of something better to do with you," he muttered unwillingly. "Besides, you'll never last. You'll be after your civilised comforts in two days, and then what do we do with you? And what do Stef and company say about you? The Islanders better not come looking for you."

"Simple enough." Kiera had been putting the plan together the previous evening, while Trethowan and I talked and drank. "They show the boat wreck, and say I was eaten by a monster. I'm borrowing your own story, but it's plausible enough. The Witch Queen will be over the moon when she hears. You three should get your stories straight. She'll want to hear it from you in person."

"Thanks a lot," Peter muttered.

"But she won't have any reason to hate you, Peter, and she won't be able to use me against you, Stefan, and so everyone wins."

"I don't win," Trethowan pointed out. "I have no damn wish to spend any more time with human beings." He did not sound quite as emphatic as he might have done, though. I think the evening spent talking with his own kind had uncovered some long-buried needs in him. Humans are social animals.

"I'm here to stay," Kiera decided, and that was that. Peter and I both did our utmost to dissuade her, but she had made up her mind, and the only ones who could have changed it were the web-children themselves. They were only too pleased to have something new to study.

Some of their scouts came through soon to say that the Island boats were still all over the place, and it was obvious that we would have to make our move. Even as Peter and Thelwel gathered up our few possessions, one of the web-children approached us. I found it next to impossible to tell one from another, but I assume it was one who had sat in the background as Trethowan and I reminisced.

"Stefanadvani," it said, with a pronunciation eerily like that other speaking animal Below. "May I show something for you?"

I nodded cautiously.

"If you will," the creature said, and closed its protuberant eyes. The webs of its hands closed up into fists, and I was about to ask what it thought it was doing when I felt it. It was like the skeleton of a dry leaf across my mind, but it was there, the faintest force of a web-child mind being projected beyond its skull. I remembered reeling out my sorry story for Trethowan, all of Helman's doomed venture, with the web-children listening, forgotten, behind us. Trethowan had told me how they had seized on our language, and I wondered if I had done the same thing. Did they all have the machinery to muster that inner force, lying dormant just waiting for someone to tell them it could be done?

"Very good," I told the web-child hoarsely. Peter was calling for me then, and I had to leave.

When we returned to our ruined craft there was already a boat lazily circling the area. As it arrowed in towards us across the murk of the water, I saw Peter regretfully empty out his flask. "Had to," he said. "People would have asked. Spoil your man Trethowan's secret." He shrugged. "I'll just have to get some more when I come to see how Kiera's doing. You're with me for that trip, right?"

I agreed that I was, as the boat coasted up, nose butting the bank.

"What the hell happened to you?" Red demanded from its deck. A few gestures at the buckled wreck and the monstrous bones (all that were left after a night's scavenging) told it all.

"The Governor wants you back now," Red told Peter. "Boat's due, and he thinks there might be passengers with business for you. I'm really sorry, Peter."

Peter swore, outmanoeuvred. He clasped the hilt of the Ropa blade like a talisman. "Let's go meet the people," he decided.

We could see the bulk of the prison ship lumbering its way across the lake even as we moored. The dock was alive with prisoners dragging up the month's catch of produce and Peter, Thelwel and I stood to watch the bustle, waiting to see what new surprise the Anteims had despatched. Red had gone off to inform the Governor that the guest of honour was not going to miss the feast after all.

"If some big-shot duellist steps off that boat," Peter decided, "I'm going to gut him there and then, and serve him right."

"The Marshal will have you then," I pointed out.

"If neither of you mind, I will go and find my father," Thelwel announced, a little awkwardly because none of this was his fight.

"Your secret is safe," I told him.

He nodded. "Good luck," he wished Peter, "if possible." Then he was slipping through the labouring prisoners and away.

The hulking iron ship pulled alongside the dock. As soon as the gap had closed, the new compliment of prisoners was herded off as the chemicals were loaded on, and more care was taken over the latter. Peter and I waited anxiously, looking over the deck for anyone other than a crewman or a new inmate. To our surprise and relief there was nobody: no new challenge came, no further vengeance of the Anteims. In retrospect we should have worried more about the absence than the presence. Peter had now added Bewley Anteim's death to the tally of Jon the Younger. It was inconceivable that they would have closed the account. Nonetheless, no emissary of death manifested itself, only that tired line of shabby prisoners.

I fixed on one, a man far too old to be out in the baking, humid air, crowded in by his fellows. His prison greys were loose on him, and at every moment it seemed that he would just collapse in a tangle of bony limbs. He raised his long face to the bruised sun and I knew him at once.

"Peter," I said urgently. "The old man, with the beard and the long hair, you have to get him into my cell."

"Oh, what?"

"Peter, please," I insisted. "I know him. He's a friend of mine from… from the city. He's very weak. He'll never survive without help."

"Well I'll see what I can do. You make yourself scarce before they get you loading sacks."

Peter went to stand with the other Wardens waiting to lead prisoners off, as someone began to call out names. Before I could get below, I was indeed collared and made to shift sacks, and so when the voice shouted out, "Arves Martext!" I was unable to see who got to lead him off. When I got back to my cell for the evening meal, though, there he was, hunched and bewildered in a corner, staring with trepidation at Gaki. I knelt beside the old man, Arves Martext, and asked him how on earth he came to be there, for he had not left the Underworld in ten years and had sworn that he would die there. He was Emil des Schartz' friend, the collector of books, and the story of how he came to be imprisoned with us was a sign of the end of the world.

PART THE FOURTH

MY LIFE IN THE UNDERWORLD

28

Ward of the Temple

I need to write about the Underworld now, both because of Arves' testimony and because it is important for later on. Cast your mind back now to that fear-ridden night in Emil des Schartz' ruined printing shop.

It was gone midnight before the man came to us. It was a long, strained wait. Emil cranked out posters for an illegal knife-fight. I made hot drinks and watched the night draw on, dreading the sight of the sun. The Angels were after me and I needed darkness to hide myself in. If I was caught, I reckoned it would be the Island for me. The fullness of time, of course, proved me right.

He came out of one of the foul mists that occasionally rise from the river, and it was impossible to see anything but a long, vague shape until he was very close. When he did reach the door he had to feed himself through it a limb at a time.

"Sergei," said Emil, a shade nervously. "Stefan, this is Sergei. Sergei, I'd like you to meet Stefan Advani."

He was surely the most freakish sight I'd seen to that point, in a life not lacking. He always claimed to be six feet tall, and yet he was taller than Trethowan by a good foot and a half, making somewhere over eight. Perhaps his feet were bigger. This incredible height was supported by a long-boned and spidery frame mostly bundled in his great coat. There were a few stars and ribbons on the front that I did not recognise, stabs of colour against the drab olive green. His face, which was trapped between the high collar of his coat and an odd kind of peaked cap, was the palest I ever saw. I have seen dead people with more colour in their cheeks, and even the web-children had a healthier skin tone. Sergei's face was long-jawed with brooding eyes and hollow cheeks on which an unfashionable bristle of stubble showed startlingly dark.

He looked down at me and said, "Why do I need to meet Stefan Advani?" His voice was more disorienting than his appearance, because he spoke very strangely. The thought occurred to me even then that he was a foreigner, not used to our language, but that was absurd. There was nowhere a foreigner could have come from and there was no other language still extant in the world. Even so, Sergei spoke awkwardly, and often had to reach for words and concepts. When he was under stress he had his own speech: a heavy, murmuring tongue unfamiliar to everyone.

He had a story to explain all of this. I cannot bring myself to believe it, but I will let you make up your own mind in due course. At the time I assumed he was a failed product of one of the cosmetics labs.

"Stefan is a fugitive," Emil told him. "He needs to go to ground."

"You vouch for him?" Sergei intoned. "The Meat Packers only yesterday hung up an Authority spy. Nobody is glad to see new faces right now."

"He's no spy," Emil assured him. "They got three of his friends a while ago. Now the Angels are after him."

Sergei stalked over to me. He would become a friend in the Underworld but at the time he terrified me. "You want there?" he asked.

"I… have nowhere to go. No money. Nothing," I told him timorously. "If there is anywhere you can take me where the Angels do not go, I have to take that chance."

"Good." That pale visage swung back to Emil. "You have my goods?"

Emil gave him the handbills hurriedly and Sergei counted out a fair price.

"What will you do with those?" I tried.

"Have them distributed. Get the message to the people." For a moment he looked deadly serious but then he smiled, and it gave his face a mischievous and altogether more human aspect. "A pastime only. Come, if you're coming."

He hunched himself through Emil's doorway and poled out into the street. Emil wished me luck as I turned to follow. "I'll see you again, if you last," he told me.

I had to run to keep up with Sergei's easy stride, and anyone looking out of their window would perhaps have seen a father and child taking a late stroll. Within twenty minutes, there was nobody to look out, because Sergei had taken a turn into a deserted stretch of city where the wells had dried. Nobody lived there, or at least nobody official. There was enough of Shadrapar still watered to house its population twice over. This derelict stretch was home only to the destitute and the outcast. I knew that the Angels made regular sweeps for business and pleasure. It was no place to hide. I put on an extra burst of speed to catch up with Sergei and asked him, "Where are we going?"

"Underneath," he told me. "The Underworld. You did not know this?"

"Well, yes, but… I never really knew it was real. It was just a story."

"The Authority likes it that way. They keep the people ignorant. If people knew that there was place to live, outside the Authority, who would want to stay? Revolution!"

The last word was shouted out loud enough to echo from the abandoned walls. Something shifted to our left and I saw a man sitting atop a cairn of fallen stones. He had a foot of knifeblade in one hand and watched us narrowly.

"Castor," Sergei named him. "All quiet?"

"As a grave," the man agreed, lingering over the last word. "Who's your friend?"

"Someone will find a use for him," Sergei replied.

We passed on with a thousand questions boiling in my mind, most of which were destined to go unvoiced. I had to deal with essentials first.

"What do you mean, a use?" I asked him.

"Underworld is a mess of factions. You must find someone who can use you, or what might happen? Dangerous place, underneath."

"Can you use me? What's your faction?" To be honest I wasn't so sure about Sergei, but who else did I know?

"I am Executive Officer of People's Collective," Sergei told me with pride. "We have all the workers we can feed. Hard work, too. I am not sure you would like it." Friends later, as I say, but at the time I think he didn't like me much.

"How many people in these factions?" I asked him.

"In Collective? Nineteen," he told me. "Others, thirty, fifty, seventy staff. Some only five, six. Very few people on their own. Someone will have use for you. You get three days' grace."

"How?"

"In the Temple: rules say every new face gets three days in the Temple. Make sure someone like you before then, or Organ Donor Boys will get you."

I wanted to ask him what the Temple was and what the rules were. I wanted to ask him who the Organ Donor Boys were and what hard work was undertaken by the People's Collective. I had so many questions I choked on them, and had to save my breath for keeping up with Sergei.

When I next opened my eyes it was to the star-studded sky, but the constellations were all wrong and some of them were on the blink. Between me and the firmament a kind of shimmering, dancing sheet of light crackled and skipped, changing colour and leaping from one edge of the sky to another. Then something like a monstrous spider cast in brass and tin crawled its way across the heavens and I screamed and sat up, because I desperately needed some idea of scale.

A face came into view as I sat up, considerately blocking most of my surroundings. It was a relatively comforting face: a woman's, round and weathered and webbed with lines. Her dark hair was cut unfashionably short, and she was ten or fifteen years my senior.

"Easy now," she said, and I felt her hands on my shoulders.

"Where am I?"

"Let's take things one foot at a time," she suggested, and another voice, weirdly inflected, called out, "He's awake then. Is he mad yet?"

"Not yet," the woman replied.

I remembered the second speaker's name and said, "Sergei," and the last night's events came back to me. "I was going underground," I remembered. "What happened?"

"You pass out on me," I heard Sergei say. "Just fell down. When did you last sleep?"

I thought back. Some time back in the Wasted God Convent. It seemed a long time ago.

The woman drew back slightly, and I saw that I was in a room designed as a simple spherical cavity, lined in metal. Two-thirds of the way down, someone had laid a new floor of jaggedly-cut plastic slabs. I let my eyes wander up. The walls were impressed with many designs that might have been decorative, or inconceivably complex and long-deceased control panels and indicators.

"This is the Temple," the woman told me. "And I am its priest for the time being, and was named Giulia Nostro."

I mumbled my own name, and then, "This does not look like a temple."

"What it was once, we don't know," Sergei intoned. "Now it is Temple. The heart of Underworld."

I saw him standing out near the edge of the pirated floor. His impossibly tall, emaciated frame brought back a lot more of my recent past.

"What is it a temple of?" I asked, craning my neck. Above was that artificial starfield, lights moving and reconfiguring as I watched, whilst that fabulous electrical discharge whirled and jumped about the bronze ring that marked the sky's edge a hundred feet above us. The Temple was huge. The spider patiently inching its way across the vault of heaven was as large as I was.

"What the hell is that?" I got out before my previous question was even answered.

"The Caretaker," Giulia replied.

"What does it take care of?" I demanded, and Giulia said, "That," and pointed behind me. I got to my knees as I turned about, which turned out to be appropriate. Before the three of us, fixed halfway up the curving wall, there was... Even now it is hard to do it justice. It was a white bubble, lit from within by a fierce argent light. Some kind of clear plastic had formed it, hollow or solid we could not tell. It was not empty, though. Through the cloudy white light there was the silhouette of a man – a giant taller than Sergei, heroically proportioned and just as naked. Through the light and the bubble's distortion no more details could be made out, but it was an awe-inspiring thing.

"This is Temple of the Last Day," Sergei pronounced. "And that is the Coming Man. They have their own mythology down here in the dark."

"It is said that the Coming Man will descend from his state

to save Shadrapar, when the end is nigh," Giulia said. "I don't believe it personally, but it's up to you."

"I thought you were the priest," I said to her, still staring at the imprisoned giant.

"Purely a transient and secular position. I'm the representative of the Fishermen in the Temple. It's my turn to be priest."

"Too much," Sergei said, striding over to us. "Give to him a chance." He gave me his unnerving grin, showing far too many teeth. "Some go mad, coming down here. They cannot take the change. Pace yourself, or you join them. Nobody wants a mad man."

"Factions…" And the remaining dregs of the previous night came back to me. "You said I needed to get myself a faction."

"Three days," Sergei reminded me. "You get three days in Temple. Have yourself patronage by then, otherwise, out into the dark. Not good thing at all."

"How—" I started, and Giulia cut me off with, "Everyone comes here to do business. Even a few from Overworld who want our services. It all happens here. They'll see you. If they want you, they'll let you know. We have two other Wards of the Temple at the moment. You're not alone." She left me then and stood under the great burning orb itself, hunched over some kind of machine.

"How do you spell your name?" she asked, and I told her automatically.

"One of the duties of priesthood is maintaining Underworld's chronicle," Sergei said. "Everyone who arrives, who leaves, who dies; all agreements between factions. That is our law. It is the thing we must hold sacred or everything collapses. Each faction puts a priest up in turn, from the great to the very least. Abuse the power, they suffer next time round. I have been priest, too, in my time. Maybe you will be."

"If someone wants me," I said sullenly. "Otherwise I get thrown to the beasts."

"Underworld has its ways with people," Sergei agreed solemnly. "A use for everyone. Even if just as organs."

I looked up at the bizarre angles of him, as he hunched over me. "Thank you for staying this long," I told him.

"We are family, underground. We all have the same enemy: the sun, the surface. We fight amongst ourselves, but learn that we are family."

The machine that Giulia was using took her words as she murmured them and brought them up in elaborate silver handwriting on a dark mirror. After Sergei had gone to attend to the business of the Collective, she showed me how she could move her hands over the mirror to call up past records. There were thousands of them, stretching back forever, priest after priest, and before the priesthood, others who had needed to record their affairs, their thoughts, their ideologies. Far enough back and most of them were in extinct languages, some of which I knew, others wholly alien. The oldest were drawn in alphabets that I had never seen before.

"People have always used this machine," Giulia said. "The Caretaker has always maintained it."

"What maintains the Caretaker?" I asked her, and she shrugged.

Later, when I was ordained as priest (as I would be) I would spend long hours searching through those maddeningly incomplete records of the elder days to find out how the Underworld society came to be. It seemed to spring to life complete and in its current form, some three centuries before, and although the names and slogans changed, the basic structure had somehow endured. There were no clues. As for the other doggerel fragments from ancient times, a last will and testament, a battle plan, a message to a loved one, they were just rags of the past preserved in that uncanny machine.

"What is the Underworld?" I asked Giulia that first day

beneath the surface. "How is it here?" She told me that there had been a city on the site of Shadrapar for longer than anyone could know, and for all that time there had been excavations deep into the earth. Underworld was archaic transport systems, sewers and old conduits, shelters and war bunkers and concealed laboratories, cellars, buried storehouses and once-secure vaults. The Underworld people lived in only the uppermost sprawl of it. Below there was an uncharted and unending tangle of deeper chambers that were no longer the haunts of mankind and which had their own dark legends. There were expeditions sometimes. Giulia had a dream, I discovered, and it made her eyes shine with a mad fire. Giulia wanted to map it all.

"It must be finite," she said to me. "It can be done." From her tone, I had the impression that only she believed this.

Later, I witnessed my first Underworld deal, between the Meat Packers and the Friendly Society. The Meat Packers' agent was a woman too perfectly finished to be natural, right down to the carefully calculated deformity of her right arm. Behind her were two muscle-packed bruisers sporting their artificially tampered bodies like badges of allegiance. The Meat Packers ran a black market surgery, and the implications of this made me shudder. The Friendly Society, conversely, were thieves, raiders of surface Shadrapar. Their man was a stocky, dwarfish creature wearing rich clothes badly tailored. He was smoking something aromatic, the smell just a stronger version of the metal-and-incense reek of the Temple.

The deal between the Packers and the Friendlies was as swift as betting over cards, and just as guarded and merciless. Giulia arbitrated between them, and in the end the final bargain was sealed within the Temple's recording machine, thereby becoming law. Neither of the factions felt that I was recruitment material. The Meat Packers' factor just looked at me once and then turned away. The little brute from the Friendly Society laughed out loud and said he didn't want any failed book-boy in his crew, but he'd spread the word. I was not hopeful.

I asked Giulia whether her faction would take me. She told me that the Fishermen were scavengers, explorers. The depths belonged to the Fishermen and a few other bold factions. They fished for the relics of lost technology, and it was dangerous work. She told me that she didn't think I would cut it. She was as kind as she could be but it was another rejection, and time was getting short. I was on the second of my three days of grace, by then. Of my fellow refugees, one had been cast out already, his time up and no faction caring for him. The other, a lean, rugged ex-Outrider hiding from retribution for some dreadful crime, had been snapped up by Giulia's Fishermen, who had first call while she was priest. At the time, "fish" and "fisherman" were just words to me. I only understood the reference after being exiled to the swamps.

As it happened, I would accompany Giulia on a fishing expedition anyway. That comes later.

Food was brought to the Temple by Giulia's confederates. It was uniformly a kind of chewy white substance a little like bread or bean curd. When I asked what it was, Giulia told me it was a fungus that grew in vast myoculture caverns beneath us, tended only by the Fermers. I assumed at the time that the Fermers were a faction.

The day after, which was my last day as Ward of the Temple, there was something called the Bazaar. I had, by then, solicited eleven different factions, and they had all discarded me as insufficiently practical. It wasn't that they had no use for a man of letters, but none looked on me and saw a man who would survive their hard life. More, the learning they were most interested in was practical, mechanical. Anyone who could breathe life back into old machines was hotly sought after. Thelwel and his father would have done well there.

There were over a hundred factions comprising Underworld and most of them had turned out for the Bazaar, setting up stock in the Temple and the halls adjacent. It was a riot of noise, shouting and the occasional fist fight. No weapons, though: like the Temple, like all of their strange hand-me-down laws, the Bazaar was sacred. I saw that the Underworld would be better called the Between-world. It was strung out in a fragile lattice of old vehicle track, pipework and abandoned mines between sunlit Shadrapar and the unmanned depths.

You could find any treasure from up above in the stalls of the Bazaar, from food (a diet of fungus was tedious) to drugs, machinery, Academy tomes and toys, anything that could be stolen from the shining world over our heads. From the depths came ancient mechanisms and scrolls, plundered treasures, curios and junk. Much of it would find its way to the surface into the ever-revolving round of Shadrapan property. There were darker things, too: live Vermin and other creatures for the labs to experiment on; preserved organs ready for transplant, and probably not cooled from their original owners. I saw the gaily-bedecked stand of the Organ Donor Boys, their wares laid out in salvaged ammunition boxes. I saw the hungry eyes of the Boys themselves, half-hidden beneath the peaks of cloth caps, and a chill went through me.

The Bazaar was a hiring fair too: many of the factions provided services. There were bodyguards and thugs for the renting (I was particularly caught by the gaudy, illuminated armour of the Electric Gangsters and the implanted hand-knives of the Packer subsidiary, the Meat Carvers). Everything was ugly, dirty, torn, rusted and twisted, yet unashamed of it. Here was not the carefully engineered misshapenness of the very rich, but a natural grime, asymmetry and disfigurement. Nobody cared for that facade of manufactured decadence the Overworlders thought so vital. Above, the world was coming to an end, and one might as well face it with poise and dignity. In the Underworld, nobody thought of the apocalypse; the next day would be challenge enough.

And I traipsed from faction to faction trying to offer my services as an expert, as a scholar, as a willing pair of hands, and nobody cared. I grew tired of reciting my credentials, and made up a new set, and then another, grander than the last. They saw through me to the frightened product of a sheltered life, and turned their backs. I was rejected by explorers, agriculturists, vandals, surgeons, soldiers and thieves. I could feel my heartbeat quickening, air hitching in my lungs, the breath of the Organ Donor Boys on the back of my neck. I have never had such an acute sense of time draining away through my fingers, and no way to bring it back. I began to believe that my only future would be for sections of me to go on living within the tissues of strangers.

The factor for Altameir's Crew, who were scavengers of Shadrapar Above's abandoned quarters (and therefore had few entrance requirements) told me I was overqualified, and anyway the scavenging business had been better and another mouth to feed would bankrupt them. The Bazaar was drawing to a close. I could see empty places everywhere, all sold up. People were beginning to disassemble their stalls and load their carts, ready for the journey home. I saw the knifeblade shape of Sergei within the crowd and tried to battle my way towards him, to plead with him to take me in. Instead, the current of the crowd whisked me aside, because it was making room for something new.

I met a lot of outlandishly tall people in the Underworld. Even Arves was taller than me. This newcomer was short of Sergei's height, but not by much, and within the dark and dusty shroud that served him as a robe, there was at least twice as much breadth. He was an odd shape in there, angles and projections as though he had bulky equipment strapped to his body. The robe was huge enough to hide four men or a multitude of sins.

Despite his height he was hunchbacked, so much so that I wondered if it was cosmetic. The hump overshadowed his bald head and brought his shoulders up higher than his ears. The one hand that dangled from a flapping sleeve must have belonged to a freakishly elongated arm, fingers hooked into a claw. He had an odd-shaped skull, long and swept-back, ears, nose and mouth all oddly delicate. His eyes were hidden behind panels of smoked glass, and from his feeling his way through the crowd I wondered if he was blind. He looked right at me, though. I was rooted to the spot. He seemed almost to unfold before me until he was craning down, bringing that face exactly to the level of my own, the shabby dark fabric of his robe curtaining out most of the world.

I had the instant understanding that everyone knew him and nobody had expected him there.

"That's the one," a voice declared, and I caught a glimpse, about the robe's edge, of the Friendly Society's agent. He had, after all, passed the word around.

The stiff claw of a hand latched onto my shoulder. It felt like a dead thing, locked in rigor mortis.

"What is your name, boy?" The lips barely moved, the sound wheezing out from some bellows deep inside. I gave my name unwillingly; I could not hold it back.

"Are you still unspoken for, Advani?" said a voice like the wind in forgotten places.

I thought of the Organ Donor Boys and made a decision. I told him I was.

"I will take you," the creature, the hunched and distorted man, declared. "I was named Greygori Sanguival, and I will take you as my own."

I had no wish to bind myself to this thing but, as I looked around, I saw something in the eyes of the spectators. They were afraid of this man, and by association they would stay away from me. In the service of Greygori Sanguival I would live in fear of him, but no other. It would be security, at a price.

"Then I am yours," I told my own reflection, doubled and smudged in the darkness of his glasses.

He seldom came out, Giulia told me later. He had not needed an agent before because he had been more socially presentable; more human. The Underworlders had their own name for Greygori Sanguival. They called him the Transforming Man.

29

The Lost Soldier and the Transforming Man

He wore the dark glasses in preparation for later developments. Behind them, his eyes were surprisingly human, with irises the colour of rusty steel.

Much later, I met an old man who remembered Greygori Sanguival from a long time before. "Weird little man," the ancient told me. "Always running about, like there wasn't enough time. Little fidgety man."

Greygori Sanguival was no longer little, although the robe hid the precise and current topography of his body. Despite the lurching and reaching for balance, he moved with a perilous grace, like a stilt-walker, as though any moment he would collapse in upon himself. He consumed a steady diet of chemicals to maintain the state and alignment of his body, and to foster further developments along his grand plan. 'Developments': that was his very mild word for them.

He was a real scientist. Trethowan would have approved of his methodology. The field of Greygori's study was Greygori. The Transforming Man was already a legend in a lifetime that had stretched over a century and a half. It was impossible to guess his age. It was difficult enough to guess his species.

"You are to perform such services as I should need of you," he told me, as he teetered through the tunnels of Underworld.

"Chiefly these will be dealing with the factions, procuring things I want. You will be my agent, you understand?"

I told him that I did, because I sensed that certainty was my best shield.

His aim, the dream into which, by carefully measured stages, he was transforming himself, was secret. His laboratory was the room into which none was allowed save the man himself. All he said was that mankind was doomed, and he intended to make himself into a shape that the world would permit to last.

He should have been a true monster, stalking the caverns of Underworld like a nightmare. Instead there was a flaw in his soul, some sliver of humanity he had not been able to pluck out. He recalled how he had been, feelings that existed in him only as memories of those memories. Striving towards his unspeakable goal, some part of him was yet jabbed by thoughts of all that he had cast away. A sculptor at the Academy once told me that she simply removed from her block of stone everything that was not like the thing she wanted. The Transforming Man had tried to serve himself in such a way, and now felt a keen wind course through the holes he had left. As his form grew monstrous, according to the minutes of his plan, so the reaction of even Underworld society had grown more towards revulsion, and it hurt him. Until this nagging splinter was removed, he would be forever haunted by the ghost of his forsworn former self. That was why the concealing robe. That was why the smoked glasses, for his eyes would soon enough be the eyes of something other than human. That was why he chose me. He no longer wished to go amongst the people of Underworld, just as, long ago, he had made the decision to eschew the surface. He needed a man to run his errands and gather the all-important components of his experiments. That was me.

There was definite cachet to being henchman (I can think of no better word) to the Transforming Man. I walked with impunity through Underworld. I had no badge, but they knew me for what I was. Perhaps some spectre of my master clung to me, tainting the air with his amorphous shadow. Once, three thugs were on the very point of knifing me, up against a wall, grim and efficient as ever the Marshal would be, when one of them saw my face and gasped out, "It's Sanguival's man!" and they ran off and left me alone. They all knew that the Transforming Man would avenge any damage done to his property.

Whilst I was the acceptable face of Sanguival on the outside, the chores within Greygori's little suite of chambers were done by the only other member of his faction. This was Arves Martext, Emil des Schartz's bookish associate.

He was probably a year short of fifty, by his reckoning, but looked far older. In a city where the rich could afford to stretch their straining lifespans to eighteen decades and more, Arves aged. He told me that exposure to the bloated, dying sun caused his body to consume itself, burning away into premature senescence. Bad debts and worse chances had led him down here, but in the darkness he aged only as others did, bit by bit rather than all at once. He was bound to the Underworld with cords as strong as his life.

The Transforming Man's suite of chambers included his ever-sealed laboratory, several small rooms that Arves and I used to sleep in (Greygori slept in the lab, if indeed he slept) and a library. This had originally held Greygori's files, and these still occupied one wall, tens of thousands of loose-leaf sheets crammed with a handwriting that changed markedly as the notes progressed. The rest of the room had been taken over by Arves' collection. He was still a man fired by books and had only increased the breadth of his reading since going underground. He surely owned more works than any other single individual in Shadrapar. Social sciences, physical sciences, satires, translated fiction of the ancients (which may have been fact, it was impossible to tell) and of course, shelves and shelves of critiques. He loved to read and to be surrounded by books, all that dormant knowledge like a warm, protective garment. He loved to run his hands over the spines. They were his life.

When I came along, I managed to broaden his life a little, in between my errands. I bartered for a shoddy chess set. It was nostalgia on my part, thinking back on my games with Helman, but Arves remembered how to play, and we sat for long hours pushing pieces across the board with an equal lack of skill.

Then, of course, Greygori discovered us playing one night. We froze up as that blinkered visage loomed suddenly in the doorway to the library, and he swung over to us, a long breath hissing out between his teeth. One hand reached down with an alien articulation and touched one of the pieces delicately.

I think he was remembering some distant sunlit time when a smaller man of more orthodox shape had enjoyed a game of chess.

After that, I played against him too, about once every two weeks when the mood took him. That remaining hook of humanity would haul him from his researches and we would play and talk. Once our miniature armies were stumbling across the board, words came out of him. It was the most he had spent in one room with another human being for a long time, and so he talked. Small talk, meaningless talk: he never spoke of his researches nor the politics of the factions that dominated Underworld chatter. He spoke of points of history and etymology, landmarks of the Upperworld, Masters he had known at the Academy (like Arves and myself he had studied there). It was all talk that would be diverting and reassuringly normal, had not the speaker been such a thing as he. I had the impression that it was only that last human vestige talking; the remainder of his augmented brain was elsewhere, plotting its own ascension.

The economy of Underworld worked on three levels. First was barter. Everyone who had something was best advised to find someone who needed it, and had something useful in exchange. Everyone who wanted something should get hold of something else worth having. It was a system that worked moderately well for day-to-day transactions, small items, low values. There were the obvious drawbacks (what if the person who has what you want, wants nothing you have?) but it was the easiest way to do anything. It was really only the next logical step to the migratory circling of Upperworld property as it was leant out and borrowed endlessly.

Secondly there was money, which was required by anyone who dealt with the surface – a surprising number of the factions had shady little deals going on in sun-side Shadrapar. Money was of relatively little use in the Underworld proper. People were only interested in trading for something that had a value in and of itself, rather than an abstract. Coins became another thing to barter for, if you needed to deal with the people above.

Finally, there was the rather arcane notion of credit. Let us say that a big deal was taking place, like the one I witnessed between the Meat Packers and the Friendly Society. In that case the Friendlies were to procure some hundred measures of a recreational drug from a surface pharmaceutical bar. If the Packers wanted to pay by barter then the Friendlies would have been taking an awful lot of bric-a-brac off with them. Instead, they used the idea of credit. The priest of the Temple would assign an agreed value to the Friendly Society's efforts, and this would be logged in the Temple's recording machine as a debt owed to them by the Packers.

Ah, you say, a debt – you've heard that one before. In the Underworld, though, the Temple ensured that debts were honoured. A member of the Friendly Society could go to the Meat Packers any time later and demand services, goods, whatever was available. They would go to the Temple again, and the priest would broker an agreed value to be taken off the debt. Had it been left to fallible human hands it would undoubtedly have failed. The Temple machine, however, could remember the state of every single debt, great and small, new or centuries old. Indeed, a vast amount of debt-trafficking went on within the machine, so that great sums could change hands without anything *physical* happening at all. It could even tell, in some mysterious way, who had recorded each transaction: frauds could be tracked down. Perhaps it read their hands as they touched its mirror. It should be obvious that, glowing frozen giant or not, the Coming Man was not what the Temple was about. The machine was all.

Sergei had a name in his own tongue for the Temple machine, translating as "something which reckons" – a poor phrase for such a marvel. According to Sergei they had these machines where he came from, albeit of a complexity several orders of magnitude less.

Sergei had a lot to say about where he was from. There, he claimed, everyone was as tall as he, and many were as pale (although none so thin, I think). Where he came from, the story ran, was the past.

"I am soldier," he told me. "Where I come from, we were at war. Not the wars you think of, not a killing war. We had only just got over the last killing war. This was hidden war. Spies, economics, a war of face. My people were locked in deadly struggle against our enemies. We stockpiled weapons, always deadlier. We must show the other side our science is better, or they think us weak and then everyone must use those weapons. They try many experiments…"

Here he paused. We were in the rooms of his Collective, drinking a liquor that his people refined from mould.

"We try anything that may help. Men study the mind, strange energies, travel into space. Then there is my project, for which I am test pilot. Top secret: only one man outside it knew. A time experiment. Travel in time, you control history. We make the war as though it never was. That was what we dream.

"We have many failures: dogs, pigs, mice. Some go nowhere. Others die from the radiations. Some disappear. Maybe they travel, who can say? We could not bring them back. In the end the project was to be shut down. We were very bitter. We want one last test."

"I was volunteer. No family, no-one to miss me. The project was life, to me. We made a machine to take a man into time, forward one hour. Easy test. If things go wrong, machine has controls so that I make it return. I was trained as space-pilot. I never got into space. Instead, I would be the first man in time.

"Obviously something goes wrong," he stated flatly. "Calculations or machinery or something. I am here, where not one soul remembers my people or what we fought for. How did war end? Who can say? I am here at arse of time with little people, with foreign language, with illness."

"And the machine?"

"Past hope. Destroyed." Sergei took a long swallow of his drink. "Did not make the journey. I survived. I am not sure it was to be wished. I do not like this time." He slammed the empty glass down. "I am a cosmonaut of Union of Soviet Socialist Republics and I want to be in year nineteen-seventy-two, not in this time of ruins waiting for world to die. I want to be somewhere with hope."

None of it made much sense to me.

Sergei had joined up with the Morlocks first of all. They were a pro-active and impolite debt-recovery crew who put his imposing appearance to good use. He spent two years with them, getting a grasp of our language. Then he chanced upon a lost cavern where the ceiling had given way, exposing a long-abandoned business office above. The premises above sported several large and grimy skylights, and in the wan illumination of these, Sergei and his new-formed Collective farmed vegetables and dwarf fruit trees. This enabled him to extract a decent livelihood from the fungus-glutted palate of the Underworld. His Collective he ran as an equal partnership of all its members.

Sergei was always on the lookout for new ways to gain credit at the Temple. He had some expensive hobbies and habits. In his spare time he was working on a vast and intricate machine. He told me that he was trying to replicate the vehicle that had transported him. Others told me he had been working on it ever since they had known him, and it had done nothing but expand into a webwork of levers, cogs, generators, pistons and valves. He was known as the Watchmaker by some.

Sergei was sick, too. About three times in the span I knew him he went off to Aleisa's House, a faction of medical engineers. He said that he had his blood and bones completely purged there, a process that indebted him to the House a frightening amount. He said that our time was unhealthy for him, that there were high levels of energy and radiations and that it had taken its toll on him: that was why he was so thin. Even the light of the sun made his corpse-pale skin burn. Like Arves, he was a prisoner of the Underworld.

I discovered the truth about the Fermers when I arose too early one day. Blundering across the room to find a lamp, my hand brushed something soft and slightly leathery that twitched at my touch. I leapt back and fell over a chair that Arves had put out, left in pitch darkness with the knowledge that there was some *thing* loose in the room. The immediate thought was that it was some experiment of Greygori's got free.

I held my breath and waited, and heard faint, scuffing footsteps as the creature made its way around the room. It was moving away from me, so I made a careful progress in search of the lamp, walking each hand carefully forwards in case there were more things in the dark. After some fumbling, I got it lit.

In the light of the pale flame was revealed a stunted, dwarfish thing, approximately humanoid in shape but with no discernible features. It was a pale sepia in colour and there were little tendrils and feelers jutting from its lumpy body. It did not react to the light, but instead made its plodding progress towards one corner of the room, where it deposited an armful of the slabby fungus-food that was the Underworld staple.

Arves joined me, woken by the light.

"What is it?" I demanded of him, and he answered, "It's a Fermer. They grow the fungus."

I stared at him, not really understanding what he was saying.

"They live in the myoculture caves," he explained, as the squat little monster began shuffling back across the floor. "They're some experiment from times past. Someone wanted to be self-sufficient down here and engineered the Fermers. Whoever made them is long gone but the Fermers go on tending their crops just like they always have."

I shuddered as the malformed little thing stumped out of our rooms and away down the tunnels.

"It's free food," Arves said. "Mostly it goes to set places for distribution, but the Master has trained them to bring some directly here, somehow. He didn't want to have to go and fetch it. Where did you think the food came from?"

"I thought it just…" I had not thought about it. "But what are the Fermers? What do they eat? Why do they keep on giving us food?"

Arves spread his hands wide and yawned. "They're fungus-creatures. The Master dissected one once. They eat rot, the rot of the ages below and the rot we produce. As for the why, why not? They do it because it's what they do."

In between the varied tasks I undertook for Greygori, I found time for a little society. Underworld was different from above, in that everyone was visibly working to survive or promote their faction. There was not the veneer of leisure and civilisation that hid the workings of upper Shadrapar.

There were moments of quiet and contemplation, though. I remember one very clearly: a sunrise. Because our business in the world above needs must be conducted by darkness, we lived when the surface world slept, and crawled to our beds at dawn. So it was that, after a hard day for us all, we were sitting out in the shadow of a ruined building looking towards the east where a faint lightening of the sky was outlining the shapes of Shadrapar. Sergei was there, and Arves, Giulia Nostro and I. Sergei was already on good terms with the other two, and I fitted into their odd dynamic easily. We all had our odd obsessions and beliefs. Giulia had her maps of the Underworld that could never be finished. Sergei had his crazy invented past, and I had my dreams of saving the world through the energies of the mind. Superannuated Arves with his bibliomania and allergy to the sun was the most normal of all of us.

On that night we sat out in the slightly chill air (which Sergei complained was humid and too warm) and looked up at a cloudless sky. We had a bottle of harsh, clear spirits from Sergei's Collective, and Sergei had a gun, too: an old projectile pistol in case of Outriders. Outriders were one of the few external menaces in the Underworld, making forays into our delvings. There had been pitched battles between the Outriders and some of the larger factions. Most of the surface citizens had no idea such things went on.

There were no Outriders that night, and we were drawn there for respite from the intrigues beneath, and for the sun. A while in the darkness and you needed a glimpse of the sun. Even Arves and Sergei craved its light, who were its victims and its enemies. The four of us watched the ebbing night out, drank Sergei's keen alcohol and talked. Sergei asked whether Arves and I had discovered what Gregor Samsa (as he called Greygori; some private joke) was actually turning into. Giulia spoke of discoveries the Fishermen had made deep down. Arves recited some poetry he had acquired. I related a good joke I had heard from the Organ Donor Boys.

It was a happy time. It was not to last. Even so, I was allowed to put down the crushing burden of Helman's death, of Jon and

Rosanna's deaths. I was allowed to forget about the Angels' persecution. It was a healing time.

Then the light on the architectured horizon deepened and the sun shouldered its way up with the dogged grind of a lame man on a long journey. It had been months, and I had forgotten what it looked like. The deep red dawn shone across the buildings of Shadrapar to light Sergei's deep eyesockets and gaunt cheeks, touch the lines about Giulia's eyes and deepen Arves' wrinkles. Another morning in Shadrapar.

There was a precious sliver of time between the sluggish appearance of the sun and the city's awakening. In that span we watched the light creep into every corner of the waking city, brightening from that deep chemical red to something like old, scratched gold. By then Sergei was already feeling the scorch of it and Arves was worrying about his longevity. We retreated to the protective dark and went our own ways to bed, and slept out the hours that the surface lived its life in, until the sun dropped from the sky once again.

30

Alarums and Excursions

"War," said Sergei, "is just capitalism by other means."

It was during the war between the Meat Packers and the Alchemical Brethren that I made my one and only descent into the depths. It may surprise you to discover that there were wars below, but even the Temple failed sometimes. In this case, the Packers had begun to move in on the pharmaceutical territory that the Brethren traditionally held. The deal I had witnessed between the Packers and the Friendly Society had been part of an overall plan to expand Packer operations into an entirely new market.

The Alchemical Brethren were distressed at this unwanted competition, and they and the Packers spent a few months trying to come to some peaceable arrangement whereby they could prosper side by side. While the leaders were talking, the men at the cutting edge were getting more and more restless: shipments of chemicals went missing, refinery equipment was sabotaged, fires were set. Then one of the Brethren's couriers was murdered and the obvious suspects were the Packers. Negotiations at the Temple went downhill sharply and war was officially declared. What this meant was that the Temple acknowledged that there was no more room to talk, and gave both factions permission to kill each other.

From that point onwards there was a careful and civilised outbreak of hostilities. The Packers and the Brethren called in favours, hired mercenaries and drew the battle lines, and then proceeded to murder each other with a free hand. It was in broad daylight, frequently in the midst of crowds and everyday business. There would be the flash of knives or the snap of a crossbow string, and a death. When I arose there would often be a body in the waking tunnels. The one rule the Temple held to – in return for giving the two sides leave to be at each others' throats – was that those not involved in the conflict must be immune. Any innocents slain or injured, any neutral property damaged, and there would be heavy duties to pay. So it was that, for everyone bar the combatants, the war was something of a spectator sport.

There were other effects, of course. The supply of chemicals dried up, and there was something of a famine where recreational drugs, medical supplies and organ repairs were concerned. Some of the lesser factions stepped up production to fill the gap but many did not dare, lest they be dragged into the war. Factions that specialised in generalised procuring, such as the Friendlies, did very well for themselves. The Fishermen also had a time of plenty: the unplumbed depths were always a good source of merchandise.

How I became involved with them was simply this: Giulia told me one day that I was going on one of their trips into the dark.

"Nothing could persuade me," I replied.

"Your boss will persuade you. He's the persuasive sort, when it comes to having things done for him."

I went to Greygori, hailing him out from his laboratory where he had been hunched around some dreadful innovation.

"They may find something I need, Stefan. With the war, they go deeper," he told me. His voice had a pronounced wheeze by then. His skin was chalk-white, and he wore the dark glasses at all times. His eyes beneath them were glossy black and round.

"They tell me, Stefan, they've a good lead, an ancient place of medicine they wish to raid. You will go with them, Stefan. I will give you a list of things I can use. Bring back all you can, Stefan. They will let you. I am paying for the privilege."

"But… the depths…" I quavered.

"The Fishermen will look after you." He had been about to slope off back to the laboratory, but abruptly a sharp-fingered hand was on my shoulder. "Besides, Stefan, we must all make sacrifices in the name of science."

I said nothing. It was not the talk of sacrifices that silenced me, but the fact that his arm had unfolded from within the robe to a length of four feet to grasp my shoulder. Neither of the two joints revealed was configured like an elbow.

It was odd: the further he got from human, the more he hung on names and other light trappings of society, as though some dying part of him was trying to anchor itself to the world it knew.

"Some freebooter from the Seekers staggered up half dead last week," Giulia told me. "He was raving, but then Seekers always are. He didn't find God this time, just got himself lost. Reckons he saw something while he was down there, though."

"Something medical, Greygori said."

She nodded. "There's a whole complex down there that was built during one of the old wars," she told me. "That's what we think, anyway. We've not explored a fraction of it. This Seeker drew a decent map of where he thought he'd gone. There's enough demand right now that we'll chance it. We've got plenty of money up front for this one. Your boss isn't the only backer."

She had taken me to the converted storehouse that was the hub of their spelunking activities. Compared to the doomed venture into the desert, this occasion was a model of rough efficiency. Giulia was in command of the venture and doing most of the organising. Her second, whom I had yet to see, was holed up with some backers, who were briefing him with their own list of what to look for.

I had been kitted out as befitted a daring explorer of the chasms of the earth. My casual clothes had been exchanged for hard-wearing canvas with pads sewn in at the elbows and knees. I had a sleeveless jerkin of some artificial cloth that was reinforced with flat metal strips front and back. On my head was buckled a plastic skull-guard which would apparently save me from cave-ins, or at least allow the Fishermen to retrieve my brain for Greygori. I am sure that he would have found a use for it. I had rope and metal spikes, a little pick-hammer and a lamp. The dozen Fishermen around me wore similar garb with many variations. Most of them were armed, too. Crossbows were an Underworld favourite, the best made to order by the Waylun Armoury. I saw a number of Wayluns around me, large and small, single shot, double-string and repeaters. One tall and broad-shouldered character bore an almost man-sized monster across his back. I had been given a knife and Giulia also presented me with a metal tube some two feet long.

"It's a one-shot," she told me. "We make them ourselves. A single bolt, a spring, trigger and trigger guard here. Try not to use it."

At that point, her second came down from the high offices of the Fishermen, taking the steps three at a time.

"He's not a Fisherman," I pointed out.

"Neither are you," Giulia said. "Sergei's good, though, and he was on the last sortie that went anywhere near our target area."

Sergei, it turned out, was an explorer as well.

"Frontiers," he told me when I asked. "All my life I push frontiers: space, time. In this backwards place everywhere is frontier. No-one steps out of doors for fear of the rain. I cannot search deserts, so I search depths. When I was with Morlocks I go off on my own, one, two weeks at a time, exploring. Back then I need to get away from you people sometimes." He turned to Giulia. "You have maps?"

"And space for more," she answered. "Carving another chunk out of the unknown."

I was given a pack of food and tools just light enough for me to lift, which was half the size of those everyone else was sporting. Even Sergei's insect-thin frame seemed, like an insect, to support more weight than was reasonable. My lighter load was more in recognition of Greygori's funding than my inadequacies.

To the Fishermen, the spaces beneath Underworld were like little principalities, small foreign states stretching out towards Sergei's frontier. Those closest to us were well-mapped, familiar to all, devoid of wonder.

On our way to new reaches of the depths I was allowed to see the myoculture caves, where vast mounds of fungus crawled and grew, tended by the busy Fermers like a scene out of some fungal hell.

There were other strange sights that everyone else took for granted. There was a great round ceremonial room with a firepit in the floor and strange, broken cables issuing from holes in the walls, coated with gold leaf when first found. There was a long hall with shelves and shelves of small plastic plates that nobody had ever found a use for. Arves had theorised that they were books, some way of storing knowledge. If so, the knowledge was forever entombed within them for none could retrieve it now.

We were a whole day scrambling and climbing through caverns and chambers already picked clean. The journey was difficult, and I slowed everybody up, not used to climbing down ropes, crawling on narrow ledges or scrambling up steeply-sloping shafts. I was continuously being helped out by the Fishermen, who seemed to regard me with affectionate contempt. At the head, Sergei stopped occasionally to confer with Giulia on the best route, and this alone gave me time to catch my breath.

We made camp around a metal sphere one of the Fishermen had. He opened it up and there was a glowing coil within that gave a little light but more heat. Even though we were on home ground, Sergei still insisted that a watch was set.

The next day we started descending into areas that mankind had never properly reclaimed. Although there was some traffic in explorers and grave-robbers through these ancient halls, there were other occupants yet that could take offence, and there were devices of the ancients that still had power to harm. "Many of the Diggers," Giulia said, using a Fisher term for those that had excavated these buried chambers, "guarded their property well, especially those who were at war. Don't wander off and don't touch anything."

I had stuck to her heels even when we were secure. I was not about to strike out on my own now.

We came, shortly thereafter, to a gaping, jagged-edged wound in the earth some twenty feet across, giving onto who knew what abyssal depths. We were going down into it. Two of the Fishermen tied ropes together to make something they reckoned was long enough, and Giulia secured it to a metal ring in the wall that a previous expedition had installed.

"We used to keep a rope here permanently," she said, reassuringly, "but something kept untying it."

I watched anxiously as one man lowered a light down on the end of a long wire, hand over hand. At first it lit nothing but itself. Then I saw a jagged circle of stone, the floor of another level that had been holed by the same unimaginable collapse. This was at the very edge of the lamplight, thirty feet on all sides from our dangling rope. I asked Giulia what was there and she shrugged almost irritably.

"No-one knows. We can't get over there from this descent, and nobody's ever found another way up or down to it. One day I'll find a way there. For now, it's just a blank among my maps."

The lowered light had illuminated some kind of floor down there, a good forty feet further down still. I saw columns, many of them fallen and broken, amidst rubble from the caved-in floors. It all looked far too distant to consider climbing down all that way. Then something scurried rapidly from one shadow to another and out of the light altogether, or perhaps it was the light's own movement. A number of the Fishermen clutched their crossbows.

"What lives down there?" I whispered.

"Sometimes you find Vermin," Giulia said, checking the mechanism of her own bow. "Seldom so deep, though. Mostly you should watch for cave spiders, Stabbers and Girricks."

I gave her a look both frightened and enquiring. "So... these cave spiders... big?"

She asked me if I had been into the deserts. "Remember the scorpions? The cave spiders are like that: some you could fit in your pocket; the biggest I ever saw was maybe a little smaller in the body than Sergei. They're a terror if you're on your own but they don't take on groups. The Stabbers are worse: less sense of self-preservation. The Diggers, one batch of them, put them together as guards. They're kind of like mantids but half-alive and half-machine. No higher than your chest, but if they get their blades into you then you're finished."

"And these Girricks?"

She looked uneasy. "Not so dangerous, just... odd."

"They talk," Sergei filled in. "Lizards that talk."

"They do not talk," Giulia said firmly. "It's just... the sounds they make can sound like they're gabbling away in some language of their own. But they're just big lizards and they don't attack unless you get too close. They don't talk, it's all just lizard noises."

"We're ready," one of the Fishermen called, which Giulia happily took as an end to the subject.

A man named Pelgraine volunteered to go first. Giulia attached a safety line to his belt, and he let himself down the rope using his knees and one hand. The other held a crossbow that he pointed out into the darkness, especially as he passed that broken, unknown level. He had to stop frequently to change arms. The climb was even longer than I had thought, and I began to wonder whether I would be able to make it. The Fishermen were toughened by previous expeditions into the unknown, from which only the strong returned. Even Sergei seemed to have within his skinny frame surprising reserves of strength. I was a soft academic who had never needed to fight for my life.

Pelgraine reached the bottom and there was a tense moment as he crouched with cocked crossbow, waiting for something to spring out into the light at him. There was nothing, though, and he waved a cautious hand up at us, a tiny insect all the way down there.

Giulia went next and roped herself to another Fisherman, who roped himself to me. I stood mute and trembling as a big man called Charno took next place, and so on down to Sergei who was bringing up the rear. By that point, Giulia was already partway down. She had a lever-worked repeating crossbow cradled in one arm in case of trouble from the air, and Pelgraine below was keeping an eye on the surrounding rubble. There was a tugging at my waist and I stood unwillingly at the very brink of the hole, looking down as Giulia and the Fisherman continued their slow descent.

"Go, Stefan," Sergei told me, and I went. I took hold of the rope, tried to clench my knees about it, lowered myself with difficulty, hand over hand. I made such poor progress that those below were constantly having to stop and wait for more slack safety line, whilst Charno above kept up a constant grumbling. I looked neither at him, nor at the distant, broken ground, but stared only at my hands as they passed one below the other. Already there was a dull ache in my arms.

I was out in the abyss now. The rope swung and jerked with every climber's movements, and if I let my eyes stray I could see the shattered edges of that forbidden and unfindable layer that had frustrated Giulia's maps. My muscles were beginning to burn by then. I was finding it difficult to support my slight weight on my arms, with the pack dragging at my back. The grip of my knees kept slipping, and there was a rising peak of fear in me as I became more and more aware of the drop. It was as if, far from getting closer to the ground, every move of mine made the chasm that much greater and more fatal. I could still feel Giulia and the other man climbing down beneath me. There was no sound from Pelgraine to suggest we were nearing the ground, and I dared not look. I seemed to have been descending forever.

"Move, you runt!" Charno shouted down to me, and I realised I had been still for some time. With a whimper I managed to lower myself another arm's span, and another. There was faint light below, and equally faint light above, but I was in a darkness peopled by all the flying monsters my imagination could come up with.

My hands slipped. It was the sweat really. One moment I was clinging to the rope, the next it was sliding through my hands, burning a neat line across both of my palms. I heard Charno swear above the racket of my own ragged breath. Then the pain registered, and I let go.

There was a moment of relief, almost, because I no longer had to continue that agonising descent.

Then I was falling into the void with a scream that cut off abruptly as the safety line snapped tight. Charno cried out in pain and alarm, but he kept to the rope, and I dangled like a spider's victim. I have no idea how much time passed before I became aware of someone tugging at my sleeve. It was the man who had been below me. I had fallen to his level. He was trying to pull me in. I grasped at his hand, and he hooked a new safety line to my belt and freed Charno from my weight. In silence, we climbed down locked together, with him doing most of the work. It was still a fair way to the ground.

I collapsed as soon as my feet touched stone and took no further part in the proceedings until Charno got down, complaining that his climbing gloves had been ruined. The rubber pads of their palms were cut deep where the rope had sawn into them. I thought that he would probably want to take it out of my hide, but instead he sat down beside me and I realised his complaining was just covering for the fact that he had been scared out of his wits too. It had been a close thing for all of us. If he had been pulled from the rope then our combined weights might have plucked the entire expedition into the abyss in one go.

Pelgraine, who had a fringe of russet hair showing under his stolen Angel headset, took point as we started off into the great pillared space. The huge columns stretched in exacting rows as far as the light shone, with the impression of an infinite rank and file of them beyond that. They were hollow and, as we approached the closest, I saw that there was a kind of window in it, edged with daggers of splintered glass.

There was a corpse inside. It was the deadest body I had ever seen, skin withered and dried to a husk, face just taut leather stretched over the skull. The shrivelled eyes were shut, but the jaw was twisted open in an endless, soundless scream. It was pitched over onto its side, part out of the alcove obviously built to contain it. Whatever had broken the glass and hooked it out had also torn one arm away, or perhaps it had simply crumbled at the shoulder. The limb was on the ground beyond the window's lip, practically at my feet.

I looked down the monolithic line of columns and saw the light glint everywhere on glass, whole or broken. An endless sequence of parched and solitary mausoleums fell away on all sides of us, and I felt a bubbling horror rising within me.

"God," I said heavily. "It's a tomb..."

But it was worse than that. As I got over my revulsion and examined the next corpse, still intact behind its glass membrane, I saw the ends of machines arrayed around the horribly desiccated body. Panels, controls, meters that showed nothing and lights that were forever put out.

"Not death, but a sleep," Sergei said softly. His strange accent made stranger echoes. "Probably it is some war, burning up the surface. They come here to be safe. Into machines they go, trusting when the war was won, their friends come wake them. Only the war was lost. Maybe everybody lost. Power died... In their sleep, their nightmares, they died too, over how long a time? The scavengers will not touch them; time has done its worst. They will lie here to the end of the world."

We passed on, our footsteps echoing loud down the halls of the necropolis, amidst the remains of ancients who had died in ignorance of the end of their world. I was constantly on edge, seeing in the darkness all the things Giulia had spoken of. Our little line stopped often as one person or another heard some movement beyond the reach of our lamps. Pelgraine eventually became so twitchy up in front that Sergei took over. When the former point man stepped back to walk beside me, I heard Giulia mutter, "Prime Stabber territory," and fumbled my one-shot out, for all the good it would do me.

Between the crypt-columns there was a quiet so intense that it could be heard, as though a single sound had been trapped in there when the place was built, a faint but eternal reverberation in the very structure of the place. Every scuff of a footstep, every exhalation, or scrape of crossbow-butt on stone, expanded out to join that almost-inaudible susurration.

We came across another rubble-strewn place where several ceilings had fallen in. There was a hill of shifting debris beneath which the occupants of downed pillars must have been pressed to dust. Sergei moved carefully up, testing each foothold. He reached ahead with one hand, pistol held clear with the other. I could hear his slightly laboured breath in the vast silence. Crouching spider-like atop the pile, he decided it was safe and beckoned for us to follow.

Of course I slipped. Needless to say, I was the one person who lost his footing and just slid off into the dark with a yelp. One moment I was picking my footholds, with Giulia ahead and

Pelgraine behind. A second later my legs were whisked from under me and I was tobogganing off into the darkness, bounding off every piece of broken stone I crashed into. Through it all I was clutching the little one-shot so close to my chest that it was a wonder I didn't shoot myself through the chin.

When I came to rest in a confusion of sharp masonry and my own flailing limbs, I could see the lights of the others only as a vague glow that threw the silhouettes of the pillars into sharp focus. I was suddenly alone and surrounded by the embalmed dead, unable to see anything but that detached illumination. I wanted to reach out and pull myself up, but then I envisaged putting my hand, all unwary, through the gap of a broken window, sinking my fingers into the crackling dry skin of a dead face. I froze up instantly, just staring towards the light.

The image that gripped me was of that body half-out of its alcove. How had it got there? Had some vermin laid hands on it, then decided it was inedible? Or had that withered ancient woken at the very end of its unnaturally prolonged life: woken, and tried desperately to escape the confines of the smothering machine. I saw, in my mind, those brittle-stick fingers clutching at the glass, forcing it out, shattering it. I saw the ghastly, dried body fall forwards, that one arm outstretched towards the stale air of the great necropolis... and if that could be so then perhaps some of those atrophied creatures were *still alive*. My thoughts conjured for me the silent snakeskin progress of one of them, freed from the confines of its machine and reaching out with wasted fingers...

"Stefan!" I heard Giulia shout, not for the first time, and I made a kind of cracked, scared bleat. I saw the shadows shift as a couple of the Fishermen cautiously advanced in my direction, and one of them threw a light towards me. It was just a stick with a bioluminant at one end, but I seized upon it as though it was life and brought it up to head height, whereupon it illuminated a head.

I screamed.

It was long-jawed and low-browed and the eyes were just plain white, but it must have registered the light somehow because it snarled and one long hand smashed the lamp from my hand and dashed it to darkness against a column. In the brief second between the reclosing of the dark and the twang of Giulia's crossbow I was left with the image of a mouth gaping open to show dagger-like incisors. I felt the movement of something very fast past my face and heard a solid, fleshy impact. When the others rushed over, bringing back blessed light to the scene, the thing was lying in a boneless sprawl at my feet with the crossbow bolt between those featureless blank eyes. Given that Giulia had been firing at a remembered target in the dark I reckoned that was actually the closest I had come to dying.

The creature was… not a creature. It was a man, or more than the web-children would ever be. I would have thought that living underground would make for dwarfish, diminished life, but the thing would have been nearly as tall as Sergei had it stood upright. The arms were too long or the legs too short, and it could have gone on all fours with ease. The nails of the hands and feet were talons, the fingers and toes long and strong. It had no clothing, tools or possessions of any kind to suggest intelligence.

"Mazen," Giulia exclaimed. "Crap."

"Pelgraine, get the light gun out," Sergei snapped out. "Everyone else ready. When did you last see only one Mazen?"

"What the hell is a Mazen?" I demanded. "You said Stabbers and spiders and maulers and whatever, but you never said anything about Mazen."

We were retreating back to the mound of rubble, all the better for a good view of our surroundings. Giulia stayed close to me, and got out the story in brief snatches.

"We never knew they could get into here," she stated. "I'll have to update my maps."

"Priorities please! What are they? As quickly and concisely as possible."

380

"They're people, Stefan," she told me. "Or they were. Thousands of years back, supposedly, some of the Diggers built a whole city deep underground, far deeper than any of us have ever gone. Probably another war, a disaster or something. They all went to live down there, cut off from the surface, and then something went wrong. They ran out of power. Their machines broke down. A whole city-full of people, soldiers and civilians and politicians and scholars and workers and children, all trapped without light, heat, food…"

"They must have gone mad," I whispered.

"Probably. Most of them. Most of them died. Maybe all but the maddest ones died. The mad ones were probably the ones who could adjust, because civilisation meant nothing to them. They lived without light or power, and they ate… anything, each other. That's where the Mazen come from. The descendants, generations later. Bit by bit they found their way out of the city, always working upwards. There are four or five points where our worlds touch, and now I must add this one."

"Are there any other people down here?" I asked her.

"No, and the Mazen haven't been people since before Shadrapar was built. We are the only people down here."

"The Shell People," Charno suggested. He was setting up that immense crossbow on a three-legged stand.

"No such thing," Giulia snapped. "Just a legend."

Charno shrugged, and that was all I heard about the Shell People because the big man called me over and said, "Look, Stefan, you'd better load."

"What?" I said, which was when the Mazen attacked. There was a sudden rustling in the darkness and the light began to fall on rushing shapes, some on two legs, some on four, glints of huge, vacant eyes and bared teeth. There was a shocking flash of light from behind us which illuminated everything and everywhere and froze the creatures with a great wailing cry. I heard Sergei's gun go off, explosive in the echoing space, and a spatter of crossbows followed.

"Put them in, pointy end forward," Charno snapped at me. There was a kind of a hopper at the top of his great crossbow, and with panicking fingers I fed bolts into it one by one. He was frantically turning a winch that dragged the string back, released and fired the bolt, then dragged it back again, over and over, while he pivoted the thing on its mount, spitting steel-tipped shafts into the dark after each searing flash of light. Beside us, Giulia steadily cranked the lever of her repeating bow back and forth, each movement slotting another missile into place and loosing it off. Her bolts were strung together on a kind of thin webbing that another Fisherman was carefully feeding to her, to stop it tangling. Behind us, Pelgraine fired the light gun at measured intervals. The Mazen looked blind, but the all-illuminating bursts of the light gun disoriented them, set them against one another, and in the aftershock of those bursts they were targets for the crossbows.

Sergei cast his pistol down and unslung a crossbow of his own, fitting a big-headed bolt to the string. "Fire!" he shouted, and the Fishermen suddenly covered their faces as he loosed. The bolt struck between two Mazen, as I saw clearly because I still had my eyes open. There was an explosion of blue fire from the impact that quite blinded me in a way the light gun had not, and I heard the screeching of Mazen with limbs torn off by the blast. My fingers kept working of their own accord, loading Charno's bow as my eyes blinked and recovered.

There were a lot of them and they were fast. Charno was swinging the great bow in a wide arc as I struggled to keep it fed. He had given up aiming by then and was just pumping bolts out into the dark. Sergei fired off his second explosive bolt and then knelt quickly to reload his pistol, pressing the shells into their chambers with an unhurried, precise hand.

The light gun went off again, showing the Mazen closer than ever, and Pelgraine shouted, "I'm out!" Then a Mazen leapt at Charno from one side, clearing the heads of two crouching Fishermen in a single bound, but getting tangled up with me on the way. I was punched to the ground, and the thing's filthy talons dug deep into one arm. I saw the jaws gape above me and tried to fold myself into a foetal position again, a process which brought both my knees sharply up between its legs. There was a shocked noise from the fanged maw, and then Pelgraine ran it through the ribs with a sword and cut its head off for good measure. There was other combat going on, but I stayed crouched down, clutching my one-shot, which had still not gone off. I fumbled the metal trigger guard away and directed it outwards. Then another Mazen sprang from behind and knocked Pelgraine back into Charno. One flailing, clawed foot raked across my leg, and I spasmodically fired the one-shot into its buttock. It screeched, and Charno gripped it by the head and, with a great effort, snapped its neck. Pelgraine, helmet gone, sat up and grinned at me. I realised that it had ended. It was over. The surviving Mazen had given up. All that was left were the dead, and the almost dead, which gave off a horrendous mewling that no human throat ever produced.

There were nineteen bodies or so sprawled about, jutting bolts or sporting burns and gunshot wounds. When I expressed surprise that there were not more, Giulia said that the survivors would have taken the rest. "They eat one way or another," she said. "It's probably the only thing that keeps the population down."

"Casualties!" Sergei called, and someone told him, "Mitch is dead, Guy Borand's next to. Pelgraine, Lombard and Stefan all got scratched."

I scarcely registered my own name. The speaker was kneeling by two human bodies amongst the sub-human carnage. Guy Borand was the man who had carried me down most of the rope, and here he was, breathing his last with his lips rimmed with blood. I wanted to tell him that I was grateful, but my gratitude would not help him. Someone was trying to put something on my wounds, but I kept shaking them off, looking down at the dead.

"Stefan!" Giulia warned. "Mazen wounds go bad fast. You need this." The unguent she was rubbing hard into my scratches burned where it touched. Pelgraine and the woman named Lombard were enduring the same treatment. Pelgraine was checking the workings of the light gun, an ancient, bronze-mounted piece of equipment with a wide, cloudy lens.

"The cell's died," he announced. "Better hope those Mazen have run a long way."

In the distance, something called out: a noise like "Girrick", and then more, similar noises. Something else answered it in a like tongue. The Girrick lizards were waiting for us to go so they could dine on the Mazen. We saw none of them, though, nor did the Mazen return.

We had more adventures, which I will not recount here. We found many interesting and valuable artefacts, and Giulia was able to extend her maps a little. We never did find that mythical medical installation, though. Either the Seeker was mad or we misunderstood his instructions. Perhaps it still waits to be found, with all the secrets of life and death interred within it.

31

Faith

You might think that I was set up nicely in Underworld. I had a place to sleep and was not going hungry. I had allied myself to someone who inspired fear and respect. I had some friends, and was not imprisoned or in great physical danger. Of course given that the Island is looming large in my personal history it should be obvious that none of it lasted.

It began when I did my stint as priest of the Temple. For a long time Greygori had ignored the Underworld maxim that all factions should put forward a candidate for the priesthood. While it was just him and Arves he conveniently forgot about it, and nobody was brave enough to force the point home. Some time after taking me on, he suddenly told me that I would be taking up residence in the Temple for a while. It makes me wonder whether he planned it, or at least had some prescience regarding it.

I was by no means loath to play priest. It was a nicely cushy position of authority where I would be able to play with the Temple machine to my heart's content. The war between the Packers and the Brethren had been brought down by a trade agreement mediated by my predecessor, and everyone was too busy picking up the pieces to make trouble. It was a nice, quiet time for the Temple, and I started each day before the machine and the light-entombed figure of the Coming Man with an easy mind. I felt that religious office agreed with me very well.

Except…

One morning, when I ambled down to the Temple from Greygori's chambers, things were different. In the centre of that rough, artificial floor, beneath the mobile starfield and the crackling flux of energy, was a woman.

She was hunched up about herself, forehead touching her knees, arms wrapped about her calves, muscles locked tight enough that you could not have uncurled her with a crowbar. I could make out little of her beyond that, save that she was of slim build, bright-haired and quite naked. And that she was something strange, something special.

The Caretaker was squatting beside her, giving a fair impression, for a metal spider-shaped thing, of bemusement.

I approached cautiously. A naked woman could be dangerous after all, especially if she were mad, which seemed likely given the circumstances.

She remained locked into her closed-up position like a catatonic. The Caretaker took a few careful steps back, as though it had been guarding her but trusted me to take over.

She looked straight into my face with wide eyes, and gasped out, "Where am I?"

I fell back from her. Granted, I had said the same when I awoke in the Temple, but this was different. Mine was a simple request for information. Her demand was the cry of the lost, the voice of someone adrift on unknown seas.

I reached out to touch her arm almost unconsciously. Her reflexive lunge away from me sent one of her feet hard into my chest and, as I sat down solidly, she tried to make her escape. She bolted straight away from me, came up against the curving wall of the Temple, skittered left and then right, trying to find an exit that was not there. The only way out was past me and she would not bring herself an inch closer to me than she had to. I was concentrating on breathing after the kick, whilst she flung herself at the walls like a trapped animal. When I finally looked straight at her, she had frozen again, back to the cold wall, staring at me with an intense fear out of all proportion to anything I could ever do to her.

She took my breath away. I was stunned by the sight of her. My mind went completely blank. It was not the nakedness. My life was not so empty of nakedness as all that, and there were three factions at least that ran men and women of purchasable virtue. It was just that she was perfect.

I do not mean that the way you think. No individual feature was unsurpassed. I had seen a more delicate nose, a more arresting pair of eyes, finer hair, curves of the body that... well. That was not it. Besides, tastes vary and one's idea of perfection is not another's.

It was the whole, the gestalt. When all those features of humble provenance were united in her, the result was unexpectedly and inexplicably perfect. All who saw her said just that. My heart leapt when I first set eyes on her and has never quite come down.

And I say 'she.' I saw her as 'she', that day, and I should know; I saw all of her there was to see. Except I do not know if what I saw was truly what was there. I knew others who referred to Faith as male, and there were days when I awoke a certain way, and he seemed male to me too. Faith was an image in that mirror we all keep within our minds to admire ourselves in, a fancy to picture hung on our arm. So she was 'she' to me, most of the time, but in committing myself, I merely betray my own leanings.

I saw what she must be, of course. She was a Rengen, taken in by the cosmetics labs and re-engineered into fresh-sculpted beauty. She had none of the normal marks of one, though; no trademark or brand name. This woman was the result of some private commission, a product of that cold and introverted love that artists and scientists alone share.

"Where—?" she said again, the words choked off. I made my voice slow and comforting.

"You are in the Temple of the Underworld." Only saying it to her did I realise quite how sinister it sounded.

Her expression was blank. She had not heard of Temple or Underworld.

"Beneath Shadrapar proper," I continued.

Her expression became blanker by degrees, and a little anxiety began to niggle at me that she would turn out to be something like Sergei, bristling with stories of impossible places and times. How could she not know Shadrapar?

"How did you come here?" I asked gently. "Did someone bring you? Did you flee here? Most of us down here are running from something."

"I—" Again that choking off, and still the blankness grew to encompass her whole body, and I read there that she did not know, and that it frightened her even more than I did.

"I was named Stefan Advani," I told her carefully. "I am a scholar, and at the moment a priest…"

She was quite still in the wake of that because of the gap I had left, for her to insert her own name. She had no name. At the core of her mind, her identity was just a brittle eggshell of the *now*, that had come into being the moment she had looked up. Whatever had brought her or driven her here had left her with a mind as bare as the rest of her.

"Let me get you something to cover you," I offered. It was for my benefit more than hers. She had not registered her nakedness, nor did she try to hide herself. Public nudity, in Shadrapar, was unthinkable. She had no sense of this. For my peace of mind I needed to anchor her in my own customs.

I returned with a large silvery sheet and found her crouching before the Caretaker, watching as it tapped across the floor. She had no fear of it, but she cringed back from me as though I meant to murder her.

"Stefan Advani," she said. There was a trace less panic in her voice. She was obviously resigned to staying put in the Temple for now. She took the sheet from me and hugged it to her, staring at me all the while.

"You are safe here," I told her. *For three days*, I thought, but that could wait. I watched as she folded herself in the sheet and then looked back at me. I was wondering what on earth I was going to do with her.

She would have no problem finding a faction, on decorative merits alone. That was the problem. She would be snapped up quickly and exploited. I told myself my reaction to this was motivated by noble concern.

I spoke with her but there was no common ground, no ground at all. She was falling into the void of her absent memories. The best I could do was try to provoke a sense of familiarity.

"Is someone looking for you?" I asked, and her expression closed for a moment, and she said that there might be something looking for her.

"Is that a good or a bad thing?" I prompted. From her expression I deduced it to be a bad one.

"Do you remember another place at all? Any other place?"

For a moment her fear was back, fear of the waste land within her mind, but then she said, "Light... there was light. There was a place... It was safe but I could not stay there. I..." For the first time she showed a little frustration at her emptiness.

"Who was there with you?"

"There were... They watched over me...?"

Again I pressed, "Is that a good or a bad thing?" and when she did not answer, I tried, "Is that why you had to leave?"

She did not know and could not say. The picture I had built up was of some unimaginably wealthy man's private laboratories where his team of experts had sweated and slaved to realise his magnum opus. Many of the Authority and others of high family dabbled in the cosmetic sciences. The idea that she was a Rengen pressed on me with ever greater certainty: some rich man's private toy and exhibit. Knowing what I do now, I have to wonder if she was *re*-engineered at all. Perhaps she was simply engineered. Perhaps she was Thelwel's sister under the skin.

And she had left the clutches of her creator or recreator. Had the escape attempt erased her memories, or had she never possessed more than the faint and gauzy recollections I was drawing from her? I envisaged some ancient guardian machine with strange rays to blank the mind. Someone who could afford to have her made could surely procure the most elaborate security.

The Fermers arrived then, and I watched as she walked over to them, the hem of the sheet trailing. She had no fear of them, and when she reached out to touch them, they did not flinch or contract into themselves as they did with anyone else.

The first supplicants to the Temple arrived shortly after. There was a dignified old man from the Meat Packers, and a bald, twitchy character from the Seekers who wanted a pharmaceuticals deal. The Seekers, in their constant quest for enlightenment, got through a whole lot of drugs.

She fell back to the wall again as they entered. The Packers' factor, especially, seemed to return to her all her desperate need for flight. The two men stopped dead when they saw her, and their expressions mirrored the one I had worn. The Seeker twitched convulsively and then averted his eyes, but there was a strange look to the Packer's man for a moment, as of lost innocence. It was common enough, around her.

"What is this, Stefan?" the Packer asked me in a low voice.

"The latest Ward of the Temple," I told him. I was waiting to see if he would take her in. The Packers were the largest faction, and one could do worse. Instead, though, he was oddly wary of her.

"What a piece of work," he murmured, for the Packers made Rengens from time to time. "Where did she fall from, Stefan?"

I shrugged awkwardly.

"I would fear to take her on," the old man said. "Who knows what her presence might bring?"

We tried to get down to the deal, but all three of us were unable to concentrate. As we talked, she crept closer and closer, skittering backwards if anyone looked at her. We were all three of us very aware of every move she made. In the end, the Packers' man suggested they come back tomorrow. It was obvious that nothing was going to be sorted out that day. That was when the Seeker made his move.

I do not know what Seekers did to their minds, but it was a common trait in them. They would look at something for an age and then suddenly see some extra dimension to it and go crazy. This Seeker, just as we were giving the negotiations up as a bad job, just leapt to his feet and ran at the poor girl, skidding down to his knees even as she shrieked and fell back.

"A sign!" the man shouted out. His face was transformed into a mask of wonder and adulation. "It is a sign! Forgive me, oh Lord, for I am a man of fragile faith, and I did not recognise you! I keep the faith, oh great God! I am a loyal follower of the True Way!"

Seekers were always doing this. They believed that God was waiting in the world to be found by the devout and they were constantly mistaking everyday items for Him. The look on the man's face was burning with awe and devotion, but Seekers could summon that up at a moment's notice.

"Get away from me!" the woman shouted, trying to force herself into the wall, limbs all hunched up. The Packer moved in to pull back his colleague, but his approach made her almost hysterical. In the end, I managed to shoo the pair of them out. The news would spread fast, though. I knew that there would be plenty of gawpers.

This was how she got her name, of course. From then on, everyone referred to her as Faith.

The reaction of the next few who came to the Temple was the same as the Packer's man. They were astounded, but oddly reluctant to have anything to do with her. Her presence in their faction would be too divisive. At this point, I began to worry. I knew that the brothel factions would be only too keen to snap her up and that was just what I did not want.

Sure enough, by mid-morning, I saw the bloated form of Virus Holms squeezing into the Temple. Virus ran the most successful Underworld brothel, the House of Lianas, and he was reckoned to be a man of influence. He was expensively lop-sided, dressed in the finest clothes of bright and artificial colours. His step was swaggering, rife with vice. Even *he* stopped when he saw Faith, but his fleshy face showed no lost innocence because he had never had any to lose.

"Astonishing, Stefan," he said, coasting over to me. "What a prize. What a spectacle. A commodity. We shall dress her in cloth of silver and teach her to play an instrument. What a unique opportunity."

I looked sullenly at him. He gave a wide, fat-creased smile.

"I'll take her," he said. "Readily. Before the competition does."

I have a sly suspicion that she would have ruined his business, to be honest. Virus was immune to that disconcerting effect, but his clients would have been thrown by it. Her appearance suggested not physical but spiritual fulfilment. All the same, I did not want to see her in Virus' clutches.

He was making his wide way over to her. He had read the surface of her faster than I, seen the loss and the vulnerability and no more. She was frowning slightly, edging away.

One plump-fingered and be-ringed hand extended to her; Virus' lips moved in some greasy compliment.

"You can't take her," I said.

I was abruptly the centre of all attention. Virus looked back at me and raised a greying eyebrow. "Whatever do you mean, Stefan?"

Even as I spoke I could not believe what I was doing. It was a course of incredible stupidity but the only one I had. "Privilege of the priesthood. I'm recruiting her for my faction."

Virus laughed deeply at the absurdity of it. "And what, I wonder, will Greygori say about that? He doesn't strike me as the womanising type. He's never been amongst my clientele. Stop being absurd and let me get on with my business."

"I'm serious," I insisted, because as priest I did indeed have the pick of any newcomers. Though I didn't think Greygori had anticipated I would be doing any recruitment when he put me forward for the post.

"Well I'm sure she hasn't agreed yet," Virus said lazily. "You can't just enslave the poor girl. We should let her choose." He struck a pose. He had an odd grace for such an asymmetrical man, a corrupt and corrupting style. "What about it, my darling? I can offer you luxuries and pleasures to fill that void in you. Stefan here has only cold libraries and laboratories. Whose hand will you take?"

She looked at me enquiringly, and I stuttered out the fact that her stay at the Temple was a short-term measure, and that she was better with a faction than alone in the Underworld, and fair game.

Her face, as she cast between Virus and me was distressed. "I have to choose…?"

"In two days, darling," Virus confirmed. "And you'll get no better offer than mine, I can assure you. Take all the time you may need. I can come back tomorrow."

"Stefan," she whispered. "I will go with Stefan."

There was a murmur of surprise in the little crowd of spectators, and a little mirth at Virus' expense. Virus' stature was a carefully calculated fashion statement, cultivated for his underworld clientele after all, and he used many expensive pheromones. He was reckoned to be nigh-irresistable when he turned the charm on. It was the first time anyone had turned him down.

Faith put a hand on my forearm. There was some contact there that I cannot describe. I was opened up, suddenly: all my intestines, organs, dreams and deep fears rifled through and put back. I met her eyes.

I would be in terrible trouble with the Transforming Man as soon as he found out. I had also angered Virus Holms who was an enemy I could do without.

I had taken her in. I had no idea what the consequences would be. I feared her, and desired her, and was mystified by her. And let me be honest, now I look back on all this. There was something in the way she was planned that made others want to own her, and I do not think I can call myself blameless when I took her back to Greygori's chambers.

32

Meeting the Family

Ignaz Trethowan wrote much about humanity divorcing itself from the processes of evolution. But then, Trethowan never met Greygori Sanguival, a man whose very pastime was his own evolution to a form more fitting. I'll never know whether Trethowan would see evolution as such a good thing, after viewing the Transforming Man.

I walked Faith through the tunnels of Underworld and, even though she was cloaked in the silvery blanket (and clothed beneath it by now), there were stares. She could not hide what she was. Every movement shouted it out. I kept to the less used passages as best I could but a ripple of awareness was passing through the very stone of Underworld. I am not sure who I was trying to keep our movements from, but I had the very definite sense that Faith should be concealed as much as possible. I would not have owned to it, but in my mind she was for me only.

Looking back at my dismal attempt at the espionage game I can only wonder what I was thinking. I was drunk on Faith perhaps.

We came to Greygori's chambers quietly. In the library there was a single lamp where Arves lurked over a game we had adjourned the previous night. The Transforming Man, unless he had transformed himself into invisibility, was not present. No doubt he was closeted within his laboratory again.

Arves glanced up once and then was back with the board. His eyes had taken a lot of the strain of his ageing and, unless he looked closely or wore thick, warped lenses, the world was a blur. He could read well, and see objects within a foot of his nose, and often said that the world beyond that was of little interest to him anyway.

"You're not supposed to bring girls back here," he murmured. "The master doesn't like it."

I waited for only two seconds, with Faith eyeing him nervously over my shoulder.

Arves' head lifted once more. "Oh what on earth have you done?" he asked, getting up. "Why have you brought that here?"

"Arves," I said. "This is Faith. For now."

She stepped forwards cautiously until his eyes focused on her. I saw them narrow, hit upon her, and then snap open wide. Arves stumbled back from her, waving his long, old hands before him as though to block out some kind of malign ray. "Don't introduce her to me. I don't want her to know," he complained. "Stefan, what have you done?" He was standing with one hand half over his eyes as though shielding them from her youth and radiance. Something had linked her with his condition, in his mind. She aged him, he felt; she burned too brightly. "Why can't you get her out of here?" he demanded.

That, of course, was the moment of truth.

"I have recruited her," I said.

Arves stared at me. With his face screwed up in so many directions at once he looked as old as he ever would.

"Oh, you're having me on. The master – have you thought of—! He won't go for it. He won't like it at all."

I was about to easily remark that I could surely manage whatever "the master" felt, when that sharp, wheeze-edged voice cut into both of our minds. "What, Mr Martext, will I not like? Arves, you have something to say? If not, Arves, perhaps you should retire for the night, Arves. Stefan and I obviously have matters, Arves, to discuss. Mr Advani, Stefan, tell me what it is, Mr Stefan Advani, that Arves feels I will disapprove of." By then he was using names in his speech as a climber hammers iron spikes into a rock face.

He was louring in the doorway to the laboratory, one elongated hand hooked around the frame. Arves retreated in double time before him, dashing off to lose himself elsewhere. I stepped forward unsteadily, rifling the contents of my vocabulary and finding nothing of use.

"I…" I managed. The dark-glassed face peered myopically at me, and Greygori lurched a step into the room.

"Stefan…?" he said. "Stefan Stefan Stefan… What is it, then…? In what way have you compromised me, Stefan?" Then Faith moved, the blanket rustling about her.

She had been holding quite still and Greygori had somehow not seen her. The eyes that he had built for himself had never been intended to see things of impossible beauty.

"What…?" he spat out, and I was gone from his mind in that instant. His weirdly jutting shoulder almost knocked me down as he turned sharply to face her.

She regarded him with naked curiosity. I cannot know what she made of that hostile, chalky face with its lipless slot of a mouth and those merciful black shades. She took it all in. She did not flinch or quail before the hunched spiderness, the superfluous angles beneath his shroud. She was calm even when one hand cupped her chin lightly, the last two fingers fused into a single misshapen digit.

"What…" he whispered. His expression could not be read but something was trying to happen to his face.

"I recruited her," I said, very carefully indeed. "They call her Faith. She just appeared in the Temple."

Greygori made a sound. It recalled the wind moaning low and lonely through deep, empty caverns, speaking of some need that the human mind could not even understand. His other hand came up to knuckle angrily at one covered eye and I wondered whether there was a tear trapped beneath all his surgery.

"Find her a room, Stefan," he snapped, shocking me out of my speculations. He was sloping off into his laboratory again, hurried and awkward, hands clutching at the doorframe to pull the bulk of him through. "Find her a place, Stefan. We will talk later."

Faith looked into the glare of the laboratory, and then at me.

"Greygori Sanguival," I explained. "He rules here. This is his faction."

She shrugged eloquently. It suggested that she had seen stranger things than the Transforming Man.

"You are to stay here," I said. "I mean… if you want to."

She had raised her arms as though to taste the ambience with her fingers, "This place means nothing to me," and while I was fumbling for something to say that would change her mind, "No place does. Where is there to go?" That apparently settled the matter.

I showed her somewhere to sleep, pilfered some sheets for her, and she curled up on them, knees to her forehead, arms about her legs. Save for the fact that she was clothed, she was just as I had found her.

She slept for two whole days. In all that time, whether I was officiating at the Temple or idling in Greygori's chambers, I was aware of her. I would have known, I think, had she awoken at any time.

The night of that first full day, Greygori came to play chess. Arves, who was happy to play with me, always stole away to his books when "the Master" wanted a game. Either he felt it would complicate the master–servant relationship he had dreamed up (surely it was none of Greygori's doing) or the transformations of the Transforming Man (of which he had seen more than I) were getting too much for him.

The chess we played was the complicated sort, with nineteen different pieces and a host of odd rules. We sat across from each other at the long table in the library, and Greygori marched his pieces about automatically as I tried to keep up with him.

After the game had started, Arves made a reappearance to sit in the corner with some new manuscript. His rustling of paper and scratching of notes made a constant foray into the silence between our moves.

Greygori had been quiet as we settled into a protracted mid-game, but eventually his narrow mouth got out the words, "What is she, Stefan?"

"I have no idea," I told him quietly, conscious that Faith might wake and hear at any moment. "She was just there, in the Temple. No memory, no explanations."

He grunted moodily, more humanity surfacing. "Just appeared," he murmured. "From the depths, Stefan, perhaps."

The thought had not occurred to me. The idea that Faith might have been a prisoner of some buried installation, released only now into a world centuries older than her own, was plausible, but I shied away from it. She was a creature of light and life, not the cold, dead depths of the earth.

"Who made her, do you think?" the Transforming Man mused, as one hand clicked a piece forward in another stage of his invisible master strategy. "She is a startling piece of work, is she not?"

I agreed that she certainly was. Arves let out a sniff of amusement that Greygori did not seem to hear. Some normally-silenced part of Greygori's mind was taking control of his voice. The names and anchors he usually relied on were falling away.

He said, "She reminds me of the sky," which threw me. He was not a poetical man, as though what poetry he had been born with had been the first thing under the knife.

Behind the panes of darkened glass and the fragments of murdered expression there was nothing to be read, but he went on, "The daylight sky. She reminds me of the sun."

I wondered how long it had been since Greygori Sanguival had seen the sun.

His warped fingers, over-jointed, with rough ridges about the knuckles, twitched another piece into position.

"I am not ready to face the sun just yet," he told me. His hand contracted savagely, knocking the piece over, and we both stared at it.

"If… If you want me to find somewhere else for her…" I started slowly.

Greygori's hand, of its own volition, replaced the fallen piece precisely in the centre of its square.

"No need," he said. "Keep her out of my way but… keep her, Stefan. She may, Stefan, be of use."

I did not like the sound of that, but the Transforming Man's thoughts were not for me to pry into.

When she awoke, I thought that our previous days had gone the way of all her memories. She did not recognise me. She was terrified of me. Then something passed over her face and my name came to her lips.

"I was dreaming," she said. "I was somewhere else…" but she could remember nothing save for that. "It's not important," she told my questioning look, though I could see it was.

When she ate, she ate sparingly. She and Arves avoided each other. To Arves she was still the sun that had condemned him to his subterranean existence. Greygori was keeping to his experiments and we saw nothing of him. Faith asked me questions about what he was doing, what his laboratory was like. I think she half-expected to find the shining place of her vanished dreams behind the door. She never asked about Greygori's physical appearance. That, of all the things around her, she just accepted.

★

She came with me to the Temple while my period in office paced itself out. Whilst never fond of crowds, she gradually became bolder, pushing the boundaries of her fear until it had retreated to the horizon. It never wholly disappeared.

I would be talking through some commercial point between Rodin's Garden and the Exceptionals (another team of thieves), and I would look up to see her talking in halting tones to a young woman of the Garden faction, or to a new Ward of the Temple. There was even a Bazaar when I lost her completely amongst the stalls and shopfronts, only to find her listening to a Fisherman telling some great tale of cave-diving adventure. He had been speaking to a crowd of the impressionable young, but by the end of his story he was speaking only for Faith. He was an old man, grey hair cut to a stubble and face lashed by two long scars that were a Stabber's work, but there was a yearning, young man's look in his eyes as he looked to Faith for some sign of approval or favour.

"You have been to many places," she said, and he nodded sagely.

"Above and below, desert and jungle. Few many places I've not been, in my time." It was as though he were stating his credentials for a job.

"Do you know of a place of gold, of lights? Where everything is cared for, and there are…" I could see her breaking down inside as she tried to externalise those wisps of memory. "There are friends." A tear splintered in the corner of her eye.

The old Fisherman shook his head slowly. "Nothing like that," he said sadly, "or I'd not be back here."

I took her to meet other friends. Giulia showed her maps but the golden place was on none of them. Pelgraine fell in love with her, an exercise doomed to failure. He scared her and she would not go near him. Eventually I even took her to Sergei's Collective. Like Greygori, she did not find Sergei strange to look upon.

She feared him less than she feared the normal run of men and women. He told her of the place where he was born, the myths he made up about himself. She heard the whole improbable fable and believed it. It was no stranger to her than the truths I gave of Shadrapar and Underworld.

"Where did you get her, Stefan?" he asked later. "What the hell is she?"

I explained my theory that she was a Rengen and had escaped or been liberated from some private clinic. "She is looking for some place... some place she belonged," I said.

"But you think she has escaped," he pointed out. "If she escapes, she will not want to be returned. Or, if she tries to return, then there was no escape. She fell, merely."

"She fell..." I considered.

"From grace," Sergei finished. "She does not fit, so she seeks some place she will."

I nodded helplessly.

"And you help her?"

"I don't know why. I feel responsible. I want to find this place for her, but... How?"

"She is like a hook, I think, and you are on it."

I tried to defend myself, but I knew that it was true. I was a victim of Faith just as everyone else was, who looked upon her. It was how they had made her.

Sergei fell for her too, in his way. "I also shall help," he decided. "We two shall seek out this place of hers."

We lived a strange kind of life over the next months. When Greygori did not want me, and when the Collective could spare him, Sergei and I took on the profession of burglars. We contacted groups like the Friendly Society, the Exceptionals, even the Ascendants whose larceny was grounded in their bizarre religious beliefs. At one time or another, Sergei had done good for just about everyone. We would go to a Friendlies factor or the like and Sergei would say, "We wish to look at some laboratories."

The factor would nod and a message would reach us a week later, that this or that team of entrepreneurs would be raiding a rich man's factory or a pharmaceuticals husbandry, and Sergei and I would sign up for the job.

I learned a lot in those months. By my third sortie I could climb up and down a rope without falling off and I could sneak across a roof without waking the sleepers below. I was taught the rudiments of how to fool a clever lock and how to pick a simple one. I cannot claim to have been a quick student, but I was driven by Faith.

You may think we were mad, to venture so far on her vague imaginings, without her ever asking us. You would be right. Blameless though she was, this was how she was made. Nobody under the effects of Faith was entirely rational.

For example, we would hook up with three of the Exceptionals an hour after dark and steal from the Underworld into the Steel Town district. By routes that they had discovered through careful experimentation we would ascend to the rooftops and make our way by a system of lines, jumps and rope-bridges (unsuspected by those below) until we reached the building in question. Below us, through skylights, we could see the heedless night shift preparing their toxins. As nimbly and silently as web-children we would find the loose panel or open hatch or sabotaged lock that would let us in. While the sleepy labourers worked around us we would grab the chemical goods and creep away as though we had never been there.

Sergei and I would describe these places to Faith in the hope of prompting some return of her lost soul. She would listen with infinite attention, sifting each word for something of familiarity. There was nothing. Each time she would lower her head a little, and thank us mechanically for what we had done. Each time we were both more determined than ever to break the lock that sealed away her mind. It became a challenge in its own right. The universe was mocking us with our impotence, and we were not putting up with it. Word got around, soon enough, that Sergei and Stefan were interested in ever more exotic targets. At the time I felt assured of her eventual gratitude and some nebulous reward arising from it. This is the dangerous fiction we spin for ourselves, is it not, that so readily turns sour. Looking back I can only think that I tired and frightened her, yet kept her beholden on me because she had nowhere else to go.

Our new hobby was not only to our benefit. The thieves could make good use of us. Sergei was an all-round cracksman: good with machines, a climber and sneaker, skilled in a fight. We had not needed to fight in our three forays, but the thieves were no soldiers and they grew nervous without some kind of backup. As for me, I was none of those things but I discovered that my education was a commodity. It had won me no friends when I was a Ward of the Temple, but now I was a known quantity and my word was trusted. The market for liberated books and papers was as lively as that for drugs and elixirs, and I found that I was a good man to rifle a bookshelf or case a library. When I went with them I could be counted on to find some piece of ancient literature that I knew would have a buyer amongst the literati. The Overworld rich asked no questions when prizes were proffered. Between my criminal ventures, the thieves began to bring their finds to me for valuing. When Greygori was deeply engrossed in his experiments I held court with Arves, the two of us talking over the value of stolen scrolls and pilfered poetry.

The Ascendants took us on their expedition into the private de Howza museum, where a gallery of horrors showed stuffed and mounted monsters from the jungles, looming and leering from the shadows. Many of them had been collected by Trethowan's own expeditions, and I located for the thieves an untouched first edition set of his bestiaries that I knew would be the pride and joy of some rich collector.

There was a factory line of ancient machines, only a few with any obvious purpose, and the Ascendants took one, which they believed had been constructed by their prophet. It triggered some alarm, so that a device at the end of the row tried to kill us with beams of cold light that froze the walls where they touched. Sergei took a wrench to it and broke off the nozzle of its weapon. It continued to glare at us with its evil little lights and lenses but we absconded with its brother and the tale of our daring.

Faith was unimpressed with this.

We joined up with a gang named the Phlegmatics to raid an underground vault maintained by an Authority man for private experiments. The Phlegmatics were a disorganised and rowdy crew operating on rumour and hearsay, and when we had cut our way into the vault from beneath (using a fearful implement that Sergei borrowed from the Fishermen) we discovered that the installation was abandoned. The books of formulae that the Phlegmatics were after were absent. We saw that we were not the first to burrow into that secure place. There was a Vermin tunnel in the far corner and marks to suggest that much of the equipment had been stolen by the creatures. As if we were Outriders, we tooled up with our weaponry and went into their warren after them. Sergei killed one, the Phlegmatics killed another, and the remainder fled before us. We found the gnawed notebooks in a nest they had made in a deeper chamber. The Fishermen went in later, I believe, to explore further. Giulia was ecstatic that her maps could be enlarged.

Faith recognised none of it.

We went with the Friendly Society on their first scouting of a big laboratory and leisure complex owned by several very powerful men, most of whom were, or had been, Authority members. I am fairly sure that Harweg had a large stake in it. We were not just slipping in by some established route. The Friendlies were "tapping" the building, seeking ingress, investigating. I had always thought they were a crew of clowns until then, from their flippant manner and general disrespect.

My illusions were shattered on this expedition, for they were the soul of organisation. They were led by a square-jawed woman named Yarmin, with short fair hair, wearing most of an old Outrider's uniform. With Sergei and myself and four Friendlies she tackled the building expertly. By the end of the night we had found a sheet of the roof that could be peeled back, a trigger for an alarm that could be pinned, and we had looked into one of their laboratories. Sergei had been lowered on a rope until he was eight feet from the floor, like some ghastly human spider. As he slowly spun in the gloom he had looked from hall to hall (for the building was vast) seeing dormant equipment, vats of chemicals. His dim lamp had illuminated fittings of brass and bronze, strange statues and ornaments. It was part-laboratory and part-state-room, and perhaps storeroom too, for all the decorative junk that the owners' townhouses could not accommodate.

When Sergei described all this to Faith she looked troubled.

"Tell me again," she said.

He went back over the details for her. I had expected her to be delighted, once we found anything that rang a chord in the void of her memory. Instead her worried look increased, as though she was on the verge of some horrible revelation.

"What do you know?" Sergei asked her.

She shook her head, shrugged, huddled into herself. "Nothing. I know nothing."

Sergei and I exchanged glances. "Probably it is nothing," he said, voice heavy with disappointment.

"I want to see it," Faith said flatly. Sergei and I stared at her.

"You… did not seem to like it, when Sergei described it," I pointed out.

"I have to see it. Your words sound familiar. I cannot visualise it, but still… Do I know it? I have to see it."

"I really don't think that you can come with us," I said dubiously.

She shrugged. "I have to see it," she repeated.

"We talk to the Friendlies," Sergei suggested. "They prepare now to make their raid. We see what they say. It is their choice."

We spoke to Yarmin, who would be leading the burglary as well. She had heard of Faith and was intrigued.

"What good is she?" she demanded.

"She thinks she may have seen the place before," I explained.

Yarmin pondered this, and I saw she thought Faith could perhaps lead them to treasure within the unexplored building. It had not been my intention to give her the idea but before I could dissuade her she had said, "Fine. We go in five days. Be ready."

33

Bride of Sanguival

Within those five days everything began to go wrong. My first warning was a conversation late one night, which was to say, around midday above ground.

I was having trouble sleeping. Perhaps it was worry over Faith accompanying us on our next jaunt; perhaps it was just prolonged exposure to Faith. I was drawn out of an extended sequence of disturbing images by the sound of voices from the library. It was two rooms away, but in the dead silence I heard every sound as though I was right there.

I heard Greygori say, "Stefan tells me you are searching." Perhaps it was my own name that awoke me. I had told him nothing of the sort but he still knew.

I assumed, in those bleary moments, that Greygori was just muttering to himself. I only came fully awake when I heard Faith say, "Stefan is searching."

"For you, though, Faith. On your behalf. In accord with your purposes, Faith. Is that not the case?"

No audible answer came, but I could imagine the shrug, that little movement of her shoulders with her face turned away.

"You are a grand experiment," Greygori wheezed at her, an odd tremor in his voice. "You are a most exacting piece of work, Faith. Really, you are a detailed creation."

I heard the oversized nails of his bare feet ticking on the stone as he advanced across the library floor. Greygori had more to say, and there was something familiar about the way he said it.

"I have not seen, Faith, such artifice beyond my own work," he murmured. I imagined him standing beside and around her, just short of touching her, whilst she kept her head carefully tilted away from him. "Faith, you are the project of a master."

"I don't want to be that," from Faith.

"You should embrace it," Greygori pressed. "You are the pinnacle of the art, Faith. You should not pretend to be one of the dying masses, Faith. You should rejoice in your nature, that you have been made into what you are. You are a special construction, Faith."

I realised that the faintly familiar tone of Greygori's voice was one I had heard in my more innocent days often enough. I recalled sitting in some fashionable dispensary or other and hearing a young student shower the object of his affections with a welter of compliments. No lover would have been won by the compliments Greygori had found, but then what pleased Greygori was manifestly not that which pleased any other.

I heard Faith say, "Don't talk about me like that, as though I am some *thing*."

"You would rather be a natural person, Faith?" Greygori wanted to know. "Have you not seen them, Faith, enough of them? Their pointless, brief and flawed lives? They're vermin, Faith. Useless, out-evolved, Faith. Doomed, Faith, they're all doomed." I heard Faith give out a little sound of fright and I deduced that he had laid one of those mutated hands on her.

I could not get up. You may have wondered why I just lay there, listening. The whole drama held a terrible fascination for me, as I listened to Greygori's long-denied human side rise up to put him through the paces of a wooer.

"And what are you?" Faith demanded faintly.

"Observe," Greygori told her, and there was a sound of flapping cloth, and I did not know whether to be horrified or to laugh. In my mind's eye – and perhaps in reality – he had exposed himself to her like any dirty old man. God, though – what abomination would be exposed when Greygori lifted his shroud? Faith was never distressed by the grotesque, though. Often she found it comforting, as she found the familiar frightening and strange.

"What think you of the fruits of my labours, Faith?" Greygori asked of her.

She said, cool and unworried, "I think nothing of them."

I heard more cloth sounds, and then the clicking of his nails again as Greygori prowled with halting gait around the perimeters of the library. I imagined his fused fingers trailing the spines of Arves' books.

"You come from a shining place, is that right, Faith?" Greygori said, and the staccato sound of his footsteps stopped.

"A shining place," she confirmed, with that same wistful air that always attended her blank nostalgia.

"I am going to a shining place," Greygori told her. "I am working my way to it, one gene at a time. Would you like to come with me?"

I was silently praying that she would say no, trying to send my mind out to warn her. My mind never reached her, for she said, "Maybe… Perhaps…" and I heard Greygori rustle and scrape his way close to her.

"I can take you, Faith, to my shining place," he wheezed, and the weight of pinned emotion in his voice was hideous. "Faith, you can come with me, but you cannot go like that, Faith. You are not dressed, Faith, for that shining place. You must cease to resemble one of these milling slaves, Faith. You must not want, Faith, to be such a thing as Arves or Stefan or the countless others. You must let me prepare you for that shining place. You must be like me."

I heard nothing for the count of a long breath. Greygori waited, his offer exposed at last. Then I heard feet, not the claws of the Transforming Man but human feet, as Faith ran past him and out of the library into the nest of rooms she shared with

Arves and myself. I saw her shadow dance past the doorway to my chamber, and then she was gone, hidden somewhere beyond.

After a long, long silence, Greygori hauled himself from the library with heavy steps. His breath, wheezy and ragged, infected the air before he closed the door to his laboratory.

I lay awake all that night, because I had heard the crippled remnant of Greygori's humanity claw its way into the light like one of the infinitely withered corpses from the necropolis. Greygori was his old, cold self again for now, but there would be further eruptions of his repressed innards and he was a man used to getting what he wanted. Sergei and I were suddenly up against a cruel time limit in which to find something for Faith.

Over those next few days, Greygori and I played an odd little game. He did not know that I knew, but I did not know for sure that he did not know... and so on. He found every excuse to send me and Arves out of his chambers in order to have time alone with Faith. Conversely, I found every excuse to drag Faith along with me. Whether or not he pressed his suit further on her I cannot say. I heard no more, but I knew the clock was counting down.

We met Yarmin at Emil's print shop with her crew of Friendlies. They were all in high spirits, excited about the coming raid. They were excited about Faith, too. They all viewed the night's venture as an opportunity to impress her, to fashion a simulacrum of themselves in her mind as she helplessly conjured one of herself in all who encountered her.

We made our way across the usual rooftop paths to that great complex and checked that our previous ingress had not been detected. We were clear, and the alarm systems were still pinned, the panels still loose. Sergei went first, the rest of us lowering him down in utter silence. He hung in a slow spin for half a minute and then signalled for us to let him all the way down to the factory floor. One of the Friendlies secured the rope, and we all crept down it. I had worried about Faith, but she climbed as though she were born to it, or as though her engineers had grafted the skill onto her. She was wearing dark, loose clothes like most of us other burglars.

Within the building it was dark and almost silent, save for the faintest murmur of activity from far away down many corridors. Sergei lit a very dim silver lamp that, from a distance, might have seemed moonlight. We had found our way into a room of fixings, unfinished housings for machines as yet uninstalled. The interior of the building was still being fitted out and the Friendlies planned to take advantage of it. In the confusion many valuable things could go missing without suspicion.

I saw now why Sergei had said the place was a money sink. There were odd works of art, statues and icons and idols, both ancient and the modern replicas that constantly flooded the marketplace. The facings of the doors and the fixings of the furnishings were all gold and brass and other precious metals, elaborately worked and ornamented and set with faceted plastics. One half-built horologium had a pendulum of solid crystal that disappeared into Yarmin's pack almost immediately.

Faith was staring about in the wan light. Her face was a closed book, but not an unwritten one.

"You know this, don't you?" I prompted.

"I know something," she whispered. "I feel the presence of someone I should know. I see his hand in this." Then she surprised me by adding, "I do not like this place, Stefan."

"You want to leave?" I asked, and she shook her head irresolutely.

"No. I need this. I need to know… but I do not like this place. There is evil here."

The word lodged in my mind and worried at it, because Faith was not judgemental. She had looked upon the worst the Underworld had to offer, Greygori included, and passed judgement on none of it. I had thought her devoid of any knowledge of good or evil.

The Friendlies had advanced to take the next room on, and one skipped back to hurry us up. They had found some documents they thought might be valuable, but which turned out to be inventories of rooms somewhere else in the complex. I murmured down the list of fittings and fixtures incredulously. Someone was spending obscene amounts of money to fit this place out: baths of alabaster, plumbing of brass and lead, locks and door furniture of adamant, a bed of costly machine-silk over intricately moulded plastics. Someone was making this building their world within a world.

"No man is rich like this without stealing from the people," Sergei observed. "The greatest thieves are always the wealthy."

I had never felt moved to defend the Shadrapan political system to Sergei. I agreed wholeheartedly that the entire enterprise was probably paid for by prying bread from babies' mouths. By that time the Friendlies were already moving on. Faith had not, though. She was shivering, rooted to the spot.

"I must go on," she whispered to herself.

"What is beyond here?" I asked her.

"Something terrible?"

"A guard? A machine? A trap?" I pressed.

"A man," she told me.

Her creator, I thought, but I said nothing. I could see the war in her, driven to know and yet what she learned could bring pain, even madness.

Beyond there was a museum or something, a collection without any taste or intent. The exhibits were all remarkable, but there was no other common link. It was a rich man's museum, a private gathering of rarities without context.

I examined a book, millennia old, copied from a work even older; Yarmin had cracked its glass case open for me. Sergei had found a small clockwork he claimed would capture images of the world. The Friendlies were swarming everywhere, prising locks and breaking fastenings.

The place was beginning to get on my nerves. It was partly Faith's anxiety, more that the halls had an echo of that underground necropolis. There was the same vast breathing silence over everything. We were surrounded by dead things and abandoned chambers, although in this case it was that they had not been inhabited *yet*. The murmur of distant activity in other far parts of the building just emphasised how quiet it was around us.

Faith stood in the midst of our activity and swayed a little: I tried to keep an eye on her, but the Friendlies kept bringing me things to value, most of which I could not begin to guess at. Sergei was stepping uneasily about the perimeter of the room, eager to move on; he had good instincts.

Two of the Friendlies were dismantling a square case on one wall, which seemed to contain silvery treasure glittering in our lamplight. I thought, in the moment before they pried it open, that Faith was suddenly energised, raising a hand to stop them, opening her mouth to speak.

Too late. With both of them leaning on the crowbar they forced the case with a loud sound of splitting plastic. Even as Yarmin was crossing to remonstrate they stumbled back as its contents cascaded onto the floor.

I thought it was a liquid at first because it moved like quicksilver, but the texture was wrong. As it piled onto the floor it seemed nothing but endless lengths of gleaming chain coiling upon themselves, like a metal waterfall. There were more reflections in that tumbled, flowing mass than our lamp could ever have struck from it. Whatever lights were shining back from that thing, they did not exist in our room, perhaps not in our time.

It lay piled in a heap at the foot of the pedestal, a mound of something shining, perhaps three feet across. One of the

Friendlies stepped in towards it, and then our collective breath caught as it flowed away from him in a fluid mass of metal links, half its bulk climbing the nearest wall.

The Friendly was intrigued and reached out to gather it up. Sergei and I, and others, all shouted at him, but it was too late. He touched it and he died. It was a quick death, a snap and sizzle of electricity and a stink of burning hair and the man was arched rigid on the floor with his hands black as charcoal. Then everything went to hell.

Almost everyone made for cover. I skidded behind an armless, headless statue and looked back to see the flowing thing fire a beam of silver chain at another Friendly, stopping him in his tracks and stone dead in an instant. In that same instant it was gone, for it had somehow fired *itself* at him, leaping down the length of its own ray or tendril, so that it was now coiling and writhing off the man's charred body looking for further victims. It moved like the lightning it contained.

Sergei dived across open ground to get to me, risking his life every fraction of a second. The thing was oozing forwards and backwards, searching. A second later it snapped itself out at another Friendly crouching behind a metal machine or sculpture. The machine exploded into pieces and the man behind was killed. The silvery killer flowed easily from within the heart of the destroyed artefact.

"We've got to get to the rope," Sergei whispered. "Look, I will run and distract it. You must go, climb."

"Suicide!" I hissed at him. "It's too fast. It'll fry you and be back for us before we blink."

"Get the Friends following you," Sergei continued implacably. "And Faith. I will—"

"Faith?" My stomach lurched. "Where is Faith?"

Sergei stared at me and swore in his made-up language.

I put my head around the statue and saw the malignant entity crawling across the floor like a puddle. It was making its steady, calculating way towards a niche where Yarmin and two of the Friendlies were crouched. One of them leant forwards, preparatory to making a break for it. The thing, machine, creature, whatever it was, licked out a tendril of itself to strike a spittle of molten metal from the nearest case, making the man drop back. It could have followed that tentacle and been on them right then, but it was playing with them. Whatever it was, it *thought*.

One of the other Friendlies took the bold but pointless move of firing his crossbow at the thing. The bolt just shattered into fragments of burned plastic, but it attracted the thing's attention. With a final flick towards Yarmin it humped itself off in the direction of the crossbowman who was—

Who was hiding with Faith behind some kind of verdigrised telescope.

I actually got a step towards rushing the thing. I cannot say what I would have done. Sergei grabbed my belt and hauled me back into cover.

The crossbowman was mindlessly slipping another bolt to the string as the alien thing advanced on him. He was almost done by the time that Faith stepped past him. Her eyes were closed and she was standing almost on tiptoe.

I glanced at Sergei and saw him as mystified as me.

I remember Faith then as glowing with her own light. It was surely not like that, but the memory plays tricks. I remember her as though her pale hair and flawless skin gave out the light to complete the chain-creature's unsourced reflections.

Her lips parted slightly, and I knew she was singing, somehow. I heard nothing, no note, but she was singing. Somewhere deep inside, she had always been singing.

The guardian thing reared up almost to the height of a man, little flickers and loops of chain arcing and dancing about it. There they stayed, she perfectly still and it in constant motion, but linked somehow. I cannot explain it but it saved all of us. Sergei hissed out in the loudest stage-whisper you ever heard for everyone to move to the rope, and Yarmin and her two padded stealthily out of their hiding place, glancing at the creature all the time. The crossbowman edged his terrified way from behind Faith and crept along the outside wall, weapon dangling from his hand.

There was an abrupt shout from a further room, and we saw several shapes, human shapes, appear from a new doorway. All the noise had not gone unnoticed; someone had called the guards. There were a good dozen of them, men in dark uniforms not unlike Wardens' clothes, each clutching a musket. Yarmin and the Friendlies were frozen for a second and then they were running even as the first guard raised his flintlock to his shoulder, tracking them.

Sergei shot him, pistol out from inside his jacket in a smooth motion, and the shot was a monstrous explosion in the echoing space. I was shouting at Faith to come on, to run while we could. I had the horrible feeling that, if she stayed, I could not have left, either.

The matter was taken from my hands. The other guards were taking aim and one let loose at the crossbowman as he tried to dash for it. The ball skipped within inches of Faith and took the poor thief in the thigh, knocking him to the ground. As he cried out, Faith awoke from her trance; her concentration shattered and I knew she would die.

I see the tableau in my mind's eye: the felled crossbowman writhing, face twisted in agony; Sergei halfway to dragging him after us; Faith's wide eyes, staring at the blood; the guardian monster or machine released and crouching down into an ugly lump, poised to lance out.

It struck the first guard as the man was reloading, and his powder magazine blew up even as the creature ricocheted from his scorched chest to the next. Sergei and I were away by then, Faith alongside us and all three of us lumping the wounded man along. We left three blackened Friendlies dead behind us and nobody had much loot to show for it. It was a dismally failed burglary but it could have been so much worse.

As we tied the injured man to the end of the rope we heard the screams and cries of the guards as the monster hunted them down and consumed them. I have no idea what it was: engineered life, some strange chemical compound or a trapped natural force, save that it thought. It was ripe with malice and it, too, loved Faith. It certainly wreaked a vengeance on those who interrupted its conference with her.

Did they tame it again, imprison it beneath glass as a mere exhibit? Or did it evade them, escape the complex, find its own alien life in Shadrapar or beyond? I may yet meet that thing again.

And Faith? Faith would say nothing? The mystery refused to unveil itself. She would talk of none of it, admit none of it.

Was it her shining place? I wanted to believe not, but it was a place from her past. She had known it and it – in the person of the guardian – had known her. If that was the place that she dreamed of going back to then, Sergei suggested, those dreams had been programmed into her in order to coerce a return.

We went on no more burglaries. There seemed to be no point. We had got as close as we would get, and neither of us wanted to hazard the guardian again, or the other horrors the building surely contained.

This left Greygori with the field. The illusion that we had a place to get Faith to, beyond the reach of his long arms, was lost. When I returned that night from the abortive raid he was in the library, leafing through some book with his narrow lips curled into an unnatural smile, though he could not have known.

Two days after the raid Faith disappeared for a whole day, and a week later, for a day and a half. It took no stretch of the imagination to guess where she was going. Greygori was taking her into his forbidden laboratory.

I eavesdropped, the once, and heard him expounding something in terms so abstruse that I could not follow him. He was talking about a process, and I realised from context that it was part of his self-engineering. He spoke about his shining place, that he would somehow reach by turning himself into a thing that should only live in darkness. He spoke of her in terms architectural, technical, biomechanical, genetic and mathematical, which for him were terms of love. And she listened.

When I found her between these episodes, her manner was changed. She was anxious and restless, and yet she seemed less and less able to leave our rooms. Greygori had planted some suggestion in her that meant he was always in her head. Either it was his promises of shining places or else he resembled – in temperament, surely not in appearance – some creator-figure lodged in the submerged part of her mind. If Sergei was right and her creators had conditioned her to return to them, perhaps Greygori had co-opted this for his own gain.

Eventually I was able to talk her into leaving Greygori's domain. I took her somewhere we could talk and I asked her outright. "Do you want what he plans for you?" Before I got her there I had been all full of crusading fury, certain in my righteousness, but perhaps Greygori had his seeds in me, too. I remembered Faith saw the world differently to others. I remembered how meagre were the options I might be able to find for her. I could not assume that some gallant rescue by Stefan Advani would be preferable to Greygori's attentions.

"I don't understand what he will do to you. I guess he'll remake you like he's doing to himself. I mean, maybe that's an honour," I rambled. "But you should have a choice. I'm trying to give you a choice." And even now I think back on that scene and wonder if I really said those noble sentiments. Or did I just want her for myself. I can't deny she stirred me, and part of me saw Greygori as a grotesque rival. Perhaps I simply didn't want anyone else to have her if I could not.

She said nothing, and then she said nothing again. We crouched in the dog-end tunnel I'd found and I listened for the click of Greygori's nails, the dragging of his ill-fitting robe. Faith's nothings built up silently around us. She was trying to speak – her throat pulsed and her lips moved – but she could not bring the words out. At last, though, she turned her face away from me. I read rejection in the motion and made to stand, but she lashed out and gripped my wrist like a vice, freezing me in place. Her other hand reached to her ear and peeled it back, and half her scalp. I may have cried out. I may, in fact, have come very close to being very ill.

It all just lifted up, that skin, and underneath I saw something that must have been her skull. The moment would recur strongly to me much later, confronted with the disseminated anatomy of Thelwel's damaged arm. The not-quite-bone she revealed was lustrous and rainbow-sheened, like the pearls the Organ Donor Boys grew. I saw there the network of recent grooves that had been ground into the surface of that substance, a complex web of channels that were too rough to be part of her design. They were Greygori's doing. He was laying the foundations for his work on her.

Her expression, when she had replaced her skin, was desperate.

34

Repercussions

Sergei and I held a council of war with the aim of liberating Faith from Greygori's clutches. Liberate to where? It was the first hurdle and we fell at it.

"Not the factions," Sergei said. "She would not be safe. Most would sell her back to him for credit. The rest would not be enemies with Gregor Samsa."

"I don't understand," I said sullenly. "He only has Arves to back him up. I cannot see him marching up to the Meat Packers and knocking their doors down with his fists."

"Gregor Samsa has played a clever game many years," Sergei reminded me. "All factions owe him, many more than they could repay. If they will not pay Faith to him, then Gregor calls Waylun and Electric Gangsters and People of the Scarlet Sash and says, 'Go get me this girl.' And they will. And the faction holding Faith knows this, and so they surrender her before he ever has to test his credit. Besides, how easy was it for you finding her a home before? You did not bring her to Gregor as first choice, surely?"

I sat, dejected. I had not seen just how much we were playing on ground of Greygori's choosing.

"What about your Collective?"

Sergei's face twisted. "My first loyalty is to my people. He crushes us to get Faith, with ease. Trouble enough sheltering you."

"Me?"

"After you steal the girl from him, you think you're going back to your old room? He will not be pleased with you, Stefan," Sergei pointed out.

Another point I had somehow failed to consider. Months of security had made me forget that the Underworld was an unfriendly place for the unaffiliated. I remembered the looming threat of the Organ Donor Boys.

"The depths?" I asked. Even as Sergei shook his head I admitted, "We could hardly just abandon her down there, and besides, I don't think the depths are deep enough to keep Greygori out."

"That leaves one place," Sergei submitted.

I looked blankly at him for far too long before he pointed one long finger up towards the hidden sky.

We went through all kinds of clever ideas for getting Faith out. We had long conferences with Giulia about secret passages and unknown ways to the surface. The three of us pored over her maps, and the only conclusion we could safely reach was that the area around Greygori's cul-de-sac was too well known and explored for there to be any hidden routes up. Greygori had chosen a hiding place long ago, and perhaps he had needed to defend it from others. There was only one way in and out.

So it was that careful planning became irrelevant. We would act one night when Greygori was closeted in his lab. We would do it at the first opportunity.

That opportunity soon arose, and I crept to the entrance to his chambers and let Sergei in. The two of us stole silently to Faith's little room, and she awoke while my hand was still an inch from her shoulder.

She stared up at the two of us, wide-eyed. Sergei signalled for her to stay quiet.

"We're going to take you away from this place," I whispered. "We're going to put you outside Greygori's reach."

She stared at us still. Time stretched out.

"That is," I stammered out, "If you want to go."

The stare continued for another three precious seconds and then she nodded.

She dressed quickly, and we were on our way.

We were halfway to the door when Sergei stopped and I saw we were not alone. It was Arves, standing in darkness between us and the wider world. He took it in instantly, short-sighted or not: the two furtive kidnappers and their much-valued charge. There was a moment filled with infinite, silent tension as his mind weighed his loyalties in the balance.

He nodded, more like the old man he resembled than the young man he was, and then stepped aside, moving towards his room and a position of plausible deniability. Whether he too rebelled against Greygori's plans, or whether it was just that he was eager to be rid of Faith, I cannot say.

Then there was a sound, the first since we set forth upon our enterprise, and it came from the laboratory.

We froze, all four, and a creeping horror like a living thing entered the room and seized us. Arves just vanished into the rooms I had shared with him, and we wrongdoers hung poised to continue our stealthy exit. We all felt it, though, that sense that within the unknown confines of the laboratory something had awoken and was moving with patient, many-jointed strides towards the door. In an instant the fear had gripped us and we bolted for the way out and pelted through the tunnels of Underworld.

We left the most frequented halls in minutes but took no step downward. We were going out. Where else could Faith be hidden from the Transforming Man's glass-covered eyes? We knew that she had enemies in the Overworld who might seek to capture and enslave her, but we believed none could have as dire aspirations as Greygori Sanguival.

We saw no sign of pursuit; we had no doubt that we were pursued. We did not slacken our pace until we saw ahead of us the iron hatch that was our destination. Only then did I shake the belief that Greygori would somehow have second guessed us, and be waiting.

The hatch opened onto an outlying district of Shadrapar, sealed with four square-mouthed locks. Sergei produced the ancient L-shaped key and the two of us laboured to free the rust-heavy mechanism. The last lock stuck and as we hung on the key's three-foot shaft we sensed again the stalking approach of the Transforming Man. Sergei, teeth gritted, put all the leverage of his inhumanly long frame against it, and it screamed as it ground open. The corroded square of the hatch cover fell down on us, propelled, as it seemed, not by gravity but by the force of light above.

I shut my eyes against it, but Sergei grabbed me by my belt and arm and bodily hoisted me into that unbearable and merciless brightness. I hit the ground blind and rolled away from the opening, palms clamped across my eyes. A moment later someone was turning me over to face the sun.

"Stefan," I heard Faith say, and realised that the hands were hers. Her shadow passed between me and the sun and I could see a little. It seemed to me that, even silhouetted against that almighty light, I could still make out the details of her face.

To one side, a crouched blur must be Sergei. He had bound his eyes over and was listening intently. Even as I was about to speak to Faith he grabbed at my arm and silenced me.

From the open hatch there came a sound as of someone dragging at the fallen hatch cover.

"Faith...?" came Greygori's almost querulous tone. "Faith? Will you go away now, Faith, when our plans are on the cusp?"

He sounded wretched, lonely, human. "Faith, the shining place awaits but you are not readied for it yet. Faith? Faith?"

He would not step into the shaft of sunlight, nor reach up to haul his malformed bulk out into the air. How long he waited down there for an answer I never knew, for we took shelter in a half-demolished house until our eyes had grown accustomed to the light, and never returned by that hatch.

I remember Faith standing, staring about her as though it was the first time she had ever seen the sunlit world. On her face was an expression of such wonder that I thought she might have found her shining place after all.

I let her go. We both did, but Sergei was always stronger than me. I turned away, because I could not have watched her depart without running after her, without trying once again to take possession of her.

I had never had her, not in the way you think. When she was there, in my power, that was all I desired. When she was gone, I felt a gnawing withdrawal in my guts as though I was pining for a drug.

It has never left me, not quite. They made her well, when they made Faith; better than they knew.

After she had gone, Sergei and I hid out in the wasteland for a few hours and then made careful tracks by the back ways to Emil des Schartz' printing shop.

I cannot say that Emil was pleased to see us, but he hid us until nightfall, when we could return below-ground and rejoin Sergei's Collective. There we waited for the repercussions of Greygori's wrath.

*

Nothing happened. There was no mobilisation of factional forces, no assaults with strange weapons, no assassins or spies, no Temple sanctions. Nothing issued forth from the Transforming Man's domain but the usual low-key business deals. After a month I allowed myself to relax into life in the Collective, which was not easy. Their agricultural pursuits were hard work, and in between they spent the time brokering stolen goods and finds from the depths. I took upon myself once more the role of valuer, which gave me a little more free time than the average Collective member. I met up with Giulia often, and she even brought Arves on occasion. Of Arves I enquired anxiously about my former master and all he was able to do was shrug. Greygori Sanguival had reverted to type. He remained closeted in his laboratory, made the same cautious and calculating deals as he had and spoke not a word of Faith or myself. With Faith removed, in fact, it was almost as though his racked humanity had sunk back to its subconscious home. Hers had been the light that had drawn it to the surface. Now it was in darkness again, forgetting. Arves patently preferred him that way. Arves had not enjoyed much about the whole Faith business.

So Sergei and I reckoned that we were safe and that we had done a good thing, and we both speculated as to what might have happened to Faith but heard nothing of her. Later, long after I was sent to the Island, I would hear of her again.

What happened was this. It was innocent enough. Some group of amateur cracksmen calling themselves the Broken Folk had come by a trove of ancient books and did not know what to do with them. Naturally, word got to me and I decided that I would go and offer my services.

I skipped along to their headquarters and noticed nothing odd until they took me into the room with the alleged books, which contained half a dozen Angels and no literature whatsoever.

The door was shut behind me but I could not have run even given the chance. Angels were the last thing I expected to see in Underworld. They were universally hated and loathed, the butt of countless jokes. They were the symbols of the society we had all dropped out of, and there they were, six of them, their varied armaments trained on me, each in full armour with point generator packs humming. I just stared. I had no sense that they were real, so unlikely was the sight.

Then one of them stepped forwards and I saw a face I had not seen for a long time. It was the Commissar of Angels and his presence broke the spell. It was his armoured car that had crushed poor Helman, he who had left Jon and Rosanna to the mercies of the mob. This was the man who, political acumen spent, would later be delivered up to the Island and executed by firing squad. Even now the thought brings me a measure of satisfaction.

There was one other exit to the room, and I was instantly pelting for it, because I wanted to make it hard for them. I was still no man of action, and they grabbed me, fingers biting into my arms. The Commissar stood nose to nose with me, cruel features displaying a rare pleasure.

"Well," he said. "This is a fine surprise. It's not often that we recapture such a dangerous radical without any sweat at all."

"Dangerous what?" I squawked.

"The man who raised the mob. The greatest threat to civil disorder that Shadrapar has seen for a generation."

"Raised the mob?" I demanded. "The mob was raised against me and mine!"

He shrugged callously. "It was raised, and someone must be to blame. You were there. The Lord Justiciar is most keen to have you before him for sentencing."

"I'll tell everyone the truth at my trial!"

The Commissar laughed shortly, "No trials for people like you, Advani. No trials for someone who runs from justice. It is an admission of guilt. It's kinder on the sensibilities of the state. Sentencing only, Advani. No trial."

"But… Shadrapar doesn't work that way. It's unjust." I barely knew what I was saying.

"Shadrapar is a machine," the Commissar said. "We keep the casing nice and shiny so that people can believe what they want about it, but if you get into the workings, expect to be ground between the gears."

He looked away from me abruptly, face shutting down. Something was coming from the tunnel I had been running for. I knew the great misshapen shadow long before the man appeared.

"So, Stefan, Stefan Advani, you are brought to justice at last, Stefan. How very sad that is." Greygori Sanguival lurched into the room and the Angels backed away, save for their leader.

"We're much obliged for this, Sanguival," the Commissar said.

"It will go well with your permanent record, Commissar," Greygori told him smoothly. "I trust, Commissar, that you have been inflating his reputation in the interim, have you not?"

"Here and there," the Commissar agreed. "He'll stand me in good stead; they'll be choosing a new Lord Justiciar soon enough."

"Commissar, who could deny you?" Greygori oiled. "Now, have you my side of the bargain, or must I take him back for my own justice, Commissar?" He showed no doubt that he could reclaim me if he chose.

"I have made sure that nobody is searching for you now," the officer told him. "Your records have mysteriously vanished."

"Well that is excellent, Commissar, is it not? And the other?"

"If you want it." The man signalled, and one of the Angels stepped forwards with a winged point generator pack in his hands. "It's not worked for ten years or more," the Commissar cautioned. "It's yours if you want it, but it's no good to anyone."

"Humour me," Greygori suggested, and one of his long arms plucked the object from the flinching man's arms. "Now,

428

Commissar, I think you and your cohorts should depart for the open air, lest those that I have bribed here forget, and tell others of your presence. Do you not think that wise, Commissar?"

I was under the impression that I was treated abominably. I was thrown into a cell scarcely twice the size of the one I would later share with four other people. The jailer would sometimes forget to replace the lamp-wicks and the window offered only a view of the Government District. The food was bland and the wine decidedly inferior. The jailer himself had a poor line in intellectual debate (he was an Academy dropout) and would just walk away if I contradicted him too much.

In short, I had no idea.

I had conceived a plan. I was going to unburden myself to the Lord Justiciar, in whose honesty I had faith. I would expose the venality of the Commissar, explain the truth behind the raising of the mob, clear my name and resume my place in polite society. I continually pressed the jailer to send a message to the Lord Justiciar that I wished to meet. The jailer, in turn, assured me that the Justiciar wished to talk to me, that he was very interested in my case, that he was a very busy man and that I should be patient. Everything would work out for the best. I should just wait.

I had one visitor and I made one visit. The visitor first, because he led to so many maddening speculations. One evening, the jailer suddenly stopped talking and moved away from me, and I heard footsteps down the corridor. There were two Angels, better turned out than the average, and there was an older man.

There was an undefinable aura of command about him. I felt he was so used to having his words taken as truth that he never even thought of it any more. He breezed through the cells of the Government District as easily as he might the gatherings of the rich or the halls of the Authority. He had a pleasant, paternal face belied by a distant, analytical expression. His hair was

429

silver and he was surely far older than he looked. His back was hunched in elegant cosmetic deformity.

"This is the man?" he enquired of one of the Angels, and was told that yes, I was indeed.

He flicked an eyebrow in the bored surprise of a man to whom all things are, in the end, equal. "I suppose revolutionaries come in all sizes."

"Please, sir, I'm no subversive," I started straight up. "I'm innocent, I—"

He made a sharp little warning gesture at me, and it shut me up straight away.

He came into the cell, all poise and control. The two Angels seemed momentarily thrown. If I was such a dangerous man, then my distinguished visitor should not be allowed so close. On the other hand, they had no power to stop him.

The old man came close, and looked me in the eyes.

"Where is she?" he said, and I knew who he meant.

"I do not know," I replied honestly. "Gone free."

The old man stared into my eyes and divined that I was telling the truth. I saw a corner of his mouth clench up, and an unhappiness surface in his eyes that must always have been there behind the mask of his power. Then he left, and I never saw him again.

I think that he was Faith's maker or commisioner, and the architect of that murderous building where the silver-lightning creature lived. Or maybe he was simply a man of vast wealth who had seen her, once, and been as covetous as we all were. Either way, I read in that iron face that he would move earth and moon and stars to find her, and not care who he trampled on the way.

A few days later I was brought out to an office smaller than my cell where a man who had been in the year below me at the Academy, and whose name I could not recall, took my details and informed me that I had been sentenced.

"Sentenced?" I demanded. "How?"

"Standard procedure," the clerk informed me. "The sentence of exile to the Island has been judged appropriate for your crimes. Have you anything to say?"

I barely heard what I had actually been sentenced to. I was more interested in the furtherance of my plan. "I need to speak to the Lord Justiciar," I said. "I have vital information that will clear my name."

"The Lord Justiciar is very busy," the clerk informed me. "I will relay your request to him, however. I am sure that he will be able to find the time. Vital information, you say?"

"Extremely vital."

"Well then, how could he refuse?" the clerk said smoothly.

I was returned to my cell in high spirits, and spent the next hour telling the sympathetic jailer that I would surely be out by the end of the week.

I was not out by the end of the week but, the middle of the week after, I was told that the boat had arrived.

"Boat? What boat?" I asked.

"The prison boat," the jailer told me. "What do you think we've been waiting for?"

"But I need to see the Lord Justiciar!"

"I'm sorry. He's very busy. Now would you mind putting these on?"

It was my first sight of the prison greys that were to become such a feature of my life.

My only consolation is that, unlike Lucian, I knew then that I was condemned. By the time I reached the Island all my illusions had been stripped from me.

PART THE FIFTH

IN WHICH I LEAVE
THE ISLAND

35

The Battle for Underworld

There was Arves, like a heap of sticks that someone had bundled into prison greys. He was leathered and creased by the cruel sun, worn to the very rounded nub of his endurance. He looked older than Trethowan ever would.

"What's the point of him?" Hermione grumbled. "He won't last."

Lucian disagreed, with his customary vacuous cheer. Why Lucian had seen people nine-tenths into death's kingdom rally and pull through. Perhaps a little food would do him good. Maybe some exercise. In Lucian's bubble-bright world, there was everything to hope for.

I thought Hermione had the right of it, and cut through Lucian's amiable chatter with, "He's a friend of mine from back home."

Hermione grunted, unimpressed, and sat down in one corner. Gaki's face appeared beside hers through the bars. The madman was unusually subdued, biding his time for something only he could name. Hermione began to speak to him, his soft replies quite lost in her blurred bass rumble.

I knelt beside Arves, wondering if he were dead already. He looked dead for some time. Even now, in the sanctuary of the Island's gloom, he was hanging by the frailest thread.

I said gently, "Arves? It's me. Stefan."

His eyes opened, the irises were sepia and the whites had gone yellow. He could not see me.

"Arves, what happened to you?" I asked him. How long had it been since he and I, Giulia and Sergei, last drank together? A year, but that year had so ruined him that nothing of the outward man was left.

"Stefan…" His voice was a croak, strengthening as he forced the sounds out. "How did you come here? Did they get you as well? No, you were gone long before. Is this where you went? You can't know, then. You can't know what happened to us. They declared war on the Underworld!"

"They did… War?" I stared into that blind face. "Who? The Meat Packers?"

"The surface. Shadrapar. The Authority. War, Stefan. All gone to war. God save me, it's all gone."

"Arves, you are going to have to slow down," I told him, because my head was so filled with horrible speculations I could not keep up with him. "Tell me what happened."

"Tell us all," Gaki's voice cut in. "I know the Underworld. Tell us all what has gone on there."

There were prisoners crowding in from the adjacent cells, and above and below as well, though Arves did not see them. I was the only thing in his life at that moment, aside from the story tearing him apart to get out.

I will not give his words verbatim. The story was so strong, and he was too frail to control it, and so it told itself in a great torrent through him. I will give you my reconstruction, then, of the war that came beneath Shadrapar, with assumptions, extrapolations and bridged gaps. There is no other account. You will have to be satisfied with mine.

It began with a death. News came down to the factions that some great man had died. None felt like mourning, and many prepared to celebrate, for the great and good of Shadrapar Above were ever the enemies of the Underworld. So it was that the factions speculated as to whom the death might belong to. A few were hoping that the President himself had died, and far more were praying for the demise of the Lord Justiciar, a most hated figure. Wagers were placed. The details trickled through the Underworld and brought a current of surprise. It was no member of the current Authority who had met his end, but a private individual of such wealth and power that it had been assumed he was invulnerable. I speak of none other than Jon Anteim the Elder. More, he had not passed quietly in his sleep but had been bloodily murdered in his private chambers.

This seems very clear to me. Someone in power, some rival of Anteim's, had reached the far horizon of their patience, and had taken the ultimate sanction. Perhaps it was even Haelen Anteim, doting daughter, who had so coolly arranged the death of her brother and was surely impatient to claim her inheritance. Back when I was still a citizen of Shadrapar the idea would have been unthinkable. The rich did not have each other assassinated. It was not done. Perhaps it was just that I was lost in scholarly innocence and did not see the way the world turned, but I think there was more. Even on the Island I had seen signs of political upheaval, the first of which (unrecognised at the time) was finding ex-Lord Financier Valentin Miljus in my very cell.

So Jon Anteim the Elder was dead, and to the Underworlders this seemed as good a reason to rejoice as any. There were enough who had suffered from him or his corrupt family. There was further news on the way, though: a public announcement by the President himself; a eulogy for the fallen statesman in which he swore to take action against Old Jon's killers. He swore that he would forever rid Shadrapar of the murderous scum of the Underworld who had dared to strike the old man down. It was the best-fitting cloak for the truth, whether Harweg was in on it or not. The Underworld was a vague terror to surface Shadrapar. Every citizen peopled it (with some justification) with thieves and killers and mad scientists' mistakes. It was easy for the Authority to blame any kind of evil on it. That was nothing new.

The mood in the Underworld when this broke was of careless bravado. Many there would love to accept responsibility for the deed.

Then a couple of Exceptionals who were on their way out for a little freelance thieving found that others were already coming in. One of the two got back and barrelled into the Temple shouting out some mad story of invasion. "Outriders!" he declared. "Outriders are coming."

Someone asked him what he meant. How many? A dozen? A score?

"All of them!" the frantic Exceptional cried. "All the Outriders there are!"

And he was right. He had seen tens of Outriders forming up in that cavern, more dropping in through the open hatch, all in full canvas and metal armour with two muskets and a long killing knife apiece. His companion had been less quick to run, and the musketry of the Outriders had got him, leaving only one to tell the tale. If the Underworld ever had a chance, that Exceptional was it. Had he not raised the alarm so soon, there is no telling how far the enemy might have got undetected.

A summons went out to every would-be general, strategist and mercenary commander beneath the earth. Actions move faster than words, though, and by the time those picked few were assembled in the Temple, gunfire could already be heard distantly through the tunnels as Underworlders put up an improvised defence.

★

It turned out that the entry point the Outriders had picked gave them three ways forward, two that led direct into the heart of the Underworld and one that led down. It was in these former two that the first organised opposition found them.

Down one tortuous tunnel, Sergei and a band of Fishermen set an ambush behind what cover they could find, and there followed a bloody and savage exchange of fire between the Outriders' muskets and the Fishermen's crossbows. The Fishermen were more used to the dark and knew the ground, but their opponents were well trained and outnumbered them heavily. The first Fishermen volley caught them unprepared and some seven or eight were cut down at once, but then the Outriders scattered to cover and began to return the favour. The skirmish was brutal with no quarter given. The Outriders were desperate to force their way forwards, for the passage widened beyond the ambush point and their greater numbers there would carry the day. Two or three at a time were constantly making a dash for the next niche in the tunnel wall under cover of their fellows' fire. If even a few could get into close combat with their wicked knives then their comrades would be able to follow up. The Fishermen were forced to expose themselves to the musket-fire to pick off each moving man. They could not afford to miss any of them. More and more were getting closer, from cover to cover. Over half Sergei's little force was dead, and the tunnel before them was strewn with fallen and dying Outriders. Another trio broke for the very rubble the Fishermen were crouching behind, the lead shot skipping and dancing from the walls. The defenders were moments away from being overwhelmed.

It was then that Pelgraine turned up on his own, a solitary reinforcement, and let fly with a charge from his light gun. The unbearable white flash of it stopped the Outriders in their tracks, just as it had the Mazen. The surviving Fishermen fell on them and wiped them out.

Then it was quiet and there were no more Outriders there, and Sergei knew something was wrong.

"Too few bodies," he told Pelgraine. "Scouts only. We find the rest." He told his men to hold the tunnel against any further comers and then he and Pelgraine made for the Temple.

The other approach that the Outriders tried was taken first by the non-combatant novices and scientists of the Alchemical Brethren, who were in no position to weather a serious assault. Some nameless innovator amongst them had brought along an explosive of his own formula which spectacularly collapsed the entire passageway and ensured that no surface-dwellers would be coming that way at all.

The bulk of the Outriders were making for the myoculture caves beneath them, Giulia's maps revealed. Once there they would have access to the myriad tunnels the Fermers used to come and go, and thus they could take Underworld as and when they wanted it. Every able-bodied Underworlder armed and ready to go was sent down to the caverns with Giulia of the Fishermen and a Meat Packer known as the Count at their head. Their advance scouts discovered a fair concentration of Outriders at one end of the cavern with more filing in. Small groups were already crawling up the Fermers' tunnels into the Underworld proper but the main body was just standing around in some confusion. The most daring of the scouts crept between the burgeoning piles of growing fungus and saw several officer types clustered about a number of charts. It appeared that the Outriders were lost.

The obvious thing to do would be to form a defended firing line at the other end of the cavern and shoot into their ranks, forcing them to take cover. This tactic would allow the Outriders to continue filing through the nearest exits, though, and sooner or later the Underworlders would be flanked and cut off by those that got out. Instead, Giulia and the Count conceived a desperate plan. Their ragged forces, bravoes from a score of different factions, would charge the unsuspecting Outriders, firing as they went, and pin them into as small a section of the cavern as possible. They were armed with a mismatched selection of flintlocks, crossbows and a few of the Waylun Armouries' special creations, and until they had forced the Outriders back they would be fully exposed to enemy fire. It was a monstrous risk, but if they hung back and sheltered then the whole of the Underworld would be opened up like a shell.

"We are at the end of our time," the Count told his troops, in words that would reach even Arves eventually. "We have lived, unnatural, between the depths and the sun. Now the jealous surface seeks to strip our heart's blood from us. We may fall, and we shall fall, but we shall drive them before us like dust. If we fail, live or die, then true darkness shall take the Underworld. If we win, though we die, then we have the freedom at last that was always promised us!"

They stormed out from their tunnels and caves like demons, each one with a war cry or scream on their lips. The front rank discharged their guns and bows into the packed mass of Outriders, and surface men and women doubled up over puncturing bolts or fell back with shafts through limbs, flintlock balls breaking bones and lashing across faces. The fighting Underworlders tore across them and continued to run without pausing to reload.

The Outrider officers fled back to safer ground, and their sense of self-preservation saved countless Underworld lives, for many of their men followed their lead. There were others with enough sense to see the folly of their enemies' move; a score or so dropped to one knee to steady their muskets, whilst a further score and more stood behind them levelling their own. I cannot say what thoughts must have passed through the minds of those at the fore of the charge. It cannot have been despair for not one of them broke or slowed. They were doomed and it was out of their hands and there is a kind of relief in that.

The volley of shot from the Outriders ripped into them and killed or crippled virtually the entire front of the charge, sending the attackers rolling limply back under the feet of their fellows. Electric Gangsters, Fishermen, Proud Walkers, Meat Packers, People of the Scarlet Sash and members of a dozen other factions, they all died together in a comradeship forged only through adversity. The charge barely faltered, the next wave vaulting and skipping over the dead. Most of the Outriders were forming up at the far wall, unwilling to be driven out of the myoculture caves altogether, but that firing line held fast, each Outrider changing to his second musket, taking aim into the storm and letting fly. The smoke from the first barrage was still in the air but they were shooting straight into the mob and accuracy was moot. The Count died in that second blast, he of the fine words, and two dozen others in the same moment. If twice the number of Outriders had stayed then the charge would have been shattered apart. Instead, the momentum of the attackers' rush carried them down the very barrels of the muskets to tear into their enemies. They struck with knives and Waylun swords, with the butts of crossbows and pistols and with their bare hands. Some of the Outriders had got their blades out, and gave a bloody accounting of themselves, the others were simply butchered. Then the surviving Underworlders were finding rocks and mounds of fungus to hide behind, reloading their bows and guns or taking the weapons of their dead foes; firing upon the main force which had taken similar cover and was shooting back.

There was a shifting stalemate for the next few minutes. There were more Outriders, but a steady trickle of armed Underworlders came to reinforce the lines. Amongst these were Sergei and Pelgraine, who joined Giulia as she tried to find a way to force the conflict home.

The news and the call for recruits was coursing through the arteries of Underworld with the speed of running feet. It even came to Greygori's door in the person of one of the Organ Donor Boys. This was how Arves became aware that his world was on the point of collapse.

Greygori was moved by the news as he had not been since Faith escaped. "So soon!" he hissed, as though he had known forever of the attack but had grievously miscounted the days. "I am not ready, Arves!"

He was halfway back to his laboratory, arm uncoiling for the door. "Arves!" he called again, but Arves was staring aghast at the messenger. One of Greygori's three-digited hands spun him by the shoulder and he looked up into his own darkened reflections.

"Take this, Arves," Greygori told him, and pressed a long-barrelled pistol into his limp hands. "Go with that man to the fighting. Buy time, Arves. I need some small time."

Arves wanted to protest: his book-bound past had not credited him with currency to buy even the smallest increment of time. Greygori was forcing him towards the door and the war, and the Organ Donor Boy gripped his arm as the Transforming Man's hand left off. Arves was hustled away to fight.

By the time he arrived things had started to fall apart on both sides. The Outriders had scattered behind four or five different outcroppings, and their officers were unable to get word between the groups without a crossbow bolt finding the messenger. Each group's impression of how the battle was doing was at variance with the others. Some were trying to pull back whilst others believed they had to forge forwards. Giulia and the others, for their part, had never dreamed that they would be able to control their troops. Each band fought on their own terms and they were united only in their common enemy. The Outriders were constantly subjected to unexpected charges and oddly-placed snipers. Giulia's tenuous authority was complicated further when a dozen or so Outriders who had been cut off since the beginning suddenly broke from their concealment and tried to fight their way back to their own lines, attacking the Underworlders in the rear. It was beginning to look as though a single unified assault from the surface-dwellers would break the defence entirely. Then Sergei arrived with a batch of explosive bolts, and began to use them, aiming high and letting them arc along the curve of the ceiling and fall amongst the Outrider officers, sowing confusion. In the gloom of the caverns it gave other marksmen something to aim at: running figures silhouetted against the sudden flash of flame.

Underworlder consensus had it that the Outrider commander was a junior officer who had risen to his position by dead man's shoes minutes before. Finding himself suddenly under explosive attack he panicked and unleashed his secret weapon.

Grinding from the back came something like a barrel on wheels, ten feet long and half that across. It was pushed by a dozen Outriders and there was a snout at the front and some machinery at the back. Crossbow bolts spanged off its curved sides and the nearest bands of Underworlders shifted nervously as the jointed snout hinged towards them.

The machinery at the back set up an urgent clatter and the weapon spat a gout of black liquid over the nearest Underworlders and the fungus mass they were crouching behind. There was some chaos, but they realised within seconds that the reeking stuff was harmless. Then something caught at the end of the snout and the jet of fluid became a sheet of flame. That first band of Underworlders went up like candles, crisping and charring even as they ran. The fungus went up too, great boils of it cracking open and shrivelling. The Outriders wasted no time changing the angle of the weapon's nozzle so that it vomited fire in a weaving, deadly arc across the defenders' lines, setting the fighters and their barricades aflame in equal measure. The Underworlders started a retreat that became close to a rout. Sergei and the other de facto leaders did their best to rally, but the fire-gouting machine was too much. It rumbled

444

forwards, invincible, and when one of its attendants fell another ran to take his place. The Outriders sensed victory. The torrent of flaming chemicals seared in a great rain over the stacks of fungus, burning and killing men and women with the sightless malice of an idiot child. Arves witnessed it all, and his voice shook as he recounted it.

The fire burned the Fermers too. It found the little creatures in their fungal lairs or as they trundled heedlessly about their business, and set them alight like torches. The results were startling: they went berserk. Stumpy arms waving in the air, spinning and hopping as the heat destroyed them, they charged and leapt at the Outriders and their machine. They clung to legs, clawed at the barrel's sides and set the firestarters ablaze. Two dozen or more mobbed the advancing fire-thrower and dragged down several of the Outriders, the others halting their advance to chop at the little monsters with knives, because musket balls just passed through them.

Sergei stood up to his full eight-foot height and levelled his pistol, newly reloaded. A musket ball scored a line of blood across his bicep, but he never flinched, firing a single round into the body of the Outriders' machine.

It seemed that he had achieved nothing, but Arves was probably too short-sighted to see the spurt of liquid from the finger-sized hole. In the seconds following there was a *bang* that deafened both sides, scything through Outriders and Fermers alike with jagged sheets of ripped metal and an all-consuming fireball.

The Outriders stayed at bay after that, keeping to their cover whilst their enemies picked them off. Their situation worsened considerably when an organised squad of Meat Packers arrived with what they called the Great Eye of Waylun. It was a glorious killing machine, a giant gun on two solid metal millstone wheels within an armoured housing of riveted plates. There was a single great central barrel surrounded by eight smaller guns that fired in turn, recoiling back into the housing and then extending

445

outwards again, reloaded. The great central eye itself remained silent but was enough of a tacit threat that the Outriders began to fall back, and then to flee under the massed fire of the defenders. Very few escaped. The Great Eye of Waylun ground forward implacably, its operators guarded by its bulk, sending shot after shot whistling across the cavern.

It looked as though things were over and the war was won, but the tide of fortune never ebbed and flowed as it did that day. Arves saw some commotion at the far end of the cavern where the Outriders were now trying to leave. A new force was pushing its way through, indeed shooting its way through, cutting down the panicked Outriders even as the Underworlders picked them off from behind. As the Outrider discipline finally collapsed in its entirety, a squad of twenty Angels forced its way into the cavern and began a swift advance on the defenders' lines. Each man had his energy shield on, and shot and crossbow bolts bounced and skipped from the crackling air before them. Their own weapons, projectile rifles, pulse and beam guns, began to rake across the Underworlders, burning through flesh and fungus without distinction.

The Great Eye of Waylun essayed a few rounds of its minor barrels, its whole iron frame shuddering with the recoil. The bullets struck the shields hard and made the Angels stagger, no more than that. At around that time the second Angel task force turned up out of nowhere, dropping from a cave mouth at the left of the defenders' positions and opening fire immediately. They had entered the Underworld at some other point and navigated their way faultlessly to the battlefield. From being on the brink of victory the Underworlders were suddenly in danger of being annihilated by forty men.

It was later found that there had been a third squad, running for the myoculture caverns with their shields down to conserve energy. Unexpectedly, Yarmin's Friendly Society had ambushed them and struck down over half before the others could activate their point generators and return the favour. It was a disorganised, hopelessly courageous attempt, typical of the Friendlies. Once shielded, the Angels shot them down, save for a couple who fled to bear the tale.

In the myoculture caverns the Angels marched forwards calmly and efficiently, putting a bullet or a beam of white light into anyone who tried to run, pinning groups whilst other Angels moved in. It was like some kind of pest-killing venture. At least the Outriders had been fighting for their lives.

As Arves crouched and hid, Sergei continued to fire off futile shots. Behind them, the Great Eye of Waylun finally loosed a shell from its monstrous central barrel. The missile impacted in the midst of the central unit of Angels and scattered them left and right, but when the smoke and dust cleared they were picking themselves up again with the same routine patience. One did not. A single armoured body lay like a discarded doll. Sergei guessed the man had fallen badly and broken his neck. Some of the Underworlders took heart from this and set up a ragged cheer. In response, one of the Angels levelled a long silvery weapon at the Great Eye. There was a shimmer and a sparkle in the air, and the wheels stopped grinding instantly, the mechanisms froze. A thin sheet of shining material condensed across the metal, and the skins of the operators. The Great Eye never spoke again.

Arves saw little more, for he was crunched up into a ball between the cavern floor and a wall of fungus as beams and bullets punched above him. His pistol was clutched, unused, in his hand. Around him the air was a thunder of gunfire as the Angels executed their prey and the Underworlders put up a powerless resistance. The Authority had mustered every Angel in the city whose shield still functioned and sent them in as a unified force. They were taking no chances.

Then a familiarly deformed hand touched Arves on the shoulder, and he looked up at the nightmare bulk that was Greygori Sanguival.

"How goes the war, Arves?" The Transforming Man bared atrophied teeth. From one claw dangled some device with straps and wings. Arves saw it was an Angel's shield generator, although he could not know by what means Greygori had obtained it. In the hand that rested on Arves' shoulder was a tiny object, small as a knife: a flat rectangle with a single button.

"Wonderful technology," Greygori was saying, as people died around them. He was letting the generator pack spin from its straps. "Very advanced, Arves, but very reliant on frequency. Point generators, Arves, produce such an inordinate amount of energy, Arves, and it all must go somewhere."

He stood up without warning and stepped from cover. Arves fully expected to see his grotesque body fall straight back down, riddled with holes. Instead there was a crackle and hum, and the firing from both sides slowed a little. Arves risked a look and saw his master standing taller than human, presenting the generator pack like a talisman. The fire from the Angels bounced and danced about him, springing away from a shield that could only be seen in the moment of contact. Greygori had managed to repair the generator; perhaps only he or Father Sulplice could have done it.

The Transforming Man strode forwards and Arves appreciated that the lurching shuffle he had affected in everyday life was not a crippling of the limbs but a conscious effort to keep to a human pace. Greygori made eight feet to a stride, advancing with great telescoping bounds on the Angels, who were beginning to back up.

Greygori levelled the bronze device at the Angel with the frost ray, even as that weapon was discharged harmlessly against him. There was no sound from the little toy, no beam of light or any other indication that it had worked, save that the luckless Angel's generator pack exploded in a violent storm of shrapnel and searing blue-red energy. There was precious little left of the man from the knees up.

In the resultant seconds of silence, Arves heard Greygori say, "Well, that worked slightly better than I expected."

Idly the Transforming Man clicked his little trigger at another two Angels with similarly pyrotechnic results, which was quite enough for the rest. Some were trying to get their packs off when Greygori destroyed them whilst others were running for cover, only to find that the mysterious medium that Greygori used to transmit his signal was not blocked by fungus or even stone. The Underworlders roared their triumph and sent shots into any Angel who managed to divest himself of his shield whilst Greygori calmly blew up generator after generator with the air of a man conducting an educational, but essentially routine, scientific experiment.

The very last Angel was spared, the final man of forty. Greygori pointed his device and clicked away but nothing happened, leaving the man to flee. Greygori seemed a little disgruntled. He returned to Arves and Sergei and Giulia and the others.

You might think the Underworld won its freedom as the Count had promised, save that of course Arves had not come to the Island for his health.

There was a sudden outbreak of firing at the far end of the cavern, and Arves saw a further mass of Outriders flooding in. These were not the ousted remnants of the previous force but new, fresh fighters. Nobody at the time could say where they had come from. My guess is that the first wave represented those Outriders immediately available for service. This second batch comprised those who had been engaged elsewhere, hunting Vermin or patrolling. The call had reached them, wherever they were, and they had been rushed hotfoot to the front. Who would have thought the Authority kept so many under arms?

There was a scattering of Angels in their midst as well, the remnants of the third detachment the Friendlies had engaged. The whole force was smaller than the first wave, but the Underworlders were in no position to stop them now. Too many had fallen, too much ammunition had been spent.

"Ah well," said Greygori. "So much for that." He turned his humped back and made to go. Arves grabbed at his trailing robes and asked him where.

"The depths, Arves," Greygori told him. "I have my eye on an old medical installation in which to continue my work. They will not find me there."

"But what about me?" Arves demanded. Greygori stared at him, and a musket ball whistled through the air between them. The Transforming Man shrugged, perhaps his most human gesture, and made off for his buried refuge in a manner that did not invite followers.

The first charge of the Outriders met with such a fierce barrage of fire that it faltered and stopped in the open. Sensing that the tide could still be turned, Giulia took up her crossbow and vaulted over the barricades with her Fishermen in tow. She might well have done it, but a beam of ruby light dissected her heart even as she called for her followers. She fell back into the arms of Charno, who died a moment later.

The Underworlders began fleeing in droves. Arves saw Sergei finally abandon all hope and retreat with his ragged Collective. Pelgraine and a few other Fishermen made a fighting withdrawal another way, running for that eternal Fishermen haunt, the lightless, Mazen-haunted depths.

Arves himself ended up in the Temple, the Underworld's beating heart, beneath the backlit form of the Coming Man who had not arisen to defend his adherents in their time of need. There, he witnessed a final stand against the invasion, armed Underworlders crouching either side of the Temple doorway and loosing bolt after bolt into the advancing enemy, while the non-combatants reloaded their weapons for them.

When the Outriders broke through into the Temple they fired at everyone they saw, even the poor Caretaker which never harmed anyone. The spider-like machine scuttled down the wall, perhaps to look at the damage the musket balls had done, and was hit four or five times. It jumped and fell onto its back, legs waving jerkily, and then let off a great cloud of choking powder from nozzles along its rim that drove the Outriders briefly back. In this confusion, Arves escaped the carnage and saw no more of it.

He was picked up by another band of Outriders minutes later. This group was less bloodthirsty and simply took him captive. He was one of perhaps a dozen taken to the surface as trophies.

While waiting in the prison boat he heard that the invasion of the Underworld was a grand civic success. The haven of the dispossessed, the lower frontier of human knowledge, had been swept away at the cost of countless lives for the sake of some rich man's lie.

36

Echoes of the Fall

Arves died in his sleep that night, perhaps the kindest thing that could have happened to him. The Island would not have permitted him to live long.

The story of the end of the Underworld spread out through the Island: from our cell to our stretch; from our stretch to the other prisoners; from the prisoners to the Wardens. A great cloud of gloom settled over the inmates as a whole; many had dealt with the Underworld and others had sheltered there, as had I. When I next saw Shon he remarked, "There goes half my client base."

The news reached the Marshal eventually. We knew this because he came to our stretch a week or so later.

"All still mourning the loss of your thieves' nest?" he remarked, stalking between the cells. We stared at him sullenly and he singled a man out at random. "What about you? Are you sad that such a place has been exterminated?" Silence. "I'm talking to you!"

The man, whoever he was, looked away and said nothing. The Marshal gestured for a Warden, holding out one gloved hand for his gun. He shot the man dead through the bars of his cell. The thunder of it broke the spell and fearful normality returned with a vengeance.

"Anyone else feel like ignoring my questions?" the Marshal asked. There was a moment's fraught silence and then a muttered chorus of negatives. The Marshal stalked two doors down the line until he was looking into the cell the other side of Gaki.

"You with the scar," he directed. "You tell me whether our Authority's righteous victory makes you unhappy."

There was a murmur from the accused prisoner that I could not catch, but it must have been an affirmative. The Marshal did not shoot the man as expected, but looked around at the rest of us. "And I suppose you others feel the same. How about you, Advani?"

I started. The Marshal skipped Gaki's cell and was bearing down on me. Hermione and Lucian contrived to fade into the background.

"I had friends there," I said, in as steady a voice as I could. "So, yes, I do mourn for Underworld."

"Do you really?" There was a change in the Marshal's tone, although not in his face. "Let me make you all an offer, a special celebratory offer in honour of our victory. If any one of you will stand now, and pledge that you are glad to be rid of the Underworld, then I will let that man off tomorrow's work. How about that, you wretches? Everyone who forswears the Underworld, come to the front of your cells. This is your one and only chance."

Everyone was staring at him. Nobody could tell what he was about. He gave nothing away, standing with the gun still clutched in one hand. "Nobody?" he said, in the same light, sardonic voice.

Someone, I cannot say who, stood up and moved to the cell door, then seven or eight others, all at once, and then twenty more. Tallan was right there, and I saw Thelwel too, who had never known the Underworld, barely even known Shadrapar. Hermione muscled past me ponderously. A moment later, Lucian was there too, and all around us was the shuffle of traitorous feet scuffing over the memory of Underworld.

I cannot say if I was the last man left, but the thought had long before occurred to me that the Underworld and Sergei and Giulia and the rest were gone, and no amount of stubborn pride would bring them back. Before the Marshal could revoke his offer I joined my two cell mates at the door with a shrug. The Marshal's eyes gleamed.

"Is this not a disgusting thing?" he remarked, although he looked anything but disgusted. "Look at this, men; look at them all. Their Underworld not one month dead and they're ready to betray it for the sake of a day's leisure." He stalked closer to our cell until he was staring directly into my face. "Even the vaunted Stefan Advani will drop his lordly airs for another crumb. Whenever I have doubts about the rightness of what we do here," and his voice made it clear that he never had such doubts, "I will remember this little display." Hermione could have reached out and broken his neck. It would have been the work of a moment. She never thought of it or never dared to.

He strode away down the stretch and his words carried back to us. "I lied. Of course I lied. There are no holidays on the Island. But I did want to see that, just for the purposes of morale." Then he was gone, leaving us all in a foul mood. All bar one.

Gaki laughed lightly. He was watching the Marshal's back, though, and I thought I saw his lips move slightly. It almost looked as though he were counting.

It was a hard month, all told. The Marshal's humour set the pace, and it was obvious he was making life miserable for the Wardens, for they were not shy of passing it on to us. Shon got beaten for some imagined infringement, and a weaker man might not have lived through it. One of the Wardens got into a blazing row with Father Sulplice and, because the old man was too precious to risk, they dragged out Thelwel and whipped him with canes so that inch-high welts rose on his back. I knew he

454

would heal as soon as he was left alone to do so, but the pain was real, for him and for his father. I saw tears in the old man's eyes.

Lucian fell ill.

It was quite unexpected; he was a robust enough little man. Something came in off the waters, though, and about one in seven prisoners were suddenly hacking their lungs out, shaking and shivering with a rainbow sheen of sweat slicking their skin. I was spared; Lucian was not. Soon enough his rasping coughs were keeping Hermione and me awake and I began to fear for his life. It was not uniformly fatal, but a few had died from it already, and the Warden running our stretch then was not a man to allow people sick leave. If anyone lingered in their cell of a morning, he would march in and kick them out into the corridor. Not that Lucian did. He was more than eager to go out and work each day, far more eager than when he was well. His manic optimism drove him to show how healthy he was. After all, was he not going to be sent for when the very next boat arrived? A few paltry germs could hardly stand in his way when he was a man of such manifest destiny. He forced himself to greater and greater extremes of exertion, all the time trying to explain how healthy he was and why people should not have any concern for him, in between great bouts of choking that doubled him over.

I made sure that he had a little extra food for each meal, and I think Hermione did the same. I tried to stay close in the workshops and keep him out of the way of any vindictive Wardens. I was not the only one looking after him. He had been on the Island longer than most and many of the staff, let alone the prisoners, had conceived a vague fondness for him.

An odd result of me being kept awake at night by his sporadic hacking cough was that I was put into closer contact with Hermione than I otherwise would have wished. It was not that I disliked her, but she could have folded me in four without effort, so I was wary. Normally she would sit like a stone in one corner

455

of the cell while Lucian rattled on at her. Now, awake and past midnight, she began to sit by me, a massive brooding presence. For the first two nights I ignored her. It seemed inconceivable to me that an introvert like Hermione might actually desire companionship. On the third night, though, I looked at her and she looked back.

"Can't sleep," she said, and to make the point Lucian launched into another great barrage of phlegm. I admitted to the same problem.

She continued to stare at me and it was obvious something was on her mind and, equally, that she was not going to bring it into the light of her own volition. I tried to out-stare her, a doomed venture. At last her weighted silence drew the words from me and I asked, "What is it, Hermione?"

The voice, when it came out, was tiny. I never knew that she could squeeze it so small. The people in the adjacent cells could not have heard it.

"You've been here a while," she said. "You know how people here are."

I put my social scientist's hat on and admitted that I did, though to be honest I hadn't been there much longer than her, and not generally to my benefit. She, however, seldom mixed with our peers, a privilege that I lacked the heft and demeanor to enforce.

"People," she repeated awkwardly, "together." I guessed where her ponderous drift was going and nodded. It was a topic I'd rather have dodged, but we were moving in that direction with the same iron momentum as the prison boat, and I had not the strength to change our course. The thought of her folding me in four for a poorly chosen comment was still in my mind.

She started her next sentence several times and then subsided. "People," she got out eventually. There was no expression visible on her face save her habitual sullen scowl.

"What is it, Hermione?" I tried again.

She shrugged her rounded shoulders. "I wanted to ask about someone."

I took my life in my hands and said, "I don't think he feels the same way." I remembered her talking to Thelwel and had seen that he had nothing for her, even before I discovered what he was. Hermione slumped into herself a little and I persevered. "I don't think Thelwel feels that way about anyone."

There was a strange kind of grunt from her that I really could not interpret. For a horrible moment I thought she was going to cry. Then came another, and I realised that it was a deep, gruff chuckle. I was about to ask her what it was when we heard a Warden's footsteps and both snapped silent. I put my head down again and pretended to sleep as the man passed, despite Lucian's choking refrain that nobody could have slept through. The man stopped at our cell and looked in to see Hermione sitting by me, staring up at him balefully. The Wardens gave Hermione a wide berth. She was one of those dangerous people who might not be put off by the threat of instant reprisal, should she choose to tear a taunting Warden's head right off. Those times when she was beaten or punished she took it like a stone. There was no joy in her for them to take. Besides, she was a hard and uncomplaining worker, asked no questions, gave no trouble, and the Marshal steered well clear of her because of his almost phobic misogyny.

The Warden decided that the curfew was not that important and walked on. By this time, I was wide awake and only too eager to continue our conversation. Hermione, though, yawned mightily and was about to lumber over and try to sleep again. Her curiosity was a short-lived beast.

"Who, then?" I hissed at her. Now she had lost interest I found I had to know.

She did not say anything, but her eyes led her face in the direction that her heart was pulling: towards that shadowed cell where Gaki sat alone in one corner, perhaps asleep and perhaps not.

Gaki? How could anyone found any attraction on the homicidal madness that bubbled in every word and deed? But then I found myself thinking that at least he was genteel, and that he had treated Hermione with courtesy, even kindness, more so than the outside world. I remembered them playing games together and talking in low voices, and at the end of it the idea was not so unthinkable. I hoped that it was a mutual thing, but I couldn't imagine Gaki having any affection to bestow. I was left with the twin unhappy options that it was all in Hermione's mind, or that Gaki, for reasons of his own, was leading her on.

And there we have it: what I see now as my greatest failure. I was scared of Hermione: she was strong and unpredictable and different and I stayed away from her. She gave me no cause but the potential threat she posed was enough. And if I had spoken to her, if I had got to know her and brought her out of herself, how things might have been different. I was no better, in the way I looked on her, than the Witch Queen.

That month the whole Island was out of sorts. People walked around as though their skins were a size too large or too small, tormented by an unscratchable itch. The one Outing we had was so obviously going to turn into a brawl that I just stayed put and chatted to Thelwel. Later we listened to the sounds of fist on flesh from down the corridor, and five men ended up Below.

Even Leontes de Margot, the Governor, was afflicted by the strange malaise. When Shon and I were working on the Trethowan manuscript he suddenly appeared behind us like a bulbous ghost. Licking his moist lips, eyes darting nervously, he craned over Shon's tense shoulder at the translated text. The two of us avoided the sight of him and stared at our hands like scolded children, but he would not go away.

"When will it be finished?" he asked us without warning. A pudgy hand slipped between us to paw at the completed sheets.

Shon deferred to my expert judgement, which is to say he turned away slightly and left me to deal with the situation.

"Hard to say, sir," I managed. "The writing is very dense and difficult to transcribe." I was hedging outrageously and for the first time he seemed to know it.

"It must be finished soon," he whispered. There was an awful significance in his voice, a man who knew some great fact that overshadowed us all. "Soon, Advani."

"I am working as fast as I can, sir," I continued to hedge.

"You. Go away a moment. Wait in the next room." He dismissed Shon with a gesture while I watched him nervously. I was used to his dreamy and bland moods, his occasional ineffectual rages, but this was different. Something was gnawing at him.

He made to sit down beside me, checked himself for propriety's sake, then paced off a little. One stubby hand fingered the rich weave of the robe he was wearing.

"You are afraid of the Marshal," he said. I replied promptly that I was and the line of a frown furrowed his otherwise unblemished forehead.

"Don't play games with me. You are afraid he'll kill you as soon as you finish."

I had not realised he had appreciated this; he was an easy man to underestimate, really.

"You have been delaying the work," he continued. I could not tell if it was an accusation or only a suspicion. "You have been stretching your life out. That is what you have been doing."

"No, sir. Of course not."

He did not seem to hear me. "You must finish. Finish soon, Stefan."

I did not trust myself to reply but just waved at the ambiguous stack of papers of the desk so as to indicate the magnitude of the task. Abruptly he was face to face with me, that bald and pallid circle blotting out my world and fixing me with its narrow and watery eyes.

"Stefan, I have to know if he had any hope at the end. Trethowan was a wise man. You must finish it soon, Stefan. Within the month."

It was not my fear that gripped me, but his. There was a dreadful, creeping horror that had grown through the man like a disease. Dead stars and ancient sciences had given place to some modern and terrible vision. Such fear is contagious.

"I will finish it as soon as I can," my mouth said.

His loose lips opened to impart something else, and then he broke and was looking, abruptly, through one of the walls. That was the Lady Ellera waking, or moving, or watching. Instead of the mingled anxiety and anticipation it had provoked before, though, the Governor's face showed only that unnamed dread. He left the room uncertainly, as though the place was unfamiliar to him. Shon asked no questions, and I was not minded to enlighten him.

The first sign of the Thing that everyone was so manifestly waiting for was Peter turning up in the workshop and telling me it was time for a jaunt.

"We're going out," he said. It was the middle of the morning and the mining expeditions were long gone. I raised an eyebrow at him.

Peter glanced at the working prisoners, many of whom were eavesdropping. "Just out. Grab Thelwel and that lawyer mate of yours to make up a boatload."

He clapped me on the shoulder and then launched off across the workroom floor. I saw him meet Midds at the far end of the room and exchange a few hurried words with him. As I was recruiting Shon a minute later I saw Midds, too, grab a couple of prisoners, and another Warden I did not know seemed to be doing the same thing. Something was afoot.

Peter led the three of us down to a low-ceilinged room on the waterside, open to the river on one wall with the floor sloping away so that the far end was lost underwater. Nudging their way up this slope with the action of the waves were half a dozen boats. One was the Marshal's personal skiff, and another was a monster, a giant version of the mining vessels with metal-plated sides and some large weapon bolted to its front deck. The other four were to the mining ships as young water-beasts were to their overweight adult relatives. They were low, sleek craft with little but the arms of their point generators and an additional contraption astern to disturb their shallow profile.

"This is what the miners were converted from, decades back," Thelwel murmured. "Beautiful, aren't they?" He was already up to his ankles in water, trailing a hand over the boat's polished lines. "They must be over a century old. My father and I, we keep them in good shape."

Peter swung a canvas bag of his gear into the boat, and I asked him, "So what is it this time?"

"The boat," Shon guessed, and Peter nodded seriously.

"Which boat?" I demanded, apparently the only person who had not realised.

"The prison boat," Shon told me.

"It cannot be that time already."

"Been and gone," Peter confirmed. "Damn thing's not been late for twenty years, they reckon. Search party. Thelwel can fix it if it's gotten broken, and your mate there has a good pair of arms."

"And me? What can I do?"

"You're welcome to go back to the workshop," Peter pointed out. I felt generally useless but said nothing.

We put out with two other boats and cruised round the Island's bulk at an easy pace before scooting off downriver. The constant and disquieting vibration of the mining boats was here transformed into a thrumming of power and, I think, joy. The boats, soulless metal as they were, leapt over the water with the sheer glee of motion and the feeling was contagious. I have never cared for machines in general and boats in particular, but I will not deny that I enjoyed that journey. The speed and nimble steering gave at least the illusion that we could escape any monster the river could throw at us. Thelwel, at the helm, was grinning into the breeze like a child.

There are only so many places on a river for a lost ship to be, and the prison ship was some two hours downstream. We all began slowing as it came in sight, because it was obvious that there was something badly, even fatally, wrong.

It was canted at an angle and the nose was buried deep in the trees of the shore where it had drifted and beached. No human beings were in sight.

Other things moved. Other things flapped over the ship or crawled with many legs up the side of the hull to pick with claws at what was on the deck. There was little left by then: the efficiency of the jungle's scavengers gave us no clue as to how long it had been. What we saw, coasting closer, were remains of some score of men strewn across the prison boat's deck. The foul smell of carrion came to us with the buzzing of the flies.

37

The Shadow of Death

Our three boats cruised up to within ten yards of the prison ship, which was close enough. The stench was making me sick to the stomach and all around I saw similar faces. Someone in Midds' crew vomited over the side and I felt that I was about to do likewise.

"You know animals, Stefan. Some river monster did this?" Peter asked me. I shrugged to indicate that there was infinite potential in the world for monsters.

"Bodies still intact," Shon reeled off tonelessly. "Weapons. Some of them are still locked together. They killed each other. If there were monsters they just finished the work."

"All of them?" I got out.

"All of them," he confirmed.

"Someone's going to have to check the boat out," called the Warden I did not know. It was obvious that he was not volunteering. "Might be some survivors."

"I'm taking downriver," Midds said definitively. "Nobody's getting me on that thing." I knew that the only thing he would find downriver would be more of the reeds he smoked. Peter and the other Warden knew the same but they let him go and his boat cut a wide arc and sped off.

Peter looked over at his fellow Warden and said, "I'll do the boat, if you want." The relief on the other man's face lit him up like a lamp. "You check upriver. Someone might have found their way along the bank."

When we were alone, Peter took his Ropa blade out of his bag and weighed it thoughtfully. "Don't want to rule out the monsters just yet. Let me go first." Nobody was going to argue with him. "After that, Thelwel tries the engines and the rest of us get to piece together what the hell happened."

The canting of the deck meant that one rail was only inches above the water line. Scavenging birds hauled their glutted bodies into the air as we approached, descending to bow the overhanging branches. Whilst I moored our boat to a rusty ring on the ship's side, Peter hauled himself over the railing and took the sword when Shon handed it up to him. He crouched on the slanted deck, one foot against the rail, surrounded by the dead. At a gesture, Shon followed him and, as they began to make their way against the slope Thelwel and I had no choice but to take up the slack.

The first thing I saw was a knot of the dead, some five or six scavenger-ravaged corpses, all bloodied limb-bones tangled together. I did not gaze on them long enough to unravel their story but Shon looked them over with a clinical eye. He shot a shrewd glance at Peter's back and stooped to scoop something up, and I saw it was a blade crusted with blood the colour of rust.

"You never know," he told me.

Peter was standing in the centre of the deck by now. There was a combative set to his shoulders and the sword hung so easily in his hand that I knew he must have activated it. For a moment I expected some monster to come bounding from the water or belowdecks. There was nothing to fight, though.

Some of the dead still sported crossbow bolts projecting from skulls or between ribs. There were the notches of blades, and between the picked sockets of the skull nearest me was a chipped hole that a flintlock ball had made.

"Prisoners against sailors?" Thelwel wondered aloud, but Peter called back, "Look at the clothes," and he was right. There were a few whose stained rags might have been prison greys, but for the most part they wore the hard-wearing garb of the crew.

I felt my queasiness wearing off from the surfeit of gore on all sides. At my feet there were two bodies intertwined like lovers, save that each clutched a hilt buried in the other's back. As I bent over them, one eyeless visage rolled up of its own accord to grin at me. I stumbled back over the strewn dead and a crab-like thing unshelled itself from within the skull and tapped away. My queasiness returned in force and I threw the morning's stew over the side.

Peter was approaching the entry to the hold, and gestured for us all to join him. The air from within was as laced with decay as that without, stale and stuffy to boot.

"There are no survivors," Shon said.

Peter shrugged. "I know, but we have to check." He led the way down the steps sword first. Thelwel produced a little hand-lamp and clicked it on, throwing a reddish glow that stretched the reaching fingers of our shadows out before us.

"Engines are straight ahead," Peter recalled. "Holds are behind us, to fore. Left and right, crew quarters, small storage…" He stepped abruptly to one heavy metal door and kicked it open, revealing a bare metal room relieved only by a grimy porthole and a table bolted to the floor. "Remember, Stefan?"

"It's been a while since we last played," I said.

"That it has."

The others looked at us as though we were mad.

"Thelwel, go check the engines out. Did they stop or were they broken, or did they just run out of something? You," to Shon, "Go with him."

"And we are…?" I enquired.

"The hold. You should remember that too."

I did. Crushed in a metal cage with a mass of other prisoners;

465

frightened, jostled, with no hope for the future and violent men all around me. Until Peter demanded a chess partner and took me from there, the first in a long line of kindnesses.

We made our way forwards less and less carefully. There were a couple of bodies in the central corridor, sailors both. The head of one was smashed almost flat. The other, one torn hand still near the chair-leg club, had a bolt in his back.

"Did they all go mad?" Peter muttered to himself. "Did they catch some brain-fever from the jungle?"

I remained silent. I was thinking about news I had heard from the city, not least Arves' tale of the Underworld.

The hold door was ajar and Peter kicked it open. Something rushed at us instantly, nothing but a sense of movement in the gloom. The Ropa blade swept round and, if I had not already been falling backwards, it would have been the end for me. It cleft the air, the metal of the doorframe, and then its momentum dragged it on through the space that I had occupied until a moment before. Two long reptiles dashed between Peter's legs and around me, birdlike on two feet. We heard them patter off down the corridor. Peter looked down at me contritely and helped me up.

"Are you all right?" It should have been his question, but it was mine.

"Just a bit on edge," he said unhappily. "I thought…"

"That it was a monster after all. Something you could kill."

He smiled slightly. "Something like that." Then we stepped into the hold and the smile was gone.

The door of the cage was broken outwards. The prisoners had forced it in utter desperation, because the crew had obviously been shooting them through the bars. A good forty men and women were heaped like rags in the cage, and there was a scattering of dead, prisoners and crew, across the floor. I could see exactly how some had escaped the shot enough to break the door and throw themselves on their executioners, killing several with their bare hands.

Peter turned and his face was expressionless. "Check the other rooms," he told me, and walked away.

I pushed open each door in turn, seeing a few other bodies, nothing much else. In the last I was confronted by a pistol aimed straight at me. Behind a desk sat the foul-mouthed captain I remembered. His head was tilted back and he started blankly at the ceiling of his cabin with a pistol ball in his head. Whichever mutinous crewman had killed him had also closed the door of his room, and so he was untouched by the scavengers. I judged him to be about two days dead. It was a subject in which I was becoming an unwilling expert.

Another link to my past had been severed.

There was an atrocious grinding noise from the rear of the ship and every rivet, plate and bolt of it shuddered and jumped. I reeled out of the room as the captain's dead weight jolted from atop the desk and slid, rigid, to the floor. I saw Peter ahead of me, and I swear that we both thought some titanic monster was battering at the metal to get at the meat inside. Then the same realisation clicked in each of our minds.

"Thelwel," Peter shouted over the din. "The engines!" and we both ran aft.

By the time we arrived the racket had stopped, and Thelwel was shaking his head at a massive block of machinery larger than the cell I shared with Lucian and Hermione.

"Damaged," he told us. "Sabotaged. This boat isn't going anywhere soon. How long can we spare to fix it?"

Peter frowned at him. "We're not here to fix it. If the Marshal wants it fixed, he can send a repair crew. We're here to see what happened."

"I think it's clear what's happened," Shon put in. There were even a couple of bodies in the engine room.

"Tell me about what they did," Peter said patiently, and Thelwel began to give him the kind of technical details that I could not follow, and that I knew Peter could not. I lost interest

467

soon enough and decided that what I needed most of all was fresher air.

Climbing up to the sunlight, I disturbed all the scavengers just settling down to feed again. Many of them hopped only feet away from their half-complete meals and then sidled back warily. At least they were making the best of a bad situation.

I found that the air closer to the jungle was heavy enough with the scents of life to counter those of death, and leant back on the rail at the branch-speared prow, taking advantage of the shade and wondering what on earth was going on. That was when I was grabbed.

Something hooked my shoulder from behind, and my mouth was stopped. I was whirled around to look into the heart of the jungle, into a face I had missed like a dead friend.

"Kiera!" I exclaimed, or would have done if her hand had not been over my mouth. She stared at me almost with disbelief and then clutched me in such an embrace my heart almost leapt out of me.

She released me a little awkwardly, sensing that she had perhaps crossed some line she had not intended to. "You have no idea what it's like to see another human being!" she said.

"Trethowan...?"

"I don't think he's even slightly human any more, not after living with them for so long," she said, all in a rush. "And they're not bad, but they're so different. I never realised how much I needed *people*." She was sitting on a branch that ran along the prison ship's rail, and there was a certain nimbleness new to her. She still wore prison greys, but cut to bare her arms and legs, and she had gained a woven bag and belt. There was a knife in that belt, scavenged from some old metal tool, and something that might have been a sling. Her delicate skin, that I had always admired, was now smeared with some greenish paste that helped blend with the greenery or maybe deterred insects. She had been working hard to fit into her new world. "You're here with Peter and Thelwel, aren't you?" she said. "And someone else. Where do I know him from?"

"He's Shon. He's a friend. He helps me write for the Governor."

"That's it." She still had not wholly let go of me, hands trailing on my hands, eyes still on my eyes. "You're here because of this. You've been sent to find the boat."

"Yes, we… Were you here when it happened?"

"Some of the web-children saw it, and I've been nearby since, to see who came."

I wanted to say something poetic then, about absence and fondness and so forth. The day had been too full of death and my customary eloquence was wanting. I was still muddling a suitable sentence together when she said, "Go and get Peter," which derailed me.

"Go and bring him," she repeated. "I want to see him, too. And I can tell you what happened here. Go."

And of course she wanted to see Peter, and of course I went.

We left Thelwel tinkering with the engine, and Shon watching him because it was a valuable skill on the Island. I had not told Peter why I needed him, I just led him to lean against the rail and we stood there in silence as he grew increasingly impatient. At last I realised that Kiera was right there amongst the leaves, practically between us, one hand pressed to her mouth to stop the laughter. I think she had adapted to her new lifestyle better than she knew.

They embraced, Peter and Kiera, but it was not such a grand affair as ours had been, I was sure.

We asked her how she was coping in the wilderness, and she said she was managing. She was a creature born of the social gatherings of the Shadrapan elite, no more used to survival than the Governor, her kinsman, and yet she had prospered where I would have fallen.

"I can find food, make shelters. I know some medicine. The practical side is all taught to me. It's when I'm not doing all these things, it starts to get to me," she revealed. "It's the stillness. Then I wonder what I'm doing there and who I'm trying to fool."

Peter was brooding over something, so I gestured to the ravaged deck and asked her what the web-children had seen.

"No more than you might think. People fighting on board, then the whole ship just shuddered and ploughed into the bank. Some escaped it, but the jungle took them, one way or another. The web-children say nobody made it far."

I wondered if they had made sure of it but said nothing. Peter made a dissatisfied noise.

"I can tell you more, though," she added. "Just from my own reasoning. I can guess what happened. You've seen the hold? The prisoners?"

Our grim expressions told her that we had.

"Did you notice the balance of them, men and women?"

"It was... difficult to tell," Peter said flatly.

"The balance was about even. That's not the way of the Island. Normally there's a single woman to a boat, if that. What does this suggest to you?"

"Politicals," I recognised, "being shipped to the Island for a quiet execution, like before."

Kiera nodded. "Only this time someone pushed too far. These prisoners had friends. Either they bought some of the crew, or the crew were their supporters already, but there was a mutiny. You can see how bloody the fighting must have been. Nobody gets that single-minded unless there's ideology at stake. The mutineers wanted to release the prisoners so some of the loyalists got below and killed them. Fanatics on both sides."

"And the mutineers must have thrown the engines, to stop the prisoners arriving. Or the loyalists did, to stop them returning," Peter said incredulously. "And these were just sailors. What business did they have caring so much? What can it be like in the city?"

"Kiera, you were in politics," I noted.

"In a way," she admitted.

"Were your family allied to the Anteims?"

"My family? No, damn them," she replied with surprising vehemence. "Not most of the time, anyway. Not as much as we'd have liked."

"Jon Anteim the Elder is dead," Peter explained. "Murdered. What does that do to the balance of power?"

She digested that, wide eyed, and I saw she must have known the old man, that his death had a particular significance for her. "Knocks it over completely. Presidents change, Lords change, the whole Authority swings from one faction to the next, but the Anteims were a constant, always pulling strings. So the old man's dead? And his son, too, of course." Her face closed up as she considered the implications of this. "And now the Authority is shipping its dissidents off to a quiet death in the jungles, but there's enough opposition to cause this kind of mess."

"And few Outriders or Angels left to keep order," I pointed out, and gave her Underworld's defeat in brief, and what it had cost the city.

At this point, Kiera drew back, for Thelwel and Shon were coming up from belowdecks. "I have to go," she said.

"Kiera." Peter leant back on the rail, nodding to Shon and Thelwel, talking out of the side of his mouth. "Have the web-children keep a watch on the Island."

"They always do."

"If they see the two of us put out in a boat again, you have to come here. We'll meet you here," he told her. She nodded slowly, and then froze and neither Thelwel nor Shon seemed to pick her out from the overhanging greenery.

Just before we re-embarked onto our own boat I cast a look back at her, but I could make out nothing but the jungle from which the birds were again descending. As I looked away I caught Thelwel's enquiring expression. I never did find out if he saw her.

The journey back was not as pleasant, both because we were returning to our prison, Wardens and inmates all, and because of the heavy news we had to tell. There had been some talk of trying to keep it silent from the general populace, but Peter had pointed out that the news would spread soon enough of its own accord. The Warden I did not know proposed having all of us prisoners shot. Peter answered that he had seen enough death for one day.

Sure enough, by the time I returned to my cell, the word was already out. By that evening, even as Peter and the others made their official report to the Marshal, everyone was anxiously speculating over what would happen next. Someone on our stretch wanted to know when they would send the next boat, and Thelwel's clear voice called, "What next boat? There is only the one boat from Shadrapar. It has always been the same one."

I had not considered that side of things. No boat, at least until the city reclaimed it, or commissioned a new one. No boat meant no more prisoners, and nobody to take away the sacks. No boat meant we were completely cut off from the city of our birth.

I was awoken maybe an hour before dawn. There was a rushing and a murmuring from the end of the stretch as some new piece of news was passed from ear to ear. I was about to put my head down again and get what sleep I could (Lucian's cough was still troubling him) when I was shocked into wakefulness by a terrible, inhuman wail like nothing I had ever heard. Everyone was quickly at their doors, clamouring to know what was going on, and above it all that horrible sound continued, something that could never have come from a human throat.

It did not. It came from Thelwel. The news had reached him and he was standing in the centre of his cell, hands pressed to

472

his eyes, shrieking out his pain to the world from a throat that seemed not to need any fresh breath.

The word reached me at last from the men in the next cell.

Father Sulplice was dead.

He had been found at the foot of a flight of stairs with his frail old neck broken, and it might have been an accident save that there were two clear thumb marks where his killer had pressed for purchase. In ancient times they had sciences to tell a man from the marks of his thumbs, but we had long lost any such. All those marks spoke of was the fact that the old man's death was no accident. Father Sulplice had been murdered.

38

The Rule of the Marshal

The news of the murder was only the faintest breeze before the storm. Even as we were talking it over; even as Thelwel's cries of grief were dying away, someone got the news to the Marshal. He wasted no time in letting us know of his displeasure.

Why should he care that some old prisoner had met his end? Because Father Sulplice was irreplaceable. Not even his son knew the machines of the Island as the old man had, and the Island was more reliant on technology than its parent city ever was.

The Marshal came to our stretch just before dawn, on fire with rage. It leaked from his eyes and the corners of his mouth and every movement he made. Behind him came a pack of Wardens, beating on doors and making sure everyone was standing to attention. Every man of them had guns and there was blood in the air.

"Which of you did it?" the Marshal demanded outright. "One of you scum killed the old man, the only wretched inmate on this Island who was worth anything to anyone." I thought he had narrowed down the killer to our stretch, but he was going through the stretches in turn, spreading his anger as far as it would go. All of his homicidal moods to that point were nothing to the state we saw him in then. He was a hollow man. There was nothing but hate in him.

"I will know the name of the man who did this," he promised us flatly. "You will tell me. You will give him up to me. One or more of you knows who it was that ended the old man's life. I am sure you think that you will stick together and keep silent. This will not be the case."

He stalked back and forth down the corridor, incapable of standing still even for a moment. The Wardens skipped to get out of his way. They were as scared of him as we were. He had shot two dead, Peter told me later. On hearing the news, he had quite literally shot the messengers. He said they were derelict in their duty, but it was just his rage pulling the trigger.

All the boundaries and rules and regulations that he lived by were straining to hold his fury, and I could see them buckling. He, whom the least challenge to his authority had sent into a killing rage, had been driven mad by the immense presumption of someone taking a thing of value from him. Father Sulplice had been under his protection. It was not for the old man's sake that he was here with his threats, but because of the challenge to his rule.

"Do you know why you will give up the killer to me?" he demanded of us, and we said nothing. Not one man moved. Anyone attracting the Marshal's attention would be a dead man in that instant.

"For each day that passes," he spat out, "I will kill a man on this stretch. I will kill a man on every stretch. What are your lives to me? Have I inspired you, now, to give the murderer up? Perhaps you are asking yourselves what happens should I kill the murderer by random chance, or if I kill the only man that can name him? Then I go on shooting you until not a man of you is left! Do you understand? It is a risk I am prepared to take."

"Can you afford to do that, Marshal?"

The Marshal froze, his general loathing crystallising into a specific hatred. He stalked over to the cell next to ours: Gaki's cell.

"What did you say?" he demanded.

"I asked whether you could afford to deplete your charges here," Gaki said lazily. "With the prison boat gone, you won't get any more toys to play with."

The Marshal stared at him. Their faces were less than a foot apart, separated only by the bars. It was a strange contrast to see the calm and sardonic face of one madman across from the rage-bleeding mask of the other. Without warning, the Marshal put out an arm and shot a man across the corridor, dead on the moment.

"It is a risk," he repeated, "I am prepared to take." He spared a glance for his victim. "That was for your insolence," he stated, and then his gun swung in our direction. "This is today's quota." He fired. The bullet lanced through our cell and missed Lucian by a hand's breadth before ploughing into the shoulder of a man in the cell behind.

"I will be back tomorrow," the Marshal stated. "You can be sure of it." Then he was gone to the next stretch with his nervous gang of Wardens filing out behind him. We heard more shots soon enough.

The man with the injured shoulder was unable to work that day, of course, and was gone when we returned from the workshops. Most reckoned that the Wardens had taken him, because when the Marshal said he would kill a man a day, he meant it.

In the workshop that day, each man was watching every other. Even the slowest had worked out that not only murderers but scapegoats might be offered up to the Marshal. I think the only reason that the man had not been deluged with them was fear of his reprisal if he chose not to believe the accuser. It was simply not wise to be anywhere near the Marshal right then, even to give him what he wanted.

I wondered what the Governor thought of it all, whether he even knew.

Thelwel got into a fight in one of the storerooms. Someone from our stretch came and told me that he was brawling, begging me to stop him before he brought the Wardens down on us. I ran along and discovered Father Sulplice's son locked in a grapple with none other than Tallan.

I assumed that Tallan had attacked him, but a moment later I saw Thelwel had one hand about the man's neck and the other twisted in the collar of his prison greys, and Tallan was struggling to get away. The larger man struck Thelwel twice across the face, without achieving anything. Thelwel was panting for breath, but between gasps he was saying something.

"You killed him! You did it!" He had let his face go slack and expressionless as a rubber mask. He was concentrating on other things. Tallan was making a half-strangled denial but Thelwel was not listening, forcing him back against a wall. "You did it! I know you! You're evil! Why not you?"

"Thelwel! Thelwel, leave him!" I grabbed his shoulders and tried to prise him off his victim. "It wasn't him. Thelwel, listen to me!"

His face turned to look at me, and for a moment there was nothing human in it, no admission of any common ground at all. He was, for a brief span, a killing machine who would not allow that we had shared conversations and expeditions and secrets together.

"Stefan," said the thing that was Thelwel.

Then it all flowed back into him from wherever he had penned his humanity. For Thelwel was human, more so than many born to the title. His grip loosened and Tallan bolted away without a word.

"It wasn't him," I said again. "Much as I am loath to defend Tallan in anything, we were all locked up in our stretch, and Lucian kept me awake most of the night. There's no way he could have got out, and besides, why would he? I know he's a bastard but I can't see him deciding to kill your father just for

477

the fun. It must have been someone from another stretch. Who had a motive?"

"Nobody," said Thelwel in a small voice. There was no sign of the energy that had filled him. "Nobody. He was so careful. Everyone knew they needed him. Who would do such a thing, Stefan?"

I had no answers for him.

The next morning we were once again woken before dawn as the Marshal grimly followed through with his promise. I could see that the strain of the situation was beginning to tell on him. Not the killing; there was never a man more able to deal out death with a clear conscience. In the light of a new day, he was beginning to realise the situation he had created for himself. He stormed in and demanded that we turn over the killer, and he got his wish. Three prisoners in one cell called him and told him that their fourth was the killer. I heard the trio of strident accusations and the solo of terrified denial. The Marshal was over there at once. I heard him say, "So, he did it, did he?" clearly over the pleas of innocence.

"How do you know it was him?" the Marshal demanded. The cell went very quiet. They were so shocked he was actually asking them for proof, they could not even come up with the obvious: "he told us" or "we overheard him boasting about it", or even "we saw him do it". The Marshal gave a snarl of frustration and his Wardens killed all three of the accusers and wounded an innocent man in the cell behind them. I heard the accused man thanking the Marshal again and again.

"But maybe you did do it," said the Marshal, and the Wardens shot him too. When the Marshal turned back down the stretch there was a fear to him. He had lost control. He could never know whether a man was the killer: we were all liars to him. Nor could he be seen to be going back on himself. He had trapped himself in a bloody spiral and I could see him thinking through the maze of it, trying desperately to find some way out. I was afraid that the only way that would occur to him would be to kill everyone and have done with it.

He had done his killing for the day, and he was about to make for the next stretch, when I visibly saw an idea take him. It came out of nowhere at all. I never saw something so strange before. I felt the ripples of the surface of his mind as the alien object struck home and made itself apparent to him.

He stopped dead, and the Wardens almost walked into the back of him.

"Advani!" he barked, and my blood stopped in my veins. There was nothing I could do but stand and wait as he approached. Lucian and Hermione melted from my side and fell to the back of the cell.

"Advani. You claim to be an educated man. Would you explain to these ignorant scum the meaning of the word, 'decimation'?"

My heart sank, but beyond that immediate fear for my life there was an almost cringing sense of embarrassment for the man. It was the poverty of his imagination, his ability to solve problems only in the same tired way, over and over again.

"It means to remove one in every ten," I said, as calmly as I could.

"Exactly so," the Marshal confirmed. "I see that you are all irredeemable, and the true killer will hide amongst you forever whilst you betray each other in turn. Sulplice's death shall be punished and the punishment shall be felt by you all. I shall bring you out one mob at a time and I shall remove, as Advani puts it, one out of every ten. Each and every one of you has that chance to die, and it shall be today."

He stared about him, and there was less of a reaction than he was expecting. Deep inside, I was not the only one who was becoming jaded. One can only live with random violence for so long before the shock wears off. At least this new terror would be over and done with soon enough.

The sun was uncompromisingly bright, as we were herded out onto the open dock. I had watched Peter fight his duel there, first set foot on the Island there, first seen the Marshal claim a life there. Now I would see the logical continuation of his policy of fear: his *decimation*. Where, I wondered, had he even learned that archaic word? Or did he have an infinite vocabulary where death was concerned?

I think there were five stretches worth of prisoners blinking and cringing in the harsh sunlight. We were packed in, shoulder to shoulder, backs to the water. Around two-thirds of the Wardens were between us and the dubious safety of the Island's innards. They had all been issued with firearms of one kind or another. I saw balding Harkeri there, and Red, and the resolutely brooding Sauven.

The Marshal kept us waiting. We had ample time to reflect on that one-in-ten chance. We were all wondering how he would make his selections. Would he count from the left, the right, the front? There was a constant silent eddying amongst our ranks as people tried to jockey for some position that would be absolutely safe from all directions.

I was close to Thelwel and I saw that he was looking out past our fellows to the line of the jungle. He was making the most of the view while he could. I had assumed that with Father Sulplice dead, they would need Thelwel to carry on his work but, the way the Marshal was behaving, nobody was safe.

Some tugging at my mind made me look up, and I saw a gallery high above us, set into the Island's wall. I had never known it was there from the outside, but I realised I had seen it from within: the Governor's window, from where he measured the waning light of the stars. Squinting into the sunlight I could just make out two faces in the shade there, looking down on us. What could the Governor and his lady think of this pointless butchery? Did they approve of the Marshal's firm hand or were they powerless to stop his rampage?

The Marshal emerged. Something had prompted him to give the event a sense of occasion. He was in some bizarre dress uniform that I had never seen: a half-cloak trimmed with gold and some decorations across his chest, with braided epaulettes at the shoulder. It was a piece of the Island's history from generations back, unearthed to commemorate his latest act of destruction. He adjusted his headband and then marched out, a one-man parade, to give his orders.

"You convicts have conspired to conceal the name of Sulplice's murderer," he called out. "You have nobody to blame but yourselves for this justice." His cold stare bit into the warmth of the afternoon. "The survivors will learn to know their place. I will have no murder done in my prison."

This was such a grand piece of illogic that I nearly choked. It was clear that the Marshal saw no inconsistency. To him, executing political prisoners or randomly shooting inmates was not murder. Lawful authority was all, and moral authority merely its shadow, to be forced into whatever shape the law adopted.

His gaze was hovering over us, seeking victims. I decided that he was going to use this opportunity to take care of a few grudges. I wondered if the Governor's writ still held. I was surely for the axe otherwise. I had a recurrence of my calm resignation. The matter was beyond my control.

"Oh stop this charade!" called a voice from the ranks. Several of the Wardens flinched and guns came up to cover us. It was a miracle that no-one was shot there and then. The Marshal waited, though, and I saw some part of him had been expecting this.

Gaki stepped through the massed inmates as though he was walking through an empty room, and came to stand in front. The sun gleamed from his shaven head, his lean, bare chest.

"Marshal, you disappoint me," Gaki said, and the temperature dropped. The Marshal was still as stone.

"Decimate the whole prison to cover up your own fear? Kill one man in ten to hide your own inadequacy," Gaki prodded gently. "And from the moment the body was found, you knew the name of the killer. You never had a doubt and yet you have gone through this ridiculous puppet show. Who are you trying to deceive, Marshal? The Governor? Yourself?"

The Marshal never moved, but I could feel something building in his mind, as one might see a swift dark mass of cloud and know that a storm was on its way.

"You've always known that I killed the old man," Gaki said lightly. I felt a current recoil through the collective mind of the listeners, prisoners and Wardens both. I gripped Thelwel's arm convulsively because I had visions of him leaping fatally at Gaki's back. Thelwel's eyes were dead, face loose. Of his mind I could feel nothing.

I had not thought of Gaki. He was a madman, but not without method. He killed for a reason, even if his reasons were insane. Why would he destroy a harmless old man? I saw it now. He did it to draw the Marshal out. He did it to force this confrontation in a time and space of his liking. That idea, that had struck the Marshal so unexpectedly, had its origin in Gaki's brain.

"Now," said Gaki, as if prompting, and the Marshal dragged a pistol out and fired at him, point blank. There was a second's hesitation, though, and Gaki had sidestepped away to let the bullet slam into a prisoner behind. With the gunshot, everyone moved. Inmates tried not to be in the way of the next shot. People pushed and jostled and fell into the water. Wardens ran forward, trying to aim at Gaki, who was circling the Marshal. No, not circling, spiralling in. I was slammed from behind and people trod on my feet and struck me, but I could not tear my eyes away. The Marshal was trying to track him, firing again and again. Each time there was that second's pause before his finger closed on the trigger, and each time Gaki was elsewhere. I saw Harkeri go down with a bullet in the leg, and a prisoner take a graze across the side of the head. Many of

482

the Wardens were keeping a line of guns between the prisoners and the doorway, still acting on their last received instructions. The men in the water were crying out for aid, and I heard the bellow of a river monster as it scented their fear. All this was background.

Gaki tucked and rolled and came up nose to nose with the Marshal, the gun pointed at his chest. He was smiling serenely. I saw a musician once, confident in his skills and caught up in his performance, wearing just that expression. He stood still for the next shot and the gun clicked, emptied out.

I recall the next moments in silence, although surely the same commotion was going on all around. I hear nothing, in my memories, see only the two men, law and chaos, the powers of the Island.

The Marshal lashed the barrel of the pistol at Gaki's face, reaching for the knife at his belt left-handed. Gaki blocked the gun with a forearm. His other hand had something in it that glinted like glass, and I could not tell what it was save that I had seen it before.

He made a graceful pass across the Marshal's stomach as bullets and beams of energy from the Wardens passed soundlessly around them. The Marshal lunged forwards with his own blade, but it stuttered still before it could drive in. Gaki turned away, kicked off into a backflip over the Wardens' guns and was gone into the depths of the Island before anyone could stop him.

That stutter, I had seen it before. I had done it to the Marshal myself to throw off a killing thrust by that very knife. Gaki had been holding the Marshal's mind between thumb and forefinger, squeezing every time the man tried to kill him.

He had learned Helman's techniques.

There were Wardens moving after Gaki, but they slowed as they reached the doorway, because the darkness within was suddenly populated by a real monster.

The Marshal stood very still, very straight, and I saw a thin line of red appear across his torso, like another decoration. He clutched at it and at last I saw an expression on his face, like marble cracking; an animal expression; pain.

The glint in Gaki's hand had been Father Sulplice's diamond-bladed knife, his tiny metal-shaping tool. In all the uproar over the old man's death, who had thought to look for it?

The Marshal lurched, then forced himself to stand straight. A Warden came to him, offering support, but he waved the man off with a stilted gesture and turned from us to go inside. His steps were too fast, disjointed. He kept having to stop and re-pace himself. We massed prisoners watched his back and thought about the future.

He gave some order to Sauven, at the door. I thought it might have been "Kill them all," but it turned out to be nothing more than, "Get them inside."

39

Requiem for a Tyrant

We were herded back into our cells full of questions. The Wardens struck down anyone who tried to ask them. They had only been taught the one way to deal with dissent amongst their charges.

And we were not taken out to go to the workshops, and that made everything worse. It was admission by omission. It told us the Wardens knew that nobody was coming to pick up our sacks of chemicals. Why should they waste their time supervising us in the work rooms, just to clog the stores with useless produce?

I missed the irony at the time: that the Marshal's injury had given us the day's holiday he said we'd never get.

Each cell petitioned the next cell for news, and the questions passed along the corridors, up and down, even reaching the waterlogged darkness of Below. Is the Marshal dead? Has anyone seen Gaki? What is going on?

Confused and contradictory rumours started: The Marshal is dead. The Marshal is unharmed. Gaki is dead. Gaki is working his way through the Wardens. The Governor is dead. Nobody knew what to believe.

Midday came and went, according to those closer to the outside, and a new concern voiced itself for we had not been fed. Someone pointed out that it would be easiest for the Wardens just to let us rot. If the Marshal was fighting for life, then the last thing they would be concerned about was us. People started stamping and shouting, demanding food. A stir of fear fluttered through us all, a primal fear, one of the oldest. Even one missed meal reminds us all that starvation is our common birthright. Soon, with nothing to eat but small creeping creatures and each other, people were trying the slats of the doors as they never had before. People were suddenly testing themselves against the very structure of the Island. The mood in the cells tilted towards revolution.

They brought us food soon after that. Wardens trekked round the whole Island with food for everyone. The prisoners relaxed: things were the same as usual. Only a few people noticed that things were really changed, and forever. For the first time ever, the prisoners had forced the Wardens into acting. We had raised a threat, and they had backed down rather than beating us. I was not the only one thinking it, I am sure.

Midds brought our food round. When he came to my cell I was bold enough to ask the question on everyone's lips.

"Midds. Tell me."

His eyes were frightened.

"Is the Marshal dead, Midds?"

"No." Most other Wardens would have struck out at me but I knew him by then. He was not one to waste his energy. "He's… resting," said Midds haltingly, and the word was passed from cell to cell in all directions. I looked into his eyes and knew that "resting" was not the same thing as "recovering".

It was a long night, and I was kept awake not by Lucian's cough but by my own fears and phantasms of the future. I could feel the structure of the Island creak around me: not the physical but the social. The Marshal was injured. The Marshal was dying.

I shed no tears for him. He was a man born of hate and a tool for nothing else. He deserved his end, if anyone ever did. His one redeeming feature would die with him, though, and that was a talent for maintaining the status quo. I had not thought that I would value the way things were on the Island. Only as the world hung in the balance with every laboured breath the Marshal took did I appreciate that things could get worse still. I remembered the prisoners on the boat, butchered through the bars because it was easier that way.

What if whoever took over had even less imagination than the Marshal? What if nobody took over?

All night, Hermione crouched by the bars of the door, perhaps waiting for Gaki. He did not come that night, or not that I saw. She was in the same patient position come morning.

That morning, Midds came down to us and hauled us all out to work again, face without expression. A lot of people asked him questions but he would say nothing. He just called out that we had already been given one day off, and that was more than he ever had; we shouldn't make a habit of it. He said that we had to get our lazy backsides down to the workshops and nothing was wrong, nothing had changed. Business as usual, he tried to convey, but his body did not believe it and his face, customarily so expressive, was saying nothing.

Things grew stranger when we got to the workshops, because there were so few of us. At first we assumed that there had been some massive silent cull and that we were the lucky survivors. Then we saw that entire stretches were absent: only some of the Island's inmates had been pushed out to work, whilst others were still sitting placidly in their cells, getting fed for free. There was no consensus amongst the Wardens.

Some of the prisoners tried to complain about this inequality. Most of the Wardens who had forced their charges to work (Midds being a conspicuous exception) were the tough-minded brutal sort. Anyone trying to claim rights was given a kicking.

I did not complain. I had been coasting on an assumed immunity that had filtered down from the Governor. The Marshal had obeyed the Governor reluctantly but without question. The Wardens had barely seen their shadowy ruler. His writ would run thin with them. I was taking no chances. I am not a brave man, but I hope you will allow that I am not a stupid one.

Then they came for me.

It was just after lunch, and I was tending one of the simpler machines, trying to make myself look valuable, although God knows it had not helped Father Sulplice. I was grabbed from behind by two Wardens, who bundled me away at speed. I had one brief glimpse of Midds' face, unhappy but unsurprised. Then we were ascending, and my feet barely touched the ground as I was hustled up flights of stairs.

The Marshal, I decided. In his final hours he was settling old scores. He had never liked me. My death had been snatched from him once, and the lost toy is always the most vividly recalled.

Then we were going higher still and I realised the Governor himself had become impatient.

Shon was there too between two more Wardens, with a black eye just starting to blossom on his face. My own captors stomped to a halt right in front of him and his escort, and there was a ludicrous little moment as everyone stared at everyone else, patently uncertain as to exactly what should happen next.

The Governor came in unannounced and shouted at them, or his closest approximation. "What are you doing out here? Get them into my rooms," and then got in their way as four Wardens tried to squeeze two prisoners through a narrow doorway simultaneously.

"You will write," he told us. "I want it finished. No more excuses. I don't care about anything else. Neither of you are leaving until it is done."

At his gesture the Wardens dragged us to the familiar old desk and sat us down with unnecessary force. They were unsure as to what was going on, but they clung to their familiar methodology.

"Now you go wait outside," the Governor told them. "Don't let them out. If they want food, get them food. That's all."

The Wardens exchanged mutinous looks but stormed out, all four of them. Neither Shon nor I felt like asking them for any food.

We had to call out for sustenance eventually. After the first eight hours, hunger began to bite. The Governor was going to be as good as his word. We were going to sit here like punished schoolboys until we had finished.

We had no idea what was going on beneath us, in the shaken and unsure corridors of the prison. Was the Marshal dead yet? I did not think that he could die without us knowing. I had some superstitious idea that the last beat of his heart would resound through his domain like a bell ringing his passing. How could there be an Island without the Marshal, and we not know?

Shon and I worked doggedly and without conversation. We were all too aware of the Governor's co-opted death squad outside the door, keen to come in and enforce their orders should we show any signs of slacking. I read through Trethowan's crabbed text and found a path through his Old School Shorthand to some kind of readable account, and Shon scratched it all down in his formal lawyer's hand.

We had been going long enough that we were both heavy with fatigue, he with cramping hand and me with hoarse throat and aching eyes. I had begun to imagine things, idle parts of my brain amusing themselves. I thought I saw movement, heard sounds, words. Some part of me was on a permanent lookout for Gaki, who had still not been seen. So it was that when the Lady Ellera came to watch us, for a long time I assumed it was just my eyes being desperate to see anything but Trethowan's writings.

She was there, though, watching us with predatory eyes. We avoided her gaze and worked as though we were alone. I wondered what she thought about the situation below. She had a strong interest in things staying as they were, but at the same time she had always hated the Marshal. He had been the sole challenge to her illicit authority. Now he lay dying, perhaps she believed that she could take the Island herself. I did not believe it. Her methods were suitable to the domination of individuals, the Marshal's to whole bodies of people. Unless she could find those amongst the Wardens who could keep the others in line, I did not value her chances.

She watched us for a long time. I am sure she still hated me for my perceived refusal to share my powers with her. With the completion of Trethowan's writings, any bar to her revenge would be lifted. It struck me, of a sudden, how similar she was to the Marshal, her self-constructed world held together with pure willpower. Neither of them could abide any resistance to their sovereignty. No wonder they always hated each other. I almost felt sorry for the Governor having to mediate between them.

Just as I had not noticed her appear, I did not notice her leave. She had simply grown bored whilst we worked (she was not the only one) and gone to amuse herself with other things. I spared a thought for the Island's female prisoners, locked up in their seraglio for the sole purpose of fueling the Lady Ellera's researches. Did she really believe in those sciences that she shed blood for, or was it just another way for her to exercise her power, lest it grow weak through lack of use?

I do not exaggerate when I say we worked on that manuscript for some eighteen hours, not counting some five hours' fitful sleep, until I began to wish that Trethowan had never been born. The only relief I had, actually having met the man, was to envisage crushing his shrivelled neck between my hands for the crime of being so prolific. I am sure Shon felt the same, and had better hands for strangling. We were still not finished, and I began to realise that I need not have wasted all that time stalling.

Shon asked me how long, and I reckoned glumly on at least nine hours more before we were done. The joke being, of course, that Trethowan himself had never completed the work, but had made his ingenious exit before getting to the last chapter. So the entire mammoth task, on which the Governor pinned such bizarre hope, was a doomed venture from the very start.

However, we were interrupted by Peter.

He came in without ceremony and said, "I've been looking all over for you."

"I've been right here," I told him, "working the Governor's word-mill."

"Well leave it," Peter told me, and I picked up on a change in his voice, an excitement.

"The Marshal—" I said, and he shook his head sharply.

"The Marshal clings to life like a persimmon," he said, and I wondered what terrifying beast his mind had attached the word to. "We're leaving."

It meant nothing to me. "Mining... or..."

Peter's face broke into a fierce predator's grin, and he gripped me hard by the shoulder. "Going, Stefan. This place is falling down and we're getting out."

Shon, too, stared at him.

"Going home," he stated.

"But..." I managed. I could not comprehend what he was saying to me. It was too big to fit into my head. I think I might have just stood there forever had the Governor not come blundering in.

"If they want food, get them food," he told the astonished Peter. "If they try to leave, stop them. Don't waste their time talking to them."

Peter looked at him levelly. "Come on," he told Shon and me.

"What are you doing?" the Governor demanded, as Shon and I got up from the desk. "You have to stay here and work. Warden, what are you doing? You have to do what I tell you."

Peter shrugged. The Governor actually stamped his foot. "Stop! Don't you know who I am? I am the Governor. That means you have to do what I say!"

In the doorway, Peter stopped and turned back to the man. He walked up until they were close enough to touch. The top of the Governor's head barely cleared Peter's shoulder. I saw then the big difference between Peter and everyone else. He had never assented to any of the Island's preconceptions. He had never acknowledged anyone as his master. He had only been biding his time and, more than any prisoner, thinking of escape. Peter stared down at the Governor and something drained out of the face of Leontes de Margot. It may have been his illusions.

"But… it's my prison, my Island," he whispered. "I'm the Governor…" but he no longer believed himself. All that reading about evolution and it took Peter to teach him this one vital lesson.

"Come on," Peter repeated, making for the door.

"Stefan," the Governor whined behind us. "You can't leave, Stefan. You haven't finished the work, Trethowan's work. His answers…"

I looked back and decided I had earned a little nastiness. "He never completed it," I told the man.

He gaped at me like something dredged up from the lake bottom.

"Trethowan had no answers," I told him flatly. "He wasn't trying to save the world." And then, because I could not resist it, "You were reading the wrong book for that."

I turned and followed Peter out. I heard the Governor start again. "Please, you have to stay, you can't leave me," and I realised that he was begging Shon.

"You don't even know my name," Shon told him, and left.

"Right," Peter said as we descended the stairs. "Now, we're going to take this calm, but fast. I've got Midds and Red

492

getting us some rations. Real food, not the stuff they sieve out of the engines. Shon, your stretch is at work. Stefan, yours is locked up. I've got the key to your stretch here. I want you two to go grab a few people, just a very few. We don't want to overload the boat. Stefan, we're going to need Thelwel. Anyone else has to be useful and trustworthy. This is going to be tough enough even without infighting. Meet me in the big storeroom off the central workshop. And don't get in the way of any other Wardens. Midds and Red are the only two I can trust."

It was a strange thing going alone to my stretch, when all the others were safely locked up in their cells. When I was very young, I sometimes crept out of bed to steal delicacies from the larder. Incongruously it was just like that.

I found Thelwel's cell first and rapped on the door to attract his attention. He had shared the cell with two others, but only one was left.

"Thelwel," I said, "I need your help." I did not want to cause a riot by saying I was skipping out on them all.

"What is it?" he asked me, coming to the door.

"I'll tell you later. Come on." When I unlocked the door there was a ripple of amazement, even alarm. Prisoners did not have keys. For a moment I thought of some flimsy story, the Governor trusting me enough and so forth, but I could not make it convincing even to myself. Thelwel's other cell mate got out too and made off down the corridor, but I did not care about that.

I had little love for any other in my stretch, save for the occupants of my cell. I felt I owed Lucian something. He had been kind to me. I paced down until I found the familiar door, as though playing at being a Warden. He was alone within.

"Lucian," I hissed, while Thelwel hovered in the background. "Come here."

He trotted over and asked me what on earth I was doing walking around free what with the Wardens being so unreasonable at the moment and...

"Never mind. Just come on."

I opened the door but he just looked discomforted and lingered within. I had no time for his chatter. Much as I had hoped never to pass that doorway again, I darted inside.

"Listen, Lucian," I told him. "Quiet now." I was whispering so that no other prisoner would hear, taking him close to the empty cell that Gaki once claimed as his own. "Lucian, I am leaving the Island. I am leaving with Thelwel and Shon and a few others. I want you to come too." Peter would not have approved. Lucian hardly fell into the "useful" category. Even so, I owed it to him.

Lucian stared at me, eyes wide, and burst out that he couldn't possibly because after all he would be out any day now, because of all the good work his friends were doing for him back in Shadrapar. He really didn't want to jeopardise his legitimate release with anything so dangerous as skulking off in a stolen boat—

"Lucian, stop," I told him, not least because the other prisoners were all staring. "Lucian, nobody is coming to get you out. I am sorry, but it is not going to happen. There is no prison boat for you to go back on. This is your chance. I can get you out of here. We can go home."

His eyes were wider and wider, as though someone was peeling his skin back from them. His patter had died a sudden death, leaving only the corpse of it in his open mouth. By now everyone else else had understood what was going on.

"We don't have the time for this." I could hear Thelwel shifting uneasily in the corridor outside. "Lucian, come on."

He was trying to tell me that I did not need to do this and that everything would be fine, I didn't have to worry myself over him and that his friends would—

"When would they?" I demanded of him. "When? How long

have you been here, Lucian? See some sense, for God's own sake."

"I'm scared," he whispered. These were the only concise words he ever uttered. "Don't make me go out there I don't want to leave here and go back to that place I'm safe here and I know everyone and please—"

I could feel something twist inside me, some worm of pity that I could not afford to indulge. "I'm going," I told him, and as an afterthought. "Where's Hermione?"

Lucian explained, voice still trembling, that she had gone.

"Gone where?"

I was told that "he" had taken her, and Lucian's glance to the empty cell behind him told me all I needed to know to identify "him".

"Gaki was here?"

Gaki had been there, selecting prisoners before me. Hermione had gone with him, and also Tallan. Hearing that put a weight back on me that I had not even realised was gone. Tallan, one of a growing number who wished me dead, was free and walking the Island in the company of the world's most accomplished murderer.

Part of me knew instantly what Gaki was about: the same thing we were. He was making his exit, to return to the place that bore him.

As I left with Thelwel, some of the other prisoners began calling for me, asking me to release them too. At the mouth of our stretch I turned and put the keys into the hands of the nearest man. "Wait your moment," was the only advice I could give. Perhaps they would riot instantly and be gunned down. Perhaps they would be wise.

Sometimes it seems my life has been no more than lighting fuses and running away.

40

An End to Cells

Thelwel was trying to ask me what was going on but I was too busy getting down to the storeroom before all hell broke loose behind us. I ran into Shon practically in the doorway and Peter was already waiting inside.

"You took your time," he said. "Thelwel, good. Shon?"

"The only man on my stretch I'd trust got shot while we were writing," Shon reported. "Let's go."

We stormed out of the storeroom trying hard to look casual, with Thelwel at the back still wanting to know what we were doing. There was no time, though. I could hear a commotion from above, as the loosed prisoners of my stretch were discovered by Wardens. Things were going to be busy from now on.

I was anxiously counting boats the moment we hit the dock. The huge gunship was still hulking there, and the Marshal's launch, surely never to feel the hand of its master again. The other vessels were just as I remembered them, not a one astray. I could not imagine Gaki putting out in a ponderous mining ship. I reasoned he must still be on the Island.

"We have to go right now," I pronounced.

"We have to wait for Middsy and Red," Peter corrected.

"Stefan, will you please tell me what we're doing here," Thelwel demanded.

"Well," I started, and then someone was shouting at us. There was a Warden crossing towards the boats, one I did not recognise. He held a flintlock pistol loosely, but his eyes were too suspicious. One Warden and three prisoners, unauthorised at the boats. He had obviously put a fair picture of our business together.

"What's this?" he demanded of Peter. "What are you doing?"

"I don't answer to you," Peter said casually, careless of the gun.

"You will," the man told him harshly. "Skipping out on us, Drachmar? The Marshal knew you were a sneaky bastard. I reckon you and me had better go see him."

"The Marshal's dead," Peter said. "I'd find a better role model."

"He is not dead!" The Warden's face contorted with something that looked like anger but was probably despair. "He is not dead. He was wounded, only." Peter gave a shrug and a little smile, as if to say that the health or otherwise of the Marshal really did not interest him anyway. This only served to enrage the man further, and I really thought he would shoot. Some vestige of order, some prohibition on killing another Warden in front of prisoners, stayed his hand. I saw then that Shon had already slipped behind the man.

"Put your hands where I can see them, Drachmar," the Warden ordered, sensing a trap, just not the right one. Peter did so with sloth bordering on insolence.

"Now, you lot get back to the workshop—" the man said before Shon came up behind him, crouching low, and smashed his elbow up into the back of the man's neck, round about where the skull joins the spine. The Warden dropped with no more words and Peter caught the gun out of the air.

"You must have elbows of steel," he remarked mildly to Shon.

"Elbow," Shon corrected. "Just the one."

"We're here!" boomed out Midds' voice, killing all attempt at stealth stone dead. "Got our provisions, got our gear right here. Did you miss us?" The big man was lumbering forwards with two sacks and a long bag over his shoulders. Behind him, the tall, stiletto-sharp form of Red carried a sleek and nasty-looking rifle. I saw that Midds had some kind of weaponish-looking thing jammed in his belt, and a big machete as well. The bag he carried was the one Peter used for his duelling kit.

"Are we set?" Midds asked us all. "I'm itching to be out of here."

"What happened to him?" Red asked, nudging the fallen Warden with a boot. He seemed entirely less sure of what we were doing.

"Rhetorical argument," Peter said, with the utter confidence of a man who had no idea what it meant.

"Excuse me," Thelwel said. "You're leaving?"

"We're leaving," I confirmed. "All of us."

"No," he said simply. "Thank you but no."

"Thelwel—" I started.

"We need you," Peter pushed in. "And you'll not get this chance again. What's here for you?"

"What's out there for you?" Thelwel countered.

"Shadrapar. Home," Peter said.

"Well then." Thelwel looked from him to me. "I never called Shadrapar home. My whole life is here."

"The Island is falling down right now as we argue," Peter told him. "Nobody's going to be safe here. You have to come with us. You'll die otherwise."

"Shadrapar is not safe, especially for me," Thelwel insisted. "I have no wish to go to that city. The Island needs me. Who will keep its engines running if not me? If things get so bad that I must leave, I'll take to the jungles."

This brought incredulous noises from Midds and Red, but I knew Thelwel. He had a love of the wild and he of all people could survive there. I could see Peter working up for another sally at him, so I spoke first.

"I'm going to miss you," I said.

"Likewise," he agreed. "No time, though, if you want to be away. Look here." He was hurrying over to one of the boats. "You too, Regenel," which I recalled was Red's real name.

"Look at this," he told us, pointing to the ugly protruding mechanism between the arms of the point generators. "This is the engine. When you leave the swamps and the chemical gradient declines, the point generators will stop working and you'll need this. Here's the ignition, to start it. Here's to turn it off. It has a solid fuel reserve and they're all topped up, but it'll run off the sun too, if you need it. Do you understand?"

I thought I did and Red was nodding sagely.

"Good," Thelwel said. "Stefan, you have been a good friend to me. Now I have to go. Forgive me but I cannot travel with you."

We clasped hands briefly, and then he was gone, slipping off to the upper levels. Almost instantly I was gripped with loss, the sense of a true companion I would never see again, and I wanted to call him back. He was gone, though, and nothing we could have said would have persuaded him to part with the Island or go to the place that had condemned his father to exile.

I got the point generators working second time lucky, and the others pushed the boat out and climbed in. Nobody shouted out or demanded our return. The Marshal did not make a final appearance to deny us our freedom. We coasted across the waters of the lake with no more resistance than the breeze, and nobody even marked our departure.

As we passed from beneath the shadow of the Island, I felt as though we had broken through some great barrier and that every sound of jungle and water came together in an echoing crash of shattered glass that would resound in us forever. We had left the Island. We had left the slavery of Warden and prisoner. After so much suffering we were finally going home.

No-one spoke until we had cleared the lake, and the bends of the river had put the Island out of sight. Whilst we still had an eye on that place it seemed that it could reach out and snatch us back at any time. As soon as it was obscured by the riverbank foliage, Midds let out a great sigh of relief.

"Not going to miss that place," he murmured. "Roll on Shadrapar."

Red looked entirely less happy but said nothing. He was a man who valued order, I guessed – even the bloody-handed order of the Marshal. He was loyal to his friends, though, and he had sided with Peter before.

"Right," Peter said. "That's that then." As though we were home already, without the miles of dangerous river. "Rule one."

He waited until he had everyone's attention.

"Rule one is: no more prisoners. No more Wardens. We're all equal. I don't want you two lording it over Shon and Stefan."

"Do you think that's wise?" Red asked, ignoring us two. "Where does it put us?"

"You've been on the Island too long," Peter told him without sympathy. "No prisoners. No Wardens. We're all just people, no rank."

"But we need some structure," Red argued.

"That's where rule two comes in," Peter told him. "Rule two is: I'm in charge."

"So everyone's equal but you're in charge," I clarified.

"That's right."

"The Marshal would be proud," I told him.

"Who organised this boat trip anyway? Red, can you live with that?"

"Yes," said the thin Warden, still not entirely happy.

"Red?" Peter prodded.

"So long as you keep a hold on things."

"Shon's a lawyer and Stefan's an Academy boy," Peter pointed out. "They're not going to go berserk on us. Brings me to rule three."

"What's rule three?" we virtually chorused.

"Weapons," Peter said. "I want everyone armed." Red was about to protest, so he added, "No prisoners, no Wardens, remember? You have a gun. I have a gun. Midds has a gun. There are no more guns, but everyone gets a weapon." He reached into his kit bag and got out the T-handled duelling dagger. "Stefan, this is for you," he said.

I took it doubtfully, trying out the grip, which was uncomfortable. Given that Peter was being so egalitarian, I did not feel I could complain.

"Shon," Peter continued, "Can you use this?" He handed Shon the heavy mace-spear combination, which was hefted critically.

"I should think so," Shon said. There was a delighted little smile curling at the edge of his mouth. He always did love the duels.

"Now, Stefan, set course for the prison boat," Peter said authoritatively.

"You mean just follow the river until we see it," I said, but I knew what he meant. A little later, when I could speak to his ear only I said, "You had all this planned out, didn't you? When we met with Kiera before."

He shook his head. "All on the spur, Stefan. All thinking on my feet. It was just that I reckoned we'd want a reunion some day." He grinned at me.

When the leaning hulk of the prison ship came into view I cut the generators and let us coast in gently.

"Why are we stopping?" Red asked me.

"We have arrived."

"This isn't Shadrapar," Midds pointed out. "You're not thinking of living out your days on that thing are you, Peter? One prison is as bad as the next."

"We're picking up," Peter told them.

"Weapons? Supplies?" Shon prompted.

"Crew," Peter said, and the nose of the boat clanked gently on the iron side of the ship. "We may have to wait a while."

"Peter, just what is going on here?" suspicious Red wanted to know.

"You'll see yourself," Peter said, "Just give it time," and other assurances. Red sat back down and sulkily guided the boat near to shore, to moor alongside the ship's grounded bows. The air was a good deal sweeter than when we had been here last. The scavengers had done their worst, and when I peered onto the slanting deck, I saw that most of the bones had gone, taken by more durophagous feasters. Here and there was still the odd glint of metal from the weapons that had enacted the slaughter.

"Someone should get those," I said. I exchanged a look with Shon, who presumably still had his stolen knife from last time.

Peter followed my nod and agreed. "Might as well make use of the time." Midds and Shon scrambled out and started putting together a collection of blades, bludgeons, crossbows and the occasional flintlock.

She came out of the jungle like a vision. I thought my eyes were playing tricks on me at first, and then I knew they had been, for I had been looking at her yet not seen her until she wished it. She locked eyes with me and gestured towards the busy Midds and Shon, asking if it was safe. I nodded, just a little.

Shon and Midds stared in slow surprise as she stepped from the branches onto the deck. She spared them a slightly nervous smile, and crossed to where the boat was moored, saving any explanations for Peter and me to make.

"You took your time," Peter said, smiling up at her.

"You had a boat. I had to walk."

He helped her down, where she nodded to Red. He looked at her guardedly, but I thought he was not entirely unhappy to see her there. He had got on with her quite well, I recalled, during her stay with the Wardens.

"Is someone going to explain just what the plot is?" Midds demanded plaintively.

"For those that don't know, this is Kiera de Margot," Peter told them.

"Former prisoner and child of nature," I added, because I liked the sound of it.

"We're complete," Peter declared. "Back in the boat, boys. We're putting off. Fire her up, Stefan."

Midds was halfway over the rail when the river erupted. A great circle of it, out in the centre, gouted up in an explosion of spray, the wake of it slamming our boat against the prison ship's side. I nearly fell out and Peter nearly lost his fingers. In the midst of the chaos Red had his rifle in his hands without thinking, looking for the monster that had surely arisen from the depths, but as he did so there was a hollow thunder from behind us all, the sound catching up, and we saw we were not alone on the river any more.

It was the gunship. The monstrous ironclad had sailed for surely the first time in a generation. Out of sight of the Island, the idea of pursuit had not occurred to us. Now the great angel of destruction was bearing down on us, too far to see who was at the helm but well within range of that huge gun.

"Get us out of here!" Peter shouted. Midds dropped heavily into the boat, doing more towards capsizing us than the shot had. I tried to stir the engine, but it only coughed and coughed again, turning over in its casing but not waking. Peter had unloosed the mooring but we were just drifting out into the river's heart. I saw Shon hesitate at the ship's rail, and decide not to jump for it.

"Stefan! Get us moving!" Peter shouted again. The boat was too small for us all to be charging about, but he and Red and Midds were trying. The engine whined briefly, and I thought something was loose inside it, but then it stuttered out a harsh cry and we lurched forwards. It was much more powerful than the point generators. We rebounded from the prison ship's hull leaving a dent the size of a man, and Midds lost his balance and bounced over the prow into the water.

He could not swim. None of us could swim. Who knew we would need to? He was out of sight in a second, then up again, floundering and splashing and keeping himself afloat more by luck than skill. Peter lunged forward and grabbed his arm, and then Red and Kiera had to grab Peter to stop him going straight in after the bigger man. As they hauled the dripping Midds aboard I tried to control the engine.

Then the second shot landed. It was closer than the first, and the swell of it knocked our little boat right into the trees. I had the engine in hand by then, but it was screaming away in the water uselessly, the boat tugging but going nowhere.

"We're hooked on something!" Kiera cried.

Peter snatched his duelling staff and pried down at the tangle of roots we were beached on. Midds was already hacking at everything green in sight with the great weight of his machete. Something juddered horribly across the boat's underside with a grinding that shook my teeth, and we exploded across the river as the engine took out its frustrations on the water. Red and I both hauled on the tiller to keep us from ploughing all the way into the opposite bank.

I will not say that we nipped out under the nose of that gunship but we were not far off. The great gun did not belch again, but they must have been cranking it hard to follow our erratic course. A few bullets skipped the waves around us. We were coming in range of their smaller weapons.

"Are they faster than us?" Peter yelled over the row of the motor.

"Depends on engine size," was all I could say.

"Get us at the prison ship's backside!" he told me. I steered the course straight away whilst everyone else argued with Peter, saying that we should just scoot straight out of there.

"If they're faster, we're dead," Peter told them. "And there's that gun. I've got a plan."

The chorus of disapproval told him what people thought of his plans in general. Something composed mostly of energy fried a hand's breadth span of water past my face. I tried to use my inner energies to speed up the engine, but I was too flustered to do anything with my brain bar the basic motor functions of steering the boat into the protective shadow of the prison ship.

"What the hell now?" It was Shon's voice. He had run over to the stern rail and was looking down at us.

"Help me up," Peter told him. He had his Ropa blade in hand. "Ambush. The only way."

"That's your plan?" Kiera demanded.

Shon hauled Peter up and then they both reached down for Midds, who was stuffing his belt with the flintlocks he had collected.

"Red, stay here. You and Stef and Kiera. Guard the boat."

"Why me?" Red argued.

"You know how to make the damn thing *go*. You're too valuable. As for Kiera—"

"Don't think I'm going to fight you for a place on your suicide squad," Kiera said sharply. Peter grinned broadly at her. A second later all three disappeared as the next cannon-shell struck the ship's side with a sound like God's last bell. It must have made a dent like a giant's punch. I could not hear a thing afterwards, just that great metal ringing reverberating to the sky and back. Looking decidedly less cocky, the three ambushers regained their feet, and ran off to hide.

"How many on the other boat?" Kiera asked us, in the quiet that followed.

"On a boat that large, there could be twenty, thirty easily," I speculated.

"Nowhere near," Red said. "How many Wardens can they take from the Island without everything going to hell? Ten at the most, probably less."

"So who's leading them?" Kiera pressed. "The Marshal?"

We explained the events that had overtaken the Marshal.

"Not Leontes," she said. "My idiot cousin's not the man for armed reprisals."

"Peter made enough enemies," Red said, sounding as though he was perhaps unhappy not to be amongst them. By this time the engine of the gunboat was a full-bodied thunder as it neared the grounded prison ship. There were no more shots, but I could imagine the railings crammed with gun-toting marksmen, ready to cut down anything that moved.

Kiera gripped my free hand, the one not hovering over the engine controls.

The first shot rang out, then two more, and we heard an unfamiliar voice cry out and something heavy hit the water. I imagined Peter and company dropping back into cover amidst panic on the gunboat's deck. There was a confusion of shouting, several other shots impacting with the prison ship's iron. Above it all, one voice came over clearly.

"Bring us about, you fools! They've gone to ground! I want men on that ship!"

"The Witch Queen," Kiera breathed, for it was the Lady Ellera's voice. She had cared enough to come after us. Probably it was not personal animosity as much as a cause she could use to unite the Wardens under her banner. The end result would be the same.

There were more sporadic shots from above, and then we heard a ferocious grinding as the gunboat shuddered along the larger ship's side.

"They're boarding," Red said unnecessarily, and then: "Move us out, Stefan. I want a shot."

"We're not moving," Kiera stated. "We're staying right here."

"They need my help," Red decided, as we heard more shots and running feet on metal. "Now let's go."

"I really don't think—" I started.

Red had his rifle out. "Move, Stefan!" he ordered. I cannot

say which was worse, his ingrained instinct to command or mine to obey. Obey I did, though, starting the engine first time and darting the boat out from beneath the prison ship's stern. This time we really were right under the gunboat's nose.

Aboard the prison ship our three friends were trying to pin the Wardens, who were making halting progress from cover to cover across the sloping deck. Peter was inching around away from the other two, trying to make his move.

Kiera crouched as low as possible amidships, and Red was levelling his gun, one eye squinting as he calculated trajectory. His long rifle spat a sizzle of fire and I registered a human shape kicking back from the gunship's rail.

"Take us round them," Red told me. "I want the Witch."

I did, so hunched that my head was between my knees. Two or three bullets whistled past us and Red returned fire, hit nothing, pulled back the bolt and fired again. Of all the pops and cracks and crackles of energy I heard, I could not tell which were aimed at us and which were at our comrades on the ship.

Something changed in Red's posture and I realised that he had seen the Lady Ellera. I dared not snatch a look myself. I had only a moment to wonder whether he just wanted to cut the head from the serpent, or whether he had some unspoken personal grudge. His rifle spat and I heard her cry out, but Red's face betrayed a sudden anger at a near-miss. He dragged the bolt of his gun back feverishly, raised the barrel again to track. Some weapon drilled a neat circular hole through the hull by my hand. Another three beams of black and white light danced past us, and the fourth struck Red in the neck and he died.

I hauled hard on the tiller to change our course, my gaze dragged to the rail of the gunboat where the marksman was lining up his energy gun with care. I felt a jolt of connection, as though by looking up the barrel I was looking into his eyes. Then he lowered the rifle with a slumping of the shoulders and I saw that it was Sauven.

I had saved him Below. We had sailed together with Thelwel and Hairy Klamp. He had killed Red without thinking, but in that moment something stayed his hand.

Then Peter leapt over the gunboat's side with his Ropa blade leading the way. Sauven turned frantically, and the last expression I saw on his face was the disgust of a basically bad man fallen foul of one good deed. Peter's blade cut through the gun he held up in a futile parry and deep into him as well. Then Peter was off again, not even realising that we were there.

"Get us back into cover, Stefan," Kiera told me sharply, even though nobody was shooting at us any more. I glanced at Red's body and saw that the river had claimed his rifle. Wrenching the tiller the other way to make a wide circle, we headed back for the prison ship's aft.

On board the gunship the fighting was fierce as Peter ran all over the deck to keep clear of his enemies, letting the irresistible momentum of the Ropa blade dictate his movements. The half-dozen Wardens knew that a mere nick could be deadly. Most of them had switched from guns to blades and truncheons in the confined space, but they kept a wide distance from him. I did not see Lady Ellera.

"Stefan!" Kiera shrieked, and did her best to push me out of the boat. I took the tiller with me and the craft spun in a circle and skidded off in another direction. When the great gun spoke it smashed the water all about where we had been. The concussion wave lifted us up onto our side, so that it was touch and go whether we came down right way up or underwater.

"Again!" I heard the faint voice of the Witch Queen. "Shoot them again!"

With one mind, Kiera and I shunted the boat back along its course, bouncing off the waves. The gun would pound us to scrap with one hit, but I could see Wardens sweating to wind it around. They would not catch us if we kept moving.

"Peter's right on the edge," Kiera announced. I spared what little attention I could and saw that Peter had indeed been backed up to the stern rail of the gunboat. Midds and Shon were still on the prison ship, trading shots with the Wardens. I saw Peter spin with his sword, throwing back his opponents and hacking the arm off the most incautious, and then he was raising the hilt high, point downwards. I had to look away then, and swing us off the tracking gun's course, but when I heard the shearing noise, I knew he had plunged the blade into the gunboat's engine.

"We have to go pick him up!" Kiera decided. I wished she would make up her mind just how brave we were supposed to be. I reckoned I had cast away my vote when I gave in to Red, though, and hurled the boat back down its own wake towards Peter and the gunboat's aft rail. This time we were seen, and a couple of gunmen tried to pin us down, bullets zipping into the water and rebounding from our hull. I threw the boat away from them to make a better pass and saw a particularly dense shot strike one of the point generator arms flat against the hull.

"It's not going to happen," I ground out between my teeth.

"You have to!" Kiera demanded. Suddenly she was the battle princess, heedless of danger. "Just go straight, they're almost on him— Who's that?"

For there was a new boat on the river, as fleet and flat as ours, lancing between us and the gunboat. There were maybe ten on board and I saw one topple from the back as it approached, shot down by the Wardens. Then someone had leapt from it lightly to grasp the gunboat's rail and vault aboard, and I knew who it was.

Gaki and his subjects had arrived. Heedless of anything that Kiera was telling me, I made sure we gave that boat a wide berth.

The gunship Wardens recoiled from Gaki. The Marshal was still a great part of their minds, and here were the bloody hands that had laid their master low. He lashed out twice and killed, with hands or with his little knife, then he was making for the great gun, scattering Wardens as he went. In the moment of distraction, Peter broke out with a great cleaving stroke and ran for the port rail and for us. One of the Wardens levelled a pistol at his back but either Shon or Midds shot the man down, and Peter was clear.

"Go!" said Kiera, and I needed no more telling. As I gunned the boat forwards, I caught sight of Gaki's stolen craft making a wide loop to come back: to pick him up or to attack us? I could not know. I did not have time to work it out.

Peter saw us coming, and he stepped out off the rail, into the air.

I slewed the boat into a turn but missed him by seconds, and I had a horrible vision of him coming up into the engine. A hand lunged from the water to grasp the side and Kiera pulled him in.

On board the gunship Gaki killed one of the gun crew and then struck down amidst the levers and gears. Father Sulplice's diamond knife glinted once in the sun and the great gun made a screaming noise and stopped. Gaki skipped away even as the Lady Ellera tried to drive a knife into his bare back. His boat was nowhere near, but he dived into the water like a water-born thing and struck out across the waves. He was probably the last human being left on Earth who knew how to swim.

The Lady Ellera screamed her fury to the sky but the few Wardens were concentrating on us, and I had other things to worry about. Peter was pointing urgently. The other boat was coming for us, and Gaki had a villainous mob for a crew. I saw Hermione and the less welcome face of Tallan, and the rest I did not know and did not want to. I turned sharply, but it looked as though they would catch us nonetheless. Then another thin salvo of shots washed over us from the two remaining Wardens. One lashed Peter across the shoulder. Another killed one of Gaki's crew, dense-packed as they were. A third struck the other boat's engine, which whined like an automatic saw, and their whole boat kicked to the left. We sped past within ten feet of them, and I saw Gaki slip out of the water to stand in their midst, their captain. He was staring back on the Witch Queen, a mad grin on his face.

"Stefan," I heard his voice call over. "Join with me."

I had no idea what he was talking about. Did he want me to become one of his pirates? Then I felt it, the reaching out of his mind. He was making something happen.

I did not want to help him but part of me wanted to know what it was, so I let my inner energies go until I found what he had found, some dim and tiny pinpoint of sluggish mind deep beneath us. There was already vague curiosity aflame there, and I helped Gaki to fan it, drawing the little spark up from the mud towards the light. I was wondering what use such a minute fleck of consciousness could ever be when it broke the surface beside the gunboat.

A tiny mote of a mind was all it took to move a monster. It was one of the eyeless river beasts, all jaws and arching neck and paddles beating at the waves. The blind head swung over us all, but there was only one on that river still making noise. The Lady Ellera's demands for our death were louder than the engines.

She stretched out her hands towards it with a great cry, as though she could control it somehow and bend it to her will. Her will was the stuff of legend and had forged a role of power and command from no better raw material than prison greys, but in paring it down to that honed state, she had pruned away that part of her that might have ventured beyond the confines of her brain.

The long jaws swept down with a crushing disregard for power or will and snapped her up. The sounds of her rage were abruptly gone.

I steered our boat to the prison ship and Midds and Shon embarked hurriedly. Before anything else could happen I had us off down the river, leaving the three other craft, one beached, one abandoned and one crippled, in our wake.

41

Tales from the Riverbank

We buried Red in the river, because it was all we had. Back in Shadrapar he would have been rendered down and shipped out to the fields to help the crops, but we were not in Shadrapar and could not perform such civilised rituals. In the Island the dead were left for the eaters of carrion, and we were Islanders still until back within Shadrapar's boundaries.

In Shadrapar someone would have words to say. Someone of the dead man's religion if he had one; someone of his family if he had one; someone.

Peter and Midds looked at one another awkwardly.

"Didn't really know him," Midds said. "He was a smart one. Very tight for the rules. Didn't like mess."

It was a poor epitaph.

"Him and you were the only ones who were with me, when we had that scrap," Peter added mournfully.

"And we got royally beaten for it," Midds recalled.

There was a pause. It was little enough for the sum of a man's life. Kiera sighed, annoyed more than anything.

"His parents weren't well off," she said tiredly. "He got some kind of patronage or something and went through the Academy, got his education. He liked things with moving parts, gears, levers. He had almost no friends there, because of his upbringing.

He was lonely. When he came out with a simple pass, nobody would employ him as anything because his family were poor and he had no connections. He had a string of menial jobs and in the end he came here because he thought at least he would be doing something worthwhile. I think he was disappointed. The Island was not the place he thought it was, but then neither had Shadrapar been. He respected the Marshal, because the Marshal made order. He liked you, Peter, because you made a difference in the way he always wanted to make a difference. That was what tipped it. You went outside the rules just like he never did, and you helped people. He wanted to be like you."

"Look where it got him," Peter muttered, sounding choked.

"Where did you get all that from?" Midds asked suspiciously.

"I talked to the man, while I stayed with Peter. I needed friends, and the best way is to be interested in someone. I *talked* to him, like any civilised human being," Kiera told him sharply.

Midds just shrugged. "Nobody ever talked to me," he said mildly. "Most people had reasons for being on the Island they didn't want bandied about."

Those reasons were our prime topic of conversation that first day down the river, along with the ways that we would deal with them when we returned. The point generators (bent back out into shape) drove us sluggishly through the water, and we watched the passing scenery and ate our rations. These were preserved food shipped in for the Wardens: fruit, grain cakes and biscuits. It was a real taste of Shadrapar and made us all think of the home that was growing closer every moment.

"What are you going to do when you get back?" had replaced "What are you in for?" as the question. Peter asked it to Midds and we got Midds' little story: his getting into trouble a girl who would surely have got out of it by now; his returning to his family and the Compassionates, mostly because they would put him up for free. He had decided to join the Outriders. After the story of the Underworld he reckoned that they would be desperate for new recruits.

"Not had enough of uniforms, then?" asked Shon.

"The ladies love them," Midds confided.

"Not had enough of ladies, then?" Kiera needled him.

"Never," Midds declared. "And they never could get enough of me. I am amazed that the ladies of Shadrapar haven't all killed themselves by now, what with me being away so long."

Shon was next, and we heard his past as a criminal lawyer. He went into the details of his last case. The people he was advocating for had been a front organisation for my old friends the Organ Donor Boys, of fond memory, who had been trying to make an alliance with a surface firm of black marketers that would have been happy for all concerned. A rival had got wind of it and had framed Shon for some misdemeanour. He had been packed off to the Island within a day, without a trial.

"And when you get back?" Kiera asked him.

"I'm going to find who stitched me up and I'm going to kill them," Shon said frankly. "After that, I'll catch up on the latest precedents and get back to business, but it's very bad form not to visit old debtors the first chance you get, don't you think?"

I told them my sorry story. We had the time and I had become quite the teller of tales by then. Something told me to leave out Faith, perhaps because she always provoked more questions than she answered. From the arching of her eyebrows, Kiera noticed the gap in the narrative.

"I may come and work for you," I suggested to Shon. "Need a clerk? I could do your writing for a change."

"What about saving the world?" Peter asked.

"I've given up on philanthropy."

Peter's turn came next: "You all know what happened to me. I killed Anteim's son. I never made a secret of it."

"We had to pry it out of you with hooks," I pointed out.

"Well, never after that," he said. "So that leaves just one, and she, I might say, has been very, very secretive. What landed you on the Island, Kiera? Don't say you just went to visit your cousin and got stranded."

Kiera looked guarded. "It's nothing much," she said.

"You were so interested in people," Peter prompted. "So we're interested in you. So what's the story?"

She sat in silence a bit while we made impatient noises. At last she raised her head and I was surprised to see that she looked less than her usual collected self.

"I was a spy," she said. Nobody found it particularly shocking.

"My family is a small one and not influential. We have no great allies and are in no particular clique. This is of occasional use when one of the major players needs a pair of eyes. My family trained me for the political game. I had a battery of private tutors. I learned all the airs and graces and small talk, how to pass myself as educated in every subject without ever wasting time reading books. I knew food, wine, music, history, fashion and genealogy. I collected a cadre of young men and women I kept keen, from families far greater than mine. They were part of the image. I was a very unpleasant person to almost everyone who did not matter, because I had to be so very nice to all the people who did, every one of whom I despised."

We were all a little sobered by this, but not surprised.

"I would attach myself to the relevant person of wealth and power and we would be seen together, and they would be happy enough with my company that they would let me into their world. Usually my targets were old men with horrible wives, because that's who Shadrapar is ruled by. They were delighted to have me as an ornament and all their friends would be very jealous. Eventually I would find out about their dealings, and the information would get back to those who had commissioned my family. Then I would break the thing off, find some pretext, make a scene at a party. Shortly after, the man's business interests would go through the floor, his deals pre-empted, his life shaken down. I did well. My family were happy with me," she said. There was no pride in her voice.

"My last target but one was a man who had half the Authority in his pocket, as filthy an old lecher as you can imagine. I latched onto him like a leech. I got paraded on the end of his decaying arm and leant on him and fed him fruit and doted on his every habit. He was into something big with some friends of his. There was some great project: a building they had fitted out with laboratories and luxuries. They were creating something he was very excited about. All this was well advanced before I came onto the scene."

I was feeling a chill rise in my stomach, because this was sounding familiar.

She continued, "I got in too late, really. The project came to fruition before I was in any position to find out what it was. Then, instead of him coming to me and being too excited not to boast about it, he just... lost interest in me. Suddenly he could not be bothered to talk to me and he stopped going to parties, and I was shut out. He hadn't uncovered me. He just no longer had time for me.

"I latched onto one of his friends, a younger man not fully in on the project. I was desperate to get things done. I used everything I had been taught, made him want me, dangled myself like a prize. I had never failed before and I wasn't going to fail this time. I waited until I had him in my palm and then I pushed him to go to the Justiciar and demand to know what was going on."

She paused a moment, reflecting on the events. "I think he found out. He went to this building that they had and confronted his old friend. There was an altercation, and the two of them had an argument, and something happened. Certainly the old man was very, very angry. And desperate, when I saw him.

"I assumed that my new man, who was so in love with me, would tell me all about it. He did not. He was angry and desperate too. Something he had seen had plucked me right out of his mind, and something else had grown there instead. He was furious with me for making him do whatever he had done.

516

He and the old man had me arrested. They called the Angels and had me thrown into prison. There were no charges; I just knew too much and they wanted me out of the way. You see how little I knew? Still, it was too much and they had me exiled because the old man had the Lord Justiciar in his pocket. And that is my story. And that, I am afraid, is the person I am."

"The person you were," Peter told her.

"The person I am," she corrected sadly. "Much as I hate it."

A cold and frightened feeling had come over me, although nothing she had said amounted to any kind of evidence. I had a building in mind, though, newly furnished and secret, with bizarre guardians and distant scientists. A building that Faith had known and recognised, and been drawn to, and feared.

"When the older man lost interest in you, was it as though there was... another woman?" I asked her tentatively.

She frowned sharply at me. "Another woman? No." And then, after a pause, "Perhaps."

They were all waiting for me to elaborate but I did not know if I dared. The whole business of Faith seemed so much like an unbelievable tall tale. Worse, when I thought about it too deeply I had the sense of vast and unseen chasms behind the few facts I knew. What great conspiracy of great men had been behind her making, and under what circumstances could she ever have escaped to the Underworld? Was that what Kiera had just told me?

I thought of the man who had demanded answers of me, after my arrest. I asked Kiera to describe her old man, and it could have been the same. Peter pressed me to reveal my thoughts, but instead I just asked her the simplest of questions. "What was his name, this old man?"

Her face went stony. "I have reasons not to say."

"You think we're going to blackmail the old boy when we get home or something?" Peter asked her.

"Sounds like a fine idea to me," Shon said. "Why not? I can put you in touch with some very discreet professionals."

Kiera shook her head. "He's not blackmail material any more," she said shortly. "He's dead now."

"Kiera, was it Jon Anteim the Elder?" I put forward, which shut everyone up.

For a moment she gave nothing away, but then she nodded shortly.

A picture was growing like a crystal in my mind: the creation of something perfect and hedonistic and never seen before; an argument resulting in something flying free that had been intended only for imprisonment and private use; a falling out of wealthy thieves over their lost prize; an assassination enacted by the richest, and blamed on the poorest. It was all speculation.

I told them the story of Faith, in the end, so much of it as I could. For Shon and Peter and Midds, it was a slice of the bizarre from the now-emptied stocks of the Underworld. They were more interested in my descriptions of Greygori Sanguival and Sergei (whom Shon had once met). But Kiera understood what I was trying to tell her. It was a secret history only we shared.

In return Midds told another strange tale also featuring a mysterious woman, in this case, leading men to their deaths in the desert. According to him she had appeared to a friend of his, begging him to free her from a ruinous pyramid further out into the white wastes than any man had ever gone. It was all the usual ghost-story stuff of ancient technologies and creeping dooms, yet no more unreasonable than my own story, I suppose.

Peter had the next, talking about a monstrous scorpion that could take the shape of (of course) a beautiful woman, and then Shon had an allegory about two rival thieves trying to top each others' larcenies. Then Midds came in again, swearing that there was a crystal machine in the President's office that spoke with the voices of the dead. And so on. We moved from the realms of the real into pure fantasy.

We spent the night camped on the riverbank and Kiera showed us how to take certain herbs and tubers and crush them up to make a paste that kept predators away, and another concoction she put on Peter's shoulder to help it heal. It was a warm, overcast night, and we used Midds' energy weapon to light the smallest of fires. The telling of false stories continued until everyone was asleep.

The next day I switched from the point generators to the engine, because the river was becoming too dilute and the former just dragged us along at walking pace.

We camped on a sandy stretch of beach that night, and that was where the attack came.

I think most people were asleep but I was still drifting on the edge of the night, and I know that Shon was on watch because it was his shout that roused us. I sat bolt upright and saw him pass between me and the fire, rolling, and then there were figures charging out from the forest edge, a good half-dozen. The firelight made them painted and hideous but I knew them: Gaki's crew.

Shon came up with a long knife. He feinted towards them and then darted aside from the lead man. A lunging blade passed under his arm and he slashed his opponent across the shoulder as he dodged out of reach. Another man came for him with a club, but he sidestepped that as well and left another long mark on the attacker.

By then Peter was up. He had time to get to his feet before the first bleeding man reached him, but no time to get to his sword. He sent an arcing kick into the luckless pirate's groin and then practically vaulted over the man to meet the next. In all this time I had managed only to stumble to my feet.

Midds' rod-weapon flashed out and killed a man stone dead, but another jumped him, and they both fell backwards, kicking and tearing at one another. Shon was circling with an enemy, a little duel of his own, knife loose in one hand. I did not see Kiera.

Then someone grabbed me and shook me so hard I thought my neck would snap. A leering and ugly face eclipsed my vision.

"Gotcha," said Tallan. He hoisted me up by my throat and ran with me until my back hit a tree with force enough to knock the breath from me. All the time he was shouting right into my face. "What're you going to do now, eh? What now, eh? Going to play your tricks on me, eh? Going to get me like you got Harro? Going to fry my brain, is it? What's the matter? Can't get it together? Can't concentrate?" By now he was slamming me into the tree with each exclamation. "I know, see! (*slam*!). I know! (*slam*!). Gaki told me (*slam*!). Told me all about your little tricks (*slam*!). Told me how you need a little peace (*slam*!) and quiet (*slam slam slam*!)." His unbearable face loomed and bobbed and obscured everything else in my world. He kept one hand about my throat, lifting me to my toes. I felt my consciousness shiver in and out as he pressed the arteries in my neck.

"What's the matter, little bookworm?" he sneered down at me. "Can't play a man's game?"

The next expression on his face was exactly the one worn by a man at a loud party I once went to, who thought that I had made some tremendously insulting remark about him but, in all the noise, was not entirely sure – that exact expression of mingled outrage and uncertainty.

With a convulsive jerk I wrenched Peter's duelling knife out of him, and the horrible warm rush of blood that followed turned my stomach. It was nothing, though. Compared to the sensation of crushing Harro's mind, it was nothing at all to kill a man with hands and a steel blade. I felt only hollow. Tallan stared into my eyes and made an unfinished word-like sound. Then I got enough purchase on the tree to push him away from me, and he staggered off clutching at the broad and spreading pool of darkness in his prison greys. He moved in a little uneven circle, and then he fell down.

There was a shot that brought me abruptly back to wider events. One of Gaki's men jerked even as he tried to stab Shon, and fell into the fire. Shon was grappling furiously with another man, slamming his elbow repeatedly into his opponent's head.

There was a hilt jutting from Shon's side, I saw. I stumbled towards him, clutching my own weapon.

Peter passed between us. He had retrieved his sword and there was an expression of fierce desperation on his face such as I never saw before or since. Another shot rang out from somewhere.

Shon brought his elbow down with a terrible crack and his antagonist let go his grip and reeled backwards. I raked my dagger clumsily across his back and, as he turned to look at me, Shon slammed his own blade to the crosspiece in his ribs. I stepped to catch my friend as he staggered, going to his knees with both hands about the jutting hilt. His face was a mask of sweat and smeared blood.

I looked around to see Peter pursuing the last of Gaki's crew with fury on his face. The man tripped back on a branch, came up with a blade, and Peter let the Ropa sword swing from the sky to the ground and slice the man entirely in two. Another victim, bisected in that peculiar bloodless way, lay next to a still form that I realised with horror must be Midds.

I grasped that Gaki had made no appearance at the same time as I heard the engine start on our boat. I lurched for the water to see our craft already out in the river's midst, shuffled slowly out with the point generators while we were all fighting. Gaki and Hermione were aboard, and the murderer even waved lazily at us before Hermione fired the engine up and the vessel sped off into the night leaving us marooned on a body-bedecked shore.

42

Tales from the Riverbank (Part 2)

Midds lay quite still on his back, showing off the long tear across the belly of his black uniform. Peter cursed over and over, furious with himself.

"I saw it about to happen, saw the knife come out, but I was too late," he spat.

Kiera appeared from the shadows between the trees. She had an armful of flintlocks, all those that Shon and Midds had culled from the prison ship. The shots I heard had been hers.

"There was nothing you could do," she told him. It was just a standard platitude. In such a chaos, who knew if anything more could have been done?

"I got him into this, him and Red. I might as well have killed them both myself," Peter said bitterly.

"Don't get ahead of yourself. I'm not dead yet." Midds' lips had barely moved. His voice was quiet but surprisingly clear. Peter dropped to his knees by the man's side.

"I'm not dead," Midds continued patiently. His eyes were closed and his body was completely relaxed, as though he was talking in his sleep. "I'm just staying very, very still. Don't want to juggle anything about, okay?"

"What can we do?" Peter asked him.

"Damned if I know. Maybe Kiera can stuff me full of herbs or something. I'm not a doctor."

"Does it hurt?"

"Now that," said Midds, "is a really stupid question. I guess I'm just lucky that I've got more junk under my belt than you guys, yes?"

"Kiera," Peter said, "What can you do?"

"Shon is hurt too," I put in.

"I'm fine," Shon said from just behind me. I jumped and saw him looking pale, with one arm clamped to his side, but otherwise as fine as he claimed.

"But I saw the knife stuck in you," I got out.

With grim amusement he showed me a hilt with a fraction of jagged blade.

"It broke off in you?"

"Outside. I trapped it and snapped it, but the bastard just kept coming with it," he said.

By this time Kiera was hunting for anything the web-children held as medicinal, and Peter was sitting mournfully by Midds. His boyish face was twenty years older. I sympathised. It had been such a simple idea to fly the Island and go home. Who would have thought that so many things would get in the way?

Shon peeled back his tattered prison greys to look at the wound, and I saw the shine of metal. With dull surprise I saw he really did have a metal elbow. It had a steely round cap that joined to a rod inset all the way to his shoulder.

"Won me a lot of fights on the Island," he told me, as he cleaned out his wound.

"Look," Kiera was saying to Midds, "I don't know what I can do. The web-children knew all sorts of things, but half the plants they showed me don't grow here and… and I don't even know if I can remember…" She stopped, frustrated.

"Just do something," Midds told her softly. "Don't care what."

"This is going to hurt," she warned him.

"I guessed."

I turned away then, because I did not want to see all that human anatomy. Unlike Thelwel's arm, it would not just knit itself together. I made the weak excuse of, "I'll go and get more wood for the fire, shall I?" and stumbled away. Shon came with me and we searched without much enthusiasm along the riverbank. We heard no sound from Midds behind, and I did not want to think of him lying in self-enforced immobility as Kiera pried into him.

"Your man Peter," Shon said. "He's finding out what being a leader means."

"I don't think he ever wanted to be one," I said.

"Sometimes you just don't get the choice," shrugged Shon philosophically. "I hope Midds pulls through. He may be a Warden but he's a good one." A change came over his face and he looked a little shaken, almost afraid. "I have to stop thinking like that, don't I?"

"I know."

He stopped walking, more troubled than I realised. "Wardens, prisoners. Us, them. I'm not going to be free until I get rid of it all, Stefan. You need to be free inside your head as well."

We trailed along another stretch of reed forest, listening to the sounds of the jungle.

"You did well," Shon told me unexpectedly. "In the fight, you did well. You must have killed one and you bloodied the man I was fighting."

"It's not a skill I want to excel at," I said.

Shon shrugged and then winced. "We're made by what's around us, Stefan. You could get away with being a peaceful man when you lived in a peaceful place, but you can't go back there now and just fit in. You're not the same."

I reflected sadly that it was true. I had done too much in my quest to survive. I would never again be the idealist who had co-written *How to Save the World*.

Abruptly, Shon ducked down and dragged me with him.

"What?" I hissed. He waved at me to shut me up. His wound was bleeding and he was gritting his teeth against it. One hand pointed forwards, and I caught the glint of metal through banks of reeds.

It came to me quickly, but I should have thought of it long before.

"It's Gaki's boat," I said. Shon shot me an enquiring look.

"His boat. They didn't walk here, that lot. I saw their engine damaged, but their point generators were fine. They would be able to get this far on them, must have gone night and day to catch us up." I crept forwards and was rewarded by a clear view of the point generator arms curving up amidst the rushes.

"So what good is it?" Shon asked.

"At the very least we can paddle it," I suggested. "If Midds can't move then we can get him into the boat, and that will be a smoother ride than a stretcher."

We crept up on the boat like hunters. It was there in all its flawed majesty, abandoned by its master in favour of a better.

"So, do we tow it," Shon asked, "or what?"

I balanced at the water's edge and then jumped awkwardly in, almost upsetting it. "Let me just try something," I said, and switched the point generators on.

They were much abused pieces of machinery, those point generators. Gaki had obviously not had plain sailing either. One arm was warped, and there were tooth marks deep into it, and the whole mechanism looked as though it was ready to fall off the back of the boat. Nonetheless, it hummed into life with that familiar vibration, and the boat began to grind forward at a snail's pace.

"It's moving!" I exclaimed, somewhat disproportionately.

Shon squinted. "Isn't that the current?"

"Get in."

"Be quicker to walk," he muttered but he made the jump and sat behind, sorting through the previous owners' left luggage.

When we got back, at the boat's infinitesimal pace, Peter had dragged all the bodies away into the jungle, where they might serve as a distraction for predators. Midds was unchanged. Only Kiera's continued supervision told us he had not died.

I introduced them to Gaki's boat.

"Is that all it does?" Peter asked me.

"We're lucky to get that much out of it. The generators are next to useless this far out and the engine's dead."

Peter looked at me strangely. "Fix it," he suggested.

"I wouldn't know where to start," I said.

"We'll never be home without transport."

"I'm no artificer," I pointed out. "I'm a social historian."

He shrugged. "Well, we're not going anywhere with Midds like he is."

But he had implanted the idea: I did so want to go home. I was owed repatriation, after all I had gone through. I had watched Thelwel and Father Sulplice. I knew what parts of a machine did what, I thought. Surely something as simple as an engine could give me no trouble.

I meandered back to the boat and looked at the abused engine. There was a massive dent and a small hole in the casing where the bullet had struck. That, I diagnosed, was probably the problem. This was the limit of my mechanical understanding. I might have hung around Thelwel and his father, but only because passing tools to someone was easier than work.

I took out the duelling knife and levered the top of the casing off. Inside I saw a rootwork of ducts and tubes and wires, all awash with murky, oily water. I was uncomfortably reminded that Kiera had probably seen something similar whilst attending to Midds.

Some of the metal pipes had been bent and broken. I ripped them out because it was obvious they were of no use any more. Beneath the debris I found another pipe with the bullet embedded in it, and so I reasoned that everything beneath that had to be fine. I prised that pipe out with the point of the dagger, and saw to my dismay that beneath it was the fuel tank. The buckling of the pipe under the shot's impact had forced it down and cracked the tank, so that the fuel was now a greasy film atop the water half the way back to the Island. No fuel, I guessed, meant no going anywhere with the engine. So much for that.

I had been a few hours at it now, and so I cleaned my hands and went to get something to eat. Kiera had been teaching Shon how to fish with a sharp stick, as the web-children did, and there was a zoologist's miscellany of aquatic life charring on the fire.

Midds had his eyes open, I saw, and they tracked to follow me as I sat down beside him. I asked him how he was feeling.

"Kiera gabe me sumpin to deal widda pain buddit sops me fom tokkin popperly," he explained thickly. There was a broad bandage of cloth swathing his entire torso, cut from the unneeded prison greys of our enemies. It was stained with old blood, still wet with new in places. He looked ashen, blue around the lips.

I was about to mutter some pleasantry when an idea struck me and I leapt up. "Thelwel!" I got out, drawing everyone's attention. I ran back to the half-gutted boat.

Thelwel had taken such pains to tell Red and me that the boats did not rely on their fuel. If they ran out, he said, we could use the sun. The engines ran on the sun. I had no idea how this was accomplished, but it was a hope. It did not matter that all the fuel was gone, that all those pipes had been broken. If the other part, the sun-engine, was still intact then perhaps I could get it working.

I stared into the engine. I had no concept of how it actually worked. I would have to work from first principles.

The fuel tank was broken. I did not need it. I borrowed Midds' machete and pried at it, eventually managing to snap it free from its bindings so that it fell out of the bottom of the engine and into the river. I could now see clear down into the water.

I reasoned that not only did I not need the fuel tank (and just as well, since I was not getting it back), neither did I need anything attached to it. It must all be part and parcel of the fuel system, rather than this hypothetical sun-system. I ripped all of that out too. By this time there was distressingly little left of the engine at all, and I was surrounded by a graveyard of broken metal.

My logic then told me that what I did need was the propeller part that made the boat go. I would magnanimously leave that in. Now that I had excised all the unnecessary pieces, whatever was left connected to that propeller must be what I needed to fix in order to make the boat go. I was dizzy with the heights of my technical achievement.

There were a lot of wires, and some solid pieces of plastic and metal that looked important. I thought about solar power, and how the sun would get into the engine. Then I followed the wires and found they seemed to link into things inside the hull.

The engine was in a metal case in the dark. For the sun to get into it, it would have to be forced down the wires. The wires were stuck into the main body of the boat, which was out in the light.

I hypothesised a system by which the sun could fall upon the metal boat and be collected by whatever batteries lay within. Then it could be put through to those compact little boxes, whereupon, by whatever magic was involved, it would be turned into motivating power to move the boat.

But the boat would not move. The engine was dead. I should look inside and find out what was damaged, and try to put it back the way it was. Unfortunately, I had done rather a lot of damage myself in removing non-essential parts of the engine, and so I was left with a lot of loose wires.

I started connecting them up, just shoving them at random into sockets or tying them together. Nothing seemed to happen. I got bored after a while, and it was getting dark, so I wandered over to the fire.

That night was cold and overcast and rainy and there was no telling of stories. All of us wondered whether Midds would still be with us come morning, Midds included. I do not think he slept at all, that night. He just lay there, concentrating on staying alive.

The next morning he was looking paler, and his face was almost thin with the strain, but he lived. Kiera had done all she could by then. Everything else would be between Midds and a God who was perhaps no better off Himself.

I returned to fiddling with my wires. The project was becoming less and less interesting as I failed to provoke any life in the engine. I was beginning to think Thelwel had been making some obscure mechanical joke.

There was a cap towards the top of the engine, a faded red plastic disc that I assumed covered yet another fuel pipe outlet. In desperation I decided to see whether I could pry it off, in case any of my wires would fit beneath. I put my knife to it and scratched away, trying for purchase, but it was reluctant to come free. That this was an unusual trait for a cap did not occur to me. I just thought the machinery was being bloody-minded. I decided to see if I could slide it off, and tried to force it with my thumbs.

It gave abruptly under pressure, sinking in, not popping off. Instantly, something like a metal whip went through me from my hands to my feet and up through the top of my head. My legs kicked spasmodically and I jolted backwards, losing my connection to the engine. Shaking slightly, I lay in the belly of the boat and wondered what had just happened to me.

It had not been a cap, it had been a button. It had been an "ON" button. With all that fuel pump clutter in the way I would never have seen it.

Thelwel had not mentioned an "ON" button. Thelwel had probably assumed that I was intelligent enough to expect one.

The engine was still not going, but the power was being charged out into the metal casing, so I found a stick and prodded the button until it popped out again. Then I connected all the wires together and pressed the button with my stick. Nothing. I turned it off and changed the arrangement of the wires.

On the fifth time around the engine suddenly sparked once, and then the propellor whirred into sullen life. It sounded far less enthusiastic than ours had with the fuel system running, but it lived and I had made it live.

Peter and Kiera came running at the sound, but all they had to say was, "What happened to your hair?" because it was sticking up at all angles from my contact with the electricity.

"I have the boat moving," I pointed out, somewhat annoyed. "How is Midds?"

Kiera would not meet my gaze, which only confirmed what I already knew.

"So we're not going anywhere just yet," Peter said heavily. He was clenching and unclenching his fists, wanting to be able to solve the situation with his hands.

Then Shon was shouting for us, sounding panicked. I shut the boat down and the three of us pelted back to the fire and Midds. Shon had a flintlock in one hand, a knife in the other.

"There is something," he said, "Out there. In the trees?"

"Something big?" Peter asked him.

"Something small, but more than one. I turned round and there was something not three feet from Midds here, but it bolted and I didn't get a good look at it."

Peter swore and unlimbered his sword. Midds had propped himself painfully on one elbow, eyes wide. "Someone get me a gun," he said urgently. "Don't want to get eaten by anything without a gun."

"Wait," Kiera told us. "Just wait." She walked a little towards the trees, squinting. I had horrible visions of some huge beast (despite what Shon had said) just smashing through the foliage to snap her up in its toothy jaws. I clutched the duelling dagger and tried to remind myself that I was a dangerous outlaw now, and not just a social historian.

"Come out," Kiera said, but not to us. "And you lot," she

530

added, for our benefit, "just put the arsenal away. You won't need it."

None of us did, but at least nobody shot anyone when the first web-child stepped from the undergrowth.

It looked as nervous as we were, clutching a spear in one webbed hand. Two more followed, one with a bow, and then another half a dozen, a full hunting party.

"What the hell are those little freaks?" Shon demanded.

"Web-children," Midds moaned. "Bloody web-children. They eat people. Little cannibal bastards."

"They do not eat people," Kiera stated.

"And that's not what cannibal means," I slotted in.

"Where do you think I learned the little medicine I used on you?" Kiera asked Midds. "Do you think I just sat out in the swamps and invented it all? They taught me. By that light, they've saved your life once already."

Midds stared at her.

"You were with them?"

Shon was still looking tense, gripping the pistol tight. He did not know Kiera at all, really. I told him softly that Peter and I had been guests of the web-children before.

"You're a strange man, Stefan," was all he said, but he lowered the gun.

A voice rang out, clear and sardonic, from within the treeline. "Can I assume that nobody is going to shoot or stab or otherwise assault me, then? If so, I shall make my entrance."

"It's your mate," Peter pointed out unnecessarily. "Tet-wotsit."

Trethowan strode into the light like a man one-third his age and stared at us as though we had all personally plotted his assassination. I was used to that instinctive glare, though. Beyond the uncontrolled whiskers and the wrinkles, I saw something more human and less hostile. I think a little time with Kiera did him good.

"For those that do not recognise me," he said grandly. "I am Ignaz Trethowan. I assume you've heard the name."

531

Midds and Shon exchanged looks of comical blankness. Trethowan's expression soured distinctly.

"How did you get here?" Peter had never really liked him.

"I got here by the paths of the web-children, which are more direct than the curve of the river. As for why..." He screwed his face into an impenetrable scowl. "My people here grew very fond of the girl while she was with us. They like her, although I'm damned if I know why. They insisted on making sure she was all right. They even insisted that I came with them, which for a man my age is as close to suicide as I care to go. After all this pointless effort, all I can say is that I hope you're all happy."

I was watching his eyes, though, and I felt that there had been less insisting than he was making out, and that Trethowan, too, had grown fond of Kiera. She was very good, after all, at making people like her.

"Drachmar," Trethowan greeted Peter. "I see you've made a royal cock-up of the whole situation, of course."

"You really came here just to have a go, didn't you, you spiteful bugger?" Peter said.

"How well you know me," Trethowan replied.

I introduced Midds and Shon.

"You finally decided to get out of that hell hole, then," Trethowan remarked. "Not so stupid after all, Drachmar. Following in my footsteps. Although why you're heading back to that stinking hive..." His harsh words trailed off uncharacteristically. "Well," he contented himself with. "Well."

Kiera had been talking to some of the web-children, and now she came and crouched beside Midds. "Look," she told him. "I've got an idea you won't like."

"Oh joy," he grumbled. "And spare me it, because I know what it is. So these little guys taught you all that doctor stuff. So you think they can do more for me than you, right?"

She nodded, and he clutched at her arm. "Kiera, I don't know what the hell they are, but nothing anyone's said about them

532

until now has been any good and they creep me out. And who's the old man?"

"Trethowan was a prisoner. He's lived with them for decades," Kiera told him. "And I've lived with them, and I'd like to say that they're just people, only they don't fuck each other over quite as much as people do. Midds, I think they're the only ones who can help you."

"I know, I know," he muttered. "Get Peter over here." When Peter had been brought (which brought the rest of us, too) he announced, "Right. I guess I'm going with the midgets. I hurt like hell and I feel worse now than I did when I got stabbed, and I know that's not good. If they can do anything for me, then I want it done. Right?"

"We are not some kind of charitable organisation," Trethowan objected sharply. "We have no intention of doing anything for your fat friend—" but he was overruled by web-children who were adamant they would do what they could for him, because Kiera had asked them.

"Well, just him, then. Not the rest of you. You go off to that damned place downriver and leave us alone," Trethowan declared. "Except for Kiera, who can come and visit if she wants, since everyone seems so bloody fond of her."

"We'll go downriver, all right," Peter promised. "We're going to catch that skinny bald bastard Gaki and cut him up."

"You have got to be joking," I objected.

"Never been more serious," Peter said. "We'll come back for you, Midds. We'll get you to Shadrapar yet."

Midds nodded weakly. I think he would have liked some company to stay with him, but my life was bound to Peter's. Despite my reservations, if he went hunting Gaki, I would back him up with my useless education. Shon was bound to me, somehow, and even more strongly to Shadrapar. And Kiera...

"I have to go with Peter and Stefan," she said carefully. "I want to see this out."

"I thought you would," Trethowan said sourly. "Will you wait until the morning, at least? My people here want to get some food for you, for some reason. It's not as though they don't need it themselves."

"It's near dark now," Peter agreed. "We'll go at first light."

43

The Cage of Souls

Late that evening, as Shon, Peter and Midds shared the fire uneasily with a gaggle of web-children, Trethowan strolled down to the water's edge and beckoned Kiera and me to follow.

He had been oddly quiet, for a man only too keen on making his opinions known. Whilst the web-children chattered at each other, Trethowan had brooded like a gaunt and bearded spectre. Now he was staring over the river, listening to the slap of water and the splash of its denizens.

"I had not thought to have my mind turn to Shadrapar again," he said slowly. "I thought I was rid of it. I have lived amongst my people for long enough, and never looked back. For ten years now I have not so much as dreamed of that city. Now, though, a journey of only a few days closer has filled my head with it."

"Do you want to come with us?" Kiera asked him, and he shook his head violently.

"No! Never! Just because I think of the place doesn't mean I *like* it. I hate that damned city and everyone in it. If not for them, my children would roam their swamps without fear, instead of hiding away. If not for them, this world might have some grain of hope. You're welcome to the place. Go, and forget all of this and pick up your lives as politicians and sociologists and whatever the hell your friends are. Go forget."

"We won't tell anyone," Kiera assured him.

"That's not what I'm worried about," he said. "Will you even remember, yourself? No, your minds contract so that nothing but that awful city is in it. You will forget that there are other ways of living. Even Stefan here, who writes brave words about how to save the world, never dreamed of living outside Shadrapar. If the city can be saved, he thinks, then save it. If it cannot then he'd rather go down with it than find another way. I despair of the lot of you."

"That's unfair," I complained.

He fixed me with a steely look and said, "Is it?" and I was not so sure. His bony shoulders slumped a little and he seemed to grow older there and then. "After all this time it still hurts, you know," he whispered. "Shadrapar, that exiled me to the stinking Island. Shadrapar, blind and deaf by its own hand, ruthless to those who tell it the truth. Shadrapar. Home, damn the place, and damn the lot of you for making me remember it."

"You heard what Peter said," Kiera told him. "We're coming back for Midds. Once we've... dealt with Gaki, however Peter intends to do that, we're coming back. Nobody said anything about staying there."

Trethowan snorted, unconvinced. "Oh you know Shadrapar. I would not trust myself, even, to go to that place and not be dragged in. I certainly wouldn't trust you."

"I may surprise you," Kiera said acidly. "I've got little enough to go back for."

"Then stay!" was his instant reply.

She shrugged her shoulders, dodging the issue. "I'll be back this way some time," she promised lightly. "Returning in triumph or shipped back to the Island. I'm sure they'll find another prison boat."

"And you, Stef?" Trethowan asked me.

I mirrored Kiera's shrug. I wanted to go home. I wanted to be amongst civilised, educated people. I wanted to leave all this riotous nature. Privately, though, I thought that if Kiera returned to the web-children then I was likely to follow. How that would actually have played out, with a city of other distractions at my hypothetical disposal, I cannot swear. I may have said that I am inconstant.

"I will dream of it tonight," Trethowan murmured. His armour of vitriol had fallen away and the old, old man inside was revealed. "In my dreams I will have forgotten my people and I will be there, back in the Academy, back in the cage of souls."

"The what?" I demanded, suddenly shaken from my contemplative mood.

"It is a name I gave to Shadrapar. If you can believe it, when first I came here I bored the web-children with tales of the city and the wonders of civilisation. I spoke to them of the place that had cast me out, the lights and the sounds, the unfathomable complexity. They did not understand, and not because of any limit to their intellect. I tried over and over to make them see the point of Shadrapar, the reason for its being there. Then there came a day when I suddenly saw things clearly myself, and I realised that there was no point. Shadrapar has no purpose, no function. It exists for itself only, its own downward spiral to oblivion. It exists only to imprison the minds of those who dwell within it, so that their world shrinks until it holds nothing but their own desires, and they fight to stop you showing what's beyond the bars. So I called it the cage of souls, so they would understand."

"I have heard the term before," I told him. "Although not from the web-children."

Trethowan glowered out at the water. "There are others besides my children... Language is now the stock in trade of rather more species than even I care to name. The world seeks someone to record its dying hours."

It was pitch dark by then, save for the cowering light of the fire, and the pairs of big, round reflecting mirrors that were the eyes of the web-children, casting back its light.

In the morning, Peter organised our departure in a businesslike manner that suggested he was avoiding thinking of other things. He took all the remaining food (Midds being provided for now) plus the gifts of the web-children. He took most of the weapons, but left Midds enough to defend himself against the terrors of the unknown jungle. Midds himself was not yet ready to concede that those terrors did not include the web-children, despite Kiera's protests.

"Are you sure they don't eat people?" he pressed her.

Kiera was beginning to get fed up. "Well I never saw any of them eying me as though I'd look better boiled, if that's what you mean, and Trethowan's been with them forever and nobody took a bite out of him. To tell the truth, I got more trouble out of that lecherous old man than I did from any of the web-children."

Midds still looked uncertain.

"Look," Kiera told him flatly. "They're people. That's all. So they live in the swamp and they look different. They're just people."

On a scientific level it was almost entirely inaccurate, and Trethowan would have been incensed by the suggestion that his beloved web-children had any connection with mankind. It made Midds relax, though.

Kiera and I joined Peter as Shon untied the boat.

"Maybe we should stay here with Trethowan," I suggested. "We can wait until Midds is better, and then all five of us could go."

"I have a plan," Peter stated. "I thought of it last night."

"You want to kill Gaki," I confirmed.

"If he crosses my path then I will kill him," Peter said. "I think that the two of us are going to have words at some point. That's not the plan, though. That's personal."

"So what's the plan?" Kiera asked him.

"We go home. We get some lads together – Shon can help with that I'm sure – and we get a boat."

"A boat?"

"A big boat. Two big boats. Maybe three. We drive them upriver, pick up Midds. We go back to the Island. We tell whoever's left in charge there that it's over."

"You are so mad," I said.

"The Island is over. It's doing nobody any good: not the staff, not the inmates, not the web-children even." His face was set in uncharacteristically grim lines. "I can't just leave it and forget it. I wish I could. It's in my head. I can't leave them all there, Wardens and prisoners, to rot in the swamps. We'll turn up with our boats and say that anyone who wants can come and join us."

"It won't work," I decided.

"It might. The Marshal will be dead by then, or I'll kill him myself. Who else is going to hold everyone in when they all want out? We'll get them into our boats and then—"

"Yes, and then?" Kiera pressed. "What next, admiral?"

"Then we go back to Shadrapar with all of those angry people and we shake some bloody sense into the Authority," Peter stated. There was an appreciative silence.

"Do we indeed?" I said at last.

"We do," he confirmed flatly. "The Angels are mostly gone, the Outriders cut down. Who's going to stop us when we've got things to say? How to save the world, Stefan, is by getting your mates together and bashing on doors."

I felt distinctly uncomfortable with this view of government.

"We've seen a hundred different signs that the old place is coming apart at the seams. Either nobody's running the place, or the people who're running it have all gone bad. It's time for a change."

"You're talking… revolution," I whispered. The ancient word, death and renewal in a single breath, sounded oddly appropriate in the jungle air. Why not revolution? I imagined President Drachmar, and found the image all too plausible. Could he be any worse than Harweg? At least Peter was starting out with good intentions.

"I don't believe any of it," I said slowly. "I can't see it working."

"It will work," said Peter, and he believed it.

Everything we were taking was on the boat except us. Peter went over to Midds and knelt by him, saying, "I promise we'll be back. I got you this far and I'll get you home. Now just take it easy, heal up and ignore that old man because he knows absolutely nothing." He said it loud enough that Trethowan, on the other side of the campsite, gave a snort of displeasure.

"Good luck, Peter," Midds told him. "You take care of yourself."

Kiera and Shon made their farewells too, and left me to have the last word.

"You were always a good Warden," I recalled. "You were the first one I met after Peter, and you've always been a friend to me, as much as you could."

He shrugged slightly, painfully. "Can't escape your breeding, I guess. Go with God, Stefan." He managed a weak smile. "Go with God."

We were all looking for the other boat, all the way home. Myself especially. I reasoned that Gaki's fuel would run out soon enough, and they would have as many problems as myself in activating the solar motors. I half-expected us to run across them paddling down the river, drifting with the current. Peter expected an ambush, Gaki and Hermione breaking out from the greenery to re-steal their boat back from us.

We did not see them on the river. Somehow they got all the way to Shadrapar before us. Just another one of life's little mysteries. Perhaps Hermione was some kind of technical savant and had never let on.

We had some days on the river, using up our stock of conversation. Kiera remained reticent about further details of her past and Peter's anecdotes seemed to have dried up as well. His speech of the morning had given a window onto a more vulnerable man than I would have guessed at. He had been made to be an amiable creature with enough easy charisma to get by without making any serious decisions. Except he had made a bad judgement call and killed the wrong man; his laid-back world had been torn apart and he had found himself on the Island. On the Island all the masks were put aside, and the ugly faces beneath were on parade. For me, it had been harsh. For Peter, it had been a forge. From the Marshal's authoritarian brutality to the infighting Wardens and sullen prisoners, he had been given all the evils of the world in miniature.

Somewhere he had got the idea that he could change them. The fact of the Island, the lessons it taught on human nature, were a worm gnawing in him, and he had to try to dig it out.

It was Shon who spoke most. Shon, who was surely made to be a cynical, hard-bitten man, had caught whatever ideological disease Peter had developed. Shon was listing people who would sail with us when we had our boats, people who might steal the boats for us, where weapons might be had from. Peter's revolution was to be founded on larceny.

I was thinking about the mob. I was thinking about Helman and Rosanna and Jon. The agitators behind that crowd had been selfish and evil reactionaries, and Peter was a good man. I was unsure that this was a material difference. I was also unsure that once a man has raised the mob (for there is really only one mob, waiting *in potentia* to be raised) whether anyone can keep it from the barbaric acts of violence it strains for. We must be careful what we become when we seek to change things. An old principle of physics: if you push, you yourself are pushed in turn.

And then there came a sunset where we all decided not to camp. We did not take the boat to the shoreline and tie it up, or make a fire. We all knew, as though we could feel the city's heart beating through the surface tension of the water, home was near at hand. The meanders of the river might keep us from seeing her, but we knew.

There was an unspoken but unanimous decision to press on, to catch the night and dock silently with the last of cities, without questions or prying eyes.

I will confess that all thoughts of Trethowan went from me. Living in the woods with savages was all very well if you were an exile and a hermit, but it was a poor substitute for home. Shadrapar, ancient widow-queen of cities, hive of corruption and vices, vessel of every ill and darkness that mankind ever conceived, and some that have simply arisen without anyone's volition or consent. To hell with living in virtue in the wilderness, we thought: let us live in sin at home.

So much for our sense of proximity, or perhaps it measured as birds fly, and not by the curved course of a river. It was almost all of the night, before we saw the blotting of the stars that heralded our city. The trees had given way on either side to fields under their canvas covers, waiting for the farmers to expose them to the rising sun. Above, the sky was studded with stars whose reflections swum below in the water. Where the stars were not, where there was nothing but the dark, that was our home.

The docks were ever an old, abandoned place and we had little fear of discovery. What river traffic was there, after all, now that the prison boat was gone? It was unthinkable that any Shadrapan would want simply to gad about for the fun.

There were great rusting hulks of ships there, which had not moved in a hundred years. Peter was sizing them up even as I guided our craft to a secluded mooring.

"They'll do," he said.

"You won't get them to move," I returned.

"We'll find someone who can," Peter announced.

"I know some artificers," Shon added. "They owe me favours."

As the boat touched the rusted spiderlegs of the docks, Shon reached up to grasp the nearest rungs and began to climb.

The docks of Shadrapar are six great jointed arcs of age-corroded metal lancing out into the water from the body of the city. Their original purpose was lost to the minds of men and, now that the prison boat had foundered, they had no purpose left to them at all. The part of the city they jutted from was all empty shells of buildings which might have stored exotic commodities from other lands, when there were still other lands.

It was light enough by then to see Shon waving at us, and so we clambered rung after rung, with iron flaking off in our hands. I was waiting for the moment when some part of my soul joined with the greater soul of Shadrapar and proclaimed that I was home. It did not come.

Instead, I saw the other boat: Gaki's boat. No craft from the city had point generators. It was docked a leg away from us, and Gaki had done some madman's thing with an upright spar and a sheet, the purpose of which I could not guess at. All it told me was that they were here already, in the maze of Shadrapar.

Dawn was almost on us. The sky above was an old, faded grey, soon to host the bloated hulk of the sun. The four of us crouched on the metal of the docking leg, ready for discovery, but there was none. The docks were deserted. The predawn city was a soundless grey mirage.

Peter made a signal, and we dashed along the leg, as broad as a street but riddled with great holes with only the oily waters beneath. The shells of a previous age's storehouses loomed abruptly before us in the gathering light. We all had a driving need to seek shelter, none of us welcome in our own city. Peter was pointing at a yawning hole in the wall of one warehouse, and we pelted for it as the sun heaved its bulk over the jutting points of the skyline. In our mad dash I tripped on some bundle that had been left on the dock and went sprawling on the ground, before clambering up to pelt after Kiera. At the time it was just an annoyance.

Inside the warehouse it was dark as we could ask, only the jagged gash of an opening to let any sun through. We huddled and watched the daylight reclaim Shadrapar from the night once more.

We could hear only our own harsh breathing in the echoing space. The city was silent.

"Where now?" Kiera was asking. "Shon, who's your best friend here?"

Shon gave a few names and discussed their pros and cons. I was looking out at the docks, at the arches of the metal legs. Probably I was thinking about Gaki.

I saw the bundle I had fallen over and for a moment I thought it was a body, but it was too flat. I stared at it and something about it communicated an urgency to me; a message.

Shadrapar remained quiet. Nobody was stirring save for us: dawn was not a time when civilised people arose. I wanted to stay safe and sheltered in the warehouse, but my mind was hauling me out to look at that abandoned bundle.

"Stefan!" Peter hissed at me, but I was gone into the light, moving at a run to crouch beside it.

I stared blankly: whatever inner voice had told me it was so important was silent. It was clothes: a scuffed tunic, old patched trousers, boots. I picked up the tunic and found the meagre weight of a purse within it. Baffled, I stared at it. There were a few coins of low denominations, the kind Jon de Baron would stuff his pockets with. There was an old brass ring on the ground as well, bare of inscription.

I looked out at the city, which had yet to wake, and I saw

something else. Ignoring Peter's urgent gestures, I went to investigate.

I found some more clothes, shabbier than the first and with no purse to keep them company. My higher mind was going over mad fantasies of disguise, but the more grounded parts were feeling a chill of premonition. At last Peter and the others came to join me in the light.

We looked down the street towards the heart of Shadrapar, the looming Old Quarter, the factories of the Steel Town and the bleak hill of the Government District, and we saw nothing in the early morning light but some dozen other forlorn huddles of clothes lying discarded in the street.

And something was wrong with the view but none of us could put a finger on it.

Increasingly on edge in the silence, Peter ran past the derelict old storerooms to a house. The door opened without resistance and we all pushed inside. I could feel a crawling sensation clutching each inch of my skin: horror, more than a fear.

In the front room of that poor little house there was a table laid for a meal. Of the four chairs, one was empty. The others were draped with empty clothes. A man's. A woman's. A child's. Their personal effects, their garments, their crockery and cutlery. Their house, but not them.

We ran out, for in that moment none of us could have stayed in that house a moment longer. We stood in broad view in the street and stared wildly at those unclaimed clothes that studded it, the only sign of a human habitation otherwise conspicuous by its absence.

Then I saw what was wrong with the view.

"The Weapon is gone," I said. The most distinctive sight of Shadrapar, the centrepiece, the symbol of our city, that twisted spire of unknown metals that had forever stood as our potential saviour in the face of the city's doom, was simply not there.

The city was silent save for the sound of our breathing.

"Oh dear God," said Kiera. "Someone's used the Weapon."

I could not imagine it, but that silence was shouting at us, telling us in no uncertain terms that we had not come home after all. Home was a place we would never know again; all there was of Shadrapar was what we carried with us. The cage of souls was empty, and all the souls had flown free.

44

Shadrapar Desolato

We did not know, and we could never know, just what events had led to which hand triggering those ancient mechanisms. The Weapon had stood longer than records, longer than Shadrapar perhaps. It had been known forever as the ineffable, definitive protection that Shadrapar had against its enemies. What enemies? Other cities, in the dim recesses of the past; more recently the deserts and the jungles.

Who could have known that Shadrapar would be its own worst enemy? Who would have thought that we would turn in upon ourselves?

"There was a coup," Kiera suggested. "There was a revolt against the Authority. Or perhaps the Authority fell into two factions. Each side had its supporters. It might just have been a shifting of power across the Authority table, people moving from one faction to another, until whoever was in charge could see they wouldn't be by dawn."

"You think it was Harweg," I said.

"I think it was someone who would rather do something unthinkable than let themselves be ousted. Perhaps they did not know what the Weapon would do. Perhaps they thought their opponents were the fabled enemies of Shadrapar the Weapon was supposed to guard against. Perhaps it was all in good faith. But rather than go quietly, they did it."

And my head crawled with pieces of a puzzle I would never quite solve: the Anteims, the Angels, Kiera's fall from grace. Faith.

We stood in that deserted street for a long time as the sun crawled up the inside of the sky and looked down at the city it had outlived. I felt as though the whole insides of me had been scraped out, nothing left but a hollow space. I felt as though I should just fall down and die. It was no place for living people.

The silence was so very absolute that it had ceased to be silence. It became for me the cavernous and unending echo of the sound that the Weapon must have made. A sound that no man could hear, I am sure, rushing through the city in all directions to vanish away, instantly and impersonally, every Shadrapan there was. That sound had rushed out to the very boundaries of the city, catching even poor vagrants camping out in the docks, leaving only the eternal ringing echo of its absence to preside over all of the other absences that now made up Shadrapar.

Peter's face was blank. What possible expression could a man be equipped with, to cope with such a concept. No great rescue for Peter. No triumphant return at the head of an army of convicts and guards. Perhaps he was thinking that, had his plan played out, his revolution might have precipitated just this. In contrast, Shon's face was afraid for the first time. He had lost his friends and his contacts and his criminal networks. Shadrapar had finally been cleared of crime. No more vice, no more laws, no more duels, no more deals. Shon's eyes glittered in the sun. He was the only one, perhaps, to love our mutual birthplace enough to shed a tear for it.

Kiera muttered, almost under her breath: an appeal to divinity, or maybe just something profane and prosaic. She had family, I recalled. They were gone. Gone too, the great game of politics and society she had trained for. Gone, her way of life, the point of her and the reason for all her skills. As a social historian I was the same. Social history had closed its final chapter.

Peter lurched forwards, Ropa blade in one hand as though he could do battle with the emptiness, slay it and cut open its corpse to let out all the sound and life that it had consumed. We all followed him through the vacated streets.

I do not think that Peter had any particular destination in mind. Every place in Shadrapar, after all, had been voided of significance. We just drifted with the dust through the alien streets we had all once known. We glanced at the emptied clothes we came across, trying to piece together the stories of their owners. Had they been running in terror? Had they been out for a stroll? Had they any warning of the catastrophe before the unimaginable force had taken them away? There were men and women, large and small, rich and poor, adults and children, all witnessed for only by what they had chosen to wear that morning. Had the wisest, the most powerful, the most beautiful man or woman gone naked into the streets in that fatal moment then they would have nothing to speak for them at all. It would be as though they had never been.

We saw a flat semicircle of clothing cast off around a metal crate on which another suit was laid in state. Some demagogue on the very moment of conjuring the mob; some prophet imparting his revelations of the end of the world? What satisfaction to the latter to discover, in one apocalyptic second, that he was right?

We saw one street clogged with uniforms. Ranks of Outrider leathers, knives in their sheathes, muskets fallen like straws. Their crisp-cut military styles opposed a great mass of coarse cloth, the hard-wearing garb of factory workers that I remembered so well. Many of the clothes were holed by musket balls, the blood without gone to the same oblivion as the blood within. There had been a riot here, in the same instant that the agitator had been orating, in the same moment that the family by the docks had sat down to their last meal.

Then Shon cried out, for he had spotted something moving at the far end of the street, and abruptly we were running. His mirage was gone before we reached it, leaving no trace of its reality or unreality, but Shon swore that he had seen someone: a living person; a survivor.

"Gaki," Peter said.

"Needn't be," Shon countered him. "I mean, who's to say everyone's dead? How many people were there in Shadrapar? They can't all be gone. They can't."

"If it was Gaki, he would let us know it was him," I said slowly. "Or we would never see him until it was too late."

"Do we call out?" Kiera suggested.

"No," Peter said firmly. "Not until we're sure."

Kiera clutched at my arm suddenly. "There!" she said, and we all saw it then: someone dashing from shadow to shadow and away from us, round a corner and out of sight. We gave chase instantly. The thought that our frenzied pursuit would not reassure anyone did not occur to us. The lure of human company was too great. Shon was fastest, in the lead from the first step. Kiera was next, and then Peter hauling the Ropa blade in his wake. I was never a good runner and had the rearguard, toiling over cobbles and clothes, over the memories of Shadrapar's last second, trying to keep up.

I tried to remember my streets and knew that we were on the Fenney Way that led from the docklands into a nasty area of decrepit housing near where Helman had rented once. Markaf Square was ahead, and the thought came to me that it would be an ideal ambush point. Even as I opened my mouth to urge caution, though, Shon had stopped so suddenly that I thought he had been shot.

We caught up with him, halted by an inexplicably horrible sight. It was just a pile of clothes, a huge pile about man-high, in the centre of the square. There was nothing innately hideous about it. There was no happy way to account for it, though, knowing what those clothes represented. They were mostly of the poorer wardrobes, as the area would suggest, but there was some bright and expensive cloth tucked in between the drab and the cheap. There was the tough canvas of Outriders and even the sombre half-cape of an Academy Master. My skin crawled. In the mind's eye was conjured the image of a mass of people clambering in mindless terror over each other, crushing each other down, climbing up into an obscene human pyramid to reach some unthinkable salvation. I felt ill at the sight of it.

Peter advanced cautiously, sword in hand. He was the only one of us that could move. He was no more than halfway to the mound when something else entered the square. For a moment we thought it was a child.

It was less than three feet tall, hunched and covered with matted dark hair. Eyes glittered above a long, whiskered snout, and a bristle-covered tail snaked out behind it. Its forelegs ended in clawed almost-hands and it was holding some vanished Shadrapan's clothes with the obvious intention of adding them to the pile. Vermin.

Something broke in me that had been under too much strain from the moment we made our discovery. From my starting position of static horror, I found myself in screaming, murderous descent on the creature with no obvious transition. I sped past Peter, drawing my knife and shouting curses and threats at the paralysed rodent. In my mind, it was responsible for everything. The Vermin had killed Shadrapar and now they were doing something unspeakable with what was left.

It fell over backwards and then was scurrying away on all fours, but I had a good start and flung myself on it, catching it by the tail. I, Stefan Advani, Academy graduate and man of peace, crouched over a cowering animal with my blade raised and nothing but hate in my mind.

You must understand that everyone knew to despise the Vermin. They were disease-ridden parasites, worthless animals.

551

They stole children. They stole valuables. The Outriders did everyone a service trying to wipe them out. They bred so fast that they would infest Shadrapar within weeks if they were not continually culled. They did not have any culture. They made tools and dwellings by bestial instinct and nothing more. We all knew this. We all had been taught this.

Peter grabbed my knife hand and dragged me back before I struck, which I am glad of in retrospect. I was shouting all manner of accusations but I will not recount them here; they would add nothing.

There were others, I saw. They had been brought by my cries, perhaps a dozen little hairy shapes. Some of them had young clutched to them; some held jagged-ended shafts of metal and plastic, but they were far too frightened of us to use them. One in the centre, grey more than black, held a plastic rod that was aflame at one end, giving off a plume of noxious smoke.

I tried to understand what it was they were about. Defiance of the master race that would no longer hunt and trap them? Respect for the dead? I could put no interpretation on it that would not force me to revise the way I saw them and so, in the end, I did not interpret it at all, just backed off from the fallen Vermin and stared. The wretched beast I had assaulted bolted away into the shadows and was lost.

I came to my senses and remembered who I was, and what I was, and that I was not that sort of man. I felt unstable. Wherever all that violence had come from, I was not sure that it had gone away.

"Help me," I said, I am not sure who to. It was Kiera who touched my arm, then held me when I started to shake. Shon and Peter had weapons drawn and ready, watching the Vermin. The creatures were clustered together, glaring at us with a mixture of fear and defiance. Poor monsters, to discover that humanity was not as dead as they had been led to believe.

Abruptly Shon fired a pistol into the air and they scattered at the noise. Moments later they were all running like animals,

552

spears and torch forgotten, offspring clinging to the adults' pelts.

Kiera was asking me if I was all right, but I was waiting for the echo of the shot to die away. It just seemed to go on and on until I realised that I was listening to that same awful reverberating silence again. She had to ask me three times.

"I don't know," I said. I could hear a raw edge in my own voice that I did not like. "I think I'm going mad."

The others were all looking drawn and pale, but none of them seemed as oppressed by it all as I. My mind had been opened up by Helman. I had gained an extra sense that people were not born with. I must have been hearing the echoes of a mass of minds every day since then, a comforting, inaudible background murmur that underscored everything I ever thought or heard or did. Now, save for the fragile minds of my companions, there was nothing. There were no human minds within the boundaries of Shadrapar save for us, and Gaki and Hermione wherever they were. Into that vast absence of mind, that intolerable vacuum that nobody else could feel, my thoughts were slowly bleeding.

Peter was moving off again with Shon following a little behind, a little to the side, keeping an eye out for surprises. Kiera hugged me briefly. "Are you going to be all right?" she asked. "We can stop here if you need it." She looked frightened, and I realised it was for me. It was enough, in that moment, to draw a little strength from.

I cannot say where Peter was taking us. It did not occur to me to ask. He moved purposefully enough that I believed in him. Looking back, I think he was just moving because it was better for a man of action than staying still.

We were making our way slowly towards the centre of the city, I realised. The great square that expeditions had traditionally set off from would see the return of the last expedition ever re-entering Shadrapar. There we would stand, as people had once said, in the Shadow of the Weapon. All Shadrapar was in the shadow of the Weapon now.

I found myself leaping forward to grab Peter by the belt and drag him down. We were just moving up a broad commercial street lined with wound-up business when something alerted me. Whether I heard a sound the others missed, or whether my flayed-open mind felt some pressure against it, I suddenly had a feeling of fear that I was familiar with, a specific dread. Peter struggled to dislodge my grip, but something in my face stopped him from shouting out. Across the street, Shon had also gone to ground in a doorway, and Kiera was crouching next to us.

It was not as close as I feared. It came from a side-road five-hundred yards down the street. Something white arched its way into view, and then another pale arc to join it, poling forward a squat, ridged body with underwater ease. Even at that distance we could see the great man-wide eyes and ragged sense organs that sprouted from the body's leading edge.

The Macathar strode through the abandoned works of mankind at last. It was a moot point whether it had come out of the deep desert, or whether the desert had come to Shadrapar.

It did not see or sense us, passing by on some mission of its own devising, meaningless to man. Even at such a distance we were left shattered in its wake.

"God," Peter got out. "So that's what one of those damned things looks like."

"But why is it *here*?" Kiera demanded.

"In the desert," I said hollowly, "you will often find them amongst the ruins. I think that they are curious."

We saw one other Macathar, at an even greater distance. It was just a white shadow drifting across the expanse of the Academy grounds. We saw many more Vermin, trekking in little lines through the deserted streets with their makeshift spears and crude sacks of possessions.

"They're kind of like the web-children," Peter suggested.

"They are not like the web-children!" I snapped. "Vermin are... animals. Pests. The web-children are people." As I was saying it I was aware of how unsatisfied Trethowan would have been by the division.

Just before dark we found the great square where the Weapon once stood. It had been a long, halting progress through dead Shadrapar. There was a great hole in the square's centre that must surely go down into some part of the Underworld. I wondered which lost faction's ceiling had been violated and I knew that it did not matter and nobody was left to care. It is a great lie of civilisation that the things we invest with our emotions are real and important, but they are not. Take away the people and they vanish into smoke. All those idle dreams: government, money, education, love, revenge. All these things are parasites that cannot survive without the host. A thousand million things had gone out of the world when Shadrapar died, and we were too few to recreate them.

We stopped in that square, in the shadow of the Weapon's absence, as if whatever driving force had drawn Peter onwards had fallen down that hole and disappeared.

"What are we going to do?" said Peter for the first time, perhaps, in his life.

"It's a looter's paradise," Shon said, "if you could do anything with the loot. Still, we could find a lot of useful things, get some power running maybe."

"And then what? Be lords of the Vermin?" I asked.

"Life is life," Kiera said, surprising me. I had thought, of all of us, that she had lost the most. I had forgotten that, first and foremost, she had been trained to be adaptable. "I think your first plan is still the best," she told Peter. "Back to the docks and get a boat. Go liberate the Island."

"And then what? If we bring them here we're going to be on the run from the Macathars," Peter said.

Nobody had any easy answers as to what we would do with several hundred people and no place to put them. The best idea was Shon's. He suggested that we just take over the Island and live there. It was a poor substitute for Shadrapar, and none of us was eager to return there, but it was civilisation. It was a defiance of encroaching nature. None of us thought it likely that the Macathars would wade up the river after us.

We slept in the square, and Peter was concerned enough about the unseen Gaki to set watches. I knew that Gaki could have walked by unseen with us all wide awake, but I said nothing. Between the Weapon and the Macathars, Peter was fed up of things he could not fight. Kiera watched first, Peter second. My turn came after the night had started on the long journey towards dawn, and this is where my problems really began.

Peter woke me to a chill darkness relieved by the tiniest fire (matchwood from the buildings lit with sparks from a flintlock). After he had settled down and instantly fallen asleep, I was left with only that fickle flame and my sleeping comrades, and the utter, utter emptiness of the world.

I held on for about an hour. For just so long did I crouch by the ember of the fire and do my best to fill my mind with thoughts: any thoughts save those of vanished Shadrapar. Thought after thought evaporated away until eventually, in the small and dead hours of the night, I was left with nothing between my naked brain and the truth of it.

I found myself staring at the familiar buildings, populating them with people that I knew. I shuffled through the deck of faces and found myself listing all those who had died here, and the worst thing was, there were so few that I could name. My closest friends had died in the riot, my comrades in adversity had died in Underworld. Who was left? Emil des Schartz, some Academy Masters, some socialites whose faces no longer even conjured up a name. The best of my life had been spent and gone before ever the Weapon fired.

The silence was closing in on me. I could hear it creeping soundlessly through forever-deserted alleyways. It stole like a predator, lured by my heartbeat and my breathing. The dark and vacant city now exhaled it into the shrouded streets and it was coming for me.

I had gone mad. Of that I am sure. Only for a moment, but in that moment I did not know myself and I was privy to an understanding of the universe grotesquely at odds with the norm. I believed without hesitating that the silence was a thing: an unliving but animate thing. I could not see it. Of course I could not hear it. I could *feel* it, though, with the extraneous senses of a mind gone awry.

I did not dare wake the others. A single sound would bring the silence down on me in an annihilating wave. I knew it when it entered the square; I recognised the clues left by all the absences of sight and sound. As I crouched in abject terror by the fire, the silence, the *Silence*, slithered from a side-street like a great eyeless serpent.

I tried to stay as still as possible but it had heard the blood hammering through my arteries. It knew that I was close. The great unseen jaws gaped, a tongue of air tasting air. It towered upwards on its coils, vast and deathly and utterly a product of my brain. When only one man perceives a scene, who is to say what it real?

I knew, with a complete certainty, that it would strike and kill me the moment it found me. I could not fight it. How can one fight a silence? Even Peter would think twice. Without ever taking my eyes from its invisible form I crept backwards, painstakingly slow. Above me, around me, the Silence swayed.

I moved back and further back, and sometimes it heard me and slid a yard closer and sometimes I made five or six paces without alerting it. I knew only one place where it could not follow me. The silence was vast, far greater than any serpent of flesh and blood. It needed the lonely sky to form it. I would go underground.

Yes, I was abandoning my friends to the mercies of Macathars, Vermin and Gaki. I should not have done it. I had no choice. In those painful dragging moments, I believed it.

My foot touched the edge of the hole where the weapon once was, with the slightest scraping of metal. Abruptly the Silence focused its attentions on me and threw all the looping coils of its insubstantial body into motion. I looked down frantically and, as I had somehow known, there were metal rungs descending into that abyss. Even the Weapon was only a machine, that had been built and maintained once. Now that it had taken itself away, all the mundane details of its construction were revealed

The Silence was rushing on towards me with its jaws agape, and I fell into the Weapon's setting, grasped the rungs and clambered down hand over hand.

45

The Underworld Desolato

The big house I grew up in could have been tipped down that hole and not have touched the sides on the way down. The Weapon's roots had been vast.

I climbed hand over hand for an unmeasured time. Looking back I can see the changes the Island had wrought in me. The man who could not descend a rope could now march on, rung after rung, without slowing or tiring. The madness drove me. I could still sense the Silence at the hole's mouth. Around me as I descended, the shaft narrowed and narrowed.

After a while the black metal that lined the shaft gave out, and I was left climbing down rungs of an unidentifiable material hammered into the rock. They were luminous, and lit the shaft interior with a queasy, greenish-yellow light. I was slowing by then, more aware of my surroundings. I was climbing through history.

Across the shaft from me, almost close enough to touch, there was a cave mouth, the entrance to some suite of caverns that Giulia's maps had never suspected. Whatever enormous drill had bored this shaft had sheared straight into those pre-existing caverns without a thought, destroying most that was in there, sealing off the rest as the Weapon was fit into place. Now I was the first man in a thousand thousand years to look into that opened space. I saw bodies. There were three of them and the conditions of their deaths had mummified them perfectly. Within another month they would be eaten away by the damp, but they were there for me: a man, a woman and a child, still cased in paper-brittle hides they had been wearing when they died. I saw no cause of death. There was a litter of small bones on the cave floor, scraps of desiccated tissue and stone tools. I wonder, now, what nadir of civilisation they represented, which of the many dark ages. How long had it been since that cave had last seen light and air?

Whatever catastrophe had forced them back to the very dawn of man, man had survived it. We had rebuilt, over and over. I could not see us building again.

I pressed on, because to be alone with the dead is never preferable to simply being alone.

Then I ran out of hole. Abruptly the metal ladder which had replaced the strange rungs came to a sheared close, and there was simply a dimly-lit space beneath me through a gap no more than six foot across. I saw a floor, and it did not seem too far. At the time I did not recognise it.

I looked up and could not tell if the pinpoints of light were stars, or fabrications of my brain. I found myself hanging at arm's length from the bottom-most rung of the ladder, about to drop.

It occurred to me that this was not a good idea, but by then I had let go.

In the fraction of a second after I dropped I was struck by a savage jolt of energy and lost consciousness. My mind came back to me as I struck the floor and I think it was the looseness of my limbs that prevented any permanent harm. I injured my ankle painfully, and it was that pain that dispelled the madness and let me realise where I was.

The hole in the centre of the ceiling was now a great void in the midst of an ever-moving starfield. The jolt that had run through me was a crackling dance of energy passing from one edge of the starscape to the other. Beside me on the floor I saw the unmoving dead-spider form of the Caretaker, lying where it had fallen. The other bodies had been removed.

I was in the Temple. The Temple had been directly below the Weapon.

I got to my feet and winced with the pain of it. The Temple lights were dim, as though in mourning, but they were still on. There was power yet.

The Temple's computer was still there. It had gained some bullet holes since I had last seen it, and the mirror in which one had read the records of antiquity was cracked beyond repair. I looked up, with that peculiar reverence the sight demanded, and I cried out.

Above the computer was an empty oval niche in the wall, from which a clear eggshell lid had been hinged back.

The Coming Man had been and gone. Too late to save the Underworld, too late to save the city, the imprisoned giant had woken, turned his back and walked away.

I have no explanation for this. It is a small thing amongst all the other unexplained events, but I still wonder.

Now that I had my mind again I thought of the fastest way back to my friends. There were no quick exits into the shadow of the Weapon, though. To leave the Underworld was to enter some little-used or derelict part of Shadrapar Above.

The fear that had been so great beneath the sky was gone now. The Temple was my place, after all. The surface had grown to be as strange and hostile as the desert. Down here there was only the restfulness that always presides after terrible deeds have been rubbed smooth by time. In this very room there had been a massacre. Only the broken metal spider and a few bullet holes testified to it.

The idea that had been nudging at my mind with the lazy curiosity of a predatory fish suddenly seized me. The Vermin, who had made the Underworld their home as much as anyone, how had they survived the lash of the Weapon?

Obviously – so obviously that I was kicking myself for not having thought of it before – they had been underground. Certainly there were Vermin in the desert, the jungles and everywhere, but the quantities we had seen suggested a boiling-up out of holes and dens and cellars. The energies of the Weapon had not reached underground.

The community of Underworld had been destroyed, but surely some others had found these tunnels before the end. There had only been a month of so, but a city can throw up a lot of rogues and malcontents in that time.

I left the Temple and my feet took me towards home automatically. Not Greygori's cheerless chambers but the rooms of Sergei's Collective, where I had spent my last month. Arves had not pronounced the death of Sergei. He might still be living out a troglodytic existence, tinkering with his machine and trying to return to that place and time that only he believed in. As I made my way, my own belief in Sergei swelled larger and larger. It was another face of the madness, I suppose. I was desperate to walk into the Collective's rooms and find him there, larger than life. I broke into a run without intending to.

The way into the Collective's quarters was lined with broken barricades. Sergei's people had put up a furious fight in defence of their home. Arves had said that Sergei had been fighting with the Fishermen down in the mycoculture caverns. Had he evaded pursuit and retreated into the deeper caverns, or had he come back here to die with his people?

I stepped over the shattered wood, the twisted metals and plastics of their last stand. The walls were scarred by musket shot and other weapons, so much so that I almost heard the echo of it.

Then I realised that there was a sound, and that it was not my overstretched imagination working on me once again. A faint, low hum: a machine sound.

The little fruit garden the Collective had tended had run wild, still bathed in its shaft of sunlight like a prisoner Below.

Beyond that illumination I saw a faint phosphorescence from Sergei's workshop. Wordlessly I tiptoed onwards. Part of me still expected the man himself; part of me was looking for his body.

I found his creation instead. When I had last seen it, it had been a bizarre cluster of rods and gears and wiring. Now it had grown to fill the room, a veritable forest of interconnecting spines and pistons and hollow bars. It was the source of the sound, and I felt that each individual part had its own tone, blended into a harmony by the whole.

I stepped into the room, ducking beneath the nearest projections. It was like some mad plumber's nightmare, and a clockwright's as well. The air was charged with the energy of it. To go further was to step into the heart of the machine.

He had left a plaque there. A roughly-tooled plate of metal proclaimed:

IT WAS FROM HERE THAT CAPTAIN SERGEI ANDREIOVITCH MAZHIENSKY SET FORTH ON THE SEAS OF TIME ONCE MORE, IN SEARCH OF HIS COUNTRY.

A second inscription might have said the same, but it was in an ancient script I could not read.

I stood a long time looking at that, and it seemed to me that, knowing Sergei, it might have been his joke. He was quite capable of that.

Then I looked at his machine, still buzzing with power, and I wondered. After the Underworld fell, after the Outriders departed, he must have come back here. He must have worked, all alone, extending and building upon his machine. Had this tortuous monster resembled the thing he had seen in his head?

Had it worked for him? Was he even now adrift on the seas of time, or simply scattered into atoms like everyone else.

I stepped in. You would have done the same.

You would have been disappointed, too. It would not work for me. Perhaps there had been power only for a single step into time. Certainly the residue that thrummed in every lever and pipe did nothing.

Sergei was gone, then: into the past of his own belief, or just gone. I had the Underworld to myself, or so I assumed.

It was on leaving the Collective's rooms that I saw her. I knew even then that she could only have been a hallucination. How else could it be that I should see Faith at the very edge of the light, just a lit face in the gloom?

I saw her face turned towards me, out there in the dark beneath the earth. Or I convinced myself that I did. I have seen prey in the jungles freeze suddenly before bolting from a predator. It seemed to me that Faith sprang away into the darkness just like those prey animals. And like the predator, I pursued.

They made her irresistible, and they made her too well. They had coveted her, and they had fought over her, and they had lost her.

It was just possible that they had fired the Weapon because of her.

And she was alive, and everything else was dead, dead, dead.

I did not see her again. I ran with all my speed but she must have been faster. She was a hallucination, after all, I realised. They can go as fast as they like.

I realised I had lost track of where I was just before I was snagged. Something like a bony hook tore into my prison greys and yanked me backwards, and only later did I realise it was supposed to be a hand.

The face that was presented to my own was fishbelly white and round and hairless, with the skin and flesh hanging at odd angles, as though no longer pinned properly to the skull. The mouth was a pinched wound. With nobody to hide from, he had lost his smoked-glass lenses. His eyes were too large to be covered anyway: great round grey-black discs that I had seen before. The smooth white brow was dotted with livid boils which were other sensory organs just beginning to emerge.

"Stefan Advani," came out of that mouth like rust speaking. "It is not safe, Stefan, to be walking in these places all alone, Stefan Advani. The Vermin, Stefan, are become uncommonly bold. Or you might meet Mazen, Stefan, or something worse."

He held me out at arm's length with no discernable effort, despite the six-foot spindliness of his arm. He had forgone the robe, I saw. The rest was abomination. His hunched shoulders were set off at an impossible angle from an exploded ribcage where all the struts had grown in different directions, stretching the skin to its limits. That was not so bad. There were all manner of tubes and pipes below, as convoluted as Sergei's machine. Some of them were atrophied and others bloated out, and the skin over these had parted long ago. That was also not so bad.

The bad part was where his spine and organs merged into a chalky, ridgy pelvis from which four legs sprouted, to arc as high as his shoulders before stabbing down at the ground. At the base of that tangle of intestines a bundle of strange projections, feelers and lifeless eyes dangled obscenely.

Greygori Sanguival's regime of self-improvement had progressed apace. He was now more than half-Macathar. That was the dream he had been chasing: a form to survive the Earth. His bright place, that he had tempted Faith with, was no more or less than the desert's white sand.

"Stefan Advani." He tasted the words again. It had been a long time since he had spoken to a living soul.

"Hello… Greygori," I managed weakly.

"It is you, Stefan Advani…" That scratchy, unused voice seemed querulous. "How is it that you come to be here, Stefan, for they told me you had died on the Island?" There was nothing to admit that he had sent me there himself. There was no indication of incipient violence either, or of anything human at all.

"I came back," I said inanely.

"Did you?" Greygori whispered. "Stefan… Stefan Advani… I have tried to forget your name, Stefan. On some days I think I have succeeded, but it sticks in me as few others do. Why is that,

565

Stefan?" He was still holding me high above the ground, and now to my horror his legs clicked into cumbersome motion, just as much of a staggering lurch as always. There was nothing of the otherworldly grace of the Macathar to him.

"Why?" came that lost, sad voice. "Why won't you leave me alone, Stefan?"

"Put me down and I'll go," I whispered. I reached one hand up to clutch at the barbed claw, but it dug its way into my shoulder, drawing blood.

"Are you come back to accuse me?" There was no anger in those plate-like eyes, which was why, when he swung me into the wall, I was not ready for it. I recognised a damaged rib instantly and then I was tumbling down to the floor. The world went black for a second and then the nightmare was advancing on me. Those many-jointed arms whipped about his head of their own accord. His exposed organs pulsed. Words forced themselves from his mouth like bullets.

"I have no guilt. I have cut it from me. Why must I always see you, Advani? Why must I see Arves? Did I abandon Arves? Did he die in the fight? I have cut the memory from me, and yet I see you always. And her, I see her. What is it, Stefan, that I must do to rid myself of you all?" At last the thin voice broke into something like emotion: no emotion I could name, but it was there.

I tried to scrabble out of the way, but a hook tore into my ankle and my shoe, and I was hoisted upside down to look into those soulless eyes.

"I have done everything," Greygori said. A rivulet of blackish blood sprang suddenly from one of his larger eyes.

I pushed calm through myself like a wave. "Talk to me. What is wrong?" Something twitched aggressively under his skin and I added, "We were not always enemies."

"Look at me, Stefan." I thought that he was lucid then, although there were precious few clues. "I am not perfect."

I had no words.

"I have done everything right, Stefan Advani. I have cut it all out, severed everything that holds me back. I wielded the knife myself. Why can I not let it go? Why am I still tied to these memories?"

He dropped me abruptly. Pain tore through my side and I collapsed in a heap.

"Is it really you, Stefan?" he asked softly.

I stared at him.

"I have seen you so many times. You, Arves and the girl. Why can I not cut deep enough to be rid of you?" One of the eyes at his groin twitched sluggishly and turned its blind gaze upon me. "Humanity, Stefan, is such an easy thing to be rid of," he said, as though he was an Academy Master lecturing me. "Many that wear human shape are yet bereft of it. It should be an easy enough thing to sever those ties that make us men, to pave the way for something greater. To become the new, one must cut, Stefan. One must take the scalpel and cut away the cords that bind our minds. A human mind is human forever. Look at me, Stefan. I am trapped in my human mind. Pity me, Stefan."

I could not find it in my heart.

Without changing tone he added, "It is your fault. That is why I cannot rid me of you. Arves, who betrayed me to you. You, that took her from me. Faith. Faith. How I wish you had never brought her, Stefan. Not guilt, Stefan, but a lust for revenge, that keeps you with me. Revenge, the most paltry of human things."

He was very still now, looking at me.

"I cannot forget her," he whispered. "I see her everywhere."

"I saw her too!" I burst out, and he recoiled.

"No, you are all my mind's things, that I can cut out. For if she, of all the people in the world, was still alive, then I could never be rid of her."

I crawled up to my knees, a fitting position for a supplicant. "Listen to me, Greygori," I choked out. What did I have to say to him, though? He was madder than I was.

"I could never be rid of her..." he mused distantly. "You, though... I could be rid of you. If you are truly here..."

It was my misfortune then to be truly there and not one of his hallucinations. One of those spider legs flicked forwards and hit me in the stomach. I doubled over and fought for breath, even as a hook caught in my collar and I was hoisted aloft again, this time strangling.

I kicked out, but I was nowhere near him. I clutched at the twisted spines of his hand but could not loose them. The other hand was coming in, a surgeon's toolkit of spines and barbs. It hovered before my face meditatively.

"Cut," said Greygori's mouth mindlessly. "Cut away. Cut it away."

His free hand made an experimental motion and scarred a line down my cheek. I screamed and he brought the claw before my eyes, almost solicitously, as though it would not be so bad for me if I truly appreciated the instrument of my dissection.

And then he stopped and skittered, swinging me along like a sack. I could not say where any of his eyes were looking, but I saw something reflected in them – something behind me that shone softly.

Greygori stuttered through his atrophied sphincter of a mouth, "T-t-t-t-t." Forgotten, I reached up and tore at my prison greys until I fell to the ground, and still Greygori did not react. The Macathar parts of him trembled and twitched as though eager to be off doing something incomprehensible and alien, but his upper half was paralysed by the sight.

I backed away from him slowly, but I did not see myself reflected in those huge dark eyes, only her. I did not look at her myself. I thought I might not be able to escape, if I did.

When I had passed three junctions in my headlong flight from Greygori, I heard his voice again. The sound of him calling her name echoed through the tunnels, as distorted as the rest of him. He sounded terribly lost and lonely, the last human part of Greygori Sanguival.

He was receding, as far as I could judge, and so I collapsed down with my back to the tunnel wall, and that was where she found me. I think she did. I remember this happening, but I was exhausted and had not slept for a long time. I did not truly see her with Greygori, only the faint image of her in his eye. Perhaps I never saw her again, at all.

But let us say I did. If so, it was at the edge of the light, just a pale glimmer of her. She would not approach closer than that. I saw the manufactured perfection of her face, her expression one of wary caution, poised to flee.

She wore a mismatched assembly of clothes: a rich woman's gleaming gown over Outrider canvas, with an Academy Master's hat covering her gleaming hair. She, who had first come to this place naked, had a whole city for her wardrobe.

I think she said my name. When I shifted position she was gone, creeping back when it was plain I would not lunge for her.

I could only stare and shiver. If I truly saw what I saw then she survived, and I wondered if it was because she was a *thing*, like Thelwel was a thing, and the Weapon had not concerned itself with things. The great men who made her had left her behind, just like their clothes and their money.

She looked well. She looked alive in a way she never had before. She looked like I felt when I put the Island's walls behind me for the last time. We had all put walls around her, after all: me, Sergei, Greygori, Jon Anteim the Elder (or whoever it was who had commissioned her making). She had been built to be an object without agency – worse, she had been built to evince just that response from all of us: that she must be protected and possessed and coveted. I could tell myself that I had been innocent and only sought the best for her, but in truth the only moment I had ever acted in her interests and not my own was when I let her go.

I could have said so much, then. I could have asked what happened when the Weapon fired, or how she made her life now, or why she had returned to Underworld. In the end I did not trust myself. If I stirred my voice into conversation then I would speak her name, and if I spoke her name I would ask her to come closer. I wanted her to come closer. I wanted to feast my eyes on her. I had let her go once, and I think it was only that Sergei was there, that let me. I valued his regard and did not want him to know what sort of a man I truly was. And perhaps he valued my regard and did the same right thing for the same wrong reason.

Faith was still waiting, and I thought of the way she had tried to return to the place where they had kept her, even though she hated it. Was she drawn to Greygori and to me because we had kept her, too? Was that a hook they had put in her?

And so I did speak, after all. I begged her to go. I told her that there were still men in the city, and that she should stay clear of them all. Even me. Especially me. Even that much wore down my good intentions, and I had to bite down on whatever contradictory words might have come next.

I thought I saw her smile before she vanished. Or perhaps she was never there, and all this is my subconscious pretending to a strength I never really owned.

I did sleep a little, then, which adds to the hypothesis that it was all imagined. After that, I levered myself up and looked to find a way out of Underworld, to search all of Shadrapar for my friends. Taking stock, I found that I was close to the portal through which Sergei and I had smuggled Faith. Still fuddled from a long and hectic night, it was a strange thing to stand in the shadows looking up at that square of light. Last time I was here, I had been looking down through that opening where Greygori had scratched and pleaded.

He was there again. Possibly he had returned there a hundred times since that day.

His voice quavered from the darkness. "Stefan...?" I froze.

I heard the tap-scrape of his arthropod legs hauling him forwards until the edge of that light touched him. "Stefan...?"

he said again. I was waiting for *Cut it away* but there was no admission in face or voice that he had any recollection of our encounter so soon before. Or perhaps the sight of Faith (if there had been a sight of Faith) had effaced it from his memory.

"I'm going now," I told him, though there was no way I could have made it through that gap had he chosen to stop me. The reach of those arms was appalling.

"But you died on the Island," he said.

I felt a sudden wash of impatience. "Yes, yes, I died on the Island and you keep seeing me and Arves and Faith and you're very guilty and you want to cut the guilt away. I know it all already."

He actually flinched back from the words. I barely made out his next halting utterance, or perhaps I misheard it – after all he had no lips to read.

"I just want to stop feeling this…"

His legs shifted, impatient to be done. Those long, deadly arms flailed a little, aimlessly, neither human nor Macathar, an error of replication.

He could lash out for me at any time, I knew. Probably he could outrun me if he could order his legs properly.

"Greygori," I said, "you're right. I died on the Island. It was a long time ago." Surely the world's weakest deception, save that he was confused and in pain and detached from anything I would recognise as reality. "But listen," I went on, "before I died, I forgave you."

He stayed still, various of his eyes upon me.

"I remembered us playing chess like we used to," which was true-ish. "I remembered you took me in. I was happy down here for a while. I'm sorry we became enemies. And so I forgave you, before I died. And Arves did, too. You don't need to think about us any more."

Perhaps he had access to all the senses of the Macathars, but what would such capabilities understand of guilt or absolution?

It was his human remnant I spoke to and I saw my words hit home.

"I'm going now," I told him. "You'll never see me again. Forget me. Forget all of it."

I stepped closer, reaching up for the hatchway, well within the reach of those hooked hands, but Greygori made no move to attack me.

"Forget," he said, and grew two extra arms. They came from behind his back and were surprisingly human. Then one of them grabbed his ribs for purchase. Abruptly Greygori was bucking and twisting his head back and forth as I stared, utterly bewildered. Then one of his arms caught me with a ridged knuckle and knocked me flat. Only then did I realise that there was a man on his back.

Greygori's long limbs jerked furiously behind him but never seemed to catch anything. "Cut!" the puckered mouth spat out. "Cut! Cut! Cut!" and obligingly, the newcomer did. One human hand moved in a flashing pass across Greygori's throat and in its wake it left a track of black fluid that was too thick for blood. The rhythm to which it gushed and pulsed owed nothing to a human heart.

I scrambled backwards as the Transforming Man's human parts collapsed back upon his arthropod parts. The four Macathar legs wobbled and folded. He went down into a pile of unrelated limbs from which a human figure stepped clear.

"Gaki," I said softly. Who else?

"You have the strangest friends," Gaki said softly, looking down at the tangled mess of Greygori's body.

"I suppose he was a friend, once," I agreed.

"And now it is no longer important what he was, for he is past and the world need not concern itself with him." He tossed the knife from hand to hand idly, the same tiny diamond blade he had taken from Father Sulplice.

He saw me looking at it. "Sing not the praises of the sword or jagged knife, for the perfect'st measure of destructive force

572

needs naught but the point and the edge, and all else is vanity." I recalled the quote from Sandor's *Lying in State*.

"A metaphor for politics," I noted.

"But here at the world's end we need no metaphors, for all the things we have left are themselves and nothing else." He was smiling at me as though I was an old friend he had not expected to meet. I was terribly aware of the edge and the point cupped in his hand.

"I have not been a happy man all my life, though you may not believe it. I owe you much, Stefan. You opened my mind and told me what was wrong with myself."

I conserved my strength for the task of standing up.

"I have been set aside from my fellow man by a pressure at the back of my brain that could not be explained. It distanced me, a burden I thought only I bore until I met you. Now I know that we are brothers and we share that burden. I wish I could have met Helman Cartier. From what I read he must have been an impressive intellect."

I nodded shortly, back to the wall.

"That pressure was my mind's sense of the world, the dreadful babble of a thousand other minds, all those mundane, pointless thoughts, that wasted intellect. We know, you and I, how many tedious ideas pass through even one poor brain. We know the drudgery of being surrounded by all that unceasing banality. I think that must be how I found my true vocation. The first time I killed, I felt a tiny lessening in that interminable pressure."

Without any warning he was right up close to me, a companionable hand on my arm. I could not see the knife.

"The Island was easier, of course, although there were still far too many minds there. I am surprised at my own forbearance in not killing the Marshal sooner. Or perhaps he is still dying; he was a resilient old man. No mercy, though, for such a strident thinker. I knew you would approve."

I had indicated nothing of my approval or disapproval. Perhaps this in itself condoned his actions.

"If I killed him sooner, though, they would have exiled me from the Island and forced me back to civilisation. But see: I have returned at exactly the right time. Is this not a wonderful development?"

I stared at him leadenly.

"I have had a dream forever that I would be alone in the world. That no mewling thoughts would press upon me and make me angry. I dream of a world in which I need not be a killer, because there would be none left to kill. And now I have my dream, or nearly. Shadrapar is a beautiful place now the rabble have gone. There are only the animals and the Silence. Isn't the Silence wonderful, Stefan?"

My expression must have disagreed with him. Abruptly the levity was gone from his face and he nodded seriously at me.

"You're right, of course," he noted. "We are not perfect yet." He smiled with genuine warmth. "I have to kill your friends, and then you. But, because you have been such a friend to me, I'll leave you until the last. Goodbye."

He was off out of the hatch then, and running. I was battered and bruised and I could not have kept up with him anyway, but I prayed to the Wasted God for a little strength. I was after Gaki as fast as I could manage and hoping I would not be too late.

46

The Reckoning

At the time the sheer effort of chasing Gaki left me with no room at all to think. I did not fear losing Gaki to the maze of Shadrapar. I did not consider that I had no idea where Kiera and the others were, though Gaki seemed to know. I just found a ragged rhythm and stuck with it, and eventually the pain from my legs, arms, side and head settled into a kind of harmony.

In retrospect, I suspect Gaki slowed his pace to be always at the limit of my vision, too far ahead to catch, not far enough to lose. He wanted me to be there when he killed my friends.

The lack of thought was a blessing. Otherwise I would have had to ask myself what I would do if I ever caught Gaki. I could not fight him. I would sooner throw stones at a Macathar than take on Gaki; sooner strike at the Silence.

I saw Peter, Kiera and Shon ahead, picking their way through a clothes-strewn street towards another square. Perhaps they were looking for me. Gaki was racing towards them and they had not seen him.

I filled my lungs and yelled out, "Gaki! Look out! Gaki!" and shattered the Silence for good.

Gaki, like an actor with his cue, was instantly still and waiting for them. Peter and the others stopped and saw him there, in the centre of the square. There was a brief debate whose tides I could not plumb, and then Peter had launched himself forwards, hauling the Ropa blade after him. He had surely known that Gaki was waiting for him to do just that. Being Peter, he must have thought that if he acted suddenly enough he might still catch the other man off guard.

Behind him, Shon was also picking up speed. Gaki was unmoving and I knew he would be smiling.

At my distance one saw the movement and not the stillness. What excuse Peter could have in not seeing Hermione there I cannot say. She must have been shadowing my friends while Gaki hunted me in the dark. Her huge, motionless form was just another piece of ruin to Peter, until she put out a massive arm and slapped him across the face. His head snapped back and he fell, Ropa blade describing deadly circles before burying itself to the quillons in the ground.

I was still running, and the next few moments had already sketched themselves out in my mind with a surprising accuracy. Peter lay still, Kiera sprinting forwards to aid him, and Shon was ahead of her. Hermione loomed before him and I imagined him breaking against her like a wave, but his hand flashed out, and the woman reeled back with a hoarse yell, clutching her face.

Shon did not stop or even slow, but ducked under Hermione's arm and lunged for Gaki himself. I wanted to shout at him that Gaki could not be beaten that way but I had not the breath. Still I powered on, feet raw, muscles searing. In my hand was the punch-dagger Peter had given me.

Shon feinted at Gaki, turning the feint into a full thrust when he did not react. Gaki was abruptly not there, a sidestep so subtle that Shon was out of position, turning his lunge into a forward roll to get clear of an answering cut that never came. The murderer stepped back lightly and said something I could not catch. Shon turned, knife and off-hand outstretched, a proper fighter's stance. If Gaki was baiting him, he was not biting.

Hermione had her back to me, so I could not see what Shon had done to her face. She was advancing on Kiera though, driving

576

her from Peter's body at some signal from Gaki. Kiera was shouting something but all I could hear was my own breathing, savage and strained in my ears.

Shon circled, feigning a thrust that Gaki again failed to believe. His knife flicked at the killer's face, scooped down for a stomach shot. Gaki bowed gracefully aside, danced his own glint of a knife past Shon's face, kicked Shon's feet out from under him, stepped back. Shon stumbled but caught his balance. He had his back to me now: I could not see his face either.

I was almost there.

Shon cut high, changing his grip so that he could stab down as Gaki moved under his blow. Gaki slid out from under the stroke, cutting with a knife that was suddenly in the other hand. Shon blocked, forearm to forearm, trying to grapple so he could get his blade in. Gaki slipped from his grasp like smoke and that tiny glint in his hand arced in again. This time Shon only got his elbow in the way of the blade. It was his prosthetic elbow and I think he was counting on it jarring the knife from Gaki's hand. I recalled Father Sulplice whittling machine parts with that knife.

It sheared straight through Shon's elbow. My friend had time for a curious cry, more of surprise than pain. His arm went limp, bone and tendons severed. His own knife came up, but Gaki grasped the wrist and held him off easily, even as the diamond blade licked out to touch Shon's throat.

For a jagged second they were poised like that, a barber and his client. Then the blade moved the tiniest space and Shon was falling backwards in a shocking shower of blood that Gaki walked through and came out clean and spotless.

I was there now, with all that momentum, my knife plunging towards the small of Gaki's back.

He backhanded me lazily away. The knife fell somewhere beyond my knowledge. My head rang with the blow but I clearly heard him say, "Don't be stupid, Stefan."

I saw Peter sitting up, shaking his head awkwardly. Kiera shouted, "Keep back! I mean it!"

Hermione went for her and Kiera levelled the gun and pulled the trigger. I think Gaki, Peter and I were all watching, waiting for the outcome.

The gun did not go off. Kiera's expression was one of rank disgust with both the weapon and her own luck. Before she could get back out of reach, Hermione had her, holding her up by her throat, her kicks and blows finding only that dense, impervious flesh.

I went to intervene, though what I could have done I don't know. I stopped well short of them, though, because Gaki was somehow ahead of me, standing companionably near Hermione, yet with the slightest air of impatience, a man with an appointment.

"Well?" he said. "Finish her."

Hermione regarded him, still holding the struggling Kiera up one-handed. She sighed massively. "Why, though?" she rumbled.

Gaki seemed taken aback, insofar as he ever was. "Have you ever needed a reason? Because she's there; because she's pretty and fragile. Or the overriding reason behind all we ever do: because you can. Because then there will be one less person in the world and the work will be that much closer to completion."

Hermione grunted. "Were you going to leave me 'til last," she asked dully, "or did you want to talk Stefan's ear off about your mind powers?" There has never been a more dismissive assessment of all Helman and I slaved for than Hermione's just then.

Gaki's stance shifted ever so slightly, and I swear I drew breath to call a warning. Hermione knew it was coming, though. She had taken the role of henchman to an omnicide, after all, and there is only one way that can ever go. Even as Gaki flicked the little blade up at the great width of her neck she was flailing down at him with whatever she had to hand – in this case, Kiera. What Hermione did not quite appreciate was how effortlessly swift Gaki always was, even from his genteel standing start. Kiera flew past him, limbs windmilling, but the murderer's body slid like a serpent aside and then he had cut, not quite the smooth and fatal throat-slitting he had doubtless intended, but enough to release a rush of Hermione's blood.

Hermione sat down suddenly, broad hands clasped about the wound. Her face bowed to her knees and I could not see it.

Gaki stepped back, an artist admiring his canvas, and then turned to me as though inviting a critique. Peter had got to his feet, though, and laid his hands on the Ropa sword's hilt. With an brutal motion he drew it from the earth and levelled it. His eyes turned once to Shon's still form, once to me as I clutched my head, once to Kiera: sprawled and dazed.

"All right," he said quietly to himself, and I remembered how he had set out against Jonas Destavian, another invincible opponent.

"When you're ready," Gaki told him. "It is not for a prisoner to rush a Warden, after all."

Before he had finished speaking the Ropa blade was arrowing in for him, towing Peter in its wake. Gaki dodged it, of course, but Peter had known that he would. He dug his heels in, so that the thwarted momentum of the blade dragged it round, forcing Gaki to hurl himself aside. He regained his poise immediately, but there had been the smallest imaginable moment when he was not in full control of the situation. I realised that he had never fought against a Ropa blade before, nor seen Peter's duel.

Peter was still moving, steering the eager blade in great arcs and curves that forever impinged on Gaki's space. Gaki continued to pace backwards and sideways to keep out of their way. I saw his face: a man glad to have a challenge at last. He made no counter-move but kept a single step outside the reach of that deadly blade. Peter's face was blank: he was concentrating.

Without warning Peter dropped to one knee with a great scything sweep of the blade, then was dragging it up fiercely even as Gaki skipped over it. The killer put a foot on Peter's shoulder and vaulted over his head with the blade in pursuit. I knew it was only a question of mass and velocity, but Peter was making it look as though the blade wanted to kill Gaki, and he was doing a poor job of holding it back.

Gaki spun, letting the blade pass to one side of him, and I thought he would get Peter then, except that Peter dragged the hilt down and the blade cut where Gaki's arm would have been. They continued their circling.

I knew Peter must tire, but I saw no sign of it. I knew I could not interfere because I could not predict the blade's movement, and it would bite into me as willingly as it would Gaki.

It was like watching a raptor take prey in the air, watching that sword. It swooped and dived, always curving back towards Gaki, always homing in. Like a good puppet show where one forgets the puppeteer, I discounted Peter from the fight, it was Gaki against the sword. I think, in the end, even Gaki saw it that way.

The blade drove down for him again, high to low, pulling up just in time to avoid the ground, bearing in for his stomach. This time, Gaki acted. He spun aside like a dancer and, as the blade was pulling round to follow him, his hand pursued it. There was a moment when it passed over or through the hilt of the sword, with that tiny glint cupped in the palm. Then Peter made a shocked sound and the sword dove into the ground and stayed there. I could not see what had happened for a moment, but Peter was staggering backwards and, after a beat, the blood started. Gaki had cut three fingers from his right hand.

Gaki bore a thin white line across one bicep, a souvenir of the Ropa sword's death-field where he had not moved quite fast enough. It was the only time that anyone had ever marked him. Peter should have been proud.

Peter was holding hard to the wrist of his mauled hand, trying to slow the bleeding. Gaki advanced on him carelessly and the glint in his hand winked at the sun.

I struck out at Gaki with all of my inner energies. The same claw that had crushed Harro's mind now seized on his, just for a vital second, and Peter whipped his knife out left-handed and ran him through.

Or that was the plan. Peter knew it and I knew it, but nobody had told Gaki. Instead, I felt Gaki's razor-toothed saw of a mind rip through me, a white-hot pain that exploded every nerve ending I ever had. In that moment I was blind and senseless, knowing only the agony and the hoarseness of my throat as I screamed and screamed. At the same time, without faltering, Gaki slapped the knife out of Peter's left hand and broke the remaining finger of his right.

When I recovered my wits, Peter was lying virtually beside me, curled up about his own pain. Gaki had not killed us because he had been distracted. Hermione had been calling for him.

There was more blood soaking her prison greys than I had in my whole body and she was staring at Gaki. He must have felt that he owed her something, for he went to her. I fancy I saw a real tenderness on his face, for all that she had only one service left to render him.

"I must be the last, after all," he told her frankly, then glanced at Kiera, who was clambering to her feet again, looking around for the gun. She made a sudden lunge for the fallen weapon, heedless of whether it would fire or not. Gaki was already there, Hermione abandoned again, effortlessly between Kiera and the weapon. She came up unexpectedly with my duelling dagger instead, and then Peter spat out some bitter words and lurched to his feet again, mangled hand held tight to his stomach. He staggered towards Gaki and I was right behind him. The killer turned on us with a delighted smile on his face, a man welcoming guests at a party.

"Just when I was losing faith in human nature!" Gaki's left hand slapped Peter across the face, open palm, breaking his nose and giving Gaki the opening to lock his right hand over Peter's finger-stumps. Kiera went for him with the knife and he rammed her below the ribs with his left elbow, driving the breath from her and knocking her down.

Peter fainted. Even he had his limits. Gaki cast him aside a little disappointedly and blocked the angry, amateur punch I threw at him. Hermione watched us dully, too weak from her wounds to stand or even move.

"What is this obsession with action, Stefan?" Gaki asked me gently. "You've had your chance to ape the deeds of others. Stick to what you know. I'd save you 'til last. What are you worried about? Now I'm going to have to do *this*."

This was a simple jab to the neck with a single finger, but all the strength went out of my body and I fell loosely to the floor. There were shivers of weakness passing through my every muscle. It was all I could do to lever myself up on my elbows.

With a 'now where was I?' look, Gaki turned back to Kiera, who was still getting her breath back, the knife lost. With no other option I cast my mind at him, expecting the same fierce flaying as before, but this time he was not bothering with me and I just slid from the greased iron of his brain, clutching helplessly for handholds.

"Since you care about her, Stefan," he called to me companionably, "I can draw this out, if you prefer…"

He choked off the word. The expression on his face, for the first and only time, was one of surprise.

Something had come ghosting into the square like a floating seed borne by the wind. I could not help but look at it, and the sight of it made me weaker and more sick than Gaki's touch had, for it was Greygori Sanguival.

That part of him that had approximated a man was thrown backwards carelessly, like a shawl in hot weather. The long arms trailed in the dust behind him. Behind *it*; there was no *him* any more. The articulated legs made their patient way over the rubble and, despite their limp burden, they had a smooth grace to them. The eyes that had sprung from Greygori's loins were now lustrous with life, and the feelers and sense organs twitched and groped. What Greygori had started, Gaki had finished. He had finally cut away the human part that even the Transforming

582

Man had not been able to transform. Now Greygori was no more, and was perfected.

I think Gaki was horrified by it more even than I, but only because it was a thing that he had killed, and it had not stayed dead. It was a disastrous precedent.

Kiera took that opportunity to scrabble back from him, dagger shaking in her hand. She ended up crouching behind Hermione's seated form as though intending to use the larger woman as a barricade. Her hand was on that broad, sloping shoulder, though, and I read some desperate camaraderie in that, though I reckoned it would shatter the moment Gaki recovered.

I had that moment, while he was distracted, and I put everything I had into it. I made my brain into a spearhead and launched it at him while he was not expecting me. He flicked me off almost irritably. The instinctive backlash of his brain laid my mind open like an autopsy, so that I had no guards or shields to protect me from the vast Silence of Shadrapar that was all around. For a moment, I was aware of everything.

Gaki was turning back to Kiera. I could feel his mind like a dark, thorn-spiked metal ball. Kiera was a winged thing struggling to fly and Hermione like a rock. Beside me, Peter's subdued mind boiled with chained rage. Shon was an empty shell, the cage open, the soul flown. Inside the half-dead half-animate thing that had been Greygori, something was unfolding like a puzzle-box.

I touched another mind, a mind vaster than mine as Shadrapar is vaster than the Island, as the sky is vaster than Shadrapar. It was a mind like huge stone blocks slamming into place, earthquakes and thunder and the lightning that destroys.

To me, it was the mind of God. I could not imagine anything else having such a breadth of incomprehensible, inhuman intellect.

Thinking it was God, I prayed; I asked for help. In my direst need I became a believer.

Gaki strode towards Kiera, on message again, the little blade in his hand casting rainbows where the sun hit it. She threw stones and pieces of metal at him, loose clothes, bags of coins. Hermione actually levered herself to her feet, shuddering, her face the colour of ash. I expected a look of betrayal on her face, recounting of shared times on her lips, but she just stared at Gaki as sullenly as she ever had at the Wardens. He was just one more tribulation her life had thrown at her.

He showed them the glint in his hand like a magician exhibiting his sleeves.

But God was coming.

God came as a sense of great calm and peace. Kiera stopped moving and stared at God and, whilst she had been willing to fight Gaki, she knew she had no chance against Him. I likewise saw the error of my ways and saw that my divinity was something else, less divine and more deadly. I touched the contours of its thoughts and marvelled. Who would have guessed that within that ridgy shell was a mind like molten lead and the shift of rock and the dance of the sands?

The Macathar must have been just around the corner all the time, but nobody had known. Now I had called it down upon us and it stretched above us all like... what was it like? I have no similies. It was like a Macathar.

Our reflections were captured in an eye eight feet across. Our signatures were written in heat, in light, in sound, in mediums unknown to man, and recorded within its mind. I was still touching it. I could not bring myself to sever my contact with that consciousness. I had some fleeting idea of what it was like to be a Macathar: more colours than mankind ever saw, more sounds than we hear, to smell the radiation and to feel the crisp vibrations of the Earth's crust and the songs of each and every star.

Gaki was expressionless. He had no response prepared for the entry of a twenty-foot, crab-legged monster into his plans.

Then he did move, and it was to conclude those plans as quickly as possible, for he was suddenly at Hermione again with the knife spearing down. Kiera darted to one side and tried to kick him, but he caught her ankle.

At last I got through. *Help*, I said.

I saw the eyes focus and narrow, triangulating, and then Gaki was on fire. The invisible beam had gripped him, and his skin blackened in patches all over his body, and he began to shrivel and crisp and char. I was no more than ten feet away and I felt no heat. Kiera would bear the white, clear impression of Gaki's fingers on her ankle until she died, but no more than that. The intense, bone-consuming blaze of Gaki's death was felt by none but Gaki alone. He was curling in on himself, cracking like charcoal. The angry coal of his face was turned from me, and I was glad. Then a breeze picked up from nowhere, and Gaki was ashes, nothing more than ashes drifting through the streets of Shadrapar.

I felt the Macathar turn its attention towards me.

It made a sound in my head: groaning and grinding, vibrating rocks, abused metal, shearing tin and the deepest thunder of the sea, so that my skull rang and my teeth ached and every bone in my body sang. It may have been asking me a question, but no man has ever encountered such a language barrier, not of words but of concepts. My world and the way I perceived it meant nothing to a Macathar, and its world was to me as mine would be to an insect. There was the tiniest overlap, though, some minute common root. It had heard my cry for help and it had come. Now I felt what in a human would be astonishment: a Macathar encountering the unexpected. It spoke to all of its fellows, scattered across the city and the desert (for they have a community, Macathars, that does not rely on physical proximity), and its meaning, clear to me in that moment of contact, was that these Vermin, these scavenging things, had some small intelligence after all, and who would have thought it?

There was no more room for communication, no common ground. I was filed in the anecdotes of the Macathars, and the creature stepped over me and away. Hesitantly at first, but then with more conviction, the thing that had been Greygori Sanguival followed it into the silence that was not Silence any more, but the unthinkable sound of vast inhuman minds at work.

Peter, when he awoke, refused to believe a word of it, but Kiera and Hermione saw it all.

47

Thelwel Through the Looking Glass

Peter and Hermione were both so weak from loss of blood that I thought they would die. It took all our fragments of medical knowledge, and my discovery of a surgery nearby, to save their lives. Neither was able to move for the next week, which infuriated Peter, and which was treated by Hermione as just one more damned slap from the world. Kiera herself could, at first, place no weight on the ankle that Gaki had grasped, but after a few days she began to get its use back. I think it was a result of Gaki's grip rather than the Macathar's power. The upshot of all this was that I had to do the running around for a while.

I got us ensconced in the nearest house and I searched for such food as the Vermin had not taken. I buried Shon, too. I found a hand cart and I dragged him to the Academy, where there was a green open space for him. It would be a good place for him to lie, a single corpse in the city's heart turning the place from a cenotaph to a huge and majestic tomb for a criminal lawyer. Perhaps in future ages, if there are future ages, some archaeologist will disinter his bones and judge him a king of times past, to have been buried so.

I buried him before the Grand Memorial, which became his headstone. Digging a hole of the requisite proportions and then filling it in was surprisingly hard and lengthy work. At the end of it I wanted to say a few words, just for my own peace of mind. I wanted to say that he was a friend, that he had died in a good cause, he had lived a full life, all of those platitudes. In the end I said nothing. I knew what he was, and he knew what he was, and God, if He yet lives and cares, knows what he was.

That got me thinking about posterity, or lack of same.

Hermione, not really trusted by or trusting us, hauled herself off to a room of her own as soon as she was able, leaving Peter and Kiera alone together to further their acquaintance. I was aware of the fact as one might be of a constant, mild toothache.

I saw several Macathars, and could still not comprehend what they were doing. I wondered if they even linked the structures with my almost-vanished kind. They paid me no heed and I was never sure enough of them not to stay still or take cover when they strode into view.

When we had enough food stockpiled to last two weeks, I declared, "I am going to the Authority chambers."

Peter raised his eyebrows. He and Kiera were playing chess with a beautifully moulded set I had found. Kiera kept winning; she cheated better than he did.

"The Governor of the Island has a mirror that he can use to talk to the President," I said. "I have seen it myself. I'm going to talk to him."

"If you think that you owe him anything," Kiera said.

"They need to know what has happened here," I decided. "Besides, I thought we were all still planning to go back. It will change the tone of our welcome if we come back as witnesses and survivors, rather than escaped prisoners and a deserting Warden."

"I suppose there's not much left in Shadrapar for us," she agreed. Peter was staring at the chessboard. While Kiera was talking to me he reached out to subtly reposition one of her pieces and she told him to stop it.

"Does anyone want a souvenir of the presidency?" I enquired. "For that matter, if I find the chain and the coronet, does anyone

588

want to be the president? We can declare ourselves the new Authority."

"On balance, I think politics has done enough harm for one lifetime," Kiera decided.

The only part of the Authority buildings I was familiar with was the part near the docks, where they kept prisoners. Everyone knew where the Authority met, though, and where the president had his offices. I was gambling that the mirror was an official tool of office rather than a private toy of Harweg himself.

The doors to the Authority chambers were wide open. Strangely, it made the place feel more occupied, rather than less. One could imagine an official bustling out at any moment, three books clamped under his arm.

As I came to the door I flushed out two Vermin that darted out under my very nose. One had been wearing a councilman's robe in great, ill-fitting folds. The other had been clutching a musket, which was an ugly trend. Whether or not they were brute animals incapable of thought, I reckoned they could work out how to pull a trigger.

The last moments of the Authority were spread through the corridors of power like a discarded fashion show, but the attentions of the Vermin had muddied their deciphering. The doors were mostly open and few of the clothes strewn about were in the rooms themselves. The passages were thronged with them. Had someone raised an alarm? Had they known the Weapon was about to fire? Why run, then? Where could you reach, in that blink of time?

I found signs of fighting, too. Musket balls had scarred the walls and there were the canvas clothes of Outriders here and there. Whether they had fallen in combat or just vanished with everyone else was impossible to say. I found Angel armour too. I stooped to take a shielding pack, strapping the unaccustomed weight to my back. If I could make it work it might be useful.

I found the president's office eventually, and the door, alone of all the doors I had seen, was closed.

It would not open for me, so I found the nearest window and checked the distance. It would be a shuffle of five feet before I reached a window into the president's office. The building was not built with serious burglar-prevention in mind, and I had served my time in the trade when I ran with the Friendly Society.

I knocked in the window with an economy of motion and it occurred to me, as I squirmed my way into the room, that in some small way I had become a man of action.

There was no president, alive or dead. I had been toying with the odd idea that this office might have been protected from the Weapon somehow; that I would find a starved and half-crazed Harweg. Instead I found, as I had joked, the coronet and the chain of office. They were strewn across the big desk, amidst random books and scribbled jottings. There were no clothes.

I was faced with the bizarre idea that either he had been elsewhere at the end, or Harweg had been in his office completely nude save for the regalia of power. I preferred the latter.

I spent too long looking for the mirror because I assumed that it would be in plain view and identical to the one on the Island. Eventually I triggered a catch which opened a panel in one of the walls, and there was a silvered oval of glass and a few brass buttons.

There was also a light that was glowing on and off, on and off, with the patience of the damned. The sight made me uneasy. I did not like the idea of this hidden mechanism calmly sending out its message for hours or days or weeks, behind its little panel door.

I touched a button, and the silver mists of the mirror parted. I stared into the dimness and recognised the gloomy confines of the Governor's quarters. Of course, there was nobody within view. I had not considered the possibility that Leontes de Margot, Governor of the Island, would not be waiting at my beck and call.

"Hello?" I called, feeling foolish. Perhaps I had to push other buttons for my voice to come out of the Governor's mirror. I really had no idea. "Anybody there?"

A face came into view without warning and from an unexpected direction. It was Thelwel's face, and not the Governor's. He was oddly slanted: while the wall behind him was straight, he seemed to have chosen to lean into the mirror at a thirty degree angle. I assumed it was some strange joke on his part.

The surprise he exhibited on seeing me was exactly mirrored by my surprise on seeing him.

"Stefan?"

"Thelwel?"

"What are you doing there?" we chorused.

There was a pause as each of us waited for the other to speak.

"Thelwel," I said at last. "I need to give you some news. I need to give everyone there some news? Where is the— Is the Marshal dead?"

"Yes," Thelwel confirmed solemnly. "The day after you left. Some people said it was the news of your leaving that killed him."

I did not know how I felt about that. Still, I pressed on. "And the Governor? Can you get him?"

Thelwel looked at me with huge eyes. "He's dead, Stefan," was all he said.

"He's dead too?" I frowned. It did not seem reasonable.

"He took his own life, Stefan."

"Thelwel, are you playing some elaborate practical joke on me? Are you drunk? Why are you leaning at that ridiculous angle anyway?"

"I... I'm not, Stefan. I'm not leaning. I'm standing quite straight." He left a careful pause at the end of the sentence.

At the end of that pause I said, "Oh," as the implications fit into place. "Tell me everything."

He shrugged. "There's not much I can tell. After the Marshal died things held for about a day – some stretches were controlled

591

by prisoners, like ours. Some were still locked up. Then fighting started. Wardens started shooting up whole stretches. Prisoners got up to the fourth floor. Wardens started letting people loose and Wardens started fighting Wardens. Everyone knew the boat was wrecked. Everyone knew we'd been abandoned. It all broke, Stefan." He shivered. "A bunch of Wardens turned up above us and started shooting through the ceiling. I was shot. It took me a while to put myself back together. Lucian was shot, Stefan. I'm sorry."

I said I was sorry, too.

"By the time I was on my feet it was mostly over. There were maybe four different groups – prisoners, Wardens, one with both, holding to different parts, and the machinery was broken. Nobody says if it got damaged in the fighting or someone did it deliberately, but the big pumps are failing and I can't fix them." That seemed to distress him more than the deaths.

"So what now?" I asked him.

"Some few took boats for the city. Maybe you'll see them, or maybe the river will take them. More have lit out for the jungle, and most likely the jungle will take *them*. But of the rest... I went to the group that held the fourth floor. They were Wardens and prisoners – a lot of the women prisoners too, the ones the Witch Queen had left alive. I told them I could show them how to live in the swamps, if they followed me. I showed them what I am, Stefan, and that they couldn't kill me. I made myself their leader." His voice shook. I couldn't imagine my mild friend from the cells doing any of these things. "We are all that's left in the Island now. And so I call on the Authority of Shadrapar. But instead I get you, Stefan."

I dodged the implicit question. "How many are with you?"

"Eighty-seven men, twenty-four women." He blinked. "All the women have guns."

I sat back and thought about how many people had been on the Island when I left it. But then I thought about how many people had been in Shadrapar when I left *there*, and Thelwel's news seemed positively good.

Then Thelwel politely expressed his surprise that I appeared to be President-elect in Harweg's absence, and so I had to tell him. There would be no help from Shadrapar for his little band. At the same time, there would be no punishment, no orders. Whoever was left in control of the Island would face no challenge from that compass point.

We sat and stared at each other for a long time after that, and I swear Thelwel listed slightly further as we did.

"What now, Stefan?" Thelwel asked me at last. "My home is broken and yours is abandoned. What now?"

I thought about that and I had only one answer.

My life is strung on a serious of fortuitous absences. I was at a party one evening, so I was not there to stand by Helman, Jon and Rosanna when the mob came, and I lived. I was sold to the Angels by Greygori Sanguival, so I was not there when the surface-dwellers descended upon Underworld, and I lived. I was exiled to the Island like a common criminal, so I was not there when some mad and desperate man fired the Weapon, and so I lived. I escaped the Island and returned home, so I was not there when the riots erupted and the massacre happened. I have made my mark on history in a series of Stefan-shaped holes and lived to write this account. At the same time, this is not the account of a reliable witness, only the speculations of a man who was not there.

"You want us to do what?" Peter demanded of me. "Finally, you've gone crazy."

I shrugged. "So what else?"

"Go to that nasty old man and throw ourselves on his mercy?"

"So what else?" We were all four of us together. I had gone

to get Hermione, who had shambled in and was sitting, separate from the rest of us, watching with extreme suspicion.

"He can't stand people, I don't know if you noticed that," Peter went on. "You think he's going to be happy to have us four and a hundred Islanders appear with begging bowls?"

"So what else?" I practically shouted at him. He blinked, hurt.

"Just… stay here… I don't know."

"I could not stay here," I told him. "I don't trust the Macathars not to destroy us absentmindedly, as we would swat flies, because that's what we are to them. I am going to throw myself on Trethowan's mercy."

"Me too," Kiera agreed, "And so are you, Peter. What is there here? What would we eat, that the Vermin haven't taken? And they won't stay afraid of us for long. What will we do, save hide for the rest of our lives?"

"Trethowan won't go for it," Peter argued.

"Trethowan will see things have changed," Kiera pointed out. "If Thelwel keeps the Islanders in line, they can set up away from his precious children. And Trethowan'll lord it over them anyway, you know him. There are too few of us left to endanger his people and so he'll get to enjoy treating everyone like a poor relation. Let him, so long as people get fed. I'll convince him." And then Hermione was finally out of patience and we had to explain to her what we were talking about, and whilst it was technically a violation of our promise to Trethowan not to do just that, I felt that circumstances had changed enough to render the vow null and void.

"I'm not ready," Peter said weakly, after that was done. "I can't travel."

"We have enough food for now. We have the time to wait for you," I said. "Besides, I have something to write down."

And so, while the two of them cheated at chess and recovered their strength; while Hermione, already further along that road, began to go on her own plodding expeditions into the city; while Thelwel ordered his diminished flock, I took what pages I had smuggled out of the Island and I expanded them into this.

I wanted there to be a requiem of sorts, for the human race. I have no idea who may come to ruined Shadrapar to read it. Perhaps the Macathars, or the Vermin, or the distant descendants of the web-children. Perhaps those races from the stars that ancient man was so fond of imagining will finally come down, too late, and discover my words.

There is a concept in Trethowan's writings about a crucial population size, below which a species simply cannot sustain itself, and is destined only for extinction. I do not know if there are enough of us left.

I am finishing now, for all the invalids are well enough to travel, and I am becoming less and less willing to stay in this city. The Silence never went away. I have felt it stalking me. I will not be able to stave off the fear of it for long, and then where might I go? And I have seen Faith again, or my mind is playing more tricks. Am I anchoring her here? Another reason I should go. When I am lonely I yearn for her. I would not trust myself if I met her again.

Yesterday I saw a strange monster in the streets. It was a black, tentacled, armoured thing that moved slowly, as though it had been taken from some other medium entirely. I found myself thinking that perhaps it had come from the poisoned and infinitely dead sea. I have no wish to meet anything from there. I hope I imagined it.

We will go tomorrow. I will leave this account here. It is decided. Perhaps it is Faith I will leave it for. Perhaps this knowledge will allow her to make informed decisions at last and take control of her world.

*

I almost didn't include this. It is my account, after all. I should have fiat over what goes in, and what details I excise and which are, therefore, lost forever out of this leaking world. But, given what was said, I have decided to be frank and honest, this one time.

I had come back to my account with the intention, perhaps, of adding or subtracting some small adventures. There is so much circumstance I have left out, so much I have put in. But it is a life, my life. Hard to know, from the limits of these eyes, what can be treated as relevant.

Except my account was not lying patiently awaiting its creator. Hermione was there reading it.

I cannot say how long I stopped and stared at her. She seemed as absorbed as a child. A chronicler could not ask for a more intent audience for his words. Peter could not read, of course. Kiera could, but she was rusty and took no particular pleasure in it. I had never even considered that Hermione might possess that ancient and arcane skill.

And yet many of the prisoners could read and write, of course. Outside the elevated social circles I had been used to travel in, many people actually needed to write things down for practical purposes, like tallying stolen goods or sending threatening messages to their fellow criminal literati.

She had been trained to keep stock in a warehouse, she told me. In fact, she pointed out that she had certainly told me exactly that at some point in our shared incarceration, but I had not paid much heed to it.

"I wanted to finish it," she said. Her face told me nothing, as broad and suspicious as it ever had been. "I could see you were done. I thought you were going to set fire to it or something."

"Why would I…?"

"The sort of thing you posh people do, isn't it?" she suggested carelessly.

"No, no it is not, just…" I reached for the pages and she took them between her hands as if to tear the whole manuscript in half, a feat she was certainly capable of. I backed off.

"What do you think, then?" I asked. I had not anticipated literary criticism with the Shadrapan publishing industry in the parlous state it now was, but apparently that was my lot.

"You missed a lot out," she told me. "What about that time that…" and she referred to some incidents that befell me on the Island that, even being as frank as I am, I have not mentioned. There were countless humiliations and hurts and frustrations in my past, and there were things I did, too: mean and petty things that I am not proud of, enacted because I was powerless and afraid.

She regarded me, as hard to read as the Marshal. "You are a shallow one."

I gaped at her. I was outraged, though not so openly that she might take offence and hit me.

"Pretty face this and posh education that. You and me, we shared more time and words in the cell than you ever did with those two. And what am I, in here? Ugly and big." She didn't seem angry, just sad. She still wasn't handing over the pages, and it was because she still had something to say. Eventually I came and sat down beside her, just as we had sat in the cell, me in her shadow.

"I'm sorry, I'll…"

"Don't," she told me. "Big and ugly, like the world. Just put in that I tore a strip off you, here and now, and we're quits. Bad things happened. Don't have to mention any of it again."

I was being let off, and at the time I thought it was because we'd saved her life, tended her wounds and fed her as she lay under the weight of the cut Gaki had given her. Or else she was setting it against having leagued herself with Gaki in the first place. Afterwards, I had a more dire thought than that, but I cannot bring myself to satisfy my curiosity.

She talked of Gaki then, who she had known was a frightful man without fearing him. He had treated her better than I, even though she'd known that becoming his companion was no more than a novel method of suicide. "But he got me out.

Better days with him than a life in a cell," she said. "He was interesting." She missed him, and she knew that she only lived because he was gone, and there was no contradiction in that for her.

I let her finish the few remaining pages and then she shoved the bundle of papers into my chest and ambled off. Only after she'd gone did I think about what else that 'bad things happened' might have referred to. She had been a factory worker, after all, at exactly the time that Helman and the rest of us had produced our doomed magnum opus. She was perfectly placed to have been within that crowd, worked up and unleashed upon the subject of her employer's ire. And she had killed before. Who knew just whose blood was on those big hands?

I have not asked. I will not ask.

The most extraordinary thing has happened!

I must expand my account, for this is worthy of record.

The four of us were scavenging some last food, on the very point of leaving, when I found someone.

I was sitting in a square, counting my containers and trying to calculate how many we needed, when I saw movement at a window. I quickly packed everything away in a sack, for the Vermin are much bolder these days and will take food from us if they can. I stood there with a flintlock in my hand, ready to fire it and scare them off.

I saw nothing more, but the Vermin are grown very clever as well. I took up my sack and my gun and I made a quiet progress by a roundabout route to the back door of the building, and slipped in. If there were Vermin tailing me, I wanted to scare them off.

Instead, I found myself creeping up on a woman. She was short, and dressed in hard-wearing clothes that I found more than a little familiar, and when she turned at my step, fumbling for her crossbow, she said, "Hey! I know you! You're that Strepan something."

"Stefan Advani," I corrected her, lowering my pistol. I recognised her. I could put no name to the face but I could see, plain as day, that she was a Fisherman. "What are you doing here?"

"Could ask you the same question. Thought you got deported."

"So I came back," I told her. "I heard the Underworld got cleaned out."

"So we went deep," she told me. "Then when we came out again, place was like this. What the hell happened?"

I seized on the salient point. "There are more of you?"

"A fair few," she agreed. "You're that weird booky friend of Sergei's, that right?"

"Sergei's with you?"

"We lost track of him in the fight," she said. "Pelgraine's in charge."

"Pelgraine," I repeated stupidly. She nodded.

"Now are you going to tell me what's going on?" she asked me.

"Take me to Pelgraine right now," I replied, and she did.

It was just as she had said. After the battle for Underworld, Pelgraine had led his survivors down into places only the Fishermen knew. They had survived there the best they could, fending off the Stabbers and the Mazen. Eventually, the need for food forced them up, and they discovered the same thing we had. They numbered twenty-seven.

I told them I had a plan, and they were shaken and desperate enough to come with us, so now we were thirty-one and not four, and the human race numbered practically a hundred and forty.

When all was ready, I sat up on a rubble mound away from the others and looked out at the city of my birth. Each landmark recalled a face to me – people I'd known back in the day. This low dive might be where Rosanna and I had embraced; that rooftop where Giulia, Sergei and Arves had watched the dawn in with me, one time. Astonishing how a species-wide extinction event can pale before the knives of personal tragedy. And it is that self-centredness, no doubt, that led some great magnate of our city to unleash the Weapon on his rivals.

So it was that, faced with the ghosts of a hundred thousand vanished people, I moped like a bad poet about my own trivial worries.

Kiera came and sat beside me. I did not know how I felt about her then, because she had spent so long alone with Peter while I gathered food and spoke to Thelwel and Pelgraine. Perhaps I felt hard done by. Yes, I am inconstant.

"You've been very quiet," she observed.

I nodded.

"What's wrong?" she said carefully. "I'd have thought that, what with this friend of yours appearing, you'd have cheered up."

I looked at her.

"Are you worried about Trethowan?" she pressed. "Now that there are more of us?"

"No," I said.

"Progress. We have speech," she remarked acidly. "Talk to me, Stefan. Nothing's going to get better if you bottle it up."

"I really do not have anything to say. You don't need to worry about me."

She put a hand on my shoulder. "Stefan, I don't *need* to worry about anyone. I know Trethowan will take *me* back. The web-children would lynch him if he didn't. I choose to worry about you."

I tried a wry and sardonic smile, such as some of the Academy students had practised to make themselves look romantic. "And Peter?"

"Peter is starting to get on my nerves," she said, and I had opened a floodgate somewhere because she continued, "I have never seen a man less able to sit still, and for all that time that he couldn't go out he had a hundred damn things he needed done, and I had to do them all. You did not get the short straw going out to find food. You didn't have Peter Drachmar complaining all the time about the things he should be doing while he was laid up recuperating. Hermione was better company. And then the moment he's well enough to walk I've not seen him do anything but chat to those Fishermen of yours. And talk about a bad loser! I have never known anyone quite so damned competitive! Every time I beat him at chess – and it was every time – he sulked like a five-year-old."

"I thought you liked him."

"Oh I like him," she admitted. "He's a great friend and a brave man and all of that." Then she squinted at me, as though trying to make out the small print. "Seriously, that's what this is about? I like you too, Stefan. I don't choose to ignore Peter because of that, or pretend you don't exist because of him. I've spent my whole life casting people aside for stupid reasons. I would far rather like you both, or neither, or however I choose, without limiting my options." She shrugged. "What can I say? I'm inconstant."

Something flowered in my shrivelled little soul then. It is always good, even at the end of the world, to find a kindred spirit. In my mean heart of hearts I choose to believe that had Peter only been a more sportsmanlike chess player then things might have gone very differently.

I do not think we will survive, as a species. I have especial doubts in view of the amount of radiation that might be burning invisibly about Shadrapar right now. Depending on how the Weapon worked, of course.

There will be the Mazen, of course, who are technically

human. They will outlive us, but I cannot envisage that they will have such a long future. They will tear themselves apart.

I have a vision of the world in several centuries' time. There are no human beings in my vision but there are the web-children who evolved, or were evolved, in our image, and they have prospered. They have made a civilisation that does not rest on energies and weapons. Instead they use the powers of their minds to build and create, and they work together.

Perhaps they are working on a way to save the dying planet or revive the sun. Perhaps they have built a great boat in which to sail the heavens and find another home, just as men may once have done.

Perhaps, too, they have legends of their pre-history, mythic figures of an elder race. That would be a fair reward for us, I think: Trethowan, father of the web-people (for the web-children will have grown by then); Kiera the clever, ambassador between the old masters of the Earth and the new; Hermione the enduring, whose supplicants ask for the strength to survive what they cannot change; the wounded god Midds (who I hope is waiting for us); Pelgraine, searcher of the depths; the terrible death-god Gaki, whose slaying by Peter Drachmar ushered in the new world (I have to allow Peter some credit, after all). And I shall be there, in some form: Lucky Stefan, perhaps, a trickster god always one step ahead of trouble.

Thelwel should have a role, but at the back of my mind I remind myself that Thelwel has not aged a day since he was made, and can repair all but the most grievous injuries. Perhaps in my dream, Thelwel is still there, a living god, not human, but a reminder of the way they, we, looked. Perhaps Faith is with him, too, amongst hearts she need not shield herself from. She and Thelwel would make a good couple, once the rest of us are gone.

I will leave this account in the Temple, beneath the opened sarcophagus of the Coming Man. Let it be theirs who find it.

Let it be yours.